THE PASSAGE

Novels by David Poyer

Louisiana Blue
Winter in the Heart
The Circle
Bahamas Blue
The Gulf
Hatteras Blue
The Med
The Dead of Winter
Stepfather Bank
The Return of Philo T. McGiffin
The Shiloh Project
White Continent

THE PASSAGE

DAVID POYER

ST. MARTIN'S PRESS
New York

 For information, address St. Martin's Press, 175 Fifth Avenue, New York, N.Y. 10010.

Library of Congress Cataloging-in-Publication Data

Poyer, David.
The passage / David Poyer.
p. cm.
ISBN 0-312-11874-0
1. United States. Navy—Officers—Fiction. I. Title.
PS3566.0978P37 1995
813'.54—dc20 94–24626
CIP

First Edition: January 1995

10 9 8 7 6 5 4 3 2 1

This book is dedicated to those who fled
And those who died.
When they demanded your labor,
They found defiance;
When they demanded your voice,
They found silence;
When they denied you ballots,
You voted with your lives.
You could not bend or compromise.
So, like sand eroding from under foundations,
You slipped away, grain by grain,
In the most grievous battle of all,
Facing them alone, or holding your children's hands
With the most desperate bravery
Until you knew freedom—or night.
As the last walls fall
It is your victory.
We will not forget your struggle.
May we be as brave
When ours is upon us.

ACKNOWLEDGMENTS

Ex nihilo nihil fit. For this book, I owe a great deal to James Allen, Joe Anthony, Mark Bakotic, Tom Bates, Jake and Ellwood Blues, Lauryl Boyles, Bill Buehler, Robert Carter, Andrew Diamond, Carol E. W. Edwards, Ann McKay Farrell, Kathy Fieler, Mark Gibson, Paul Golubovs, Frank and Amy Green, David Grieve, David Helmold, Milo Hyde, Robert Kerrigan, Larry Lane, Lloyd Lighthart, Rene Maynard, Frank McCall, Jim McIngvale, Will Miller, Lenore Hart Poyer, Alan Poyer, Jason Poyer, Lin Poyer, Miguel and Maria Roura, Angela Speranza, George Witte, and many others. All errors and deficiencies are my own.

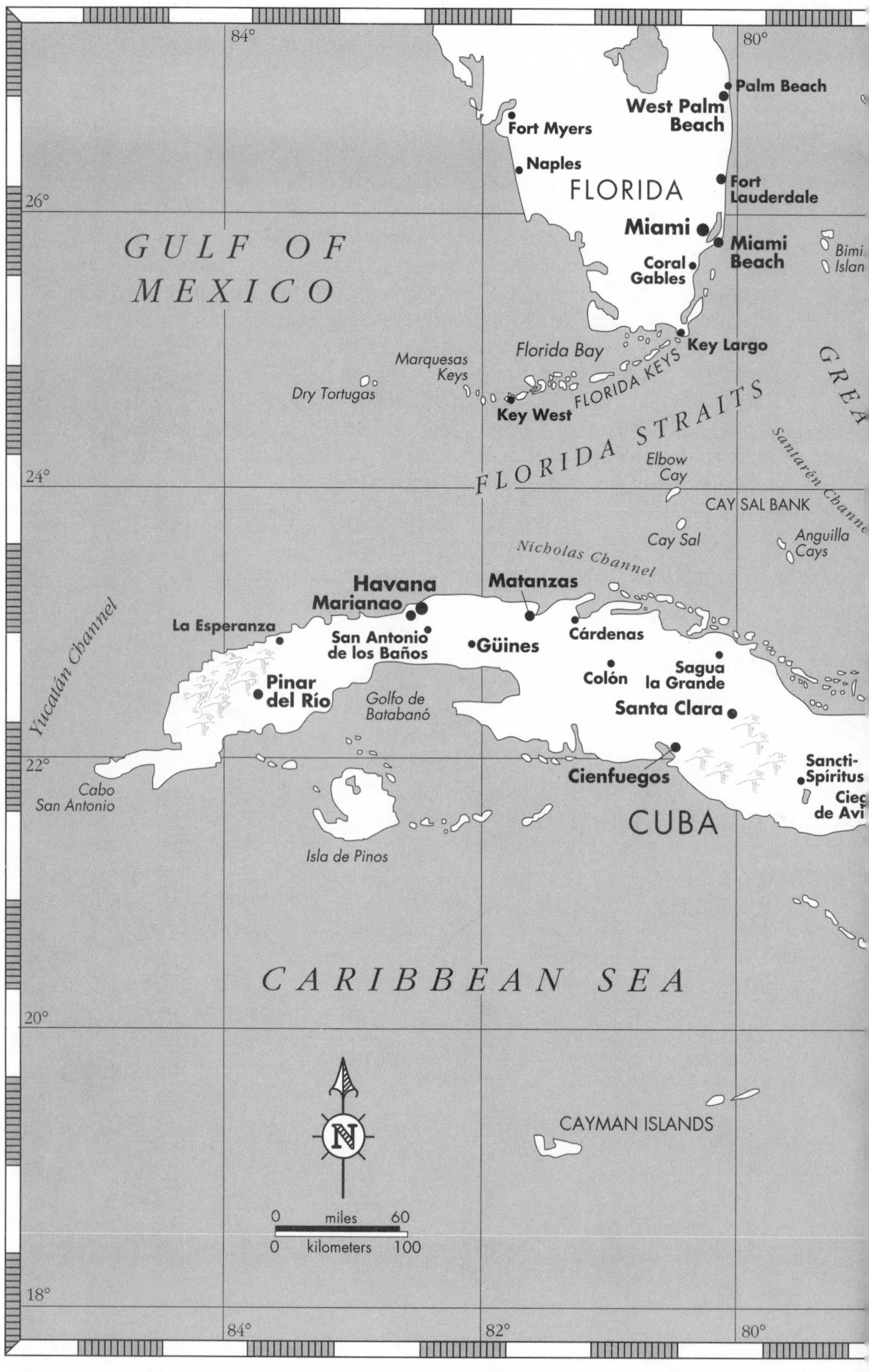

84°
80°
82°
26°
24°
22°
20°
18°
Palm Beach
West Palm Beach
Fort Myers
Naples
FLORIDA
Fort Lauderdale
Miami
Miami Beach
Coral Gables
GULF OF MEXICO
Key Largo
Florida Bay
Marquesas Keys
Dry Tortugas
FLORIDA KEYS
Key West
FLORIDA STRAITS
Elbow Cay
CAY SAL BANK
Cay Sal
Anguilla Cays
Nicholas Channel
Havana
Marianao
Matanzas
La Esperanza
San Antonio de los Baños
Güines
Cárdenas
Colón
Sagua la Grande
Santa Clara
Yucatán Channel
Pinar del Río
Golfo de Batabanó
Cabo San Antonio
Cienfuegos
Sancti-Spíritus
CUBA
Isla de Pinos
CARIBBEAN SEA
CAYMAN ISLANDS
N
0 miles 60
0 kilometers 100

78°
76°
74°
72°
26°
24°
22°
20°
GRAND BAHAMA
GREAT ABACO
B A H A M A S
ELEUTHERA
ATLANTIC OCEAN
Nassau
NEW PROVIDENCE
ANDROS ISLAND
CAT ISLAND
Exuma Cays
Exuma Sound
SAN SALVADOR
Tongue of the Ocean
Rum Cay
AHAMA BANK
Deadmans Cay
Crooked Island
Old Bahama Channel
Cayo Romano
RAGGED ISLAND RANGE
Crooked Island Passage
Mayaguana Passage
Caicos Passage
rón
Esmeralda
Nuevitas
Puerto Manatí
Puerto Padre
rtientes
Camagüey
Chaparra
Victoria de las Tunas
Holguín
GREAT INAGUA
Punta Maisí
Bayamo
Guantánamo
Windward Passage
Cap-Haïtien
Santiago de Cuba
Guantánamo Bay
HAITI
Port-au-Prince
JAMAICA
Jamaica Channel

Every sin arises from a kind of ignorance. A man's will is secure from sinning only when his understanding is secured from ignorance and error.

—St. Thomas Aquinas

Prologue
The Sea of Okhotsk

FIFTY miles off the coast of Siberia, the sea was a wind-scratched, ash-colored desert, heaving almost imperceptibly under a steely sky. Here and there, calm patches reflected the passing clouds like old mirrors. A faint cold wind off the Gydan Mountains moaned as if bereft, unheard by any ear.

Four hundred feet below the surface, a shadow slipped slowly through the dark.

The submarine milled northward at a pace no faster than a leisurely stroll, balanced on the knife edge of a thermocline. The huge machined-bronze propeller rotated its seven blades once every two seconds. Only the faintest blue filtered down to it through the cold and murky sea.

It was not the darkness that hid the three-hundred-foot-long, thirty-foot-diameter steel hull of USS *Threadfin*. It was silence. Pumps silent, plant silent, the hot radioactive water seeped through the vertical core of its reactor without throb or hum. Like a trespassing cat, she placed paw after paw, barely breathing, eyes wide and ears up, through the deep silence.

Standing behind the plane control stations, not looking at the diving officer, her captain murmured, "Woody, sure we're not getting too heavy?"

"No, sir," said the junior officer. "We're trimmed out right. But damn it, I'd like to try it, one of these missions."

"It's not going to make much difference at this speed. We're putting out more decibels from the screw than any kind of flow noise."

"It'd work," said the diving officer stubbornly. "I was talking to the sonar officer off one of the six-eighty-eights; they were playing around with it at Tongue of the Ocean. Regular two-part epoxy, got it from Servmart. They laid it in all the hull gaps, the safety tracks, retractable cleats, forward escape trunk. Then ground it smooth. Same-same with the flood ports, except one flush-closing valve—"

"But think how hard it'd be to get it out after the mission was over. And flow noise is a squared delta. Right now, there isn't anything in the ocean quieter than we are—except maybe a jellyfish."

The conversation was interrupted by a chief auxiliaryman. He reported that the problem with the rudder emergency-mode valve had been resolved. It had been clogged by a Kimwipe. The captain examined the frayed cloth absently. Under normal circumstances, he'd have exploded, asked who had inspected the last maintenance job. Now he just said, "Thanks. We'll talk about it later, Chief." He was still watching the diving-control station, staring through the dials. A grease-penciled placard above the panel read: DAYS OUT OF PEARL: 91. DAYS TO PEARL: 36.

Eighty feet aft of the control room, locked into the five-foot-diameter escape trunk he'd spent the last three days in, a thirty-year-old master diver from Eugene, Oregon, took a test breath off a Mark 16 closed-circuit underwater breathing apparatus. The 7 percent helium-oxygen mix tasted like stale ice. He was sweating under waffle-knit underwear and a dry suit. He blew out, trying to relax, and peeled a scrap of Saran Wrap—from the sandwiches they'd been living on since they went into saturation—off the number two diver's leg.

Two decks down, a sonarman sucked his lip, hunting through the static of overamplified noise for the sound he'd heard, very faintly, fifteen minutes before. He didn't want to report it too early. As soon as he spoke, the captain would want a bearing, range, classification. His fingers nudged the dial a millimeter left. Finally, he reached for the intercom.

In the control room, a speaker said, "Conn, Sonar: probable pinger bearing three-five-one. Contact is very faint."

"Sonar, Conn aye," said the officer of the deck.

"Ease us over there, Woody," said the captain. "Remember, we're hitting freshwater strata up here; we're not far from the mouth of the river. Slow and easy. No transients, no knuckles, let's oil our way in. Take her under the layer for the approach."

"Aye, sir. Come left, steady course three-five-zero," said the OOD. He wiped his hands on his trousers. "Dive, make your depth six hundred feet."

"Make my depth six-zero-zero feet, Dive aye," repeated the diving officer. He was a slight blond twenty-five-year-old from Bow, New Hampshire, and had left a pregnant wife behind in base housing. Submerged, *Threadfin* could copy broadcast, though it could not, on the current mission, transmit. Two weeks ago, a ten-word

Red Cross message had told him he was the father of an eight-pound, seven-ounce girl. But there was no word in it about his wife, and he worried in well-worn grooves about her as he maintained the bubble between up one and down one.

In the sonar room, the technician stared at a screen of green light. A voice said in his headphones, "Hey, officer a' the deck wants an estimated range?"

"Tell him five to ten miles."

"That a good range?"

"What you want up there, want me to run out with a tape measure?"

"Sonar estimates ten to twenty thousand yards, sir."

"Silence the boat."

Four discreet tones sounded in berthing compartments and in the engine room, in the sonar room and the wardroom and the long low-overheaded space smelling of oil and canned air where the torpedomen lay beneath the weapons, staring upward. In the scullery, the cooks slipped off their shoes and moved quietly about, securing pots and soup kettles. The engineers eased circuit breakers out on air-conditioning units. In the fan rooms, the blades slowed in their cages, whirring down to a stop.

The captain lifted his head, sensing the cessation of air movement on the nape of his neck. He unzipped the collar of his coveralls and took another deep breath. "Drop her to three knots."

"Maneuvering, Conn: Make two-zero turns."

The chief of the watch muttered into his sound-powered phones, relaying the order aft.

Back in the escape trunk, the divers pulled Navy Special Warfare–issue fins and masks over dry suits already sodden with trapped sweat. They checked watches, buddy lines, weight belts, duration/depth computers, and pony bottles. They wore no snorkels, no inflatable life preservers. If they saw open sky on this dive, they'd die in agony, coughing their lungs up in scarlet foam.

The sonarman nudged his dial left, then right. He frowned.

"Conn, Sonar: new DIMUS trace, Sierra four-seven, bearing two-five-eight."

DIMUS was digital multibeam steering, the equipment that gradually sampled noises too faint to hear out of the random crackle of the sea. "Bearing drift, classification?" the OOD asked.

"Sierra four-seven classified warship. Making three hundred turns on, uh . . . two three-bladed screws. Drawing left slowly. We're picking up an occasional fifty-kilohertz pinging, sounds like the fathometer."

"Probably out of Kamenskoye. Put a tracker on him. Notify me if there's any indication he's sniffed us."

"Sonar aye."

A long period of silence. The sonarman watched the screen as the prickle of ship sound ebbed, till it merged back into the hiss and crackle of the never-silent sea. He listened at the same time to the pinger, now dead ahead, as every ten minutes it emitted its low, short-burst narrowband signal, nearly undetectable unless you knew exactly where to look.

"Estimated range to pod, one mile. Permission to take a sounding?"

The captain considered. He needed to know how far above the seafloor he was. But to do that, he'd have to put sound in the water. Contrary to the three cardinal principles of submarine stealth, which are: one: Be as quiet as possible. Two: If you must make sound, try to disguise it as something else. And three: If neither one nor two is possible, then go ahead and make the noise, but don't repeat it, and move away as quickly as consistent with principle number one.

In this case, each submarine assigned to Operation Northern Bells had been equipped with, among other special gear, a fathometer that operated at the same frequency as the depth-finding gear installed in the Soviet trawler fleet. A hunting sub or destroyer would likely classify it as from one of the dozens of small fishermen that dotted these far-northern waters.

He nodded silently to the officer of the deck, who kept his eyes on the fathometer. The display came on, flickered, registered 0000, then, for a moment, 80 M, then 0000 again. Then it went off.

"All stop! Diving Officer, I need her about two tons heavy. Do it slow, no transients, no pump noise."

The chief of the boat bent over the ballast-control panel. He pressed two circular symbols, which changed to red open circles; waited thirty seconds, his eye on a slowly rising column of light; then pressed again. "Two tons flooded."

"Retract pit sword." The OOD glanced at the captain, who was staring forward again, deep in thought.

He was seeing it all in his mind.

To his left, perhaps fifty miles to port, was the Soviet mainland, the barren, isolated Magadan Peninsula. To starboard, seventy miles away, was Kamchatka, a dangling, even more godforsaken appendage of Siberia that had no value the Russians or anyone else had ever been able to find. Save one: a harbor, Petropavlovsk-Kamchatskii, now home to the ballistic missile submarines of the Soviet Pacific Fleet and control center for the SS-12 ICBMs of the Rocket Forces based there. This narrow neck of sea was all that separated the two.

For the last eleven hundred miles, since threading La Perouse

Strait, *Threadfin* had been in Soviet territorial waters. For the last six days, she'd run silent, sometimes at seven knots, sometimes at five, sometimes at two, and sometimes at a dead stop, drifting with the deep currents; and once at twenty knots, racing westward as Soviet sonars searched and probed the sea behind her.

Now she approached her goal, and he rubbed his chin and stared blankly at the readouts. This was sticking your crank under the guillotine, he thought. The Soviets had shot down a civilian jetliner that strayed over this area. They'd not let a submarine escape once it was detected.

But the reward . . . that made the risk worthwhile. Or at least those who'd sent them thought so.

"Sir?" said the diving officer, and the captain nodded, once.

"Pass the word to the divers: It's up to them now."

INSIDE the escape trunk, sealed in with a closed hatch below and another above, the master diver heard the order without change of expression. He sucked the empty space where a tooth had exploded years before, when he came up too fast from five hundred feet. The helium atmosphere distorted speech, so he said nothing to his partner. Just held up a finger, tapped his watch, then pointed at the four-inch-thick screw-sealed hatch above them. He reached up to spin a valve wheel open, bent, and cracked another. The smell of the sea hit his nose, cold, dank, as water began gushing in.

His hands moved with the familiarity of long practice, checking the oxygen bypass valve, the straps and nonmagnetic buckles, the lighted oxygen/CO_2 readouts clamped to his mask. As the rising water chilled his thighs, he sealed tempered glass over his face, twisted the bottle valve handwheel to full ON, and took a deep breath. He set the outer ring on his TAG/Heuer to twenty minutes past the hour.

Ten minutes later, the hatch lifted from the flush curvature of the submarine's hull. The lead diver pulled himself through, into darkness. He fumbled at his belt.

The light showed the black torpedo shape of *Threadfin*'s hull stretching back into darkness. He pulled himself along it, keeping his breathing slow. The indicator inside his mask stayed green. He felt the number two diver behind him, heard a clank and scrape as he fended off. They fell together, linked by the buddy line, toward the bottom.

As they dropped, he fumbled at his waist. The box came on, red light–emitting diodes flickering as he swung it left, then right.

His knees hit bottom, sinking into cold ooze. He angled up again and finned westward, following the device held out at arm's length like a compass. A faint green radiance in the enormous night marked the number two diver following him, off to his left and slightly above.

BEHIND them, hunched in front of the sonar stacks, the sonarman was tuning slowly across the band between 2 and 3 kilohertz. Occasional transients spiked the display. There was no periodicity, though, and when he tuned closer, he saw only random dancing light, heard nothing but the steady hiss and crackle of the empty sea.

THE lead diver swam steadily through the dark, sixty beats a minute, following the green LEDs like an aviator on instruments. Gas rasped in his ears and parched his throat. Eight hundred feet, he thought. That means, if you don't find Big Mama sub again, there is no way you don't die.

A section of the panel previously dark suddenly came to life. A blue LED flickered, strengthened, became steady; then another. When the third flickered on, he immediately stopped swimming, sank toward the bottom, brought his fins under him, and swam back the way he had come.

Twenty feet back, he collided with a thin nylon cord. He seized it, waving the number two in with the phosphorescent wand. The other diver's hand fumbled over his, found the cord, too, and followed it down—into the silt.

A muffled clank told him the other diver was unsheathing the trenching tool. He had one, too, but the way they'd planned this, one man dug and the other stayed alert. He didn't know what for, though. He couldn't think of anything that might happen that they could do anything about.

When he pointed the light down again, the beam went about two inches and stopped. Murk, and lots of it. He heard the scrape and hiss and clank as the other diver dug. That was the miserable part of the job, on your belly in the muck, scraping and clawing your way down into what seemed like the most remote part of the most remote sea in the world, in the utter cold of however many thousand lost aeons had laid down this ancient silt.

Down to the cable.

The line pulled at his wrist. He flinched, then angled down, eeling himself into the black quicksand that was the roiled, undulating bottom of the Sea of Okhotsk.

THE man in chinos and button-down short-sleeved shirt wandered nervously down the corridor aft of the wardroom. This was the first time he'd ever been to sea. He didn't like it. Being aboard a sub was a lot like being in jail. He'd been in jail once, in London, when an overzealous bobby had found him replacing the cover of a phone switch box outside the Chinese embassy. (The next day, a polite sort from MI5 had come round and persuaded the Metropolitan Police to let him go, friendly relations and all that, thank you, disappear now, no fuss please, there's a good chap.) He grinned faintly, remembering.

Only this jail was 278 feet long and very training-conscious. The crew had made him qualify on everything from emergency air-breathing masks to submersible pumps, not to mention the goddamn toilets.

He clenched his fists suddenly, checking his watch for the hundredth time since the divers had locked out. *Christ,* he thought. *Let's get the fucking pod aboard and get out of here.*

The pod was a tap, just like the one he'd put on the embassy phones years ago. Two months back, *Threadfin* had attached it to the undersea telecommunications cable linking the Kamchatka Peninsula to Moscow. This cable carried all the traffic between the command, administrative, and technical authorities in Moscow and the Pacific Coast submarine and missile bases. The Sovs knew that NSA monitored all their radio communications. So they used land lines for the stuff they didn't want intercepted. They buried them deep, put armed guards on them, one every mile, and bingo: They were secure from tapping.

So secure, in fact, that most of what went over the cable wasn't even coded.

The kicker, though, was that for 120 miles, the cable ran underwater.

The civilian grinned, then stopped, looking at the thick curved ribs of the overhead. He shivered, feeling suddenly cold, and looked anxiously, for the hundred and first time, at his watch.

THE number two diver grunted as his spade hit something hard. He reversed the trenching tool and probed. The buddy line fouled the handle and he had to stop to untangle it, by feel in the dark, his hands numb now, freezing cold. Goddamn it. . . . Goddamn this silt. . . . He dropped the tool and dug with his hands, furiously, like a crazed beaver. Then reached for the Ping-Pong paddle jammed under his weight belt.

The pod emerged from the silt under their lights, the muck melting in slow-mo as the divers fanned it away. It was three feet long, black, and shaped like one of those oval pieces of foam that are supposed to keep your keys from sinking if they fall overboard. Down its center ran a groove about eight inches wide.

In this groove, free to lift out of it without hindrance or binding if it was hoisted from the surface, ran the cable. It was black, too, new-looking and smooth. There were no barnacles or coral. Not this deep, this cold.

The number two diver knelt. Like an acolyte performing a sacred rite, he hesitated, then worked his gloves under the cable.

The lead diver was ready with his tool. Levering the handle under the cable, he pried its deadweight out of the groove. The pod remained, still half-buried. The ooze had crept back a little, almost like a live thing, though it was the essence of lifelessness—of death, black and cold, every trace of sun energy sucked out, till the empty atoms were useless to even the humblest life.

Suddenly, he lifted his head. He snapped his light off, and the other diver, startled, did, too. For a long minute, they stared into the mighty dark.

Did I imagine it? thought the number one diver. I didn't hear anything. But I thought I felt something. Something . . . watching us?

Finally, he decided he was getting spooked. There was nothing else down here. His light clicked back into life, fainter now as the cold leached chemical activity from the batteries. Got to hurry, he thought, and anxiety made his hands clumsy as he inserted the butt of the tool into a slot, turned it, and caught the puck-shaped module as it came free. The number two slapped a new one into place. The lead diver replaced the sealing cap, turned it twice, and bore down till it clicked.

Done. The spades clanked and scraped as they dug silt back over the pod. Gloved hands passed over it, smoothing the cold, furrowed bottom. The lead diver caught the number two's eyes. He nodded and jerked his thumb over his shoulder.

"MANEUVERING reports divers locked back aboard, sir," said the chief of the watch, letting go of the switch on the muted intercom. "Pumping the trunk down now."

The captain straightened instantly from his too-careless slouch

Winter Park Public Library

Renew by phone: 407-623-3300

Hours: M-Th 9-9 Fri & Sat 9-5 Sun 1-5

Renew online: www.wppl.org

Date: 12/7/2019 Time: 2:45:48 PM

Items checked out this session: 2

Title: Downton Abbey. Season 4
Barcode: 39677201109166
Due Date: 12/14/19

Title: The passage /
Barcode: 39677100144385
Due Date: 12/28/19

---

against the ballast-control panel. He crossed the control room with four long strides, slid down the port ladder, turned in a two-foot landing at the bottom, went down another ladder, turned, and headed forward. Crewmen flattened themselves against the sides of the passageway as he slid by, turning, too, so their chests brushed lightly as they passed. Grabbing a handhold above a massive door, he levered through and ducked under a hoist arm just as a torpedoman swung back a heavy machined-brass inner door. A little seawater ran out, dark with suspended silt. At the far end of the empty torpedo tube, circles of reflected light cupped a black object. The torpedoman reached for a battered pool bridge someone had racked on glue-on plastic brackets above the tube face. Its worn handle read: SONNY D'S, IMPERIAL BEACH. He slid it into the tube, then followed it, crawling in till only his feet stuck out into the torpedo room.

When he wriggled back out, pulling out the pool bridge, the module came with it. The civilian pushed past the captain, saying, "Excuse me, gentlemen." He wiped the black disc with a bandanna from his back pocket and laid it on the head of a torpedo. An electric screwdriver whirred, and the cover came off with a pop.

They stared down at an empty reel and a small, complex tape drive and recording head mechanism. Under it was a second reel. The second reel was full of two-inch-wide magnetic data-storage tape.

"It's good?" said the captain.

"It's all here." The civilian closed his eyes. "It worked. The son of a bitch worked."

The captain grabbed a pair of phones hanging near the tube. He clicked the circuit selector. "Woody? Skipper here. Let's get the fuck out of Dodge."

BACK in the control room, the chief watched a gauge column drop as pumps drove water from the fore and aft trim tanks, replacing it with air. The bubble of the fore-and-aft clinometer tumbled slowly forward as the bow lifted. The helmsman eased his aircraft-style wheel back into his lap, and the lee helm rang up ahead two-thirds. Two hundred feet aft, one of the enginemen released a locking gear; with a faint hiss and sigh, the shining shaft began to rotate. The prop eased into motion again, slowly, slowly.

Threadfin began to move. Her rudder swung ponderously on its pintles, and she curved left, continuing her swing till the blunt bullet of her bow pointed south by southwest, back toward international waters, over a thousand miles away.

Within her hull, the word ran from mouth to mouth: The mission was over; they were headed home. In the sonar room, two enlisted men were talking about the surfing on Oahu when one caught sight of the screen.

"Conn, Sonar: new DIMUS trace, Sierra four-eight bearing two-seven-zero. Sierra four-eight classified warship, making two hundred turns on two fours."

The OOD frowned. Two screws with four blades each meant a Soviet destroyer. He called the torpedo room. When the commanding officer got to the control room, Sonar was reporting another contact, this time from dead ahead.

The captain stood by the periscope stand, rubbing his chin as he did relative-motion solutions in his head. "Left fifteen degrees rudder," he said.

"Captain has the conn."

"Steady one-zero-zero. Slow to fifteen turns. Rig ship for ultra-quiet."

"Conn, Sonar: gain Sierra five-zero, bearing zero-nine-five. Sierra five-zero is a warship."

"Shee-it," whispered the captain.

"Conn, Sonar: Sierra four-eight and four-nine are active on eight kilohertz."

"They're warships all right."

"I knew that," said the captain. "What I want to know is, why are they pinging?" He crossed to the intercom, but before he touched it, it spoke. "Conn, Sonar: suppressed cavitation in the baffles."

The captain's nostrils widened and his face went tense. Suppressed cavitation meant another submarine. "Bearing?" he asked quietly.

"Can't get an exact bearing, sir. Too much background noise. Somewhere on the port quarter."

He took a deep breath. "Okay, man battle stations. Make tubes one through four fully ready with the exception of opening the outer doors."

For twenty minutes, they twisted and turned in a narrowing circle. Sonar reported more active sonars, then helicopter flybys and sonobuoy drops. Sweating, the skipper ordered turn after turn, changed depth and speed, tried to keep his bow to whichever pursuer seemed closest. The beat of the screws, the pings hemmed them in closer and closer. At one point, something hissed along the side of the hull, making the deck sway beneath their feet. "Submarine screw noise, close aboard," reported Sonar. "Opening now, bearing one-one-five."

The diving officer muttered, "The son of a bitch almost hit us."

"They've got us boxed, sir."

The captain looked around. It was the boat's exec, a stocky lieutenant commander from Gibson, Louisiana. "It's a box," he said again. "They're trying to force us to surface."

The skipper thought this over. "Get the spook up here," he said.

"I'm here."

The civilian's head appeared at the top of the ladder. The captain beckoned him to where he stood by the scope.

"They're trying to force us to surface," he said.

The man in chinos went white. He shook his head slowly. "I can't believe I'm hearing this."

"It's not a decision I'd want to make. But the op order's clear about who's in command."

"I didn't mean to say you *couldn't*. But this program's too important to compromise."

"It's compromised already. They obviously know we're here."

"They don't know what we're doing. What we *did*."

"It's that important?"

"It's that important. Yeah."

"I think I understand what you're saying," said the captain. "But do you understand what I'm saying? Let's make real sure. Tell me what you think I'm saying."

"You're asking me if it's all right for you to surface, to give up."

"No. I'm saying I may have to shoot my way out of this one."

The civilian licked his lips; his eyes darted around the control room.

"Captain, here's an opening," said the OOD.

The captain swung instantly back to the plot. The exec put his finger silently between the green and the blue traces.

"Seems to be a gap developing between four-eight and four-nine. Back to the northeast."

"We're not going to get out of this jam going northeast, Paulie."

"No, but an end run—if we can shake them—"

"You're right; it's worth a try. Let's go for it. Shit a decoy. Soon as you hear it trigger, kick her up to flank and we'll try to drive between them."

The *Permit* class were the fastest U.S. submarines ever to go to sea. As the reactor coolant pumps went to full power, *Threadfin* began accelerating with incredible smoothness, smoother than a train on welded rails, but so rapidly that the planesman felt himself pressed back into his seat. The glowing numerals of the rpm indicators flickered upward. A faint vibration grew over their heads, a fluttering roar like wind tearing by at great speed. It was the sound of 15,000 horsepower converting itself second by second into velocity.

As they passed twenty knots, Sonar reported losing all contacts due to self-noise. The acceleration continued. The captain leaned on the plotting table, looking down at the moving spot of light and the penciled tracks that hemmed it in. The paper was blistered. He wondered why, then saw another drop of sweat hit it.

"Answering ahead flank, sir, thirty-five knots."

"Very well. We'll run for fifteen minutes at high speed, then cut the go juice and slew right, coast out to listen."

Seconds ticked by. The diving officer and the exec and the plotting team members stood around the table, watching the lighted rosette creep across the paper. After five minutes, the captain said, "You know, a few more minutes here and we just might make it out of this catfight with our shorts intact."

"We're making a hell of a racket."

"I know that. The question is, now they know we're not going to surface, if they're willing to—"

The sonarman's voice crackled through the room. "Water impact! Multiple water impacts, three-sixty degrees, all around us!"

Every man in the compartment strained his ears, listening for the whine that meant an incoming torpedo. But complete silence succeeded the warning.

"Hard left rudder!" shouted the captain suddenly. "Now!"

But the helmsman never had time to acknowledge the command.

THE first salvo of RBU-25 rocket-thrown depth charges fell in a four-hundred-yard diameter circle imperfectly centered on *Threadfin.* Sinking through the sea, set to explode on impact, the closest one passed her madly milling screw fifty yards astern. The second salvo fell two hundred yards ahead of the first.

The first hit landed on the sonar dome. The molten jet of its shaped charge penetrated the inch-thick fiberglass. The seawater inside changed instantly to steam and exploded. The ruptured dome caught the high-speed laminar flow along the hull and peeled outward like a tulip blown apart by a jet of compressed air. The curved shards clattered and banged along the length of the speeding submarine.

The second hit detonated on the port stern plane, blowing half of it off the boat and bending the rest downward. A fifteen-foot chunk of steel spun aft into the prop, which was still driving at full speed.

The crew heard both explosions as muffled thuds, less than a third of a second apart. Then they felt themselves grow light as the boat nosed over, still at thirty-five knots, and headed for the bottom, two hundred feet down.

The third shaped charge punched through the pressure hull just aft of the sail. The two divers, still locked helplessly inside the escape trunk, heard it as a deafening slam, followed by the roar of pressurized water blasting into the engine room.

The men forward of the engine room transverse bulkhead heard it, too. They knew what it meant when the overhead lights went out and failure alarms flashed from every indicator. In the two or three seconds before they plowed into the bottom, some of them wondered what the Soviets would do with their bodies. Others wondered what would become of their souls. The comm officer, in the radio/crypto room, spent the last seconds of his life pulling the red toggles that would detonate the destruction charges.

The captain and the OOD, crouched in the hammering, slanting din, stared at each other in the weird red glow of emergency lighting. The younger man said, "Did we screw up, sir?"

"I don't think so."

"What I want to know is, how the fuck did they *know*? We were quiet! *How did they know we were here?*"

"I don't know, Woody," said the captain. Turning to the rest of the men in the control room, he said the only thing he could think of to say. "Thanks for everything, guys. You all did a super job."

I

THE COMMISSION

1

Pascagoula, Mississippi

THE gull gray hull towered up suddenly a mile from the sea, its main deck rising two stories above the sluggish eddies of the East Pascagoula. The squared-off, high-volume superstructure went up another fifty feet, topped by two rectangular stacks with screened intakes and cooling baffles. An echelon of pelicans slanted past the forward mast tip, 140 feet above the river.

It looked like a warship, but it wasn't—not yet.

Alone on the bridge, a thin, bearded man with gray eyes glanced at his watch, then at a walkie-talkie. He wore service dress whites, with choker collar, sword, and gloves.

Propping a shoe on a cable run, Lieutenant Daniel V. Lenson, U.S. Navy, looked down at the paved area inboard of the quay.

Half an hour to go, and the bunting-draped grandstands were filling. Above them, the flags of the United States, the U. S. Navy, the state of Mississippi, and Ingalls Shipbuilding stirred in a warm wind. On a raised dais, a technician chanted, "Testing, testing." Below her, men in work clothes pushed brooms past TV vans, sending welding grit and paint chips sifting down into the muddy water.

Aft of the stands, the white-hatted mass of USS *Barrett*'s prospective crew was shuffling itself into order like a pack of new cards. Dan didn't envy them, broiling down there on the asphalt. It would be a long ceremony. Politicians and flag officers loved commissionings. No better way to get your name in the papers.

He stretched, rubbing his shoulder, and glanced at the radio again. Then he strolled forward and looked down at the ship.

Barrett was at attention for her first day in the Navy, launchers and guns aligned fore and aft, brightwork polished to a jeweler's glitter. Every flag she owned, a two-hundred-yard display of fluttering color, stretched from the bullnose aloft to the masts, then aft to the stern.

With a teeth-rattling crash, the band swung into Sousa, selections from *El Capitan.* Dan picked up a set of binoculars and undogged the starboard door. The thud . . . thud . . . thud of the drums echoed back seconds later from across the river, out of joint, out of step, as if two bands were playing, one real and true and the other false, counterfeit, always somehow lacking or lagging behind.

As he stepped out on the river side, the wind snatched his hat off. He lunged and caught it at the deck edge, just before the long drop to oily water, where anhingas bobbed like dirty bath toys. He jammed the cap viciously onto sandy brown hair, set the glasses to his eyes, and searched up and down the channel.

The shipyard surrounded him, lining both sides of the torpid estuary with an industrial ghetto of docks and plate yards and construction sheds. On the east bank, steel towers rose like rusty castles: jack-up rigs being built for offshore drilling. They'd delivered one last week. Without much ceremony, Dan thought. Just flood the dock and off it went downriver behind a tug.

The Navy did things differently.

The channel was clear except for a barge anchored upriver, where the Pascagoula moseyed east before wheeling south, oozing past the yard and surrendering to the Gulf of Mexico. He swung the round magnified field of the glasses past welding generators, stacks of steel plate, coils of cable, and mobile test equipment and steadied on Port Road.

The radio babbled into speech. "Bridge, XO."

"Bridge aye."

"Dan, keep a sharp eye now. Just got a call from the ship supe's office. The official party's en route."

"Yes, sir, I have my glasses on the gate. Stand by—here they come."

The sedans and limos rolled in like a funeral cortege, headlights on. Marines snapped to present arms as aides and chauffeurs opened doors. A saluting battery detonated dully across flat water. Amid handshakes and salutes, gold braid and gray suits searched for their seats. A frail woman with bouffant blue hair teetered at the edge of the dais and was hauled back by an usher.

The band crashed to a halt. The crowd quieted for the invocation. Dan stepped back inside the pilothouse. He didn't bend his head or close his eyes. He stared out at the river, then beyond it at the milled-steel edge of the open sea.

DAN had joined *Barrett* two days before, his third duty assignment. His first tour out of Annapolis had been aboard USS *Reynolds Ryan.* After the court of inquiry following her loss in the North

Atlantic, he'd finished his division officer tour aboard *Bowen*, a *Knox*-class frigate, then reported to Commander, Amphibious Squadron Ten, for deployment to the Mediterranean.

With his fitness reports from Commodore Isaac Sundstrom added to the letter of admonition for *Ryan*'s loss, he'd been surprised to make lieutenant. But he knew why. After Vietnam, the officer corps had decimated itself in a mad rush to leave a shrinking Navy. Now that the fleet was building up again, there were billets galore, but not many bodies to fill them.

Not that he was due anything wonderful. His detailer had explained that he could forget the good jobs—cruisers, destroyers, and the flag aide billets and postgraduate schools the golden few were picking up. He was headed for a tender or an oiler, the bottom of the surface Navy's pecking order.

He'd thought about whether it might not be better just to get out. But the trouble was, there wasn't anything else he wanted to do.

He decided to give it his best shot and see what happened.

After his wife left him, he'd sold the furniture, hauled the leftovers to the dump, and moved into the Bachelor Officers' Quarters. Transient personnel got a twelve-by-twelve room with a dresser, desk, and bed. He didn't feel like dating. So he stayed in nights and weekends and plunged into his textbooks like a man leaping into the sea from a burning ship.

Department-head school was six months long. First came administration, then antisubmarine, antiair, and antisurface warfare, then tactical action officer training—four weeks of high-pressure memorization and drill in handling a ship in combat.

But halfway through, a funny thing happened. His midcourse grade put him in the top 10 percent of the class. The day after that, the school's commanding officer called him in. They talked for a while about what kind of ship he really wanted. Then Captain Chandler had pointed to his phone. "Call your detailer, Lieutenant. I believe he has something to discuss with you."

Lieutenant Commander Veeder had the clipped glibness of a man who spent eight hours a day on the phone talking people into things. He said he had an unexpected opening aboard a *Kidd*-class destroyer. Dan said, buying time, "That's one of the Iranian *Spruances*, right?"

"Same hull as a *Spruance*-class, but the Shah wanted more bang for his buck. The beauty is, it has cruiser weapons, but you don't have to deal with the fucking nukies. With that weapons suite, it's a second-tour department-head job."

Dan stroked his beard as he tried to figure out whether this was a good deal or a trap. Lieutenants did two eighteen-month tours as department heads. The first was on a simple, technically less demanding ship, a frigate or auxiliary. The second tour you fleeted up to a bigger ship, with more complex weapons and systems.

He said cautiously, "You're considering me for a *Kidd*? What job?"

"Weapons officer. Combat systems, they call it now. I know we were talking a gator freighter or oiler, but when this opened up and I called Chandler for a recommendation, you were the highest-ranking guy with the lowest-ranking expectations."

"Where is it?"

"USS *Barrett,* DDG nine-ninety-eight. Commission in Pascagoula, home port in Charleston. Beautiful city. Sue'll love it."

"Sue?"

"Isn't that your wife's name?"

"She goes by Betts. Anyway, we're divorced. What happened to the regularly scheduled guy?"

"Divorced? Sorry. . . . What happened was, he fell off the brow. The ship was in dry dock, fixing seals on the sonar dome, and he went sixty feet down and splattered himself over the concrete. . . . Before you answer, uh, downside: Trying to learn all the systems while they're in predeployment work-up, it's gonna be easy to fall on your sword. Hear what I'm saying? You don't wanna sweat blood, work thirty hours a day, say no and I'll send you to an oiler."

"I hear you, sir."

"Be make or break careerwise, but I figured you might go for a gamble. . . . We'll cut you two-week orders to Weapons Direction System school. That'll get you to Pascagoula for the commissioning. Okay, you talk now. Want it or not?"

Dan remembered how he'd gone quiet inside. He looked across the desk at Chandler. The old man was watching him, eyes narrowed.

"Yes, sir," he'd told Veeder. "Thanks for the chance. I want it, and I'll give it everything I've got."

THE wind changed, carrying the public-address system up to him more clearly, and he came back to the present. One of the suits from the shipyard was speaking.

"We are here today to deliver the last of five ships built under a contract awarded six years ago. Originally, these were not intended as U.S. Navy ships at all. Under the military sales program, the *Kouroosh*-class destroyers were to be built to U.S. standards, equipped with U.S. weaponry and sensors, and sold to the Imperial Iranian Navy. Ironically enough, all the *Spruance*-class destroyers were originally intended to be armed as heavily as these ships are. Due to cost considerations, however, the U.S. units were cut back to one short-range missile launcher apiece, and many other items were deleted.

"But events supervened. The lead ship was nearing delivery when revolution broke out in Iran. Following the new government's demonstrated hostility to America, Congress and the President authorized purchase of all five destroyers to fulfill the Navy's requirement for increased general-warfare capability.

"The basic *Spruance*-class hull and propulsion, already proven in fleet service, will provide *Barrett* with speed, maneuverability, and extremely quiet mobility. She is powered by four General Electric gas turbines, the same engines used in commercial airliners. Their eighty thousand horsepower can drive the ship in excess of thirty knots. Her weapons include five-inch guns, triple-barrel torpedo launchers, Harpoon surface-to-surface missile launchers, Phalanx close-in guns, and fore and aft twin launchers capable of firing surface-to-air and antisubmarine missiles. The ship is equipped with highly capable sonar, radar, and a remarkable new weapons-control suite. . . ."

DAN stared down at the audience—at the female guests, at the wives and girlfriends and mothers. Wind rippled their dresses, contrasting with suits and uniforms.

His white-gloved hand struck steel.

Betts and Nan had been taken hostage when he was in the Med. She'd done what she'd thought she had to to protect their daughter. After her release, they'd seen a chaplain; talked it out; cried over it. And for a while, he'd thought it was over and that their marriage was stronger for it.

He'd only slowly realized something else was wrong. She subscribed to feminist magazines, then joined a group. The more meetings she went to, the angrier she got. It seemed to him they were designed to make women unhappy with men and marriage. He'd tried to explain that to her, but she'd turned on him, angrier than he'd ever seen her.

He'd fought to keep her, tried to become what her magazines said a man should be like. He didn't object when she went out or ask where she'd been. But it didn't seem to work. Somewhere in there, the sex had stopped, too. Then one day, she gave him a choice. He was gone too often; it wasn't what she'd had in mind when she married him; either he left the Navy or she was leaving him.

It hadn't been an easy decision. But if it was that kind of choice, he'd lost her already. They'd had five years—not long by civilian terms, but a good run for a Navy marriage.

He'd come back from a two-week underway period to find the apartment empty. The note said she and Nan were going back to her parents till she decided where to live. She'd left his things, half the furniture, and the new vacuum was still in the hall closet.

He'd gone out and gotten a fifth of scotch, then sat on the floor, holding an old pair of her jeans and an old, outgrown set of Nan's jumpers, and cried. He drank till it didn't hurt anymore, till he felt nothing at all.

That had been months ago. He didn't miss his ex-wife now. In fact, he felt angry whenever he thought of her. But he missed his daughter, missed the little stocky body cuddled against his chest; the way her skin smelled, like sugar and butter; the way she saw the world new and fresh and told you about it, all excited, in ways that made you laugh and at the same time see it new again, too. When he thought about her, he had to stop or go somewhere so the men around him couldn't see. He missed feeding her and even changing her diapers, though she was long out of them now. He called every Sunday to talk to her, sent things on her birthday and at Christmas, but already he could hear forgetting in her voice. Who could blame her? She had so much to think about, school, new friends. . . .

Yeah. He'd drunk himself into oblivion that first night, and a lot of nights after, too.

He couldn't understand, even now, how anyone could *stop loving* someone else. But apparently women could. Women . . . No matter what you did, they wanted more. They wanted you to devote your life to them, change for them. But if you did, they turned away in disgust; you were weak.

Since the divorce, he'd decided he didn't need anything from women he couldn't get in one night.

All is for the best. Wasn't that what Alan Evlin had told him as *Reynolds Ryan* fought thirty-foot Arctic seas, the old destroyer foredoomed to a fiery death, and Evlin doomed with her?

Fucking Ay, Dan thought bitterly. Like Seaman Recruit Slick Lassard used to say on the old *Ryan.*

Fucking Ay, it is.

AN admiral was speaking now. Which one, he didn't know, or care.

"The commissioning ceremony marks the acceptance of a ship as a unit of the operating forces of the United States Navy. At the moment of breaking the commissioning pennant, USS *Barrett,* DDG nine-ninety-eight, becomes the responsibility of her commanding officer. Together with the wardroom and crew, he has the duty of making and keeping her ready for any service required by our nation in peace or war.

"The first USS *Barrett* was a response to the worldwide catastrophe of World War Two. Named for one of the first Navy men to fall at Pearl Harbor, she fought throughout the war in the Atlantic, Mediterranean, and in the closing campaigns in the Pacific. We are delighted to welcome several of her old crew here today.

"These, too, are dark years. We stand guard against a determined enemy around the world. Just as we stand guard against another, more ancient enemy: the sea itself. No matter how advanced our technology, going to sea is an inherently dangerous venture. Today, in the North Pacific, Navy units are searching for another ship—USS *Threadfin,* a nuclear submarine overdue and presumed lost on a routine training cruise. Let us pause for a moment, thinking of them, and pray that the news will be good.

"The newest *Barrett,* built to face and outlast any sea and any enemy, is a symbol of the resurgence of America, of her return to the world scene after years of withdrawal.

"Not long ago, the Navy was in trouble. The mood of discontent was reflected in the fleet's decline to a low of two hundred and eighty-nine ships. By wide agreement, this number was inadequate to fulfill our commitments in two oceans. And with recent events in the Persian Gulf, the Indian Ocean has been added to our responsibilities.

"Today the Navy is coming back strong. We now number five hundred and forty total ships in the operating forces, and the fleet will stabilize at six hundred, centered around a powerful striking force of fourteen carriers. *Barrett,* with her ability to counter enemy attacks in every dimension, will be a stout shield to the battle group she is designed to defend.

"The ship we are commissioning today is the most formidable warship of her size ever to patrol the oceans. She blends the hull of a destroyer with the combat systems of a nuclear cruiser. The result is unique: a ship so quiet, she can operate offensively against submarines; the most sophisticated antiaircraft systems in the fleet, quick-reacting and highly accurate; and a deadly antiship weapons capability, as well. Able to deal simultaneously with air, surface, and subsurface attacks, she is designed to go in harm's way—and win.

"But even that does not completely describe her. *Barrett* is the first ship to incorporate a new automated combat direction system. So new that even its capabilities must be classified, it is truly a tremendous step toward the warship of the twenty-first century."

* * *

DAN'S gaze moved to the faces in ranks below—his new shipmates: his division officers; the other department heads, his peers aboard *Barrett;* the chiefs and senior enlisted; the sailors, rank on rank. At parade rest in front stood the exec, Lieutenant Commander Vysotsky. Weird, he thought, having an XO with a Russian name.

He shifted his eyes to the dais. Behind the admiral, legs crossed, hands folded on the pommel of his sword, sat the slight, relaxed figure of Commander Thomas R. Leighty, USN, *Barrett*'s prospective commanding officer. Dan had met him only once so far, not long enough to form much of an impression.

He crossed to the starboard wing and swept his glasses up and down the channel again. The barge was still anchored. A crew boat was coming in, hugging the east bank. Satisfied, he looked into the sun, welcoming its warmth after a bitter Rhode Island winter. It seemed like a pleasant place, the Gulf Coast, but they'd be leaving right after the commissioning.

That was one thing you could count on in the Navy: You never served with anyone or went ashore anywhere for the last time. How many of the wizened geezers down there on the dais had figured they'd be back forty years after the big WW II, commissioning another USS *Barrett*?

WHEN he went back to the port wing, the senator was speaking, his tones booming out over the audience even when he turned away from the mike. He was saying something about how the Navy, and the nation, faced a critical time in world history. Dan watched the crew flexing their knees surreptitiously. Now the senator was off on how they stood at a crossroads of world events; how if America could stand up to this last pulse of Soviet expansionism, it might be the last gasp of the Evil Empire; but how the last innings were always the most dangerous, and the other team might still come from behind and win.

There was a stir in the ranks as someone toppled, buddies on either side catching and easing him down, corpsmen carrying him off to the ambulance.

At last, with a scattering of polite applause, the speeches ended. Everyone on the platform stood. The officers and men came to attention.

The supervisor of shipbuilding read the orders for the delivery. The dry official words bounced off steel and reverberated in expectant silence. The shipbuilder, in sentences just as arid, turned her over to the Navy.

The admiral turned to Leighty, and said quietly, "Commission USS *Barrett*."

The bugler sounded attention. Eyes swung as flags broke snapping against the sky: the national ensign, the red-and-white whip of the commissioning pennant, and, on the bow, the white stars on dark blue field of the jack.

Leighty strolled to the dais. He slowly unfolded his orders and read them. Finally, he faced the admiral. "I assume command of USS *Barrett*, sir."

A salute, a handshake, then Leighty barked, "Commander Vysotsky, set the watch."

A dozen boatswains' pipes keened and, simultaneously, the white-uniformed ranks broke into a run. Boots clattered on steel. As each sailor reached the main deck, he broke left or right. The chiefs followed, slower, heavier of foot, and then the officers. When the thunder finally subsided, 350 men stood at parade rest along the main deck, the flight deck, the 03 level, the bridge wing. Leighty paused at the microphone, running an eye along them, before he announced, spacing the words dramatically, "USS *Barrett*—come alive!"

And together, all the train warning bells began to ring, the horn droned out a deep note, the radars began to rotate. Missile mounts elevated, signal flags leapt up their halyards, and every light came on from the stern to the man overboard and task lights high on the pole mast. The audience broke into applause.

THAT was the high point. After the benediction, the stands emptied; the limousines swung in again, embarking the guests for the reception. Dan wiped out his hatband with a glove. "Okay, that's it," he told the enlisted. "You guys want to go over to the tent, punch and cake yourselves, make your bird. You can knock off from there, unless you're in the duty section. See you tomorrow."

"Not coming, sir?"

"Think I'll stay aboard, get some reading in on the combat systems doctrine."

A kid who looked about eighteen lingered shyly. He said, "Guess we got us a ship now, Lieutenant, huh?"

"Yeah, Sanderling. A brand-new one."

He watched the technician look around proudly. Being part of a ship's first crew, a "plank owner," was a title a sailor carried all his life—like the old men who'd put the first *Barrett* in commission when the skies were dark with war. Funny how he kept thinking of them. Had they ever been as young as Sanderling, as trusting, as thrilled, as dumb?

He grinned to himself, amused but also bitter. He'd been like that once himself.

The buzz of the A-phone brought him back. "Bridge, Lieutenant Lenson," he said into it.

"Dan, this is the XO. I've been looking over this inventory, what you came up with versus what Sipple signed off for before his accident. Are you sure these figures are right?"

"The chief warrant and I counted everything twice, sir."

"Well, I got some questions. Can you come down to my stateroom?"

"Yes, sir," he said. "I'll be right down."

2

Cooperative Cane Production Facility Number 176, Camagüey Province, Cuba

THE land sprawled like a sleeping child under the blanket of night, a vast plain unbroken by hill or mountain or city—only the land, naked to the wind. Across its black expanse, no cars, no vehicles moved in the last hour before dawn. Only at a huddle of concrete and tin buildings, at an intersection of the roads that led through the great plain, were a few lights coming on.

The woman woke drenched with sweat, a distant whistle still sounding in her ears. She lay unmoving on her pallet, looking up into the darkness as if listening to a voice only she could hear. Then she swung her bare feet out and set them gingerly on the floor.

The bed was pushed against the wall of a one-room house of unpainted palm boards, uninsulated and with one shuttered glassless window on the south. A colored picture of the Virgin, the kind that had been for sale everywhere before the revolution, was pinned up beside it. The floor was bare, swept concrete. Faint rustlings and scratchings came from the peaked darkness. Thatch from the *palma real* made a tight, waterproof roof, but it hosted mice and scorpions. For this reason, she slipped her feet into a pair of rubber-soled sandals, then got up. Moving quietly about the room, she lighted a small charcoal fire, poured water from a jar in the corner, and put a pan of it on to heat.

The woman was very thin. Her dark legs were scarred with a pale map of old cuts. She had wide shoulders and a short muscular neck. The arm she stretched up to screw in a dangling bulb was long and sinewy, the hand calloused. As harsh light stabbed into the corners of the hut, it cut the planes of her face from darkness. Her angular cheekbones and long eyes she owed to a Chinese grandfather. The rest of her features were a blend of African and European, mixed for centuries on an island without barriers between races. Her narrow lips were set, her expression sad, as if she'd been waiting for something too long and now despaired of ever seeing it.

The water was warm now, heating quickly above the blue and yellow flames dancing on the charcoal, and she dipped a little out and set the rest back till it should boil. She washed her face carefully, then under her arms, her neck. Crossing the room to a row of nails, she took down a work shirt and cotton trousers. Then, easing a door open, she went outside, under the stars.

When she came back, the water was hissing and bubbling. She measured out a little ground coffee into a sieve, poured the water carefully into it, and set it aside to steep. She flicked a metal box open and set the bread on the table, which was, aside from the pallet and an old rawhide-and-hardwood chair, the only furniture. Then she took out a mirror. In the quiet, broken only by the steady drip of the coffee and the chirp of an awakened cricket, she brushed her hair back and tied it in place with a strip of red ribbon.

She sat at the table and ate the bread and drank the strong black coffee, stirred thick with two spoonfuls of coarse raw sugar. She didn't speak or look about, just stared in front of her as she ate.

When she was done, she washed the mug in the remains of the water and hung it on a nail. She put the other things back, the sugar, the remaining coffee, and scooped the crumbs off the table and tossed them into the fire. Sitting on the pallet again, she pulled on a heavy pair of black military boots with worn-down heels and tears in the sides sewn up with twine.

Getting up again, she took down from the thatch a two-foot-long, slightly curved blade of spring steel. Its cutting edge was wavy, concave and then convex, nicked and scarred with long use. From a handmade wooden haft dangled a loop of green cord.

She sat again at the table, poured water out on a small flat stone, and set to work sharpening the machete. Each stroke began with a grinding rasp and ended with a faint musical singing. From time to time, she tried the edge with her thumb. Finally, satisfied, she fitted a slit-open length of rubber hose over it, thrust it into her belt, and opened the door.

The hot dark wind came out of the night and fanned her sweating face. It brought with it the smells of smoke and dust and drying urine, but above all of the soil—a crisp checkerboard of cracks at the end of the dry season, *la seca*. The sky was gray to the east, over the next house, the door of which opened, and two shadows stepped out, as she just had.

"*Buenos dias*, Augustín, Xiomara."

"Graciela. You're working today? Feeling better, then?"

"Better, yes, thank you."

A woman's voice, concerned: "Are you sure? If you don't, we'll let the comrade brigadier know—"

"I'm well enough to work," she said again, sharply now, and they said nothing more.

As they spoke, more shadows emerged from other huts. They did not linger in the open area in front of the *batey*, the cluster of workers' dwellings, but turned up onto an unpaved dusty road that led away between the still-dark fields. She moved with them, unspeaking. Bare feet and shoes and boots scuffed along as a faint light began to diffuse downward from the eastern stars, gradually bringing out the silvery surface of the road. Gradually bringing into view the nothingness that surrounded them, great expanses of flat earth stretching off till they met the sky. A month before, she remembered, the cane had hemmed in the road like two black walls. Now the fields were stripped bare, shorn, littered with the detritus of harvest; the cane leaves were like discarded corn husks, crackling-dry on the parched ground, rustling like a million insects as the predawn wind scuttled over them. She moved with the other shadows at a steady pace, not brisk, not slow, following the deep powdery dust as it wound left and then right and then came out in a wide plaza lighted by bare bulbs on high poles. Beneath their light, huge shapes grumbled and chattered in the saurian speech of diesels. Wordlessly, the workers queued at the tailgates, the men climbing up first, then hauling the girls and boys, old people and women up by their arms.

"*Listos. Vamos,*" someone shouted outside, and, jolting and grunting, the trucks jerked into motion.

COOPERATIVE Cane Production Facility Number 176, Alcorcón, covered seventy-five square miles of fertile flatland that had been divided among fifteen small cattle ranches before the second agrarian reform law. Number 176 produced almost a hundred thousand tons of raw sugar a year, although this year it was running behind schedule. Cane did not sweeten fully till it dried, and an unseasonally wet January had extended the harvest a month beyond its usual termination. The *central* had its own worker housing, offices, machine station, railroad station, warehouses, store, staff housing, garage, and barracks for the army units, school groups, and urban workers who rotated through on "voluntary" work assignments during the cutting season. At the height of the *zafra*, the harvest, a thousand human beings rode out to the fields each morning before dawn.

One of them this dark morning, sitting silently on a wooden bench in the back of a swaying Soviet-made two-and-a-half-ton truck, was Graciela Gutiérrez.

* * *

THE trucks stopped at the edge of one of the last still-standing fields. The tailboards slammed down and the *macheteros* spilled off. Not speaking, they ranged themselves out across the road, facing the cane like soldiers staring down an enemy. Drawing on a pair of worn gloves, lacing on leather shin protectors, Graciela looked down at it from the road; a vast, slowly tossing green sea half a mile across. Her expression was hard, but she did not feel as determined as she looked. She felt a heaviness in her stomach, a steady pressure. It was unpleasant, but she didn't ask to be taken back to the *batey.* It was a heaviness; that was all.

The *jefe de brigada,* the overseer, glanced at his watch, then shouted, "Time to go to work, *compañeros.*" And in a ragged wave the workers moved forward, stepping down off the road and into the cane.

As she let herself down the slope, Graciela picked out the place she would begin. The cane, seven feet high and brownish green, came up from the dry soil in clumps of five or six stalks. Two feet away was another clump, then another. She took a deep breath and bent, folding herself awkwardly.

Stooped, she seized a two-inch-thick stalk in her left hand and slashed it through half an inch from the soil with a quick stroke of the razor-sharp blade. Then, lifting it, she quickly trimmed the leaves off. She lopped off the leafy top, laid the cane aside, took a step forward, and reached for the next stem.

Gradually, sweat broke under her clothing. Above her head even when she stood, the tops of the cane danced in the wind, but it was as if they absorbed the breeze. The air between them was dense and hot and filled with mosquitoes. They found her mouth and face. But the tender parts, the ankles and the back of the hands, she had covered. And she ignored the rest even as they settled and stung. Only occasionally did she pause long enough to blot the sweat from her eyes with the frayed cuff of her shirt.

When she had eight or ten trimmed stalks laid aside, enough that it was heavy to carry, she began a pile. As she cut on, moving slowly deeper into the field, the initial stiffness ebbed away. The machete hissed as it sliced through the cane, and drops of pale sugar milk bubbled at the cut roots. Such a useful tool, she thought. You could saw through the tough stalk, like the volunteers from the city did at first. Or, if you had a sharp-enough blade, you could slice through with a sudden, nearly invisible wrist flick that clipped through the tough fiber like a razor blade through a stalk of celery.

And gradually, her tight lips relaxed. She forgot what was past and what might come and swung the flat blade, dust-streaked now, again and again. She merged with the work and the dry heat, the smoke and dust that drifted in golden sparkling, itching clouds between the stalks; with the endless stoop-slash-trim-toss, the steady progress across the fields, hearing and sometimes glimpsing at the edge of one's own gradually lengthening clearing the knotted kerchief or the plaited straw hat of a neighbor, the quick grin or averted eyes of another worker. Till all that existed in the world was the swaying, waiting cane, darker green at the base, then lighter, and finally a withered brown at the leaf tips. Each stalk shuddered as she grasped it, as if it sensed the moment had come when it would lose its grip on the earth and become raw material for the mills. She worked in silence, without joining in the shouts and encouragements of the other workers, or the songs. Although she listened, and sometimes her lips moved with the refrain.

¡Venceremos! Venceremos!
¡Guerrillero adelante, adelante!

After an hour, a boy made his way through the stalks, carrying galvanized buckets carefully balanced, one to each hand. When he came to her, she paused and lifted her head to the bright blue sky, put her hands to her back, wiped her face, and only then bent to the dipper of cool water that she drank a few swallows of, a few swallows only. She smiled at the thin, shy youth with the gap-toothed smile and big dark eyes that searched the ground as she spoke.

"Miguelito, this water is fresh? You didn't let the men piss in it?"

"No, Tia Graciela. How are you feeling?"

"I'll get through the day. Go on, along with you." She gave him a playful tap with the back of the blade, then reached for the next stand of cane.

When she saw the shadow stretching forward from behind her, she thought at first that it was the boy again. She was thirsty, and she said sharply, not pausing, "Miguelito, bring it up here. I don't want to take one step backward today."

"Spoken, at least, like a daughter of the revolution," said an unfamiliar voice. Her hand went tight on the stalk it had already grasped, then released it.

He stood with the sun behind him, so she couldn't see his face. She could see that he was a large man, though. And what they called a *gallego*—light-skinned. He wore boots but not a uniform. His clothes didn't look ragged, though, as hers and all the other workers' did.

Suddenly, she shivered. A cold wind seemed to blow over her, like the icy breath from the heart of the approaching storm.

"Are you speaking to me, *compañero*? I'm working now."

"I've been watching. You're a good worker."

"Who are you? What do you want with me? I have a *meta* to meet."

"I have a question for you, *mulata*—a question about certain worms."

"What worms?"

"The question is: 'The guitars, why do they sing to me of your tears, O Cuba?' "

She blinked sweat out of her eyes, staring into the sun and in front of it this blackness, this shadow, and suddenly she was so frightened, it was hard to breathe. He wasn't in uniform, so he wasn't from the army or the police. He carried a machete, but his boots were new and his clothes fit him and were not torn or patched, and he was muscular and well fed. So there was really only one thing he could be.

"Graciela Gutiérrez?"

"You're speaking to me. But who are you?"

"What do you say to my question?"

"I don't know anything about guitars. I don't have a guitar."

He came a step nearer, and she caught his face as the shadow of the cane brushed it. "You're not stupid. You have no education, but you're shrewd. Then why do you act stupid, like a *hija boba*?"

"I don't know what you're talking about, guitars," she said stubbornly, flicking her machete over the stub of a stalk. The flies started up at the motion, circled, settled again, feeding on the sweet ooze. Their buzzing seemed very loud. In the distance, men began a *décima*, a folk song.

"You are Graciela Lopez Gutiérrez. Born on a sugar estate near Esmeralda. Your father was a *tercedario*—"

"Yes. He was a sharecropper."

"You began living with Armando Guzman Diéguez, a son of a mill engineer, when you were fourteen. You have never been married. You have borne him three children, of whom one is still living. Diéguez has been convicted as an enemy of the revolution—"

"Not so—"

"He is an enemy of the people and of the revolution. In 1967, he was condemned by a tribunal and sentenced to five years in prison for setting fire to standing crops, an act of CIA-inspired sabotage. He pretended to reform and in good faith we released him and assigned him to productive labor at Central Number One seventy-six, with his family, just as he wanted. Then last year, he was caught stealing state property and sent again to prison for a further term of seven years." The man waited, then added, "Is all this correct?"

"It's correct. But it's not all."

"What do you mean, 'it's not all'?"

"I mean that yes, he stole, but this is not a just act, to condemn a man for stealing a bag of corn for his family."

"You are also a worm, the woman of a worm."

"You know nothing about my husband. His brother was killed by the Batistianos. Beaten, his legs broken, driven over with a jeep—"

"His brother would be disappointed in him."

"No, he would be proud. Armando fought against them, too. He took up a gun and fought."

"I find that hard to believe. All you worms are good for is talk."

"I have never spoken against the revolution."

"Someone is lying, then? All your neighbors are lying to us?"

"A measure of sand for a measure of lime."

"What does that mean?"

"That if you pay people for lies, you will get lies for your pay."

The man said harshly, "A woman with a tongue like yours should keep it firmly in her mouth. What were your people before the revolution? Sharecroppers. Now you have a free house and food. Your daughter's books, food, classes, everything paid for. Would she have gone to school before Fidel? Would she not be cutting cane like you or bearing bastards for the pleasure of some fat *latifundista*?"

She said reluctantly, looking at the dusty ground, "No, *compañero*. She would not have gone to school; that is certain."

"Yet still you people continue to speak against us, carry out thefts and sabotage. . . . I warn you, our patience is at an end. You can tell that to your fellow counterrevolutionaries."

"I know no other—"

"Be quiet. The revolution cannot be opposed. It moves from victory to victory, marching toward a future we only glimpse. Well, perhaps it will have one final gift for you." He laughed, a muted snort of contempt. "For you and the rest of the blind worms."

She glanced up in sudden fear, but where he had stood was only the sun now, shining so brilliantly between the swaying tassels of the cane that she could not look into it.

THE confrontation left her feeling ill and dizzy. So when she bent again, the water sprang into her mouth and she swayed to one side and vomited. She wiped bitter acid from her lips with her sleeve, staring at the ground with open, unseeing eyes.

Then her gloved hand reached out for the next stalk of cane.

She worked through the morning and when the sun was high had sheared eighty yards of field twelve feet wide and left eight huge square stacks of stalks behind her along the rows of what were now stubbled fields. Each stalk was sheared off close to the ground so that next year it would grow again.

A distant whistle signaled the end of the morning. She carefully put the hose back on her blade, took off her gloves, and turned and trudged back to the road. Other figures came out of the fields with her, most in ragged cotton work dresses or trousers, a few in army fatigues. They gathered by the road, squatting and exchanging a few words, and presently the trucks came into sight.

They rolled into the buildings at the crossroads and eased themselves down. No one could work now, at the peak of the day. Those who were too hungry to wait joined the line in front of the dining hall. The others found shade and huddled in it, waiting their turn to eat. Graciela looked at the line, then headed for the shade. When she had settled in it, a man joined her.

"Tomás."

"Feeling better today, Cousin?"

"I'm well, but . . ." She examined her cousin's familiar swarthy face. She wanted to tell him about the man in the cane field, but something held her back. What was it he'd said . . . "Someone is lying"? He meant the informers, the *chivatos*. Now she feared to speak her mind even to her relatives.

"They say this is the end of the harvest—the last day of cutting."

"I thought there were some fields left over by Alcorcón."

"They moved in an army unit and cut those yesterday. No, this is the last field, the one you're working."

"What are you doing today?"

"Work assignment. Cleaning out the hog pens."

"So that's why you smell like a pig."

She liked his quick grin. "I don't care. As long as they pay me, I'm happy. If that makes me a pig, I've been called worse. Any letters from Armando yet?"

"No."

"He hasn't written once since they took him."

"No," she said, wiping sweat from her hair. "I worry, Tomás. He wasn't well when they came for him. The first time he nearly died, and now he's not a young man."

"He'll return," said Tomás fiercely in a low voice. "If the Batistianos couldn't kill him, the Fidelistas never will. Are you eating? There's no line now. . . . What are they giving us today, *chico*?" he called to a passing boy.

"Rice, beans, a shred of pork, coffee, Comrade Tomás."

"Shall we go in?" Tomás said, offering his arm like a gentleman to a great lady. She smiled sarcastically and struggled up, grateful for his strong arm under hers.

"Thank you, Señor Guzman. Let us go in to dine."

* * *

THE afternoon was like the morning, only hotter, as if the whole earth itself was baking and nearly done. A group of older workers grew in the shade of the trucks, those who'd fainted or cut themselves, or couldn't finish for whatever reason. Graciela worked on, though her hands had gone numb and her shoulders felt like lead. Now she no longer thought about the man in the cane or about her missing husband, but only about the next stalk to be grasped and when the water would come around again. She finished her quota but kept on without slackening. The men and women sitting glumly by the trucks would not be paid today, though they'd labored through the morning. They hadn't made the *meta.* But once you had, you didn't stop. You had to keep cutting, for the revolution.

When at last the whistle sounded, she staggered back, straightening with a great effort. Her back was iron, twisted with pain. Her clothes were soaked dark and her hands shook as she fitted the hose back on the pitted, dulled blade.

SHE sat outside that evening on the rawhide *taburete,* which she'd taken out in front of the hut to escape the closed-in air that lingered from the day. And truly it was pleasant now, with the night coming, the breeze no longer a breath from hell, laden instead with the green perfume of spring flowers. She sat exhausted, not speaking as the children ran past her barefoot, only staring across the cropped dry fields that surrounded the *batey.* Her hands clutched her stomach, feeling, or perhaps imagining, a fluttering within.

She sat hunched, mind a hollow bowl, watching the coming of darkness. It was almost undetectable, the way evening came in the tropics; presaged only by an almost-imperceptible shadowiness, then, in seconds, the sudden descent of night.

Just then, she noticed something white off across the bare cut fields, out on the road. It was eclipsed by some ragged trees, then emerged again, closer. It was a person. No, two, one taller, one shorter.

Something about the tall one seemed familiar. She frowned but couldn't make it out. The darkness was falling swiftly now, like a black machete blade, and she was getting nearsighted; she'd noticed that.

But it *did* look like him. . . .

The two left the road where it cut away across the fields and they crossed toward her along a bare path.

She slowly put her fist to her mouth. The next moment, the chair tilted and fell, and she was on her feet, stumbling as her tired muscles gave way, but recovering and running, running toward the man who approached over the barren field. She screamed hoarsely as she stumbled over the cutoff stalks on the littered, hard-baked ground. Thought surfaced in her mind, then vanished in the manic tumbling of joy. *It was him.* They'd let him go. But why didn't he wave? Why did he stand waiting; why didn't he run to meet her?

Then she saw the boy.

Miguelito, looking sad and frightened, supported him under one arm; he was leading him.

Before she understood it, she had reached them, thrown her arms around him, screaming and sobbing in joy. She felt his arms come up around her, hesitantly at first, as if they could not believe what they held, as if her sturdy body were delicate as blown glass. He was so thin beneath the old white shirt. She thought, I must feed him. They didn't feed well at the prison. Those who had been there did not like to talk about it, but they always mentioned that. There were yuca and beans in the patch back of the house, but they weren't ready yet. . . . She'd fry plantains for him. He was really here, home! Oh Lord, she thought, you have delivered him.

"Graciela," Armando said then, in a strange voice. It was his, but thick, strained, saddened as she'd never heard it, even at Victoria's death. And when she looked up, she saw why the boy had been leading him, saw that his eyes were open, yet could not perceive her, or the open fields, or the curious children who came running; could perceive none of it; could see nothing at all of the world of light.

3

Johns Island, South Carolina

THE light leapt out at them long before they reached the grounds, wheeling and dipping and blazing with vibrating electric brilliance; and the music, too, loud ludicrous hurdy-gurdy amplified through buzzing speakers till it boomed out across the cars and pickup trucks and the rapt open faces of the children and the wary suspicious faces of the adults, closed and defensive, as if they feared and grudged themselves any part of wonder or joy. The circus had set up on a plot of empty land, an old pasture or cornfield somehow left unbuilt on while all around it suburbs had crept out. Now, as they neared, the boy tugged at the man's hand. "Let me go, Dad."

"No, buddy, better hold on. There's a crowd; I want you to stay close to me."

"The Ferris wheel! A Tilt-A-Whirl! Keen!" The boy tugged again, and the man smiled, looking down at the top of his head. "Dad, let *go* of my *hand. Please!*"

"Okay, but stay in sight. We'll need tickets to get on those, anyway."

Released, the youngster darted ahead, looking back only when he'd wedged himself into line for the first ride. He waved wildly to his father, who waved back. Touching his wallet lightly through his slacks, he looked around for a ticket booth.

He was standing in front of it, smelling the roasting peanuts and the caramel coating of the apples and the sulfur reek of gunpowder that drifted from the shooting gallery, when he saw them.

Suddenly, a dry feeling came in his throat, a faint falling away behind his chest as he stared out.

They stood on the open field beyond the last row of stalls. The glaring garish electric lights on the wheeling rides, the strings of incandescent bulbs that lighted keno and bingo and the games of chance and skill made the evening out there even darker. As he watched, money clenched in his damp hand, he saw two of them merge, melt, and then slowly dissolve into the darkness, till he could no longer make them out at all.

"How many, Mac?"

"What?"

"How many tickets you want, Mac?"

"Oh. Let's start with five dollars' worth."

Tearing his eyes from the dark, he said, "Thanks," then turned back toward the music, toward his son, hands clenching and unclenching as he looked openmouthed up at the Rocket to Mars.

Later he watched as the boy rotated high above him, fists white on the safety bar as the make-believe rocket twisted and rolled. Just watching it made him feel sick. But he was glad they'd come. This would be their last time together for a while. When he returned, the boy would be older; he'd have missed part of his life, and he regretted this even as he knew that he couldn't stop it, and wouldn't if he could. He had to grow up. Nothing could change that. But tonight they were together at the circus, and they were going to have fun.

When the ride was over and the attendant clanged up the safety bar, the boy struggled out. "That was great!"

"You liked that?"

"Hell yes. Why don't you go on it, Dad?"

"You're not getting me in one of those things. Maybe the Ferris wheel, though."

They went on a couple of the easier rides together and had withered greasy hot dogs. They pitched pennies and the boy won. At last the man glanced at his watch. "Ten o'clock," he said.

"Aw, Dad, we just got here. Can't we stay longer?"

"School day tomorrow, big guy. C'mon, Mom'll be waiting up for us. You remember where we left the car?"

WHEN he dropped the boy off, his wife was at the door, smiling at them both, and he winked as he turned away, calling, "I'll be back in a little while, okay?"

"Where are you going?"

"We need some milk. I'll pick up a quart at the Piggly Wiggly. Anything else we need?"

"We're out of your cereal," she said.

He stopped at the corner and got milk and cereal, then sat in the car with the engine running, there in the lot. His hands felt numb, gripping and releasing the padded plastic of the wheel.

You shouldn't do this, he told himself.

But he knew even as he thought this that he was going to. It had been too long and he would not be able to resist. He had tried not to want to; he had even, once, prayed not to want to. But it was something inside him that was different and unalterable—not something that he did, but something he was and would always be.

THE fairway was almost empty, dying back now toward night. Darkness trickled like black blood between the naked transparent bulbs. His loafers scuffed up dry dust that smelled of cotton candy and stale popcorn and old cowshit and oil from the engines that powered the wheels and rides and the sharp scared smell of his own body. The barkers and roustabouts and sharp-voiced stall keepers glanced incuriously past him as he strolled, sleeves rolled up in the lingering heat of the summer night. The grinning and crying masks leered down from the carousel; the painted horses nodded knowingly as they swept round in endless circles, the music jangling and bleating out into the night with forced desperate joy.

The shadows waited—out there, beyond where the last parents tugged the last whining kids toward the cars, past where the last teens threw baseballs at cascades of milk bottles.

He stood under the light and bought a Coke he didn't want. He drank it with a dry mouth, tossing the ice cubes back and crunching them as he looked blankly at the grinning faces of stuffed dinosaurs, rag clowns, cheap stuffed dolls. If they found out, he would lose everything. He'd seen it happen to others, men he knew and respected. Decades of work, sacrifice, achievement, none of that mattered. They'd been cast into the outer darkness, and there was no way back.

And his family—he *did* love them; he loved his wife, his son, his daughter. It was not their fault that love was, somehow, not enough. He could lose them, too. No, this was madness, idiocy. It wasn't too late to turn back. He tossed the empty cup toward a trash barrel and touched his slacks lightly. Wallet, car keys . . . he had only to get into his car, return to his wife, his home, his family.

Touching his lips lightly with the back of his hand, he walked slowly out from the circle of light. His chest was tight with mingled fear and yearning. Fear, because you never knew exactly what or whom you would encounter. He moistened his lips, eyes flicking around in the growing darkness around him. Avoid groups. Look for cover. Sometimes he thought it might be wise to carry a knife. But he never had, and up till now, he'd been lucky.

And yearning, because if just once in a long time you could take off the mask and breathe . . . then you could stand it. You could stand all the rest.

He walked slowly on, back rigid, as his shadow grew longer out in front of him and the field grew dark and the music faded to a whisper, a jangling discordant rumble—until he heard the whisper, so close and intimate, it seemed to come from within some secret chamber of his own divided heart.

II

CHARLESTON

4

U.S. Naval Base, Charleston, South Carolina

TWO months after *Barrett*'s commissioning, Lenson squinted into his stateroom mirror. His head pounded; his teeth hurt; his hair smelled like smoke. He'd been out late attacking the Fleet Bar's fifty-cent double martinis. His bike was still there. Fortunately, the ship was moored at Pier Juliet, close enough for him to stagger back to his bunk.

He closed his eyes, remembering Palma de Mallorca, when he'd stayed at the Brasserie till the taxis stopped running and had to walk eleven miles back to fleet landing. He'd made it just before dawn and collapsed on a bench by the seawall, waiting for the early boat. He'd come to with an old man groping him, muttering love Spanish.

He grimaced, felt around in the cabinet, and swallowed three commissary aspirin. He pulled on khakis and headed down the passageway.

Barrett's wardroom was luxurious compared with those of the ships he'd served on before. The carpet was deep blue. Armchairs covered in blue leatherette ovaled a dining table. The sitting area had a coffee table, corner sofas, and built-in bookshelves, though the only books yet were Crenshaw and Knight and *Customs and Ceremonies.* The bulkheads were off-white and the overhead pierced steel, with fluorescents too bright for a hangover. A gray joiner door led out to officers' country.

"Mr. Lenson, what can I get you? Hash bacon eggs, grits corn muffins."

"Just coffee. And some battery acid."

As he waited, he looked down the table. The other men at it wore khakis, the usual in-port uniform, except for Giordano, who was in coveralls.

Dan remembered the light cruiser he'd served on during his

third-class cruise. The wardroom was lily white then; a Catholic or a Jew was exotic. *Barrett* reflected a changing Navy. The majority was still Caucasian, but Burdette Shuffert, Dan's fire control officer, was black; so was Glenn Crotty, the main propulsion assistant, and Martin Paul, the first lieutenant. The operations officer was Felipe Quintanilla, a dark stocky man with a Hispanic accent that got stronger when he was excited. He'd grown up in a family of migrant farmworkers and managed to get himself appointed to the Naval Academy.

His musings on sociological change were interrupted by one of the ensigns, talking to Ed Horseheads, who was scanning the morning paper. "What's the news, Mister Ed?"

"The usual shit. Castro's making hostile noises again."

"Anything else?"

"*Threadfin*, that sub they lost. There's an article says it was probably a flaw in the welding."

"Welding, shit! The fucking Commies sank it." A lean, grizzled man in an old-style foul-weather jacket stenciled USS ENTERPRISE pulled out a chair next to Dan. He wore a knife and a flashlight in a black leather holster, aviator-style glasses, and had whitewalls to his haircut, though he was going thin on top. "Caught it out there alone and dropped the hammer on it. Morning, shipmates."

"How's it going, Chief Warrant?"

"I've had it better, but I've paid more."

CWO3 Jay Harper was the C3M officer, short for command, control, and communications maintenance, though most still called him the electronics maintenance officer. Dan had seen a lot of him since commissioning, since Harper was also the combat systems test officer, responsible for accepting the sensors and weapons as the yard finished installing them. This had made it awkward for Dan, taking over. The captain had developed reflexes, and even now, when something was wrong, he'd pick up the phone and call Harper. Dan was trying to cure him of that.

"Look like you got up on the leeward side, Lieutenant. Out steaming last night?"

"Cracked a couple. You, Chief Warrant?"

"Pussy and booze don't affect me like it does you young guys. Want me to take officers call?"

"I'm on deck. We ready for the conference?"

"Right after quarters."

Horseheads, still deep in the paper: "Christ, you see this? About the chief getting murdered?"

"What's that, Mister Ed?"

"Told you, J. J., call me that again and I'll shove a horseshoe up your ass."

"One of our chiefs?" said Dan.

"No, no. Yeoman chief on the *Biddle*. His wife was banging this guy who works at a Seven-Eleven. When the chief's in port, the guy works nights. He's at sea, the guy works days. Chief deploys, he moves in. Finally, he gets back from the Indian Ocean a week early and finds them both there. The wife hands the guy a knife, he ventilates the chief about twenty times, and the cops catch them hoisting him into a Dumpster."

"Any kids?"

"A boy. He was at Scout camp when they whacked his dad."

Shuffert grunted, "Why do we keep people like that around?"

"Now you're talking, Hoss," said Harper. "Microwave 'em both."

"Her, too?" said a slight man with a black beard. "Then who raises the child?"

"Hey, the cunt's been screwing the guy all along, gave him the knife. What kind of mother's that? You always was a softy, Mark. Being liberal, does that go with being kosher? It's genetic, or what?"

"Some of the most right-wing assholes I know are Jews," said Deshowits. "What's your excuse, Chief Warrant?"

Antonio and Pedersen, the stewards, came out of the pantry and ranged themselves on either side of Ensign Paul. He stared at the coiled brown mass that had materialized in front of him. A single pink candle burned on top of it. "What the fuck's this?" he said, pushing himself away.

Harper leaned forward. "Looks like shit. Smells like shit." He scooped a fingerful out. "Tastes like shit. Must be shit," he announced.

"You bastards—"

"All together now." And the table burst into:

"Happy birthday to you,
Happy birthday to you,
You look like a monkey,
And you smell like one, too."

"Gee, thanks," muttered Paul.

"It's chocolate and peanut butter, sir," Antonio offered. "Want a scoop of vanilla with it?"

A stocky man with lieutenant commander insignia came in. His blond hair stuck up on one side, as if he'd slept on it. "Hello, XO," somebody said, and George Vysotsky half-smiled. "Happy birthday, Martin," he said. His voice sounded hoarse.

"Did you hear the one about the bus driver?" Harper said to Deshowits.

"The what?"

"There's this bus driver, see? And it's the last part of his route, it's real late, and finally there's nobody on the bus except this nun. So they're talking, and he's asking her where she's going. She says back to the nunnery, that she only gets to go out once every ten years. And he says, 'That sounds terrible. What's it like being a nun.' And she says, 'Oh, it's not that bad, except that.' "

"Except that what?" said Horseheads.

"That's what the driver said, 'Except that what?' And she says, 'Well, sometimes we wonder. You know, about men.'

" 'Yeah?' says the bus driver.

" 'Are you married?' she asks him.

" 'No, I'm not married,' the driver says.

" 'Well, it's late, and we're all alone, and nobody will ever know. So why don't you show me what it's like?' the nun says.

"So he parks the bus and they go back where the bench seat is, and it's dark. And she says, 'But you know, we have to still be virgins when we go to Heaven. So I want you to do it the back way, all right?' So he does.

"So they're done and the driver's zipping up and he says, 'You know, I got to tell you something. I lied. I'm really married and got two kids.' And the nun smiles and says, 'Well, I lied too. I'm a queer, on my way to a costume party.' "

Vysotsky glanced down the table at Harper, but he didn't say anything, except to Antonio: "One over easy, bacon."

"Right away, XO."

Harper launched into a long story about an ex-skipper of his on the USS *John R. Craig*, DD-885. "The old 'hatchee-hatchee-go,' they called it. A chain-smoker, smoked filter tips, and when he was done with 'em, instead of stubbin' them out, he used to eat the butts. He only had two sets of khakis. He used to inspect them, when he got them from the laundry, for wrinkles along the seam, and if he found any, he'd have the supply officer up on the carpet and scream at him for hours.

"He got pissed off at the XO once. Left him on Hilo Hilo, wouldn't let him back aboard when they sailed. Something about letting the Filipinos steal all the wing nuts. He used to put the officers in hack and take the chiefs waterskiing behind his gig. Once he ran it up on Diamond Head, he was drunk as shit. But it was okay—none of the hookers got hurt."

Dan grinned at the ensigns and jaygees. "The old Navy," he told them. "The chief warrant's your living link with it."

"Yeah, I was on the fucking *Nautilus* with Captain Nemo. . . . Pass the go juice, Ensign."

Dan had another cup, too. He was starting to feel better as the aspirin kicked in. But he'd noticed it before in hangovers: Things occurred to you that didn't when your head was straight. Ideas came loose and drifted around, made different connections than they usually did.

Like now . . . He found himself musing as he looked down the table how they all seemed the same at first, and how then when you looked closer, all different. Horseheads with his baby face and hurt expression. Kessler, big and slow, in an old green cardigan with a piece of masking tape spotted with blood stuck to his chin. Harper, Deshowits, Vysotsky . . . He thought about the military people you saw in the movies, in books, how one-dimensional they seemed—either evil or heroes, but either way, without complexity or depth. It was probably true that they seemed simpler than civilians. They spent too much time with other men, for one thing. They didn't lead examined lives. But beneath that, they were as divided and contradictory as any other human beings.

He sipped coffee and looked thoughtfully around at them, feeling like them, yet unlike; one with them, yet separate. As he had all his life. Nor did he have the faintest idea why.

"NOW all hands to quarters for muster, instruction, and inspection. Officers' call," said the 1MC, the general announcing system. As they clambered toward the weather decks, Dan shivered in the morning wind, wishing he'd worn a jacket.

The exec held officers' call on the 03 level, in the sheltered area between the stacks. The department heads—Dan, Quintanilla, Cannon, Giordano, and Cash—aligned themselves in front. The others fell in behind them, spaced around antennas and lockers.

It was a clear morning, and he looked out past the black shoals of submarines and the gray bulks of other ships, over the sheds and cranes of Charleston Naval Shipyard. An oiler loomed in Dry Dock Five, her underwater hull hairy with weed. Beyond that sprawled North Charleston, one of the most depressing places he'd ever seen. To his left rose the spires of St. Michael's and the other churches.

And behind him was the Cooper River, sliding like melted silver slowly out to sea.

It felt as if he'd spent half his time aboard in shipyards. But that was usual for new construction. The first year saw you in and out constantly for tests and trials and availabilities. And since she was the last of her class, *Barrett* had a lot of catching up to do, installing backfit gear.

Backfit was tearing perfectly workable new gear out and replacing it with something even newer. Over the years a class was in production, new gear didn't stop coming out. But instead of trying to keep up, the Navy accepted the ship as it was originally ordered. Then, after commissioning, it put it back in the yard, tore out the gear that had to be changed, and installed the new stuff. It had always struck Dan as a no-brainer way of doing business.

But after a while, being in the yard got to you. First was the endless noise, a nerve-torturing cacophony of grinders, chippers, the shrill of warning bells, the hiss of compressed air. There were always strangers in the ship, and they left behind dirt and trash. They were stripping an old *Gearing*-class at the next pier, getting it ready to sell, and the wind carried grit and paint down every time it blew from the north.

Dan ran his eyes over her, feeling nostalgia and fear as his guts recalled *Ryan.*

Suddenly, before he could throw up his guard, a black wedge drove itself silently between himself and the world. At its foot, a line of white gleamed like bared teeth: the bow of an aircraft carrier, towering sudden and tremendous out of what had been utter blackness.

No, he thought. No! His fingers dug into his shoulder, fighting memory, hallucination, nightmare, with raw pain.

Ryan had been in company with a carrier task group, late at night, several hundred miles west of Ireland. Dan had been junior officer of the deck.

And someone had made a mistake.

He arm-wrestled will against memory, gritting his teeth, till at last the North Atlantic, the screams of burning men thinned and vanished. He took a shuddering breath, becoming aware of someone next to him: Quintanilla, brown eyes concerned. "You okay, Dan?"

"Yeah. Yeah," he said, swallowing. Christ, he had to get a grip.

"Attention on deck!"

"At ease," Vysotsky said, returning their salutes. The exec was wearing one of the new green nylon jackets, with his name stamped in gold. "Who's command duty officer today?"

"Me, sir," said Shuffert.

"Don't we have a CDO name tag?"

"I have it, sir. Sorry, I forgot to put it on."

"Take a look at the starboard side after quarters—about frame sixty. Okay, everybody, progress on yard work is the big number one today. . . ."

Vysotsky conducted a fast officers' call. He reminded them that the parking lots outside the shipyard were unsafe; another sailor had gotten mugged the night before; the men should use the buddy system after dark. Radio message traffic should be held down, a worldwide Fleet Minimize was in effect. When he dismissed them,

Dan huddled with his division officers. He glanced around at them—three young faces, one older: Horseheads, Kessler, Shuffert, Harper.

"Okay, first order of business today, like the XO says, look over what we got left to do before going to sea. Progress conference after quarters. Casey, I need a sonobuoy inventory today. Write it in message format for transmittal to Gitmo."

"Check."

"There's something dicked about the results we got off the self-noise test. Chief warrant will help you if you need to tear down the equipment."

"I'm not touching shit in that sonar room till you get your chief ping jockey squared away," Harper told Kessler.

Dan waited, but neither gave any inclination of telling him what that was about, so he went on. "Ed, here's a message about servo controllers. Check it out and see if it applies to us. Burdette, the test van—"

"It's on the pier. The chief's down checking out when they want to roll the scenario."

"Chief Warrant, what's broke?"

"Wacky two, fleetcom downlink."

"ETR?"

"Back to you on that."

"Okay, everybody," Dan told them, "XO's inspecting Zone Three today. Make sure your guys have their names on their bunks and one locker. Any locks on blank lockers get cut off. Go to it." He returned their salutes as they scattered, carrying the word to every man in his department.

THE progress conference convened in the wardroom a few minutes later. Dan pulled out a chair, joining the XO, the other department heads, and a middle-aged civilian in coveralls.

"Attention on deck," said Vysotsky. Dan got up again hastily.

"Sit down, gentlemen," said the captain, taking his chair. He wore trop whites, contrasting with everyone else in khakis. Antonio put a cup of coffee at his elbow, centerlined the server, sugar, and cream, then closed the pantry door. Leighty added two cubes, considered, stirring, then lifted his head.

"Good morning, everyone. We're not far from the end of our availability. Mr. Grobmyer's here to discuss what we have left to do."

They waited as he sipped, then set the cup down. "Now, I know things have been high tempo since commissioning. Independent operations off Florida, weapons loadout, structural test firing. Then the final contract trials and the shock test. The delay in Key West wasn't our fault, but we end up paying for it in missed sleep.

"But in just three weeks, we'll be in Guantánamo Bay, Cuba, starting refresher training. It is very important that we achieve a good score the first time through, as I think the XO has explained."

He waited till the chuckle spluttered out. "But one thing I do *not* want is for us to take on the kind of hurry-up attitude that lets the men cut corners on safety. There's time to complete everything, if we do it right the first time instead of rushing to get a block checked off. That's not how *Barrett*'s going to operate."

He nodded to the shipyard representative. "Mr. G., have at it."

"Combat systems first today—forward and aft Mark twenty-six missile launcher guiderail modification. . . ."

HE stood in the passageway, wondering what was going on. As the meeting broke, the captain had bent to the XO's ear. A few seconds later, Vysotsky had said, "Dan, Norm, can I see you a second?" He and Cash had moved up a couple of chairs. "The skipper wants to see you two later. Eleven hundred, his stateroom."

"Yes, sir. Anything we should bring?" the supply officer said.

"I don't think so."

"We'll be there, sir." And Dan had nodded, too.

Now he glanced at his watch. Time to get moving. He liked to see all his spaces once a day, every day—especially now, when they were getting ready for sea.

He started all the way forward, in the handling rooms for the forward five-inch. The gunner's mates were lubing the projectile hoist. Dan went over the Gitmo checkoff list with them, how they were going to fix the way the batten pins were secured in the projectile magazine. Aft of that was the handling room and magazines for the forward missile launcher. Horseheads and Chief Alaska were helping the yardbirds replace the guiderail. He observed briefly, then headed aft and upward.

In the data processing center, two computers hummed in the chill air. The others stood silent, shut down or racked open for maintenance. The bulkheads were lined with shock-mounted tape drives, memory units, racks of data tapes. His breath was a plume of white. "Coldest computer room in the fleet, sir," said Chief Mainhardt, looking up from where schematics and circuit boards were spread out over the spotless gray diamond-tread matting. "Want a Coke?"

"Sure," he said. One of the DSs reached up into the air duct and handed him an icy can. Dan drank half at one swallow, then looked around, shivering as frigid air crept under his khakis.

The DP center was *Barrett*'s brain. The five general-purpose mainframes, gray machines each the size of a refrigerator, ran four major systems. The first was the Naval Automated Communications System, which processed messages in and out through the high-frequency fleet broadcast and the new geostationary communications satellites.

The second was the Naval Tactical Data System, which shared target data automatically by radio among ships and aircraft over long distances.

The third was the sonar. Modern sonars depended on computers to filter distant sounds out of noise. So when *Barrett* was operating against submarines, one computer was devoted full-time to signal processing.

Most warships had these systems, or some variation of them. But the fourth, the newest and most sensitive, was one only *Barrett* had.

Surrounding him in these humming gray machines was the first operational installation of the Automated Combat Decision and Direction System in the fleet. ACDADS evaluated the threat picture from NTDS, calculated how the ship should react, and generated engine, rudder, and weapon orders.

After two months aboard, Dan was familiar with all this. But the thought of what it actually meant, when you put it all together and flicked the switches to automatic, still sent a chill up his spine. Because ACDADS didn't just advise you what it thought would be good tactics. *It could fight the ship without assistance from human beings.* Since ordnance now moved mechanically from magazine to gun or launcher, or else fired from sealed canisters like Harpoon, it didn't even need sailors to throw shells in the hoists.

In automatic mode, *Barrett* would be the first truly autonomous war machine ever created: a 560-foot, nine-thousand-ton fighting robot.

Of course, ACDADS was also incredibly complex; it had a mean time between failures of about an hour and a half. But past it, he could glimpse the dim shape of futurity: a warship with no men aboard at all.

"Sir, can I talk to you a minute?"

Dan turned. He studied the young, uncertain, yet somehow impudent face; the hand, holding out a special-request chit.

"What is it this time, Sanderling?"

"Application for Boost program, Lieutenant."

"Have you run this past the chief?"

"All I got to do is take the test; I got the time in rate."

One of the other men said, "Hell, Sanderling, you haven't hardly been off the dock yet."

"Shipyard counts as sea time. I'm eligible, the career counselor says."

A black petty officer said, "Yeah, maybe you better try bein' an officer. You sure ain't so hot as a seaman."

"You got to talk to me with respect, Petty Officer Williams. It ain't that hard. Is it, Mr. Lenson?"

"You get all the respect you deserve, you no-load pecker-puffer—"

"Knock it off, people," said Mainhardt.

When Dan let himself out into the passageway, he almost ran into Casey Kessler. He looked pensive, but he snapped his head up when he saw Dan.

Dan liked Kessler. His antisubmarine officer was Academy, too. When he said he'd check something out, he did; he had common sense. His wife was Navy, too. "How's Candace like the new billet?" Dan asked him.

"Good, but she's always hopping up to Norfolk or D.C. or Mayport."

"Your mom doing any better?"

Kessler traced a chill waterline with a finger. "She's still about the same. She hates the dialysis, but she'll die without it."

Dan couldn't think of anything to say but "Hang in there. Maybe it'll work out."

"Yes, sir." He looked back along the passageway, to see the big lieutenant still standing there, looking blankly at a fire alarm box.

He stopped at a scuttlebutt and drank as much icy water as he could hold. He had several more spaces on the 01 level, but they were unmanned. He made sure they were locked and then climbed the ladder.

The hangar smelled of isobutyl ketone, rubber, and cleaning compound, aircraft, MIL-C-43616C. It was empty and echoing, a huge cube of space that on deployment would house two helicopters. The 02 level was built around the five-foot-wide interior passageway leading forward from it. It was nonskidded instead of tiled, so supplies could be forklifted from the helo deck straight to the stores elevator for strikedown. The whole ship was built that way so weapons, food, parts, and fuel could be loaded without all-hands working parties. In the passageway, he stopped at a plaque that read: RESTRICTED AREA. KEEP OUT. AUTHORIZED PERSONNEL ONLY. A smaller plaque read *Crypto and Registered Publications Room.* When he tried the handle, the vault was locked from inside.

The lights were on in the Combat Information Center. Dan looked around, blinking at tote boards and radio remotes. Usually CIC was dark as a cavern. Lieutenant (jg) Lauderdale, the CIC officer, was thin and ash-blond. Dan asked him if the exercise had started yet. Looking surprised, he said it was over, that the guys were down decoupling the van. Dan squinted at the bulkhead clock, surprised to find it almost ten. "How'd it go?"

"Okay, except the ASWO console keeps going down. I called Harper; he's sending a guy up."

"How was the training?"

"Rough. Bombers and fighter attacks, an antisurface action, then more bombers simultaneous with a low-level missile attack from a patrol line of *Echo*-class subs."

"Did we survive?"

"No, but the carrier did."

He was feeling better now; the massive infusion of fluids helped. He ran up another ladder and went forward to the bridge. The IC men were reassembling a gyro repeater; the quartermasters were correcting charts. He went up another, external ladder and talked briefly to the fire controlmen working on the Phalanx. Then he continued aft, checking the rest of his spaces and lockers as he went.

AT 1100, he found Norm Cash waiting outside the commanding officer's stateroom. Dan knocked and went in, the supply officer following him.

Leighty's cabin was pretty much as issued: low table, sofa, armchair, desk, with bedroom through another door. There were books, though, secured in a steel rack, and a brass desk lamp tempered the overhead lighting. A studio portrait of the captain's wife and children was mounted over the desk. They stood waiting as water ran in the head. Then Leighty's voice: "Sit down."

Close up, Commander Thomas Leighty looked smaller than he did from a distance. His bearing was disciplined, but with the faint air of conscious poise Dan had noticed at the commissioning—as if he was acting the part of a commanding officer in a movie about the Navy. He was still in whites. Dan counted the rows of ribbons: five. The top left one, the highest earned, was the Bronze Star. He recognized the Purple Heart and several Vietnamese decorations as Leighty took the armchair and crossed his legs.

"How's the guide replacement going, Dan?"

"Okay, sir. They're fitting the new rails. We'll get them finished over the weekend."

"Good. How are you, Norman? . . . The subject today is missing funds."

Dan's head pounded again as he recalled the bucket of worms Lt. Marion Sipple had left him when he plunged to his death. Harper and Kessler, trying to handle their own work as well as that of the department head while they waited for Dan to report in, hadn't inventoried the controlled gear. Not till after Dan arrived had anyone realized what they had aboard didn't match what Sipple had signed for.

"Norm, what are we on the hook for, how much, and who to?"

"Sir, do you want that bottom line, or in excruciating detail?"

"How about medium density?"

"We've finished a complete inventory of the CS department. There's fifteen thousand, seven hundred dollars missing in the consumables accounts. In controlled equipage, we can't account for two night-observation devices, one portable radio, and some of the chemical warfare detection gear. Total value there's another twenty-two thousand, seven hundred and eighty-six dollars and eighty cents. Five silver bars are missing, total value nine hundred dollars—"

"What in God's name were we doing with silver?"

Cash looked at Dan, who said, "Sir, those are actually silver anodes. They're used for electroplating on tenders. They're a supply system item, but you're right. There's nothing we use them for on *Barrett*."

"Go on," said Leighty, supporting his chin on his hand and looking unpleasant.

"The biggest discrepancy," said Cash, "is the missing MAMs. Our allowance is almost three hundred items, three hundred separate cards. We've located two hundred and fifty-one. The last signature for the missing ones was Sipple's."

Dan was feeling more and more uncomfortable under the captain's stare. "MAMs," maintenance assistance modules, were kits of replacement components the techs used to do part swapping to isolate casualties. Each major system had about thirty spare cards. Typical ones were circuit boards, loop assemblies, and reference generators for the fire-control systems.

"How much are they worth?"

Cash said, "Uh, the total cost new was a hundred and seventy-six thousand, two hundred and eighteen dollars."

"Now try the bottom line."

"For everything that's missing, two hundred and fifteen thousand, six hundred and four dollars and eighty cents. Sir."

The captain let that bounce between the overhead and the carpet, then looked at Dan. "And the XO tells me you have no idea where it all went. That right?"

Dan felt guilty, then indignant. *He* hadn't lost the stuff. He hadn't even been aboard. But he just said, "No, sir."

"Norm? How about you?"

"That's about it, sir. When Lieutenant Lenson came to me with the discrepancies, I thought, well, maybe the yard burned something out installing it and used them for spares, something like that. But we went through the records and got zip. The very last record we have on those serials—it's a quarterly requirement, to inventory MAMs. The last chop on them was Marion's."

"So where are they?"

"I don't know, sir."

"Are they worth stealing?"

"Sir, obviously the night scopes and the radios were, and the silver. But MAMs, I don't think so. There're minute amounts of gold and silver in the contacts, but it wouldn't be worth much even after you melted it out."

"Dan?"

"I agree, sir. It's not something you can take down to the pawnshop. Unless you got your own personal busted SPG-fifty-one D fire control radar, it's not a lot of use to you."

"How are we doing on replacements? And who's going to pay for them?"

"I was talking to the N-four at squadron, sir, and he says we are."

"That's going to be a hell of a chunk out of your budget, Dan."

He was horrified. "Sir, that shouldn't all come out of my hide. That gear's used for repairing Operations equipment, too."

"It's your gear, Mr. Lenson. Suppose the screw falls off. Are you going to volunteer part of your budget to pay for it? On the basis that it pushes the whole ship around, not just the Engineering Department?" Dan couldn't think of a response, so Leighty turned back to Cash. "As I recall, we notified the Supply Center as soon as we realized we had a discrepancy."

"There's an audit scheduled next week, sir."

Leighty tapped the tips of his fingers together, then placed them on his upper lip. As if, Dan thought, to illustrate Deep Thought. "All right," he said at last. "Mr. Lenson, I got a call this morning from the chief staff officer. He asked if you could report to squadron this afternoon at thirteen hundred."

"Me, sir?"

"Yes. I assume this is what it's about, which is why I wanted to clarify it before you went over. Will you see what they want?"

"Uh, yes, sir. I'll be there. Who should I—"

"Report to Chief Hone. I'd suggest whites."

DAN stood outside, feeling as if his pocket had been picked. Leighty was sharp. He communicated well. He made decisions. But there was something Dan didn't like, didn't trust about him.

Get real, he told himself. The real reason you suddenly don't like him is that he's (a) asking you questions you have no answer for and (b) making you pay for stuff this poor bastard Sipple either lost or stole before he bit the weenie. A quarter of his budget . . . hell, he was doing everything but recycling toilet paper already.

And what was this about reporting to squadron?

"Hey, shipmate. You okay?"

He looked up, to find Jay Harper studying him. "Yeah, Chief Warrant. Just a little . . . session with the skipper. About that missing gear."

"It's hurt us on this availability. They expect us to have the full allowance when they come to plug in the new cards."

"I was thinking, while he was asking me . . . who would want MAMs? They're not good for anything; you can't sell them. Could another *Kidd* or *Spruance* use them?"

"That's about all I can think of who'd want spare boards. But selling them to another ship, that's kind of out of the cumshaw league."

"I guess so. Hey, got your jeep here?"

"My jeep? Yeah, why?"

"Can you run me over to the club? I left my bike there, and I'm going to need it this afternoon."

"Sure. Oh, and hey. I was going to ask, how about coming over for dinner tonight? Meet Bonnie and the girls. We'll barbecue some ribs—"

"Sounds great, but I've got a date. Rain check, maybe?"

"Sure. Need that ride now? How about we grab lunch, knock down a beer?"

"No beer. But lunch sounds good, if we make it fast. Meet you on the quarterdeck."

Whites, he thought, rattling down the ladder. Shit, did he have a clean set of whites?

5

TO his relief, the bike was where he'd left it. He threw Harper a farewell-and-thanks salute, then exchanged hat for helmet and swung a leg over the seat.

He'd started riding last year, knowing even as he bought the bike that it was a classic male response to divorce. The first time he took it out on the road, he realized why. When you blasted up through the gears, engine howling between your legs, there was no way you could be depressed. It was so much fun, he was surprised it was legal. He rolled out of the lot and gunned onto Hobson Avenue, swerving sharply to avoid a pickup full of marines. You had to *be there* on a bike every second, nowhere else, or some granddad would turn left without signaling and you'd end up an inattentive grease spot.

Destroyer Squadron Six headquarters was in a concrete-block building at the head of Pier Sierra. He parked behind a fence made of anchor chain painted white and replaced his helmet with his combination cap. He checked his shoes, centered his buckle, and walked in.

Chief Hone told him to go right in, that the Commodore was expecting him. Dan's heart sank. He'd never met the squadron commander. He fingered his ribbons, took a deep breath, and knocked.

"Lieutenant Lenson, Commodore. Captain Leighty said—"

The man behind the desk glanced up angrily, as if Dan had interrupted him. Suppressing his surprise—the Commander, Destroyer Squadron Six, was not only extremely large and heavily muscled but also the first black senior officer he'd ever seen—he stammered, "—to report over here. Sir."

Commodore Barry Niles placed two large hands flat on his desk. He stared at Dan, freckled lids lowered, mustache downturned over a scowl. His eyes were small and black and hostile. Then he nodded to someone behind him. "I believe you know Commander Byrne."

"Hello, Dan."

The other officer had been standing by the window, which was why Dan hadn't seen him. He was barrel-chested and swarthy in whites, still wearing the amber-tinted sunglasses he affected even indoors. Dan blinked as they shook hands.

He'd met John Anson Byrne in the Mediterranean, where they'd suffered together under Isaac Sundstrom. Byrne was still tall, still distinguished-looking. He had a master's in international law, and Dan had seen him translate flashing light between two Soviet destroyers.

"Jack! How are you? What are you doing here?"

"I'm Commodore Niles's N-two. Would have looked you up, but I didn't realize you were on *Barrett* till now."

N-two was Intelligence. "Well, it's nice to see you again, sir. Congratulations on making commander."

"Congratulations to you, too. Those railroad tracks look good on you."

"Please sit down, Lieutenant," rumbled Niles, behind them.

Dan sat, his mind running data at a high bit rate. As Commander, Destroyer Squadron Six, Niles had the commanding officers of twelve destroyers working for him. For him to see Dan . . . He hoped Niles hadn't noticed his surprise. . . . He shut his brain off and concentrated on what the commodore had to say.

"Commander Byrne and I have been discussing you," Niles rumbled. His diction was high English; Dan thought he spoke like a lawyer. One of the big hands moved to a glass dish, selected a red spheroid, and inserted it slowly into his cheek. "I don't know if you realize this, but you have a modest notoriety in the fleet. There is a story going the rounds about a statement you made before a court of inquiry."

"Uh, yes, sir."

"It's rare for a man to have the . . . courage to make a statement like that. Demanding to be held accountable, when he had already been acquitted."

"The Commodore was wondering," Byrne said, still looking toward the window, though he was seated, "what made you say that. Of course, you were injured at the time. Under medication. But why exactly did you insist you were responsible?"

Dan thought about that. It had been years ago, and he wasn't sure it had been courage that made him do it. But they were waiting. . . . "I guess just what I said to the court, sir. That it was unfair to pin all the blame for *Ryan*'s loss on a dead man. Commander Packer couldn't answer for himself. I thought there was a lot more blame lying around than anybody was picking up."

Niles rumbled, "Rear Admiral Hoelscher and Captain Javits were issued letters of admonition for negligence. Commander Bryce and his associates were found guilty at court-martial and sentenced to prison."

"Yes, sir, but what about the Chief of Naval Operations—who sent us up into the Arctic when we could barely cross Narragansett Bay? Congress—the people who made us steam without repair parts, without proper manning—"

"I see what you mean," said Niles to Byrne, cutting across Dan in midspeech like a battleship cutting across a frigate. "Yes, I do. In a sense, it is admirable—but in a sense, it is not."

They both regarded Dan, making him feel like something misshapen in a jar. Then Niles pressed an intercom. The chief answered. "I need that letter now," he said. "Lieutenant, it was interesting meeting you. I'm glad your career and your motivation have survived the—vicissitudes of your naval service. Thank you for coming by."

Dan stood for a moment, unsure what to do. The Navy didn't salute indoors, and neither officer extended his hand. Niles solved it for him, saying dryly, "That will be all, Lieutenant. Dismissed."

BYRNE led him through an office into an inner sanctum. Its door was steel and had a push-button combination lock. There were no windows, just locked filing cabinets, a microfiche reader, a hot plate. "Coffee?" he said to Dan. "Cups in the drawer. That your cycle out front?"

"Yeah."

"New?"

"I got it after Betts left."

"You two split? I'm sorry to hear that. She showed a lot of guts in Syria. And your little girl—what was her name?"

"Nan."

"Cute as hell. Anything I can do?"

"No."

"It's rough. Rosemary and I—it takes a special kind of woman to stay married, raise a family when you're not there half the time. I assume she got custody?" Dan nodded. "So you're alone here."

"Basically."

"Seeing anybody?"

"A girl I met, a teacher."

"Serious? Bring her over."

"It's not that serious." Dan sipped at the coffee, burned his mouth. "Commodore Niles—he's uh, different."

"Quite a character, eh? One of the few ex-football players I've ever met who astonishes me intellectually. I wouldn't be surprised if we pick up the paper in ten years and he's Chief of Naval Operations."

"Where's he out of?"

"University of Georgia, surface nuclear engineering; he's had *Barney* and *California.*"

"What are those red things he was sucking?"

"Atomic Fireballs. He calls them 'the Devil's eyeballs.' "

"Uh, Jack . . . you mind telling me what this is all about? Because you seem to know, and I guess he does—but I don't. Is it about the MAMs?"

"The . . . oh, the spare parts you lost—"

"*I* didn't lose them."

"Tender spot, eh? No. Basically, he just wanted to meet you."

"Why does he want to meet a lieutenant without his commanding officer present? Am I that much of a freak?"

"As a matter of fact, there's a reason." Byrne went around his desk and sat down. "Relax! Mind if I—"

"It's your office, sir."

Byrne toyed with a pipe, then decided against it. "We were looking over the complement on *Barrett.* I noticed your name and mentioned that I had served with you. He asked about you and I told him. Then he asked some more questions, such as when you had joined the ship."

"Why would he care?"

"Dan, let me start off like this. Most Navy people are like the fitness report form says, typically excellent, top ten percent, et cetera. The kind you want around you in case the balloon ever goes up."

Dan remembered Byrne habitally circled a topic before approaching it closely enough to bite. "Yeah," he said cautiously.

"Yet you and I have both occasionally run into some off-the-wall puppies. Sundstrom, for one. Yes? No?"

"True."

"Well . . . I wonder if you have noticed anything like that recently."

"Like Sundstrom?"

"No, not necessarily. Anything out of the ordinary."

"I don't know, Jack. That's a pretty broad question."

"Have you noticed anything strange aboard *Barrett* since you joined her?"

"Anything *strange*? Jack, what *is* this? Why are you asking *me* this stuff?"

"Because I'm the squadron N-two?"

"I mean, talking about strange, *this* is *strange.* Has Commodore Niles asked Captain Leighty if he noticed anything 'strange'?"

"He may have. I can't say. Are you saying we should?"

Dan was feeling more and more unreal. He trusted Byrne, but jumping the chain of command like this was not the way the U.S. Navy operated. Then again, every surface line officer knew that the 1600's, the intelligence corps, marched to a different drummer—one only they could hear.

"You know, Jack, if I didn't know better, I'd read that as asking me to be some kind of informer."

Byrne laughed and picked up the pipe again. "Dan, the Navy's not such a big place. Stay around a few years, you get a rep. Especially if you've been involved in anything . . . controversial. Want me to tell you yours?"

"If it's the answer to what I asked you."

"You have a rep for honesty, but not diplomacy. Put another way, you tend to speak up in situations where the intelligent—meaning safe—thing to do would be to keep a low profile. What I am asking today is, if you saw a situation developing that felt wrong to you, would you be willing to give me the nod to send in the elephants?"

"Elephants?"

"The Naval Investigative Service."

Dan thought about that. The NIS was one of those agencies nobody liked, because its main job was to keep the rest of the Navy in line, like Internal Affairs in a police department. Usually, you only heard about it after it had wrapped up a case, and not much then. He said cautiously, "You think there's something going on aboard *Barrett*?"

"Not specifically. If we thought there was, we'd be aboard right now grilling everybody from your skipper on down. It's Navy-wide. I'm discussing this same issue with people on other ships, and the same thing is happening at Desron Four and Group Two and Subgru Six and the minesweeps, too." Byrne hesitated. "I didn't tell you this?"

"I never heard it."

"What this thing is, certain quarters are starting to wonder if there's a hole in our crypto."

"In our *codes*?"

"Yeah. See why they're going to general quarters? If somebody could penetrate those, we wouldn't have any more secrets. They'd be able to read everything right off the air, ballistic missile targeting, alert condition, execute orders, position of our submerged submarines, anything they wanted."

"But I thought our codes couldn't be broken. They're so random, and we change them so often—"

"Theoretically, that's true," said Byrne. "You'd need two things to break our message traffic. Both a current key list and a complete operating model of the decrypting/encrypting equipment. Neither of which the other side has. But the question always remains: Is the theory right?" He waved a match over the pipe, exhaled aromatic smoke.

Dan put two and two together. "Does this have anything to do with the Fleet Minimize?"

Byrne shrugged, a gesture Dan remembered from the Med when someone asked him something he didn't want to answer. Behind the amber glasses, like barriers against those not cleared for access, he didn't give anything away for free. "So, can I count on you?"

"I still don't know what you want."

"Let's go over it again, then. Certain people we all work for are getting an uneasy feeling. I can't be more specific, okay? But if there's something wrong, it means that our normal ways of preventing 'accidents' aren't working. So we want a back channel in place to catch any vague suspicions things may not be the way they're supposed to be."

Dan started to ask, Why can't you go through the chain of command? Then he thought better of it. He could figure that out himself. If they weren't using the chain of command, that meant they weren't sure they could depend on the links.

"This is all about as clear as bean soup, sir."

"Well, let me elaborate," said Byrne, rubbing his long nose thoughtfully. "Officially, what I am asking you to participate in is called the Passive Listener Liaison. It's a security-awareness program that operates covertly within the command structure. Certain key individuals are selected for their alertness and trustworthiness. We train them on what to look out for—certain indicators, certain profiles that may point to trouble. We want people we can rely on to detect suspicious activity and report it directly to us." Byrne looked away. "You won't be expected to testify against anyone. Your name will never be made public. The PLL just acts as a watchdog. If he signals us there's cause for concern, then we start a formal investigation."

"This is pretty . . . surprising, sir. I didn't know the Navy did things like this."

"Wouldn't do us any good if everybody knew about it, would it?"

"Probably not. Would I be the only one aboard *Barrett*?"

"You'll never know if there's another, or more than one. But, how about it? Feel like helping us out?"

Dan shook his head. "Better count me out of this one, Jack. Don't take it personally, but I just don't like the sound of it. It doesn't sound real . . . honorable."

"Whoa."

"I know, that's irrelevant. . . . If NIS wants a mole inside the ship, why don't they put an agent aboard? Give me a little credit, Jack. *Barrett*'s being singled out. Why?"

His chair creaked as Byrne leaned back. He relighted the pipe, which had gone out as he talked. Finally, he locked his fingers behind his neck and met Dan's eyes again. "*Barrett*'s a brand-new ship, a very valuable ship. It has systems aboard that are of considerable interest. It might be a target—or become a target—for that reason alone."

Dan grinned. "Sir, remember Comphibron Ten? On the flag bridge, trying to grease the right decision past Double-Nuts without him noticing? I can tell when you're bullshitting me. I can hear it in your voice! What's really going on?"

"Okay, you asked for it. How do you feel about homosexuals?"

"*What?*"

"Homosexuals. Gays. Queers. How do you feel about them?"

Dan remembered to close his mouth. "I don't know any."

"Oh, you probably do."

"I don't think so. Anyway, I've never met one." He remembered the groper in Palma. "That I knew, I mean. How do I feel . . . well, my experiences to date have not been real pleasant."

"Childhood? Youth? Navy?"

"On liberty . . . and a couple guys got me in a basement once and felt me up. I must have been about eight."

"Those would be pederasts, not homosexuals. They go for children, regardless of sex."

"Well, I don't know about the fine distinctions."

"So the reaction is negative but uninformed."

"I guess so. There aren't any in the Navy, I know that."

"Really," said Byrne.

"Yeah. Why are you asking me that?"

"Because maybe you're right. Maybe you need to know why we're concerned."

He nodded, and the N-two said, "Let me flash back to something that happened a couple of months ago. *Threadfin*."

Dan said, surprised, "The sub we lost in the North Pacific?"

"Right."

"The papers are saying it was one of the welds."

"We don't think it was a structural failure."

"What do you mean?"

"There's a rumor that one of the torpedomen aboard was gay. He had a big insurance policy made out to his shoreside lover. There are those who think he tampered with one of the warheads. If a Mark forty-eight went off in the torpedo room, at depth, that would be it. They all got blown to hell. Of course, we won't know till we actually find debris."

"Holy smoke." Dan reflected on that. "But what has that got to do with—"

Byrne shrugged. "Maybe nothing. Or maybe just that, if we'd

had a PLL aboard that boat, we could have saved a hundred and twelve men."

"Jesus, Jack! So if something happens on *Barrett* and I don't blow the whistle, it's my fault?"

"No, not exactly. I guess what I'm really saying is, we really, really are concerned about this. We know there's something rotten, but we don't know where. And I'm asking you to get on the team and help us out."

Dan rubbed his mouth, hoping he wasn't making another bad decision. "Sir, I want to help, but this is just not the kind of thing I think we ought to be doing. I thought we were supposed to trust our people, not spy on them."

Byrne studied him for a couple more seconds while Dan tried without success to interpret his expression, then shrugged. He tapped out the pipe briskly, ran a cleaner through it, and propped it on a rack. "All right. That's clear enough. I'll just remind you that this is all classified, everything we just discussed. And I expect you to treat it as such under the provisions of the relevant statutes."

"What, that's all? You're not going to tell me what you mean?"

"Well, you've made it clear you don't want to cooperate. So there's no point in going any further, is there?" Byrne glanced at the door, got up. "It was good seeing you again. That invite still stands. I know Rosemary would love to see you again."

"Well . . . thank you, sir." He wanted to backtrack, try to find out more, but Byrne didn't give him a chance. He just led him out to where yeomen and officers were working, gave him a card with his home number, shook hands again, and said so long.

Standing outside, he buckled his helmet as the bike idled, drawing glances from passing sailors. He was trying to mesh it together in his mind. But no matter how he tried, the gears didn't mate. All he ended up with was that something was loose somewhere—something that was making the top brass nervous. And shit, as everyone who'd ever been in the service knew, rolled downhill.

He rolled the bike off the stand, swung aboard as he let in the clutch, and gunned it back for the ship.

6

RACKS of glittering bottles reached higher than his head, aisle on aisle. GIN. SCOTCH. VODKA. SAVE WITH SUMMER PRICING AT YOUR NAVY EXCHANGE. Dan rubbed his mouth, considering. Enough for the weekend, and Beverly would probably expect him to take a bottle to this thing tonight. . . . He got a fifth of White Horse, a fifth of Smirnoff, and two of Seagram's gin, then added a clay-colored bottle of Lancer's at the wine section. Standing in line to check out, he remembered and went back for two cartons of Benson & Hedges 100's.

Outside, the late-afternoon sun slammed off four lanes of hoods and grilles and fenders locked together like a Rubik puzzle on Rivers Avenue: shipyard traffic, base traffic, rush hour. Hot air sucked through engine after engine until it was a brown roiling haze. He oozed with it, blipping the throttle and dragging his boots along the potholed concrete. Sweat matted his hair under the helmet and ran down his back. He thought about stopping for a cold beer on Spruill. Cars were pulling left toward it at the light ahead.

There was a Spruill Avenue outside every shipyard and naval base in the world, though they went by different names. They smelled the same: stale beer, stale butts, urine-soaked alleys. What old-time sailors had called a Fiddler's Green: hookers and hoods and two-for-one drafts in smoke-filled pool clubs, pawnshops and tattoo parlors, go-go clubs and used car lots with fluttering plastic banners. The North Charleston police liked to put a policewoman in fishnets and fuck-me heels at the corner of Spruill and Reynolds, just outside the gate. They took down twenty or thirty guys on a good night. The locker clubs had gone once civvies were allowed aboard ship, and the all-night greasy spoons and live sex shows were falling to fast-food franchises and video clubs. But though the shop fronts changed, the feeling never did, and maybe never would as long as there were sailors and those who preyed on them. He extended an arm to turn. But then he remembered the bottles shock-corded to the seat, that he had a woman waiting for him, so he dropped it and went straight when the light changed.

When he pressed the buzzer of the town house, she opened the door as if she'd been waiting just inside. She was barefoot, wearing a green embroidered dressing gown. He held up the bag. "Got you something."

"Two cartons! Thanks." He felt her naked leg engage his. Some faint revulsion made him want to pull away. Then, behind her, he saw the kid watching from the door of his room. He took his hand off her ass and said, "Hi, Bartholomew."

"Hi, Lieutenant Dan." His face lighted up and he ran out into the living room.

His mother said something about getting a drink and disappeared into the kitchen. Dan looked down at the boy, then picked him up. He yipped and clutched. "Whoa, don't grab the uniform, okay? How are you, Bartholomew?"

"Billy, Lieutenant. You smell like motorcycles."

"Sorry, I forgot. Billy."

"Did you fight any Russians today?"

"No, we just mainly fought ourselves today."

"Scotch and water? Or something with gin?"

"Scotch, with ice. Look in the bag—"

"I still have some you brought last week."

Billy wanted a ride, so Dan gave him a merry-go-round for a couple of minutes. His head whacked into an overstuffed chair, but he didn't want to stop. Dan grinned, planing him up toward the ceiling.

His mother came out with glasses. "Oh—don't be too rough. He loves it, but . . . Now don't mess his uniform, Billy. You'd better go back to your room."

"Oh Mom, do I hafta? Lieutenant Dan and me—"

"Your room, I said, young man. Jennifer will be here in a little while. Dan, want to come upstairs? I'm still getting dressed. Billy, stay down here. You can watch TV till we come back down, okay?"

Dan looked back as they climbed the stairs, to see the boy's saddened eyes watching him.

"DID you like that?" She rolled over, tucking the sheet between her legs, and propped her head on her arm. He kneaded between his eyes, wishing the knot would go away. Fucking depressed him, he didn't know why. "Yeah, it was great," he said, glancing at the door. The boy's eyes—he couldn't get them out of his mind.

"Yeah," he mumbled, looking upward to where chandeliers glittered through a beveled fanlight.

A butler showed them down a narrow, creaking hallway, past rooms of fragile-looking antiques. Gentlemen in neck cloths and ladies in bonnets stared down from the walls. A dumb anger welled in him. He felt out of place, out of body in someone else's clothes and his bike-riding boots.

"Mind the step, ma'am, sir," said the butler, holding the door, and Dan followed Strishauser's erect, expectant back down again into a walled garden dark with greenery and shadow. Lights glittered above gentlemen in tuxedos and ladies in cocktail dresses, and behind them, in darkness that stretched back and back, fireflies sparked and drifted in evanescent reflection. Flambeaux flared over white-draped tables glowing with old silver. Hearing the soft Charleston accents, he felt even more like a just-arrived immigrant.

"The bar's over there—"

"What do you want?"

She said gin and tonic, then went smiling toward hands that reached out to touch, to welcome her.

He got two drinks, but instead of taking hers to her, he stood at the edge of the crowd, gulping his own till the alcohol warmth flicked on and slowly spread, relaxing, comforting, till he felt no more out of place here than anywhere else.

"Saw you come in with Beverly."

An older man with thinning hair and a supercilious smile introduced himself, but Dan responded in monosyllables, till the man excused himself and went toward a knot of people beneath a palm.

Time went by. He had a couple more drinks, talked to an old lady who quizzed him about when the Navy was going to admit women. He told her he didn't know, said he was only a lieutenant.

Later he found himself in line at a buffet table, staring at Strishauser's back. He touched it with his glass, and she winced and turned a displeased face. He stared blankly at her. Her face came back, concerned now. "Are you having fun?" she asked him. "Where did you go? I turned around and you were gone."

"You didn't tell me this was going to be dressy."

"It's not 'dressy,' Dan. The Densons came casual."

"Everybody I've seen's been in a suit. I don't know any of these people."

"You've met the host and hostess. And I know I introduced Tony and Bess, and Mrs. Chassen, Mr. Parkey. . . . There's someone—isn't he in the Navy? You could talk to him—"

"He's a *rear admiral*, Beverly."

"That sounds so funny . . . 'rear' admiral. . . . Well, does that mean you can't speak to him? Why don't you go down into the gallery after you have something to eat. Maybe you'll like it better there."

He liked the gallery better. It was a basement, and the low overhead was arched and the floor old hand-laid brick. There was a band and he smelled pot smoke. He got a beer out of a tub of ice and cracked it, looking around at the art that covered the rough walls, and at the women. There were dozens of them talking, drinking, looking at the pictures and sculptures, which were on pedestals, in niches that must once have held candles or lamps. He leaned against the curved wall, thinking about women.

The divorce had been like being released from prison, or from many prisons. The first was what they'd drilled into him in church: that women were chaste vessels to protect and worship. And against that was the way his father treated his mother: the shouting, the bullying, the beatings. And in some kind of weird rebellion, he'd built the last one himself: his self-imposed faithfulness to Susan.

Betts had been the first girl he'd gone to bed with, and the only one till after the divorce. Closing his eyes, he saw her again . . . hair dark as oiled walnut . . . legs tanned dusky, breasts with a hint of saffron. Compared with her, other women still seemed oversized and hairy. Other men took advantage of being overseas. He never had. Instead, he'd done what he had to do; done it thinking about her, eyes fixed on her picture, pinned to the bunk above his. There hadn't been much emphasis on chastity at the Academy, but there was on honor. And if a wedding vow wasn't giving your word, then what was? Back then, he'd thought that if he did what was right, nothing bad could ever happen. . . .

You fucking fool, he thought, draining his beer. Right or wrong didn't make any difference. They fucked you one way or the other. His hands shook as he fished out another brew, cocked it, and put it to his head.

Since then he'd become like everyone else. If you could get it, take it. And it seemed like you could. That changed everything, the heady prospect of sex with every woman you met.

"Excuse me, friend, can I get to the beer?"

He yanked his tie down and strolled through the rooms, drifting from picture to picture, looking over the women more than the art. They glanced back boldly or dropped their eyes; he imagined each naked. Then his eyes, flicking around the walls, suddenly froze.

At first glance, it was crude, angular and stylized. But its misshapen figures huddled in the corners of blank white spaces conveyed alienation and fear. It looked like something drawn by a battered child. A short woman in a green dress was standing in front of it. He looked around, saw no Beverly, and walked over. "That's quite a piece," he said.

When she looked up, he saw she was drunk, breasts falling out of her dress. Green velvet and soft white flesh, lost eyes that attracted him instantly. Flushed cheeks, a hand that trembled as it held a martini glass. Or maybe not *drunk*—she had a hand-rolled cigarette in one hand.

"You like it?"

"It's grim."

" 'Grim' is good. I like 'grim.' So you like it?"

"I guess so."

"I did it."

"Did what?"

"This."

He realized she meant the painting, and he looked at it with new eyes. "You're an artist? *This* artist? Wow. You're"—he leaned to read the signature—"S. Bond?"

"Baird. Sibylla Baird. I was probably stoned when I signed it." She chuckled and swayed. "I know who you are. Saw you with Beverly. I know Carl, her ex. Isn't that his jacket?" She touched his lapel.

"Uh-huh." He looked at the painting again. The figures were childlike, stick trees, a round yellow sun with lines coming out of it, a corkscrew of smoke spiraling out the chimney of a house. But there was no comfort, only alienation and loneliness and horror. "It's not fun to look at. But I can't look away."

"You know why, don't you? Because that's the way you feel inside."

"I guess," he said slowly, still staring at the stick figure in the corner. It was a child, he was pretty sure. "It makes me feel . . . like I did when my dad would come to beat me. I hid under the bed once. I thought it'd be too narrow for him to come in after me. But he just lifted up the whole bed and pulled me out from under it."

"You know what it reminds me of?"

"No."

"Looking in the mirror when I was fourteen. Lying on the bed, with my stepfather fucking me from behind."

"Jesus," he muttered.

"I saw you by the beer tub. You looked like you wanted to kill somebody. Was that who you wanted to kill? Your father?"

"I was thinking about my ex-wife."

"What did she do to you?"

"It's a long, boring story."

"She fucked somebody else. And you can't forgive her."

"I pay too much alimony," he said bitterly, looking away. Why was he telling her this?

"If she fucked around, why does she get alimony?"

"It was simpler no-fault. There's a kid involved, my daughter."

"You *do* sound bitter. What about Beverly? Are you in love with her?"

"No."

"Sleeping with her?"

"I don't understand why you're asking me all this stuff."

"You don't screw and tell. That's unusual. Interesting. A close-mouthed type."

He looked down at her breasts, and she said, "They're a lot bigger than hers. Is that what you're thinking?"

"Well . . . yeah."

"You ever read Erica Jong?"

"No."

"She has a fantasy. A man she's just met—she doesn't even know his name. They have what she calls a 'zipless fuck.' Because there are no zippers, no buttons, everything just falls away. Do you have fantasies like that?"

"I'm having one now."

"Oh my God. We have to do something about this."

She glanced around, then drifted toward the exit. He hesitated, looking after her. She didn't look back, just went slowly up the steps, holding the wall for support.

He followed her up, out into the garden.

It was late now. The flambeaux were guttering low and the bar was empty except for elderly men. He followed the green shadow of her dress back and back, along a path between the live oaks, until it faded away into leafy, cricket-racketing blackness. His heart began to pound, making him feel breathless.

For a moment, he wondered if he should turn back, find Beverly. Then anger and contempt for himself and her and the woman ahead, for everything human, made it impossible to look back. The world held no faithfulness. Why should his heart? Between the wandering beacons of fireflies, he staggered, hands extended, till they found her, leaning against something that glowed white in the starlight. His fingers tightened on her shoulders and she pulled his head down to kiss her.

The white gridwork was a trellis. As he lifted green velvet, her outstretched arms twisted into it like ivy. A little later, it began to shake, raining down fragrant petals in the warm and windless night.

7

Dorchester County, South Carolina

IN the night, the highway rolled down across the flat land like a concrete river, leaping impatiently over the narrow country roads with immense wide-legged overpasses. Straight as a ray of light, paved with moving light, the interstate arrowed down from Washington, Richmond, Fayetteville, Florence on its way to the cities of the south. Along it in the darkness roared a torrent of metal a hundred yards wide. Each driver intent only on the vehicle ahead, the trucks and cars and huge tractor-trailers bored blindly past the pine forests and palmetto swamps around and beneath them, as if they had moved beyond the need for anything but the next fuel stop, the next rest stop, the next Exxon or Days Inn or McDonald's.

On a forest road not far from an exit, a dark-colored car rolled quietly, lights off, to a halt along the berm. Its tires whispered on sandy soil just past a curve, engine murmuring beneath the black masses of the tall straight pines.

The door swung open to admit a windless heat. Footsteps hissed through pine needles, kicked aside the cones that littered the road.

The beam of a flashlight stabbed out under the stars. It touched the rusting shell of a gas pump, gleamed off the shattered windows and sagging tin roof of a long-abandoned service station. Swept around, then steadied on the reflective letters it pulled out of the dark ahead.

The call of an owl, the chirp of peepers were joined by the faint hollow shriek of thin metal being penetrated.

The figure moved back, and a momentary burst of light illuminated an empty Dr. Pepper can impaled on the post of a bullet-punctured NO HUNTING sign. A moment later, the note of the engine rose. The car lurched back onto the pavement and moved off, headlights flashing on a few hundred yards away.

Half an hour later, another set of lights separated themselves from the stream of southbound traffic. They swept down the off ramp, hesitated at a crossroads, then turned left. They probed into the forest, pausing occasionally as the driver flicked on a courtesy light and consulted a map or checked his watch. At last, they rounded the curve. They swept over the abandoned building, the sign, the bent can. Then, as the first car had, the second rolled to a halt.

The driver, a large, heavy man, got out hurriedly. Despite the heat, he wore a dark overcoat and a hat. He ran back to the sign, lumbering through the undergrowth that bordered the woods. Sweetbrier and blackberry thorn cut at the legs of his trousers.

Then he stopped. He looked searchingly for several seconds into the shadows of the trees, wiped sweat from his face with the sleeve of his coat.

Finally, he decided. Reaching up, he seized the can, crumpled it with a powerful grip, and thrust it deep into a pocket. He bent and groped around at the base of the signpost.

Returning to the sedan, he unlocked the trunk. The sudden brilliance of the interior light made him squint. Under it, in the clean empty trunk of the rented car, lay a plastic trash bag, full and taped shut. He jerked it out and laid in its place the neatly wrapped package he'd just retrieved, then slammed the trunk closed and ran back to the sign. Bending, he nestled the bag carefully against the base of the metal post, then brushed the tall grass up to conceal it.

Straightening, he peered around again, listened to the strange creak and whirr of hidden insects from the darkness. He wiped his face once more, then pushed himself back into motion, back to the car.

When the growl of its engine faded, the woods lay in silence and darkness for an hour. No other vehicle passed. An owl hooted occasionally, questioningly, and a faint wind began to ghost through the treetops.

Then the first car returned, this time with headlights on. It passed the curve and the abandoned shack. Its lights steadied on the sign. The brakes locked and the tires skidded a few feet in the soft sandy ground.

The door made a soft thud as it opened, creaked faintly on its hinge, coming to rest; then it creaked again and closed with an echoing slam.

The car moved off. It made a sharp right at the next road, then a three-point turn. It doubled back and made two more abrupt turns before passing beneath Route 95, heading east.

* * *

THE rental car was thirty miles to the north before it turned off the interstate at a roadside rest outside Manning. The man in the overcoat carefully slit the masking tape and peeled the white wrapping back from the stack of paper beneath.

The topmost sheet—a photocopy, but perfectly legible—was labeled TOP SECRET. SPECIAL CATEGORY. Along the left margin was a list of dates, one line for each day of the month. The rest of the sheet consisted of column after column of numbers, closely ranked.

The heavy man nodded slowly, as if satisfied, but no hint of a smile touched his mouth.

THE other car doubled back and made two more abrupt turns before passing beneath Route 95, heading east. A mile farther on, it crossed a state highway. At this point, it swung off the road, losing itself in the crowded parking lot of a truck stop.

Walled in, surrounded by trucks and vans, its driver tore open the green plastic membrane of the trash bag with an eager swift motion. In the dim yellow glow of the lot's lights, empty bottles, soda cans, candy wrappers spilled out onto the seat. But the bottles had been washed and carefully recapped and the wrappers were clean, free of food detritus. Beneath them was a brown paper-wrapped bundle. As a tank truck snorted and grunted past, his hands hovered for a moment over it, then tore down one side, revealing the green-gray edges of a stack of currency. He ran a thumbnail down it, as if preparing to cut a deck of cards. Fifties and hundreds—all used.

There were four more identical stacks in the bag, each wrapped the same way. He didn't open these, just pushed them aside. One fell off the seat onto the floor. Beneath it was a floppy disk in a white paper jacket—unlabeled, unmarked.

As if it could be read by sight, the driver held it up, peering at it in the dim light filtering through the windows.

A few minutes later, the seat had been cleaned up. The bottles and cans lay at the bottom of a Dumpster at the truck stop. The disk and the bundles of cash lay locked in the glove compartment. The jeep swung out of the lot, flicked on its lights again, and pulled up at last onto the road that led back to Charleston.

8
Alcorcón, Cuba

THE windless night spread over the land, turning the stars to shimmery blurs. Voices murmured from rectangles of yellow light as men and women squatted on the stoops of *bohíos*. From the dark around them came the endless vibrating song of insects, the tapping of a *bongó*, the far-off roar of the generator at the *central*.

Graciela listened to the summer night as she sat beside the pallet where her husband lay. Three flies circled under the bare electric lights. They landed in turn on the table, the floor, the sleeping man. When they brushed his face or hers, she moved a hand abruptly and the buzzing resumed, endless, thoughtless, a mindless futile searching through the dark.

She'd nursed him since the night Miguelito led him home across the fields. For the first two days, she'd stayed in, but on the third she'd been forced to act by the realization they had nothing more to eat. The tin box was empty; the rice sack hung limp from its nail; the last *malanga* had been boiled. She'd dressed him, then helped him up. Armando didn't walk well. It wasn't just that he couldn't see; he couldn't make his legs go the way they had to. He'd leaned on her arm as he had on Miguelito's. She cut him a stick to grip, and together, with many pauses to rest, they'd walked the dusty road down to the *central*.

Cooperative Number 176 had its own dispensary, actually one room in the long steel-roofed building that held the offices. She took him there first, signed him in, and told him to wait until the *médico* came in.

Then she went into the deputy superintendent's office to explain why she wouldn't be able to work for a while. She hadn't looked forward to this—he was not a warm man—but it went off all right. The cutting was over; there was slack time now before planting began. But he wouldn't give her an advance on her wages and refused anything at all for Armando, since he was no longer officially attached to the cooperative. She started to argue, but he turned away. Graciela picked up her pay for the two days she'd worked that week—ten pesos, the worn bills with the picture of José Martí—and stopped by the cooperative store for rice, dried beans, a little cornmeal. Then she went back to the dispensary.

When the *médico* came in, she helped her husband into the office, then waited, looking blankly at an old map on the wall as he examined Armando, peeling back his lids and peering into his eyes with a flashlight. Finally, he washed his hands gravely in a sink and dried them on a threadbare towel.

"Well, señor? What is it, do you know?"

"Don't call me 'señor,' I'm a comrade like you," said the man. To Armando, he said, "*Compañero,* I will have a word with your wife, if that is all right with you."

In the corridor, he put his hands in his pockets. "How long has your husband been unable to see?"

"Since he returned from prison. I told you that."

"But there was a loss before that, no? As if there was a part of the world that to him, was no longer there?"

"No. He could see perfectly when he went away—like a hawk, miles away."

"In that case . . . The paralysis of the eye muscles, lesions . . . I'm sorry, there's nothing I can do. He's blind."

"I can see that, but why? Have they beaten him so badly?"

"I see no evidence of trauma," said the doctor uncomfortably. Then, seeing that she did not understand the technical word, he added, "Of beatings. Much of what they say about prisons is exaggerated. . . . At any rate, I don't think—"

"Then what causes it?" She cut him off angrily, looking down the hall to where two of the managers were talking with the secretary. All three were smoking. They glanced at her and chuckled.

"It's what we call *neuritis óptica.* It's a disease of malnutrition. The nerve damage leads to blindness. Why did your husband go to prison?"

"He stole a sack of ground corn to feed his family," Graciela said, loudly enough that the managers stopped speaking. "They caught him and sent him away. They fed him nothing, so he went blind. So they let him go. How merciful they are."

"Comrade, *por favor* . . . You are upset, but remember yourself, no?"

"I'm sorry. You're right, I'm upset. . . . I didn't mean to speak against anyone. . . . What medicine are you going to give him?"

"This disease is not well understood."

"There must be a medicine. Tell me what it is. I'll get it if I have to walk to Neuvitas."

"We could give him thiamine, if we had any. But that wouldn't help his heart." The *médico* shrugged. "It's plain he cannot work. I'll give you a sick pass. He'll get the ration for the sick, and some dried milk."

"Should he go to the hospital?"

"It can be done, but not right this minute. You can leave him here if you like. Then when transport is available, we'll take him in to Camagüey."

She turned her face from the *médico*'s and said, "I'll take care of him at home till you're ready to take him."

"Whatever you say," he said. "I will arrange for transport, the hospital. . . . Now, if you please, others are waiting. Is that a machete cut, *compañero*? Come in. Don't drip blood there; that is clean."

BUT of course he never had arranged any transport or any care. And he didn't come to the house, not once.

So there'd been nothing for her to do but go back to work, walking behind the harrow that disked up the fields where the cane had to be replanted, pulling up the uprooted stumps and piling them for burning, or digging out irrigation trenches with shovels and hoes. And in the nights, she would sit up with him, and pray when she could. He's always been strong, she told herself. He wasn't old. He was only fifty-five.

But he had become weaker and finally took to the pallet. She fed him as well as she could, but now he didn't seem to care whether he ate or not. He complained of pain in his legs and couldn't bear to have a blanket over them. Then he'd say he was cold, although she was sweating in the closed hut. Sometimes she got angry, but then she'd catch herself. As long as he complained, he was alive.

The light flickered and a second later she heard the falter in the far-off drone of the generator. Then it stopped. The filament faded to orange and then red and then the darkness flooded in all at once through the door and window, and the silence echoed out over the land.

A tap on the door made her sit up from her drowsing, catch her breath. The hinge creaked. She half-rose, reaching above her head, then dropped her arm as a voice whispered, "Mamá. Mamá?"

"Coralía. What are you doing here?"

"Uncle Tomás wrote me that Papa was sick. Oh, poor Papi."

"Close the door, child," said Graciela in a low voice, feeling her way to the table.

A match scratched and a candle sketched the interior in flickering shadow. The girl hesitated, then came into the light. She smiled uncertainly at her mother, then knelt by the bed. When she looked up again, her expression was frightened. "Oh, Mamá. Was he really released?"

"What do you mean? He's here. Of course he was released. How other?"

"But are his papers stamped? If he escaped—"

"The police would have come days ago. You know that." Graciela slumped back into the rawhide lacing, looking at the daughter she'd borne seventeen years ago.

Her firstborn was lighter than her mother but unmistakably mestizo. Coralía wore a uniform; blue trousers, blue shirt, blue cap with a little red star.

"I'm surprised you came."

"Why should you be surprised?"

"You never write."

"I have to study, Mamá. All the time."

"How are you doing at school?"

"It's tough . . . very difficult."

"You look thin. Are the studies hard?"

"I don't mean that. I can learn anything they put in front of me. You know that. But to know your father's a criminal, a *plantado*—"

"He accepted the revolution long ago."

"Not if he stole from it. You don't know how humiliating that was, when they called me in to tell me. I had to stand before the others and confess my father was in error." She raised her head in the candlelight. "Mother, there is something I must tell you. I had to renounce him."

"You renounced your father? Then what are you doing here?" Graciela got up suddenly, and her arm went up into the thatching. With a hiss, the machete slid out.

"Put it away, Mamá," said the girl, sighing. "You always have to make everything so dramatic. It doesn't mean anything, only words. It wasn't easy to get here. You don't know."

"I know you put on airs, but you're a *negrita* like me."

"How old-fashioned you are. Why do you say things like that about yourself?"

"Because they're true."

"And you reject the revolution, even though it's all for you."

"For me? All for *me*? Oh my God! What have they given *me*?" Graciela waved the blade wildly around the hut. "*¡No hay nada!*

What do you see that we have but hunger, work, fear? It was bad under the old regime, but there was always something to eat—even if it was nothing but sugarcane during the *tiempo muerto*."

"Put the machete down, Mamá. You'll hurt yourself."

"I'll hurt someone else first!"

"And don't make threats. I would give my life for the revolution tonight if they asked me."

"Why not? You've already betrayed your family. Why not give them your life, as well."

"You sound so bitter. You don't love me anymore, Mamá?"

She looked at her daughter for a long time, then sighed. She sat down at the table and put her face in her hands.

Coralía stood above her, fists on her hips.

"You see, you have it backward. You wanted me to stay here and swing a machete with you and Father's relatives, live in huts, and never go anywhere and never see anything. I can't live like that, Mamá. I can't live like a campesino."

"And your father, what of him?"

"He made his choice. If the camps couldn't reform him, what can I do? As a person, I feel sorry for him, but I won't throw away my life for some futile gesture. It's not good that I come here again. My home's in Havana now; that's where I'll live when I graduate."

Graciela sat at the table. Bitterness like a wall was rising in her heart. She hadn't wanted this wall. She didn't think she was the one who'd built it, but it was there.

A mutter from the bed interrupted their whispers. Coralía knelt again. "Yes, Papi? It is I; I am here!"

"I remember the day Raimondo died," Armando murmured in a voice scarcely louder than the scorpions rustling overhead. "Do you remember Raimondo?"

"No, Papi. Papi, it's Coralía. . . . Does he know me, Mamá?"

"He's confused," said Graciela. "He speaks to his brother, his grandmother. His mind goes back to the past. Yes, *mi vida*, I remember him, your brother."

The man on the pallet murmured, "The Batistiano soldiers surrounded the village. The officer announced that they were looking for enemies of the regime. Then they began going from house to house. They pulled the people out and lined them up on the street. They shot into the air. Then some of the people, they began setting their houses on fire.

"Now the village echoed with shouts and screaming. They shot the pigs, the chickens, burned the houses. It was then we realized they were not looking for enemies of the regime. This was to terrify us.

"But Raimondo was one of the revolutionaries. He had been with Fidel in the mountains and was back home trying to persuade the young men to go back with him, to join Che in the Sierra Maestra. So he knew that they would kill him, and he tried to hide. We wanted him to hide in our house, but he said no, they would kill us, too, if they found him there. So he ran into the house of a neighbor.

"Yes, my brother tried to hide, but the soldiers saw him running. And they came and looked, and when they did not see him, they set the house on fire and waited outside with their guns. And finally the heat was too great and he ran out.

"When they saw him, they seized him and dragged him out into the square so all the village could see. They beat him with the whip they call the ox's prick. They broke his joints with the butts of their guns, then drove over him with their jeep. They killed Raimondo in the street like a dog. Then again they shot their guns, and I heard the bullets go *whick, whick* through the walls.

"After the soldiers left, we all came out and looked around. I, too, came out, and I sat down beside Raimondo, who was still alive, but not for long.

" 'Armando,' he said to me, his mouth crushed from where they beat him, 'it's no good. We've got to make a change here. Everybody together, we've got to make a change.'

"Then he died. And that night, I went into the mountains to take his place."

Graciela passed her hand over his face again and again. She thought she should be afraid, but she wasn't. Her heart didn't know what to feel—just as it had been when the children had died, the children after Coralía.

"His brother gave his life for the revolution," Coralía said. "You see, Mamá?"

Armando muttered, "It's true. And because of him, I believed. But the bearded one betrayed us. People said he was going to bring democracy, but Fidel, he's just the same as Batista. And the prisons . . . decent people cannot imagine such things. It's not for this my brother died."

"Things will change, Papi."

"That's what I've heard for twenty years. And they don't. They only get worse."

"I can't listen to this," said Coralía. Her face was hard in the candlelight. The door clacked behind her, and they were alone.

"We lost her," he said, and his voice was so sad, it made her feel like crying now at last.

"She'll always be ours, Armando."

"No, her soul belongs to them now." He sighed, glanced around with his sightless eyes, then gestured her closer with a little motion of his fingers. "Do you remember when you tried to kill me with grandfather's machete—"

She smiled. "Yes."

"Are you glad you missed?"

"Yes."

He'd been smiling, but gradually it faded. "There's something I have to tell you. You remember when I was in the camp—not this time, the first time, on the Isle of Pines—"

"You never talked about it."

"I know, because I was ashamed. I was afraid; they beat and threatened us." He paused. "They released me because I gave in."

"Armando—"

"Three years was long enough. I surrendered. I went to their indoctrination. I memorized Marx and Che; I signed petitions against the Yankees. Who cares, right? What did they do for us at the Playa Girón? But there were others who held out till they died. For giving up, I was ashamed . . . but in my heart, I never was one of them."

"I know, Armando. You don't need to tell me that."

"I thought I'd outlive them . . . someday it would change . . . but now I don't think I will." He squeezed his eyes shut, and she looked away, understanding that he was weeping.

"Then what do we do, *mi vida*?"

"For me, it's too late," Armando whispered, staring into a darkness that must, she thought, be blacker than any night. "For me, the time has come to leave this place. But my son—" He put his hand out, and as if he could see, it came to rest lightly on her, right where the baby was. "My son—I want him to be free."

She watched his face in the guttering light of the candle, not believing for a long time that at last Armando Guzman Diéguez, cane cutter, son of a mechanic, and the man she had loved all her life, was dead.

down, and I think the problem's in the feed from the sonar stack. You want that ping jockey homesteading his equipment, sitting on a four-decibel loss? Or you want me to take him down on the pier and show him what's inside the fucking piñata?" Harper held up a fist.

Dan sighed, looking down and across the pier to where the old destroyer was getting her final coat of haze gray. He wished abruptly that they were all far at sea, away from the yards, the heat, everything that fucked up a sailor's life. "Neither. I'll talk to him. But you've got to make an effort, too. He's right about one thing: It *is* his gear. He sits on it twenty-four a day under way."

Harper sucked a tooth, leaning out. Dan followed his eyes down. At the bottom of *Barrett*'s sheer, like a moat at the foot of a castle's wall, a ribbon of river separated her from the pier. A gull floated in that narrow strip of calm water, oblivious to looming steel and concrete. Harper took out a quarter, bombardier-aimed it, and let go. Halfway down, the wind caught it and it curved away and hit the water a yard from the bird. It swam toward the splash and dabbled its bill.

"Well, sometimes maybe I do come on too hard-assed. Want me to go scratch his ears, make him purr?"

"That might not be out of place."

"I'll take care of it. Hey, you like to sail?"

He remembered as if from another life sailing in Newport with Betts and Nan—the baby just big enough for a life jacket; the hard wind, cool-edged even in summer up there; the sail, struggling like a living thing in the sunlight; her arms, tanned dark as a Polynesian's; body outlined by the sun under thin cotton. . . . "Yeah. Haven't done it for a while, though."

"Saturday's supposed to be nice. Want to slam a few brews, do a little sailing?"

"You have a boat?"

"A little one. Fun to kick around in." Harper clicked the knife closed and put it away. "What you say? Not gonna be a lot of free time once we hit Gitmo."

"Might be fun. I'll get back to you. Okay, I'm going to go see Fowler now. Next time you go into his space, make a point of asking permission in front of his guys if you can work on his gear. Got that? A sense of ownership, that's good. Let's make it work for us."

Harper nodded, passing a hand over his bald spot. Dan left him standing there against the lifelines.

HE found Fowler pacing outside his stateroom. "Come on in, Chief," he said, opening the door. His roommate frowned up from a pile of papers. Dan closed it and said, "Well, maybe we can talk out here. Look, I told the chief warrant to back off. It's your gear; he can't work on it without your say-so. But you need to lighten up, too, Chief."

Fowler stood silent, molding invisible spheres with his hands. Finally, he said, "Sir, I don't want him in my spaces—*at all.*"

This was unexpected. He studied the chief's face. Sonarmen were all a little strange, true. If they didn't start that way, staring into a screen twelve hours a day made them weird. And now that Harper had pointed it out, Fowler *did* seem sort of . . . fussy. In one way, that was good; he was great on the paperwork end. But Dan didn't know yet whether he was going to cut it as a supervisor, running the stacks watch after watch. Dan remembered the cramped, dirty sonar room of USS *Reynolds Ryan.* He remembered in the soles of his feet the week they'd spent tracking a submarine that refused to surface, refused to identify itself as a winter Arctic storm gradually tore the old destroyer apart. He blinked and said harshly, "What the hell are you talking about?"

Fowler wilted. His narrow shoulders slumped and his eyes slid aside. "I don't know," he mumbled. "Just don't like it."

A seaman came around the corner and they stood apart to let him pass. Dan said, "Look, I don't know what the two of you have going, but we won't have time for personality conflicts at Gitmo. You guys are going to have to work it out. Any questions?"

"No, sir," Fowler said, still shifting the invisible balls from one hand to the other.

HE didn't go to lunch. Instead, he changed into gym gear and went for a run, dodging forklifts and trucks. He ran hard and felt pleasantly tired when he climbed the brow again. As he faced the ensign, then showed the petty officer of the watch his ID card, he resolved to cut down on the drinking and try to get more sleep.

He started the afternoon by clearing out his in box in the department office. He signed off on changes to quarterly maintenance schedules, looked over the revisions to a tacmemo, signed three outgoing speedletters. At the bottom of the box was a special request chit from ETSN Sanderling to get Thursday afternoons off to take a class at a junior college. Harper had checked "disapproved." Dan started to, too, then stopped. He got two or three chits a week from Sanderling. It was annoying, but that shouldn't mean each one didn't merit consideration. He put it in his hold box to think about.

He gave the other things to Cephas, the departmental yeoman, to distribute and then checked his wheel book. Time to see how yard work was wrapping up. He grabbed the clipboard off the bulkhead and went out.

Things looked good up forward. Horsehead's gunner's mates were greasing the new guiderails for sea. The other jobs were on schedule or close to it. His spirits rose a bit. A centerfold in one of the missile-maintenance rooms reminded him of Sibylla Baird. He'd called twice but hadn't caught her in yet.

But as soon as he walked into the computer room, he knew something was wrong. A portable air conditioner was whining, but the air was still close. All the equipment fans were on. Mainhardt and Dawson and the other DSs were staring at logic diagrams, plugging and unplugging boards. He propped an elbow on a workbench and waited till Mainhardt glanced up. "What's broke, Chief?"

"Can't get these subprograms to run, sir."

"Which system?"

The data processing chief blinked, bringing himself back to the world around him. "New Version Three software for the ACDADS. It's supposed to have a self-installation feature; you just get it talking to the operating tape and it erases the old code and writes the new in. But it ain't working."

"Why not?"

"Williams, answer the lieutenant. He's been on it all night, sir, trying to get it to run."

DS2 Williams was tall and black. He wouldn't look directly at Dan. He paused after every few words. The pockets under his eyes were deep enough to sink a cue ball into. He said, "I figure it's a configuration control problem, Lieutenant. The . . . software contractor has got a computer lash-up that's a little too unique. The system they built this version on don't look quite like what we've got here."

"You mean different computers?"

"No, Lieutenant, I mean just little differences, like the RAM configuration, or the interface lineup. Maybe they're using a different version of operating system software. Things can get fouled up easy, sir. They ain't supposed to, but they do, and more often than they should. The result is, they make a tape and send it out to us, we try to load it, and it craps."

"Can you locate the problem?"

"Trying, but we don't have the tools the whiz kids got. I think it's in the software interface between the operating system and the NTDS module."

"Go back a step," said Dan.

Williams blinked at the far wall. "Okay, sir, you know how NTDS works. The net control station does the roll call . . . polls each participating unit in turn for bearing and range to its contacts."

"I'm with you so far." Dan knew the basics of the Naval Tactical Data System. After the Pacific Fleet's hammering by kamikazes in World War II, it was obvious that grease pencils, plot boards, and voice radio nets would never cope with jets and missiles. So NTDS did it electronically. The radar operators on each ship identified and tracked incoming aircraft on their consoles. Computers derived the track data (course, speed, altitude, identification, threat level) and transmitted it automatically to the net control station. The carrier put together the big picture and rebroadcast it, so that if one ship got a contact, everyone in the task force knew about it in seconds.

"Okay, and you know that the most common problem is that the NCS and the PUs can't talk to each other, usually because the crypto gear ain't set up right. But it's all . . . gotta be encrypted because if the bad guys can read it they can see where our defense is, our combat air patrol and missile ships, and skate around them and plaster the shit out of the carrier."

Williams took a breath, but he was wound up now, not hesitating anymore. "OPSPEC-four-eleven sets the protocols for the handoff. That's maybe where the screwup is. Something in there is scrambling the data."

"Great," Dan said, hoping to cut to the chase. "Can we get it running? Or do we need to ship it back and stay with Version Two till they fix this one? We've got to have everything up by next week." That was when they were going to test-fire the guns and missiles.

"Well, sir, it's like this. . . ."

He spent several minutes trying to pry the bottom line out of Williams and Dawson, but they were still going in circles when the 1MC said, "Lieutenant Lenson, Lieutenant(jg) Deshowits." Mainhardt punched buttons into the phone and held it out. "Quarterdeck," said a voice over the clatter of a needle gun.

"Lieutenant Lenson, you just passed the word for me. What's up?"

"XO wants you an' Mr. De Shits—I mean Deshowits—in his stateroom, sir."

"Got it." He rattled the phone down. "Okay, stay on it. If it looks like something serious, let Mr. Harper know we need to start screaming."

"Aye aye, sir," they muttered, already reabsorbed.

Dan turned back from the doorway. "Where's Sanderling?"

"Captain's stateroom."

"What's he doing up there?"

"Fixing the entertainment system."

"Yeah, sure . . . been a lot of trouble with the captain's stereo lately," said Williams, blinking with reddened eyes at a printout as it chattered out.

HIM and Deshowits in the XO's stateroom . . . Dan wondered as he rattled down the ladder why Vysotsky needed both of them at the same time. Only thing he could think of that he and the damage control assistant had in common was they both had beards. Outside Vysotsky's stateroom, a petty officer was tagging out an emergency power panel. Dan stopped to make sure the OOD had signed the tag-out. Deshowits came around the corner and Dan tapped on the door. "Come in," came Vysotsky's gravelly baritone. Then, as they stepped inside, he said, "Uh, give me another minute with this. Have a squat on the settee."

George Vysotsky was medium height, with a squarish head and blond hair that stuck up in back for a day or two after a haircut. He had full lips, strong white teeth, strong-looking hands with golden hair on the backs. Right now, he had reading glasses on. His broad shoulders hunched over the desk as he rapidly scanned down the unit manning document, making corrections and insertions in #2 pencil. While they waited, Dan looked at the swords racked over the doorway. The bottom one was a standard Navy dress sword. The others were older, one a saber with a broad nicked-up blade, the other with a basket-style hand guard.

"How'd the audit go?" Vysotsky asked him, not looking up from the roster. His voice was hoarse, as if his vocal cords had been damaged. Occasionally, Dan had noticed him massaging his throat after he spoke.

"Nothing new, sir."

"No rabbits in the hat?"

Dan shook his head. "They're talking about some kind of suit. Sipple left a house and some insurance, apparently. The auditor said they were going after his wife."

"Be tough on Jerrie . . . but if he misappropriated funds . . ." Vysotsky pulled a stamp out of his desk, stamped the roster, and pushed it into his out box, then leaned back like a gun going into battery. "How about the CMS inspection?"

"Classified materials, that's Felipe's department, sir. The comm officer, Mr. Van Cleef."

"Mark, how's that lagging job going?"

"Bulkhead's done. Two days' work left on the lines."

"We be ready to steam next week?"

"Steam, sir? We'll give you something a lot better."

Vysotsky grinned back but looked tired. That seemed to be all the time he had for pleasantries, because he bent forward again—to his in box, from which he extracted a message. While Lenson was reading the headers, the XO said, "You've both already seen it—the one about beards."

"I haven't seen this."

"Beards, sir? No, sir," said Deshowits. Vysotsky looked displeased but just said, "I told Radio to slot you copies. Bottom line is, those beards are history."

Dan said, surprised, "It's regulation, sir. Trimmed and everything."

"There's a revision to uniform regs coming down the pike. The new CNO's cutting out a lot of the stuff Zumwalt let go by. Part of that, he's banning beards aboard combatant ships."

"On what grounds, sir?" said Deshowits.

"The message sets out the reasons, Mark. Uniform appearance, adherence to tradition, and you can't get a proper seal on oxygen-breathing apparatus or gas masks."

Dan said, "*Beards* aren't traditional, sir?"

"A clean-cut appearance is traditional," said Vysotsky patiently.

"Sir, I don't want to step out of line, but whoever said that had better go back and look at Farragut and Porter."

Vysotsky sighed.

"Well, that's secondary, sir. I just don't think the Navy's necessarily got the right to tell me how to do everything. Isn't that what we're on duty for—to defend freedom?"

He felt the ridiculousness of the words even as he said them. Vysotsky wasn't interested in arguing; he just wanted them to shave. And sure enough, he didn't bother to answer. He just cleared his throat and said, "Mr. Deshowits? Any comments from your side of the settee?"

"On the mask issue, sir. I went through fire fighting last month and I've been to chemical, bacteriological, radiological school. I never had any problem getting a seal."

"That it?" The XO slammed his chair down. "Okay, I heard you out. Blowing off steam is all well and good, but there's no point arguing. You want to haggle about tradition, how about the tradition of a cheery aye aye?"

Dan found himself getting mad. It wasn't so much the beard—he hadn't had it that long—but so far he hadn't heard anything like a reason. Just that an order was an order. Maybe that was good enough at the Academy, and he'd obeyed as fast and unreflectingly as the next guy there. But a few years in the fleet had changed his mind about blind obedience. He tried a joke. "Well, we're kind of attached to them, sir. And I'm as cheery as the next guy, but this is a little sudden."

"You sound like a sorehead right now, Dan." Vysotsky glanced at the swords. "Let me tell you a story.

"My grandfather was in the Tsar's Navy. But one day, the fleet mutinied. He came this close to getting shot by his own crew. He picked the wrong side when the civil war came, fought with Kolchak, and when the Whites lost, he never could go back home.

"We had to make it here. And we did, but it hasn't been easy. I was at comm school, and one day the head honcho from Schools Command is reading the roster. Suddenly, his eyes get big. He says, 'Why are we teaching a Russian?' and he sends the master-at-arms to pull me out of class. I had to be twice as good as the guy in the next seat whose name was Smith. Understand what I'm saying?"

"Well, I certainly do, sir," said Deshowits.

"Maybe you do at that. . . . Dan?"

"Uh, I understand about your name, sir. But I'm not sure what the point is that you wanted to make."

"The point, Dan, is that the Navy is not an organization that exists to dispense perfect justice. We all have to live with that fact. Okay? Think of it like an egg."

"An egg, sir?" said Deshowits, sounding interested. Or maybe, Dan saw, he was leading the XO on, flicking the cape in front of him. Whichever, Vysotsky nodded and said, "Yeah. We're the hard shell. Inside, it's soft. But if there wasn't a shell, the guts would run out.

"When you join the Navy, you give up certain rights other Americans take for granted—what to do, what to say. And what you look like, damn it: uniform and grooming. But we go along with it to protect the rest of America."

"We have to have clean chins to protect America?" said Dan, but not loudly enough to stop the XO, who was still going. "The Navy gives us security and opportunity. But it's a trade-off. You want to express your individuality, this is not the place. The service is going to a more professional image. So beards are out. End of message."

Deshowits spoke up. He explained calmly that he had no problem with that reasoning but that he was also responsible to another, higher authority. "I have to choose between obeying orders and the dictates of my religion. Do you remember our yarmulke discussion, sir?"

Vysotsky looked uncomfortable. "Uh, yeah, I remember that. . . . The message doesn't say anything about exemptions. . . . I'll have to get back to you on that." He switched blue eyes to Dan. "You got a religious problem, too?"

"No, sir," he said, swallowing his suspicion that there was no reason, that it was arbitrary and meaningless. It didn't matter what he knew or how well he could do his job. What mattered was whether he scraped his chin with a piece of steel every morning.

Vysotsky said hoarsely, “Okay, we’ve had our little discussion. You’ve got three days to comply. You have people working for you; pass the word to them, too. Clean shaves on USS *Barrett.* Mark, I’ll get back to you on your question.”

Bitter at heart, he slammed the door on the way out, knowing Vysotsky would remember it, but not caring. Christ, he thought. What a petty, asinine two-bit order. What a petty, asinine organization.

Suddenly, he needed a drink.

10

Thirty Miles North of Charleston

"ACCURIZED that baby myself. National Match barrel, hand-lapped to the muzzle bushing; recoil buffer; Bo-Mar sights; hand-tuned trigger," Harper said as Dan wrapped his hand around the grips of the .45 Colt automatic.

The blast rolled back from the pines of the Francis Marion National Forest. "Not bad," said Harper, bending to a spotting scope. The chief warrant was in civvies today—a khaki bush jacket with shoulder tabs, twill pants, shooting glasses. "You're flinching, though. Go on, fire off the clip. I brought plenty of ammo."

"Thanks, once is enough." Dan laid it gingerly on the shooting bench, massaging his hand as Harper showed him the next gun.

"Now, this is an AK-forty-seven, Chinese-made. We can't fire it full auto, not with these rangers around."

"Isn't that illegal? Where'd you get that?"

"Took it off a dead gook. I was walking down this trail and there he was. I got a long piece of bamboo and poked him. Then I went through his pockets. Then I took out my Ka-Bar and cut his nuts off."

"You cut his—Why?"

"To eat," said Harper, then threw back his head and cackled. "Joke, shipmate. I bought it off a guy when we put in to Saigon, delivering helos."

Dan cleared his throat and looked away, around him. The morning sun fell through the pines and glittered off hundreds of spent cartridges littering the ground. Saturday morning, and the first thing Harper wanted to do was hop into his red jeep and go shooting.

No doubt about it, the chief warrant was a marksman. The .45 automatic was notoriously hard to handle, but he'd put six rounds offhand into the black bull's-eye. "Out of practice," Harper had said, pulling the punctured target down and stapling another up. "The National Match, Camp Perry, I was chewing the guts out of Tommy Ten-ring."

"Where'd you learn to shoot like that?"

"On the Navy–Marine Corps Pistol Team. Would have gone to the Olympics, but fucking Carter pulled us. Can you believe it? The one time Jim boy stands up to the Reds, and who has to pay? The people who trained for years to beat 'em. What a clown."

"You like Reagan, huh?"

"Ronnie's a politician, too. There's not a lot of difference, just what brand name."

"So what are you?"

"A libertarian. There's only one person knows what's best for you."

"Your mother?"

"Funny. *Yourself,* shipmate. The government's not going to solve our problems. What can government do? Only two things: redistribute wealth or take away rights. Right?"

"I guess."

"So they do. The fucking Democrats got the welfare sluts and all the fucking liberal bureaucrats standing around with their hands out. The Republicans, their fat-cat banker buddies are three deep at the trough. And funny, no matter who's running things, the government keeps getting bigger. I think government *is* the problem." He held up the rifle. "Mao Tse-tung: 'Political power grows out of the barrel of a gun.' A fucking Commie, but on that he was right on the money. They take these away from us, God help America."

"The range is clear," someone yelled, and Dan stood back as Harper slapped in a magazine and the pop and roar swelled into a rolling rumble of gunfire as sand dust and pine needles spurted off the embankments.

WHEN they were through, Harper suggested they stop at his house on the way to the marina. They pulled off at the Mount Pleasant exit, and a few miles on left the pavement for a gravel drive that wound toward a brick ranch. Water glittered beyond dogwood and forsythia. The garage door was up; a Triumph and a late-model wagon were parked inside. Harper braked and swung down. "Hungry? Let's grab a sandwich. Maybe see what game's on."

"What are all these flowers, Chief Warrant?"

"Red salvia, uh, coneflowers, I think—the pink and white in the shade, that's impatiens. You into flowers?"

"Not really, but they're pretty."

"Yeah. Bonnie does that," Harper said, unlocking the door and holding it for him.

The living room had a big fieldstone fireplace with glass doors. "Hell of a place," Dan said, looking around.

"Four percent VA mortgage. I borrowed everything I could. Wasn't hard to figure where inflation was going after Vietnam. Plus, I don't know if I told you, I own a bar in Subic and one in San Diego. Bought 'em when I was stationed there. Bonnie! Come on out here. This is my department head, Dan Lenson."

"Pleased to meet you." The heavy woman in the apron was carrying a tray with beer and pretzels. Harper waved at armchairs in front of the TV and Dan let himself down as Mrs. Harper set out the glasses. Harper went through several channels till he found a game. "Hey, get the girls down here, meet Mr. Lenson," he said to his wife. She left, and Dan heard her calling. A few minutes later, she ushered in two quiet, pretty teenagers. "Emily, Shannon, Mr. Lenson works with me on the ship," Harper said.

They smiled and said hello politely. Harper let them each have a sip from his beer, then patted their behinds. "Okay, now let the men watch some ball, okay?"

Dan watched them go. "You got two well-behaved kids there."

"Bonnie's done okay, considering how much I been gone. She's turned kind of sloppy, though. Doesn't take care of herself. Hey! How about fixin' us something to eat, sandwiches or something?"

"BLTs, Jay?"

"Yeah, that's good. Pack some chips and stuff. The lieutenant and me are going out for a sail."

"Are you coming, Mrs. Harper?"

"Naw, she's no good on a boat. . . . I took her diving once. Got her the tank and regulator and everything. And she got twenty feet down before she figured out she forgot to turn her air on. Is that stupid or what?"

Dan felt uncomfortable. Harper talked as if his wife wasn't ten feet away, in the kitchen, where as far as he could tell, she could hear every word. To change the subject, he said, "This is a beautiful house."

"I'd like deeper water, but it's okay. I sure couldn't afford it now, I'll tell you that."

"You've been in Charleston how long?"

"Three tours. They offered me a job in D.C., but I turned it down." Harper shrugged. "I'll retire out of here. Do some serious sailing then. Hey! *Oki-san, touchi-ne!*"

As his wife brought another drink, Dan felt envious. Harper had a nice house, polite daughters; nothing flashy, but it was a home. Maybe he didn't treat his wife very well, but at least she was here.

Harper hoisted himself out of the chair. "You done? Had enough? Let's di-di out of here and do some sailing."

HARPER kept his boat at the base. They stopped at the beverage store, then pulled into the marina. "There she is," Harper said.

Dan looked out over the jostling rows of sailboats and motor cruisers. He couldn't see which one Harper meant, but it was a beautiful day, clear and sunny, with a good wind. Engines rumbled as a sportfisherman slid away from the ramp. He pulled a case of Bud out of the back, tucked it under one arm, grabbed a ten-pound block of ice with the other—his shoulder was okay, unless he reached above his head—and followed Harper's slouch down the pier to a kelly green–hulled yawl. The chief warrant looked around as if searching for someone, then hauled in on a bow line. As the boat rolled to his weight, two heads showed at the companionway.

"Come on, come on, they won't bite." Harper waved him aboard. "This here's Big Mary, and this is Little Mary. Girls, Dan works with me on the ship. Hell, he *lives* on the damn ship. Had to pry him off like a damn barnacle."

Big Mary was a green-eyed blonde with skin like old leather from too much time in the sun. Older than Dan would usually stare at, but she was built. Little Mary was Filipina, small and slim and brown. They were in bikinis and thongs, both smoking, and they'd helped themselves, apparently, to whatever liquor was aboard; he smelled rum and coconut suntan lotion. Suddenly, they both pulled out guns. They squirted him and then each other, laughing and scuffling in the cockpit.

Harper hadn't said anything about women. Dan felt embarrassed, tried not to stare. He looked at the boat instead—not new, but she seemed well-maintained. He put a hand on the boom. It was a solid, heavy light-colored wood under the varnish.

"Sitka spruce, that boom." Ice crashed as Harper, down below, threw it into the icebox. "You like her?"

"What is it?"

"Alberg. Thirty-five-footer."

"What's the hull? Wood?"

"Fuck no, fiberglass. All bronze fittings, though. Stainless rigging. Lead keel."

"Buy her new?"

"I don't buy much new stuff, Hoss. You can get a lot of used boat for not too much, and the nice thing is, taxes are next to nothing." A whine came from below their feet, then the engine fired, sending a puff of black smoke milling over the pier. "I reengined her, brand-new Westerbeke—now I got a boat that'd cost you a hundred grand new. Okay, I'm in command now, Lieutenant. Hands off those girls! Get forward and cast us off."

HARPER motored them out into an easterly wind, then gave Dan the tiller. He unfurled the jib and sheeted the main tight. When they came right, the boat heeled and began slicing her way through the water. "Cut the engine," he yelled from the bow, and Dan was still groping when Big Mary reached between his legs and did it for him. The sudden quiet was a shock. He leaned back, holding the sun-warmed wood of the tiller while one by one the piers slipped past.

"There's *Barrett.*" She looked different from seaward. Already her paint looked slightly faded. Faint lines bled down from her scuppers. He'd always thought of her as new, but he suddenly realized she wouldn't always be. One day, she'd be as old as *Ryan,* that last cruise. . . .

"Cut in toward her," Harper said, coming back from where he'd been making up lines, and Dan put the tiller over. As they went by, they waved to the men on deck. They were looking disconsolately out over the water, the duty section. One raised a finger.

"Where to?"

"Wherever you want, Mr. L. We could head for Fort Sumter, maybe duck out to sea for an hour or two."

"Sounds good to me, Chief Warrant."

"Hell, call me Jay. Long as we're on the boat."

"Okay, Jay."

"Is he senior to you, Jay? I thought you told everybody what to do aboard your ship."

"We work together," Dan told Big Mary.

Harper took the tiller, and for a while the only sounds were the cries of seabirds and an occasional flutter from the sails. Dan put his arm over his eyes. The sun came bright through his skin, red and warm. Then he felt a hand on his leg. "Want a cigarette?" said Little Mary. She shook out a match and flicked it overboard.

"No thanks."

"I like your beard."

"Feast your eyes, babe. That chin fuzz is going the way of the dodo." Harper chortled.

"What does he mean?"

"I have to shave it off. Just got the word." Resentment stirred beneath the sun sleepiness. "Can you believe it? It's 'unmilitary.' "

"That's too bad. I like it," said Little Mary, petting it.

"They don't. And they own me, not you."

"I don't wear one, but I know how you feel." Harper's voice came from the red warmth. "I mean, when you join up, you realize you might have to put your life on the line some day. I saw my friends fuck up and die. But that's not enough; they got to unload chickenshit on you, too.

"Way I figure it, you can't expect loyalty from an organization, any organization. Ask the guys it owes the most . . . poor bastards stuck in the VA hospitals . . . ask them."

Dan said, "It's not a big deal, but damn it, if you don't happy happy aye aye first time you hear it, you're some kind of disgruntled asshole."

"That's the Navy—rigid adherence to the cosmetic bullshit, and no attention to the important stuff."

"What important stuff?"

"The really important stuff. Like, you heard about this strategy, where all the carriers go up to Norway, right down the Russkies' throats. What's it called—"

"The Maritime Strategy."

"Right. Right. Crazy as hell."

"It makes sense to me. Bottle up their subs north of the Greenland-Iceland-UK Gap—"

"I'm going to get some sun," said Big Mary, sounding bored. "You dump me in the water again, Jay, so help me I'll skin you, you hear?" Without waiting for an answer, she went forward around the cabin. Little Mary looked at Dan, then got up and followed her.

Harper said, "It's crazy, that's why. Say we go up there, steam four carriers and all the cruisers and destroyers and shit, and there's this huge all-out battle. The Reds lose, then what? They're out nothing; they're still rolling their wagons across Europe. But we lose four carriers, we've lost the fucking war. What if the admirals dick it up?"

"I don't know. They probably modeled it—"

"Sure, but what I'm saying, they don't know everything. Everybody thinks he's gonna win, or there wouldn't be a battle, right? But somebody's gotta get his butt kicked. All I'm saying, maybe we ought not to go sticking our dick into the pencil sharpener."

"Well, you might be right—"

"Fucking right I'm right. And then, Christ, we go and publish it in the papers, tell them exactly what we're gonna do—so they can have everything ready when we show up."

"Maybe it's a trick. Get them set up for an attack around the Kola Peninsula, then hit them from the Pacific, or through the Med."

"Maybe. *I* don't think we're that smart." Harper looked aloft, then aft, and put the helm over. Dan ducked as the boom came around; the boat heeled, then steadied on the opposite tack. "What I think, it's all theoretical. There isn't gonna be any war. . . . Hey!

Mary! Better tuck those in. You're gonna fall out— Oh shit!" He folded, laughing, as Little Mary waved her top at a passing boat full of fishermen. Their heads snapped around, beers spilling, faces gaping at *Blow Job*, where Big Mary, too, was pulling her top down, breasts rolling out like white cannonballs into the sunlight.

DAN shook his head and came awake with a start. But when he sat up, nothing had changed—except that a half-nude Little Mary was steering now, a beer in one hand and a Salem dangling from her lips. Pointed breasts swayed, pale with a hint of saffron, reminding him of his ex-wife's. Harper and Big Mary weren't around. He sat up, started to ask where they were, then looked down into the cabin.

Later they came up, flushed, and Harper took the helm again. He and Dan chatted while the girls basked like cats. The brick battlements of Sumter slipped by. They were west of the main channel, with wooden poles sticking up marking, Dan assumed, shallows. Harper didn't have a chart, just glanced at the compass once in a while.

"Having fun yet?"

"This is great . . . Jay."

"So how come you don't have one? It's sick to live here and not have a boat."

"Can't afford it."

"Your paycheck's bigger than mine."

"Not after alimony."

"How long you been divorced, Dan?" Little Mary asked. She had a sweet voice.

"Not long enough."

"How much you get shafted for?" Harper asked him. "I thought they knocked that off . . . women liberated and all."

"Well, we went to the hearing. The judge said, 'Mr. Lenson, I'm giving your wife eleven hundred dollars a month.' And I said, 'Okay, Judge, maybe I'll kick in a couple dollars, too.' "

Harper laughed, then the women. "Funny. But *eleven hundred*? A month? Shit, she raped you, man. For how long?"

"Permanent, till she remarries. Get this: The judge was a woman."

"Yeah, she filleted you and put you on the table." Harper looked up at the rigging, then said to Big Mary, "Get me another brew, okay, bitch? And bring up that cheese stuff."

"Don't call me that, Jay. I'm not your wife."

"I'll call you what I fucking like on my boat. Get the beer, bitch."

She passed one up for Dan, too. He sucked deeply, knocking his head back against the coaming. He was exaggerating, inviting their sympathy. Six hundred of the eleven hundred was child support. And there'd be a review after five years. But still, Harper was right: It didn't leave much.

"Which is why you're livin' on the ship," said Harper, chiming in uncannily with his thoughts. "Yeah, I can see where you'd be pissed."

THEY picked up the tide around two. Sullivans Island slid by and they headed between the jetties, out to sea. Harper crossed the channel and hugged the port side as containerships and trawlers plowed past. *Blow Job* began pitching as she passed buoy Romeo 14, rusty bell clanging dolefully. The sun glared off the water in a million scintillating points. Little Mary asked Dan to sunscreen her back, then turned, offering her breasts. He felt dizzy and his bladder was full. "There a head aboard?" he asked Harper.

"Below and forward. Hey, and long as you're down there, bring up a towel. Should be some in the V-berth."

He let himself down the companionway gingerly. It would be smoother outside the bar, but right now she was going up and down so hard, he felt queasy.

Belowdecks, the Alberg was roomier than he expected: a deep main cabin with settees and a galley; gimballed lamps and a hatchway that he guessed accessed the engine. "Beer in the icebox," Harper shouted down from the blue cutout of sky, and Dan remembered the head. He went forward and found it. It was small but had everything he needed, and he sagged into the teak, closing his eyes as he drained used beer.

He was in the V-berth looking for the towels when the door closed behind him. He whipped around in the sudden dimness, feeling himself grow heavy, then light, almost floating, as the bow reared up and then dropped away.

A slim silhouette curved against the sliced light that filtered through the louvered door.

The sea pounded and swished against the hull as Little Mary, not saying anything, pushed him back onto the damp briny-smelling cushions. She unbuttoned his shorts and jerked them down with firm, practiced motions.

Suddenly, tears stung his eyes, and he put his hands on her hair, cradling her head in the reeling, plunging darkness.

* * *

WHEN she led him back up into the cockpit, she said to Big Mary, "You were right."

"I was?"

"Yeah. Like a horse."

Dan blushed as they laughed. His head felt empty, as if his brains had been sucked out. He looked out to where the land was a black line. They were pretty far out for a small boat.

"Yeah, I figured you was one of us," said Harper.

"What do you mean?"

"A cunt hound," he said. Big Mary slid her hand up Dan's leg and into his shorts from beneath. "Not like some I can name."

"What do you mean?" He didn't feel comfortable with her fondling his balls. For one thing, she had long fingernails. For another, he didn't feel comfortable having sex practically in front of another guy, especially one who worked for him. But it was a little late for second thoughts. He took the cold one Little Mary handed up from below.

Harper drawled, "I ever tell you I was on the *South Carolina*? They used to call her 'the Love Boat.' Want to know why?"

He didn't care, but because it was Harper's boat and his party, he said, "Why?"

"Because they had queers up the ass. There was a yeoman, and he started ordering other queers in. They spread the word, and guys started requesting transfers, and finally there was a hundred and ten out of six hundred crew. They called themselves 'the Family.' I was a chief then."

The girls had gone below, and Harper lowered his voice as if he was telling a dirty story, although he hadn't when he actually *had* been telling dirty stories. "There was this guy in Combat—if you put your hand over his mouth, he looked like the most beautiful woman you'd ever hope to see. Remember when they came out with the fifty percent bigger Mars bar? He used to put two of them together and swallow them. Put 'em in his mouth, then take them out—dry. The master-at-arms finally caught him sixty-nining another guy.

"That's the only way you can get them, see—you either have to catch 'em actually fucking each other or else make them admit it. . . . The strangest one was a storekeeper. A couple of Navy docs came aboard and took him off. Stripped his rack with rubber gloves and put everything in plastic bags. I'm still not sure what that was all about." He looked aloft, then turned to check the horizon. Dan did, too.

"And the *Kearsarge*, an *Essex*-class carrier out of San Diego, they used to call her the 'queer barge.' They had a boiler technician chief, they found Polaroids of two hundred sailors in his locker.

He'd get the young kids down there in the hole, feed them jungle juice, then his guys would strip them and tie them up. The kids weren't queers, but they got made into queers.... And *LaSalle*, the flagship in the Persian Gulf, another nest of 'em." Harper searched the cockpit for cigarettes, found Big Mary's pack. He lighted one, looking off at the now-dropping sun as it gilded the sea. "Shit, just thinking about faggots makes me want to dump my lunch in my briefcase. But it's funny. There were guys who didn't believe it. I guess just not everybody sees things like that. And some of them, it's hard to tell."

Dan said, "Why are you telling me this, Chief Warrant?"

"Why? Ain't no why, Lieutenant. Just that I was glad to see you ain't got knee- pads on your trousers. What about that little brown fucking machine? She's got a nice body, a nice attitude; she takes care of herself. I figured you'd like her."

"She was something."

"Know how to tell you got a good blow job? When it's over, you got to pull the sheets out of your ass."

"It's not just the sex. She's nice. How'd you meet them?"

"The usual way. Hit 'em with a monkey's fist." Harper chuckled. "I was standing on the pier when one of the other ships left for deployment. One pulls out, another slides in, you know? Big Mary had this see-through top on. I asked if I could buy her a drink. The rest is history."

Dan felt something; he wasn't sure what. "And Little Mary?"

"They're friends. They're in some kind of wives' club together."

"Some kind of—" He went tense. "You mean she—"

"Sure, they're married, if that's what you mean. Little Mary, her husband's Air Force in Japan. Don't sweat it; he's having a good time, too. Ever been to Yokosuka? USS *Newport*, an old patrol frigate they built for the Russians. We'd ask the girls, 'You got clap?' 'Yes.' 'Syphilis?' 'Yes.' 'Gonorrhea?' 'Yes.' 'You got VD?' 'No, me no got VD.' Short time was a hundred yen; all night was two hundred yen, and your blues were clean and pressed in the morning. Three hundred and sixty yen to the dollar. I thought I'd died and gone to heaven."

Dan didn't laugh. They were on a reach now, still headed out. The wake chuckled under the counter, smooth yet slightly roiled, as if things were moving under the surface of the sea. "I didn't know she was married," he muttered.

"I ever show you the old shell game?" Harper said. He was drunk, Dan realized, even through his own beer fog. But the man carried it. He didn't reel or glaze, just got more intense. "Hey! Bitch!"

"Yeah, asshole?"

"Hand me up some of them plastic cups." Harper fished in his pocket, broke the foil pack. He arranged the cups mouth-down on the cockpit seat and put one of the condoms under one of them. "See which one I put it under?"

"Yeah."

"This one here?"

"Yeah."

"Now watch close. You take this one and move it here—and that one and move it—and—" He lifted his hands. "For twenty bucks: Where's the rubber?"

Dan considered. Harper's hand had hesitated, then reversed direction. A little faster and it would have fooled him, but the chief warrant was drunk, just the tiniest bit slow.

"Come on, which one?"

"That one."

Harper grinned. He lifted the cup, and Dan stared at nothing.

"Forget the twenty, Lieutenant. You never seen this? Here's how it's done." He put the cups back and did it again, and this time Dan saw that the hesitation was not an accident but that it drew the eye while the other hand twitched the right-hand cup aside. "Classic misdirection. Make 'em think they've won. Then, when they lift the last cup—*nada.* They're dicked."

Dan looked at the dropping sun. "How long we staying out? We don't want to go back in the dark, no radar—"

"I know the channel," said Harper, grinning. "And we got loran. Hey! Little Mary! Your man needs another *ba me ma.* Enjoy yourself, shipmate. Next week, we're going to sea."

11

THE house was a five-bedroom on a cul-de-sac in a quiet subdivision, one of many carved out of the flat piney land west of the Ashley as the city had grown. Leighty, in slacks and a cotton sweater, was in the kitchen slicing carrots when he heard the door chimes.

"We're a little early," said George Vysotsky.

"I'd be surprised if you weren't. Come on in. Hi, Carol." He shook Vysotsky's hand, gave his wife a hug. Then he followed them into the high-beamed living room. An older couple smiled up from the sofa. "George, Carol, I'd like you to meet the Kavanaughs; they live down the street. Robert's retired. Joan, George is my number two on the ship. Carol has three little ones at the moment, but she runs a framing shop in her spare time. Grab a chair, the sofa, whatever. Jeannette's warming up dinner. How about a drink? We've got wine, beer—"

"Beer for me," said Vysotsky, settling himself into a recliner. He looked casual in a sports shirt and slacks. Carol stood at a floor-to-ceiling window for a moment, then said, "I'll see if Jeannette needs any help."

"George, what'd you think of the game?"

"Not much. I had guys on my team back on the *Shangri-La* that could have outpitched that Reasoner. Say you were ex-Navy, Bob?"

"Army, does that get me thrown out?"

"No, hell. Europe? Asia?"

"I'd date myself if I told you," said Kavanaugh. "But what the hell. North Africa, Sicily, south of France, Germany. Then a very cold place called Korea. I got out after that, started a food-service business."

They talked about baseball for a while, then Leighty cleared his throat and caught Vysotsky's eye. The XO followed him out into the backyard, where dusk was falling. They looked across the pool to a metal framework draped with vines. "You get any grapes on those?" Vysotsky asked him.

"A few, but the birds get them first. I never seem to be around at the right time."

"I know what you mean."

"I don't like to take business home, George."

"I know that, Tom."

"When I walk off that brow, I try to put it out of my mind till the next day. But we've got to do something about this yeoman-personnelman situation, and we've got to do it soon."

"Benner's trying hard."

"He does okay, but he's a three-oh sailor at best, and shorthanded he's getting further and further behind." The captain took a pull off his mug of beer. "I mentioned it to Fieler—he's got the *Ingram*. They're getting ready to go into overhaul and he says he's got a second-class personnelman he'll let me have outright. Straight transfer."

"What's wrong with that gift horse?"

"My thoughts exactly. You might call his exec and check it out, though. It could be the guy just doesn't want to go to Philadelphia in the winter."

"That would still leave us short. I was thinking of pulling Cephas out of the Weapons office, but then what does Lenson do? I don't want to throw any sticks in his wheels."

"It would be great if we could get somebody aboard before we shove off for Gitmo. Make them part of the shakedown."

"I'll call *Ingram*'s XO first thing in the morning, sir. But I want to get on the phone again with the squadron."

"Sure, keep pushing that button. The system's supposed to man us to a hundred percent for deployment." Leighty thought for a moment, hands thrust into his slacks. "There was something else I wanted to—oh, the beard issue. Is that put to bed?"

"The men have the word. The usual bitching and moaning, but they'll show up clean-shaven. The only hitch is Mr. Deshowits."

"Religious objections?"

"Yes."

"That could be difficult."

"I called Chief Hone; he's checking it out. I know there's a medical exemption for people who have that ingrown beard problem. But he said he didn't think they'd be making any other exceptions."

"Dinner's ready, guys," said Mrs. Leighty, coming out into the backyard. She picked up a tricycle, moved it out of the way. Smoothing her hair, she said briskly, "I hope you all like lamb."

* * *

"SO long, thanks for coming." He shook Kavanaugh's hand, slapped Vysotsky's back, smiled at the women. Leighty stood with his wife as they went down the walk. "Good dinner," he told her. "I think they enjoyed themselves."

"I like Carol. We ought to see more of them."

"Maybe we need to start thinking about a predeployment party. We haven't had the wardroom together since the commissioning."

"I could make chili—"

"No, I don't want you to do it. See if that woman can cater it—what was her name, the one who did the crab bisque?"

"Peggy."

"We need to look at a night and get it set up for when we get back from Gitmo. Maybe do a pool party. . . . How's Dougie doing?"

"He's not feeling well. He went to bed early."

"You're not coming down with anything, are you?"

"No, I feel all right. And Heather's still fine."

"How did you like the Kavanaughs?" he asked her, looking at a stairway that led off the living room.

"They seemed all right. Quiet."

"He's ex-enlisted. He probably felt a little ill at ease."

"Really? After all those years, and having his own company?"

"I've seen it before," Leighty said. "Look, I'm going up to the office for a while. Got a lot of stuff to read through before we get under way."

"Are you going to be up late?"

"Not too late."

"I'm just going to put these things in the dishwasher," she said.

He patted her and went up a narrow flight of stairs and turned on a light at the top.

The third floor was almost a separate apartment: a large room with a table in the center stacked with books and official references in binders, a set of weights and a rowing machine; a wall mirror. The rug was old, greasy, smelling of dog. A door led to a bathroom and shower; in an alcove was a single bed with a reading lamp clipped to the headboard. A long table held a Radio Shack computer and a printer converted from a Selectric typewriter. Leighty flicked them on as he walked by, stripping off his shirt, and sat at the rowing machine. He fitted his feet to the straps, and for twenty minutes there was no sound but the rapid click of the machine, the barking of a dog downstairs, the hum of the computer and printer as they waited, screen empty. After that, he did a hundred push-ups in sets of twenty, seventy-five sit-ups, then finished with twenty fast pull-ups on a bar in the door to the bathroom.

He stood in front of the mirror, looking at his body, the muscles hard and defined, engorged with blood from the fast, hard workout. He touched his chest lightly, feeling the resistance of muscle. He looked into his eyes. Me, he thought. This is me. Now is now. I am at home. Everything I need is right here.

He turned away, looking angry, and sat down in front of the computer.

LATER he stood in his bare feet, listening outside one of the bedrooms. His hand rested on the doorknob. Then he turned it silently and eased the room within into visibility.

The boy lay amid rumpled covers, legs flung out. In the dim light coming through the window, the man stood looking down at him. The faint roughness of the boy's breathing was just discernible. He'd had a virus for the past few days, been cranky and tired. His hand reached out to the boy's forehead, brushed his hair lightly. The child turned his head, drew his limbs in, flung them out restlessly, turned over. He waited motionless till all was silent again, then eased the door closed. He looked in on his daughter next. She was sleeping with a large stuffed clown. He knew it was silly—she was fine—but he still watched the covers till he could see the rise and fall of her chest.

He padded down the stairs into the darkened living room. Moving silently, he policed up glasses and ashtrays and carried them in and left them in the sink. Then he went back to the stairwell.

He paused at the second floor, looking out the window at the end of the bedroom hall. He just stood there, looking out.

The streets in this subdivision were empty at night. Only occasionally did a car roll past. But from up here, he looked down on a square of light several houses over. Leaping shadows moved back and forth across it. He couldn't see faces, just bodies. Only when he leaned close to the glass could he hear very faintly the distant shouts, the faint scrape and thud and thump as a basketball was lofted, missed, kissed asphalt, lofted again, shuddered off the backboard into a flurry of young lithe bodies that knotted, then broke again into a run.

Watching the leaping shadows, he remembered the first time his brother had taken him to the Y to swim. He'd undressed in the cold cubicle and come out, to find everyone naked. Then they'd gone through a little tunnel and come out into a wide white echoing place. Sun streamed down from high windows, outside which you could see the upper parts of trees. And all around the pool were naked young men—diving from a low board, clinging to the edge of the pool as they talked, jumping from the sides, seeming to float in the air before plunging down into the foaming, slightly murky water. The chlorine tang made his eyes smart. He saw their penises glistening, water running from them as they climbed out of the pool. Arms, muscles, legs, thighs, ribs, flesh. He hadn't even swum that day, not till his brother threw him in. He'd wanted nothing but to stand by the pool, shivering, and look.

It was the first time he'd realized that men were beautiful.

"Tom?"

He turned and saw his wife standing in the doorway to their bedroom, holding her housecoat closed at the neck. Her hair was down and her bare face shone, floating in the darkness.

"You startled me. I thought you were asleep."

"I'm sorry. I was waiting for you. Are you coming to bed?"

"I've got a couple things to do yet. I don't want to bother you. Maybe I'll just take my shower upstairs."

She didn't answer and he added, "Is that all right?"

"I guess so," she said.

"Good night, if I don't come down before you go to sleep."

"Good night."

At the top of the stairs, he stopped and leaned into the wall. He held his hand over his face, then took it away, breathing rapidly several times. Crossing the room, he sat down again in front of the keyboard.

12

WITH all due respect, you don't want to do it, Captain. It's too close to your sailing date."

"I'm not sure that's the right approach, Mr. Grobmyer."

"Sir, we see this day in and day out. NAVSEA tells you this; type commander tells you that. You can waste a lot of time and money running back and forth on that treadmill."

"You're saying these specifications may change?"

"Hell, I'll flat out guarantee they will, Captain."

Leighty leaned back. His eyes followed Pedersen as the steward bent with the coffee server. "What do you think, Jay? Is this a major project? What exactly's involved?"

Shit, Dan thought angrily. There he goes again, asking Harper.

Another day in the yard. They were in the wardroom, progress conference again, and in the middle of a wrangle about electrical repair benches. The Naval Safety Center had come out with new requirements, and the question was whether *Barrett* had to meet them now or wait till the next yard period. He tuned back in as Harper cleared his throat. "According to *Ships Safety Bulletin*, you got to insulate all vertical surfaces with eighth-inch plastic laminate. That means the knee knockers under the table, the ends of the workbenches, the back panel, the top shelf—"

"What about horizontal surfaces?" Leighty asked him.

"They're already insulated. Then you got to cover the foundation with either rubber matting or more laminate, and check the hinges, door handles, and catches to make sure they're nonconducting material."

"What about the sign?"

"We can do the sign for you, Captain," said the shipyard rep, doodling on his pad. "Not a problem. But all this laminate has got to be hand-measured, hand-cut, hand-fitted. That's four, five man-days we're talking, times three workbenches, and you're pulling chocks out of here day after tomorrow."

"I'm aware of when we get under way, Mr. Grobmyer."

"Yes, sir. Sorry."

"But I'm not sure this is something we don't need. Jay, how about it, do we need this?"

"No, sir," said Harper. He tapped the message. "We're grandfathered. Paragraph four. 'Commands meeting specs of NAVAIR drawing sixty-three A one fourteen'—that's us—'may defer action until the next regular overhaul period.' "

"There you go, sir," said Grobmyer. "Now, let's go to the helicopter deck-edge net modifications—"

"Hold on," said Leighty. "That's not what I meant. This sounds like something that could protect our guys." His eye snagged Dan's and he blinked. "Uh, what's your take on this, Lieutenant?"

"I tend to agree with the Chief Warrant, sir."

"How many volts are they playing with on those benches?"

"There's around twenty thousand volts on the CRTs, sir."

"That's a lot of juice."

"The guys know it's dangerous. They ground everything."

"I'm sure they do. But what if we have to make repairs in a seaway and we're rolling? I can see somebody losing his balance, falling." Leighty turned to the civilian. "We'll comply with the new directive, Mr. Grobmyer."

Grobmyer doodled, then shrugged. "Your call, captain. But like I said, I got to get ship supe's chop. An' I don't think I'm gonna get it for anything you get grandfathered for, like your chief warrant says."

"How about this, then: Cut us three sets of the lucite, or whatever it is, and our guys will install it themselves. Can you do that for us?"

"That's gonna take time, too, to do the measurements, do the cutting—"

"I seem to recall my men assisted yours on the reinstallation of the launcher guiderails," said Leighty.

"Yeah, they did." Grobmyer looked startled, then his jowls went bland again and he made a note. "Okay, sir. Can do. Okay, next issue. We got the nets rewired, put them on starting tomorrow. Crane'll be here Thursday for the weight test. . . ."

Dan half-listened to the rest of the report. He wondered why Leighty was making such a big deal out of the workbench issue. Generally, if you had any leverage over the yardbirds, you saved it—there was always something critical they forgot to do or had to do over. But Leighty had just cashed in his chips.

A flicker of motion caught his eye. He looked at the bulkhead, then through it, through the porthole, to where the mast of a sailboat was tracing slowly across the circle of inch-thick glass.

He remembered Little Mary's hands, firm and expert, her lips.

He still felt badly that she was married. But he hadn't known. She didn't wear a ring or anything.

Anyway, so what?

The captain got to his feet, and Vysotsky and the other officers jumped up. "Carry on," Leighty said.

The meeting broke. The joiner door slammed as some officers left, and others who'd been waiting outside came in. One was Mark Deshowits. Dan nodded, noticing he still had his beard.

"I heard a good one," said a voice behind him.

Dan swung. It was Lieutenant (jg) Van Cleef, the communications officer. He would have been movie-star material, but his jaw jutted too far, making his face seem deformed when you first met him. His nickname was "Cowcatcher." "What's that, Keon?" he said.

"There were these three gay guys in bed together, professional athletes, and they're shooting the shit. And the conversation turns to what game's the most fun. And the first guy says, 'Basketball. It's gotta be my game. I love it when you go up in the air and just rub up against all the other players.' "

Dan cleared his throat, glancing involuntarily toward a white-uniformed back at the coffee urn.

"And the second faggot says, 'Naw, it's gotta be football. You can't imagine how good it is in a huddle, everybody pressed together, and then—a pileup! I come every time it happens.' "

The other officers had gone silent. Was it his imagination or were their eyes making the same traverse . . . from Van Cleef to the man who stood, back still to them, at the coffee urn? "And then the third guy says, 'You're both full of shit. The best sport's what I do. Baseball.' And they both go, 'What!' 'You're putting us on, man! What's so great about baseball? Shit, you play way the hell out in the outfield!'

"And the guy says, 'Yeah, that's right. And when a fly comes out my way and bounces and I catch it, and the guy's tearing ass for second base, and I'm standing there tossing the ball up and down and looking where to throw, and there's thirty thousand people yelling, "Throw it, you *cocksucker*!" See—I love the *recognition*.' "

A snigger ran around the wardroom, then stopped. Dan eased his head around.

The captain had turned around to face them, coffee cup lifted from the saucer, hanging in the air like one of those floating magnet toys for bored executives. He didn't smile. And for that frozen second, Dan felt as if a door had come open, and he didn't want to look inside. Beside him, Vysotsky began, "Look, you people—" but Leighty interrupted him: "Mr. Van Cleef."

"Yes, sir?"

"What was the result of the classified-materials inspection? I don't recall getting a report on that."

"Uh, I sent it up via the XO, sir."

"Have you seen it, George? What were the results?"

"Uh, there were some discrepancies."

"Such as?"

Van Cleef stammered, "There's a . . . a card supposed to be on the outside of all of our safes. That you initial who opened it every day, who closed it. A Form eight thirty-three. And—"

"And what?"

"And we needed to change some of the combinations—and the letters of access, we've got them being retyped—"

"What was your overall grade, Mr. Van Cleef?"

"Satisfactory, sir."

"Not outstanding?"

"No, sir."

"Not excellent?"

"No, sir, Captain."

"Was there a number grade, Mr. Van Cleef?"

"Seventy-two, sir," said the comm officer miserably.

"*Barely* satisfactory, I would say. I'd like to see a copy of the original inspection report, along with your section of the Fleet Training Center inspection guide."

"Yes, sir, I'll . . . I'll bring it right up."

Taking his time, Leighty finished his coffee, replaced the cup on the sideboard, and knocked twice on the sliding door. Pedersen's face showed for a second before it and the cup disappeared.

"I'll be in my cabin," Leighty said. He went to the joiner door, opened it, and left.

The comm officer sat down. The other officers looked at him curiously, then, as if by tacit agreement, drifted away. Dan saw Harper sitting by the aft bulkhead, a copy of *Navy Times* on his lap.

Slowly, deliberately, the chief warrant winked at Dan.

THE rest of the day went by in a blur. There were dozens of things to be done to get ready for sea. A bright spot was the report from Chief Mainhardt. DS2 Williams had gotten Version Three of the ACDADS operating software to run over the weekend. Dan was glad to hear it. Without a running combat system, they couldn't do the at-sea gun and missile shoot. But they had to in order to align systems before going to Gitmo, and they had to pass Gitmo before deploying overseas. Everything was scheduled so fucking tight, he thought. But now it was up.

So he was on a high, standing on the forecastle, actually feeling pretty good, when the police car and van shot past him on the pier and squealed to a halt by the brow. He went to the lifeline and leaned out to see around the bulge of the ship. Chief Glasser was on the quarterdeck. He said something to the petty officer of the watch, then strolled down the gangway. Glasser leaned into the lead car as behind it the doors of the van popped open and two uniformed base cops got out and went around to the back.

Dan put his hands in his pockets and drifted aft through the breaker.

It was Sanderling. The slight seaman looked as if he'd been washed too hot and dried on high. The husky cops, ex-marines probably, flanked him, made him look about ten years old. One was showing Glasser some paperwork. The chief bent to sign it, the cop tore it off and handed it to him, and Glasser nodded curtly to Sanderling.

Dan was waiting when they reached the quarterdeck. "What's going on, Chief?"

"Morning, sir. Sanderling here, they caught him over in the Exchange shoplifting cassettes."

"No, sir, that ain't it at all." A hot, unjustly accused face turned toward Dan. "They got it all wrong. I was getting some tapes for the captain. I was lookin' at 'em, and I got six or seven. My hands was full, so I put two in my pocket. And they was watching me and they—"

"What are you doing in civvies in the middle of the day, Sanderling?"

"Captain told me to pick them up on the way in, take my time."

"But it's three hours after quarters—" Dan cut himself off; he wasn't Sanderling's division officer. "That the charge sheet, Chief?"

"Yes sir. Want to see it?"

"No. Get Mr. Harper up here."

"Aye aye, sir. Flipper, pass the word: Chief Warrant Officer Harper, quarterdeck."

"Sir, just ask the captain. He'll tell you—"

"We'll see, Seaman Sanderling. You'll probably be telling him about it at mast, anyway."

"Chief Harper, lay to the quarterdeck," said the 1MC. Glasser closed his eyes in exasperation. "Stay here," he grunted to Sanderling, and went inside the quarterdeck shack.

"Damn it, Sandy. You're damage control team–trained, fire fighting–trained—we're going to need every man in Gitmo. Didn't you think about that?"

"But they got it all wrong, Mr. Lenson. Like I said—"

"Chief Warrant Officer Harper, quarterdeck."

The phone beeped and the petty officer snatched it. "Yeah. One of your guys up here, base police just brought him back . . . Sanderling. . . . Yes, sir." He hung up. "He'll be right up, sir," he told Dan.

Looking at the seaman's hurt face, his torn pockets, he felt a momentary doubt. Then he remembered the mutterings in the computer room.

"I'm gonna talk to him a minute, okay, Chief?"

"Suit yourself, sir."

When they were out of earshot, he leaned against the king post for conrep station number 3. "What's the story on you and the captain, Sanderling?"

"What do you mean, sir? I been fixing his entertainment system."

"Seems like it's needed a lot of fixing lately."

"It's broke all the time, that's why. It's a shitty system; they bought low bid." Sanderling's eyes went still. "Or are you askin' me something else, sir?"

"You seem to be friendly with him."

"We talk. He's okay." The seaman's eyes slid off Dan's toward the pier. "What you want me to say, sir? He's the captain. I'm a seaman second. Sometimes we talk about music."

He couldn't tell if the man was being evasive or just defensive. He thought for a second of asking him something along the lines of "Does he ever try to touch you?" But that sounded like something you'd say to a child. Anyway, what could Sanderling tell him? If he admitted something and Dan reported it, ship's office would start discharge proceedings tomorrow.

So he didn't ask. He just turned, and there was Jay Harper on the quarterdeck. "There you are, you little son of a bitch," Harper said furiously. "I got him, Glasser. Sanderling, you little pansy thief. I ought to cut your nuts off."

Dan said, "Report to me later and tell me what this is all about, Chief Warrant." Then he walked aft, forcing himself to detach even as he heard Harper shouting.

HE picked Beverly up at her apartment and took her out to an Italian place. He felt her warmth against his back as they rode, arms wrapped around him, tightening every time he leaned into a curve. But dinner felt strained. He was tired and she didn't have much to say, either. He kept catching her eye, but when he looked right at her, she dropped her gaze.

"How's Billy?"

"He's fine. He wanted to know if you were coming over tonight."

"Yeah?"

"He wanted to stay up till we got back." She smiled. "You've got a fan."

"He's a good kid."

"You look tired."

"I guess I am. We're coming down to the wire on the availability."

"That's one of those weird Navy words that means something else, right?"

"It means being pierside at the shipyard—so they can fix stuff."

"I see. Well, we don't have to go to the movie if you don't feel up to it."

There it was again, her fucking agreeableness. "You wanted to see that one, didn't you?"

"Yes, but I can go anytime. I can see it with a girlfriend when you're at sea." She smiled faintly. "I'll have plenty of free time then. Why don't we just go home? You can lie on the couch. I'll rub your neck."

The sitter met them at the door, a finger to her lips. "Oh, he fell asleep?" Strishauser said, pulling off her linen jacket. "He wanted to stay up and see Dan. Here, is this enough? Thanks, Jennie."

She turned to Dan. "Just let me look in on him. I'll be right out. Wine in the refrigerator." She went off and he strolled into the kitchen. A roach—no, he corrected himself dryly, in Charleston they were "palmetto bugs"—froze on the sink as he flipped the light on. The Lancer's was in the fridge. He found glasses and poured two tall ones.

She came out in a pale flowered robe, not silk, but padded cotton. A housewife's cover-up, he thought. She wasn't wearing her glasses, and her eyes blinked, making her look puzzled. They settled on the couch, and the quiet grew longer, till it was a living thing one of them would have to kill. Beverly finally did. "Can I ask you a question?"

"Shoot."

"I know how you feel about . . . your ex-wife. But don't you think all this bitterness is hurting you more than her?"

"Bitterness?"

"Yes, I know, 'What bitterness?' I don't think men know half of what goes on in their own heads. You're full of anger, Dan. So full, it spills over on me. Sometimes it makes me mad. Most of the time, it just makes me sad."

"Well . . . I'm pissed, yeah. I got hurt. She gets my daughter and two-thirds of my fucking paycheck. You call that fair?"

"Don't you think she might have been hurt, too?"

"She didn't have to leave."

"She must have felt she did."

"I can't control what people feel. We had a house, furniture, a car. A hell of a lot better than my parents ever had it. We had Nan. Betts was going to school part-time. She could have done anything she wanted. I'm not the most in touch with my feelings kind of person. I'm not spontaneous, but I was trying to change. I *was* changing. What does she do? Fuck some asshole she meets in a bar." He tossed the last of the wine off, got up, and got another. She shook her head when he held up the bottle. "Her parents are rich. I couldn't match what she grew up with. And then she got into this feminist stuff—"

"You know, I don't drink very much—except when I'm with you. Then I always get up with a headache the next day."

"Well, your cigarettes give me a headache, too."

"You didn't notice." She sounded hurt.

"Notice what?"

"I haven't smoked at all this evening. I thought you'd be pleased." He couldn't think of anything to say to that, so he just felt guilty, then angry because she made him feel guilty.

"Did you ever ask her what she needed to be happy?"

"Who?"

"Your ex-wife."

"I don't know. Look, I really don't want to talk about this stuff now."

"I'm sorry. I just wanted to help. I don't see how you can—it's hard to be happy when you keep all that bottled up inside you."

"Now you sound like her."

"Do I?"

"That's what she was always saying—that I bottled everything up till my brains fizzed. She called it 'rigid Academy bullshit.' Hey, if it wasn't for the Navy, I'd be back in Pennsylvania wiring houses." He got up and went to the window and pulled the curtain aside. His bike was sitting at the curb, under the light. Shit, he thought, I got to get that turn signal fixed.

"I know," she murmured.

"What do you know?"

"How it feels, having someone tell you what you're like, belittle you. Carl made me feel like I couldn't do anything right. He'd criticize me at every opportunity, tell me I was helpless, that I exaggerated my feelings. I hated myself because I believed what he told me. Then I found out about his affairs."

Dan looked out the window. "Yeah?"

"My friends all knew. I finally opened my eyes and saw what had been right in front of me. That's what made me realize that I had to get out. For my own sanity and for Bartholomew—for Billy's." She paused. "Is that what your wife did? Have an affair?"

"I told you that."

"Not till tonight."

"I told you that first time I met you."

"So you know how it feels," she said in a faint voice.

He thought, What is this? He jerked the curtain closed, went over to her, ran his hands down her back under the robe.

"I locked his door," she murmured.

He uncovered her long pale body, her hollow thighs. He thought of Baird's heavy white breasts, of Little Mary's dark nipples. He pushed her down on the rug and plunged into her, riding the bone at the bottom of her belly with his weight till she tightened in a choked, shuddering murmur.

THEIR clothes were scattered over the couch and the coffee table. They lay together on the floor.

She whispered, "Have you been seeing Sibylla?"

"What?"

"I said, have you been seeing Sibylla Baird? The artist?"

"I don't know what you're talking about."

She stretched out a blue-shadowed arm for her wine. She sounded cool, but her hand was trembling. "Where did that come from?" he asked her.

"She's a friend of mine. Have you been dating her?"

"Does it matter?"

"It matters to me. I'd like the truth, please."

"Well then—yes."

"How many other women have you been seeing, Dan? Since you started dating me?"

"I don't know."

"You must *know*, Dan. You must keep score. In your head, at least."

"Holy shit." He sat up. "What is this? Do you want a list?"

"Yes. Why don't you make me a list, Dan. Just so we both know."

"All right. Jesus. Three."

"That you dated?"

"Yes."

He saw her ribs rise and fall as she took a deep breath and let it out. Her fingertips gripped the skin of her belly into faint pale wrinkles. "Did you go to bed with them?"

"I don't know."

"Oh God. *Did* you, Dan?"

". . . Yeah."

"With Sibylla?"

"Yeah."

"And the others . . ."

"Yes."

"Do I know them? The others?"

"No."

She reached out suddenly and he flinched, but she only grabbed at her robe. She shook a cigarette out with quick nervous motions and lighted it, and he saw that she was weeping.

"I'm sorry. I didn't mean for you to know."

"Is that supposed to be thoughtful? Am I supposed to thank you for that?"

He didn't answer. She went on, "I know. You didn't promise anything. Maybe I'm being naïve about all this. I guess that's the way things are these days . . . the *dating* scene. . . ." She tilted her head back and breathed smoke into the empty air. "Maybe I'm the trouble. I need a man as part of my life. And Billy does, too. . . . Believe me, I know I shouldn't love you. But I'm afraid I do. Maybe it's my fault that you felt like you needed the others. If I'd said it sooner, maybe you wouldn't have needed to look elsewhere for whatever—whatever it is they gave you."

He felt sorry for her, but it was irritating, too. He'd never promised her a damn thing, and she was acting like it was the end of the world. "I don't want you to love me."

"Why not?"

He couldn't tell her what the real reasons were, that he just didn't like her enough. She was too clinging; she smoked; her accent, the ugly dress shields . . . "I don't know. I just don't want to love anybody anymore."

"Didn't it feel good, what we just did? Don't you want to keep on doing it?"

"Sure, but now you're talking about something else, okay? It's just not on my list of priorities right now. You're acting like my mother—"

"Your *mother*? What just happened was not exactly maternal, Dan."

"The way you want to know every little detail of what I'm feeling."

"Oh my God. When you love somebody, you want to know. You don't want to just be bodies rubbing in the night."

"Cute. But I don't feel like being owned, Bev. Can't we just enjoy each other?" He rolled over and got up, looked around for his shorts, found them under a cushion. "That was what I liked about you. That we could just be together and you wouldn't start demanding stuff."

"I knew that before you told me, Dan—that you didn't want me to love you. You're right, sex is good, but I can't leave my feelings at the door. I might as well go to an aerobics class."

"Well, you're not getting any more out of me than that," he said, knowing it was too blunt and too coarse, but she just wasn't getting it.

"But I can offer *you* more, Dan. Companionship. Friendship. Billy needs a dad. And I can offer . . . what your ex-wife didn't. I won't do what she did to you."

Something huge and painful was welling up deep inside, something that wanted to tear its way out, but he couldn't let it. He kept getting dressed. He was crying, too; he couldn't tell why, whether from her pain or his own. "But I don't want that," he said. "Not now."

"What do you want, then? Whatever it is, I can do it. You don't have to leave. Dan? Where are you going?"

He didn't answer, just pulled the door closed. He slammed his boot down again and again on the bike, kicking it into life as if he was kicking something else to death.

HE ran the dark streets as fast as he dared, gunning through yellow lights and red, too, if he didn't see anyone coming. After several miles, the wind dried his tears to itchy trails of salt. At the gate he flicked the lights off, held up his ID as he rolled through; the guard gave him a bored wave. He headed down to the dry docks and turned right. He slowed when he came opposite the football field, lighted and empty under the stars, then gunned it again. Instead of turning, he headed down Hobson, shifting up and booting it till the engine boomed back from the slab concrete of the enlisted quarters and engineering buildings.

The Fleet Bar was almost empty. He hung his helmet and jacket and got a seat. His mind was a foam of self-loathing and anger, so seething that he couldn't tell how the hell he felt. Fuck her! What did she expect from him? He'd never promised her a thing; then suddenly, surprise, time for the prostate examination! "Double martini," he grunted, and the bartender pulled the bottle of already-mixed off its bed of ice and topped him up till the clear liquid bulged. Dan slapped a dollar on the wood and the guy went away, came back, left two quarters shining beside his glass.

He took his time sipping it, sitting there looking out the window, letting himself cool off.

Below was the river. The Fleet Bar was out on the point where Naval Base, Charleston, poked out into the curve of the Cooper. Beyond it was nothing, just low marsh and spoil that at night was only a black void smelling of dead fish. After a while, he got bored with it and swung around on the stool and looked at himself in the mirror behind the bar.

Looked at his beard.

He'd grown it during the divorce, when he didn't like what was happening, who he was, or anything else and wanted to change everything. He remembered when he'd stopped shaving, the standard Navy razz: You look like a movie star with that beard; do you smoke cigars? No, why? Too bad, you'd look just like Lassie taking a shit.

He contemplated it now from between the stacks of shot glasses, the hangers of Beer Nuts. It looked all right, looked good, in fact. A couple of people had said it made him look older, but most women liked it. Little Mary liked it.

"Another, friend?"

He nodded. A basket of popcorn rocked to a halt beside him and he reached out for a handful, chased it with cold gin.

He could refuse to cut it.

Sure, and then what? Like somebody had said—he forgot who—the Navy didn't care about big fuckups. But a little thing like not shaving . . . Was it worth losing his career over?

Career, he thought viciously, what career? He'd made it this far, but how much chance did he have of making the cut for lieutenant commander? Or screening for XO? Not much, with the lousy fitness reports from Sundstrom in his jacket and the letter of reprimand he'd gotten—that he'd *demanded*—after *Ryan* went down. Now, looking back, he couldn't believe he'd done that. He'd really shot himself in the foot on that one.

It was time to get serious.

And if he wasn't going any further, maybe he ought to think seriously about what came next.

FINALLY, he'd soaked up enough that he didn't give a shit about Beverly Strishauser or the Navy or anybody else. He staggered outside and fumbled with the key. It wouldn't go into the ignition. He forced it, then heard a snap. When he held it to the light, the break gleamed. "Fuck," he said, and kicked the bike. It wobbled, then fell over, and he heard the crash and tinkle as the other turn signal went.

A long storm-tossed time later, he came to in front of his mirror, in his stateroom. What was this, the world was made of fucking mirrors? His roommate stirred. Dimly, he remembered slamming the door open. "Sorry," he mumbled.

He stared at himself in the harsh light from the fluorescent a foot above. Black shadows half-erased his face. It seemed to shift from moment to moment, as if there were another, deeper visage beneath what shimmered in the silver surface. Through the roar of alcohol, he dimly knew and dimly feared what he'd feel like tomorrow.

That bitch. Fuck them. Fuck them all.

He leaned, staggering, over the stainless bowl and hit the tap. Air sucked in an expiring hiss, then water stammered out. It was spring-loaded like all shipboard taps and he had to hold it open till the bowl filled. As he searched through the cabinet, bottles fell out, clanged on the sink. His roommate turned over. "Hell you doing," he grunted.

"Don't care," he mumbled. "Go back ta sleep." He found what he wanted and sprayed his hand full, then rubbed the cold foam over his chin.

He didn't feel anything when he dragged the razor savagely through the beard. It didn't want to come off. He had to go over and over the tender unexposed skin. He didn't feel anything. It wasn't till someone naked and unfamiliar stared back at him that he noticed the blood. All the blood.

13
Alcorcón, Cuba

THE palms clashed restlessly in the gusty wind and small animals scuttled frantically away through the leaves. A full moon blinked through tumbling clouds. Palmetto fronds slashed like living machetes at her hands. It had rained heavily that day; the dry season was over. As she followed the other shadows, Graciela breathed what was less air than a compound of water vapor and marsh stink. And millions of mosquitoes, she thought. They droned and whined as boots and bare feet scuffed over the wet leaves. They brushed her face like the webs the great crab spiders wove between the trees, across the footpaths that threaded the canebrakes and thickets and broken unfarmable salt ground that bordered the edge of the Bahía Jigüey.

As she stumbled after the vanishing forms ahead, gasping for breath, she remembered burying Armando.

They'd put him in the ground behind the abandoned church, near his grandparents. There were no prayers. It had been a long time since there were priests at Alcorcón. So in the end, they'd just stood at the grave in silence, then placed their flowers and left.

Her bare foot stepped on something that jerked and writhed to escape her weight. The snakes of Cuba weren't poisonous, but it startled her. "Quiet," someone muttered, and she collected herself and shut her lips firmly and went on. How much farther? Her legs were growing heavy. She'd worked all day planting cane, and now the baby kicked and it was hard to breathe.

"*Estoy cansada,*" she murmured. And the whisper came back, "Tell those who are tired to keep quiet; we're almost there."

And in truth, they came out into the open only a few hundred meters farther on. The moonlight silvered a grassy hillside above a darkness that could have been a brush-filled ravine. Then the clouds slid closed again and the world was only sound: the trickle of water, the throaty baying of frogs. She sank to her knees, gasping shallow breaths around the other body within her own. Maybe she shouldn't have come. But she couldn't have stayed away, either.

She knew what they were going to discuss tonight, far from those who listened and punished.

Around the clearing, the others settled to their haunches or sat, brushing the grass first. The moon emerged, fingering their faces with swaying palm shadows, then waned again.

"Have the *policía* talked with you?" a man said from the far side of the circle. Those were the first words.

"They came to my house."

"Colón spoke to me at the store. Took me aside there and spoke to me." Ramón Colón was the head of the committee of vigilance for the *batey*.

"Of the guitar?"

"Yes."

"What is this guitar of which they are speaking?"

"It must be a code. They want to know what it means."

"Why ask us? We're peasants. There's no place in the world farther from anything than Alcorcón."

"All we know is to work and stand in line for beans, meat every nine days. A man can't live on that."

"It's not healthy for the children," said a female voice. Good, she wasn't the only woman. It was strange, this circle of the shadows, like the old stories of the assembly of spirits, the unhappy dead . . . but these were living voices—neighbors, relatives, people she'd worked beside for years in field and mill and warehouse.

The first voice, the one that had mentioned the police, said now, "Something's going to happen. What have we done, that they're afraid? Nothing, right?"

"Right, Tomás."

"Tomás" was Tomás Guzman Arredondo, her husband's younger cousin. He'd been in the army, had fought in Angola under the famous general Arnaldo Ochoa, had left a hand behind in Ethiopia.

"Don't use names. Just say 'man,' all right?"

"*Perdón.*"

"Like I was saying, we haven't done anything, but here they are trying to frighten us. They don't come around like that unless they're getting something ready."

The men talked on, the low voices of a card game or a life-and-death discussion. Graciela rocked, wincing as the baby dug its heels into her ribs. It didn't know that hurt her. It didn't know there was anything beyond the warm dark that surrounded it. But one day, it would be driven out, angry, screaming, terrified, into a world that would kill a child without remorse, that rewarded with survival only those who were willing to fight for it every second of their lives.

"So we talk, and talk. That doesn't change anything. He talks, too, the bearded one. Eight million tons of this, forty thousand hectares of that. Four hours you listen, then when he's done, you wake up and say to yourself, 'What *mierda.*' If everything's so great, how is it we still have nothing? Can every grain of rice be going to the stinking Russians? But still you have to stand and clap just like you believe such garbage."

Someone said, "Remember Silvio? I wonder what happened to Silvio."

"He left, *chico.*"

"Disappeared."

"He ran."

"What do you mean, ran? He escaped, that's what he did."

"I will explain the difference, *amigo.* If a young man leaves, a person without ties, to make himself a better life, that's escaping, no? But if someone like Silvio Padrón leaves his family here for us to feed, five kids, his *pobre* wife too sick to work—that's running. What kind of man would leave his family at the mercy of wild beasts?"

"I disagree. Who is to say what was in his heart? Maybe he just couldn't take it anymore."

"Elisa's right. Why judge him? He had to leave, and maybe we do, too."

No one spoke for a while, then someone murmured, "You're right. I say so, too. *¡Irnos para el carajo de aquí!*"

"It's all very well for you to say let's get the hell out of here, but what about those of us with families?"

"We take them, too—unless we are truly worms."

"I don't know about you, but my kids are little. They shoot people trying to escape. I hate the fucking Colóns, too, but I'm a father."

"So what, you son of a bitch? We're all fathers."

"What do you think, *abuelo*? You've seen all this before, with the Batistianos."

An aged voice, whispery as the wind in the palms: "Us old people, our lives have been lived. But Tómas is right. It's never been this bad before. If you young people can find a way, go."

"You're all crazy. How are we going to leave? Grow gossamer wings and fly away? There's no way out of here."

"Oh yes, there is. By boat."

"That is evident, my friend. It is also evident that we have no boats," said someone else sarcastically.

"They have them at the *playa.* I saw pictures—"

"We are not permitted to visit the *playa.* That is for foreigners only, and those in the Party. My son worked at the power plant there one summer, at Nuevitas, and they took him to the beach at Santa Lucía. They scrutinize your documents and take you off the bus at once if you do not have the proper pass. During the day, airplanes fly up and down the coast. At night, the guards patrol with dogs. If they catch anyone on the beach, they shoot to kill."

"Forget the beaches. If people could leave from there, Fidel and his fucking brother would be the only ones left in Cuba."

"Anyway, how can we do anything? The Colóns probably have a *chivato* here right now. When he gets back, he'll slip them a note and we'll have to explain all this to the Committee for the Defense of the Revolution."

"We're all family here, Tomás. No one here's an informer."

"Then where do they come from?"

"Perhaps they would inform on others, but not on their own family."

"I don't know—I think Tomás is right."

"On the contrary, my cousin."

"This is desperate talk. No one escapes. You hear what happens to those who try. They shoot them, there in the water. Or the sharks eat them. That's why we never heard from Silvio."

"Not according to the American radio."

"We don't know if those are lies or truth, Cousin. They mention people who make it, but those could be just names they make up. Do any of us know anyone who fled who ever wrote back? The only one we know of who tried was Silvio Padrón, and like you say, we never heard from him. He could be in prison, or shot, or eaten by the fish."

"Or perhaps he owns a gas station in Miami."

"This is all foolish talk."

"They flee from the cities. How can we flee from here?"

"*¡Mierda!* Fool, we're closer to the sea here than they are in the cities."

"Let us not curse each other, my children. We are all God's fools."

"Thank you for wise words, grandfather," said the sarcastic voice.

"Anyway, it's not true Silvio was the only one. Do you remember Juan Davalos? He and another man from Cayo Sabinal were working here with the tractors. Then one day they were gone."

"We don't know if they made it."

"*Carajo*, how can we know *anything*? The government radio says those who reach Florida are put to work in the fields without pay. The Americans call them *negritos* and treat them with contempt. There is much crime and great poverty. Do we want to live that way, without pride, without safety?"

"The government radio lies."

"Undoubtedly, but who knows if the Americans are lying, too, with their stories about how wonderful things are in Miami? Such a voyage would be dangerous. They may catch us and kill us. And we are not familiar with the sea. We could all die, you know. That must be considered, in my opinion."

Graciela had sat silent, as was fitting for a woman, listening to the arguments as rain began to fall, rustling in the leaves before patting cold drops on her back. Now she felt them all tasting the harsh truth in what the last man had said. Yes, they all could die.

"We're all dying here," she said then.

"Oh, Graciela."

"No names, Cousin."

She felt the baby's heels thud against her heart, uncomfortable and at the same time thrilling. She'd forgotten what it was like. So long ago, Coralía, then the two lost ones. She said, louder, "We are all dying now; the only difference is, here they do it slow. My husband, they killed him. If my baby Victoria had had food and medicine, she'd still be alive. The food goes to the Bolos; we have nothing. If I die on the way to Miami, that's better than living here. That is what I have to say. I'm leaving. Are there any men to go with me?"

"Be silent, woman. Don't speak of what you don't know."

"She's crazy, that one."

Only Tomás's voice, slow and serious, didn't ridicule her. He said, "If we decided to go, we'd have to have a boat. Find one, or build one."

"This is true."

"Can we build one?"

"Out of what?"

"We could decide to go if we found one, and if we did not, why, then we'd know it wasn't possible."

"It's also a crime to plan to leave. If they catch us examining boats—"

"Nothing can be done without risk. It'll take some *cojones, chico.*"

"And we know nothing about boats. We're farmers."

"Gustavo used to be a fisherman," someone said.

"That was long ago, *compadres.*"

"I know how to build a boat," said a high, young voice suddenly. Graciela wasn't sure, but she thought it might be Manuelito's.

"What's that, boy?"

"I have a book that shows how. It shows how the hull is put together and everything."

"A book?" said someone doubtfully.

"What's your boat made of, *muchacho*?"

"Wood."

"Where would we get wood?"

"It doesn't have to be wood," said Tomás. "It can be anything we can scrounge up—plywood, metal, anything. Palm boards. Sheets of tin."

"Where would we get tin?"

"If we're leaving, what will we need our roofs for, *chico*? Look, we are not stupid people here in Batey Number Three. If we all put our minds to it, I'm sure we can build a boat."

"I don't want to piss in your milk, my friends," said the sarcastic voice, "but even if you build a boat without the police or the CDR getting suspicious and sail it away without anyone seeing you, you are still only on the *bahía*. Beyond that are the cays. How will you cross them without the security forces seeing you? And beyond that are the border guards and then the maritime guard. Only past them all is the sea, and then you will need a second boat, for you can not carry the first one across solid land."

"These cays, they are islands, no? That means there must be a way through them by water, no?"

"But who among us knows it?"

"Your cousin's right. We'll need a map."

"There are many things we'll need. Food, water, a compass. How would we make a boat go? Sails? Oars?"

"There are motors in the warehouse," said a voice. "The Russian ones, for the pumps. They're shit, but perhaps one could be fixed to drive a boat."

"We should have a sail, too."

"This is all a dream, a fantasy," said the unhappy voice.

"It's not a fantasy," said Graciela. In the dark, it didn't seem out of place to speak up, even if she was a woman. She felt the child stir again under her heart, and somehow that gave her courage. She could not bring another life into this place. "It's true: We may not make it. We may die. But is this living, without food, without hope? We've been slaves too long. I say we have to leave while there is still breath in our bodies."

"She's right," came the strong, deep voice. "You know there's no other way. So let's agree now to try, and set a date, too."

"Why?"

"I learned in the army if there's no date, there won't ever be a plan. I propose the twenty-sixth of July."

Scattered laughter from the dark. It was the most famous date on the revolutionary calendar, the day Castro's forces had attacked the fortress of Santiago. "Why then, *chico*?" the sarcastic one asked.

"It's the holiday. Everybody off work, drinking and dancing in Alcorcón. That's the time to go."

"Wait. Wait," said the frightened voice. "You're going too fast.

This is dangerous. What if they find out what we're doing? We can all go to prison."

"Things can happen on the sea, too," someone else put in.

"Yes, yes. I don't think it's a good plan, and I don't agree with it," said the frightened voice.

"That's fine with us if you don't want to go, but you have to keep quiet. Understand? You have to swear."

"That's not enough," Graciela said.

"Yes, sister? Speak up."

She said loudly, "It's not enough to have that person swear. We all have to swear—not only not to talk but to kill any *chivato* who goes to Colón or the police. Even if he's our brother, cousin, father—the machete. One by one, we must give our names and swear it, by the Virgin or by Ochún, and by our blood."

Tomás's shadow loomed as he stood. "*Sí. Es verdad.* We'll swear that we will never tell who met here or what we're planning, and that we'll kill any informer, no matter who. After that, those who do not want to go to Miami with us can go home. Everyone understand? I'll swear first. I, Tomás Guzman Arredondo, swear to this by the Virgin, by the blue goddess, and by my own blood: And should I break this oath, I ask you to kill me swiftly, as I will no longer be worthy to be called a man. Now you, to my right."

The next man's voice cracked, but he coughed and spat and then spoke out. Beneath the palms, beneath the flickering shadows chased by the racing moon, they spoke on, man after man, woman after woman, old and young, some in a mutter, others loud and angry. And in the end, even the frightened voice added after the oath, "I, too, will go. I can't stay here if you all leave. What would they do to me then?"

"There. It's done," Tomás's deep voice said slowly, heavily. "*Y que el Señor nos proteja*—and may God help us all."

14

U.S. Naval Base, Charleston

NOW station the special sea and anchor detail. Make all preparations for getting under way," said the 1MC.

"Fog, damn it."

"I hate this fucking river."

Dan rubbed his hands on his trousers as he half-listened to the enlisted men behind him. They were getting under way this morning for the test shoot, and it was foggy as hell. Well, at least he hadn't been worrying about it for days. Vysotsky had only mentioned it at breakfast, as in "Oh, by the way, you'll be taking her out today, Dan."

He liked shiphandling, but he wasn't used to the river, and he wasn't used to handling *Barrett* yet, either. She was a lot bigger than the destroyers and frigates he'd learned on.

Moving his mind on, he looked down at the forecastle, where men scurried in the mist, getting the lines ready to take in. White tendrils blew between the vertical arms of the missile launcher. He could make out the bullnose, but past that, milky haze curtained the river. Not as thick as the Arctic—he remembered times he couldn't see *Ryan*'s forward gun—but heavy enough that he couldn't make out the channel buoy a hundred yards off the pier. Fortunately, this was a low-key under-way—no brass bands, no families. If the tests went well, they'd be back in tomorrow night.

Behind him, the bosun piped, "Attention," then announced, "Damage control petty officers check the setting of material condition Yoke. Make Yoke reports to the boatswain's mate on the bridge." Dan glanced up at the alert console above him, then around at the gradually filling bridge. With a new wardroom, the senior lieutenants carried the burden of sea and anchor details. Ed Horseheads, the junior officer of the deck, was finishing the checklist. The talkers were hooking their phones over their ears, faking the cords to run clear. Just then Dave Cannon, the navigator, touched his shoulder. "Dan. Papa Jack's here."

He turned to salute a heavyset older man. "Good morning, sir. Lieutenant Lenson."

"Will you be conning her, Lieutenant?"

"That's right, sir."

He hung on every word as the pilot began explaining the courses they'd steer. The pilot would advise him if he was standing into danger, but the responsibility for any mistake or accident was still the ship's.

And Charleston was the toughest channel on the East Coast, so narrow and shallow a dredge worked 360 days a year to keep it open. The river wound like a corkscrew, with a tidal current that clipped along at up to eleven knots, though usually it was more like six. If it caught you broadside, you were helpless; you'd just have to spin around as you were swept downstream, praying you didn't hit anything before you headed fair again. Two months before, the captain, OOD, and navigator of a nuclear sub had been relieved for going aground off Shutes Folly Island. They'd been only twenty yards outside the channel.

An unfamiliar face distracted his attention: pale, round, with gold-rimmed glasses. "Who's that?" Dan asked Horseheads.

"Name's Lohmeyer, sir. He's fresh off an amphib."

"What's he doing here?"

"He's Deshowits's replacement."

"His *replacement*? What happened to Mark?"

"They're holding him ashore for out-processing. Wouldn't shave off his beard, what I heard."

Dan rubbed his own chin, torn between anger and awe at the speed and ruthlessness of the Navy's response to what it perceived as insubordination. They'd obviously done a one-for-one ethnic swap to avoid the appearance of being anti-Jewish. "That's not gonna help us at Gitmo, having a brand-new damage control officer."

The boatswain said into a microphone, "The following is a test of the general, chemical, and collision alarms from the bridge. Disregard." He pressed colored switches one after the other, sending an assortment of bongs, blips, and wheeps through the ship, then announced, "Test complete. Regard all further alarms."

Papa Jack put a tobacco-stained finger on the chart. "Watch this left turn off Drum Island. The bar's creeping farther out every year. Got a current behind you going out. We wait too long on that, we'll be in trouble." He fixed Dan with a gimlet eye. "Sure you want to get under way now? Can't wait till she clears?"

"All the services are scheduled," Vysotsky said, behind Dan. "We pretty much have to get out there now, yeah."

"Okay . . . but I tell you it's time to get your rudder over, best not be occupied with anything else."

"I understand, Captain," Dan said. You addressed pilots as "Captain," which led occasionally to confusion at critical times. He studied Cannon's penciled courses on the chart: twelve different courses and turns.

"Captain's on the bridge." Leighty returned a general salute to everyone and swung himself up into the starboard-side chair reserved for the commanding officer. He adjusted his cap carefully, peering into the window. Dan wondered if he was judging the fog or just admiring his reflection. Then he was swung back by voices clamoring for attention, acknowledgment.

"Draft report, sir. Thirty-four feet, two inches forward."

Horseheads: "Yoke is set throughout the ship, sir. All preparations completed for getting under way. Bridge, CIC, and nav detail are fully manned. Forecastle and fantail report ready to get under way."

"Who's on the fantail?"

"Lieutenant Kessler."

"Sir, you have bridge-to-bridge on the walkie-talkie, charged and tested."

"Main Control reports ready to answer all bells."

He said "Very well," told Horseheads to test the rudder and lee helm, and took another deep breath. No point getting nervous, he told himself. This was just another evolution. He glanced toward Leighty. The captain was leaning back, reading his morning traffic. He looked relaxed. It was his head, too, if Dan dicked up, but he didn't look worried. That's my problem, Dan thought. I don't have any fucking confidence.

"Now all hands to quarters for leaving port."

"Combat, Bridge: how's traffic look in the channel?"

"Two small contacts downriver. Upriver is clear."

Dan saluted Leighty. "Sir, we're ready to get under way."

"Let's go."

"Mr. Lenson?" He turned, to find Sanderling at his elbow, holding out a chit. "Sir, yeoman said if you could sign this before we cast off, he could get it in today's mailbag."

"Get out of here, Sanderling! Get off the bridge!" He stared after the seaman, then forcibly erased him from his mind. He looked around one last time, at the captain, the pilot, the fog French-kissing the windows. Then took a deep breath. "Take in lines two, three, four, and five," he said. "All engines, back one-third."

* * *

HE had a few anxious moments getting *Barrett* away from the pier. The current pinned her against it broadside. He had to spring the bow out by hauling in on the stern line and pivoting her on a camel, a wooden float, between her and the pier before giving a standard ahead bell. She responded faster than he'd expected, shooting out into the channel. Then he had to stop nine thousand tons of rapidly moving ship before she went into the mud on the far side. By the time he got her headed fair, his shirt was soaked. He'd trained on steam-powered ships, where it took time for a command to take effect. Not only did *Barrett*'s gas turbines respond faster but she had controllable-pitch screws. The shafts rotated at a constant speed, and you simply changed the pitch to vary the thrust or back down. You could go from full ahead to full astern in seconds. He knew that, but his shiphandling reflexes hadn't adapted yet.

But what that also meant, he told himself, was that they had the maneuverability and power to get out of just about any jam—as long as he could see. . . .

The fog thinned as they approached the Patriot's Point bridge, but just to keep the pucker factor constant, river traffic picked up. The horn of a ship casting off sounded from starboard. The pilot pulled out a portable radio. He called the freighter, telling him to hug the west side of the channel for a two-whistle passage. He wanted *Barrett* farther to port, but Dan kept thinking, Yeah, and what if there's a trawler or something else small coming upriver; he doesn't have a pilot and he won't paint on the radar, either? Sweat trickled down his back.

So far, though, they had enough visibility to navigate by. The fog was thinning. Cannon was getting bearings off each pier they passed, and the lookouts could see the top of a TV tower. Plotting those on the chart, he gave Dan updates every two minutes on their position relative to the channel.

A bridge coalesced out of white opacity and swept past overhead, clearing *Barrett*'s mast top, it seemed, by inches. They were moving a lot faster than the five knots he'd rung up. The current. He wished they could have waited for slack tide. But as Vysotsky had said, their services were already scheduled: aircraft, targets, electronics. The operating area had been declared off-limits to mariners. They couldn't postpone; they'd be on their way south in a few days.

He sensed the current changing direction, shouldering them left as the bridge passed overhead. Then suddenly, the fog closed down again, heavy, beading the windows with trickling droplets. He could smell it, damp and ominous.

"Navigator reports: lost all visual marks."

"Resume sounding fog signals. Stand by to let go anchor." Dan pressed the intercom. "Combat, Bridge: Visibility has decreased to zero. I'm depending on you now."

Lauderdale's voice from a speaker grille. "Combat, aye. We've got a clear radar picture. Fix in thirty seconds."

Dan glanced at the pilot. The old man looked tranquil, almost asleep, like he'd been born out here on the river. Hell, maybe he had.

"Bridge, Combat: Based on a radar fix at time oh-nine, we are fifty yards left of proposed track. Nearest aid to navigation, buoy Romeo eighteen on port bow range two hundred yards. Nearest hazard to navigation, shoal water ninety yards off port beam. Depth sounder agrees. Three hundred yards to next turn, two minutes at this speed. Recommend coming left to course one-three-three at time thirteen."

"Very well," he muttered. He glanced out to the left, conscious of the shoal water out there, and froze. Something huge was taking shape behind the mist.

The tremendous black silhouette of an aircraft carrier.

His brain stalled, unable to accept what his eyes insisted they saw. Was he hallucinating? Was all this a dream, getting under way, the fog-shrouded river? But no, there it was, emerging more solid and real every second from the blowing fog. The long flat line of deck, the vertical antenna-spiked island amidships . . . it *was* a carrier. But it *couldn't* be, not to port; that was shoal water; that was *land.* Why didn't anyone scream? He opened his mouth; his hands trembled.

"Slack off, Lieutenant," the pilot muttered. "That's the old *Yorktown,* tied up at that museum they got over there. You're headed fair, just goin' to have to turn sooner than the radar's tellin' you. Fog's gonna lift once you get out to sea. Coming up on it. . . . Start turning now."

He felt his legs shaking. Of course, the maritime museum, how could he have forgotten . . . but it had been so much like the last minutes of the doomed *Ryan.* . . . The pilot cleared his throat warningly and Dan raised his voice to the helmsman. "Left fifteen degrees rudder, steady course one-three-three."

"Left fifteen degrees rudder, steady course one-three-three . . . My rudder is left fifteen, coming to course one-three-three."

"Better steady to port of that, current's setting you south something fierce here."

"Continue left to course one-two-seven."

"You're doing fine, Mr. Lenson," said Leighty casually. Dan glanced at him in surprise, wondering what kind of answer you gave to that. Finally, he just said, "Yes, sir."

Behind him, the talker said, "Combat recommends steadying course one-three-zero. The course just ordered will take us out of the channel to port."

"They're not taking the current into account," muttered the pilot. "Steady as you go."

Cannon's voice cut through the click of the fathometer, the steady hum of ventilators. "Navigator concurs with combat. Sir, recommend coming right now to one-three-zero."

Dan glanced swiftly at him. The navigator had his faced buried in the hood of the bridge radar repeater. So he was getting radar, too. And the two fixes agreed. "Nearest shoal water?" he asked him.

"Combat, Bridge: Based on a good fix at time thirteen we are one hundred yards left of proposed track and at the edge of the channel. Nearest shoal water is Hog Island, *ten yards to port.* Depth sounder reading agrees. Sir! Combat recommends hard right rudder, come to course one-four-zero immediately to avoid grounding."

"Captain, navigator concurs with that," said Cannon, pitching his voice past Dan to where Leighty sat, legs crossed. Dan turned, too, looking at him, waiting.

But Leighty didn't say anything, didn't even move. Dan felt cold. The captain had frozen. He'd seen it happen before to men faced with the necessity for decision. Leighty wasn't going to do a goddamn thing.

It was up to him.

He took two long strides out to the port wing and leaned out over the splinter shield. Whatever his decision, it had to be fast. The fog had closed in again and he couldn't see a thing. All he had was the sense of it pressing on his face, cold and clammy, a white spongy solidity all around. He could see the river below, whirling brown eddies hurrying *Barrett* inexorably toward whatever lay ahead. Whom to believe? The radar, the navigator, or the pilot? Nothing to go by but his gut.

"Steady as she goes," he called. The helmsman repeated the order in a nervous shout: "Steady as she goes, aye, sir; steadying new course one-two-nine."

The bridge, the fog, the world was silent for perhaps two minutes. Dan listened with his feet, waiting for the sibilance of steel on mud, waiting for the slowing, the easy deceleration, that meant they'd touched. Then a black shape took form ahead.

The shadow took on a pointed silhouette, then a color, becoming a red cone-shaped buoy moving swiftly down their port side. It lay over on the end of its anchor chain, dragging a heavy wake as the current swirled past. As *Barrett*'s bow wave hit, it began thrusting itself slowly in and out of the silvery river.

"Navigator, how far to our next turn?" Dan said, trying to keep his voice steady. Past Cannon's shame-faced look, he caught the captain's head, tilted back, staring expressionlessly out the dew-beaded glass.

THEY threaded the rest of the channel out in the same tension. They passed the dredge at work off Crab Bank, a black fog shadow of booms and stacks, the long, humped pipe of the outflow leading away into the shallows. The channel widened after that and Dan added a few knots, but he paid for it with a near miss with a motor yacht crossing from the Intracoastal. It loomed up suddenly white as the fog, not sounding any signals and not registering on radar till the forward lookout was actually shouting and pointing. He had to order back full and right hard rudder to miss it.

Just as the old man had said, the fog lifted a few miles past the sea buoy, raising the curtain on a calm morning Atlantic. He eased out a long breath, feeling now like he could deal with anything as long as he could see it coming.

"Sir, navigator recommends course one-one-zero true, speed twenty to reach operating area at fourteen hundred."

"Very well," he said. "Captain, permission to secure sea and anchor?"

Leighty nodded. Dan gave the new course and speed orders and the lee helm pinged. *Barrett* accelerated and turned southeast, toward the sea horizon. The boatswain's pipe shrilled. "Now secure the special sea detail. Set the normal under-way watch. Watch Section Two."

Burdette Shuffert came up and said he was ready to relieve. Dan leaned against the gas mask storage locker as he brought him up to speed. When the black officer relieved him, they went over to the starboard side and waited till the captain looked up from the message he was reading. "Captain, I've been properly relieved by Lieutenant(jg) Shuffert as OOD."

"Very well."

"I have the watch, sir."

"Very well." Leighty tossed a salute back and swung himself down, scribbling on the file and handing it back to the waiting radioman. Dan was turning for the ladder when he said, "Mr. Lenson. Could you join me for a moment?"

On the wing, Leighty glanced at the lookout, who had his glasses welded to a school of porpoises and his headphones clamped over his ears. Dan waited, wondering how the captain was going to justify the fact he hadn't made a decision there in the fog. But instead, he just said, "You did well, taking her out."

"Thank you, sir. Sorry about that carrier—"

"I could see that startled you, but you recovered. No, I meant the moment when you were getting conflicting recommendations. The only criticism I have is that you hesitated a bit too long before taking action."

Dan looked at him. *He* had hesitated? When the captain hadn't given him any guidance, any direction at all? It was stepping over a line, but he said it anyway. "I was waiting for you to tell me what to do, sir."

Leighty said mildly, "You're my OOD, Dan. If I didn't think you could do the job, I wouldn't have signed your appointment letter. One of these days, you'll be sitting in my chair. Nobody'll be around to tell you what to do then. I like to train my people with that day in mind."

"Yes, sir," said Dan, but at the same time he was thinking, Where is this guy coming from? It sounded a little like something he'd heard once at the Academy, but it sure wasn't what he'd seen in the fleet.

He understood Thomas Leighty less every time he talked with the man.

HE went from the bridge to his stateroom, rinsed his face, picked up a checkoff sheet, and began getting ready for the test firing.

He started at the muzzle end, the launchers and gun mounts. He made sure the gunner's mates and fire controlmen were finishing the prefire checks, that each was witnessed by an officer. He climbed up to the directors and watched the Daily Systems Operability Test from there. Then went down to the magazines and confirmed that the instrumented birds they'd loaded at Goose Creek were lined up properly in the big rotating drums that fed the launchers. Chief Alaska assured him he'd checked out each missile. They were alive, they answered up, and they gave the right responses. He spent the last half hour before lunch in the computer room, going over system procedures with Williams and Dawson.

Harper came in while he was finishing up, looking irascible. Dan asked him how the DSOTs had looked from his end. He grumbled that nobody listened, nobody used the checklists. "Yeah, but how did they go?" Dan persisted.

"All my shit's gonna work. I don't know about the assholes operating it, though."

When the 1MC said, "Lunch is now being served in the wardroom," he tore himself away reluctantly. But it would be a long afternoon. He needed to eat. He went out on the flight deck to check the weather first, though.

Barrett was charging steadily along through an enormous calm flatness. A blower roared softly above his head. Through it, he could hear the giant hollow flute note of air going into the stack and exhaust blasting out. The faintly heaving polished glass of the sea, reflecting nothing but soft blue sky, told him there was really no wind, though he felt a hot breath on his cheek and arm from *Barrett*'s passage through the waiting air. Aft of him, men were lowering the deck-edge nets. Behind them, two decks down, he caught a glimpse of the gunner's mates laying out the hemp mats that prevented spent shell cases from chipping the decks. Behind them was the fire-ax abruptness of the stern, then nothing but the wake. From a gray-green central turbulence, it rolled outward into the flat silver, spreading to either side like unfolding wings, then gradually merging with the heat haze and the topaz blur of stack gas until everything shimmered, everything melted together, nothing was definite or clear.

He stood there for ten or fifteen seconds, knowing he didn't have the time to spare but giving it to himself, like a gift. At sea . . . he couldn't really say why it was so different, but it was. Detached from the billion-voiced roar of the shore, maybe there was less to distract you. Not that going to sea on a warship was a cruise on Walden Pond. This was as solitary as it got, snatching a couple of seconds with your boot on the scuppers, letting the sea-doubled sun scorch your face.

He wondered how many more times he'd go to sea. Three years in this billet, then he'd be in line for a shore job. But then he'd be facing XO screen and the lieutenant commander board. Unless he did a stellar job on *Barrett,* he wouldn't make it, which would leave him firmly screwed to the bulkhead, passed over, without enough time to retire on.

He smiled bitterly. He'd given up his family, and now he'd probably get booted, anyway. No, that wasn't exactly so. Betts would have left regardless. Her dislike of the Navy would just have shifted to something else. He still didn't understand it. Maybe he never would. But he thought of the wreckage of his marriage now as inevitable, fated, unavoidable.

The trouble was, he still missed a little girl with all his heart.

He looked out over the sea and blinked sun tears out of his eyes.

WHEN he let himself in, Pedersen was dealing out the main course, sloppy joes and fries and pink stamped-out circles of plastic tomato. Dan took his seat, muttering "Excuse me, Captain" to Leighty, who nodded absently, his eyes following the steward around the table even as he kept talking to Vysotsky. Dan noticed a strange lieutenant commander sitting next to the XO, but nobody introduced him. The new damage control assistant sat beside Harper at the bottom of the table, looking awkward. He had short black hair, tentative eyes behind the gold rims. Lohmeyer, he remembered. "Peanut butter and jelly," Dan said to the steward.

"It's sitting there ten miles from the eastern edge of the op area. Picked it up just before I got off."

"What's that, Felipe?"

Quintanilla said, "There's an AGI sitting out there waiting for us."

"An AGI. A Russian?"

"That's right. One of their little spy guys with all the antennas. Hiltz picked up his signature just before I got off watch."

"How do they do it?" Dwight Giordano said. "They're always there when we're going to do a shoot or an exercise."

"It seemed like that in the Med, too," Dan said. "Or maybe it's just that we only notice them then. There're always fishing boats around, wherever you go."

"I'd buy that sometimes, but it's like I've heard it too often."

The lieutenant commander pointed a spoon at Quintanilla. "When we were doing the development testing on the Aegis, whenever we had a shoot scheduled or beam-tracking exercises, there was a trawler there when we got out to the op area. Finally, we had to reserve four areas and decide which one to use the morning we got under way. That solved the problem."

"Yeah, it's like they had our schedule."

Harper murmured to the new officer, "Maybe the XO calls them up the night before. Says, 'It's Comrade Vysotsky. Come on out and join us.' "

"*Jesus*, Jay," Dan muttered.

"Keon, are they reading our traffic?" Vysotsky asked the comm officer. Van Cleef said hastily, "Not ours, sir."

The captain said, "We'll hug the western edge of the area. Stay as far away from him as possible."

AT 1300, the 1MC announced, "Prefire brief in the helo hangar." Dan heard it in the department office as he was going over the exercise op order once more, highlighting call signs, frequencies, and aircraft on-station and home-plate times.

When he got back to the hangar, he looked around to make sure his players were present. Dawson, Harper, Mainhardt, Horseheads, Shuffert, Alaska, Boyer, Glasser—all here, sitting on the crate of spare blades or lashed-down boxes of aviation supplies. He leaned against the bulkhead as Mister Ed passed out the firing plan.

Through the open hangar door, the sea astern gradually slanted left, then right as *Barrett* rolled.

Vysotsky introduced the lieutenant commander who'd been at lunch as Cal O'Bierne, the exercise observer, straight from the Naval Missile System Engineering Section. O'Bierne went right into the plan for the shoot, shouting to overcome the ambient noise in the hangar bay.

"This is the prefire brief for the first stage of the combat system sequential qualification trial, the CSSQT. The purpose of the trial is to test your ship's radar, combat system, and antiaircraft team training against a UVS—"

The captain lifted a finger. "Yes, sir?" said O'Bierne, breaking off.

"What's a UVS?"

"Sir, unmanned vehicle system."

"A drone?"

"Yes, sir. The BQM-thirty-four simulates a typical antiship cruise missile profile, like a Styx or an Exocet." He waited for another question, then went on. "As I said, the purpose is to test your effectiveness against a simulated cruise missile attack. The trial will proceed in three phases. The first events, oh-six-oh-one to oh-six-oh-four, are alignment exercises using a wire-towed drogue. Once you're tweaked and peaked, satisfied your system's operating at a hundred percent, we'll do three tracking runs.

"Finally, event oh-six-oh-eight will be a live fire against a high-speed drone launched from a mother plane. *Barrett* will be firing special instrumented Standards, with telemetry but no warheads. I will grade the exercise and submit a report."

O'Bierne looked at Leighty. "Captain, about the only other thing is to make sure you'll have a boat and crew and a thousand-pound davit available to pick up the UVS—I mean, the drone, after the exercise. It'll soft-land in the water, and we'll send a truck over for it when you get back to Charleston. Are there any questions?"

Leighty deferred to Vysotsky, who asked Dan what his tactics were going to be. Dan said, "Sir, I've checked out NWP-sixty-five and the class tactical manual, but there are no tactics developed yet for the ACDADS. I recommend an adaptation of the *Kidd*-class Block-One tactics as follows. . . ."

When he was done Vysotsky asked if anyone else had comments. Finally, Leighty nodded. "Okay, George, let's get to it."

"General quarters, sir?"

"Why not. Let's make it as realistic as possible."

* * *

"THIS is a drill; this is a drill. General quarters; general quarters. All hands, man your battle stations. Set material condition Zebra throughout the ship."

The electronic bonging was still echoing through the passageways when he got to CIC. He strapped on gas mask and life jacket, buttoned his sleeves and collar, tucked trouser cuffs into his socks. A seaman handed him the gray helmet stenciled TAO and he swung up into his chair.

CIC was dark now, dark and cold and packed with people. The black bulkhead and overhead disappeared, making it seem like the backlit displays and tote boards floated in interstellar space. From the TAO chair, centered in the compartment, he had a clear view of every plot board and display. Action flowed outward concentrically from the TAO. He could speak in a normal voice to the officers who controlled the sensors and weapons: the surface-subsurface weapons coordinator, the antiair weapons coordinator. They, in turn, were in voice range of the petty officers who ran the launch consoles for Harpoon, Standard, ASROC, torpedoes, and guns. They were tied together by intercoms and screen-to-screen computer links, and if all else failed, there were the time-tested sound-powered phones. A dedicated intercom by Dan's hand gave him direct talk to the officer of the deck, one deck up, so he could maneuver the ship.

If *Barrett* ever went into battle, he would fight her from this chair. No longer did a captain fight his ship from the bridge. From there, he could see ten or fifteen miles. The net of sensors and electronics woven from CIC covered thousands of square miles. And the skipper, though he retained overall command, delegated the actual employment of the ship in combat to younger officers, recently trained in up-to-the minute threats and tactics.

As if conjured up by thought, Leighty appeared out of the dark and swung up into the chair next to Dan. Lenson nodded to him—formalities were relaxed here—and clicked a focused light on above him. He flipped open his wheel book. You could look things up in tac memos and naval warfare publications, but he didn't like to accept cookbook answers. His handwritten notes read:

1. Place FC radar in sector scan along threat axis.
2. Detect target.
3. Designate to a weapons system and launcher.
4. Launch.
5. Reengage—shoot, shoot, look, shoot.

He kneaded his forehead, remembering how much calculation it took to get to the seemingly bonehead-simple step five. If a cruise missile was coming down the pipe at you, you didn't fire one missile and wander happily away with your finger up your butt. An 80 percent kill probability was the best you could hope for. So you figured to fire more than once. But how many times? And how fast? The formula for overall probability of kill with repeated shots was:

$$Pk = 1 - (Pf)^n$$

Pf was the probability of failure and *n* the number of rounds fired. If you fired one round, *Pk* was 80 percent, two rounds would be 96 percent, and three rounds somewhere upward of 99 percent.

But balanced against that was the need to conserve ordnance in battle. Successive attacks would deplete your magazines, letting the attacker break through. Also, you couldn't fire too rapidly; the missiles would interfere with one another's radar. And there wasn't much time to get your rounds out there, not with the enemy missile boring in at ten miles a minute. He'd finally worked out a solution using a system of simultaneous linear equations.

Now Leighty was asking him, "Three-round engagement, Dan?"

"If we have time, sir. If not, we get two rounds off fast."

"Do we make that decision?"

"Not anymore, sir. The threat-response algorithm is programmed into the ACDADS auto mode."

Leighty grunted something and picked up a phone. Dan heard him talking to the XO, then tuned out as the airborne intercept controller, who directed aircraft assigned to *Barrett*'s control, yelled, "Tango four four reporting in, requesting permission to start runs."

"That the S-three with the sleeve? Permission granted."

"Tango four four wants commanding officer's guarantee no live ammunition is loaded."

Leighty grinned. "Sounds like they've been burned before. Check it out, Dan."

Dan clicked into the fire-control circuit, confirmed bores clear with the gun mounts, then did the same with the missile launchers. He pointed to the AIC. "They're safe. Give him an initial vector to make the first run in from zero-zero-zero relative. SSWC, place ACDADS in mode two and commence run one."

The first events went smoothly. The tow aircraft made run after run from ahead, abeam, astern. Behind it, a drogue wobbled through the sky on five thousand feet of cable. At each run, the system gave a threat warning buzzer, assigned a director, and locked on. As the range closed, it assigned launchers, displayed an ordnance selection, and sent train and elevate orders. Shuffert, who was antiair coordinator, kept giving him thumbs-up. They did a quick huddle at the end of the fifth run. "How's it looking, Shoe?" Dan asked.

"Everything seems to be running normal." The black lieutenant sucked his lip. "I noticed some delay on the bow-on run, though. It was in to fifteen miles before we got a detect signal."

"It was real low on that run, I noticed," Chief Dawson put in. "Maybe a hundred feet above the water."

"That's where an Exocet's gonna fly. Do you want to tweak some more, try to get more energy out there?"

"No, it's in parameters. Let's go with it."

"Shoe?"

"Concur."

Dan said to the captain, "Sir, we're ready for a firing run."

The jet drone was carried by another plane, call sign Lima two six, which had reported in during the tracking runs and was now orbiting thirty-five miles to the north. He called O'Beirne, up on the bridge, and advised him and the OOD this would be a firing run, for grade. Next he checked the surface track console, making sure there were no stray fishing boats or crossing merchants in range. Except for the trawler to the east, the sky and sea were empty. He told Shuffert to signal event 0608.

"Time to find out if all this shit we bought works," said Leighty. Dan glanced at him. It was the first time he'd heard the fastidious captain use a four-letter word.

He looked at Shuffert, sitting tensely at the weapons-control console; at Dawson, at the systems-monitoring panel, one earphone slipped off. Both were watching him, hands hovering over the proper switches. The door from the bridge undogged. It was O'Beirne, the observer.

"Archer turning inbound. Now bears zero-zero-four, range sixty-eight thousand yards."

Dan said quietly, "Put her in auto."

"Automatic, aye . . . mode three enabled."

Leaning forward, he could see the glowing symbol that was the launch aircraft, thirty miles out. He and Dawson and Harper and Williams had done all they could. It was up to the computers now.

"Lima two six reports drone separation . . . engine start . . . control test . . . drone under control. Commencing run."

"Have we got a separate paint on the drone?"

"Yes, sir."

The deck shuddered beneath their feet, and he tensed before he remembered the computers were controlling the helm now, too—controlling the engines, controlling everything.

"ACDADS has identified an incoming threat, level two, bearing zero-zero-six, range fifty-two thousand yards, speed four hundred and sixty knots. Altering course to unmask weapons."

He looked out across the room, feeling ice touch his spine. No one was *doing* anything. Dawson turned his palms outward, eyebrows up, a "Look, Ma, no hands" routine.

The ship was moving, thinking, acting on its own.

The rudder-angle indicator swung to counteract the momentum of the turn, then centerlined. The gyro repeater steadied, presenting *Barrett*'s port beam to the incoming drone. Designation lights blinked on. "Threat level one. Locked on," a petty officer called. "Very well," Dan murmured, thinking, Next they'll give it a voice. All we'll be good for then is typing up the after-action reports.

"Target bears zero-zero-eight, range forty-five thousand yards, speed four hundred and eighty knots, altitude, three hundred feet."

Dan watched the second hand of his watch creep around. It wasn't all peaches and cream, having the ship think for you. You had all the same worries, but there was nothing you could do.

The intercom at his elbow said, "Uh, TAO, Bridge: Why are we training the guns out to starboard?"

"Say again, Bridge? This is a missile run, to port."

"Well, the guns are training out to starboard."

He was opening his mouth to ask Dawson what was going on when he heard the unmistakable slam of a five-inch going off, then, a second later, another from astern. "Cease fire! Cease fire!" he yelled. "Abort the run. Break track. Take back control. Centerline all the launchers, *now*."

A minute later, a jet engine howled past overhead, muffled by the superstructure. The observer shook his head, making a note on a clipboard. Dan wiped sweat off his face. He felt Leighty's look like an icicle laid across his cheeks.

"I thought the guns were unloaded, Mr. Lenson."

"Sir, they *were*. Adamo checked the bores himself. They shouldn't have fired, anyway; this was a missile run."

"Okay, obviously something's hosed. Can we refire? Or should we scrub the trial? How much longer have we got the drone for?"

"One second, sir, I'll check. . . ." To Shuffert and Dawson, he said tightly, "Okay, something's screwy. *What?* Think fast; we only got this drone for another fifteen minutes."

Neither seemed to know. He picked up the FC circuit and barked, "Why did you fire?" But as far as the gunner's mates knew, the guns had done exactly what the computers were telling them to. He made a fast decision.

"Okay, forget full auto. Put ACDADS in mode two."

"You're going to try again?"

"Yes, sir, but in semiauto this time. It'll give us a threat buzzer and recommend action, but the console operators actually designate targets and approve loading ordnance to fire position."

"I know that, Dan."

"Yes, sir, I know you do. Just making sure everyone's using the same dance card."

Leighty nodded, approving another firing run. Dan told the AIC, who relayed it out to the drone operator on the plane.

"Commencing run two. Target inbound."

At fifty thousand yards, the threat buzzer triggered. "Designate to forward launcher," Dan said, leaning forward to watch the big SSWC screen.

This seemed to work better. The system locked on in semiauto and tracked. It assigned the incoming threat to the forward missile launcher, with the aft launcher in backup. When it recommended fire, he glanced at Leighty, who nodded curtly. Shuffert flipped up the switch cover and depressed the red switch.

The drumming roar made them all jump. Caught up in symbology, procedure, drill, you forgot there were real weapons out there. The first missile was on its way. Dan scratched itchy armpits as another bellow announced the second round had leapt off the aft launcher. The angular separation meant they could fire round two from there a second and a half sooner than a refire from the same launcher.

"Bird one away . . . bird two away."

"Check fire bird three. Stand by." He'd see if two would do it, maybe save the expense of an extra instrumented Standard. On impulse, he hit the intercom. "Bridge, TAO: Can you guys see the drone yet?"

Vysotsky's hoarse voice. "Negative, got our glasses on the bearing but no joy yet."

"How's our birds look, XO?"

"Number one and number two both normal fly-out. . . . Wait a minute. . . . *Oh no.*"

Simultaneously, the petty officer at the fire-control console yelled, "Missile number one, no tip-down! Passing over the target!"

"What the hell happened?"

"Target still incoming, bearing zero-nine-eight, range nine thousand yards."

"Fire number three, Mr. Lenson?"

"No. Check fire. Check fire—"

"TAO, Bridge: I hold the drone visually. It's low—"

"Stand by for number two intercept, now now now—lost track!"

"Ah, *fuck*," Dawson groaned.

The intercom from the bridge said, "It's still coming. Hey, right at us. Hey, this thing's way too fucking low."

The captain reached up. His hand went to the radio circuit to the launch aircraft, still orbiting to the north. "Lima two six, this is Echo November Actual. To the drone controller: Pull up. Increase altitude immediately or turn away. You are headed *directly for us* with no offset."

No reply from the plane. Two seconds . . . three. "Still coming at us," said the 21MC. "Right at us—"

Leighty cut it off in midsentence. "Left hard rudder, turn into it! Phalanx in AAW auto, *now!*"

"Phalanx in auto," Shuffert shouted.

The low bass *brruummmp* of 20-mm slugs going out washboarded the bulkheads. Then it cut off.

Dan closed his eyes. CIC was silent, waiting.

The 1MC crackled, keened, then announced: "This is not a drill. Ah . . . fire. Fire, fire! Class bravo fire on port side. Repair Three provide."

FORTUNATELY, the drone was lightly built and had been almost out of fuel when it hit; the repair party, already dressed out and on station at general quarters, had grabbed their gear, run fifty feet, climbed a ladder, and snuffed the flames with water mist before they got well started.

Dan went down as soon as the ship secured from GQ. He picked his way over three-inch hoses as the damage-control party rolled them up and carried them away in flat heavy cartwheels. The smells of kerosene and smoke coated the back of his throat. He swallowed nervously. They reminded him of another ship, another fire. . . . The light airframe had punched a jagged hole through the shell plating abreast and below the aft five-inch mount. The fire had been contained within the boundaries of the laundry and, near it, the master-at-arms shack. Smoking debris littered the deck. Looking out through the smoking hole, he saw the sea slipping by as *Barrett* dawdled along at steerageway.

He looked up, to see Vysotsky in the doorway. "Anybody hurt, sir?" he asked.

"One of the laundrymen."

"Not . . . dead?"

"No, no. Second-degree burns, smoke inhalation." The executive officer touched a bulkhead, then examined his soot-smeared hand. "Good thing there's no warhead on a drone. What the hell happened?"

"We're not sure yet, sir. Either we had two missiles fail the exact same way or else we've got a bug somewhere."

"Your troops working it?"

"Yes, sir. We'll have a report for the skipper and the observer as soon as we find out what went wrong. Uh, what did it look like from topside, XO? You were up there, weren't you?"

"Yeah. Hell, I thought everything was going fine. Both rounds looked sweet off the launchers. They were flying the normal up-and-over profile. One of the lookouts yelled that he had the drone. I saw it just for a second, a little red guy way out there a couple inches above the waves.

"Then suddenly, we all realize the missiles aren't tipping down. They're way the fuck up there and still climbing. They go over it, way over it. The drone keeps coming. Tracks in like it's on rails. It starts to nose up the last couple seconds, like the operator's reaching for altitude, but then the Phalanx cuts loose. Just about blasted my ears off—I was out on the wing. The drone's hit. Starts to wobble. The engine starts cutting out. *Blatt, blatt, blatt.* Then it quits and just kind of tumbles down into the side." He smacked his hands together. "Flash. Boom." He looked around at the wrecked machines, soaked tile, toppled racks of wet, filthy uniforms. "We're going to have to get this cleaned up, get a patch on the hull. . . . I'm just glad we had everybody at GQ. Anyway, what now? We've still got a gun event, don't we?"

"I recommended we call it off, sir. There's something wrong, and if we don't know what, it's not safe to shoot."

"That doesn't leave us looking very good to start refresher training next week," said the exec. "Is it too late to rethink that decision? We could shoot in local control, couldn't we? There's a casualty mode for NTDS—"

"Yes, sir, we can plot by hand, but not fast enough to track an incoming drone. And we can't launch a missile at all without the fire-control system up." Dan looked at the dirty oily water on the deck, a stray black sock crumpled like something small and dead. "I'll check again, sir. But the skipper seemed to agree—with calling it off, I mean. Something's out of whack."

"Well, in that case." They looked at each other. Then the XO added, "He's very . . . concerned about the men."

"Seems that way, sir," said Dan, suddenly alert. The way the XO was holding his gaze, there was something else, another message or question behind the words. But he didn't know what it was. He cleared his throat. "Is there, uh, anything else, sir?"

"Anything else? No, I guess not."

"I'd better get back up, find out what went wrong."

"Yeah, do that," said Vysotsky. When Dan looked back, the XO was still watching him.

15

THE blast of a whistle. "Moored. Shift colors."

Dan sagged against the splinter shield, watching as the line-handlers paid out five-inch nylon, doubled it, busy spiders webbing *Barrett* back to land. They'd raced the setting sun up the Cooper, and now security lights buzzed and popped and one by one hammered down green light like a thin sheet of corroded brass over the deserted shipyard.

When he went back inside, Leighty had left the bridge. He handed the binoculars to the quartermaster and stumbled toward the ladder. His feet hurt. His whole body felt sticky. His stateroom, clean uniform, shower . . . Instead, he went aft through an emptying ship.

The DP center was icy as a walk-in freezer and silent as a medieval library. The whisper of the air conditioning, the click of keys, and the occasional whir of tape drives only deepened the hush. Dawson and Mainhardt and Williams were snapped to pubs and computers. Sanderling was packaging cards for mailing. O'Bierne was sipping coffee at the workbench.

Dawson glanced up. "Hey, Lieutenant."

"Evening, sir," said Chief Mainhardt. They didn't look happy at being interrupted, but to hell with that. He gestured Dawson over behind one of the computers.

"Yes, sir," said Dawson, his voice falling on the last word.

"Okay, Chief, we've had to scrub two days' worth of exercises—which I don't know when we're going to be able to make up. We're scheduled so tight between now and deployment, we don't have time to pull our socks up."

"I know, sir. We thought the system was operational. But I think we got it squared away."

"Already?"

"Well, it's not up yet, but I think we figured out why it went down. A bad card. We'll swap it out, see if that does it."

"Sounds reasonable." He looked around, met the observer's eyes. "Commander, helping us out?"

"I'm an interested party. If it isn't something wrong with your system, then we've got a problem with our missiles."

"Well, hopefully we'll have it back up before too long. Chief, where's Mr. Harper?"

"Chief Warrant's down eating chow, sir. He's been working it with us."

The 1MC said, "Now lay before the mast, all eight o'clock reports. Eight o'clock reports will be taken by the XO in his stateroom."

"Let me know how things work once you get the new card in." He remembered something else, looked around for Sanderling, but he'd left. "Chief, when's our man going to mast?"

"He's not, sir. The XO dismissed it."

"He dismissed a shoplifting charge?"

"Said it was a misunderstanding."

"Oh." He thought about that. Then said, "Well, I'll be aboard tonight. Give me a call in the department office when you get the system back up."

AT eight o'clock reports, he told Vysotsky that the techs had the problem with the combat system isolated and should have it fixed soon. The executive officer said in that case, he was going home—it was his son's birthday; call him when he knew for sure. Dan started to ask him about Sanderling, but there were too many other people around.

There were chicken sandwiches in the wardroom. He helped himself to one, ate a piece of chocolate sheet cake, and then went down to the weapons office.

He worked for a couple of hours, taking advantage of the quiet. He kept expecting a call from Dawson, but it got to be nine-thirty, then ten. Finally, he locked up and went back up to the computer room.

Dawson and Mainhardt were still there, only now Chief Alaska, the chief missile-fire-control technician, was with them. They all had that thousand-yard stare. "Well?" he asked them.

"That wa'n't it," Dawson said.

Mainhardt said, "Mr. Lenson, it might not be a hardware problem."

He looked from one face to the next. "Software? Well, that's easier to fix, isn't it?"

"You want to come over here, take a look? . . . There it is. This's what was running this afternoon."

Dan looked at the computer. There were two ways to see what was going on inside an AN/UYK-7. There was the monitor-control console, a screen where you could read code during maintenance. Or you could read the lights on the front panel. A lighted bulb was a one, a dark bulb was a zero. He slowly spelled out, "Two, three, five, four, six, three, two, zero."

"Pretty good, sir, didn't know you could read binary. That's cell number five twenty-three on the engagement program."

"So?"

"Petty Officer Williams," Dawson called. Williams came out of the back with a looseleaf book.

Dan said, "Short and simple, please."

"Short and simple, aye, sir. Okay, you know we . . . got the operational program and the subprogram."

"The operational program runs the top-level ACDADS system, and hands off to subprograms for a given task."

"That's right. The op program just . . . runs and runs till we turn it off, we're in port, or we need the computer for something else. But as we . . . go from detection to tracking to identification and so forth, it calls other modules up. Computers can only do one thing at a time. They load up, it hands them the data, and they run till it's time to hand back. Now, we didn't have no problem today with detection or identification, did we, Lieutenant?"

"No, everything ran fine right up to the engagement phase."

"So that's where we started looking. We put in a break point and started checking it out. Now it says here—you see here in the listing what we . . . ought to have, where it come time to hand off to the final guidance-to-launch module. And that on the box is what we do have."

Dan looked at the programming in the book, then compared it to the lights. "It doesn't match."

"That's right, Lieutenant. The hard copy in the listing don't match what's in the machine."

"How does it translate to missile commands? I mean, are you telling me it's giving bad commands?"

"No, sir," said Dawson. "It's not giving it *any* commands. There's nothing in there anything like a command, good or bad."

Dan rubbed his chin. The naked skin still felt strange. "But how did it get changed? The programming's off a tape, right?"

"Yes, sir. Tape came from the Fleet Programming Center. That's the Version Three we told you about, the one Williams worked so hard getting to run for us."

"So in the shoot today, the system's running fine, then it hits this and goes haywire."

"Right, sir. So when the fire-control system asks the computer what to do next, it gets this read to it as instructions. And it is just totally confused. It doesn't know whether to shit or go blind, or do like it did today, tell the missile to find the nearest seagull and blast his ass."

"So it wasn't hardware or operator error; it was a bad tape. Have we got the original?"

"This *is* the original, sir. This is what we loaded up with before we got under way."

"Can we get a copy from somebody else in the nest?"

"Not ACDADS, sir. We the only ones got this system."

"So we order a new tape, reboot from that, and we're back in business."

"I hope it's that simple."

Dan turned to O'Bierne. The lieutenant commander sloshed his coffee around, took a slug, pointed to the screen. "It might not be just a bad line of code."

"It sounds to me like that's exactly what we've got, sir."

"I'd check the rest of your system out before you assume that."

"Lieutenant Lenson, quarterdeck," said the 1MC. "Shit," Dan said. "Excuse me, sir."

He called on the J-dial phone and got the petty officer of the watch. "Mr. Lenson. What you got?"

"Sir, outside call for you."

"Who is it?"

"I don't know, sir."

"Take a message, okay? I'm in the DP center working a major problem." He hung up and turned back to the conversation, to find that Harper had come in and was talking to O'Bierne.

"They're under tight security. Locked in the vault the minute they come aboard. I'm the custodian, so I can guarantee nobody but me, the comm officer, and the guys right here in this space. That's all that's had their hands on them."

O'Bierne said, "Still, I'd recommend checking your system out thoroughly before you spin another reel."

"Attention on deck!"

Everyone stood as Captain Leighty came in. Dan fought down tired anger. When something was royally screwed up, everybody had to get his two cents' worth in.

"Carry on, everyone. Just thought I'd stop by before I went home. Jay, how does it stand?"

"Excuse me," Dan said. "Captain—"

"Mr. Lenson. Didn't see you at first. Have we got a fix on the problem?"

"I think we've got it located, sir—in the software that tells the missile where the target is. Part of the code in that module is bad."

"Can we fix it?"

Dawson said, "Sir, once the program's loaded, we can patch it by hand. Put in a break point at the bad line, look at the listing, and use those on/off buttons on the front panel to reset the code in that cell."

"But that doesn't fix the tape," said Dan.

"No, sir. We'd have to patch it again every time we rebooted."

"Can we modify the tape?"

"Not with the gear we have aboard, sir. We'll have to get a reissue."

"How long will that take?"

Harper said, "Sir, if we put a hot priority on it, they can probably get a new piece of programming to us in a day or two. Stuff that important, they fly out."

"But Mr. O'Bierne thinks we shouldn't assume that's all that's wrong just yet," said Dan.

Leighty took off his cap and aligned it on the workbench. "Cal, I'm glad you're here to advise us on this."

"Sir, I don't really know a hell of a lot about it. I was just saying, if it was up to me, I'd check the rest of the program against the listing. Make sure whatever failure mechanism altered that line didn't alter any others."

"If we do find more glitches, can we get any help from NMSES on this?"

"Sir, I'd like to, but I've got a red-eye back to the West Coast, I need to ask somebody for a ride to the airport. And strictly speaking, we're only responsible for the part that flies away and blows things up."

The phone buzzed again. Williams said, "Mr. Lenson, for you."

It was the petty officer of the watch again. "Sir, I got that number for you, you want to call her back. Says she'll be home."

"Shoot." He jotted it down on his hand with the Navy-issue ballpoint, recognizing it halfway through as Beverly's. He hung up and went back to the discussion.

The captain was saying, "If this doesn't fix it, we don't have a lot of time to kick it around. We're getting under way for refresher training, and looking at a six-month deployment two-blocked to that."

O'Bierne nodded. "Yes, sir, I understand. Only thing I can say is, if you need help, let your squadron N-four know what's going on. If you keep having problems, have the type commander go to the software support activity for you; let them beat on whoever developed the tape. Meanwhile, have your guys shut the system down, let everything you've got running evaporate, then reload it piece by piece with your eyes locked on the screen."

Leighty nodded abruptly. "Okay. Dan, I'll make that call to squadron. Keep me informed."

"Aye aye, sir."

O'Bierne left with the captain. Dan sighed. "Well, Chief Warrant. It's going to be a long night."

"Not for me, sir. I'm going home."

Dan glanced at the chiefs. "Let's go out in the passageway."

The corridor was deserted except for a duty-section seaman listlessly steering a push broom. Dan said, "What is this? We need you here on this one."

"And I got a family I won't see for the next six weeks." Harper squinted. "This isn't wartime, Lieutenant. I seen the shit hit the fan in Vietnam, and this don't start to compare."

"The combat system's down. That's a major problem."

"Okay, but let's not get twisted into the ground on it. Piece of hard-earned career advice from the King Snake, okay?"

"I'm listening."

"When the pressure's on, people get tunnel vision. Don't get so tied up on any one problem you lose the big picture. Back off. Leave it to us. We got a week before the training team comes aboard. We'll get it shaped up before then. So unless you give me a direct order not to, I'm going home. Are you giving me a direct order?"

Dan hesitated. "No."

"Okay, then. See you tomorrow."

Dan remembered Sanderling. "Wait a minute. Chief Dawson said something about the charges against Sanderling being dismissed."

"Not exactly." Harper gave him an ironical smile. "The XO had a little informal screening mast in his stateroom. Just Sandy, me, and him. Result: The captain's friend is to consider himself counseled on being careful with his hands in the Navy Exchange."

Dan said slowly, "He dismissed it. Why?"

"Maybe you can answer that, shipmate, if you think about it a while." Harper slapped him on the shoulder.

Dan looked after him as he swung down the passageway, made a left to the quarterdeck, disappeared.

He wasn't really sure how he felt, but it wasn't good. His gear was down, the ship was crippled, and the captain and the exec were playing games over an enlisted pretty boy.

Instead of going back into the computer room, he went to the wardroom. It was dark and he had to flick on the lights. The bulkhead clock read midnight. The galley was unlocked and there was a round barrel of Rocky Road in the freezer. He wolfed a bowl standing up, drank a cup of thick tepid coffee, then stood looking out the porthole.

Finally, he went back down, to find Dawson, Mainhardt, Sanderling, and Williams still at work.

"Sir, quarterdeck was after you. A Mrs. Strishauser, calling back. Says she needs to talk to you tonight. Said it was urgent."

"Okay, damn it." "Urgent" with Beverly? The way she exaggerated? It would keep. "What's the outcome? Is the rest of the tape clean?"

"Bad news, sir. We found more nonfunctional code."

"By nonfunctional, you mean—"

"It's full of this gibberish. Or not full, but—the funny thing is, you get a patch, then some good programming, then seventy or a hundred lines later, crap again."

"So what do we do now? Patch those, too?"

"Sir, we could, but we got a quarter million lines of code here. We're getting beyond what we can patch manually. Williams here got another idea. We're gonna dump this whole program and load up Version Two again. Maybe somebody just left that new tape too close to a magnetic field or something."

He sighed and looked at the screen, the lines of green-glowing code. "Okay," he said. "And we'd better send Hofstra up for some more coffee, okay?"

THE DSs shut the system down, shut everything off, the mainframes and the magnetic drum memory units, let all the Version 3 programming evaporate. Then they brought them back up again and loaded the Version 2 tape.

It ran, but they found scrambled code in it, too.

When Vysotsky called at 0300, Dan told him they needed help. The exec said he'd already called the squadron duty officer. "They don't have any organic assets smart on software, but they can maybe scramble somebody," he said, sounding half-asleep. "If it's really beyond the capability of ship's force."

"Sir, I'm shutting everything down. I got a bad feeling."

"About what?"

"That more than one tape is bad."

"Maybe we got a bad shipment."

"Sir, these tapes came from different commands. I don't think . . . " He heard his voice trail off; it sounded weak, but he didn't know what else to say. He was stumped.

"We can't just tag out the computers. What's your best guess on time to repair? Over forty-eight hours?"

"At least, sir, unless some major-league bit brain shows up here tomorrow with a magic wand."

"Okay, we got to CASREP it." The casualty report message would tell the world USS *Barrett* had a major problem and needed help. Vysotsky added, "Have a draft ready to hand to Felipe first thing tomorrow—this morning, I mean. I want it on the street by ten hundred."

"Yes, sir."

"It sounds to me like readiness is going to drop to C three. Maybe even C four if we're honest. What's your take?"

Dan felt uneasy discussing the ship's readiness on a commercial line. "Uh . . . can I think about that? Brief you in the morning, when you come in?"

"I guess. . . . Goes without saying, this doesn't make me feel warm and fuzzy, Dan. Without those computers, we don't dance, don't sing; we just sit in the water and attract shit from everybody."

"Yes, sir," he said, thinking, That's right, XO, screw it down a little tighter.

When he finally left the computer room, dawn was breaking over North Charleston. The bulkheads glistened with dew. Gulls were mining the Dumpsters, whirling up in screaming melees when one found a morsel too large to eat in one gulp. He stood watching them as his mind formulated a shadowy image, too shifting and vague to see clearly. Could nonsense be malevolent? Could chaos reproduce itself, feeding on meaning and logic? Gradually destroying what was whole and healthy, converting it to the stuff of its own diabolic, meaningless life . . .

He shook his head as if to shake off biting flies. It wasn't possible. Computers did only what they were told. It was his brain that was generating nonsense, from lack of sleep and too much coffee. He looked at his watch again, thinking he might snatch a nap before officers' call, and noticed only then the ballpointed numerals of Beverly's phone number, obliterated now to a meaningless and unreadable smear.

III

CUBA

16

Alcorcón

AND now it was the wet season. The sky poured rain on the empty fields, lying flat and untended under the drumming downpour. They looked brown and dead. But beneath the glistening soil, the cane was growing, putting out silent secret roots so that one day soon it would shoot upward into the light.

And like the cane, something secret was growing in Batey Number 3, as well.

Graciela stood at the *central*, under the dripping metal eaves of the machine station. Shivering, she looked off across the water shining dully in the wheel ruts, and beyond that at the empty fields and the palely glowing sky.

The men had begun work on the boat. She hadn't seen it yet; it was too deep in the swamp, too hard to get to through marsh and mangrove. Mangrove was nearly impenetrable; you had to chop your way in, then wade through water filled with leeches and snakes—not for her, not now. Her other pregnancies hadn't bothered her this much. She'd worked in the fields right up till the pains began. But this time felt different. Perhaps because she was older. Or the shock of Armando's death . . . Whatever the reason, this baby seemed restless, disturbed. It kicked as if to punish her. And where before she'd been able to work all day, now she felt fatigued even as she woke. Some days, she was so exhausted that it was all she could do to drag herself to the clinic for the ration of German dried milk, reserved for children, pregnant women, and nursing mothers.

Today, the *médico* had told her it was gone, that the supplies were exhausted. But as soon as she'd stepped out of line, there was more for the others, behind her.

To hell with them. She was leaving. She hadn't seen the boat yet, but Miguelito had come, full of himself, and told her about it—how

Tomás and the others had studied his book, a child's book about boats, only that one picture showed how the ribs and stringers were put together. The men had discussed this picture and measured it and finally started stealing materials and smuggling them piece by piece back to the marsh at night.

"And what does it look like now?" she'd asked him.

"Right now, two curved sides and no bottom."

"It has no *bottom*?"

"Not yet. Tomás is building it upside down. The bottom will go on last. It'll be tin. Then they'll turn it over and put the deckhouse on, just like it shows in the book."

"This tin bottom, it won't leak?"

"Where they nail it, sure, but Xiomara stole inner tubes from the tractor shop. They'll glue rubber over the nail heads to keep the water out."

"Can *they* see this?" she worried. "If an airplane flies over—"

"It can't. They cut fresh branches each time they go and put them over the boat. Julio says that's what they taught them in the Young Pioneers. And Uncle Augustín, he says he'll make that motor run."

"And you? What will you do?"

"Oh, I just provided the plans," the boy said, shrugging, but she could see how proud he was. "And I carry things and cut branches and help."

Now she sighed. The downpour roared hollowly above her, arching off the corrugated metal roof in evenly spaced streams. It didn't look as if it would ever stop. Settling her palm-leaf hat to shed the rain, she stepped heavily out into the yard.

Tomás had taken leadership of the plan to escape, just as she'd known he would. He'd assigned each person something to do: this one to steal plywood from the sugar mill, where they were pouring new footings; that one to get a compass; another to get gas and oil. Since she could neither go into the marsh nor carry anything heavy, he'd given her three tasks. First, collect foods that would not spoil on the trip. Two, find a map. And three, stitch rice sacks together to make a small sail.

Food—she'd found a little today. It was in the bag at her waist. The map was more important, though. They were peasants. They could go without food, even water, but without a map, they'd be lost out on the *bahía.* Beyond the marshlands lay the Camagüey archipelago, a labyrinthine scatter of deserted cays, islets, reefs, and lagoons that sealed off the interior of central Cuba like a great barred gate. She had to find a map. . . . Where had she seen one? . . . Pinned up on a dirty wall . . . Where was her mind going? She didn't mind being pregnant, but she hated what it did to her thoughts. Like scrambled eggs. She wished she had an egg; it would be good for the baby. . . .

"Compañera Lopez."

She came to a halt, recalled to rutted earth, the smell of pig shit, the rain that soaked her thin jacket, the pain in swollen bare feet she could no longer force into boots. To the serious, slightly puffy face of Nenita Colón Marquez, wife of Rámon Colón and a member like him of Cooperative Number 179's Committee to Defend the Revolution. Her black hair was pinned up under a uniform cap. Her wet fatigues were smeared with mud at knees and elbows, and she had a semiautomatic rifle slung over her shoulder. The muzzle was pointing down. To keep the rain out, Graciela supposed. A smear of soot on Nenita's cheek made her coffee-colored skin look pale.

Graciela felt her knees start to quiver. A word from this woman and she'd be in a truck, on her way to the police station in Alcorcón.

"You look confused, comrade. Are you all right? Do you need a hand?"

"No, gracias, *compañera.*"

"Are you sure?"

"Oh yes, oh yes." She dropped her eyes to Nenita's boots, forced a stupid smile. "You've been out in the mud. Militia duty?"

"A surprise recall. Fifteen minutes to dress and muster. You don't have to go every time, but I try to do my duty when I can, with the children and my husband and all. . . . We get in trucks and they take us to the range for shooting practice. It makes my ears ring." She looked at Graciela's bare feet. "Have you had your tetanus shot?"

"Yes, comrade, but thank you for the reminder."

"How's the baby?"

"The baby . . . he's not sitting comfortably today."

"It's a he, eh?"

"They say when the baby sits low, it is a male child."

The smile ebbed from the other woman's face, leaving a cold regard. "I was sorry to hear about your husband. I knew him only a little, but I regret his death. Do you hear me?"

"Yes, comrade."

"I understand you've been buying food. Is this true, what they say in the store?"

She stood motionless. The militiawoman's eyes held hers with a faint smile, as if she knew everything, as if she dared Graciela to admit it. Then she thought, It's a trick; all they know is that I've been in the store. She shrugged. "Isn't that allowed, to buy something to eat when you are hungry?"

"Certainly, but what's wrong with your rations?"

"The rations are quite generous. We are well provided for. But I am *embarazada,* no? You're a mother; you know how it is. One craves other things—tinned meat, chocolate." She nodded to the bag she carried. "The little pickles in the glass jars. I think and think about these things, and finally I have to have them. And baby food, that might be gone when I need it, no?"

"But the money, *compañera*? Such things are expensive."

"My husband was thrifty. I have a little money he saved from his wages."

"Interesting," said Marquez, "that he had money hidden away at the same time he was stealing food, isn't it? But it's not wise to keep cash. You should deposit it at the office. No matter how close we are to neighbors and relatives, we never know who can't be trusted, do we? With money, with a husband—with a secret."

Graciela kept her eyes down and her expression bovine. Was Marquez playing with her? Did she know about the midnight meeting, the plan? But if she suspected, why didn't she just let the police know, or the pale *gallego* who'd spoken to Graciela in the cane? She knew she should keep on playing the idiot, act like she didn't know anything. But instead, maybe just from being tired, a little flame flared. "Nenita, why do you ask me these questions, *por favor*? Is it really the business of the CDR to concern itself with a pregnant woman's little treats?"

"Everything in the cooperative is our business, dear. But believe me, whatever your husband thought of us, we want what's best for you. Your daughter Coralía is a dedicated socialist woman. We still remember when she addressed our Marxism-Leninism study circle. I want you to consider me a personal friend."

"Thank you, Nenita. I appreciate that."

The militiawoman looked around casually, as if, Graciela suddenly thought, she, too, was afraid to be overheard. The next moment, she was astonished to hear her mutter, "I'm worried, Graciela."

"Worried, comrade? What about? We're a little behind schedule, but—"

"I don't mean that. I'm afraid hard times are coming."

"They're not going to cut the rations again, are they?"

"I mean politically. There were other prisoners released along with your husband. These other men were not as law-abiding. They were antisocial elements, enemies of the revolution. They swore to abandon their opposition, but apparently had no intention of keeping their word. They've burned a tobacco warehouse in Pinar del Río. They burned a movie theater in Havana, with two hundred people inside, women and children." She tapped the stock of the rifle. "It's being coordinated by the CIA. That's why we're stepping up our training. If there's fighting, we have to hold the line till the army arrives."

"You think there might be trouble here?"

"Let me ask you something. If you knew people who were plotting against the state, what would you do? Would you inform the authorities?"

"What kind of plotting, Comrade Marquez?"

"I don't know. Sabotage, rebellion, hidden arms, attempts to escape. Would you tell me?"

"Of course, *compañera*. Instantly."

"You're not just saying that?"

"No, Comrade Marquez."

"I would be grateful. No one would ever know it was you. And it could help your situation. You know, you are under a cloud now with the manager. Because of your husband."

"Armando paid for his mistakes."

"For stealing food, yes, but you see the cooperative no longer had his labor. They don't lower the production quotas when our labor supply goes down."

"Then they shouldn't have sent him to prison."

"That's not the point. We've all gotten lax. Private vegetable plots, economic crime of all kinds, theft—a line has to be held. Otherwise, the campesinos would loot the state blind."

"Instead, it is the campesinos who go blind."

She could have bitten her tongue; it wasn't smart to taunt a committee member, especially now. Sure enough, Nenita gave her a strange look. "Graciela, is something going on in Batey Number Three? What's happened to Xiomara's roof?"

"It was leaking. They're replacing it with thatch; it lasts better and it's not as noisy."

"And I saw Tomás Guzman with his cousin a little while ago and they were carrying a sack. I asked them what was in it and they said they didn't know. So I made them open it. Scraps of red cloth, and cooking oil. They said they'd found it and were taking it home. Well, of course it had to come from somewhere, and I had to be quite strict with them. If they try such things again, I shall have to report them."

"Examples have to be made," said Graciela. "Nenita, I'm getting cold; my legs hurt—"

"Oh, I'm sorry. Keeping you out in the rain, in your condition! I have some Bulgarian wine. I will open it and bring you a cupful."

She looked after Marquez as she crossed the yard and disappeared into the office. She didn't know what to make of what the committeewoman had said. What did it mean, there might be trouble? Marquez couldn't mean their escape preparations. Everyone had been very careful. Even Tomás and Julio getting caught with the sack—unless you knew what it was for, you wouldn't know it had anything to do with escape.

Or did she mean something bigger? "Counterrevolutionary activity"—everybody knew about the rebellions in the Escambray and the Sierra Maestra. The army had put them down—killed hundreds of peasants, relocated thousands. Could that happen here?

The thought of the army, war, killing made her feel faint. She began picking her way through the mud again. We have to leave, she thought. Maybe we'll die, but we have to leave as soon as we can.

Wet, fatigued, and cold, she turned onto the lonely rainswept road that led to her *batey*.

But that thought, that she might not be here much longer, made the familiar muddy road look new to her as she trudged heavily along. It gave the glistening soil, the wide fields scattered with the tiny green shoots of new cane, such bittersweet beauty that she found herself wanting to cry. Her tears and her sweat had fallen in those fields; years of her life had passed in them. This was her home, and poor as it was, she would not leave it without regret.

Then the baby kicked and she thought quickly to it: I will tell you of this one day, of cane fields and mangroves. But you will not eat the bread of slavery, to fear and obey, to work all your life for distant masters. Your father fought till he could fight no more. I owe him that, that his last wish for you be granted, even if it has to be in a foreign land.

Either this child would be born in freedom or it would never see the light of the sun.

17

U.S. Naval Base, Charleston

THE sun burns through the noon sky in a blaze like a near-death experience. Below it lies a ship. From across the pier, through chain-link fences, a renewed burst of cheering and waving comes thin and already faint from three hundred throats. Kids flourish flags, pretending to one another they can send semaphore. Women wave with their free hands as hip-slung babies suck their thumbs. Carefully made-up girlfriends twist glossy fingernails into metal mesh, searching the ranks that line the rails. A nearly invisible rush of brown-tinted gas shimmers above the stacks. On the bridge, a knot of men lean out, looking down on it all.

On the starboard wing, standing with the captain, the starboard lookout, and two phone talkers, Dan drummed his fingers on the varnished ash bolted on top of the splinter shield.

Where the hell was the tech rep? The quarterdeck had taken a call last night that he was flying in, would be aboard before they got under way. But since then, nothing. Leighty had held up getting under way for nearly an hour now. Now he turned from the crowd, shaking his head, and said to Dan, "I guess he's not coming. We'd better get out in the stream."

"Aye aye, sir. Fantail: take in the brow. Forecastle, Fantail, Midships: Single up all lines. Engine Room: Stand by to answer all bells." And a little while later, after sweeping his eyes down the pier one last time, he ordered, "All engines ahead one-third. Ship's whistle, one prolonged blast."

"Under way. Shift colors."

The forecastle detail, spotless in summer whites, puts their backs to the last line. A moment later, the eye splice slithers through the chocks, dripping. At the bullnose, a petty officer hauls down the jack, folding it with quick stiff motions like a *Nutcracker* Suite toy soldier. Others detach the jackstaff toggles. As they finish, the deck division falls into ranks, facing where slowly, slowly the space of water between USS *Barrett* and the land widens. The sun glitters across the murky water. From other quarterdecks, other ships, men watch with professional interest, and something else: a reluctant fascination, affected by beauty almost against their will.

In an ancient festival, the people of Venice tossed a gold ring into the waves. The most beautiful thing they could make, they gave to the sea.

To the sea . . .

"Navigator recommends come right to course one-seven-five."

Dan checked to starboard, then up and down the channel. It was clear—no ships, no barges, no pleasure craft. The radio, set to the harbor channel, hissed unmodulated, a voiceless somnolent sibilance. They had a different pilot today, not Papa Jack. Dan had told him he'd try taking it out without direction. The pilot had nodded and went out on the port wing. He was out there now enjoying a cigar; the men inside the pilothouse could smell it, that and the damp rich smell of the river. . . . God, it was nice being able to see. And slack tide, they didn't have to fight the damn current this time.

From his chair, Leighty murmured, "Boot her in the ass. Get out of here, Mr. Lenson."

"Aye, sir. Right fifteen degrees rudder, steady course one-seven-five. All engines ahead standard, indicate pitch and rpm for fifteen knots."

Barrett accelerated smoothly and stood tall down the channel, rendering honors as she passed the senior officer present aboard USS *Shenandoah.* The buoys slid by like street signs, and after the forward marker of the Mount Pleasant range passed down the side, Dan turned the conn over to Horseheads. A cannon boomed out from Fort Sumter, and they rendered honors again, in case it was meant for them. The Park Service ran Sumter now; maybe they were doing some kind of historical thing.

The long arms of the jetties released them, and *Barrett* nodded slowly, remembering the rhythm of the sea. Then they, too, lay astern, and the sky fell unhindered to meet the dark flat blue. Dan stood on the wing as the pilot climbed down into the pilot boat. He looked up, gave them a casual salute, and Dan tapped one off to him. The boat cast off and curved away, throwing spray, and he told Horseheads, "Put her on base course and speed, what the navigator recommends. Make sure you run the dead-reckoning line out well ahead and check it on the chart."

Horseheads nodded and went inside. A little while later, Dan watched the bow swing to a southerly heading. He went in then, too, and looked over the charts.

Morris, the chief quartermaster, pointed out their track: a thousand-mile great circle course from Charleston to the Caicos, where they'd alter course southwest to run through the Windward Passage to Guantánamo, on the south coast of Cuba. "Twelve hundred miles," said Morris. "Speed of advance twenty knots, take us three days."

Dan studied the Bahamas, the shallow sounds and islands where Columbus had struck land—San Salvador or Eleuthera or some other island, but somewhere in there the Old World had ground its keel on the sand of the New. He picked up dividers. They'd pass twenty-three miles off Punta Maisi, the eastern tip of Communist Cuba. He looked around the pilothouse, studied the surface plot—two contacts well astern, another with a closest point of approach of 11,000 yards—then went out on the wing again.

He stayed there for half an hour, letting Horseheads get a taste of being in charge. He leaned on the splinter shield and watched the sea go by fifty feet down, the deep summer blue-green of the Atlantic, frothed by *Barrett*'s skin friction as she drove through it.

The land had dropped out of sight when the radioman came up with the message that a helicopter was inbound to them, two hundred pounds of cargo and one passenger.

DR. Henry S. Shrobo looked down from the hurtling aircraft, staring through the plastic window as beneath him land gave way to a wrinkled, blazing sea. He'd used the bathroom three times waiting to take off, but now he needed it again. He squeezed his eyes closed. It wasn't healthy to compress the sphincter, but he didn't seem to have a choice. He was pretty sure there was no bathroom anywhere in the vibrating aluminum cylinder that curved now in a clattering circle out over the glitter. Sunlight flickered over his sweating face. The way the men in flight suits had pushed him into his seat when he started to ask a question, roughly strapped him in when he tried to explain he needed out again just one more time . . . well, he just didn't think he'd better unbuckle the straps.

It was hard to believe he'd been at work yesterday, secure in his routine, and that now he was hurtling outward to sea off South Carolina. Headed farther than that, to Cuba. The first hint was when he'd been asked to step into the office of the commanding officer, Fleet Combat Direction Systems Support Activity, Dam Neck, Virginia.

"Hank, I'm sorry to have to say this, but it sounds like our prototype ACDADS has developed a glitch. Who've you got available for a little on-scene consulting?"

But as he'd told the captain, all his senior programmers were in Hawaii, at the annual Advanced Combat Direction Systems Fleet Working Group conference. He'd have gone himself, but Hawaii was one of the most polluted areas of the country, as far as agricultural chemicals and insecticides went.

"You didn't go because they spray the pineapples?" The captain sounded incredulous.

"Those are *organophosphates*, Ted. They don't just stay on the crops; they contaminate the air, the roads, everything. And they don't have a good effect on the body."

That night, he was in a C-12 headed for Charleston. And then this morning, the helicopter had arrived, and they'd bundled him in—despite his changing his mind—and the well-padded, double-wrapped, nylon tape–strapped box with him.

He sat crouched in the seat, six feet three, thin as a rail, breathing hard and saying his mantra over and over.

Half an hour later, someone clapped his shoulder. He flinched and opened his eyes. The crewman was pointing out the window. He looked out and saw the boat.

It was so little and so far down. It moved steadily through the blue sea. He stared down as they approached. How were they going to get him down there?

"Get up, man."

The crewman again, smaller than the others—and without much caring, Hank noticed he wasn't a man; she was a woman. She flicked his buckles open and helped him up. He started to collapse back into the seat, but she swung him bodily and jammed him against the wall. Then she was putting a round yellow collar around him and another crewman was clacking a safety harness on beside the door.

Suddenly, he realized what they were going to do. He would have fought, but he knew it wouldn't do any good. He closed his eyes as his bowels let go.

The woman was screaming something from a contorted face. He couldn't make it out over the suddenly world-filling roar as the outer door slid back. He stared out into blue blinding space.

They shoved him through the door like butchers handling a side of beef. His legs kicked helplessly at the air. He swung out, back, helpless in a blast of hot air and sound, dizzy, sick, terrified. Then steel slammed up under his feet. Hands pulled off the collar. His legs gave way and he fell. The hands tightened under his arms. He felt the rough steel surface grind at the knees of his suit as he was dragged across it.

THEY took him down to a clean, well-lighted place deep in the ship. Two men helped him out of his dirty torn suit. He told them he had clothes in his bag, but they just exchanged looks. "We didn't see any bag, tall guy. They dumped a box and a briefcase with you, that's all."

He closed his eyes again. He'd shoved it under his seat as he got into the chopper, then forgotten it; the crew hadn't seen it, and now here he was without clothes or toothbrush or even his vitamin supplements. They were all still aboard the helo—wherever it was now.

After a shower and a change, he climbed the ladder behind one of the sailors. He was surprised how large the ship was. It had looked so small from the sky. There were a lot of people aboard, too. Somehow he'd thought of boats as smaller, with just the computer systems and, of course, a few men to handle the ropes and motors and things.

The "bridge" turned out to be a control center high up in the ship. Several men were standing around, not doing much of anything. "Sir, here he is," the corpsman said, and he was led over to someone in a chair.

"Welcome aboard *Barrett.* I'm Thomas Leighty, the captain."

"Hi. Hank Shrobo," he said. "I don't shake hands, but I'm glad to meet you. Nothing personal. It's just that rhinoviruses propagate that way."

The captain, a small man in a white uniform, looked down at his own extended hand, then put it back on the arm of his chair. "Did sick bay take care of you?"

"Oh, yes. Just shaken up a little." He swallowed. "It was a rough flight."

"Just out of curiosity, why are you wearing scrub greens?" the captain asked him.

"My clothes didn't make it, and my suit's torn. The nurses loaned me these."

"Nurses? Oh, the corpsmen. George! Come over here. This is the tech rep just came off the helo. This is George Vysotsky, my exec."

"Did you bring the tapes?" the blond officer asked.

"Yes. Version Three-point-one ACDADS. A new version of the NTDS operating system, with double the track capacity. New comm and sonar modules. And a new Link Eleven tape, too, though your message said yours was okay."

The blond guy was looking him up and down. His voice sounded hoarse. "You're what? GS-eleven? GS-twelve?"

"I'm not a civil servant. I'm with Vartech Research, Incorporated. We support software for all NTDS-related systems."

"Are you sure you're all right?" the exec asked him.

"No, I don't feel too well. Actually, I've never been out in a boat before." Shrobo swallowed, catching their exchange of looks: amused, condescending.

"Normally we call her a ship. Well, anyway, welcome aboard. George, have you got a place to put him?"

"We'll fix something up, sir."

"Dan, can you step over here? This is Lieutenant Lenson; he's the combat systems officer. Dan, the tech rep from Vartech. We should be in Gitmo three days from now, uh, Hank. Hopefully you'll have everything fixed for us then. Just in case you don't we'll get a message out, have them hunt your bag down and get it to us in Cuba."

As he followed the exec down ladders and through passageways, all alike, till he no longer had any idea where he was, he wondered if he'd done the right thing. He hadn't said he was not just a technician but also a Ph.D.; not just "with" Vartech but the head systems analyst, too. It would have sounded like he was puffing himself, but it was also something else.

He resented the way they looked at him, amused, pitying, as if knowing how to work with your mind wasn't as manly as working with your hands. That had always enraged him, but he'd never really known how to react to it.

DAN stayed on the bridge till 1145, phasing into the normal watch rotation. Quintanilla came up and posted a four-section watch bill with Dan, Dave Cannon, Burdette Shuffert, and Jay Harper as OODs, and Van Cleef, Cash, Paul, and Kessler as JOODs. The engineers were off the watch bill, preparing for the arrival inspection. Dan told Morris to advise the navigator he had the next watch. The chief said Cannon knew, that he was eating early and would be right up.

The boatswain's mate said, "Sir, Ensign Lohmeyer wants to have the at-sea fire party muster on the helo deck."

"Make it so," said Dan, thinking it was good to see the new officer taking hold. He'd seemed bewildered when he first came aboard, almost slow. "Ed, take another look out there at that freighter. Does he look like he's coming right to you?"

When Cannon relieved him, he went down to lunch, feeling better than he had for days. Just being at sea made his problems seem less pressing. He dealt rapidly with spaghetti, pizza, canned beets, and steamed broccoli, then took a quick shower.

When he stopped by the computer room, Harper was briefing the tech rep. He watched them for a minute, amused at the contrast. The chief warrant, grizzled but fit, in his faded khakis, knife sheath, and steel-toed boots. He laced technical terms with the salty obscenities gleaned from a life at sea. The civilian—why was he wearing scrub greens?—was going bald, though he couldn't be very old. He didn't look like he got much exercise. His long, knobby fingers rested lightly on a panel as he listened, as if he could sense through them the streams of data coursing through the humming gray machines.

"Excuse me. I'm Lenson, the combat systems officer. We met on the bridge."

"Hank Shrobo."

"Glad to have you aboard. Anything you need, ask Mr. Harper here, or Chief Dawson. Got a bunk? They show you the mess decks?"

Shrobo said quietly that they had. Dan felt something strange about the guy. His color wasn't good, as if the motion of the ship didn't agree with him. Maybe it was just the scrub greens, though.

"Got him up to speed on our problem?"

"Just about." Harper looked worried. Dan wondered if the glitch was worse than he thought. He wanted to ask, but he knew he was interrupting, so he just said he'd be back later and left, dogging the door quietly behind him.

HE got an hour in with Cephas on the administrative package. They got through the rescue and assistance bill, the replenishment at sea bill, and the visit and search, boarding, and prize crew bill. Then they started on the departmental correspondence file. Around 1400, the boatswain's call shrilled "attention."

"This is the captain speaking.

"In three days we'll be pulling into Guantánamo Bay for the toughest training the Navy provides. I want all division officers and chiefs to take one last look at the admin package. If there are any problems, let your department heads know now.

"This afternoon, and each morning and afternoon till we arrive, we'll practice basic fire fighting, damage control, and engineering casualty control under the direction of the XO. He and Mr. Giordano have designed a series of walk-through drills to refamiliarize us with the basics. We'll go through each one slowly and explain each step. Please ask questions and give all your attention to these drills.

"We will now go to general quarters, then break for training from there."

The bong of the alarm. Dan reached for the phone and dialed the computer room. He told Dawson to have the guys working on the computers stand fast but to break off the others to the drill.

He found CA, CF, and CG divisions sitting in a circle on the fantail, in the swaying shadow of the after launcher. The props rumbled under them as the sea marched by. The air was very warm. He squatted, joining them as a damage controlman lifted a mass of black rubber, straps, tubes, and buckles. "The Model A-four quick-starting oxygen-breathing apparatus consists of four parts—one: airtight face piece with eyepieces and speaking diaphragm, two: exhalation and inhalation tubes; three: oxygen-producing canister; four: breathing bag. . . ."

THEY secured from GQ at 1630. He put in another hour in the office, stopped in the computer room, then went up to his stateroom.

The buzz of the phone woke him. He had the watch, the 20–24, eight to midnight. He told the messenger he'd be right up.

The bridge was almost dark and he felt his way around at first. Then, gradually, stars appeared beyond the windows; pilot lights on the radio remotes; the faint radiance from the binnacle, occluded as the helmsman leaned against the console, talking to the boatswain. Frowning—the bridge was supposed to be silent—he checked the chart, then the surface plot.

They were two hundred miles out of Charleston, off the Florida-Georgia border. It would be a long run now parallel to the Florida coast, then the southeasterly tending string of the Bahamas. There weren't many ships out here. The glowing circle of the radar repeater showed him only two flaring pips. The radio circuits hadn't changed since his watch. The ship was on split-plant operations, port steering system in operation, starboard in standby.

He was ready to relieve, but he couldn't find Harper. He bumped into someone beside the bridge scuttlebutt and said, "Who's that?"

"Hey, your quartermaster of the watch, Mr. Lenson. Quartermaster Third Class Lighthizer."

"Evening, Lighthizer. Where's Mr. Harper?"

"Check the port wing, sir. He's been out there most of the watch, the guy I relieved said."

Dan stopped in the door, looking out into the night. The wind flowed by steadily, warm but not uncomfortable. The stars looked blurry and huge; no moon yet. Two silhouettes stood at the port pelorus, and he heard the murmur of conversation. As he stepped out, it clarified into words.

"I just don't see how she could do that, go out there, get her picture taken with them. Remember that, her with the antiaircraft gun? Shit, why didn't the Commie bitch pull a trigger on our guys herself? I never bought a ticket to one of her pictures after that. Fuck her!"

Something inaudible from the lookout. The shadow turned, and a red glow came into view, brightening, then dimming.

"Oh yeah? Try SEAR school. Escape and Evasion. They put you in this mock concentration camp. The guards are sadists. Army Special Forces, Marine Corps, Air Force MPs. Hit you with the side of their fists. No food. A cup of rabbit soup. Some of the guys cooperated. Did whatever they told them to, spit on the flag, sign petitions. Not me. I escaped. Got under the wire, walked all night through the fucking swamp, turned myself in the next morning at the post headquarters. Nobody ever made it that far before—"

"Excuse me," said Dan.

"Just a minute. So they give me a Spam sandwich and a glass of milk and take me back in a truck. The guards beat the shit out of me and throw me in the cage. Example to the others." The shadows separated and Harper said, "You're late, Lieutenant."

"I was here. I spent fifteen minutes getting familiarized. Now I'm looking all over the bridge for you. What is this, you're out here telling the lookouts sea stories?"

"It's a long watch. So I passed a word with the guy."

"He's also smoking. You don't let them smoke, and you don't distract the lookouts, Chief Warrant. Where are the binoculars?"

"Binoculars . . . Hey, Lighthouse, where's the fucking binoculars?"

Dan controlled himself. "Never mind. I'll find them. What's the engineering status?"

"It's all on the board, night orders."

"The night orders aren't up yet." Dan suddenly became conscious of other ears around them. "Who's got the conn?"

"I do," Kessler said from the darkness.

"We're going in the chartroom for a second, Lieutenant."

The red light in the little attached space made Harper look emaciated and diabolical. "Another ass-chewing?" he grunted.

"You rate one, Chief Warrant. You don't know where the binoculars are because you haven't been using them. You don't know the engineering lineup, electric load, or what tonight's ops are going to be. Do you?"

"What kind of Mickey Mouse bullshit is this?" said Harper. "Look, I've been OOD-qualified on ten ships and every CO gave me four-oh evals. You can chew the fat with the guys without breaking discipline, long's they know you'll turn around and beat their fuckin' ass. Why don't you just chill the fuck out?"

"I'm not going to match sea years with you. And chewing the rag—that's not the point. They're smoking outside the skin of the ship. That'll cost us points in Gitmo, not to mention it ruins their night vision."

"I've been to Gitmo five times. Robinson knows he can't smoke in Condition Three. And he won't."

"And I'm telling you, you condone smoking on watch now, he'll sneak a smoke later. And the next time I relieve you, I expect a proper turnover from a properly organized watch!"

"I stand relieved," said Harper, tossed him a contemptuous salute, and left. Dan stood in the chartroom, so taken aback he didn't respond. But when he went out, Harper was already gone. He said loudly, "This is Lieutenant Lenson. I have the deck and the conn. Belay your reports. Boatswain's mate!"

"Sir."

"Check all the lookouts. Any of them smoking, give the JOOD their names. Quartermaster! Inventory the binoculars and report to me if any are missing. Combat! Recalculate all contact courses, speeds, and CPAs. I want a complete update on the board by time fifteen. Mr. Van Cleef, call Main Control and update the plant lineup board. We'll be doing a lost-steering drill this watch, then a maneuvering-board drill."

When bridge and lookouts and combat had settled down again into the dark silence that meant a tight, alert watch, he checked the surface picture one last time, then turned the conn over to his new junior officer of the deck, Van Cleef. He leaned against the XO's chair, looking out at the passing sea.

It was so black, it seemed to pull all light into itself. Yet even this long after sunset, a glow lingered far to the west. Water crashed and rumbled as *Barrett*'s ax-sharp stem cut it apart and peeled it back. Beneath it whirled the blurry luminescence of the suddenly exposed deep, mysterious and beckoning, more profound than any man could ever know and still live. The Gulf Stream, he remembered. They were breasting the greatest river on earth, the shoreless stream that carried the heat of the equator from tropic to pole.

But he was remembering another night, the shriek of the storm in an old ship's top-hamper as Alan Evlin had explained the world and human life to him. Looking out now, he seemed to see again a huge Arctic comber, moving in on them out of the north, black on deeper black, a green phosphorescence rippling and flickering along its crest.

"There are things you can't say in words," the gentle lieutenant had said, Dan so green then that he'd hardly known his way from one side of the bridge to the other. "Just look out there, and think about it."

The wave was almost on them. "Get ready, Ali. Here comes a big mother."

"Got her clamped, sir." The strong black face behind the wheel.

"Coffee, sir?" muttered Pettus. Yeah, he remembered Pettus, too.

The sea hit them square, so hard that the old tin can's bones shook. He reached out to grip steel, but it was *Barrett*'s fabric he gripped, not *Reynolds Ryan*'s. It was tonight and not years before. He was older now and not nearly so naïve, so trusting, and so idealistic.

He suddenly missed Evlin, Packer, all the guys who'd died in *Ryan.* Did their spirits linger over the sea, as their bodies had become part of it? Because they were all still out here, in the greatest graveyard on earth—or at least the dissolved atoms that had once been their bodies. Maybe they were spinning through *Barrett*'s screws right now. Atoms remembered nothing; they were changeless and eternal. But what had happened to their spirits? Was there such a thing as an immortal soul, or, as Evlin had thought, a little splinter of the infinite within each creature that had the capability of choice?

Van Cleef, beside him: "Night orders, sir."

He clicked on the red light over the chart table. The captain's handwriting slanted big and bold across the form. He read down the own-ship and weather data, noting moonrise later that night; temperatures in the mid-eighties, visibility unlimited; independent steaming, remain alert for small contacts not registering on radar. Sonar to conduct self-noise testing at midnight. The engineers to do casualty control exercises from 0130–0500. He signed the 20–24 block and passed it back.

Yeah, this was what the Navy was all about: going to sea. Or was it? Maybe it was really about the stuff they spent 90 percent of their time doing—paperwork, messages, drills, inspections, administration. Was it about responsibility and honor? Or about making decisions he didn't want to make, serving under people he didn't trust, making compromises he hated?

"Say, sir," said a voice beside him, and he flinched, but it was only Van Cleef. "I was wondering . . . when you were getting under way the other day, you used the mooring lines to get the ship around. How do you know how much force to put on them? Is there any trick to that?"

"You have to have the lines over right. If you can get the bow and stern lines perpendicular to the pier, you can control the lateral position of the bow and stern. Then take in on the spring lines to move you fore and aft. . . ."

He thought again of Evlin and Norden and Packer as he tried to pass on some of what he'd learned to Van Cleef. For just a moment, staring at his silhouette in the dark, he saw himself again in the young man: eager to learn and contribute and perform.

And when someday the Cowcatcher was standing here, explaining shiphandling to someone else, where would he, Dan Lenson, be then? He'd always remember the nights at sea, the camaraderie, the fatigue, but one day he'd go ashore for good, and all this would be memories or less than that. His passing was as inevitable as that of every wave under the keel. All that would remain of him was what he could hand on to others—the knowledge and the craft—and beyond that what meaning he could wrest or guess at from the world and the sea, the glittering of Sirius and Deneb and the faces of human beings, each clouded or bright in his own way, like the stars.

"Mr. Lenson."

The rough-edged voice could only belong to one man. He turned quickly, to find Vysotsky's shadow between him and the helm console. "Yes, sir. Good evening, XO."

"Evening. Everything quiet?"

"Yes, sir. I was just telling Keon how you use warping lines to get under way."

"I don't think you can do better than emulate Mr. Lenson, in terms of watch standing and shiphandling."

"Yes, sir," said Van Cleef. Dan didn't say anything. Praise made him feel uncomfortable, especially from someone who would dismiss a set of charges at his superior's say-so.

The executive officer stood motionless for a while, then hoisted himself up into his chair. "How's the computer expert doing? Shrobo?"

"He doesn't have any sea legs, but he seems to know his way around a YUK-seven, sir."

"Any progress?"

"He's down there working the problem, but it'll take a while to get the new programming loaded and checked out."

"I want your guys to pick up all they can from him, in case it happens again after he leaves. And it's a great training opportunity for them."

"Yes, sir. They're down there, Dawson and Williams and the others."

Vysotsky didn't say anything for a time. Dan glanced back as the phone talker began jotting up data on a new surface contact. "You have that on radar, Mr. Van Cleef?"

"Yes, sir. Closest point of approach, eight thousand yards at two-two-zero."

"Very well."

"Has Mr. Harper been helping him?"

"Sir?"

"I said, has Jay been helping out with the ACDADS?"

"Uh, I believe so, sir. As much as he can with watch, running his division, the classified accounts, and all the other things he's got on his plate."

"What's your opinion of him?"

"What, of Jay?" Dan considered. They'd had their frictions, especially lately, but he didn't feel like going into that with the XO.

"He's a real asset to the ship, sir. He's a good electronics czar, knows the systems. He gets things fixed."

"How about as a division officer?"

"Well, he has his own way of doing things, sir. Kind of the old-style 'square the fuck away or I'll kick your ass myself' kind of leadership. But it seems to work for him. Why?"

"No reason," said Vysotsky. "Just asking."

Dan raised his glasses and leaned against the window. A diffuse light like a faraway fire glowed off to port. The moon, still below the horizon, was advertising its impending presence.

"Well, I'm going to turn in." Vysotsky swung down; Dan moved aside to let him past. "See you in the A.M."

"Good night, sir."

After the XO left, Dan checked the radar and satisfied himself the contact ahead would pass clear. He looked out to starboard for a while, then drifted over to the chart table and stared down at it. "Lighthizer," he said. "This last loran fix you took, is it—"

From out of the darkness, the suddenly energized voice of the JL phone talker cut in: "Aft lookout reports—man overboard! Starboard!"

"All engines stop! Hard right rudder," he and Van Cleef shouted at the same second. Dan kept going, dodging shadows on his way to the wing, yelling as he went: "OOD has the conn! Sound six blasts. JOOD, call the captain. Boatswain, pass 'man overboard.' "

He was startled but not terribly excited. It was probably a drill, get the guys shaken down for Gitmo. As the horn blasted into life, he reached the wing, jerked the ready float off its holder, pulled the pin, and heaved it overboard. It ignited as it hit the water and fell rapidly astern, disappearing as the stern wake swept over it, then flaring up anew, bobbing crazily. *Barrett* leaned into the turn. The horn stopped, started another blast. Simultaneously Dan saw another flare astern, more distant, but on the same line of bearing as the one he'd just dropped. Good, the after lookout had popped a float, too.

The last blast cut off and other sounds became audible. "Combat reports, shifting to two hundred yards to the inch, commencing man overboard plot."

"Very well. Keep an eye on that contact, see if he's going to embarrass us if we heave to."

"Man overboard, starboard side. Man overboard, starboard side."

Dan bent to the pelorus and lined it up on the glowing marks to the reciprocal of their original course. The night orders said the wind would be ten to fifteen knots from the east. The ship was slowing rapidly. He saw it all in his head and made his decision. "Port engine ahead full," he called in. The rapidly swinging bow eclipsed the first, more distant flare. He waited, then a few seconds before it came in line with his own, he shouted, "Steady as she goes. All engines ahead one-third. Mark your head."

"Engine room answers, all ahead one-third. Steady as she goes, aye. Mark my head, zero-two-three."

Dan hit the 21MC button for the signal bridge. "Sigs, Bridge: Get our lights fired up. Man in the water, port bow, five hundred yards ahead."

The captain came out on the wing. His torso glowed strangely. He was in his undershirt. "Where is he?" he said. Dan pointed ahead to the guttering flares. "The far one, the after lookout threw as soon as he saw him. I placed the other one."

"What's your plan?"

"Modified Anderson recovery. Line up on the two floats, take him aboard with the boat."

"Bridge, Midships: Boat crew's mustered. Request permission to lower to the rail."

"Hold off," said Leighty. Dan repeated the order into the pilothouse. The captain said, "It's calm enough for a shipboard recovery. The water's warm. Go in slow along the reciprocal. Don't run over him. Any idea who it is?"

Dan said, "No, sir," realizing only then that this was a real man overboard, not a stuffed dummy to be hauled back aboard with a grapnel. The phone talker shouted, "Bridge, Combat: Man bears zero-one-eight, three hundred yards." Leighty disappeared inside. Dan heard him yelling, "Is the XO here? Have you got a muster yet, George?"

Part of the normal response to a "man overboard" was to muster the crew at stations for a quick head tally. Dan wondered for another second who it was, then dismissed it from his mind. They were closing in on the southernmost flare. When it passed down the port side, tossing on the waves, he could hear it hissing and sputtering as its flame fought the sea. It cast a fitful glitter on the black waves around it. Then it moved past and aft. "Left hard rudder, starboard engine ahead full, port engine back full," he yelled into the pilothouse.

The boatswain's mate of the watch said, "Sir, the lookout says—"

"Which lookout?"

"After lookout. He says he wasn't really sure it was a guy."

"What!" Dan rounded on him, and the man shrank back. "What do you mean, he isn't sure it was a guy? He just told us man overboard!"

"Sir, he says he saw something white go over from the helo deck. It hit the water hard, but he couldn't make out in the dark what it was. So he called in—"

"Yeah, yeah, okay, he did right." Dan debated passing that to the captain, then noticed suddenly that his bow was swinging too fast. He yelled, "All stop! Right full rudder, steady course three-four-zero." At that moment, the little twinkling star ahead of them winked out suddenly.

"Aw fuck," Van Cleef muttered beside him. Dan asked him, "Have you got a report from the fo'c'sle?"

"Yeah, they're ready down there."

Dan leaned forward, confirming that they were indeed ready, five men spaced along the side of the ship. Only it was the wrong side. He cupped his hands and yelled down, "Port side! Port-side recovery!" They waved back and ran to the opposite lifeline.

The searchlights had been playing ahead, searching here and there across the gently heaving blackness. Now they all swung to one point and steadied. Dan checked the wind again and corrected.

"There he is! See him, sir?"

"Yeah, there's something there all right. Can't tell if it's a man. Okay, let's shift to the port wing for the pickup. Get some paper cups from the chart room."

But as they coasted in the final few hundred feet, the white patch disappeared. Dan gave the engines back one-third, then dropped a cup overboard. It sailed down fifty feet, hit the water, then drifted slowly aft. The captain and XO came out and they all three stood there, searching the water. The lights held steady a few dozen yards off the bow, but they couldn't see anything. "What the hell?" muttered Leighty.

Above them, a signalman leaned over the rail, gripping binoculars. "Didja see him?" he yelled.

"No. Where is he?"

"He was right out there—a guy in whites. When we came up on him, he dived down. You could see him a little while in the lights, under the water, but now he's not there anymore."

Vysotsky pulled another float off the rack, stripped the waterproofing tape off it, and pulled the pin. He heaved it over in the direction of the focused lights as it ignited. A sulfurous cloud enveloped the wing, then blew away downwind.

Dan yelled up, "You're sure it was a man? Not a bag of trash that sank when we came up?"

"No, sir. We could see his arms moving. He was looking up at us as we came in. Then he dived down, like he was trying to get away."

They stared down into the water. Finally, Leighty said, "Lower the boat. Do a careful search all around where he . . . went down."

Chief Oakes came out, *Barrett*'s chief master-at-arms. He handed a piece of paper to Vysotsky. The XO read it, then looked up.

"One of yours, Dan. ETSN Benjamin Sanderling."

The snort of a motor, and the whaleboat charged around the

stern. Then it slowed, purring out toward where the beams were drifting apart now, growing uncertain, groping over the unmarked surface of the sea.

Dan put his flashlight on the 21MC and punched the call button for the computer room. Williams answered. He said, still hoping it might not turn out that way, "Petty Officer Williams. Sanderling turn up yet?"

"No, sir. Ain't here, and his rack's empty."

"When's the last time you saw him?"

"Just after he got off watch. He had the second dog in Combat."

"How'd he seem to you? Anybody else see him after that?"

"Chief Dawson here, sir. He was acting kind of down. Said something about going to the XO about something. I didn't ask him what. I guess I should've, but he's like always in your face about something or other."

Dan told him not to blame himself, then punched off. He looked out to where the boat was searching, the pale thin beams of the battle lanterns probing down into black depths. Beyond, below, around it, only the black.

CANNON came up early and relieved him. Dan went to combat systems berthing, where Sanderling had slept. Its other occupants squatted in the passageway. Inside, all the bunks were empty and all the lights were on. Harper, Oakes, Dawson, and the departmental yeoman were waiting in one of the bays.

"Here's Mr. Lenson."

Dan said heavily, "Okay, Senior Chief. This everybody we need?"

"Yes, sir. Actually the inventory board just needs one officer, according to—"

"Cephas, what're you doing here? Oh, the secretary. Okay, Senior Chief. Cut it."

Oakes positioned the bolt cutters and leaned on the handles. The jaws slipped through the hasp of the padlock and met with a click. Dawson hoisted the mattress, exposing the under-bunk locker, a three-by-six-foot slab of six-inch space. He started sorting things into a cardboard box, giving Cephas a running description. "Web belt, black, one. Blue chambray shirt, four." In the personal compartment were a marking kit, a wallet, a key ring with three keys, the USS *Barrett* stationery kit that the ship's store sold, Sanderling's boot camp copy of *The Bluejacket's Manual*, and a mending kit.

"That's it. Mostly class-two and -five stuff."

"What else we got?"

"Hanging locker, then the seabag locker," said Dawson.

The upright locker held a reefer jacket and two sets of whites still in their dry-cleaning bags. By the time they were through inventorying it, the master-at-arms had the seabag locker open. The duffel stenciled B. G. SANDERLING USN held civilian clothes and carefully folded winter blues. It didn't look like it had been opened for a while.

"Anything else?"

Cephas cleared his throat. "Sir, there's a luggage locker some of the guys keep stuff in."

They found a green suitcase with a chain tag marked "Benny Sanderling, 205 West Fifth Street, Eugene, Oregon." It was locked, but a little stamped key on the ring opened it.

"Yeah, I figured we'd find something like this," said Harper.

Dan looked down silently as Oakes snapped on a set of rubber gloves. He started laying the magazines and objects out on a piece of plastic.

"What do we do with this, sir? We don't want to send this . . . stuff back to his family, do we?"

"No," said Dan. His face felt rigid. "Dump it overboard. Leave it off the inventory, Cephas."

"Yes, sir," said the yeoman.

"How about these magazines?" Harper picked one up, displayed a foldout page to the others. "How about it? Turn you guys on?"

"Put it down," Dan snapped, and the chief warrant grinned and dropped it.

Oakes took the last magazine out of the suitcase, and there was the book. It said DIARY on it.

"Overboard," said Dan. "Don't even open it."

"Wait a second," Harper said. "This might be evidence."

"Senior Chief? What's the regs say about diaries?"

"Uh, I guess class five, sir. Miscellaneous personal stuff—"

Harper picked it up with the tips of his fingers, just as he had the magazine. He thumbed through several entries. He cleared his throat, then flattened it so they could read, underlining one passage with his fingernail.

> July Fifth. Today me and the captain made love for the first time. It was not like what I expected. He is a tender man. . . .

"Uh-oh," muttered Oakes. His old face looked furrowed and resigned.

"I knew it," said Harper. "I knew it. He's been cornholing this kid, and he couldn't take it anymore. So he jumped overboard. This is dynamite."

"We better get the XO in on this," Lenson said.

"Fuck we do! He's covering for him, if he isn't one himself. If it goes to Vysotsky, it'll disappear." Harper turned to the master-at-arms. "Oakie?"

"I don't know, Mr. Harper. I don't know what to do."

They looked at Dan. He picked the diary up and made himself look through it. It was Sanderling's all right. He recognized his handwriting from the special request chits, applications for officer training, protests of his evaluation marks. He turned to the last entry, dreading what he'd find. A farewell message, a declaration of love, a cry of revenge? . . . But there was no entry for that day, and not for several before that. The last entry was a poem he'd copied from somewhere: "Invictus."

Out of the night that covers me,
Black as the Pit from pole to pole,
I thank whatever gods may be
For my unconquerable soul. . . .

He took a deep breath and put the diary in his back pocket. The others looked at him.

"The rest of this stuff, throw it overboard," he said. Cephas rolled up the plastic, hefted it.

"Off to the fantail," he said, and left.

18

Guantánamo Bay, Cuba

THE hills loomed up like a rampart built across the sea. They stretched off gradually, dropping below the limits of sight, with no sign of human habitation except directly ahead. There, east of where the land opened, a water tower and antennas rose on the far side of what the chart named the Cuzco Hills.

Dan stood on the flying bridge, looking down and forward over the venturi bulwark. Behind him, two enlisted were cracking jokes as they greased the rotating barrels on the Phalanx.

"So the boatswain's mate gets a blow job from this fireman in the after machine shop. And when he's finished, the fireman spits the come into a jar. The boatswain asks him why he did that, and he says, 'One of the radiomen's doing the same thing, and whoever gets his filled first gets to drink them both.' "

He moved away, feeling sick, but not just at the joke. He'd felt that way for the last two days, since the night Sanderling went overboard.

He'd read the diary, read it unwillingly, but he didn't see any other choice now that he'd taken custody. He'd thought he might send it back to the seaman's next of kin with the rest of his personal gear, maybe with a page or two missing. But now he'd read it, he knew he couldn't do that. He'd have to tear out most of the diary. He couldn't send it back to Mr. and Mrs. Dennis Sanderling, Eugene, Oregon—not with the things it described.

How strange that he knew the young seaman better dead than he'd ever known him alive.

Shit, he wished he could stop thinking about it. He leaned over the bulwark as *Barrett* passed between the two points that guarded the entrance to Guantánamo Bay and wheeled slowly right. Burdette Shuffert had the watch. Shuffert would be the general quarters officer of the deck during the training. Dan, of course, would be TAO most of the time.

Now he looked down as *Barrett* felt her way in, the world rotating about her pivot point, Leeward Point Field and Hicacal Beach walking down the port side. A freighter came into view upriver, steaming down from the upper bay. The hills gradually moved apart to starboard, revealing behind them the buildings and water tanks of the harbor proper, inside Corinaso Point.

He'd been here before, and looking up at the dry steep hills, he remembered the history. Guantánamo was a small but strategically situated harbor on Cuba's southeast coast. The U.S. presence was a relic of the war of 1898, when the marines had landed to support operations against the Spanish at Santiago. A few years later, Teddy Roosevelt had leased the bay, not for a hundred years, like the bases in the Philippines, but without any terminating date, as long as the Navy needed it and paid the rent.

The gates dividing the base from the rest of Cuba had closed the day Fidel Castro took power. But the Navy had stubbornly maintained its toehold, building desalinization and power plants when the Cubans cut off electricity and water, and both sides had fortified and mined the boundary between the base and the rest of hilly, dry, sparsely populated Oriente Province.

Since it lay on both sides of the harbor entrance, the base was divided into Leeward and Windward sides. The main piers and repair facilities lay along the east, shielded from hurricanes. It wasn't entirely an armed camp. Dependents lived here; there was a high school and a fishing tournament. But it wasn't like being in Charleston or San Diego, either. The base only covered forty-five square miles, most of that water or rugged hills. And it was the only U.S. military installation actually in a Communist country.

That isolation made it a good place to train, and that was Gitmo's primary mission. Ships could go out in the morning, train and shoot all day in deep water, then be back pierside the same night—something they couldn't do anyplace else on the East Coast. Every ship in the Atlantic Fleet had to complete refresher training here before it deployed, shaking down crew and systems into a battle-trained whole. And as almost any sailor would tell you, deployment usually turned out less stressful than the four to six weeks at the hands of the Fleet Training Group.

The marks of the Hicacal Beach range began to diverge as the bow swung slowly right. The piers came into view, with another destroyer, a *Coontz*-class, and a *Newport*-class LST with its unmistakable "horns" at the bow. An oiler lay opposite the destroyer, and a small craft that looked like a PT or hydrofoil, but not a type he recognized.

As *Barrett* shaped her course the last few hundred yards to the pier, the freighter upriver grew larger. Dan saw the hammer and sickle on its stack. On its bridge, a stocky woman focused a camera. Dan glanced down; *Barrett*'s officers, Shuffert, Leighty, Vysotsky, were on the starboard wing, concentrating on the pier.

He lifted a hand as the merchant swept past. He'd seen Russians at close range before, in the Med. Usually, you could get a wave and sometimes a grin out of them. But the stolid round faces looked through him as the stocky woman snapped off pictures. Then they were past, dwindling away, the wake rolling *Barrett* as she lined up for the final approach.

Sanderling's diary was a look into a world Dan hadn't known existed: of furtive couplings in bus station toilets, night-shrouded beaches, cheap motel rooms; of fear and longing, but also a kind of desperate joy, a passion that sometimes transcended itself into an existential freedom.

Some of it, Dan couldn't imagine. But some was the way he'd felt himself at Sanderling's age, the desperate, awkward, searching time when you looked for everything you needed outside yourself.

What he found strangest was the anonymity, the rapid succession of partners—strangers, maybe not even seen clearly. He couldn't understand it at first. Then he remembered Sibylla Baird. He'd met her . . . gone out to the garden. . . . What was so different?

No, the only real distinction was that Sanderling had loved men.

He wished now he'd tossed the diary overboard with the magazines. But Harper and Oakes knew he had it. If it had been purely a matter of Sanderling, he wouldn't have hesitated. He'd have called the other witnesses back to the fantail, shown them the diary, pitched it into the white boil of screw wash.

But it wasn't just Sanderling now.

And he had to decide what to do about it.

He resolved to do it now, today—to bite the bullet and get it over with just as soon as the lines went over and the brow went into place.

A battered white pickup was waiting for them at Pier L. Dan stood by it, waiting for Oakes. He looked down the side of the ship, *under* the ship. There were the twin rudders, the twin screws. Incredible how transparent the water was. He could see every pebble on the bottom. *Barrett* seemed to hover, not float, suspended in a medium only a little denser than air. From there, he glanced up at dry-looking bluffs dotted with cactus. The palms and the verandas gave the harbor a tropical feel.

"Ready, sir?" Senior Chief Oakes, already sweating, was coming down the brow carrying Sanderling's gear. Dan took the suitcase from him and threw it into the bed of the truck.

Commander, Naval Base headquarters, was a mile south of the piers, up the hill from the Blue Caribe Club. It was a World War II–era two-story, white paint flaking, with a tower that must have had something to do with the airfield once. The duty driver dropped them in front of the concrete-roofed entranceway. Dan told him to go back to the ship, figuring they could walk back once they got rid of the luggage.

A female petty officer was typing at a steel desk on the quarterdeck. He said, "Lieutenant Lenson, USS *Barrett.* We just pulled in. Is there a legal officer here?"

"Do you want that for a will, power of attorney—"

"No, this is official. We have to turn in some personal effects of a man who died en route, and I need to ask a couple of legal questions."

"That would be the judge advocate general on the staff. Lieutenant Commander Arguilles is the officer in charge."

ARGUILLES was a mountain in sloppy khakis. He had a big mustache and dark hair. Looking at Dan's name tag, he said as they shook hands, "Lenson. Lenson . . . You know a guy name of Johnstone? Stanley Fox Johnstone?"

"Yeah. The *Ryan* inquiry. He was the counsel for the court."

"I served with him on the COMNAVFORCARIB staff. He mentioned you—the guy who asked to be punished, after they told him to go and sin no more. What do you think about that, Senior Chief?"

"The Navy ain't that big of an organization, sir."

"I don't mean . . . well, never mind." The JAG officer told them to sit down, said they could smoke if they wanted. "What can I do for you?" he said, propping his shoes on the desk.

"Well, sir—"

"Call me José."

"Sir—José—I think we've got a problem aboard *Barrett.* And I thought maybe I'd better get some advice."

"We got your message. About the kid who went missing, right?"

"Yeah."

"This his gear? You sanitize everything? Take out the rubbers and cunt books?"

Dan took the inventory and forwarding letter out of its messenger envelope and handed it over. Arguilles glanced down it, nodded, and flipped it into his in box. "Page two, next of kin's address, beneficiary form, looks good. Stack the stuff in the corner, my evil dwarfs will take it from here. That all?"

"Senior Chief, I'll see you back at the ship, okay?"

Oakes looked disappointed, but he stubbed out his butt. When he was gone, Dan cleared his throat.

"Ice water?"

"No thank you, sir. I don't know how to start this. I'm not sure I ought to be here. But I don't think keeping quiet is the right thing to do, either. And it might have a bearing on why Sanderling jumped."

The phone rang. Arguilles picked it up, listened, said, "Tell her to come in. No, I can't advise her over the phone. Hold my calls, okay? Sorry, go ahead," he said to Dan.

"Yeah, well . . . I don't know, like I say, if this is the right thing to do or not."

"Why don't you tell me in confidence," said Arguilles. "You say it's related to Sanderling's death."

"It might be. We found . . . homosexual literature in the kid's effects."

"You mean cock books—naked guys with big, big hard-ons."

"Right. We also found a diary."

"Go on."

"The diary describes his acts with other people." He cleared his throat again. "Including the captain."

"Go on."

He was puzzled by the lawyer's lack of reaction. "Well . . . that's about it."

"Was there a final message, a note or letter? Anything that mentioned his intention to do away with himself?"

"No."

"What did your commanding officer say when he saw this diary?"

"He hasn't." Dan took it out of his pocket and placed it on the edge of the desk. "I didn't tell him or the XO about it."

"Why not?"

"I wasn't sure it wouldn't disappear."

"What happened to the other material?"

"I had it thrown overboard."

"You this kid's division officer?"

"Department head."

"He a good sailor?"

"Not the best I've ever seen. But not the worst, either."

"Why do you say it might be related to his death? Does he write that in the diary?"

"No. The last entry was four days before he jumped. The diary was kept in the luggage room, by the way. So he couldn't get to it every day. He must have gotten the key now and then and brought it up to date." Dan shifted in the chair. "The relationship to his death . . . well, it seems like you could make that inference."

"That he committed suicide because he fucked the captain? Or that the captain fucked him? Or that the captain fucked him once but wouldn't do it again?" Arguilles grimaced. "Let's go back to why you didn't turn the diary in. Why did you think it might 'disappear'?"

"I don't know."

"You don't trust your CO or XO not to destroy evidence."

"I guess not," Dan said. "Did you want to look at it?"

"No," said Arguilles.

"You don't want to see it?"

"For the moment, I want to be able to say I've never seen it. Okay?"

"I guess."

"So what do you want me to do?"

"I need some advice. That's why I came in."

"Advice? Let's not say I did that. I can point out some choices, though."

"Okay."

"One: You go out the door, then turn around and come back in here with it officially. Turn the diary over to me, get a receipt, and file Article One twenty-five charges against your commanding officer."

For some reason, Dan remembered his interview with Jack Byrne just then. "What's Article One twenty-five?" he asked cautiously.

"Sodomy."

"Whew."

"Yeah. Make yourself popular, plus, if he's found guilty, all he's got to do is call you a jealous lover and down you go with him. Choice number two: Lose this hot potato over the side next time you get under way. Punch a hole through the middle of it, get a shackle from the boatswain's mates, make sure it never sees the light of day again."

"Any other choices?"

"You can make an anonymous complaint."

"What happens then?"

"The Naval Investigative Service investigates anonymous complaints of homosexuality. They'll come in like a ton of bricks if it's the CO, an alleged participant."

"What's your feeling on that?"

"I don't want to put anybody down," said Arguilles. "But they're not bound by rules of evidence on homosexuality investigations. They get one pansy, they lean on him for names. And I mean, they lean hard. There's gonna be enough mud flying around to splatter everybody aboard. You start a witch-hunt, you're gonna lose some of your best people."

"None of those sounds like good choices, sir."

"I hate faggot cases," said Arguilles. "Avoid 'em whenever I can. The first case I ever handled—'the Night Crawler.' Guy used to crawl into guys' racks after taps and blow them. Never alluded to it in daylight. He said he did it for years and nobody ever turned him in. Finally he went down on this nigger boilerman and the guy just about killed him with a piece of wire rope. You think your CO's really a fag?"

"I don't know."

"Does anybody else think so? Or are you a voice in the wilderness?"

"I've heard remarks."

"Is it affecting good order and discipline?"

"It might be starting to, sir. That's really why I'm here." He looked at a colored print on the wall: sailing ships in battle, powder smoke billowing above shattered spars. "If I didn't, I might not think it was any of my business."

"*Is* it your business? Order and discipline are the captain's and XO's responsibility."

"They're everybody's responsibility."

"Yeah, but who appointed it specifically yours? Oh, I get it." Arguilles peered at him. "Same as with the *Ryan* thing, huh? You appointed yourself."

Dan said, irritated, "Call it whatever you want. What should I do about it?"

Arguilles leaned back and locked his hands behind his head. "Well, there'll be an investigation of the suicide. Diehl is wrapped around the axle now on this bad-check ring over at the marine barracks; it might take him a few days, but he'll be over. Is this diary evidence leading to suspicion that the captain or others named or unnamed contributed to that suicide? I'm not sure. The thing is, from the legal point of view, anything in it is either hearsay or unsubstantiated—if not fiction. The kid's not around to answer for it. Does he name anybody else aboard the ship?"

"No."

"No other partners?"

"He mentions a couple, but no names. The only one he names is the captain—and actually he doesn't use his name either, just calls him 'the captain.' Most of his uh . . . activity seems to center around a bar in Charleston. That's our home port."

"Uh-huh. You realize he might have made this up? Whatever he says he did with your skipper? Like you or me daydreaming about going to bed with Farrah Fawcett, okay? A sex fantasy, power fantasy. He might even have put it in on purpose, to protect himself if anybody else ever got hold of the diary. See what I mean? I've seen that before in cases like this. First thing defense counsel is going to bring up."

"I don't think—"

"What?"

"Nothing," said Dan. He'd started to say, "I don't think Sanderling would do that," but he knew now he'd never known the first thing about Sanderling. Maybe he didn't know any of his shipmates, or any human being, not deep down, as they really were. It was a bitter knowledge. He reached out for the diary, weighed it for a moment, then slipped it back into his pocket.

"I ask you one question?" said Arguilles. "In confidence."

"Sure."

"Are *you* gay?"

"No!"

"Take it easy. . . . I know, soon as you start talking about them, that's like the next question, isn't it? But there's something else eating you, isn't there? Other than this Sanderling thing. You got something against 'em?"

Dan sat hunched over, giving it a few seconds' thought. He *didn't* like homosexuals . . . didn't like the idea; it made him feel ill to think about doing the things Sanderling had described . . . but sometimes it got to be too much, the jokes, the sniggers that were common currency aboard ship, the relentless official indoctrination about their undependability, their vulnerability to blackmail, their danger to discipline. Then he remembered Byrne, what he'd told him about the torpedoman on the *Threadfin.* So maybe it was true that they could be dangerous aboard ship. But Sanderling hadn't seemed dangerous, just immature and screwed up. He honestly didn't know how to answer the lawyer's question. So he just muttered, "I don't know, not particularly."

"Then why fall on your sword over it?"

"I just want to do what's right."

Arguilles blew out like a surfacing dolphin as he hoisted himself to his feet. "Ohh*kay.* You just wanna do what's *right.* . . . Well, Lieutenant, do us all a favor. You let us know when you figure out what that is."

THE sun outside was incredible—like a tanning salon. By the time he got back down to the pier, his khakis were soaked.

Leighty was standing on the quarterdeck in whites. He looked through Dan as if he knew everything he'd said to Arguilles. He returned Dan's salute, then motioned him into the shade of the helo hangar.

"Dan, where have you been? The FTG team's here; we're starting the arrival conference in ten minutes. Where were you?"

"Sorry, sir. I was over turning in Sanderling's gear at Base Legal—and asking them some questions about how to proceed."

"What did they say?"

"Uh, there'll probably be somebody from the local NIS detachment coming down to check it out."

Blinking in the sun, he tried to see Leighty clearly. For a moment, he had the feeling, the illusion probably, that if he could see him clearly, he'd understand somehow what to do.

Thomas Leighty wasn't much bigger than a boy. His face was small and his forearms, exposed in the starched short-sleeved trop whites, were almost like an adolescent's. He stood straight, balancing himself on the balls of his feet as if about to lunge for a ball. The way he cupped his left elbow in his hand might be effeminate, or might not. The captain's uniform was spotless, ribbons new and precisely aligned. A hint of silver glinted at the temples under the gold-crusted visor. His eyes crinkled at the edges, narrowed against the sun.

He imagined himself saying, "Sir, did you go to bed with Sanderling?" Or maybe, "Sir, was there anything between you and Sanderling?" What would Leighty say?

"Sir, did you notice anything strange about Sanderling?"

"Strange?"

"You saw a lot of him, I understand he was working on your entertainment system."

The captain blinked, but it could have been the glare. "He didn't seem very happy, but he didn't talk about it to me. I wanted to ask you, how's our fire-control system doing? Has our civilian made any progress?"

Dan started explaining it to him. Midway through the 1MC interrupted: "All officers and chiefs assemble in the wardroom."

THE table was cleared and bare except for pencils and lined notepads. Four men in blue coveralls sat at the foot, and another was passing out a document, one copy to each officer and chief.

"Attention on deck."

Everyone stood as Leighty took his seat at the head of the table, then sat with a scraping of chairs. "Can we have that ventilator turned off?" the captain said to Vysotsky. "All right, let's begin."

The man who stood had lieutenant's bars on his coveralls, a blue breast patch with FTG embroidered in gold, and above that the gold ship-and-crossed-sabers insignia of a surface warfare officer. "Good afternoon, everybody. I'm Wes Woollie, Lieutenant USN, and I'll be *Barrett*'s training liaison officer, the TLO. I represent the Commander, Fleet Training Group. I'll monitor and grade your progress and provide liaison between the ship and the commodore. My mission is to make sure you get trained right, and that anything that hinders that is dealt with fast. I'll ride the ship for the major training evolutions and then for the 'final exam.'

"Captain, I've arranged calls for you on the Commodore, FTG, on COMNAVBASE, and on CO, SIMA. The car will be here at fourteen thirty."

Leighty nodded and Woollie went on, addressing the room now. "Guys, I know most of you have been to Gitmo before, and those who haven't have heard the stories. There's no point telling you what is or isn't so, because starting tomorrow you'll see for yourself. Our mission is to train you, and in order to do that, we impose some stress. A guy once called us 'boot camp for the ship.' Very true.

"We like to say there are only two ways to do things: the wrong way and the Gitmo way. What we give you's the latest gouge; it's how Sixth Fleet or COMIDEASTFORCE or wherever you're deploying will demand you do business. But we're open to criticism. Any disagreements, forward them to me through Captain Leighty and we'll get them solved so we can move forward."

Woollie introduced the chiefs, Schwartzchild, Bentley, Narita, and Ferguson. "The senior instructor—we call him 'senior rider'—is DCCS Schwartzchild. He'll act as TLO in my absence and will report to you, Captain, when all instructors are aboard each morning. He will also notify you if any unsafe or unready condition precludes commencing a training event. Today, they'll be giving first-day briefs and looking over your lectures. I understand we have a main space fire walk-through, CIWS upload training, and they'll be going over your closure logs and some other documentation. Tomorrow, we'll all get under way. Reveille at oh-four hundred, under way at oh-six hundred.

"A couple of things to note about the base. Are you giving liberty tonight, Captain?"

"Yes. I thought, Let them get ashore for one night, see what it's like—"

"Yeah, let 'em see they aren't missing anything." Woollie smiled with them. "I did want to say something about the security status here. Emphasize to your men not to stumble around in the dark or go for hikes. You always want to know exactly where you are around Gitmo, sea or land. The Cubans took a sailboat crew prisoner and kept them for a year as spies. You don't want to screw with them."

"You get a lot of refugees?" Dan asked him.

"Not so many by land, since Castro planted the Cactus Curtain. We still get people who swim across. That's no joke, swimming Guantánamo Bay. We figure half of them make it. The rest, they drown or get eaten. There're a lot of sharks."

"What exactly is the readiness status?" Vysotsky asked.

Woollie swung to face him. "It's Condition Bravo. We use ships' guns to back up the marines along the perimeter. We'd like to have one of your five-inch batteries at standby and have you monitor the fire control coordination net twenty-four hours a day."

"What's the threat?" Leighty asked. "Why's the readiness been upped?"

"I'm not sure I can answer that to your satisfaction, sir. There've been indicators of increased activity in the Cuban armed forces; that's all I can say. It happens occasionally and we respond. It may not mean anything, but we'd rather play it safe."

"I understand. Can you handle that, Mr. Lenson?"

"Yes, sir." Dan made a note.

Woollie went into the schedule. The four-week cycle would start with basic damage control and engineering exercises, battery alignments, tracking drills and close-in live firing exercises, then move on week after week into more complex antiair, antisubmarine, and engineering drills. It would end with a battle problem, a flooding, battle damage, and mass conflagration drill, and an engineering operational readiness examination, all conducted simultaneously for a final score. Then he asked for questions. Giordano had a few about port services. The exec asked about pier security, mail, and recreation, and Quintanilla wanted to know about the radio guard.

Finally, Leighty said, "What's the latest on the Soviet battle group here in the Caribbean? The *Kirov* and her escorts?"

"Uh, sir, last I heard, they were in port at Cienfuegos. But I'm primarily training; you could get the latest from the commodore when you call on him."

"Good idea. Well, is that it? I guess we'll go ahead and break now, get training started. And I've got to make those calls. Thanks, Lieutenant." He stood and everybody else did, too, as he left.

DAN had a little more preparation, but it wasn't the kind of frantic catch-up he'd had to do on his last visit, in *Bowen*. The ship was quiet; most of the crew was over at FTG getting the initial classroom briefs. He had to admit, Leighty had prepared well. If only Sanderling hadn't jumped overboard, if only they could get the ACDADs running . . . maybe it would all work out somehow.

The ear-drilling keen of the boatswain's pipe came over the 1MC at 1600. "Liberty call, liberty call. Liberty commences for Sections Two and Three to expire on board at oh-two hundred."

Dan took his sweaty uniform off and pulled on shorts and a polo shirt. He went back to the fan room, jingling his keys, and unlocked his bicycle and carried it down to the quarterdeck. They had maps there and he studied one, then carried the bike down the brow, did a couple of stretching exercises, and headed up Sherman Avenue, the winding two-laner that ran the length of Windward.

He pedaled for a long time, miles, past the clubs and the phone exchange, base housing and hospital. The road reached open country. Gradually, his muscles warmed and he started taking the hills in higher gear, pumping hard—till he looked up, to find his way blocked by a closed gate. He slowed on the dusty road, then stopped. Suddenly, he realized he was alone; there was no traffic here, nothing but the sigh of the wind as it bent the bushes that littered the dry hills. He'd never been out this far before. He got off the bike and walked it up a little rise. A green line of cactus and wire came into view a hundred yards off.

"That's it," said a voice behind him. "Castro territory."

When he turned, a marine lance corporal was standing twelve feet away. His M16 was unslung, not exactly pointing at Dan, but not pointing away, either.

"This area's off-limits, bud. How'd you get here?"

"On my bike. Came up that road."

"Don't you read?"

"Read?"

"Yeah, like 'Off-limits beyond this point' signs?"

"I didn't see it. If I had, I'd have turned back." He swung a leg over the bike and started turning it around. "That's the perimeter, huh?"

"Uh-huh," said the marine, relaxing a little. He lighted a cigarette, looking up at one of the guard towers. "See that hill? The one with the bunker on top of it? Sometimes you see a white Mercedes parked over there. They say that's Castro's; he comes down once in a while to make sure we're still here."

"Is that so?" Dan looked again. "What's on our side?"

"On our side? The biggest fucking minefield in the Western world, that's what's on our side."

"I don't see any."

"You're not supposed to," said the marine. "Tell you a story, though. Couple sailors get drunk at the club, decide they're going to walk back to the ship. They walk for a couple miles in the dark—

they're lost. Suddenly the guy in front hears this terrific explosion behind him. He starts running, but he runs fill tilt into a sign. He lights his Zippo and reads it. Knows enough Spanish to figure out it says he's in the middle of a minefield. So what's he do? The smart thing: lies down right there and sleeps it off. We saw him out there in the morning. Had to send a chopper out for the son of a bitch."

"How about his buddy?"

"Chili burger." The marine jerked his head down the road. "Take off, buds. Don't let me see you around the perimeter again."

He cycled back slowly, cooling off. The shadows of the hills lay long across the dry dust. When he came to the turnoff for the officers' club, he swung right and coasted down a steep hill and then out a narrow point surrounded by the bay. He locked the bike and went in.

He treated himself to a martini—one, he told himself, just to relax—and went in to dinner. They had fresh grilled tuna and he had a leisurely meal alone. When the waiter asked him if he'd like a refill, he said why not. Two martinis with dinner weren't going to hurt him.

When he came out, he saw unfamiliar uniforms at the bar. They turned out to be Venezuelan, off the patrol boat he'd seen coming in. It was a Venezuelan Navy missile boat named *Federación*. They were there for joint training, they said, and would be doing some exercises later with *Barrett* and the other destroyer, USS *Dahlgren.*

"Dahlgren?"

"That's right."

He had a classmate aboard DDG-43. Shoot, he thought, I'll have to stop over and see Larry while we're here.

"You will have a planter's punch with us?"

"Sure," said Dan. "If I get to buy the second round."

Around eleven, some of the other officers from *Barrett* came in—the XO, Quintanilla, Shuffert, Lohmeyer, Horseheads, Martin Paul. Dan weaved over, glad to have an excuse to say *hasta la vista* to the South Americans. They drank like they'd never seen alcohol before.

Vysotsky called for dice from the bar and they played ship, captain, and crew for each round, slamming the cup down, the dice spinning out over the table. A six was the ship, five the captain, four the crew. You had to have a ship before a captain, and a captain before a crew. The XO kept the conversation light—sports and jokes, teasing Paul about his new kid. After a round, Dan got up. He told them to save his place and went to find the head.

He was standing at the urinal when another body slid in next to him. Then the XO grunted in relief. "I needed that."

"Yeah. Same here."

The exec cleared his throat. "You know, I've been meaning to say, I'm glad you went along with the shaving issue. I'd have hated to lose both you and Mark."

"Yes, sir," said Dan, though the bare mention of it made him angry all over again.

"I know it got your goat. But I figured that after you thought about it, you'd see I was right."

"About what, sir?"

"About the issue, especially for officers. If we expect a seamanlike appearance from the men, we've got to look good. If we expect performance, we've got to know our jobs, too. If we expect honesty and dedication, we have to show them we're dedicated, too."

Dan peered drunkenly down at the urinal, trying to keep the stream steady on the little white cake. "I can't disagree with that, sir. I just didn't see the linkage between any of that and a well-trimmed beard. It just seemed like—like somebody's blind prejudice."

"Well, I thought about that after you and Mark made your arguments. I sort of had to consider what the difference was. And you know, I found it."

Dan said unwillingly, "What's that, sir?"

Vysotsky zipped up, then paused, hand on the flushing lever. "I think the prejudice, if that's the right word, comes in when you judge somebody on the basis of something he can't change. Like that fellow at the Schools Command was judging me on the basis of my name being Russian. I think the only fair way is to judge every man on the basis of his performance, not things he was born into, like his race or his religion or how his name sounds." He shrugged and flushed. "And a beard, that's a voluntary choice; that's just grooming."

"Maybe so, sir. But my reaction was just that here's another rule telling me what I've got to do."

"But we already had that discussion, right? About how it's an even trade?"

"I guess we did, XO."

WHEN he got back to the table, there was another round waiting. Dan kept drinking. He kept winning, too. Again and again, he slammed the cup down and lifted it, seeing six, five, four, and then whatever the number of the crew would be. Then he rolled a perfect score: three sixes, a five, and a four. He laughed and ordered again, and somewhere in there he stopped remembering anything at all.

19

THE night spread out on every side, from the calm black bay to the looming hills to the east. Here and there, a lighted window shone from base housing, and the beacon flashed steadily from the airfield across the harbor.

All the way forward on the main deck, forward of the ground tackle, a lean dark figure stood with a boot propped on a chock, bent forward against the lifeline at the very bow. It looked down into the black glossy water, in which the stars flashed from time to time. A flashlight came on and played idly along the mooring lines. It ran along the pier. It probed down into the water, spreading a fuzzy, unfocused glow. Then it snapped off, and the figure straightened as another shadow came out of the breaker and climbed the rising slope of foredeck. When it got forward of the gun mount, it tripped in the dark, cursed, and then stood still, looking around.

"Over here. Jesus. Took you long enough."

"I had some things to do. What, now I've got to drop everything when you call? Like I'm some fucking dog?"

"You sound hostile tonight, shipmate. On the rag?"

"I don't have anything to say to you. Just this: I'm out."

A low laugh from the darkness. "You don't remember too good, do you? I told you when we started, don't sign up unless you're sure you want it. 'Cause once you're in with me, there's only one way out. The way Marion took, or our little pansy friend Sandy."

"What are you saying?"

"I think you understand what I'm saying."

"I ought to blow the whistle on you, you lying asshole."

The lean man slowly took out a clasp knife. Clicking it open, he started cleaning his fingernails deliberately. He said, "You turn me in, you go down the tubes five seconds later. Remember? Our little deal? You had a nice taste of what that brought in, as I remember. What, now it's all gone, you're getting an attack of conscience?"

"I had time to think about it. That's what happened. Who did those kits go to, anyway?"

"I told you. Raytheon makes that system. There's a company that wants to bid against them. They want to make 'em, they need to take apart some of the cards, figure out the manufacturing tricks. That's how America works. Hey, what you sweating it for? It ain't no big deal, Lieutenant. All it'll do, bring the cost of spare parts down a little bit."

"Yeah, but this stuff you're talking about now . . ."

"All the same ball of wax, shipmate. All the same ball of wax."

The taller figure's voice fell suddenly as a party of sailors passed by on the pier. Both men looked down at them, then off across the calm starry bay. "Pretty night," said the taller one.

"Yeah, this isn't a bad place to spend time."

"You should have been here in the old days, before Castro. We used to put into Havana then. Tell you some stories . . . Shit, don't change the subject on me. You want out? No problem. Only, hey, all of a sudden somebody might find out what happened to those parts. Then you can kiss your career good-bye. And kiss off about ten years of your life, too. Cause that's gonna be how long you spend in federal prison for grand theft."

The other didn't answer. "But you ain't gonna do that. You're going to hang with the program and keep on collecting that little supplement. You're going to keep on helping us out. And keep on helping yourself out, too. Right?"

The other didn't answer for a time. Together, they listened to the far-off sound of laughter, of boisterous singing, the sudden screech of brakes far off.

"What do you want me to do?" the voice murmured at last.

WHEN the second man left, the first lingered at the bow, looking out at the hills. He considered going over to the club later. But then thought, No, it might be best not to.

He had a great deal to do and not a great deal of time left to do it in. Thinking of this, he took a notebook out of his back pocket and turned the flashlight on once more, ran down the list of names, checked his watch. Then clicked the light off again and stood pondering in the darkness.

And after a time, another shadow detached itself from the superstructure. It hesitated for a time, looking searchingly around at the forecastle, the pier, the distant hills. A match flared and lips drew nervously on a cigarette. Then it made its wary way up to the man, who waited casually for it to draw near, one boot propped on a chock, his upper body leaning easily forward on the lifelines, looking off toward the waiting shore.

20

AND three hundred feet aft, another man, balding and gawky in too-small scrub greens, stood too, blinking down at the inky tropic shadows, the dark hills, at a flashlight spot that someone shined on the pier for a little while from up forward, before it went out. And above everything were the stars, caught in the black cage of *Barrett*'s masts and antennas.

Hank Shrobo blinked slowly and pulled his glasses up, rubbed his eyes. The eyeballs felt like hot ball bearings. When did we get here? he thought. Was this Cuba?

He stood motionless for a few minutes, mind still seething with the convoluted syntax of computer language. But his eye muscles spasmed at the thought of reading another line of code.

Standing there, swaying-tired, he massaged his face and then his neck as his mind moved back again to square one. Sometimes that helped you break out of a logic jam, going back to the start. He needed some new ideas. Because right now, he was locked up solid.

Back when he'd come aboard, still feeling ill from the helicopter ride, he'd started in the DP center, the "computer room," as the sailors called it. Already it sounded dated; soon there'd be computers in every room, and not long after most likely embedded in everyone's skull. Trying to push the queasiness away, he'd settled on a stool as the men there gathered doubtfully around him. He'd caught the whisper behind him. "Shit. Who's this? Mr. Peepers to the rescue?"

"So what's the situation?" he asked the black man in dungarees, who stared at him, then turned to look at the monitor, as if he could talk only like that, face-to-face with the data.

"Well, we got a . . . major glitch here. I've been working this thing for four solid days. Thought I could patch code, but when I do the software runs okay one minute, then it wanders off into the weeds and the system locks up. Takes a full-system reboot to get it running again. I can't make shit out of it." He told Shrobo how they'd discovered it, about the missile shoot and the way everything had gone haywire. Told him how they'd found the bad code, corrected it, but then found more, not just in the Version 3 but in the older version, too.

He pondered this. "Did you run the module-level diagnostics that come with the op tape?"

"About fifty times. Every time it reports a different glitch. When I take the recommended action, the system just hangs solid."

"Have you got the problem in other modules? The communications program, the satellite navigation program, the Link Eleven?"

"Haven't gotten that far."

"Have you taken the system down completely and reloaded it? I mean down all the way—cold start."

"Mr. uh . . . Shrobo," said one of the men in khaki, and Hank swiveled the stool slowly to him. "I'm Chief Dawson. This is Chief Mainhardt. And, 'scuse me, but we aren't idiots. Every time we do that, it comes up clean for about an hour, then craps in the NTDS module."

"I know you're not idiots," he'd said carefully. If only the compartment would quit rolling . . . "I just like to start the fault-location logic from block one. Does it lock up in the same segment every time?"

"No, it jumps around inside the module."

"Have you looked closely at the source code when it does?"

"Shit, Mr.—"

"Hank," said Shrobo.

"Matthew," said the black man. "Shit, Hank, we been banging our heads against CMS-2 so long, we're about done in trying to do this manually."

He thought about this for a while, looking around at the compartment, the memory units, the hulking gray slabs of the shock-mounted, water-cooled mainframes. CMS-2 was the standard Navy programming language. But the executive program itself was written in assembly language, computer-specific code, because it ran faster. It had to run fast because of everything it had to do: schedule and dispatch program modules, manage memory, service input/output communications requests, as well as the internal stuff, the redundancy, fault tolerance and alternate configuration schemes built into the system architecture.

These men were just technicians, but they sounded competent. So he could assume it wasn't the kind of problem that could be solved by swapping cards or patching a few lines of code. He rubbed his face. It felt wet, though ice-cold air was blasting out of the ceiling. His stomach felt like he was still in the helicopter. That sensation of utter terror, then swinging around at the end of the line—

"Grab that swab bucket, quick," said Dawson. "Get his head down. Take him out to the deep sink, Matt."

When he felt better, he rested in the little broom closet, then wiped his mouth with his sleeve—there was nothing in the closet he felt like touching—and followed the one they called Matt back down the hall.

"Sorry I got sick."

"No problem, Hank. Hey, call me Ted, okay?"

He looked rather shakily around the room. "Yeah, sounds like you got a problem. My box—there it is. I brought some software tools from the lab. Maybe we need to load those and take a look at this thing."

"Okay by me." Williams pulled a knife, sliced through the strapping tape.

As he loaded the program, Shrobo opened his briefcase and put on his working glasses. Thank God he hadn't left *them* in his suitcase. He perched on the metal chair in front of the screen.

"Uh, you gonna be a while? We're thinking of breaking for chow—"

"Go ahead," he mumbled.

"Somebody better stay with him."

"I'll stay," said Williams. "Bring me a sandwich. Chicken, if they got it. You want one, Hank?"

"Half the chicken sold in the United States is contaminated with salmonella," Shrobo told him.

"Say what? That mean you don't want one?"

"I prefer organic foods."

Dawson said slowly, "Oh. What—you mean like liver?"

"No." He swallowed again, wishing they'd abandon the subject. "Look, I'm not really hungry. You go ahead."

When they finally left, he ran some of the test tools. Williams sat close to him, staring at the monitor. Occasionally he asked a question. Hank replied absently, tapping in commands, then twisting to watch the lights flicker across the face of the computer. He pulled a pad toward him and started jotting numbers in columns. "Huh," he said at last.

"What's that?"

"Take a look. See this segment here?"

"Uh-huh. What about it?"

"There's something strange about it. Look at these pointers."

Williams looked at it. "This pointer here," Hank said, putting his finger right on one line.

"What's wrong with it?"

"This WRITE instruction here creams whatever instructions are in that location." He swallowed again as the room and the console took a lean and his chair tried to skid away across the deck. "Do boats always roll like this?"

"Naw, this is nice'n calm tonight," said Williams. "I better make us some fresh coffee. Sounds like it gonna be a long night. Or would you rather have a Coke?"

Hank thought of the herbal tea he'd tucked into his suitcase. "Yeah. Coke," he muttered.

NOW, standing by the rail, Shrobo remembered that night and the long nights and days at sea after it. At first, he'd been intrigued, then entranced, then fatigued, and now he was starting to feel angry and bewildered. The loud warrant officer, Harper, coming in two and three times a day; and his boss, the serious-looking lieutenant; and twice the XO, the one with the Russian name. That didn't bother him; he just shunted them off to one of the chiefs to explain things in one-syllable words. What disturbed him was that he couldn't figure out how so many errors had gotten onto the tape.

The first thing he'd tried was to systematize what the sailors had already attempted randomly. He'd loaded the new Version 3.1 tape he'd brought, ran it for an hour, then done a diagnostic. To his surprise, it tripped over several bad segments, although this same tape had run perfectly back at Vartech. He marked them with break points and started patching line by line, comparing what was in the computer with the printed source listing. That had taken two days, stripping in correct code everywhere he found bad.

But today when he ran it, the computer had locked up on a section he *knew* he'd already fixed.

Something was wrong, but he didn't know what. That was what was so disturbing. The great Henry S. Shrobo, B.S. from Brigham Young, M.S. and Ph.D. in applied physics from Johns Hopkins, senior analyst for Vartech and sometime member of the JHU/APL Advanced Computer Architecture Working Group, stopped in his tracks by an elusive bug in an already-fleet-approved system architecture. If he couldn't crack this one, he'd better start thinking about running an organic vegetable farm.

He stood staring out into the dark, no longer seeing the stars or the hills. The warm wind fanned his face, bringing the scents of the land. But he didn't smell them.

Sometime later, the door opened behind him, and he started, surprised. "Sorry," someone said.

"Matt?"

It was Williams, startled, too. "What you doing out here, Doc? Thought you'd be ashore."

"Doc?" He didn't see how they knew. He still hadn't told them.

" 'Doctor DOS.' You picked up a nickname, man."

"Are we permitted ashore? I didn't know."

"Remember when they passed the word—'Liberty call, liberty call'? That's what it means."

"Why are you here, then?"

Williams grinned painfully. "Duty section. Yeah, you get over and grab you a beer while you can."

"I don't drink. Maybe I'd better just stay aboard, get back to that bad code in the tracking module."

"Jesus, Hank. You're like one of those Guild Steersmen, aren't you? Can't get enough of that spice." Williams punched his arm. "How about a workout?"

"I don't think I'd be able to—"

"Be *able* to?"

"I'm not what you'd call a physical person."

Williams punched his arm again. "We got us a nice weight room—machines and everything. Me an' Baby J and some of the other dudes, we go down there every night, break a sweat. Get you down there for a couple weeks, I bet you'd be pressing two hundred."

"Two hundred pounds?" He had to smile. "I don't think so."

"Give it a try. It's organic, man. Like that good Navy chow."

He had to laugh at that. He'd been appalled at the food on the mess decks. Milk and hardboiled eggs, that's all he'd found that looked safe to eat. "Okay. Maybe a little exercise will clear my head."

Taking a last breath of the sultry air, he followed the petty officer below.

21

THE next morning, Dan slumped nervelessly in the TAO chair, grateful for the cool dark. CIC was dim and quiet, the ideal place for a guy with the hangover of the decade.

He couldn't remember it all, but he had to have had at least six planter's punches with the fucking Venezuelans and four or five drinks playing dice after the other officers arrived. After that was a black curtain. He couldn't remember where his bike was. Had he left it at the club? Like he had his motorcycle in Charleston? He didn't think he could have kept it pointed straight all the way downhill to the pier.

Reveille had jerked him awake at 0400 with a feeling of horror at what he'd done to himself. He took one look at breakfast and had to leave and barf in the urinal. Fortunately, he had a break now as *Barrett* got under way.

How could he have done it again? Going into the club, he hadn't planned to get drunk. He'd told himself, One martini with dinner. But that first one had softened his resolution, and the second had washed away any idea of restraint. After that, he'd just drunk and drunk, not caring what, just that the glass was heavy in his hand and then light and that there was another behind it.

I've got to stop drinking so much, he thought. Maybe cut out the hard liquor. It was stupid to get plastered the night before he had to think fast and make the right decisions.

Now he leaned forward. The big SSWC scope showed the land as a green fluorescence, the channel as jet studded with jade. They were second in the morning parade going out. *Dahlgren* led, then *Barrett, Federación, Manitowoc,* the LST, and last the oiler, USS *Canisteo.*

Lauderdale, the CIC officer, came by and Dan said, "Herb, what have we got this morning?"

"I taped a schedule up between your chair and the skipper's, sir."

He blinked at it. Right now, the bridge team was conducting a low-visibility piloting exercise. Offshore, they'd do test firing, engineering drills, a CON-1-EX—whatever that was—seamanship, tracking and electronic drills, and finish with general quarters for chemical, bacteriolocial, and radiological training before heading back in.

"Herb, this CON-one—"

"That's a general quarters, then whatever they assign. Usually like rocket hits or shell hits, to get us spun up for damage control and casualty repair."

One of the blue coveralls passed through, and the atmosphere seemed to chill. Dan recognized the senior instructor, Schwartzchild. He didn't stop, though, just kept going, swinging his clipboard. Headed down to the engineering spaces, most likely.

"Coming up on the sea buoy," said Chief Kennedy.

"Then what?"

"We'll be coming left to one-three-seven and slowing to conform to the swept channel. Stand by—"

"Now secure the special sea and anchor detail. General quarters. General quarters. This is a drill. All hands, man your battle stations—"

Life jackets flew through the air to outstretched hands. Dan buttoned his collar and settled his helmet. Into the meat grinder, he thought. It was going to be a long morning.

THEY went from the swept channel transit to a main space fire drill, simulating a mine hit. Combat and Radio were tied down with system control, tracking, and electronic surveillance and countermeasures drills. The training team moved them along, not very fast yet, but without letup except for a half-hour lunch break. Dan kept chugging coffee and Cokes and gradually lost himself in the exercises.

In the afternoon, they moved farther offshore for tracking and comm drills with *Dahlgren.* At first, they were miles apart, then joined up for the seamanship exercises. When the 1MC called the replenishment detail to stations, Dan got a break to go out and observe.

The day was so bright it hurt his eyes, closed down from hours in the cave. The sky and sea blazed as one, luminous with tropical light, and the deck was baking-hot. He found a vantage point on the Harpoon deck as First Division rigged for under-way replenishment.

His first job in the Navy had been as first lieutenant. It felt strange to be looking on as they sweated and swore, frantically rigging for a high-line transfer as *Dahlgren* edged closer. He saw himself in Ensign Paul, saw old Harvey Bloch when he looked at Chief Giles. Over the young taut faces seemed superimposed those of his old division—BM1 Isaacs, "Popeye" Rambaugh, Petty Officer Pettus, the loose league of bad boys that called themselves the "Kinnicks." As both ships steadied up into the wind, the sea went mad between them, leaping and frothing as the two hulls closed on it. Then the line-throwing gun cracked.

At 1400, they broke off and headed for their assigned firing area. Dan checked their coordinates carefully against the surface grid warning areas before requesting "batteries released" from Leighty. Shortly afterward, he heard the tapping of the .50's as they fired the antimine exercise.

The GQ alarm bonged again at 1500 for the chemical and nuclear attack drill. The ventilation died as all over the ship intakes closed and fans stopped. The *Kidd*s were the first U.S. ship class that could completely seal themselves off from outside air.

"Now contamination has been detected inside the skin of the ship. All hands don gas masks."

They started heading back in at 1700, but the drills continued till they were pierside. When the 1MC announced, "Moored," Dan took off his earphones and sagged in his chair. Maybe he could snatch a shower, lie in his rack for thirty seconds—

"Now all chiefs and officers assemble in the wardroom for post-exercise critique."

"OKAY, next, the chemical attack."

Woollie sat and Chief Schwartzchild stood. He read off his clipboard with a poker face, every word the same inflection, so you couldn't tell what was important from what wasn't; you had to listen to it all. Dan, on the settee, made a note in his wheel book.

"It took seven minutes to set Zebra throughout the ship. Nonessential people were still present on weather decks. Ventilation was secured and Circle William was set expeditiously. The damage control assistant passed the word properly and the team was in appropriate dress. However, it did not exit the ship or carry out rescue or decontamination of the wounded. Overall grade, unsat."

Lohmeyer sat openmouthed. Vysotsky said, "Mr. Lohmeyer, why in God's name didn't you send the decon team out?"

"Uh, I was waiting for orders, XO."

"Don't wait on normal procedure! In future, just do it, and inform the officer of the deck they're going out. If he has a problem with it, he'll have to let you know."

"Aye aye, sir."

The next chief, Narita, stood up. "I was inside the skin of the ship when Chief Bentley dumped the wintergreen into the intakes. I checked four interior spaces ten minutes after GQ went. I found fifteen people without Mark five masks on or with bad seals. Both gun crews and Aux-One personnel were deficient in putting on masks. Number three switchboard operator has a broken mask. Overall grade, unsat."

Hell, Dan thought. Woollie was saying something about how this wasn't for score yet, but the way the XO glared around, *he* was grading, even if FTG wasn't. Leighty leaned back, looking detached.

Dan tuned back in to Schwartzchild. "The nuclear burst casualty and decontamination drill. Initial notification and water wash-down activation satisfactory. It took one hour for the external survey team to find the hot area on the Harpoon deck. One reason may be it isn't on their route chart. The chart is supposed to show all vital equipment. Is Harpoon vital?"

"I'd say so," said Vysotsky, staring at Dan. "Mr. Lenson, is the Harpoon a vital system?"

Clenching his teeth, he said, "It'll be on the route chart tomorrow, sir."

"First aid was not rendered to casualties. No attempt was made to help them until prompted by the observer. Forward decon team did not know assignments or procedures for decontamination. Forward decon station was unusable, with no supplies in place. Overall grade, unsat."

"Chief Narita?"

"I observed from aft. Eleven men were caught on the weather decks when the blast went. Repair Three didn't know how to rope off or scrub down a hot spot. You need to map out other routes to the decon station; you can't carry wounded up thirty-foot ladders. The damage control officer did not know how to do a log-log of radiation decay. Overall grade aft, unsatisfactory."

Lieutenant Woollie said, "The overall grade was unsatisfactory. Next was the casualty drill under conditions of nuclear contamination. Chief Bentley?"

"The after director casualty was troubleshot quickly and creatively. However, Petty Officer Fisher was sent for a part. He requested a battle route to supply but decided to take a shortcut over the weather decks. Chief Schwartzchild nailed him on the hot spot. So the part didn't get to the casualty and it didn't get fixed, and the overall grade is unsat."

"Fuck," Harper muttered beside him. "Are these guys for real? Fish would have gotten back fine. It was only—what, a hundred rads an hour up there?"

Vysotsky glared, and Dan elbowed Harper into silence. The warrant officer sank back sullenly.

"Attention on deck." They rose as Leighty got up, nodded to Woollie, and left. Then he stuck his head back in. "Lieutenant Lenson, could I see you in my cabin, please."

"TAKE a seat. Be right back," said Leighty, disappearing. Dan squatted on the settee and looked blankly at the picture of the captain's family. He had a knot in his stomach already.

Leighty came back in T-shirt and trou, combing wet hair. "It gets hot in that damn wardroom when the AC's off," he said.

"Yes, sir, it gets pretty ripe in there."

"But if you leave it on, you can't hear a word anybody says. Maybe I'm going deaf?"

"No, sir, it's hard to hear in back even with the blowers off."

He'd expected Leighty to take the seat opposite, but instead the Captain settled beside him on the sofa. "I need to know what's going on with the fire-control system, Dan. We're doing air tracking tomorrow and live firing the day after. Will we be able to shoot without having it go crazy on us again?"

Outside, the 1MC announced: "Sweepers, sweepers, man your brooms. Give the ship a clean sweep-down fore and aft. Sweep down all lower decks, ladder backs, and passageways. Now, sweepers."

Dan said, "Sir, my guys have been working on it eighteen hours a day. Dr. DOS has tried several things—"

"Who?"

"Mr. Shrobo. That's what the guys call him. He seems to know what he's doing, but apparently this is new to him, too."

Leighty extended an arm along the back of the sofa, and Dan sat forward to avoid it. "So what is it? Operator problem, hardware problem, software?"

"Sir, we're pretty certain it's software. But Shrobo swears nothing that dicked up would have left FCDSSA."

"Can it have happened in the supply system?"

"They don't run the tape in the supply system. I don't think they can. They have computers but not UYK-sevens."

"So it happened here. Who has access to it? Only your guys, right?"

"Sir, it's like this. The ETs and DSs fix the hardware when it's down. The DSs put the tapes on and alter the software routines, usually with the menus, when they have to. The other rates actually operate the programs—the STGs the sonar programs, the FTs the fire-control modules, et cetera."

"But it's all in your department."

"Well, no, sir. Dave Cannon's people run navigation programs. The radiomen run the comm system. ACDADS is the first place we noticed the problem. But that doesn't mean that's the first system it hit, see that, sir? Only that it showed up there first."

Dan felt a trickle down his back. It was hot in the captain's cabin, too. Leighty's foot, propped on his leg, was nearly touching him. The captain's bare arm lay right against his back.

"Okay, tell me how we can shoot without the computers."

"Can't, sir. Not and have any chance of hitting anything." Dan took out a pen and pulled a copy of the plan of the day toward him. He turned it over and drew a hierarchical diagram.

"Sir, you remember how it's set up. ACDADS proper is just the controlling program. CDS processes the fire-control data. WDS directs the weapons systems to engage and destroy the target. All three have to be running in order to go to automatic mode. WDS is the only leg that can stand independently. We could fight the ship with just WDS, but we'd have to detect, track, and designate manually." He looked at the diagram. "Shrobo may have something better to suggest. Can I get back to you after I discuss it with him?"

"Okay." The captain reached out then and patted Dan's leg, and Dan tensed. Yet it seemed innocent enough, the kind of thing any CO might do to encourage one of his men. He got up. "Uh, is that all, sir?"

"Almost. One last thing," Leighty said, looking up at him. "The investigator spoke to me. Diehl. He mentioned a diary. Did Seaman Sanderling leave a diary?"

"A what?" said Dan. He knew it sounded stupid, but Leighty had blindsided him. He'd been thinking about the ACDADS, had that program loaded in his brain, didn't have his Sanderling file ready to run at all.

"A diary," Leighty said patiently. "He said Sanderling kept a diary, and that he was going to interview you tomorrow and find out what happened to it." The captain gave it a beat, glancing at the clock as it chimed eight bells. "Have you got it?"

There it was, point-blank, and he'd played dumb long enough. He cleared his throat. "Yes, sir. I have it."

"I didn't see it on the inventory. Why not?"

"Sir, there were several things that weren't on the inventory. You know the procedure. Certain things we don't send home to the family."

"Okay, but the presumption is that we destroy those items. Did you destroy the diary?"

"No, sir."

"Why not?"

"I . . . Diaries are personal items, like letters. I didn't want to just throw it away."

"But you didn't inventory it either. Which is it, Dan? Is it a personal item, in which case you inventory it, or is it something scurrilous, in which case you destroy it?"

"Neither, sir . . . or both." He struggled in the vise Leighty was gradually closing on him.

"Okay," said the captain. He jiggled one white shoe. "Neither, and both. So, are you going to turn it over to NIS?"

"I don't know, sir."

"Sit down. Go on—sit. Dan, I have the feeling we're dancing around something here that maybe we both know but for some reason you don't want to talk about. Why don't you trot it out and we'll at least have it on the table."

Dan started to sit on the settee, hesitated, then took the chair opposite Leighty, with the coffee table between them. He rubbed his hands together. His palms were as wet as if he'd just taken them out of the sea.

"Okay, sir. Judging by the stuff we found, Sanderling was a homosexual. In the diary, he named you as one of his partners."

The silence was suddenly deafening in the little cabin. Dan felt detached, unreal, as he waited for the captain's response. For a moment, there wasn't any, though. He added, thinking maybe the captain hadn't heard him right, "He named *you*, sir. In the diary."

"And you think that I'm homosexual, too," said Leighty. "Which is why you kept it. Correct?"

Dan took a deep breath. "Sir, it's not something I could rule out. Because of the diary, you see."

"What if you knew that the accusation was false?"

"If I *knew* it was false? Then I'd destroy it," Dan said.

"Okay," said the captain. He got up and stood looking at the portrait of his family.

"Tell me, Dan, what *is* a homosexual? Can you answer that for me?"

"Well . . . I guess, it's somebody who engages in homosexual acts."

"How do you know someone engages in homosexual acts?"

"You see them?"

"Without actually witnessing it, I mean. Are they effeminate? Do they wear women's clothing? Hold hands with other men? Wear earrings in the right ear? Tell me how we *know*, Mr. Lenson."

"They tell you. That's how you know."

"Ah." Leighty put his hands on his back and stretched, as if his spine hurt. "So a homosexual is someone who admits that he engages in such acts."

"I guess so," Dan said. Then he thought, What? "Sir, let's cut through this 'how do we know' stuff, all right? I'm sorry to be blunt, but is what he says true? Were you his lover? Or partner, whatever?"

"That's blunt all right. But maybe you're right; maybe that's the best way—cut through it," said Leighty, still looking at the portrait. "Okay, I'll answer it. I'm a family man. I love my wife. I love my children. I did not engage in homosexual acts with Benjamin Sanderling."

Dan stood up, feeling his heart physically lighten. "Thank you, sir. That's a relief—a *big* relief."

"And now you'll destroy it?"

"Yes, sir. That's good enough for me."

"Good," said Leighty. He patted Dan's shoulder, then put his hand on his back, steering him toward the door. "It's going to be another long day tomorrow, so—"

"Yes, sir," said Dan, shaking the proffered hand. "Thanks. This is really a load off my mind."

AS he left the captain's cabin, the 1MC intoned, "Now taps, taps. Lights out. All hands, turn into your own bunks. Maintain silence about the decks; the smoking lamp is out in all berthing spaces. Now taps." The lights waned from white to red along the passageways. He felt tired but relieved. The channel ahead was narrow, but the fog had burned off and it lay marked and navigable. It hadn't been a bad day, he thought. Not a bad day at all.

22

ARMS throbbing, Shrobo sidled warily through the passageways, glancing into doorways. His tall, awkward form lurched and zigzagged as the ship rolled around him, and he put a hand out to the bulkheads from time to time to stop himself from staggering.

He moved warily because from time to unpredictable time the whole ship became a madhouse. A bell would start ringing, and within seconds the passageways were jammed with running, shouting men in various stages of undress. Once he'd been climbing the stairs when it happened, and suddenly about twenty people had appeared from nowhere, all headed down while he was still trying to go up. The language had been shocking.

He mused on it as he drifted along, rubbing his arms. They felt numb from half an hour at the workout machines that the black technician, Matthew Williams, had introduced him to.

It wasn't that the men didn't accept him. When he went into the dining room, they made room for him, then stared in disbelief at his tray: raw vegetables and bread—the only things he figured weren't loaded with nitrates and pesticides. When he went into sick bay for clean greens, they greeted him like a long-lost brother. But the Navy was a foreign country, a foreign language. He still wasn't sure which was fore and aft and port and starboard—how did you know when you couldn't even see the water? What about the strange things they kept saying over the public-address system? What was "material condition Yoke," and what did all those whistles mean? He knew the difference between officer and enlisted, but where did chiefs fit in? They were older than most of the officers and seemed to know more, but they called even the youngest officers "sir."

He recalled himself with a start and turned around. Lost again. The Kafkaesque corridors all looked the same: narrow, lined with complicated masses of pipes and wires, roofed with the horrible fluorescent lights. He snagged a passing sailor. The man had a shock of dirty blond hair in front, tapered close in back, and a Band-Aid on his nose. His thin shoulders were hunched under a short blue jacket; he sniffled as he stared at Shrobo. "Say, uh, can you tell me how to get back to the computer room?" Hank asked him.

"Go forward to frame two hundred, take the starboard ladder up to the oh-one level."

"Thanks," he said. "But which way is—"

"Forward? That way. Say, you're that dude come to fix our computers, ain'tcha? They running yet?"

"Uh, not really. But we're working on them."

"I heard a you. Hey, welcome aboard. Glad to have ya." The boy seized his hand before he could react, pumped it twice, then dropped it and disappeared around a corner. Hank looked at his hand, remembering the boy's sniffle. His resistance was down anyway; lack of sleep and the omnipresent fluorescent light reduced immune system activity.

He went forward, trying to remember not to touch his lips or eyes with the hand he held out in front of him. The thought made his nose itch, of course. He twitched it like a beleaguered rabbit. Passing sailors eyed him strangely. Behind him, a speaker announced: "Now the seabag locker will be open for approximately twenty minutes." Finally, he saw a rest room. A sailor looked up angrily from a swab and bucket but shrugged when he pointed to the sink. He squirted liquid soap and worked up a froth, staring into the mirror as his mind reverted once more to the problem.

He just couldn't understand how you could ship perfectly functional taped programs, then have them degrade when they hit the ship's computers. Things simply did not work that way. A computer was an incredibly complex but totally dumb machine that was capable of doing only what it was told. The program didn't change. What was on the tape couldn't change. And once it was used to program the computer, *that* couldn't change, either.

But it did aboard *Barrett*. Was he dealing with some kind of computerized poltergeist? Something that transcended normal physical laws? Ridiculous. It had to be an error of some sort, an error of replication—

Then he stopped.

He looked at his hand, where the sniffling sailor had touched it. Slowly, he rinsed off the rest of the soap.

Why had he just washed his hands?

Because that was how rhinoviruses were passed.

Cold viruses.

Viruses were replicating molecules.

His mind shifted now to a discussion he'd participated in on Arpanet. Arpanet was a secure DOD-wide network of computers, interconnected in a wide area network. It serviced major defense labs and research facilities with electronic mail and file-transfer services. It also connected to mainframes in the academic and business world via a much larger network called Internet. Internet was the exchange media for a number of electronic forums and debates on the burning technical issues of the day. A typical query from a scientist seeking information or ideas, for example, could generate literally thousands of comments from all over the world.

What he remembered now was a debate about a new and rather sinister development beginning to plague university computer departments. A few malicious computer-science students, called "hackers," had unleashed a new kind of mischief. They got their giggles from making computers do things they weren't supposed to do, or getting into computers they weren't supposed to have access to. At the cost of hours or days of intense, tedious work, the hacker could break into it, apparently thereby gaining some sort of rush or excitement. Using techniques born of the innate cleverness of the kind of people drawn to computers and programming, some didn't stop with gaining access. Instead, they disrupted the system's operation in a number of interesting and sometimes catastrophic ways.

He also recalled an Internet conversation with a doctoral candidate at USC, Berkeley, who was doing a dissertation on what he called "virtual disease emulators." Their conversation had been theoretical, but the student had made some thought-provoking speculations about how a properly written program might be able to propagate itself—

"Hey, you okay?" a voice behind him asked. It was the sailor with the swab.

"Excuse me?"

"Said, you okay? You just standing there, like you froze or something."

"Yeah," he said. "Yeah. Just thinking, thanks."

WHEN he got back to the computer room, Dawson and Williams were looking at the new code for the weapons-assignment module. Their faces were appalled. Shrobo said, "What now?"

"It's lousy with it, Hank."

"Bad code?"

"Are you kidding, bad? It's . . . garbage, garbage, garbage, garbage." Williams turned a suspicious eye toward him. "And it's in the sections I already patched. We got gun shoots and tracking drills tomorrow. What are we gonna do? This ain't gonna cut it."

"I know." He sat down and took a breath, thinking about it. The more he thought, the more certain he felt. Everything fit—the good tapes that mysteriously went bad; the patched code that over time slowly degenerated back to noise; the origin of whatever it was in one module of the tape, but then, as they looked, gradually revealed itself in more and more segments, more and more cells, more and more modules. It was as if the very act of looking for it spread it.

"I think I have an idea what might be going on," he said tentatively, looking up at the rows of flashing lights. "And you know what? I sure hope I turn out to be wrong."

23

THE machinists stopped talking the second he stepped through the door the next morning. Dan looked around the shop: racks of hammers and mallets, machines for bending and cutting metal. Smells of oil and acid flux and hot coffee surrounded him.

"Morning, sir. Help you?" said a tired-looking first-class; his dungaree shirt said BAKOTIC in Old English script.

"Wondered if you had any scrap wire, strapping iron, anything like that."

"We got rid of most of our good scrap before we got here, sir. Inspectors don't like a lot of crap layin' around the shop. . . . Studie, can you help the lieutenant out? What you need it for, sir?"

"I just need some scrap wire, but it's got to be heavy."

He left the shop with five feet of battery wire, soft copper cable half an inch thick. He twisted its heavy ductility into a coil as he went aft. He stuck his head into the laundry as he passed. Despite fresh paint, the smell of fire still lingered.

He emerged on the afterdeck, into the lingering cool of dawn. The sun bulged out of the sea like a thermonuclear detonation, glinting and winking off glass or metal far down the coast in Cuban territory. Dan rubbed his eyes. He'd been up past midnight fixing the casualty routes; then at 0400, reveille again. . . .

The *Kidd*-class destroyers, like the *Spruance*s from which they'd inherited hull and machinery layout, had a dropped weather deck at the stern. The twin tapered rails of the Mark 26 launcher rose above him, pointed straight up; the tapered barrel of the after gun aimed at the departing land. He stepped over flemished-out mooring lines and around bitts and scuttles. After so long locked inside, in CIC and office and wardroom, he had a moment almost of agoraphobia as he stopped on *Barrett*'s broad, open fantail.

Back here, at fifteen knots, the rumbling vibration of the screws was like riding a tractor over a potato field. Twin whip antennas drew circles on the sky. The wake tumbled under the counter, a white-green maelstrom thirty feet across. The sharp-cornered stern dragged little whirlpools after it, then left them spinning and rocking in a sea the color of chrysoprase till they dissolved into a welter of hissing foam.

Dan half-trusted his weight to the rail. There was one patch of turbulence about ten feet back from the stern where the sea seemed to be sucked downward, as if into a huge open mouth just below the surface. He nodded to the after lookout, who gave him one incurious glance, then lifted his binoculars again.

Wondering if he was the one who'd spotted Sanderling, Dan took the diary out of his pocket. He wrapped the cable around it tightly, then twisted the ends together till they locked.

He looked out at Cuba, the low hills sinking astern. A dark speck caught his eye above a gleam of white. He frowned, then understood; it was the submarine, following them out. *Barrett* was headed straight out to the operating areas today. As he recalled the chart, the hydrography was fairly steep here. The hundred-fathom curve was only about half a mile off Windward Point.

Leaning out, he tossed the diary into the sea. It curved out and fell into the vortex and disappeared, sucked down into the continuously beating froth. He shaded his eyes, watching for it to reappear farther aft, but it didn't.

It was gone. When he straightened, it felt like some heavy yoke had been lifted from his shoulders. He should never have kept it, never have read it. Maybe the legal officer, Arguilles, was right. He was too quick on the trigger when it came to taking responsibility.

He turned from the lifeline, to find a man in civilian slacks and short-sleeve shirt watching him from the deck above. He had close-cut dark hair and muscular arms crossed over a middle-aged paunch. They stared at each other for a second. Then the man looked around, found the ladder to the afterdeck, and let himself down it.

He held out his hand. "Lieutenant Lenson, I presume."

"That's right." Dan met flat blue eyes. "Who are you?"

"Bob Diehl, Naval Investigative Service. Looking into ETSN Benjamin Sanderling, USN, decease of." Dan looked at the ID card and nodded; Diehl flipped the case closed. "Pretty morning."

"Yeah."

"I like riding the ships. Put in eight years in diesel boats myself, *Carbonero* and *Medregal*, then the old Rocketwolf. Ever heard of her? USS *Requin*, SS-four eighty-one?"

"I don't think so."

"I remember I was the lookout in a hurricane once. Nineteen

hours stuck on the bridge. Couldn't get down. We had twenty feet of green water breaking over the top of the windshield; that fiberglass sail kept shuddering like it was going to break off. Well, I know you have a busy day planned. I thought I'd try to talk to some of the men who knew this fella jumped overboard, in the in-betweens. The XO—hey, what kind of name is Vysotsky? Sounds Russian."

"It is," Dan said, wondering why every ex-sailor you met had to tell you all about his old ship.

"That so? Well, he said okay. That all right with you?"

"Sure," Dan said. He gave the guy a second to ask anything else, unsure whether he'd seen him get rid of the diary. When he didn't, Dan added, "Will you want to interview me?"

"I don't think that'll be necessary. Division officer, leading chief, the guys bunked with him—that's the usual procedure. I don't imagine you saw much of him."

"No. Not much." Dan checked his watch. "We'll be going to GQ for a local firing pretty soon—"

"Sure, Lieutenant. See you later."

DOORS and hatches slammed as he went through the by-now-mindless motions of donning battle dress. He checked the gas mask, making sure the snap on the cover didn't stick and that the rubber "spider" was prefolded so he could slap it on his face, pull the webwork down, and have an instant seal. The requirement was fifteen seconds from "go" to breathing through the activated-carbon canister.

"Harpoon, manned and ready."

"SSWC, manned and ready."

"UBFC, manned and ready."

"Sonar, manned and ready."

"AAWC, manned and ready."

Lauderdale hit the intercom near Dan. "Bridge, Combat; Combat, manned and ready. Can you give me a visual range and bearing to the sub?"

"Roger, stand by."

"Mr. Lauderdale, I'll be in Sonar," Dan told him. The CIC officer said, "Aye aye, sir."

The sonar room was separated from the rest of CIC by a black folding curtain. When he closed it, he found himself in a blue-lighted space the size of a camping trailer, completely filled with the three huge sonar stacks, chairs, safes, racks of pubs and tape reels, and the sonobouy and passive-tracking cabinets. A Barbie doll in a sailor hat, naked legs spread, dangled from an overhead light.

Fowler glanced up as he slid in. "Mr. Lenson, howzit going? . . . Start a standard beam-to-beam search. Depression angle two."

There was the eerie song of the outgoing pulse, three notes repeated over ten seconds, then a click from the speaker by the port stack.

"What are we doing in active, Chief?"

"They're starting us out in active mode, sir. See how good the tracking team does, I guess."

Barrett carried one big SQS-53 sonar. The radiating elements were far below the waterline in the bow dome, a huge bulge beneath the sharp overhanging cutwater. The sonarmen "listened" from up here, but not with their ears. On the number one console a ring of white light expanded slowly from the center to the limits of the round scope, then disappeared. Below it on the B-scan, amber lines marched from the bottom to the top of the screen. The number two console operator sat glued to a jade shimmer like moiré silk, fingers resting on a joystick. He looked drawn. Dan leaned against the safe, thinking they were all going to be exhausted before this was over. He noticed the sign on it. NO ONE WILL REMOVE ANY PUB FROM THIS SAFE WITHOUT MY PERMISSION. CHIEF FOWLER.

"You and the chief warrant getting along better these days?"

Fowler molded an invisible snowball. "We got an understanding, sir. He stays out unless I ask him in. He comes in, one of my guys stays with him. Hey! Freeze that, around two-one-six. Tweak your gain up."

The curtain rattled back and then closed again; Lieutenant Woollie loomed up through the dimness. "Got a track yet?" he asked briskly.

Fowler pulled the mike down. "Evaluator, Sonar: Active contact bears two-one-six, two point five kiloyards, bow aspect, up doppler. Recommend we come left; he's nearly in our baffles."

"It doesn't do any good if we're the only ones know about it, Chief," Dan told him. Fowler grimaced.

Woollie quizzed the sonarmen about equipment settings, power out, depression angle, and pulse length and asked to see their sound-velocity profile. Then he left. Dan searched around for a place to perch, and someone handed down a folding chair.

Corpus Christi dived shortly after that, and they did sonar detection and tracking exercises through the morning. Active pinging went okay, but when they went to passive, to listening, everything fell apart. *Corpus Christi* was a new boat. Everybody expected her to be quiet. But when they passed within five hundred yards of her without a detection, the captain called down and roasted Dan. As soon as Leighty hung up, Dan dialed the computer room. Williams answered. "DP center."

"Lieutenant Lenson, in Sonar. We're not getting shit on passive tracking here. How's the program look?"

"Sir, all you're getting on the fifty-three is straight-stick passive output. I told Sonar that."

"Are you telling me we're not running any digital processing?"

"Sir, the Doc says we run those programs, we lose them. Until we get the diaphragm in place—"

"The *what*?" Dan said to Fowler, "What the hell's he talking about?"

"I don't know, sir."

"Stand by. I'm coming down."

When he got to the computer room, he looked around for Shrobo. He was about to ask for him when he came out from behind one of the UYK-7s. His glasses gleamed blankly, filled with light. "Uh, Hank," Dan said, "I know you're trying to figure out what's wrong, but you can't just shut the computers down till you find out. We've got to keep working with what we've got, okay?"

"Sorry. Can't be done that way."

"Uh . . . sir, I'm gonna break the guys for lunch, it's almost time for the mess line to close."

"Okay, Chief." When they left, Dan turned on Shrobo. "What is this? You're supposed to be here to help us, not shut us down!"

"That's what I'm trying to do. But if you keep running these computers, there's not going to *be* any system."

"What do you mean?"

Shrobo gazed at the overhead for a second, as if receiving divine guidance, then reached for a pencil. "Let me show you."

DAN sat in CIC, worrying about what Shrobo had just told him. Things were worse than he'd thought. Everything was affected, not just the fire-control systems but everything that the computers controlled. And it was getting worse.

Finally, he clicked the light on and checked the schedule.

They were well offshore now, fifty miles south of Guantánamo Bay. The afternoon's drills would begin with antiaircraft target designation, followed by tactical antiaircraft exercises. A-4 Skyhawks from Fleet Composite Squadron Ten would simulate attacks on the formation while the ships practiced tracking them and handing off engagement responsibilities. At the same time, an EA-6 over the horizon was testing their electronic surveillance capabilities. On completion of the tracking exercises, the ships would split into two parallel lines and another plane would report on-station with a towed target, making runs on each ship in turn for live firing.

He clicked the light off, slid down, and leaned over the surface scope. It showed four pips on a line of bearing, steaming southwest at fifteen knots. *Dahlgren* was guide, followed by *Barrett, Manitowoc,* and *Canisteo.* "What's our watch zone?" he asked Lauderdale.

"Port and starboard, thirty degrees to one-five-zero degrees from the bow."

"And how are we tracking?"

"The usual way, sir, on the UYA-fours—"

"We'd better practice our manual plotting. Shut down the consoles. Get the guys up on the phones. I want a surface status board, tote boards, and air plot."

"We can't just shut down the NTDS, sir. They're going to be throwing a lot of targets at us during the battle problem."

"We've got serious problems with the combat direction system. I don't know if we're going to be able to count on having it up."

"It'll be awful slow."

"Not if we get them drilled right. Anyway, I want to give it a try. Get them all up on the phones. Use red for hostiles or unknowns, white for friendlies. Plot everything inside two hundred miles. That includes commercial air out of Jamaica and Haiti. Draw big—I have to be able to read it from here. Get on it fast, Herb; they're gonna start the first run in seventeen minutes."

One by one, the edge-illuminated boards came on and the men took their positions behind them. Dan caught more than one doubtful glance through transparent plastic. Hell, he thought. I don't know if it'll work, either.

If antisubmarine work was chess, antiaircraft defense was jai alai. It took more computer power and electronics than anything else a surface combatant did.

Modern warships weren't designed to fight alone. They fought in formation, defenses interlocking to form a vast shield hundreds of miles from edge to edge. But to take its place in that phalanx, each had to drill and report to a common standard. Radar, radio nets, patrol aircraft, lookouts, electronic sensors, and intelligence estimates all fed the stream of data. The task group commander stationed his ships to make the best use of their weapons and sensors. The force antiair warfare coordinator controlled the combined air defense. The outer edge of the shield was carrier-launched jet interceptors. Then came long-range missiles, point defense missiles, and last, gunfire.

It all moved so fast that Dan wondered if manual plotting was still possible. The plotters worked from behind the boards, so everything had to be written backward. You got used to that, but updating everything every three minutes, a skilled plotter could still only keep six contacts current. Two could work at one board, ducking and whirling around each other, but still that made twelve the upper limit of human ability.

In three minutes, a Soviet SS-N-7 cruise missile traveled thirty miles. Launched from a submerged submarine, at a maximum range of thirty-five miles, it would be manually plotted once before it crashed into the ship.

As the first event started, a murmured chant began behind the hum of the blowers, the crackle of radio transmissions.

"Mark, bogey track three, green zero-six-zero one-five-zero, altitude thirty-five, course zero-six-four, three-fifty knots."

"Say again, didn't catch that . . . no . . . gimme the next one."

"Bogey track four designated to Alfa X-ray."

"Bogey track five in a fade, handing off to Sierra Lima."

"EW reports racket, Ice Drum radar bearing two-five-three."

The men leaned into the boards, eyes abstracted as they listened, then intent as they etched in symbols and information. They gradually warmed to the task, but it was still dreadfully deliberate. Midway through the exercise, one of the instructors came in, clipboard under his arm, sat down near Dan, and began writing.

THE faces in the wardroom that night were haggard. Leighty looked exhausted. Dan, looking at him, realized the captain had been everywhere; the engine room, the hangar for fire-fighting drills, then the bridge again as they came in at dusk. Vysotsky looked just as wrung-out. He blinked, making himself concentrate as Woollie started to speak.

"The exercise with *Corpus Christi.* Active tracking was adequate, but the passive tracking was unsat. Based on your grades to date, I don't think you're going to stand a chance of passing the antisubmarine portion of the battle problem."

"Mr. Lenson?" The captain pointed at him, and for a second Dan regretted he'd broken him of his habit of calling on Harper. He stood up.

"Sir, what he's calling a degradation in performance is due to the fact that we weren't running any digital processing. It's part of the overall problem in the ACDADS." As he spoke, he wondered where he should stop. It was never good to give the commanding officer bad news in front of the troops. But then he thought, Hell, he asked me. "It's worse than we originally thought, sir."

"What's our new ETR?"

"We don't really have an estimated time of repair yet, XO," he said, turning to face Vysotsky. "If you don't mind, I'd like to let Dr. Shrobo brief on the problem."

Leighty raised his head from the test results. "Is he here?" he said. Shrobo stood up in back. "Can you enlighten us as to what's going on?"

"I'll try, Captain."

As the angular figure stalked forward, Dan realized how out of place Shrobo looked. "Dr. DOS" was still wearing scrub greens, which apparently had become a uniform for him. At least he had a clean set on, but he still hadn't shaved, and his hair dangled, snarled around his bald spot. Half-inch-thick glasses transformed his eyes into polished gemstones under a magnifying glass. As he reached the front, he unsnapped a rubber band from a scroll. He handed one end to Vysotsky, who looked surprised and not overly pleased, but he stood up to help display it.

"This is a block diagram of the subordinate modules of the Automated Combat Decision and Direction System, Block One, Version Three-Point-One," Shrobo muttered. "I drew it out when I was explaining things to Lieutenant Lenson today. The first thing I need to tell you is that I think I know now what we have in our system. There's a short name for what we've got."

"What's that?" Leighty asked.

"A virus."

"A *virus*?"

"A computer virus. That's what they're called."

Leighty said mildly, "I'm drawing a blank on that, Doc. How can a machine get a virus?"

"Not a biological virus. These germs are actually little programs. They ride in on a tape or a disc and burrow into memory. Then they multiply—erase the original programming and write themselves over it, or lock up the keyboard, or display a message—whatever the programmer who wrote them wants them to do." Shrobo glanced at Leighty. "It's something that's started around the fringes, since they started making personal computers. We've never seen one in the Navy before, but I think that's what we've got."

Leighty said, "Some kind of rogue program that goes around eating memory . . . sounds like science fiction, doesn't it?"

"Oh, they're real all right," said Shrobo.

"I see. Well, how do we know if we've got one? And if we do, how do we get rid of it? And are we talking just the fire-control system, or—"

Dan said, "It'll depend on what we find, sir."

"What do you mean? What could we find?"

He took a deep breath. It was always better to let your seniors know the worst that could happen up front. And now that Shrobo had explained how the thing worked, it was easy to visualize how badly it could damage a ship that depended on computers for almost everything it did. "Well, sir, it depends on how long it's been in there replicating itself. From what Hank says, it may have infected everything the computers handle—the message-processing system, pay records, personnel, admin, sonar programs, navigational programs. And of course the fire control and combat direction systems."

"This may be serious, then," said Leighty.

Shrobo said, "It's like the lieutenant says, depends on how long it's been in there. Thing is, like for the message processing, you've got tapes with all the back messages on them. The virus could be on those tapes, too. You've either got to eyeball every piece of data you own or else try to put some kind of routine together to search for it and tell you where it is."

"Can we do that? Eyeball it, I mean?"

"I don't believe it's possible to sanitize everything manually. There are a quarter of a million lines of code in the operating programs, but there are millions more in the memory units and data tapes for radio messages and the other records. All we have to do is miss one iteration and the virus will regenerate and crash the system again."

Everyone looked grave. Finally, Vysotsky said, "Then how about the search routine? Dan? Is that within our capabilities?"

"I don't know yet, sir," said Dan. "We really need to get deeper into how it's done. Dr. DOS is going to have to lead us."

"But how did *we* get this?" Vysotsky asked him. "Where'd it come from?"

"We don't know that, sir," Dan told him. "But we'll try to find out."

Shrobo said, "I need to emphasize one thing. I wouldn't waste any time. Every hour you run your system, you lose more data. The thing's growing in there right now. I've been trying to isolate what I've tentatively named the '*Barrett* Virus'—"

"I don't like that name," said Leighty.

"Well, some of the sailors call it the 'Creeping Crud.' "

"I'm glad you're here, Doc," said Leighty. "No disrespect to you, Jay, and Chief Dawson and the rest of the DSs, but it sounds like this is beyond them technically. Okay, go on. You were talking about counteracting it. How?"

"I'm not sure yet." Shrobo took a turn back and forth, hands behind his back, looking more like a stalking heron than ever. "First, I have to isolate it. Break it, read it, and understand how it works. Then maybe I can write a program that operates within the computer to protect it."

"Have you done that before?" the XO asked him.

"No one's ever done it before. You have to understand, this is a new field. Of course, you can trace it back to Von Neumann and Turing's work on automata and Shannon's work on information theory—"

"That's all very interesting," said Vysotsky, "but how long will it take you to fix the computers?"

Shrobo said, in the tone used to placate a child, "How long it takes is not important. Understanding what's happening—*that's* important. I don't want to wipe out this virus. I want to capture it alive." Vysotsky looked incredulous, started to say something else, but Shrobo went on. "To address your immediate problem, I propose a short-term fix. It may be possible to erect an electronic fire wall or placenta between weapons control and the rest of ACDADS. The interface to designation and identification functions will be manual. But it should control the guns and missiles well enough to permit engaging one or perhaps two targets simultaneously."

Woollie spoke up then. "Sir, I don't think we can go along with that."

Leighty looked at him. "Why not, Lieutenant?"

"Sir, it's not that we don't want to cooperate. It's more of a point of philosophy. You're the first ACDADS ship to go through refresher training here."

"That's right, so?"

"So . . . Sir, we have no objection to your doing the preparatory exercises any way you want to. The question is how you do the battle problem. Our philosophy is, you train the way you'd fight. Normally, you'd fight in full auto mode, right? That's why this jury-rig mode the man here is suggesting—I don't think we can go along with that. If things are really that bad, maybe you should be back in the yard, not here getting ready for deployment. I'd be glad to set you up with the commodore, though, let you argue your position."

Leighty placed two index fingers to his lips. Then his eye caught Dan's. "Mr. Lenson, you're the combat systems officer. What's your recommendation?"

"Sir, I did a practice run-through today in CIC. Plotting by hand."

"And?"

"Sir, I recommend we start training everyone that way. Full manual, plotting and everything, right now."

"Tell me why."

He sat for a second marshaling his thoughts, then leaned forward. "First, if they want us to do the battle problem in a standard mode, manual makes the most sense. We'd have to fight that way if we had battle damage. The battle problem's three weeks away.

That gives us time to train the talkers and evaluators. By then, we should be able to isolate and run the weapons control systems independently. And, best case—Shrobo gets everything up and running again—we switch to auto, but we're still well trained on the backup mode."

"Then what's the point in having this class of ship?" Vysotsky said. "Without the computers—we've already proved we can't detect a sub even with his nose up the crack of our ass. We'd never be able to operate as part of a carrier battle group."

"But we can't depend on the computers in automatic," Quintanilla said. "Last time we shot at a drone, it hit the ship."

Dan glared at him across the table. Thanks, you son of a bitch, he thought.

They discussed it back and forth for a while. Finally, Leighty held up his hand. "Okay, here's my decision. I believe Commander Vysotsky is right. Your recommendation is noteworthy, Mr. Lenson, but I'm not going to step back in time."

"I don't think it's—"

"Let me finish," said Leighty mildly, and Dan bit his tongue. "The Japanese lost at Midway, maybe lost the whole war, because one squadron of dive-bombers got through unnoticed. In a general war at sea, we'll have upward of a hundred Backfires, Badgers, and Blinders in a strike, all firing air-to-surface missiles, and more cruise missiles from their Echoes and Charlies. The results of the Velvet Hawk series of fleet exercises are pretty consistent. Screen units—like *Barrett*—can expect to engage up to twenty incoming missiles at once in a major strike."

Leighty paused, then went on. "This ship is the future, and we've got to make it work. If we can't, if the computers have become a liability instead of an advantage, maybe it's best we get that on the record by failing the battle problem."

Vysotsky looked stunned. Dan couldn't believe what he was hearing. Leighty didn't seem to register that failing refresher training could mean both he and the XO would be relieved. The captain continued, "We have three weeks. Mr. Lenson, I want you to pass off as many of your duties as you can to Mr. Shuffert, then supervise the effort to get ACDADS back up."

"Uh . . . aye aye, sir."

"It's in your hands. Maybe Gitmo can help, though I don't know how much smarts they have on software. But bottom line is that we'll do the final battle problem in full auto. The system *will* work by then in mode three, or we will accept a failing grade."

Harper looked grave. Shrobo shook his head slowly, gaining him a virulent look from Vysotsky.

Woollie broke the pause. "That's a risky course of action, Captain. Really, if this new software's the problem and a senior software engineer says it's not working right, maybe I can persuade the commodore to grant you some kind of waiver on the—"

"I see what you mean, but I don't think that's the issue." Leighty tapped his lips with a pencil. "These ships are going to have to fight someday—without software engineers aboard. You can't ask for a waiver in the middle of a battle. Thank you for the offer, but I believe I'll stay with what I just said."

"All right, sir, I'll notify the commodore of your intention. Otherwise . . . today's exercises were unsatisfactory."

"Thank you," said Leighty. He stood up, and glancing at one another, the officers and chiefs got up, too, and filed out.

DAN was sitting glumly in his office, contemplating the fact that the captain had just bet his career and the possible future of a whole ship class on him and his team, when someone tapped on the door. "Yeah," he called.

It was Diehl, the NIS guy. "Lieutenant. You said if I had any questions . . ."

"Yeah. Come on in." He tried to force a casual tone as he cleared off a chair beside his desk.

"This a good time? You look busy."

"I'll probably be here all night. So you might as well ask whatever it is you want to ask me now." He forced a smile. "Cephas, how about getting Mr. Diehl some coffee. Me, too. Sugar? Cream?"

Diehl said black, and the yeoman left. He and Dan were alone, with the upper half of the Dutch door open. Diehl reached over and closed it. "Keep it private," he said.

"How's the investigation going?"

"It's an interesting situation. Did you know Sanderling was a fruit?"

"You mean did I know before we went through his belongings, or—"

"Before."

"No."

"No hints to that effect? No suspicions?"

"I'd hear the guys make jokes occasionally. He was kind of the runt of the litter in the division. But they talk that way all the time."

"Sailors, you mean? Enlisted?"

"Not just enlisted."

"The kind of 'suck my dick,' 'whip it out' kind of stuff?"

"Yeah."

"Uh-huh." Diehl sat slumped, looking vaguely around the office. His eye lingered on Dan's desk. "That your daughter?"

"Yeah."

"No picture of your wife?"

"We're divorced."

"Uh-huh. Tell me, did he have any special friends he hung out with, went ashore with?"

"Not that I know of. The leading chief, Dawson, or Petty Officer Williams, they might know."

"Uh-huh. I sure wish we had a body, or a note. You know, eighty percent of suicides leave notes. The stuff the signalmen are telling me, just that they saw something white, that it was moving, then it sank—that he jumped overboard, then finished himself off when the ship was making up on him—that's like only one way of looking at it."

"What do you mean? They saw him go down."

"They saw someone struggling in the water, then sinking. How about this: Somebody knocks him on the head and throws him over. He comes to, tries to swim. Maybe he's hurt. He almost makes it, but he goes down just as the ship's getting ready to pick him up. It would look exactly the same."

"Now taps, taps. Lights out," announced the 1MC. Diehl waited till it was silent again. "You sure this is a good time for you? Now, you were on the effects board for his stuff. Who was there? You, that chief warrant—"

"Harper. It was me, Harper, Oakes, Dawson, and Cephas, the recorder."

"Uh-huh. Cephas says you told him to bag and dump all the boy mags."

"Right."

"Why'd you keep the diary, Lieutenant?"

Dan blinked, suddenly angry. They couldn't keep quiet, like he'd asked them to. The question was whether they'd also told Diehl that Sanderling had mentioned the captain. He was starting to answer when the door banged open suddenly, as if kicked from outside. "What is it?" he said sharply.

"Sorry, sir." The yeoman stopped halfway in. "You *asked* for coffee. . . . Should I come back later, sir?"

"No, leave it here. Thanks," Dan said. Then, to Diehl: "You already talked to the yeoman here?"

"Yeah, hi," Diehl said. "You want to give us a couple more minutes? Thanks. Close it. . . . Man, this is shitty coffee. Okay, why'd you keep it?"

"I couldn't decide if it was better to throw it away or forward it to his family. So I decided to look through it."

"Why didn't you look through it there?"

"I thought I'd do it later."

"Uh-huh. Where is it?"

"I finally destroyed it."

"Uh-huh. That's what you were doing back on the fantail this morning?"

"Yes. I wrapped it in—"

"Five feet of copper wire and threw it overboard."

"That's right." The guy had done his homework, Dan thought.

"Let's see, you were court-martialed once, weren't you?" Diehl asked him, offhand, sipping coffee as he waited for an answer.

"Not a court-martial. Court of inquiry."

"Letter of caution, not good. And according to your service record, you had to respond to some of the fitness reports you got as a jaygee."

"I didn't know you were allowed to go into our service records."

"Sure I am. Anybody I think might be subject to charges."

"So I'm a suspect?"

"You got to admit, it looks suspicious. The kid's queer, he dies and you steal his diary and throw it away. Makes me wonder what it said."

"I took charge of the diary as the ranking member of the effects board. I didn't 'steal' it."

"This could just be a murder investigation, Lieutenant. Why don't you can the coy act and tell me what the book said. It could save us both a lot of trouble."

"It was a record of his feelings. Part of it, he wrote about his sex life. Like anybody does in a diary."

"He's open about being a faggot? In the diary?"

"Yeah."

"Mention partners?"

"Sometimes."

"Anybody on the ship?"

"It mentioned some contacts on the ship."

"This ship. *Barrett.*"

"Yes."

"Now we're getting somewhere. Names?"

Dan said carefully, "It gave no proper names."

"That's hard to believe. Are you in there?"

"No."

"No reference to you at all?"

"Only that I kept turning down his special-request chits."

"Come off it, Lieutenant. Where did you fuckee-suckee this kid? Your stateroom? The office here? You didn't do it down in the bunkroom with the enlisted."

Dan controlled himself. This was the guy's interrogation technique, that was all. "I told you, I didn't have relations with him," he said.

"You got a girlfriend, Lieutenant?"

"As a matter of fact, yes."

"Show me a letter."

"Wait a minute. Are you really asking me to prove I'm heterosexual by showing you a letter from my girlfriend?"

"Maybe. How about it?"

"I don't have any letters from her. She's in Charleston; we only left last week. And I don't think she'll write, anyway. We had an argument before we got under way. Anyway, does that mean a guy's not gay, if he's got a girlfriend? How about a wife and daughter?"

"You'd be surprised, Lieutenant. I personally think there's a hell of a lot more guys out there go both ways than anybody thinks. Anyway, you ain't got a wife; you said you were divorced. How about if I call the ex–Mrs. Lenson, find out why?"

"Why we broke up is our business. I'm not giving you her number."

"Not cooperating, that's not the way to clear things up, Lieutenant."

"That's outside the scope of this investigation."

"Maybe, maybe not," said Diehl. "You sure you never snuggled up with this Sanderling kid? When your shoreside pussy wasn't available?"

"No."

"Who are you protecting, Lieutenant?"

"I'm not protecting anyone."

"You don't lie good, Mr. Lenson. Fact, you lie real bad."

"I've told you the truth. I read the diary; it couldn't be returned to the next of kin; it had no remarks indicating an intention to commit suicide; it gave no names of partners aboard ship."

"One, two, three, four, six," said Diehl. "What's five? I don't need a polygraph machine to tell me you're speaking me *sau* about something. Ask you this: If it isn't that you like to suck boys' dicks, is it worth flushing your career down the toilet for? 'Cause I'm gonna find out what it is sooner or later." He sipped coffee and looked at the overhead. "What exactly is the problem here? Have we got some kind of personality conflict going?"

"I don't think so. I just find your questions offensive."

"Oh, I'm the bad guy because I'm asking questions? Clue you in, Lieutenant. I haven't even started asking them yet. I'll tell you something else, something I learned in submarines. 'Don't sink the boat.' Everything else is secondary to that. But these asshole bandits can do it. It's not a matter of one guy. That, maybe we could live with. But these buddy fuckers start linking up. They get this chain going, and it grows and spreads. . . . When the roaches get out of hand, somebody's got to come in and spray the kitchen." Diehl took out a Skilcraft and a pad of paper. He put them beside

Dan's hand, on the desk. "Now, I'm gonna leave you alone here for a while. I want you to write down what you know. This is your last chance to get straight with me. After that, cross your legs; I only got one more nail."

"Take your paper with you," said Dan. "I don't have anything to add to what I said."

When Diehl closed the door, Dan sat without moving. His mouth was dry. Shit, he thought. I handled that *all* wrong. Well, at least he'd kept suspicion away from the captain.

Yeah, real good work. So now he suspects *me.*

A tentative knock turned out to be Cephas. Dan waved him in, seeing from his face that he'd have to mollify him now for yelling at him. He sighed. The Weapons Department yeoman was either ingratiating or else sullen; he seemed to want something, some acceptance or approbation, but even when Dan complimented him on a typing job, it didn't seem to be enough. . . . He started to reach for the growing stack of paper in his box, then remembered that as of now, when he wasn't on watch, he was on the ACDADS problem full-time. He said the necessary few words to Cephas. Then, hoisting himself wearily to his feet, he made his way through darkened, empty passageways toward the computer room.

24
Alcorcón

THE first rocket detonated with a flash and roar, showering hot sparks down over the crowd. The glow washed over the still-wet streets from the rain that had just ended. Then all at once, the searchlights came on, the bands started to play, and the first float rumbled into the square to a gasp and then a wild, tumultuous cheer. Burning white shafts clashed like sword blades, then focused on the goddesses who waved from it. Gold and white plumes nodded from their heads, making them eight feet tall. As their dazzling smiles beamed across the plaza, the air throbbed with ecstatic rhythm, amplified till it made all thought impossible.

Graciela stood against the side of a building, crossing her arms over her stomach to protect herself as the dancers whirled by. Greasepaint and sweat melted down their faces in multicolored rivers. The smells of perfume and sweat and popcorn, dust and rum and the choking exhaust from the Hungarian trucks made her feel like throwing up.

The people had spent months preparing for the Carnaval, stitching together costumes, floats, decorations out of wood and papier-mâché, colored paper and cloth and tinsel laboriously cut from foil. All stolen from the state, yet the Party looked the other way. Tonight the bands played Silvio Rodriguez and Pablito Milaués, not the "Internationale," and no one wore militia uniforms.

Tonight the worn-out engines of the dented trucks rumbled beneath immense and gaudy wedding-cake disguises, and on them perched workers and peasants who for three heady nights would be kings and queens. They passed in regal splendor, retainers throwing candy and flowers to the screaming crowd. Chinese-made firecrackers ripped the night apart in a stitching of flame and smoke. The beat of "Yolanda" grew faster as the floats glittered and flashed with sequins and rhinestones. Behind them gyrated

Santería dancers, dressed in the red of Changó, god of lightning, fire, and war, or the yellow and white of Ochún, goddess of love. Then came students, workers, teachers, but now they were Spanish dons in cocked hats and swords, showgirls, magicians' assistants. Smoking fusees smeared scarlet light over the face of a strutting Red Death with the back of his hand on his hip. By the hundreds they danced and pushed in a slow peristalsis into the heart of town, a thickening gruel of robots, eyeless reptiles, zombies, fairies, giant rats with the faces of Reagan and Kennedy.

As each float reached the plaza, its riders dismounted, joining the crowd that gradually jelled into a quarter mile of partying flesh. Though she fought for the safety of her wall, she gradually found herself squeezed out into the circulating mass. A skeleton thrust a bottle into her hand, its black maw soundless in the massive, solid impenetration of music and noise. She put it to her lips, tasting the raw sugar spirit, then thrust it back, staring over his head at the cathedral tower that loomed like a ghostly reproach of centuries past over the riot in the square. The hands of its ancient clock pointed to nine. Undertakers, Arabs, mummies rocked and tottered under the green putrescent light of exploding fireworks, the dazzling arcs of militia searchlights. Between low clouds, the stars swayed crazily above the drunken pullulation.

Gradually, the beats of the different bands melted into one another as their members, too, dissolved into the swirling, bobbing mass. It was the rhumba and the conga, the bolero and pachanga, the mambo and the son bembe, every African and Cuban beat blaring together at once. Half Spanish, half African in origin, now the Carnaval was supposed to commemorate the beginning of the revolution. But one glance at this seething mass told her that for four days now revolutionary discipline was gone. It was the perfect time to escape.

Clutching hands circled her; a hot breath scorched her cheek. She pushed herself away, screaming at the packed, swaying crowd. Eyes glared through masks, dropped to her belly, slid away.

For a moment, she thought she saw one mask turn to follow her, thought she saw someone threading the melee behind her. But when she searched the crowd, it was impossible—there were too many faces, too much noise. And so she turned again, cursing and striking out as the mass pressed in, as anonymous hands felt her buttocks and slipped boldly between her thighs.

At last, the crowd broke apart and she staggered out, dizzy but free. She ran awkwardly, till she couldn't run anymore, then walked on, breath sawing in her throat. At last, she saw the dusty green ZIL where it had pulled up to let the workers from Cooperative Number 179 join the revelers.

Julio stood tensely by the tailgate. He saw her and gestured furiously. "Come, hurry!" he shouted. "You're the last one. Where have you been, Tia? Have you been drinking? Get in at once; I'll boost you up."

Inside, the others sat in anxious silence on the board seats that ran the length of the bed. Tomás, Xiomara, Gustavo, Julio, Miguel. As she settled uncomfortably on the hard wood, Tomás banged on the cab with his stump, yelling, "Everybody's here. Let's go, *chico,*" and a moment later the engine started and the wheels slammed and the truck lurched, throwing her into the others as it jolted down off the sidewalk.

Suddenly she was filled with pure fear, simple physical terror so intense she almost vomited in the swaying darkness. Was this really it? Was it really tonight at last? The first night of Carnaval, the Carnaval that would end with them all free, or dead.

FOR the first part of that night, things seemed to go very swiftly. The truck rumbled through the dark, rain pattering on the canvas top from time to time. It stopped at the *central* to pick up the gas and the motor, and twice at Batey Number 3, once for old Aracelia, again for Augustín and Xiomara's twins, Temilda and Gracia. Everybody was ready, dressed and with their little bags with them. The children were quiet, obedient, little faces frightened. Then it stopped one last time to let them off at the path that led into the marsh.

When they were all out, Augustín leaned out of the cab, talking to Tomás. Then Guzman stepped back and he gunned the engine and put it into gear. They heard it blundering down into the swamp, through the brush, till at last the snapping and crashing died away. Augustín limped out a few minutes later, cursing; he'd hurt his foot jumping down from the cab.

Then they went into the woods.

As the vegetation closed around her, her fear returned. Her heart was pounding and her hands and feet felt like the prickly leaves of the *guao* were sticking into them. Now there was no way back—not after destroying the truck. Now, if light shot suddenly out of the darkness, backed by angry shouts and the rattle of gun bolts, they were lost. The *batey* would be broken up ruthlessly, its members scattered to labor camps and corrective farms. She'd lose her baby to a state foundling home. If anyone had informed on them . . . She shoved the fear back, sucking in her breath as sharp fronds sliced at her swollen legs. The men cursed in low voices ahead of her, carrying the engine on poles. The path seemed endless, and she had to stop and rest. When she did, Xiomara and the girls squatted with her, none of them speaking. Finally, they had to bend over and feel their way. Not even the stars penetrated into the tunnel bored through the mangrove.

Water splashed under her feet. The mud was slippery and she fell, but the twins helped her up. The warm water deepened swiftly. She felt the things living in it fastening themselves to her flesh. It reached her waist, but she waded on. If it got any deeper, she'd drown; she couldn't swim at all.

Then there was nothing above her head but sky, clouds, the black palms bent by the wind. She stopped, panting, listening to the thudding in her chest. Then she forced herself on.

The boat was only a shadow under the eclipsing stars. A faint light flickered. She heard murmurs, the clank of tools. When Tomás called her name, she got up and felt her way to the side. Hands pulled and boosted her up.

In the little cramped cabin, she unclenched her fingers from the bag with the canned meat, fish, formula, and the folded double-stitched sail. In the light of a candle, Tomás glanced through it, then passed it to Julio. More hands steadied her as she moved toward the stern, picking her way clumsily over hard sharp things in the bottom of the boat.

"Aracelia": The name went around the waiting circle of men, women, and children.

Aracelia was the oldest among them, an ancient crone dark as the bagasse pressed from the cane. She shuffled forward as Tomás held up a small object that squealed. There was the rapid murmur of an invocation, a sharp, terrified scream, then silence and the drip of blood into black water.

The piglet's throat slit, wrapped in red cloth, it was set adrift now on a little raft. A sacrifice to Yemayá, the ferocious and unpredictable god of the sea. Graciela muttered a prayer to the Virgin of Cobre, too, and Santa Barbara. . . . The gods had many faces, many names. But her heart had always told her they would listen no matter what you called them, like a mother who answers any cry in the night. The old *santera* blew the conch shell, calling the wind to aid them on the voyage. The muted mournful moan sent a shiver up her spine.

"No more noise, that's enough." Tomás murmured. "Are we ready to board?"

"I think so, *chico.* It feels like more rain, though."

"If it rains all the way to Miami, I'll be happy. Okay, everybody get in—one at a time. Then move all the way back."

She felt the boat start to move, start to slip down the mud and into the water.

Then someone said, from the darkness of the shore, "Stop."

"Oh no," someone whispered. The men sucked quick gasps of breath and rolled out again, quietly. She heard the scrape of machetes being drawn from leather scabbards. She squeezed her eyes shut, waiting for the lights, the shouting, the flash and crack of bullets.

"Who is it?" Tomás called.

"It's us."

They stared into the darkness as shadows took on shape. "Who is it?" Tomás said again, louder.

"It's us, the Colóns. Is that you, Guzman?"

"You bastards! What are you doing here?"

"Don't be frightened! We knew you were going to escape, but we didn't turn you in. We want to come."

"What the hell are you talking about?"

Now they were close enough that Graciela could recognize Nenita Marquez's heavyset form. Rámon said, "We only figured out you were going tonight. Why didn't you tell us? We could have helped."

"Bastards, who told you? We'll kill them."

"No one. But too many things were missing, too many strange things going on. We saw Graciela leave the Carnaval, and we followed the truck. It's true, isn't it? How are you getting away? Is the CIA coming for you?"

"Are you joking? You have everything, you fucking Communists. Why would you want to come with us?"

"There's a crackdown on the way. We want out too, damn it! Look, we've got money, if that's what you want."

"Forget it. We don't have room; we've got ten people here. That's all this boat can carry."

But Rámon insisted that they had to come. As they argued, Graciela suddenly understood something else. If Tomás didn't let them come, he had to kill them. Otherwise, they'd go back, sound the alarm, and everyone would be captured out in the bay. So they couldn't just let them go.

They had to know that, too, Graciela thought. It took *cojones*. The men could simply slit their throats, the kids, too, and leave. Or pretend they agreed, then kill them at sea and feed them to the fish.

And Tomás must have reasoned just as she had, because she heard his faintest whisper to Julio and Augustín: "Get around behind them. Strike when I say the word."

There was a single faint splash as a foot slipped into the water.

The two groups of shadows stood apart, melting second by second into the darkness, only a desperate whisper stretched tenuously between them.

"Tomás, you won't regret it. We'll paddle all the way to get away from here."

"No."

"You say no, Guzman. But what do the others say?"

"I'm the leader; I speak for them. We don't have room or food. You want to escape, good luck. Build your own boat."

The round shadow made a sudden motion, and Rámon shouted, "All right, you chose this. Nenita's got her rifle aimed at you. I've got a gun, too. Tell those men behind us to drop their knives or we'll kill you, kill all of you, understand? Then we'll take your fucking boat! We're in charge now."

Julio, from the darkness: "What about it? Kill them?"

Guzman hesitated. "No. They're just the kinds of bastards who'd do it."

"That's good. Now you're being smart! Get in, Nenita. Arturo, Pilar, Leonor, get in. *Okay*, are we ready to leave?"

Graciela felt the boat roll beneath her, then slide into the black water with a sucking sound and a splash.

THE sharp things under her feet turned out to be concrete blocks. She didn't want to think how hard it must have been to carry them all out here, and the motor, which ran unevenly and incredibly loud just behind her back. Over them hovered the stars; around them slapped the shallow, choppy water of the Bahía Jigüey. She could put her hand over the side into the water, they sat that low. It was warm, and when she sucked her fingers, it tasted bitter, just like tears.

"A little to the right. Pick out a star and steer by it," came a mutter from the cabin. From time to time a glimmer escaped from where Tomás, Julio, and Rámon bent over the map she'd stolen from the *médico*. She smiled gleefully in the dark, remembering how she'd just walked in, just before they left for town, and torn it down off the wall of his office. It didn't tell how deep the water was, but it showed the cays and the passages between them, and that was what they needed, wasn't it? Someone else had contributed a toy compass. And so they were setting out.

Only there wasn't enough room.

With five more shoved in than it had been designed for, the boat was packed so tightly that it was hard to breathe. Without the Colóns, they'd have been cramped, but they could have moved around a little. Now no one could move or stand up—Tomás had forbidden that—and sometimes the waves splashed in. Behind her, Augustín handled the little motor. They'd wrapped it in rags to keep down the noise, but it still sounded terribly loud.

But they were moving; they were on their way. She could hear water chuckling past the hull. In the dark, it wavered with a greenish spirit glow, and she wondered if this was good. Was Yemayá protecting them? Or was it bad, a curse? She tried to pray, but the baby started kicking so hard, she had to lean back and try to catch her breath. It had dropped the week before. Its head was pointing downward, and she couldn't eat more than a handful of rice at a time. And she had to pee all the time . . . like now. She fought it, but finally there wasn't anything to do but let it go right there, on the hard seat.

The murmuring from the cabin drifted back, became words. "It's getting rougher. This wind's kicking up the waves."

"It'll be worse at sea."

"We'll worry about that when we get there, all right? We're a long way from the sea, Rámon."

"Morning in five hours. We'll be across the bay by then if Agustín can keep the engine going."

"Then what?"

"Hide. Then go on when it's night again." Sarcastically: "You agree, Comrade Colón? After all, you have appointed yourself *comandante,* no?"

"What about the border guard? They patrol the cays with airplanes, boats—"

"We'll look for mangroves," Tomás said. "That's good cover."

"Is that a boat?" Augustín called in a hushed voice.

"What?"

"I thought I saw something out there."

"Whatever it is, steer away. Stay low, everybody. Throttle back; go slow."

She stopped listening, her attention concentrated now not on what lay ahead but on what was happening within her body. Gripping the gunwale, she stared up into the racing darkness, hoping that the child would wait until Miami to be born.

25
Guantánamo Bay

SILENT, darkened except for running lights, part of the shore detached itself from the black loom of the hills. Black upperworks wheeled through the scarlet tatters of dusk. Water began a muted chuckling as the bow swung in a long outward curve. From the bridge, eyes and binoculars peered into the heart of night.

Dan strained his eyes, fighting to stay awake. Sweat oozed from his armpits, crept down his back. The night air was stiflingly hot, like an oven on low. Beside him, the lookout straightened, muttering into his phones, "Yeah, I'm awake, Rectum Face. Are you?"

Two weeks into training, they were all walking in their sleep. They fought fuel fires, topside damage, flooding, loss of power, fractured piping, helicopter crashes. They treated compound fractures, chest wounds, abdominal wounds, amputations, burns, mass casualties. They evaded torpedoes, cleared shells jammed in hot guns, rigged emergency power, towed and were towed. Then the exercises compounded: loading weapons and treating wounded while the decks were contaminated by fallout, meanwhile conducting an attack on a surface raider. And every moment he wasn't on watch or on deck, he spent in the computer room with Mainhardt and Dawson, Williams and Shrobo and sometimes Harper, when the chief warrant wasn't on watch. Living on two or three hours of sleep a night . . .

Dan saw the NIS agent talking to men in the passageways, and once, in the wardroom, talking to Harper. They'd gone silent when Dan came in. Diehl smiled when they met and turned sideways to slide past. But they hadn't talked since their discussion in his office. And then for the last few days, the agent hadn't been aboard at all.

He stared into the dark, mind scraped clean. By now, every action, every moment and phrase had been scripted and drilled and corrected and drilled again. When they weren't drilling, the men just stopped, sat down on the deck wherever the last order had left them, or stood vacantly, waiting for the next command. *Barrett* was no longer a machine manned by individual men. She had become all machine.

Dan wondered tiredly why it was men resented becoming machines. They didn't think or suffer. They never agonized over what to do. They didn't have moral quandaries or feel sad or afraid.

It was easier, being a machine.

Around him, *Barrett* turned slowly, and the lightless mass of Fisherman Point wheeled past like the night around the spinning earth. A muted bell pinged and the chuckle of water increased to a roar.

He stood at the rail, staring out at the passing shadows, then turned away, feeling his way aft, fingertips tracing hot, smooth enamel, till they brushed the raised coaming of the watertight door.

CIC met him with a blast of air like the wind off a glacier. After the featureless night, the tote boards and displays were a carnival fairway of blinking green and yellow. His wet clothes stuck to his skin as he hauled himself into his chair. He'd slammed his leg into a hatch coaming, running full tilt down a passageway, and his shin ached so that even when he had an hour to sleep, sometimes he couldn't. Most of the men around him had shaven heads. A gunner's mate had started it and now half the crew looked like Zen zombies.

"Dan."

"Evening, Captain."

Leighty checked the surface scope. "Feels different, getting under way in the dark," he muttered. "What's the order of events?"

"Night sea detail; one-on-one against *Corpus Christi* for area search, passive tracking, close-range attack; long-range antisurface gunnery; night helo refueling."

"Are we set for this SEPTAR shoot?"

SEPTARs were self-propelled targets, high-speed radio-controlled boats. "I think so, sir."

"But we're not sure?"

"We've isolated the missile and gunfire-control systems from the rest of ACDADS. It'll run slow; we have to do manual inputs when the program asks for data, but I think it'll work."

"That's the electronic placenta Doc was talking about?"

"That's what he calls it. We'll detect with the SPS-forty-eight and hand off tracking and identification manually."

Dan examined his profile as Leighty asked a couple more questions—nothing he didn't know the answer to. The captain hadn't shaved his head, but his haircut was shorter than it had been in Charleston. He had black circles under his eyes and his hands shook as he flipped the board closed and hung it up again.

"When's the prefiring brief?"

"As soon as we secure from sea detail."

"I'll be there."

"Aye aye, sir."

THE brief was just that: brief. By now everyone knew the procedures. Dan put out the essentials—times, safety bearings, openfire ranges—and repeated the mandatory safety precautions. The men listened dully, making ballpoint notes on hands or arms. A few minutes later, the GQ alarm went.

THE ship no longer thundered with men running, hatches slamming. They were already at their stations. Setting material condition for battle took only seconds now. Sealed, alert, darkened, *Barrett* glided out into the open Caribbean.

In Combat, Dan gathered with the plotting team around the dead-reckoning tracker. He watched the lighted pip of the ship creep down a sketched-out lane as Shuffert briefed that night's play.

Tonight they were matched one-on-one against *Corpus Christi*, which had sortied during daylight and now lay submerged somewhere along a transit lane starting twenty miles southeast of Guantánamo and stretching sixty miles into the Windward Passage. The nuclear boat was restricted in speed and depth to simulate a Soviet *Juliet*-class diesel submarine. That was loading the dice, Dan thought as Shuffert covered the rules of engagement. But *Barrett* was handicapped, too; during deployment, she'd have two helicopters dropping sonobuoys and sweeping magnetic anomaly detectors across the surface of the sea. This exercise was one-on-one, hand-to-hand, and Leighty was determined to win. He wanted to detect the sub first and attack it before they knew *Barrett* was there. Just as the skipper of USS *Corpus Christi*, SSN-705, was going to try to close to torpedo range without *Barrett* hearing a whisper.

Dan rubbed his face. They weren't deaf anymore. They could run digital signal processing now, so they could hear. But the sub's ears were sharper. *Barrett* had only two choices: to steam as quietly as she could, searching in passive, and hope the sub screwed up or to go active, pinging her way along, and attract the sub like a cat to a squeaking mouse. Crap, he thought, his tired mind searching for alternatives.

Then he had one.

ON the forecastle, the electricians mates cursed the boatswains, who cursed them back. Then they all hoisted together, and the twenty-foot spar rose into the darkness. "Forward stay fast" came back on the wind.

"Aft, fast."

"Okay, give her power."

The erected pole blazed suddenly into brilliance. *Barrett*'s sidelights and masthead lights went to full brightness. Then her sides, too, flared up as the dress ship lights, draped along her lifelines, glowed on, each bulb backed by a paper plate taped to the socket.

On the wing, Dan blinked in the sudden glare, sweeping his gaze from bow to stern. The deck-edge lights shone in gay colors behind plastic filters from the signal shack. The paper plates glowed just like the round cheery disks of lighted portholes. He ducked back inside and asked Harper, "Okay, how about the screws?"

"Starboard engine, stop," the chief warrant said. "Left five degrees rudder; carry left rudder to steady on course zero-four-five." He pressed the intercom. "Secure the radars. Secure all electronic emissions. Boatswain's Mate, start the music."

A hiss, then the strains of a marimba band boomed out from all the topside speakers. And suddenly *Barrett* was a cruise liner, portholes glowing, the pool area lighted, the slow beat of a single screw throbbing out into the ocean.

"All we need are some women out on deck in bikinis."

Dan turned, to find the captain looking out beside him. Another shadow looked like Vysotsky. The XO was muttering something that didn't sound too positive. It finished, ". . . not in the manual."

"The class tactical manual is not the universe of tactics, George," said Leighty mildly.

"It's an artificiality. There wouldn't be any cruise liners out here in wartime."

"It's a stratagem, George," said the captain. "A *ruse de guerre*, like sailing under a false flag. They're acceptable in war, why not in exercises? Anyway, lighten up. The worst that can happen, the sub lets us go by. The best case, he picks up our screws, can't decide what we are, and comes in close for a visual ID. We get a passive detection, ping once for a solution, and nail him."

Dan excused himself and slid down the ladder.

In CIC, men leaned back from dead displays, faces blank as their screens. Only at the SLQ-32 did a petty officer frown as he listened for the whine of a submarine's periscope-mounted radar. The "Slick-32" told you instantly if anything within a hundred miles emitted an electronic signal, identified it, and gave you a bearing. In Sonar, Fowler and his men were equally intent on the passive display. A yellow tag-out hung on every switch that would put sound in the water identifying them as a warship.

The captain came in and stood by the DRT. Dan joined him and Kennedy and Shuffert. They leaned silently, like late-night drinkers at a quiet bar, watching the rosette creep northeast. *Barrett*'s course meandered left, then right, a shallow zigzag toward the Windward Passage. If *Corpus Christi* was here—

"Racket," said the EW operator. "Mark! Time three-three: a Snoop Tray radar, bearing one-nine-seven."

"There she is!"

"Suckered 'em in. Stupid bubbleheads."

Chief Kennedy was drawing the line of bearing in red pencil when Dan blinked. "You mean a *simulated* Snoop Tray—right?" he called to the operator.

"No, sir. Racket ceases! Time three-four, Snoop Tray ceased radiating."

"Check the characteristics."

"L-band radar with a pulse repetition rate and frequency match. It's a Snoop Tray all right."

A Snoop Tray was a Soviet submarine radar, carried on their latest nuclear-attack sub classes. "Can *Corpus Christi* alter the output characteristics of her radar?" asked Leighty at last.

Neither Hiltz nor the sonarmen had any idea if a U.S. sub could detune its radar to imitate a Russian boat. Dan remembered the *Kirov* battle group. It was still reported in port, in Cienfuegos. But what if it had a sub attached and they'd decided to do a little scouting?

He went over to the 32 and put a hand on the EW's shoulder. The petty officer lifted an earpiece. "How many sweeps did you get before he shut down?" Dan asked him.

"Four, sir."

"Was there a bearing drift?"

The man typed in a couple of commands and regarded the screen. "There was a right drift."

Behind him, Leighty said, "So he's headed down the Passage."

"Toward us, yes, sir."

"Okay," said the captain slowly, cocking his head in that slightly theatrical way. He walked his fingers across the chart, measuring.

"Here's my reading. He's doing the same thing we are: trying to fox us. He popped up, radiated a Soviet signature, and went deep again. He's on this line of bearing. Got to be at least twelve miles off Haiti, right? That puts him . . . here." Leighty laid a finger across an area of sea that did, if you looked at it right, block the lane *Barrett* had to transit. "Actually, he's playing fair. He's imitating a Soviet. He's running slowly southwest, popping up and looking for us, then going back down."

"I vote we go over there," said Vysotsky.

"What's predicted active sonar range?" Leighty asked Dan.

"Ten thousand yards."

"So we'd have a detection diameter of ten miles. He can be anywhere in this roughly thirty-mile area. If we go in and suddenly start pinging, we've got a thirty-three percent chance of nailing him."

"Unless he's under the layer," said Dan.

"Let's head on over," said Leighty. "If he radiated once, maybe he'll do it again. Then we run another line of bearing and up our probability. Drop a bathythermograph. Whoever's our best guy on gram analysis, get him up here."

"Increase speed, sir?"

"Hell no. We're the Love Boat. Let's cruise on over and play him some marimba."

THEY steamed slowly east, burning all their lights, for forty-five minutes. The sonarmen listened till perspiration glowed green on their faces in the light of the screens, but they got nothing. Dan wished again they had a helo aboard. Drop a line of sonobuoys ahead of the sub and nail him. Minute by minute, the lighted rosette of their position neared *Corpus Christi*'s estimated position.

Finally Leighty lifted his eyes. "Are we set to go active?"

"Yes, sir."

"See if Woollie's on the bridge. Underwater Battery, stand by to simulate firing."

When the senior observer joined them, Leighty explained what was going on, how he planned to carry out the attack. Woollie nodded noncommittally. "Sound like a good plan?" Dan asked him.

"Anything that works is good. This is a free-play exercise."

"Sounds fair." At Leighty's nod, Dan said, "Simulate deploying the Nixie. Go active."

The sonar sang out. Seconds later, Fowler's voice came through the speaker above their heads. "Evaluator, Sonar: sonar contact! Bearing one-niner-five, range five thousand, two hundred yards. Classification: possible submarine. Confidence value: high."

"Remember, I want an ID before we shoot," Leighty muttered.

Dan went over to the curtain. The sonarmen looked back at him. "Hey, can you guys get anything on passive? A turn count, blade count?"

"We'll give a listen, sir. But those six eighty-eights are awful quiet."

Kennedy plotted the datum as Dan told the bridge to put both engines on the line, come right to 195, and increase speed to fifteen knots. Casey Kessler hovered tensely as his men set up the shot.

"Up doppler. Bow aspect. Contact's increasing speed."

"Can we get any kind of identification?" Leighty said again.

"They're trying to, sir."

"Evaluator, Sonar: contact has two props, strong radiated noise level, broadband machinery noise—"

"That's not *Corpus Christi*," said Shuffert.

"All stop," said Leighty. "Secure pinging. Come about!"

"You backing off, sir?" said Woollie.

"We've got to. The Agreements for Preventing Incidents at Sea. We're not supposed to ping on a Soviet boat, track it, or harass it."

"Are you sure it's Soviet?"

"There's no way a six eighty-eight can fake two screws. Dan, make it clear we're departing the area. Come all the way around and increase speed."

"Range, three thousand yards. Still holding a bow aspect."

"Bridge, this is the TAO. Come about. Come about—"

"Reciprocal is zero-one-five—"

Leighty barked, "Come to zero-one-five; go to flank speed. *Now!*"

Barrett shuddered as her spinning props suddenly went to full pitch, chewing into the sea. She rolled as she came beam to the easterly swell.

"Green flare! Two green flares, fine on the starboard bow!"

"Turn toward!" Leighty barked, then, instantly: "Belay my last—do *not* turn toward. Steady on zero-one-five."

"Sir, that's *Corpus Christi* over there. We've got to evade—"

"Steady on zero-one-five, I said."

Green flares meant a simulated torpedo attack. Woollie raised his eyebrows, made a note. Dan couldn't help grimacing. That was a major gig, not taking evasive action. "Sir, why are we—"

"That's a Soviet boat astern of us, Mr. Lenson. For some reason, he's conducting a submerged transit. We just snuck up on him and pinged him out of the clear blue." Leighty swung on Woollie. "Lieutenant, gig us if you like on the exercise, but I don't want a real torpedo up my ass, okay?"

Dan clutched the edge of the DRT, wondering if the next words out of Fowler's mouth were going to be "Torpedo in the water." A minute stretched by, long as a week, and then another.

At last Leighty sighed. "I guess we're clear. Dan, draft a Firecracker message."

"Aye aye, sir." The Firecracker system reported contacts with Soviet and Warsaw Pact vessels at sea.

THEY resumed pinging twenty minutes later, well to the north, but never made contact with *Corpus Christi.*

At 0300, they broke off play and set course for the firing area. *Barrett* ran at flank speed for nearly an hour. Dan sat in Combat as the ship rolled and buzzed.

He had to admit it, he was tense. Would Shrobo's fix work? Or would the system crash again, exposing *Barrett* as a billion-dollar high-tech paperweight? Maybe it would be better just to engage in manual, forget about the weapon direction system. . . .

Fuck it, he thought then. Let's do like Leighty wants. Take a risk for a change.

When they crossed the border of the firing area, they made radio contact with *Evelyn Kay,* the control tug for the self-propelled targets. Dan told them *Barrett* was ready, that they could start the event at their pleasure. "Attention in Combat!" he yelled. If he'd overlooked anything, it was too late now. "This will be a long-range radar-controlled gun engagement. Mount fifty-one will fire first."

As the others rogered, he fitted the earphones to his ears and clicked the selector to the fire-control circuit. He made sure all stations understood the revised designation procedures. Then he turned the shoot over to Horseheads, watching the screen anxiously as the glowing pip of the remote-controlled boat drilled inward at them. It wasn't a big target.

"Stand by to illuminate."

"Intermittent paint. Growing stronger."

"Designate hostile, priority one. Illuminate," said Dan. The man at the weapons-control console reached for the track ball before he remembered this was a manual designate, then pressed the button of his phones instead.

"Fire Control, Combat: your target, drone boat, bearing three-zero-eight, range nineteen thousand yards."

"Designate to forward director, mount fifty-one."

"Forward director reports acquisition. Lock on."

"Load fifteen rounds BL&P ammunition to the transfer tray."

BL&P was an inert-loaded target round that would splash but not explode. "Hold fire," Dan reminded them, then pressed the intercom. "Bridge, Captain: Request batteries released."

"Batteries released," said the captain's voice.

The slam of the five-inch going off shuddered through the deck. Twenty-five seconds later, it slammed again. Dan thought for a second he saw the splash on the screen, but it faded too fast. They were firing by radar, walking the rounds onto the target. But the drone boat was maneuvering, skating back and forth as it drove toward them. "Speed, twenty-five," Kennedy reported.

"Fire for effect," Dan muttered, but he didn't press the button. It was up to Horseheads, Glasser, and Adamo now.

"Fire for effect," Horseheads shouted.

Slam . . . slam . . . slam.

A voice shouted over the radio, "Cease fire. Cease fire! Target destroyed."

The compartment erupted in jubilant shouts. Dan, grinning, punched up the DP center on the intercom. "Computer room, Combat: Good work, guys! Tell Doc he just earned his coffee bill."

AFTER two more runs, Woollie said he'd sign them off on the exercise. The gunners begged to keep shooting, but Dan told them they still had the helicopter refueling to do before they went in. He called the control ship and thanked them for their services as *Barrett* secured from GQ.

The helicopter reported in as early breakfast was being piped. The air control petty officer relayed it to him. "Mr. Lenson: Mike twenty-eight reports, bustering inbound from homeplate with forty-six hundred pounds of fuel."

"Ask him what's bingo fuel." Dan, feeling more cheerful than he had for days, searched the pub shelf for the checklist and wind envelopes.

"Mike twenty-eight says bingo fuel twenty-five hundred pounds."

"Have we got a true wind, Chief Kennedy?"

"Zero-eight-zero, fifteen knots, sir."

He looked at their course and came up with five knots of wind, on the starboard bow. The anemometer agreed. It was 0447, still dark outside. After some quick figuring, he hit the intercom. "Bridge, TAO: Make this a port approach. As soon as he's in visual range, come right, steady up at two-nine-five."

"Bridge aye."

It was Casey Kessler's voice, not Harper's, but Dan figured Jay was in hearing range. He pressed the lever again. "Let's go ahead, set flight quarters."

"Bridge aye."

He called the captain's cabin and told him the helo was inbound for the refueling exercises, that the checklist was complete; they were within the envelope and had no surface contacts. Leighty yawned as he acknowledged. "Sounds like you got it covered."

"Yes, sir, he's got plenty of fuel even if we dick up."

"We aren't going to, though, are we?"

"No, sir."

"Okay, commence the evolution. I'm gonna get my head down for an hour. Keep a sharp eye out."

"Yes, sir." Dan hung up. He had the ship now. He checked the radar and then the chart. Do the refueling as they steamed in, then, when the helo left, steer for the bay entrance for the precision anchoring exercise.

"While *Barrett* is at flight quarters, all hands are reminded to refrain from throwing objects over the side. Remove caps; stand clear of weather decks aft of frame one sixty. Smoking lamp is out topside."

"Helicopter bears two-seven-two, forty-two thousand yards, radial inbound."

"Pass it to the bridge. Are we up on—"

"Yes, sir," said the air controller.

Dan told Lauderdale he was going out on deck for a second.

"Red deck," said the 1MC as he let himself out onto the 03 level. The night wasn't as black as he expected—moon and stars, and a faint pinkish radiance to the east that presaged day. *Barrett* drove through the sea with a hissing crash. He strolled aft, stopping under the steel web of the after mast, looking down.

Work lights illuminated the refueling party, crouched in colored jerseys along the narrow deck-edge outboard of the hangar. The landing signal officer waited quietly, lighted wands dangling as he watched a distant flashing star.

"Green deck," said the 1MC. A few seconds later, the flutter of rotors came across the sea.

The pulsing star reached *Barrett*'s stern. Then suddenly it became not flashing lights in the sky but a huge unsteady machine dropping slowly toward the deck. The rotor blast battered at his ears. It veered off at the last moment and dangled unsteadily thirty feet up. It only took seconds before the hose was connected and the huge clattering aircraft, dipping and swaying like a drunken hummingbird, began sucking fuel aboard.

When he let himself back into CIC, nothing had changed. He checked the scopes again, then the coffee situation. He got a fresh cup, and punched the intercom to the helo control station. "Tower, Combat: How's it going?"

"Ninety percent fuel transferred. Six minutes to break and waveoff."

He clicked the lever twice, acknowledging, and leaned back, thinking about their brush with the Soviet sub. That could have turned nasty. But what was it doing transiting so covertly? Was it related to the *Kirov* group? Had it known *Barrett* and *Corpus Christi* were out there too, due to operate in the area? And if so, how?

"Refueling complete. Stand by to pop and drop. Mike twenty-eight requests permission to depart."

"Permission granted. Notify the bridge."

He dimly heard Kessler acknowledging. The whine and clatter of the rotors increased outside, and he heard it pass to port and decrease ahead. "Give the officer of the deck a course and speed to reach Fisherman's Point at oh-six thirty," he told Lauderdale.

"Bridge, Combat: Recommend come left to two-seven-eight, speed eighteen." A moment later, the deck leaned in a turn.

"Alfa Sierra, Mike Twenty-eight: We seem to have a little trouble here," said the nonchalant voice of the helo pilot.

"Ask him—" said Dan, but he didn't get to finish his sentence. The air controller said, "Mike twenty-eight, Mayday, going to autorotate; engine failure, power failure—"

"Son of a bitch," said Dan. He sat frozen in the chair for an endless second. Then he remembered. Mike 28 had taken off to port; *Barrett* was *still turning to port—*

"Bridge, TAO: Do you have the helo in sight?"

No answer. He didn't call again. Instead, he hit the deck running. Radarmen jumped out of his way. He slammed through the door, pounded up the ladder, burst out onto the bridge. "OOD!"

"JOOD, sir!" Kessler said, turning to him.

"Where's the chopper, Casey? Where the fuck is *Harper*?" Kessler goggled at him. Dan swept the bridge with his eyes, then leaned to look out. A shadow that had to be the helicopter, all lights off, was settling into the water dead ahead—so close, he could hear the rotors, powerless, windmilling down.

"This is Lieutenant Lenson. I have the deck and the conn. All engines back full! Left hard rudder! Flight crash alarm!"

The pilothouse broke into shouting, alarms. Harper ran in in the middle of it. Dan didn't stop, just kept yelling orders, dreading the crunch and slam that would mean they'd hit the chopper. But it didn't come. Then the starboard lookout shouted, "Helicopter, in the water, passing down starboard side!"

"Meet her! Steady as you go! Engines stop."

"Mr. Lenson, I have the deck—"

"No, I do. Radio, Bridge: Patch helo control circuit to position six. Boatswain, call the motor whaleboat away."

"Captain's on the bridge—"

"What in God's name is going on?" Leighty's voice cracked like a shot. Dan explained, pointing out to where the helicopter rolled violently in *Barrett*'s wake. "He just called engine failure, sir, then autorotated in with his lights out."

"Do you have comms?"

"Not since he went in. Sir, he came down directly ahead of us. I thought we were going to hit him. I took over and maneuvered to avoid." He glanced at Harper and raised his voice so that everyone could hear. "I will now give Mr. Harper back the deck and the conn."

Leighty frowned but didn't say anything. He went out on the starboard wing with Harper. The chief warrant called back, "This is Mr. Harper. I have the deck and the conn. Engines ahead one-third, right five degrees rudder. Boatswain, have you got the motor whaleboat on the line?"

TWO hours later, the tenor voice said, "Come in." Dan opened the joiner door and stepped in, taking his cap off.

The captain's sea cabin looked the same as it had last time, except messier. The blackout drapes were drawn so tight none of the morning light bled in. Only the corner lamp was on. In the lowered light, it looked more intimate and less official.

Leighty swiveled from his desk. "Dan. How's the hook look?"

"It's holding, sir."

"Grab yourself some joe. Make a head call, then I'll be right with you. By the way, we got some good news. Mr. Cash brought the message up. We've gotten a reprieve on the missing gear."

"A reprieve?"

"Funding-wise, I mean. Since Sipple can't answer for it and the investigation dead-ended, the type commander decided to cover most of it out of his discretionary fund. Norm has the accounting data, but the big picture, they're picking up the tab for the controlled equipment. We're still stuck with the missing cash and the silver bars. That's sixteen thousand some—"

"Sixteen thousand, six hundred, sir," said Dan. He'd worried over it for so long, he knew each sum to the dollar. "That's great news. It'll be a lot easier to cover that than a quarter million."

"Good," said Leighty. He seemed about to add something but then didn't.

Instead, he went next door and half-closed the joiner door. Dan heard water rattle while he poured himself coffee. The adrenaline rush when the chopper went down had evaporated, leaving him shaky and prone to snap at people. That *was* good news, about the funding, but if only he could get a little sleep. . . .

Leighty came out, toweling his face, in uniform trousers and undershirt. "Hairy there for a couple of minutes."

"Yes, sir. But it turned out all right." They'd stayed with the helicopter till the pilots located the problem, then maneuvered to provide a lee as they tested the engines and finally lifted off again in a blast of spray. Then they proceeded on in for the anchoring exercise. Leighty had decided to stay anchored out, swing around the hook and give the men rope-yarn Sunday.

"The shoot went well. How's the ACDADS effort progressing? Have you got the Crud tracked down yet?"

He cleared his throat. Yes, the shoot had gone all right, but only by blocking out most of the combat system and feeding in their designations and spotting corrections manually. Tracing the Crud . . . they'd found its telltale damage on every tape that had gone through the computers. That included operating systems, modules, and data tapes, navigation, radio, and sonar. Everything except, for some reason, the Link 11 module, the one that linked *Barrett* to other NTDS-equipped ships. Then they'd hit an invisible wall. Though they could see traces of it everywhere, in the wreckage it left in the code, when Shrobo had tried to isolate the virus itself, it slipped through their fingers, vanishing like a ghost. He told the captain all this, and Leighty nodded somberly, listening. When Dan was done, he just said, "And the battle problem?"

"I can only say it's going to be close, sir. Mr. Shrobo has some new ideas he's trying. Maybe we'll have a breakthrough."

Leighty nodded again. "I hope so, too. There's a lot riding on it. Keep me informed. . . . Next subject. You took the deck from Jay this morning."

"I felt I had to, sir. We got a transmission from the helo indicating they had engine trouble. I called the bridge, but there was no answer, so I left Combat and ran up. The officer of the deck was not in evidence. The JOOD, Mr. Kessler, is a good performer, but I judged that we were in extremis, so I took action."

The phone buzzed. Leighty snatched it off the bulkhead. "Captain. . . . Hi, Dwight. . . . How many gallons? Are the evaps in limits? Send it to potable and bromate them. Yeah." He hung up and rubbed his eyes. "So, where was Mr. Harper?"

"He says he was in the ET shop."

"He had the deck, and he was in the electronics shop?"

"He said he was there only a moment, sir. It's fifty feet aft of the bridge and on the same level. He wanted to find out our grade on the radar-repair exercise."

"I don't buy that. That's not the way I want my bridge run."

"No, sir—but he's always been a good shiphandler, in my estimation."

"Mine, too. But I've noticed a falloff in his level of performance, his level of interest lately." Leighty pinned him with a glance. "The exec has noticed it, too. Mentioned it to me. Have you?"

"Maybe, sir," he said reluctantly.

"Have you discussed it with him, this decline? How close are you to him, Dan?"

"I've been to his house. Went sailing with him once." He sipped coffee. "But I think you're right, sir. He's not an easy guy to tell he's wrong. But I'll give him a talking-to."

The captain sat down. He said, closing his eyes, "Okay, let me know how it goes. . . . We're all locked down on Gitmo right now. And that's as it should be. But I don't want to get so focused on the drills that we lose track of what's going on in the real world."

"No, sir."

"You know, I don't entirely believe in the way the Navy runs things, Dan."

Dan thought this was an abrupt change of subject. But maybe the captain had made some sort of transition he hadn't followed, tired as he was. "You don't, sir?"

"No. It's as if we can only do one thing at a time. Engineering readiness, or shipboard security, or racial awareness—they're all good, but we need to do them all the time, not just two weeks before the inspection. I'm not even sure we ought to have inspections."

"You get what you inspect," Dan said. "Isn't that what Admiral Rickover said?"

The phone buzzed again. "Captain. What? Permission granted. Make it so." He hung up and stared blankly at Dan. "What were we talking about? . . . Oh, inspections.

"I'm not sure who said it, but it's exactly right—and exactly wrong. The XO and I should spend half our time preparing the ship for battle—tactics, intelligence, training. Instead, we spend all our time preparing for the next inspection. Here in Gitmo's the only time we actually train to fight. And even here, there's too much emphasis on doing things the approved way." Leighty frowned. "I'm a radical in a lot of ways, Dan. I think we micromanage too much. We strive for control, but what we get is bookkeeping. We say we want tacticians and innovators, but what the system selects for is adminstrators and inspection-passers."

Dan wondered why the captain was telling him this. It seemed like a conversation he ought to be having with Vysotksy, or better, with another skipper at the club. "I agree with some of that, sir," he said. "But I'm not sure why you're telling me."

"You're one of my best officers," said Leighty, shrugging. "You seem like a serious person, someone who reflects on things. You have ideals, but they're not inflexible. But you also seem lonely. I know you've been upset about losing your wife."

He couldn't help sighing. "I guess it takes a while. Actually, I miss my daughter more."

"You're dating?"

"That didn't work out too well, either."

"You know, friendships are important in the service."

Dan looked at Leighty's leg, crossed toward him, and at the captain's bare arm. For a moment, everything seemed relaxed, commonplace, homelike—not at all like sitting with the commanding officer. It was more like having a talk with an older buddy. He could smell the captain's aftershave. The skin on his arms looked smooth and pale.

For just a moment, he saw that skin as not belonging to another man, or as not belonging to either a man or a woman, but simply as bare flesh. He imagined what it would feel like: warm, slightly hairy, slightly damp.

Suddenly, the compartment seemed dim. The air was cool, air conditioning blasting out of the diffuser, but he started to sweat. "Sir, I feel uncomfortable about this," he blurted.

"Uncomfortable. Why?"

"I have a good deal of respect for you, sir, but I just feel . . . uncomfortable."

"I wasn't talking about much of anything, Dan. Certainly not about anything I thought would upset you. You mean about friendship?"

"Sir, I'm not sure it would be appropriate between junior and senior."

"I know what you mean," said Leighty. "But I don't see anything inappropriate about two officers having a private discussion. You know, when you get a little older, get some shore duty under your belt, you'll understand how things are done. You've heard of the 'rabbi' system, I'm sure. Well . . . there are different kinds of rabbi systems."

Dan looked at Leighty, his heart hammering. "What about Diehl? The investigation?"

"Diehl's been satisfied. I don't mind telling you, he suspected you—"

"He suspected *me*?"

"Oh yes. He came to me with that, including some statements he'd gathered from others aboard ship. I told him that whatever they thought, they were wrong; that I had the highest confidence in you; that in destroying the diary, you undoubtedly acted in accordance with the most honorable intentions; that his suspicions about you, *whatever they might be*, were groundless."

Dan stared at the captain. Leighty looked back, holding his eyes.

He lurched to his feet suddenly, onto legs that felt numb and separate. Without saying a word, without being dismissed or asking for dismissal, he let himself out, closing the door quietly behind him.

He stood in the corridor, heart shaking his chest so hard he felt dizzy. Then he heard a movement from inside. He flinched, went around the corner to the ladder and slid down it, and jogged aft till he had several compartments between himself and the sea cabin. Sailors walked by, giving him quizzical glances.

Had the captain just made a pass at him?

Or was he weird from fatigue, imagining things?

Had he actually been attracted to Leighty for a few seconds? Had he really wanted to *touch* him?

He thought again of Diehl, realizing with horror that what he'd done with the diary, and everything he'd said to the NIS agent, had been based squarely and solely on Leighty's word that he wasn't gay—Leighty's *unsupported* word.

A naval officer didn't lie. Everything was simple that way, clear—like ice, thick clear ice that you could walk out across without worrying about whether it would crack under you.

But now he wondered if he'd been naïve.

If he couldn't trust the captain's word . . . then not only might Leighty be gay but he might be the reason Sanderling had killed himself. And Dan had helped him cover it up.

What was the meaning of Leighty's offer of friendship? Of a friendship that could help his career?

Suddenly, his legs gave way. He leaned against a stanchion, buffeted by alternate waves of rage and fear as he struggled to understand.

26

Bahía Jigüey

THE humid heat surrounded them, close as a blanket over their faces. Above them, the wind made the dangling black runners clack like castanets. But not a sigh penetrated the nightmare branches that knitted an impenetrable canopy of dense green. Only shadow, a rotting smell, and the sounds of hushed furtive beings living and dying: the creak of frogs, the ripple of tiny fish, the whining cloud of biting mites that had tormented them since dawn.

Graciela lay with her head pillowed on her arm, looking over the side of the boat. Like a thick, flexible mirror, the black water pulsed slowly between the prop roots the trees dropped to support themselves. Such a clever plant, the mangrove . . . so shallow she could see the bottom, a sticky-looking tangle of roots, mud, and debris that bubbled as if heated from below. Gone abruptly noisy, then deathly quiet as they'd pulled in, the swamp had gradually resumed its normal life around them. Finches flitted between the branches, scarlet bills sharp and impeccably clean, as if polished that morning. Butterflies vibrated like flying flowers. Shrimp stirred the water like tiny silver spoons, and striped snails measured roots centimeter by centimeter. She watched a crab hunch patiently, then lunge for a tiny fish so fast that the eye couldn't follow.

She was the fish, and the planes that droned overhead from time to time, they were the crabs.

They'd reached the patch of mangrove just as the sun rose in a bloody boil of cloud. The motor had run out of gas during the night, but when Augustín put more in, it wouldn't start. For the last few miles, the men had paddled savagely toward the dark line of cay, racing the sunrise. As the great bay had gradually brightened, making their hearts racket with fear, they'd seen three other boats in the distance, black silhouettes against the delicate shimmer of dawn. They couldn't tell what they were—patrol boats, fishing boats—and Tomás had ordered them tensely to row, row till their lungs burst; they had to reach cover before they were seen.

And at last, they had. Julio and Tomás and Miguelito, on the bow, chopped furiously with machetes as Augustín and old Gustavo and the women, Nenita and Xiomara and even the bent, ancient Aracelia, pulled on the bulging humped roots to move them forward. The tin bottom boomed and scraped over root clumps as parrots exploded from the trees like screaming green-and-yellow fireworks. Branches trembled as steel sang through them, then collapsed onto the huddled children. Till finally they'd come to a halt. The twins had been throwing the fallen branches overboard, but Tomás ordered them to stop at once. Woven back together, they'd serve as a screen, shielding them from both the sea and the air.

Breakfast was a mug of *guarapo,* warm cane juice, passed from hand to hand. Tools clicked as Augustín disassembled the motor. The other men conversed in the cabin, jabbing fingers at the map and pointing shoreward. Finally, Julio and Gustavo and Miguelito swung down into the mud and slogged away, sawing through the thickest patches with their machetes instead of swinging them—the pock of a blade on a hollow root could carry for hundreds of yards.

And now she and the others were waiting, sweating in the windless heat, trying to ignore the insects, so thick sometimes that you couldn't help breathing them in. Xiomara smeared gasoline on her skin to discourage them, but Graciela couldn't stand the smell. So she just pulled her dress tighter around her and closed her eyes.

For years, she'd dreamed of escape. When Armando had closed his eyes forever she'd sworn she'd get out at any cost—even if she never saw Coralía again. But you lost her long ago, she told herself coldly. No, even if she had to leave her, and two tiny graves, even if her heart shattered like a dropped bowl, she had to go. No matter that she was pregnant or that she felt like throwing up. She'd had enough.

But part of her still wanted to stay.

Cuba, beautiful Cuba, it was still her country and always would be, and she longed for it even as she left it behind: the cry of the owls at night; the thud of bongos and cricket click of the *guayo;* the smell of the fields in the spring, of mariposa and frangipani. . . . Did they have mariposa in the United States? She didn't know. She wished she didn't have to go. *Lo hago por ti, hijo,* she thought. I do it for you, loved one, child.

Eyes closed, she put her hand softly on a mysterious hidden movement only she could feel. Did it understand that it was leaving its native land forever?

Mi hijo. Again and again she said it, and after a long time, the fear stepped back a pace.

THE boy threw dripping hair back, trying not to think about what lived under the lightless spotted surface, brushing his bare legs as he plowed through the black water. Lizards ran like iridescent mercury up misshapen roots. Birds waited till he was inches away, then burst shrieking from concealed nests. Each time, he froze, gripping the slippery handle of his machete. He wanted to run away, back to the boat. But he couldn't. Tomás had sent him out, two hundred paces along the water's edge, to stand picket. He had gripped his shoulder and said quietly that he depended on him. That meant that no matter how scared he was, he had to do it.

He circled to skirt an immense tangled mass of roots and fallen trees, finding himself at the edge of an open bowl of water so black and still it mirrored his frightened face. He waded into it, then scrambled back, flailing his arms for balance. The bottom had dropped away, the mud crumbling under his toes. Strange, this empty crater. As if the mangroves had been blown apart . . .

His eye picked the skiff out of the debris before he realized what it was. It was lying on its side in the tangled roots, vines twisted through the hull. His head came up and he waded the rest of the way around the pool. He grabbed it and tugged, experimentally, to see what was inside.

It rocked down and splashed into the black water, then slowly started to fill as he stared at the tumbled mass inside—crude hand-carved paddles, plastic bottles of water, still capped, just like the ones their own boat carried. But along with these were faded cloth, white bone, a skeletal hand gripping a crucifix, a boiling of black insects within a skull that regarded him for a long time, staring into his eyes, into his soul.

He turned away at last, unable to meet that chill and distant regard. Miguelito Guzman swallowed hard, not because he was afraid of the dead, but because he was afraid of joining them.

THE patrol boat came that afternoon, in the hottest part of the day.

She lay there, her mouth parched, panting for water. In the moist heat, you wouldn't think you needed it, but she did. Finally, she asked old Aracelia to hand her the bottle. The water was warm and tasted of resin. She held it in her mouth, letting it seep into her tongue, but when it was gone, she was still thirsty. She looked at it again longingly, then capped it and wedged it down beside her. She was used to going without in the fields. She put her hand over the side of the boat, wet it, and drew the moisture over her face. It cooled her a little as it evaporated. Beside the boat, the little *chalana*, the skiff, was drawn up, the one Miguelito had found in the mangroves. He and Gustavo were working on it, plugging the bullet holes with whittled chunks of wood and patches of inner tube.

At that moment—maybe because her cheekbone was resting against the wood and the sound came through the water to it, not through the air—she heard something. It grew nearer slowly, out beyond the whispering screen of the mangrove leaves.

"A boat," she murmured, and the others lifted their heads. Barefoot, moving in a crouch, Tomás stepped between the packed children and squatted on the stern. Extending his machete, he parted the hacked-off branches, slowly, slowly.

Looking past him, Graciela saw it. Framed by the leaves, as if she was looking out at a moving picture. Not sharp, to her nearsighted eyes, but she could make it out.

The motorboat was painted camouflage brown and green. A curl of white rippled along its bow. At the stern fluttered the Cuban flag, blue and white stripes, red triangle, white star. A man in a shoved-back cap was scanning the shoreline with binoculars. A soldier in fatigues leaned on a machine gun.

Tomás turned his head very slowly, so slowly it might have been swayed by the wind. "*Silencio*," he whispered. "*¡No se muevan!* They're looking for us."

A moan from one of the children was instantly stilled by its mother's hand.

"Rámon. Nenita. You're the only ones armed. If they discover us, what?"

"I say we fight," said Colón, his throat moving as he swallowed.

"What of the children? The women?"

"You'll just go to prison, but they'll shoot us. We can't let them take us."

Aracelia spat. "Why you ask him, Tomásito? These lousy Communists. They found out about us; maybe they turn us in already. Why you listen to them?"

The big man with one hand looked back at Colón for a while, his face thoughtful. Finally, he said. "So they were Communists. And I was in the army, grandma."

"That's right, amigo. They fooled us all, the bearded ones," said Rámon. "The only question, how long it took us to wise up."

"Which 'bearded ones' do you mean, exactly?"

"All of them—Marx, Lenin, Castro. Ever notice? They've all got beards."

Tomás said, shrugging, "Okay, we fight. Nenita, you any good with that, or is it just jewelry?"

"I can shoot it."

"We'll see. Better get up here, get sighted in."

As she squirmed back, Tomás told Graciela, "Get as low as you can. The children, too."

"Shouldn't they get out, Tomás?"

"Even better, but wait a minute. Let's see if they keep coming this way."

They waited. The buzz of the motor came through the leaves like the drone of a huge and remorseless mosquito. Then it changed.

"He's altered course. Toward us." Guzman narrowed his eyes. "Think you can hit the officer? The pale one, the *gallego*?"

"I think so, but I'm not much good at judging distance. At the range, they always tell us how far it is to the target."

Guzman raised his handless arm to shield his eyes. "Call it four hundred meters," he said.

Nenita Marquez flicked the leaf on her sight forward, settled the stock on the gunwale, and turned the safety down. Graciela, looking up at her from inside the boat, saw beads of sweat quivering on her upper lip. Nenita took two deep breaths, then settled her cheek to the lacquered wood. "You want him first? Or the one on the machine gun?"

"You choose, but try to get them both. Everybody else, quietly now, into the water. Miguelito, Tia Graciela's your responsibility, okay? Stay with her. If we have to split up, run, swim, get as far away as you can. When we stop shooting, come back. If we're dead, go ashore, find a militiaman and give up. Say we forced you to come, okay? Nenita, three hundred meters."

The motor droned louder. Graciela felt the boy tugging at her. She knew she was supposed to get out of the boat, but she couldn't. She wasn't going to get over that thwart without a lot of noise. "I'd better stay," she whispered. She looked up at Nenita again, at the bottom of her chin. A drop of sweat gradually gathered, then dripped off it. Over both their heads, a seedpod hung above the boat. It looked like a miniature plant, and she realized the tree must spread that way, the seed growing till it became a little tree itself, then dropping into the mud and rooting itself another few inches farther out from the shore. How perfect, how clever, how beautiful! She stared at it for a long time.

The click of the safety going back on made her flinch. Tomás sighed, and Marquez slid back down into the boat. She mopped sweat with the sleeve of her shirt. "He didn't see us?" Graciela asked her.

"Apparently not. But I don't see how. He had the glasses right on us."

"It's dark in here. He couldn't see past the shadow."

Tomás, rocking the boat as he dropped down to where the women were, said, "Okay, he's gone. Everybody back in! Let's try to get some sleep; we'll be awake all night."

TOMÁS squinted at the plug, then reversed his machete and tapped it. He asked Gustavo, "You'd trust your life to it?"

"*Sí, jefe.* Wood swells when the water hits it."

"Don't call me chief, Uncle; we're all equal here—even those who think a gun makes them a king." Tomás straightened and passed his hand over his hair, looking once more out at the darkening bay.

His stomach felt like a ball of concrete. It was like the hours before an assault. Remembering Africa made him think of his hand. He examined the stump clinically. It looked like the puckered end of a chorizo, the spicy Cuban sausages he'd loved in the days you could still get them. Some said when you lost a limb, you could still feel it, like a ghost. He never had. It was gone as if it had never been. Four years now since the South African mortar shell had taken it off.

It had crossed his mind that maybe in Miami the doctors could do something. Perhaps one of the metal claws, or a plastic hand? But *mierda,* he was lucky to be kicking around at all. Too many guys had died there. And for what? Once he'd believed it, that they were fighting for the poor and starving of the world.

"*Mierda,*" he whispered again, and his thoughts left his missing hand and moved remorselessly ahead. It was a miracle they'd found cover in time. If they made it to sea tonight, it would be another miracle. If they could find Miami, yet a third.

He hoped old Aracelia had done her ceremonies right. They were asking an awful lot of the gods.

Colón came climbing over the huddled, waiting women and children, his cheeks quivering like jelly. He levered himself over the side, splashed into the water, and waded back to join Guzman. "That was close. They almost saw us," he muttered, looking curiously at the skiff.

"Yeah. But they didn't."

"Who you putting in here?" he asked, adjusting the pistol holster around his paunch.

"Whoever wants extra room. You?"

"Fuck no, not us. That's all you want, get us in there, then cut the rope some night! What's wrong with the big boat? Get rid of the cement, it'll ride better."

Tomás said patiently, "We need it for ballast, but this boat will not stay afloat with fifteen people in it. You hear that wind. It'll be rough out there. We'll just turn over and sink, and the fucking sharks will eat everybody. *¿Entiendes?*"

"Maybe we can't take everybody," said Colón, fingering the holster. "We don't have much food."

"I figured you'd come up with that sooner or later, *compañero*. That's why I got the skiff fixed. And speaking of food, let's not forget, you didn't bring a fig, not one mouthful of rice, not one bottle of *cerveza*. You didn't bring a thing but that gun and your big mouth, and you want us to abandon somebody else so we can take you? You're an asshole, a *culo*. Get out of my sight."

"My family's staying in the big boat," Colón repeated.

Tomás shrugged. He waded over and looked in. The old woman sat staring at the twins, who were playing with a lizard they'd caught, making it run around inside the hull. It could not escape, and so darted here and there in frantic silence. It had already lost its tail. Graciela lay with her eyes closed, sweat shining on her face like a coat of varnish. He gnawed his lip. She couldn't take much of this. And the way she looked, the kid could arrive any second.

Augustín straightened and wiped his hands on a piece of rag, grimacing at the motor. "Will it run now?" Tomás asked him.

"Think so. But it used a lot more gas than it should last night. Half of what we brought . . . in only three hours. These Russian machines are shit."

"We can put the sail up once we're out of sight of land. Okay, listen, everybody: Some of us are going to get in the *chalanita*. We'll tow it astern. That will give us more room and be safer." He glanced at Colón. The fat man shook his head, scowling. "Okay . . . Gustavo, you patched it. Get in. You can fix the plugs if they work loose. Uh, Tia Graciela, do you want to stay where you are?"

She opened her eyes slowly. "I can if you want me to, Tomás."

"Yes, but you have a choice, okay?"

"Room to stretch out would be nice."

"You can lie on the bottom; it's flat."

"Maybe it would be better there. Yes."

"Help her up, Miguelito. That means you go, too, and Julio—he's the best swimmer we've got. That's four—no, five. I want Aracelia with her, in case the baby . . . Give them a bottle of water, food, a paddle. Hand me the rope. Is this all we have? Okay, tie it tight; we don't want it to slip."

All at once, it was dark, like a great eyelid closing on the world. Tomás swallowed again, wishing the lump in his gut would dissolve. Looking at the dead bones had made him afraid. Those bones had dreamed of freedom, too. Had come the same way, across the Bahía

Jigüey. Only the patrol had caught them. No burial, nothing. Just shot them like dogs, like animals.

How many thousands lay along the shores of their country, at the bottom of the sea, buried in mass graves, victims, victims? . . . One man had aborted the glorious revolution into bloody tyranny. And then like an infection, it had spread. Bolivia, Venezuela, Zaire, Angola, Somalia, Nicaragua. "One, two, many Vietnams," Castro had ranted. And darkness and terror, murder and war had stretched their shadows from Havana across the world. How long would it last? He'd given up asking. It was time for him to go, that was all he knew.

"Okay, let's get moving," he said.

They emerged with a clatter and rustle, a scrape and bump. Paddles splashed. Then they were afloat, and the wind came gusty and faintly chill. Blowing from the east, he thought. That would help.

During the day he'd memorized the chart. He didn't know the ocean, but he could read a map and judge distances. He figured they were three or four kilometers from a passage between Cayo Romano and Cayo Coco. It was narrow; on the map, the two almost touched. There had to be guard posts there. So he didn't dare use the motor. He didn't dare put up the sail, either. It would be too easy to spot through binoculars or a night-vision device.

No, they'd have to paddle.

They moved through the darkness, helped by a wind that felt heavy, cold, stronger than he'd expected. The boat was pitching already. The skiff was a black wedge astern. He worried again about Graciela, then put it out of his mind. He couldn't help, if this was her time. He didn't see how women stood it, blood, pain. . . . All he had to do was get them through. If they could just do that . . . if they could only do that.

He figured they had about an even chance.

THREE hours later, hours of paddling and drifting and anxious peering through the dark, he figured they must be near the passage. The sea had smoothed, which meant they were in the shelter of land. He clambered up onto the corrugated-metal roof of the cabin and balanced there, opening his eyes wide.

He gradually became aware of two darker masses hemming in the black of the water: two points of land, stretching out to meet ahead of them. Only the map convinced him they didn't, that there had to be a way through, however narrow.

Suddenly, a light stabbed out, swept around ahead of them. A string of red balls arched up, hung in the sky, then went out. Finally, the searchlight went out, too, slowly, fading gradually back into the somber, chill darkness. Only then did the tap-tap-tap of the gun reach them.

He stood there for a long time, watching, listening. Tracers, but what were they firing at? Was someone else trying to get through? If so, they'd send out a boat to check for survivors, no? But the only sound was a muffled *thunk* as a paddle, thrust by tiring arms, knocked against the hull. Then came a whisper that might be the wind in palm trees off to the right. The searchlight stabbed out again, scribed a semicircle across the black water, the beam clearly visible in the humid air; then it faded out. He wished desperately that he could run the engine. But that would be fatal. They'd be out after them in minutes. No, they had to paddle. Too bad he had only one arm.

But looking back and down, he could tell even in the dark that one man wasn't rowing. He leaned down and grabbed. Colón's shoulder quivered under his grip.

"You son of a bitch! Why aren't you rowing?"

"I'm tired. Let the others row!"

"*Gordo hijo de puta,*" Guzman said in his most intimate ex-sergeant tone. "I don't give a fuck who you used to be; you're a worm now, a *gusano*, just like me. And if you don't put your back to that paddle, I'm going to kick your ass overboard and let you swim in to your border guard buddies. And I don't give a fuck if you shoot me or not." He shook him. "Grab that paddle, *cabrón*!"

FIFTY feet behind, in the skiff, Graciela lay sprawled under the thwarts. Her back lay flat against the bottom. It felt good, being able to lie down. But she felt so huge, so swollen, as if she were ready to split apart. She was barely aware of the cold hand of the old woman gripping hers.

AHEAD of her, Miguelito stared into the darkness. His hands hurt where they clenched the wood. He wished he was in the bigger boat. But Tomás had told him to stay with Tia Graciela. But what if they started firing? All he had was a machete. Maybe he could cover her with his body. . . . Would that stop the bullets? He shivered in the cold wind.

* * *

A drop went *splat*, then, sometime later, another.

It began to rain, gently at first, then with increasing force. And gradually the two boats started going up and down, only a little at first, a suggestion. Then they began to roll.

Tomás swung himself down from atop the cabin. He crouched behind it, squinting out as the rain stung his eyes like cold wasps. He couldn't see what was ahead, only that it was black. The boat rolled harder, a strange heavy motion, and someone screamed as a wave broke over the side and showered them all. "Start throwing the blocks over," he ordered. "Hurry. Hurry! Not all, about half of them. Not you, you men keep paddling!"

"We can't, Tomás. We're exhausted."

"Can't we put up the sail?"

"Not yet. This wind'll push us right back on the shore. Just keep paddling, damn it!"

"We really can't," Julio said. "Tomás, we really can't. It's really hard; we're finished."

Tomás didn't answer him. It was too dangerous. But in the end, he couldn't think of anything else to do.

"Okay, Augustín, start the engine."

The clatter when it kicked over was incredibly loud. Tomás felt cold sweat wring out all along his body. The wind would blow the sound west. If the border troops heard them, they'd either fire or else send out a boat. It wouldn't be that hard to find them. They couldn't evade. They could still end up like that other boat, only on the sea beach instead of the bay. Like those skeletons . . .

After a long time, the light stabbed out again. Only this time, it had crept aft a little.

"How far out do the patrols extend?"

"I don't know," Tomás said. "Rámon, you know that?"

"Ten miles?"

"And after that?"

"We're clear, I think."

"There they come," said Julio quietly.

Tomás whipped his head around and saw the lights come out from the shore. Red and green and white, startlingly bright against the black land, they moved rapidly out across the water. The light smeared off the waves in long trails. They could hear the motor, too, a deep grumbling song of power.

"What do we do, Tomás?"

"Guzman? Now what?"

"Shut up. Just keep going," he shouted at them, but his bowels felt loose. They'd gambled and they'd lost. No chance of fighting them off out here. The patrol would stand off and shoot them to pieces. If they surrendered, they might save the children's lives, at least.

The motor ran and ran. The boat rolled dizzyingly in the dark. Clutching the top of the cabin, Tomás stared alternately into the lightless gulf ahead and back at the lights behind. They grew steadily brighter. They were gaining. He couldn't think of anything else that he could do, though. Just hope Augustín could keep their worthless motor running, that some current wasn't pushing them backward, that they wouldn't capsize or smash themselves on some reef unmarked on the rudimentary map they sailed by. And that the beasts that guarded the perimeter of their cage would blink or yawn or look away.

After a long time, it started to rain again. The lights of the other boat stopped closing. They dimmed, then faded as the rain pelted down.

Staring into the darkness, he listened tensely to the uneven, faltering throb and hum from aft.

BUT when the sky grew light at last, the motor was still running, and they saw that they were surrounded by the open sea. When a wave lifted them, they could glimpse a dark low line astern. That was all that remained of the cays, of the border guards, of Cuba. Looking at each other, they tried tentative haggard smiles. They'd made it. They'd escaped.

Then, as the light increased, they looked out to the east, to the north, at the low, sullen, tumultuous sky. And their smiles faded to horrified stares.

From the east, from the north, waves beyond anything they'd ever conceived in nightmare toppled in endless ranks. The boat rolled with sickening jerks, slamming down with a hollow metallic thunder. Already vomit stained the gunwales, and the fragile boards and plywood and nailed tin that cupped them groaned as they worked.

They weren't sailors. Most of them had never seen the sea before. They hadn't expected green waves taller than houses, or a sky gray as poured lead, with the flicker of lightning from low, menacing thunderheads.

But to their surprise, they weren't alone.

They'd expected that, to be alone. But other boats dotted the waves around them. They disappeared and reappeared as the waves shouldered under them. Some had sails up. Other were only specks. But they were all headed west. And they were all moving, borne along on an immense river in the sea itself.

Seasick and afraid, the fifteen people in the two little boats faced the ocean with a hand-stitched sail, a toy compass, and a motor that against all expectation ran on and on, steady save for a choked, bubbling snarl when the violently pitching stern plunged it down into the foaming sea.

27

THE metal gangway that rattled under his boots, the quarterdeck he paused at were low compared with *Barrett*'s. The fantail was small and cluttered. But the OOD looked squared away in summer whites. Dan saluted the flag, faced left, tapped off another. "Permission to come aboard?"

"Permission granted. Help you, sir?"

"Here to see Lieutenant Prince. He aboard?"

Waiting, snatching an hour away from the ship, he stood looking down the length of USS *Dahlgren*, DDG-43.

The *Coontz* class had started life as "destroyer leaders," DLGs. Now they were guided-missile destroyers. Whatever you called them, he thought, they looked like warships. They had the big raked stacks that had descended in U.S. destroyers in a straight line from William Francis Gibbs's great liners. They bristled with guns, antennas, masts, directors. Most striking of all was the beautiful curve of their main deck. It swept in one rising line from counter to bullnose, then terminated abruptly in a bow like the nose of a mako. They looked capable and dangerous, as if they could punch through a sea or an enemy with equal ease.

And *Dahlgren* had. Her waffle-ironed hull plates showed where the seas of decades had hammered them in. Her rows of combat ribbons and the stenciled symbols on guns and directors showed that she had bombarded hostile coasts, guarded convoys, shot down enemy aircraft.

"Dan?"

"Hey. Larry!"

Larry Prince was one of the greatest épée fencers the Naval Academy had ever produced: Eastern Intercollegiate, NCAA, three times Maryland state champion, Princeton-Cornell Memorial

Fencing Champion. "Good to see you," he said, shaking Dan's hand. "You're keeping yourself in shape."

"Heard you were over here. Thought I'd come over, say hi."

"Glad you did. How's Betts? Didn't you have a kid?"

"She left," said Dan, and Prince looked at him for a moment. "Took my little girl with her."

"I'm sorry to hear that. Well . . . come on up. Meet the guys."

They ascended through decks and passageways, Dan feeling steadily more oppressed, as if the low cable-festooned overheads were pressing down on him. The hot fan-stirred air smelled of food and oil. Finally, Prince held a door open. Dan hung his cap on a wooden peg and went in.

The wardroom was half the size of *Barrett*'s, with worn carpets and comfortable-looking metal chairs. Officers in khakis were sitting around drinking coffee, smoking, reading the *Guantánamo Bay Gazette* and limp worn copies of *Playboy* and the *Naval Engineers Journal.* They glanced up as Prince introduced him. "Dan came over from *Barrett*," he finished. "What are you over there, Dan—Operations?"

"Combat systems."

"What, plain old weapons officer ain't good enough anymore?" one of the men said.

"We don't have mess decks, either," Dan said. "Now it's the 'enlisted dining facility.' "

"You guys classmates?" a heavyset black guy asked, getting up, holding out a big soft hand. "Leo Abbott. I was a plebe when you were segundoes."

"Not another frickin' ring-knocker," said one of the smokers in the chairs.

"You're surrounded. Dan, this is Wilson Benedict, our tame mustang. Jaze Walberg, he's in charge of keeping all the scuttlebutts broke-dick." Dan tried to register names as he shook hands. It was always disorienting going aboard another ship, as if the people you knew so well, the chief engineer, the comm officer, the bull ensign, had been reincarnated with different faces, different voices. It made you wonder how much of what you knew of any man was just a role.

"Want some eggs? Mess decks do eggs benedict Sundays, with hollandaise sauce. Gonna win us the Ney award one of these days. We grind our own coffee, too."

"Sounds good. Thanks." The messman set him a place and for a while they didn't say much.

"When you doing your battle problem, Dan?"

He said around a mouthful, "Friday. You?"

"Tomorrow."

"Good luck."

"I think we're ready," said a lieutenant. "The skipper got Ming to promise the guys three days in Jamaica if we pass. I think we'll make it."

"Ming?"

"Well, you call the chief engineer 'Cheng,' right? We call the weps officer 'Wang,' the ops officer 'Fang.' That makes the exec—"

"Ming the Merciless. I get it." Dan grinned with them. "How about the captain?"

"He's just 'the captain.' "

"We got some sheet cake from last night. Want a piece?"

The others came over as Prince dipped a knife in a glass of water and subdivided the cake with navigational precision. The steward poured more coffee.

"Hear you got trouble over there," said Abbott. "On BFB."

"What's BFB?"

"Butt-fucking *Barrett,*" he said. The others laughed.

Dan laid his fork down. "What the fuck's that mean?"

"Take it easy. We heard you lost a queer, that's all. Isn't that why the kid jumped overboard?"

"We're not really sure."

"Did you know him?"

"He was in my department. Yeah, I knew him."

A lieutenant (jg) said, "Be tough on his parents, but you know, it was probably the best thing for him."

"I don't see how," said Dan. He didn't like hearing his ship put down, and he didn't like talking about Sanderling as if he were some kind of defective part best disposed of over the side. "I wish he'd talked to me before he did it. I've been . . . wondering how to look at it."

"How to look at queers? Shit, it's unnatural."

"Tell 'em, Marco."

"What's it say in the Bible? I forget exactly, but it's against it. Like, isn't that why God destroyed Sodom?"

" 'For even their women did change the natural use into that which is against nature; and likewise also the men, leaving the natural use of the women, burned in their lust one toward another; men with men working that which is unseemly.' "

"Wayne's our Protestant lay leader. Isn't it the worst sin there is, Wayne?"

"Not exactly, but you can't be a Christian and a practicing homosexual."

"You mean God won't forgive them?" Dan asked him.

"God will forgive everyone, but only if they repent and have a sincere determination never to repeat their sin."

"I'm not religious myself," said the lieutenant (jg) they called

Marco. "I don't know about the theological stuff. I look at it from an evolutionary viewpoint. Like, nature doesn't do anything doesn't help the species to survive. You ever see two gay mallards together? Or a lion sucking another lion's dick? Faggots are sick, that's all. Doc, what do you think?"

"This is Doc Gehlen," said Prince, nodding to the civilian who'd just come in, "our resident shrink. He's teaching one of those extension courses. What do you think, Doc? Ever run into any queers?"

"Lots," said the civilian, helping himself to the cake. "Is it a sin? I don't believe in sin. Is it a sickness? The ones I've seen have all been disturbed individuals in one way or another. I would call it a . . . personality disorder. A compulsion, like pyromania or bestiality." He took a bite, considered, then added, "Of course, my sample may be skewed. The happy ones might not bother coming to see me."

"Are they born that way?"

"I don't buy Freud's theory that it's rooted in the relation with the maternal figure. But it happens early."

Marco said, "Hey, whatever. I knew a guy—he was standing in the shower on the *Iowa* when this pansy comes up and just grabs his dick, you know? He told me they caught eight guys in a daisy chain on the Oh-four level one night. Every one of 'em tested positive."

"Yeah, they all got that gay cancer. They just don't show it yet."

"I don't want them around. What if they sneeze on you?"

"That's not what I joined the Navy for. I thought it was one place where you didn't have to put up with the fucking feminists and lesbos and gays."

"They're security risks. Every spy we've ever had has been a homo."

"Dan, no offense, but I heard there was more than one over on *Barrett*."

Dan put his fork down again.

"Mr. Marco didn't mean that," suggested one of the senior lieutenants.

"Uh, I guess not. It's just scuttlebutt, you know."

The lieutenant turned to Dan. "It's not a complicated question. Homosexuals don't fit in, because the other guys aren't going to accept them. You get one in the berthing compartment, the other men don't want to sleep with him. They don't want to shower with him, or take orders from him, or have anything to do with him. Now, you feel guilty about your guy, the one who jumped. Think about this. If they'd have kicked him out, he'd still be alive."

"Jack's right. I was on an LPD once; they found out they had some. They had marines embarked. They pulled liberty in Sydney, and the marines went into this bar and found them there in drag. And they just beat the shit out of them."

"They'd be happier on the outside, with their own kind."

"Unless they had one ship, made it all gay."

"Sure, put 'em all on one ship."

"Then sink it."

Dan said slowly, "But isn't that what they used to say back when they didn't want blacks in the service? And then women?"

"Hey." The black officer put his hands on the table. "I resent that, man. I resent comparin' me to some faggot. It's natural bein' black. My dad was black. My ancestors was black. Guarantee you, their ancestors wasn't faggots."

Prince said, "I see what you mean about women. But you keep men and women apart. You don't have guys showering with the girls. You want to bend over, with one of them behind you? Or four or five of them?"

"Let me tell you about the discharge board I was on," said a supply officer. "Lebanon was getting hot; we just kept ironing out the water in the east Med. The captain was the junior skipper, so we kept getting hosed on liberty. We had such lousy liberty, we thought Soudha Bay was great. And this commissaryman starts seducing the kids in the galley. Eighteen, seventeen years old, they'd get detailed to mess duty. He'd take them down in the storeroom and tell them they didn't cooperate, they'd be there forever. Then he'd fuck them, till another kid came along he liked better. Finally one of them turned him in."

"That's not seduction. That's rape."

"Call it whatever you want. You just can't have seventeen-, eighteen-year-old kids in crowded berthing compartments with these people. Doc?"

"You've got a point. Young men often have profound doubts about their masculinity."

"How are we gonna recruit? Nobody wants their kid going to sea with a bunch of fags. Maybe it ain't their fault. I don't know. But if they can't help hitting on them, that means you got to keep them away from normal people."

The senior lieutenant said, "Bottom line: What are we out here for? Ships exist to sink other ships, okay? We need to focus on that, not get diverted by affairs among the crew. The day they let them in, they can let me out."

"Not on my ship. Not in my Navy."

"Yeah, at least with women you can put them all in the same compartment and have them indifferent to one another."

"You never been on the *Norton Sound.* Fucking bull dykes, all of them."

Dan looked around the table, at a wall of faces that had turned hostile.

" 'Scuse me, gentlemen, I got to clear the table now."

As they rose, he glanced at his watch. "Larry, I'm going diving this afternoon. Want to go? Any you guys want to come?"

"Not me. I don't go under the water unless I got a submarine around me. We got any divers?"

"Jonesy, but he got mono."

Dan said so long, shook hands. A couple of the men left before he got to them. Prince grabbed his cap off the peg and held it out.

"I can find my way out. You got things to do."

"No way. Gotta escort you, man. You could be one of those security tests."

"Thanks for coming over," Prince said when they got to the quarterdeck. "Stay in touch, hear? You goin' to the game this year?"

"We're going to be deployed for Army-Navy."

"Oh, yeah, us, too. What'm I thinking about? Well, we'll catch it on the tube. So long, buddy. Oh, and—"

Dan stopped as Prince did, looking up at the aft launcher, then glancing casually around. It was incredibly hot. The steel absorbed heat and radiated it again, cooking you from all sides. "What?" he said.

Prince extended an imaginary blade. He went to *en garde in quarte,* waited for Dan to respond, then lunged. Dan did a half-circle parry and riposted to the inside; Prince beat parried, laughed, and they disengaged. Dan felt slow and clumsy. He'd fenced for only one semester before going to lacrosse, mainly because Prince had beaten him every time they put the masks on. He saw the OOD watching in astonishment from the far side of the quarterdeck.

"A touch, I do confess it."

As they shook hands, Prince said in a low voice, "Dan, better lay off this homo stuff. It doesn't take much to make them think you're one."

"I'm not."

"I don't care if you are."

Dan's gaze locked suddenly with his classmate's. "You don't? In there, you said—"

"What else am I going to say in front of everybody? Like I said, I don't care. But if you are or think you might be—that happens sometimes—do what you have to do. But don't talk about it . . . to *anybody, ever.* Understand?"

Dan stared at him, catching his breath—at Larry Prince, the deputy brigade commander the year they'd graduated, someone he'd known for years.

"Thanks for the advice," he said quietly.

* * *

THEY were waiting by the brow when he got back. Jay Harper was standing by a pile of gear. Gary Lohmeyer was talking to the messenger. The damage control officer had asked to come along, said he was a diver, which had surprised Dan, since it didn't jibe with the impression he gave. Maybe he had misjudged the kid. Harper looked irritated as Dan trotted down the pier. "*There* he is. You about ready to go, shipmate?"

He and the chief warrant had had their "talk" out on deck one morning as a squall moved across the face of the water. To his surprise, Harper hadn't flared back at him. He just said quietly that yeah, he'd been in the wrong, that he wouldn't leave the bridge again. Dan had asked him then if there was something bothering him.

Harper had just shrugged. "I guess just that the King Snake is looking at punching out of this flea circus."

"Retiring?"

"It's getting to be time." The older man had looked off across the sea to where the sun braced the clouds with golden beams. "It's like after a while, the challenge is gone. There's nothing you haven't done a hundred times. No thrill, no kick."

"And?"

"I'm just thinking about when," Harper had said.

Now Dan told him, "Yeah, I'm ready. Let me run down, get my gear. Did you reserve tanks?"

"Waiting for us over near Base Ordnance. We'll swing by and pick 'em up in the truck."

He was in his stateroom, pulling out fins and mask, when Hank Shrobo put his head in. Seeing him, eyes like used ashtrays, brought back all the last two weeks, deep in the complexities of signal-flow diagrams and fault isolation: the anxiety, the ever-present sense of urgency, the glimpses of hope, then despair as once again the solution eluded them. "Yeah," Dan said. "Make my day; tell me you caught the Crud."

"Not quite. But we're nailing the fence closed."

"The battle problem?" Dan unwrapped his regulator, examined the hose.

"Oh . . . that. The program's almost finished. Then we'll load a clean tape and boot Elmo up." Elmo was what Williams had started calling the ACDADS. "We just might make your captain's deadline."

"Do you need me down there?"

"Not right now. Maybe for a test run later."

"Good. But you look like shit. Want to take a break, go swimming? I got a spare mask—"

"I'd better not, but thanks. I don't swim very well." The civilian seemed embarrassed by the invitation. What a strange guy, Dan thought. Could he be gay too? Or was he getting tunnel vision, like Harper had warned him about?

HARPER and Lohmeyer were waiting in the truck when he got back to the quarterdeck. He ran down the brow and threw his gear in, and climbed up.

Harper picked up the charged tanks at the Reef Raiders' shack, wedged them into the bed so they wouldn't roll, then headed south along the bay. The road clung to the hills, and as they bounced along, he could look off across the entrance to the airfield, and beyond that to the hills. They pulled off onto the sand not far from the lighthouse on Windward Point.

"Here it is," said Harper with a grand announcing gesture, as if he owned it or had discovered it. "The best fucking diving in the western hemisphere."

Dan looked out at it with the same mixed anticipation and dread he always had before a dive. Beyond the surf, the sea was a light blue, clear and pure, darkening rapidly to azure. Between blue and blue was a darker mottling, which meant sand between patches of grass or coral. Harper was telling them how nobody fished here, how clear it was. He pulled a speargun from behind the seat.

"They allow spearfishing here?" Dan asked him.

"You see anybody keeping tabs? There're groupers down there that'll swallow you alive." He grinned. "Kind of like my fucking wife, you know?"

The surf creamed among dark jagged rocks. Lohmeyer went in first, balancing on his fins till a sea reared in front of him, then diving in over it. Harper waded in, skinny legs gradually submerging but perfectly visible, bent, as if they were both broken. Dan waited for a wave, then swam out through the surf line. When he put his mask under, he could see powdery white sand engraved with riffles and small white fish the color of the sand.

He followed the others out, watching bubbles swirl as their fins pulled air down into the water. White sand crept past beneath him. A pale fish with spines drifted a few inches above it. It didn't swim off as he approached. It just waited, lifting its spines slightly. He decided anything that confident had to be poisonous, so he angled back toward the heaving silver surface.

A greenish shadow took shape: a coral head. Beyond it was another. The sand made fine white paths between them, like a Japanese garden. Angelfish browsed among the sea fans, and a school of blue tang angled away into the haze.

Silver bubbles drifted up. Lohmeyer and Harper sank slowly, hands to their masks. Dan felt for his mouthpiece, cleared it, and sucked a breath: air, cold and dry. He jackknifed down and the sea sealed over his head.

His breath squeaked and bubbled in his ears. He cleared them as he sank, then again. A sea turtle swam past a hundred feet away, thrusting itself through the water like a round rowboat. It trailed a huge appendage Dan hoped was its tail. They swam together over the coral heads, looking down. He kept craning around, looking for a 'cuda or a shark. But the enormous blueness seemed empty. Aside from the turtle, he didn't see anything at all, just the little chaetondontidae, bright as butterflies, that drifted in clouds above the coral heads.

Ahead, Harper pointed. Lohmeyer followed him around, angling left, and Dan, too. And they saw the wreck.

It lay at the base of a rock pinnacle. Reels of rusty steel cable sagged from the afterdeck. Hundreds of fish moved in and out of a black gape in its side, as if the wreck were breathing. The anchor chain stretched out across the bottom. Dan saw what looked like a circus wagon upright on the sand. As they closed, he saw it was a motor-generator truck, sitting on the bottom as if it had been parked there.

They investigated the wreck for a few minutes, then Harper pointed seaward. They followed him along the sloping bottom. Dan checked his depth gauge, then his watch.

As they dropped, the sea grew cooler against his skin. The light grew green, then blue. The vegetation dwindled. Again he noticed, with a thrill of apprehension, that there weren't any fish around at all now.

Then he saw where Cuba ended.

It was a drop-off, a sharp one. He checked his gauge again as they crossed the ragged rocky lip: 120 feet. Lohmeyer stopped and hovered, looking down. Harper glanced over his shoulder but kept swimming outward. Dan hesitated, then followed, feeling the upwelling in his face like a cold slow wind.

As they descended, a shudder crept up his back—a primeval fear of being trapped, of the dark, of the cold. It was deep blue above him; below, only an immense darkness. Was something moving down there? He imagined falling away into that abyss, being crushed. . . . No, the pressure wouldn't crush him; he'd just run out of air . . . a thousand feet deep out here. . . .

Something took shape from the blue-black. He blinked, not really comprehending what he saw. A steel hawser, big around as his thigh, stretched parallel to the cliff face. Coral festered slowly in brainlike knots. Harper hovered above it, looking off to the right and then the left, to where it stretched into invisibility again.

Something jabbed his side and he almost cried out. But it was only Lohmeyer, holding up his tank gauge and pointing upward. Dan wasn't sure he wanted to go back up. Part of him wanted to keep swimming down till he understood the dark, fathomed it, grasped it, knew.

But maybe you couldn't understand it till you were part of it. . . .

Harper turned, saw them, and at last nodded slowly to Lohmeyer's urgent pointing toward the light.

HE ran out of air and surfaced half a mile out. He turned on his back and finned slowly shoreward, trying to relax as the sea washed over him and came down the snorkel. It tasted bitter and warm. He felt vulnerable, like a lure being trolled slowly across the surface. He couldn't think of anything that was likely to look better to a shark than he did, silhouetted against the surface.

But at last the bottom came into view again, and he rested, letting the waves toss him around. He couldn't see the others. He'd lost them when he had to surface. Finally, he decided to go in on his own.

He came in at a bad place and got knocked around, but finally he staggered out. He looked up and down the beach, but he was alone. He was wondering if he ought to go back in and look for them when he caught sight of two black dots far out. He waved and the sun flashed off their masks and after a while one of them waved back.

When they came ashore, he helped them with their tanks. Lohmeyer pulled his mask off and blew his nose. A red thread mingled with the mucus. "A little squeeze," he said. He looked at Dan's leg. "You're bleeding, too."

"Lost an argument with one of those rocks."

Harper pulled the cooler off the truck. "Beer, anybody? Chips?"

The beer tasted great and so did the salty snacks. They stripped the rest of their gear off, then lay around and popped cans till Dan felt light-headed and detached. He forgot about the battle problem and the computers and Leighty and lay on the hot sand with his arm over his eyes and his mind as close to being turned off as it could get. Only the sand fleas kept him awake.

"Man," said Harper, "this is great. Isn't this great? All we need is some cunt bitches and we'd be in hog heaven."

"Did you see that manta?"

"You saw a manta ray, Gary?"

Lohmeyer fitted his glasses back onto a reddening nose. "On the way back in. I saw him from the side and I thought he was a shark.

Then he sort of canted over and I saw the wings. Jay tried to get close enough to shoot him, but he couldn't catch up."

Harper was still talking about women. "Ever teach a fifteen-year-old to suck cock? San Juan, when I was a radioman . . . Hoss, I got somebody I want you to meet, we get back to Charleston. Little lady name of Mary." He winked at Dan. "The lieutenant knows her *real* well."

He felt annoyed. "Isn't there anything else you can talk about but pussy, Harper?"

"Oh sure. Gash and twat and cooze and poontang. And bearded clams, come holes, fur burgers, beavers, nooky, muff pie . . ." He went on for at least five minutes while Lohmeyer giggled in admiration. Dan gave the younger officer a disgusted look.

"So," he said, hoping to change the subject, "you're really thinking about getting out?"

"Yeah. I've seen it all so many times, nothing's new anymore. And I need to put some time in on the bars."

"I think you put too much time in at the bars."

"I mean the ones I own. Need to show that forty-five to a couple people. Fuckers rip me off, I'll jam it up their assholes and pull the trigger."

Dan looked sideways at Harper's weak-chinned profile. He'd put his glasses back on after the dive, and his bald patch was getting burned. Sometimes he couldn't figure the chief warrant. "You better cover your head," Dan told him. "You're gonna burn."

"Hey, ask me if I give a fuck."

"You'll make this deployment with us, though, won't you?" Lohmeyer said anxiously.

"Oh sure. Don't worry about that, shipmate. There's a bar in Istanbul I'll take you to. Best belly dancers in the world, and you get a free massage after you get your ashes hauled."

"How are you ever gonna give the Navy up?" Dan asked him. "You enjoy it too much."

"There's some good times, Hoss. Never said there weren't. But it'd be different if they paid us. You might not notice. Officers don't do too bad, but half the junior enlisted are on food stamps. You know Chief Alaska? He works at a pizza place when we're in, evenings and weekends, to make ends meet. I shit you not, he's the goddamn guy flings them up in the air."

"Like that Marion Sipple," said Dan.

"Sipple? What about him?"

"I figure that's what he was into. You know, stealing the funds, the stuff. I figure that's what happened to the silver."

"What happened to the silver?"

Dan blinked. He was a little toasted, but he'd racked his brain long enough over the audits to have an opinion at least. "I figure, I never met him, but say he needed money for something. Maybe he was into gambling. And so he stole the cash from the operating funds, and then he saw silver anodes in the supply catalog and ordered them, then took them to a jeweler and sold them. Then he goes after the night-vision scopes and stuff. Ever been to those pawnshops down on Spruill? You see binoculars and stuff there all the time; you know it's off the ships."

"You could be right," said Harper. "And you know what? That's going to keep happening just as long as they don't pay us a comparable wage. This is shit, scraping along from paycheck to paycheck. And guys like you, got three-quarters of what you make tooken out before you ever see it. I don't see how you stand in line for that."

"It sucks all right," said Dan. He felt bitter about it again. Why couldn't *she* get a job? She was so fucking independent, sure, till it was time to fend for herself. Then she was happy to run to the judge and take the biggest handout she could get.

Harper said, "Say, did you see that movie about the guy and the girl who find the treasure? What was it? They were divers. Jacqueline Bissett was in it."

"*The Deep*," Lohmeyer muttered.

"That's it, *The Deep*. Remember when they find the gold? I was really into that. Did you see that?"

"Everybody likes those kinds of movies," Dan said. "It's like wish fulfillment."

"You want to go in again, Jay?" asked Lohmeyer. "Try to catch one of those waves?"

"Naw, I'm just gettin' dried out. Watch those fucking rocks or you'll break your fucking head."

The ensign went down to the water again. Dan turned over, watched the black dot of Lohmeyer's head bobbing around.

Harper said, "What you think of that kid?"

"Gary? He seems okay."

"He's kind of slow. Always around, but he never says much. Kind of a klutz."

"He's got a tough job, taking over damage control right here in Gitmo."

"Yeah, maybe," said Harper. He belched. "You know, stuff like that—finding treasure—sometimes it happens. Sometimes it really happens." Ice rattled as he rooted out another beer. "Lemme ask you something. What would you figure, you were in that guy's shoes?"

"Lohmeyer?"

"No, fuck Lohmeyer. I mean the guy in the movie. Say you could make a pile of money. Nobody knows about it; nobody gets hurt. Only thing, it's illegal. What would you do?"

"What, if I found a wreck full of gold and jewels?"

"Yeah. Would you turn it over to the cops?"

"Hell no."

"Course not. And what would you do with it?"

Dan said, knowing it was a fantasy but warming to it, "What would I do? First thing, get my own place. I'd like to have an apartment, not have to make out on the damn couch, wondering if the girl's kid is going to come down in his jammies. Then I'd send some money home to my mom and my brother."

"Didn't know you had a brother."

"Yeah, two. One of them's trying to work his way through college; he could use some bucks."

"What else?"

"I'd probably save the rest of it."

"You don't have very expensive tastes," said Harper. "No boat? No big new motorcycle?"

Dan shrugged. Already the momentary gloss had worn off the daydream.

"What's the matter?"

"Nothing. Just that there isn't any cargo of gold and jewels. And even if there was, my fucking ex-wife and her lawyers would end up with three-quarters of it."

"Yeah, but there's other ways to make spending money."

"Like how?"

"There's some things I could let you in on," said Harper, "if you wanted."

"What kind of things?"

"That would depend on what kind of risk you wanted to take on. What if I let you in on the bar business?"

"What, you mean invest money? I don't have any."

Lohmeyer came back then, and Harper fell silent. Dan thought about his proposal for a little while—if it was a proposal—then dismissed it. He didn't have anything to invest, and if he did, it wouldn't be in anything Harper ran. The sun beat down as they dozed, and his thoughts drifted. Harper's raunchy talk and the sun and the beer made him wish he was somewhere he could at least see a woman. He'd have to make some kind of decision when he got back about whether to see Beverly again. Or maybe Sibylla Baird. His prick went hard between his belly and the warm sand as he remembered the garden, the smell of roses.

A battered station wagon turned off up the beach and a black woman and a little girl got out. The child ran toward the water, and Dan's eyes followed them. The woman swung past them, carrying a picnic basket. "Man, you see that?" muttered Harper.

Dan said, "Nice legs."

"But not great," said Lohmeyer. "A little fat—"

"You're wrong, Ensign. They're perfect," said Harper lazily, lifting his head to watch. Sand coated one cheek, like a sugared doughnut. "All women got perfect legs—feet on one end and pussy on the other. Man, look at that. It'd be just like licking the cream filling out of an Oreo."

Dan lost it then. His sorrow and his apprehension dissolved, and the others grinned at him as he quivered on the hot sand, holding his stomach in helpless laughter.

They were interrupted by the sound of engines snorting and echoing from the hills. Dan rolled over and looked.

Two jeeps were bumping along between the dunes, followed by a truck. They turned before they got to the station wagon, the woman watching them, shading her eyes, and braked at an observation tower. The gate of the truck came down and several marines jumped out, then slid out a long box.

"What the hell?"

"They're setting up a machine gun."

"M-sixty, looks like," said Harper. "Fuckin' Commies'll be sorry, they try and come ashore here." He got up abruptly, mimicked tommy-gunning the sea. He howled, "Nuke 'em till they glow, then shoot 'em in the dark!"

"We better find out what's going on." Dan got up and trudged over. The sand was hot on his bare feet. But before he got there, one of the marines cupped his hands and yelled, "This beach is closed. Leave immediately. The beach is secured."

The woman called to her daughter, waving her in from where she stood examining a dead fish. "We better get back to the ship," said Lohmeyer, and his voice held a note of alarm.

WHEN they got back, they found that the base had gone to full alert. Dan immediately checked that the ready mount was manned and that CIC had comms with the Fire Direction Center. He made sure Adamo had the Phalanxes loaded and that they had war shots lined up in the launcher drums and that Horseheads was setting up a watch rotation. When he was satisified they conformed to the new alert status, he stopped by his room, pulled some clean khakis on, and went down once again to the computer room.

28

LEIGHTY shoved himself back from his desk in sudden irritation. The notice he'd just read directed all ships' commanding officers to form a communications security review board. The board had to meet immediately, review all records and clearances pertaining to classified materials, and make a letter report to their respective type commander. It had to be comprised of the exec, the operations officer, and at least two other officers or chiefs, none of whom could be the primary or assistant CMS custodians.

More lost hours, more pointless palaver and time-eating correspondence. His teeth set in helpless anger. Every year, it got worse. Higher authority's reaction to every failure or shortcoming was to impose a straitjacket of reports and checklists on subordinate commands. Each new fleet or type commander instituted new programs, inspections, requirements, but the old ones were never canceled. And of course no one ever considered that the total number of man-hours aboard ship was finite. He glanced at the next document in the stack the yeoman had brought up. It was the pre-overseas movement inspection checkoff list. An accompanying letter requested an initial report no later than August first and weekly progress reports thereafter. He stared at it, shaking his head slowly.

He rolled his chair back a few more inches and rubbed his face, then kneaded the nape of his neck. A headache throbbed at the rear of his skull. I'm letting it get to me, he thought. Can't let myself get too stressed out. Back in port, he'd have strolled down to the basketball court, burned it out in a fast pickup game. But right now, he was juggling several anxieties at once: the NIS investigation, refresher training, the problem with the ACDADS, the alert status, and whether the presence of a powerful Soviet task force in Cienfuegos had anything to do with it. And whenever he tried to deal with any of them, the paperwork began to pile up. . . . Well, it's only for a few more days, he told himself, digging his fingers into the knotted muscle of his shoulders. Then they'd leave Cuba and hopefully more than one of his problems behind.

He rested for a few minutes, trying to calm himself, but the headache pounded on. Finally, he got up and went into the bedroom. He stripped off his uniform and bagged it for the steward, laid out fresh khakis on the bed. He did a hundred push-ups and a hundred situps, then stepped into the shower. He turned it on, wet himself down, turned it off. He soaped down, working it into a lather in the distilled water the ship's evaporators made, then rinsed down again with fifteen seconds of steaming water.

When he came out, he felt better. He put on a dressing gown his wife had given him and sat on the sofa.

At least they were doing better training-wise. Their overall score was rising after a lackluster start. Making progress here and there. . . . But it seemed that as soon as he defused one situation, another grew worse. The Sanderling thing had worried him most. For a time, he'd feared it would explode, tearing apart crew, ship, wardroom.

He'd seen it happen before, and had carried that horrifying example in the back of his mind ever since. He'd been a junior officer then—in Vietnam, in a riverine squadron, the Brown Water Navy: not massive ships, but landing craft and PBRs; not missiles and computers, but men in fatigues with .50-caliber guns and grenade launchers and M16s, patrolling the shallow swampy tributaries of the Mekong. Ninety percent of trade and traffic in the Delta moved via river and canal, not by road, and the Delta covered nearly a third of the Republic of Vietnam. He'd arrived in-country in the middle of an ambitious attempt to blockade the Viet Cong's southern logistic pipeline out of Cambodia. After six months setting up and leading sweeps and strikes, establishing bases deep in VC-controlled territory, and nearly getting his ass shot off several times, he'd gotten orders up to the COMRIVRON, to squadron headquarters in Saigon.

He'd known almost at once about the commodore and his staff. And there had been opportunities. But that had been when he was still uncertain. Homosexuals wore dresses and imitated Bette Davis. He could not be one of them. In heat, humidity, fatigue, and danger, in the shared risk and terror of combat, there was emotional closeness to other men that didn't necessarily result in physical affection. Yes, he'd loved those he served with. He'd wept when they died. And so had the other men. Then, too, something about the senior officers at his new command put him off. They were too obvious. It was tolerated; that was the unspoken message. But something about it had made him wary, so he'd rebuffed their advances.

Only two months later, his self-imposed isolation had saved him. In a moment of mistaken judgment, the commodore put one of his friends on the staff in for a Bronze Star. Said friend, unfortunately, had never been out in a Swift, never been in the field, never been shot at in his life, in fact. The resulting investigation, initiated and controlled directly from COMNAVFORV, had torn the staff apart and reached out into the operating forces, uncovering a network of liaisons that had ended dozens of careers with dishonorable discharges. A career marine, a master sergeant, had gone out into the center of the command compound and pulled the pin on a grenade, then stood looking down at it as people shouted to him to get rid of it. Before a burst of smoke and dust obliterated him.

Yes, he'd learned from that.

So when Diehl had come aboard, he'd given him full access, full cooperation. He could talk to anyone about anything, Leighty had told him. If there was a homosexual ring, no one aboard was more eager to uncover it than the commanding officer. And the agent had done his snooping, collected a dredgeful of innuendo and rumors. But when they sifted through it, nothing was left. There was no evidence of murder and no evidence that anyone aboard had been sexually involved with the seaman. As far as the Navy was concerned, Benjamin Sanderling could lie quietly in his watery grave.

The outside phone rang. He started, then crossed the room. "USS *Barrett*, commanding officer speaking," he said.

"Captain, this is the base duty officer. Do you have a moment to discuss your readiness status?"

Leighty briefed him on his weapons status and readiness to get under way. Then he asked if there was any new word. The duty officer didn't know of any, said he was just verifying that they were on alert. He asked about the tropical depression. The duty officer said it was tracking to the north and that they wouldn't even feel it in Guantánamo Bay. He sounded hurried, as if he had other ships to call, so finally Leighty let him go. He looked at the desk again, file folders, messages, the blue covers of official correspondence, and made himself sit down and pick up the pen.

Instead of working, though, he found himself thinking again about Sanderling.

Yes, he'd been attracted to the boy. Sanderling, too, had been trying to come to terms with his sexuality, but in incredibly risky ways. He'd tried to advise him. But it hadn't worked, and the boy had destroyed himself. And he could not even cry about it, locked in his carapace . . . could give no outward sign or demonstration of his rage and sorrow. He himself had always felt life was a gift, something to be grasped and prized. Everyone had pain; no one had a monopoly on that. Accepted for what it was, life was full of beauty.

Like Lenson . . . clean-limbed, spare, even graceful in a way, with those steady, serious gray eyes. Losing the beard had made him even more attractive. Sitting next to him during their interview, he'd felt the temptation. And for a moment, he'd fancied Dan felt it, too. But then he'd taken fright, rushed out. Well, he hadn't meant anything by his offer of friendship. He'd tried to keep it professional.

He rubbed his chin absently. Or was he fooling himself?

He blinked and found he was still at the desk and that he had not yet made even a dent in his evening's work. Sighing, he picked up the POM checkoff list and started to read, absently rubbing the back of his neck.

AN hour later, he let himself quietly out of the cabin. He spent a few minutes on the bridge, talking with the officer of the deck. At this ready status, the OOD stood on the bridge, not the quarterdeck, and the engine room was skeleton-manned, too. Everything looked good for a quiet night. He looked out at the other ships ranged along the pier, the way the shadows stretched out from them as the afternoon waned into evening. "I'll be taking a turn around the ship," he said. "Maybe half an hour. Then I'll be back in my cabin."

"Yes, sir."

He went down to the main deck and strolled aft, stretching his legs as the dusk stole in, and he reached the stern at the same time as it did. He stood there with the evening smokers, looking across the bay as some duty boatswain in the sky flipped the stars on one by one. They shimmered in the flat water, hanging above the black hills to the west. Somewhere beyond them was Havana. One more week, he thought, if we pass. Hit their liberty port for a few days of R and R, then back to Charleston, back to Dougie and Heather and Jeannette.

The ACDADS was the big question mark. He'd wondered on and off whether he should go over and see Captain Grieve. It was probably not too late to retract his commitment to run the battle problem in Mode 3. Woollie had offered the out. But he still felt he'd been right. If the concept of an automated ship had validity, there should be a test—preferably before the ultimate test of battle, and before vast amounts were sunk into follow-on classes. A version of ACDADS was being considered for the new *Ticonderoga*-class Aegis cruisers, and no doubt it would be incorporated into the next destroyer class, the as-yet-unnamed DDG-51's. If the concept was faulty, now was the time to find out. True, he was running some personal risk, but he had covered himself with a speedletter to Commodore Niles explaining his reasoning. The commodore had acknowledged it rather tersely, but he hadn't disagreed with his decision.

He stood with his hands in his pockets, revolving it all in his mind. And again his thoughts drifted back to the interview with Lenson. Had he acted honorably? Telling the younger officer what he had?

He didn't enjoy lying. But you could evade questions only so long. At some point, you had to answer them. But what choice did they leave you? If he admitted what he was—and it wasn't *all* that he was; he was also a father, a family man, active in the church and the PTA, a dog lover, and a professional naval officer—if he was honest, he'd be pulled from command within hours and find himself out of the service as swiftly as a board could be convened.

He had decided long ago that if the only way he could serve his country was under false colors, then he would accept that as a condition of service. What had he said to George not that long ago—that a stratagem, a *ruse de guerre,* was not considered dishonorable? When you were on your own in enemy territory, no one condemned you for lying, not if it was the only way you could accomplish your mission.

The point at issue, really, was whether his sexual orientation affected good order and discipline. If it made no difference in how well he did his job, then he could defend a certain level of subterfuge as a justifiable circumvention of an unenlightened and mistaken policy. It was a trade-off: his family, position, and career in exchange for his silent acceptance of the mask. But all of human existence consisted of trade-offs. Life did not consist of choices between good and evil. It was a buffet-table selection among a multiplicity of goods, a plethora of evils. If what was within his heart remained there, what difference did it make? None at all, as far as he could see. . . .

Two men were talking not far from him, back by the antenna-service platform. He wasn't really listening, but whatever part of your mind stood watch while you wool-gathered thought he heard his name.

"Yeah, he's one," the mutter came, barely interpretable on the sultry wind.

He turned his head slowly. He couldn't see who was speaking, whether they were black or white, only that they were both smoking—two red coals, like dying stars transmitting to each other in the dark.

"If you ask me, all the fucking officers need a goddamn testosterone transfusion. This fuckin' ship is full of fuckin' pansies."

"What can we do about it?"

"*We* can't do a fuckin' thing, man. Just watch your ass when you pick up the soap. The fuckin' skipper, he'll suck your dick, anybody goes up at night, knocks on his door."

"I knew something was funny . . . but the skipper? You're shittin' me."

"I shit you not, Jack. You can tell there's something sick waiting to blow on this banana boat. Hey, one of 'em touches me, I'll beat his fucking ass, you know? I'll fucking kill the fucker. Just among us chickens, they ought to round them all up, put 'em in a camp. Then we figure out what to do with them. . . ."

He couldn't tell who they were, even what department. All he knew was that his hands tightened on the lifeline. He cleared his throat and they fell silent. The coals wavered, then described outward arcs. The butts hissed in the still water. When he looked back again, both shadows were gone.

He stood motionless in the hot darkness, looking across the bay. He panted shallowly, quickly. When he was sure he wasn't going to throw up, he headed back to his cabin.

29

ON-SCENE leader! Cooling compartment two-fifty-four-Echo!"

The instant the water spray hit the dogged-down door, it flashed into steam. Dan manhandled the nozzle into the porthole, angling it to play around inside the compartment on the other side. He counted ten seconds, straining to hold the heavy nozzle up, then jerked his head. The access man knocked the dogs free with six fast hammer blows and jerked the door open. "Compartment door cooled and undogged!" he bawled.

Staring into the wall of yellow flame, blinking behind the mask, Dan had a moment of wholehearted fear. His lungs pumped pure oxygen in and out rapidly.

Sweeping the blast of water from side to side, he gathered his courage and jumped through.

At his feet, a black pool glowed with a faint blue unearthly flame. Then, faster than the eye could follow, it ignited with a hollow *whump* into a roaring lake of white fire. Fluttering yellow tongues raced across above his head, into a webwork of soot-blackened pipes and I beams. He wheeled, trying to quench it before it reached the crack in the pipe. But he couldn't turn fast enough; the heavy hose resisted him.

The fine oil mist ignited with a hollow boom that knocked his mask askew and blew him into the men behind him. He got a lungful of the lighter-fluid stink of distillate fuel before he could clear and restart the OBA. "Water curtain," he coughed, then yelled, "On-scene leader! Class Bravo fire, compartment two-fifty-four-Echo. Advancing! Move in!"

The fire roared around them now, licking up through the gratings under their boots. The heat scorched his face even through the shield. Suddenly, a halo of water appeared around his head, snuffing back the writhing torch of burning oil. The men behind him surged forward. Dan dug his boots in to avoid being pushed into the flames. Squinting into the glare and heat, he hauled desperately at the unyielding iron-stiff canvas of the charged fire hose.

Around the scared, sweating men, the flaking concrete of the firefighting training building was blackened by decades of burning oil. Above them, inky smoke rolled away into the bright sky. A jeep marked with a red cross waited on the apron. The instructors hovered just out of range of the flames, which were directed and controlled by valves. One was yelling, but Dan couldn't make it out over the roar. His mask was still awry and he was getting more smoke than oxygen. His skin felt like frying chitterlings. But he held his ground, sweeping the blast of mist steadily across the base of the flames that leapt up from beneath his feet, from above, from all around them.

TODAY, the last day before the battle problem, *Barrett* lay pierside while the crew tweaked and peaked before the final test. The alert condition only added to the sense of urgency. Transports screamed in, wheeling over the piers to touch down at Leeward Field. They were landing advance elements of the 38th Marine Amphibious Unit, and they screamed out filled with dependents and civilian personnel. A squadron of Air Force OV-10s had reinforced the armed A-4s, and he saw them orbiting occasionally, low-winged two-engine jets that looked slow but that could maneuver amid the low dry hills like crop dusters.

The funny thing was, there was no official word as to what was going on. There were rumors, of course. Castro was dying; there was going to be a civil war. Or that he'd sworn to take Guantánamo Bay at last. But officially it was just that "intelligence sources" had detected increased Cuban activity and the alert and buildup were purely precautionary.

It looked like a lot of activity for a precaution. But like everyone else aboard, he didn't have time to think about anything but what was in front of him at any given moment to do or solve, and when lights-out went, he fell on his bunk without taking his clothes off or brushing his teeth. Only another five days, he'd think before the black closed over him. Only another four. And last night: Day after tomorrow, and that'll be it.

And now it was only one more day.

* * *

WHEN the last flicker was extinguished, he started backing his team out. "Line One, level out. . . . Water off at the Y gate. . . . Don't kneel down; you'll get a grate burn." When they were all out safely and the open sky burned above him, he stripped his mask off and leaned against a bulkhead. The steel scorched his shoulder through the suit and he flinched upright, staggered, almost fell.

"On-scene leader: Fire is out throughout the compartment."

"Set the reflash watch," Dan bawled, then started to cough and couldn't stop. He dropped the hose and doubled over. He could breathe out fine, but he couldn't inhale without setting it off again. The corpsman ran over with the green cylinder of oxygen, but he waved him wordlessly to wait. Finally his breath came back a little, then a little more. The others bent or squatted on the shimmering asphalt, sweat running off their faces as if they'd just emerged from a river. Finally, he was able to croak, "Get the gear off. Get in the shade and drink some fucking water before you guys pass out."

HE showered and changed, feeling weak, as if he'd been fasting. He had a steam burn on his neck, but it didn't seem bad enough for sick bay. He was sitting in the department office looking vacantly at his crammed-solid in box when Ensign Steel stuck his head in. "Mr. Lenson, got a second?"

"Yeah. What is it, Ron?"

Steel let himself in. "I got my maintenance hat on today, sir." The electrical officer was also in charge of reviewing and running the ship's planned maintenance system. "Okay," said Dan, trying to refocus. "What is it?"

"Jeez, what's wrong with your throat? You sound like the XO."

"Sucked some smoke over at the trainer. What you got?"

"Sir, Chief Narita was aboard doing spot checks this morning. He hit on CE division."

Dan glanced up. Harper's division. "They failed," Steel said, then explained why.

"You mean they're not doing the maintenance? Or that—"

"Not the item they spot-checked—the filter on the UCC-one teletypewriter converter. The monthly record said they'd been changed, but when the instructor pulled them, they were dirty."

"I'll take care of it," said Dan. Steel nodded and left, and Dan started punching buttons on the phone. The filter itself wasn't a big deal. But saying it was done when it wasn't, that was bad news.

Harper wasn't in the computer room, the electronics repair shop, or his stateroom. Dan frowned, then dialed the quarterdeck. "Hi. Mr. Lenson here. Can you pass the word for Mr. Harper, please?"

The 1MC said, "Chief Warrant Officer Harper, dial two-three-four." Dan's phone buzzed two seconds later.

"Jay, where are you?"

"In the crypto locker. I'm classified materials custodian, remember?"

"You're also the electronic maintenance officer, and I just got a report about gun-decked maintenance."

"Oh, fuck me. . . . Cool your jets, Dan. The guys've been busy as a dog with two dicks."

"I understand that, but you don't mark maintenance done when it isn't. Who's your PMS petty officer?"

"Williams, and you know how busy he is. Anyway, those filters, the periodicity's wrong; they change them way too often."

"If the periodicity's wrong, submit a feedback report and get it changed." Dan felt his temper going. "Look, I'm not going to argue with you. I want your maintenance either done or properly postponed in accordance with the manual. Is that clear?"

Harper didn't answer. A second later, to Dan's astonishment, came the unmistakable click of the phone being hung up.

"You bastard," he muttered. "Okay, let's have this out."

The red light was on over the vault door. Dan pulled a wrench off a bracket and hammered on the thick steel so hard, a chip of gray paint came off. But no sound came from inside. Enraged now, he went down to the quarterdeck, looked up the number of the registered publications room, and dialed Harper there.

"Crypto, Harper."

"Did you just hang up on me?"

"I think we got cut off."

"I was beating down your door. Didn't you hear me?"

"Nobody has access to this space but me and the comm officer, Lieutenant."

"I want you out in the passageway in four seconds or you're going to spend your next liberty restricted to the ship."

"Working," said Harper, and Dan heard again that sardonic, insolent note.

When he got back to the centerline passageway, Harper was locking the vault. He turned coolly to Dan. "Okay, what you need?"

"First, I want that weekly schedule fixed. Then I want you and Williams in my office with your maintenance records."

"I'll do that, Lieutenant, but I got something to say, too. I don't like being threatened with the loss of my liberty. You do that to some fucking seaman, not to me."

"Oh," said Dan. A tide of fatigue-fed anger was obliterating his self-control. "Is that right? Or else what?"

"Or else you and me go down on the fucking pier and go head-to-head, shipmate."

Suddenly, the fire curtain descended between him and his anger. He knew what it was made of: the fear that he was like his father. "I've got a better idea. How about this: You shut the fuck up and do as you're told," Dan said coldly, turning away.

But to his surprise, he felt Harper's hand on his shoulder. He whipped around, doubling his fists. But just at that moment, the 1MC said, *"This is a drill; this is a drill. . . . Security alert! Security alert. Away the security-alert team and the backup alert force!"*

HE froze as Harper sprinted away. The chief warrant was in charge of the security-alert team, the force that responded to unauthorized personnel attempting to board the ship or to intrusion alarms in the missile magazines or Radio Central. When they were called away, everybody else stayed in place or else got "shot." Within seconds, two gunner's mates stormed forward from the hangar. One carried a .45, the other a pump shotgun. "You see the intruder?" the guy with the riot gun yelled.

"No."

When they were gone, he sidled cautiously to the nearest door and let himself out onto the weather decks.

Below him, the sound of boots on metal told him they were sanitizing the main deck. A whistle blast echoed, followed by Harper's shout. Dan looked down, to see him standing by the lifelines, gesturing furiously. "Move, move, move, move, move, move! Secure each area, then move on! Stay out of your partner's goddamn line of fire! He can't shoot through you!" Faces running with sweat, Chief Miller, Cephas, and Antonio broke from behind a bulkhead, one by one, the two others covering the runner, crossed an open area at a sprint, and skidded to cover behind a coaming. A second later, their weapons leveled and a sharp series of clicks sounded as they steadied and squeezed off at an imaginary opponent.

Dan had to admit that usually the chief warrant was dedicated, sharp, effective. But lately, he seemed to be dropping the ball, getting a short-timer's attitude. Like this maintenance thing . . . but how important was it? Maybe Harper was right, changing filters wasn't that big a deal.

And maybe even gun-decking your records wasn't that big a deal, either, considering some of the other things that went on aboard *Barrett.*

He stopped, blinking in the sunlight, wondering what was happening to him.

* * *

THAT evening at 2100, all hands met in the helo hangar. Dan went up early, but everybody else had the same idea; the hose reels and boxes were all occupied. The men squatted, heads in their hands. They looked tired beyond caring, and he heard voices raised in the midships corridor. Angry shouts were quelled by Chief Oakes's roar. Yeah, everybody was on edge.

He found a place he could perch. As he did so, something crackled in his pocket. He felt around for the letter and opened it again.

It had come in that afternoon at mail call—a plain envelope, his name and the ship's name in pencil. An adult hand had added the Fleet Post Office zip code. Inside was a piece of lined school paper.

Dear Leutenant Dan,

I hope it is all right if I write to you on your ship. I asked the lady at the post office and she said it will get to you okay like this.

I miss you, Dan. Wish we could go riding on your motocice. Could you send me a hat so I can wear it at school? From the ship. I would like to go with you and see your ship sometime when you get back.

We got our school pictures today. Here is one for you on the ship the USS *Barrett.*

Sincerely,
Your friend,
Billy Strishauser

He folded it again. Poor kid. He'd send him a USS *Barrett* hat, and a T-shirt. . . . The smile left his lips gradually. He leaned back against the bulkhead and closed his eyes.

"Sir . . ."

He flinched awake. Ensign Paul took his hand off Dan's thigh and said, "Sorry, sir. You were about to fall off."

"Thanks, Martin." He straightened and saw the XO fiddling with a mike. The next moment, Vysotsky's voice rolled out.

"Can I have your attention, please."

Men shook the sleepers awake. Dan frowned, glancing around, but didn't see the captain.

"Okay, listen up," said Vysotsky. He paused, glancing at his watch, then went on. "Tomorrow morning is the final exercise, what we've all been waiting for. The instructors will test everything we've learned and see how well we put it together under stress. To pass, we've got to show we can fight the ship, take a hit, extinguish fires, stop flooding. We've got to show them we've learned our first aid and self-aid and that we can transport and care for a large number of wounded.

"Now, remember, there won't be a single thing they ask us to do that we haven't drilled over and over. The only new element will be the mass conflagration. Again, we've drilled all the damage control and fire fighting. The difference will be that tomorrow there'll be live fire hoses, foam and smoke generators to make things more authentic. It will be as close to battle as we can get without actually taking a hit. There'll be fifteen evaluators, so don't even think about breaking your seal or sneaking a cigarette.

"After that, if we pass—I know you've all been waiting for this—the next port is . . ."

The crew was riveted. Vysotsky milked the suspense before he finished: ". . . Guadeloupe, in the French Windward Islands."

The crew murmured as the exec went on. "Not a port the USN visits a lot, but Senior Chief Oakes has been there. He says it's a great place to relax and unwind. I think you'll enjoy it.

"Okay, Mr. Lohmeyer, over to you."

The damage control officer looked daunted and sleepless. He adjusted his glasses as he said, "Okay," cleared his throat, said louder, "Okay! I went over last week and talked to the DCA on the *Canisteo* after their mass conflag to get a feel for what they're going to throw at us. They're basically going to try to burn us and then sink us. First will be the fighting portion, when the ship goes to full auto and defends itself against air and surface threats—whatever they decide to heave at us.

"That'll be graded separately, but it'll end with either a torpedo or a missile hit. That will knock out all comms except for the sound-powered phones and messengers. We've got to find the holes and plug them, find the fires and put them out. The damage control chief and the XO will track damage from the bridge. I'll be in DC Central working the structural-strength and overall stability problem.

"Now, we may think we got this stuff memorized, but it's gonna be different when we're taking water, injured guys are screaming and running through the compartments, and the smoke's so thick that you can't see your hand in front of your face. In the middle of everything, they're gonna rupture our fire main, and we'll have to patch it. There's gonna be shoring needed, and it's gonna be someplace with a curving bulkhead, so we got to figure it out right the first time.

"The good news is, that last part is only about an hour. When they're satisfied, they'll pass 'silence' over the 1MC and Woollie will come on and announce the grade. So we'll know right away if we've passed or not.

"Okay . . . that's all I have, sir."

Vysotsky took the mike back. "Thanks, Gary. Okay, where are my department heads? Instead of eight o'clock reports tonight, let's do them right here, let the whole crew know where we stand. Mr.

Giordano, are our engineers ready? How do we stand on the louver intake heaters?"

"We got the parts kit, but the bolts are the wrong size, sir. Anyway, that won't hurt us tomorrow. We got a problem in the number one gas turbine generator, the fourteenth stage bleed adjust valve, but I think we can get it fixed tonight. The fire pumps—"

"What's wrong with the fire pumps?"

"Number three motor is grounded. We can maintain loop pressure, though."

"Even in a casualty mode?"

"Yes, sir," said Giordano. "Aside from that, my major worry's water. SIMA overhauled the pumps in the distillate plant, but we broke the flex pipe putting them back in. That and the way the safeties keep lifting on the waste heat boilers means we may have to go on water hours in Guadeloupe."

"We'll be able to get fresh water there. I'm more worried about tomorrow. Mr. Quintanilla?"

"Sir, the starboard anchor windlass is back in operation. No other casualties in the Operations Department. Comms will be set up in accordance with Annex K of the CTG forty-three point two opgen."

"Combat systems?"

Dan stood and said, "Phalanx electronic cooling system, the water low-flow switch is inoperative. Parts are on order. No operational impact."

"How do we stand on alert status, Mr. Lenson?"

"Sir, all the ships in port have been issued new targeting plans, comm plans, and call for fire procedures. We can control aircraft, as well. If they want us to come on-line to defend the base, we can."

"Okay, the big question: Are we going to be able to fight the battle problem in full auto, like we committed to?"

Dan took a breath. "We're going to try, sir."

Vysotsky went down the other departments, then looked around. Dan did, too, but Leighty still wasn't there. The XO cleared his throat. "Well, that's about it. The overall score so far is forty of forty-eight evolutions sat. Not terrific, but enough to pass if we ace this bear tomorrow. If we don't . . . we'll just do it all over again.

"I guess that's all. . . . Any questions?"

"Any word on that hurricane, sir? Is that going to hurt our liberty?"

"Lieutenant Cannon?"

The navigator: "Don't worry about the weather. It'll be a little rough, but the storm should pass to the north of us."

There were no other questions. Vysotsky dismissed them, and the men stood slowly and began to file out.

* * *

DAN made a last check of his spaces, telling people to knock off, get some sleep. Shrobo and Chief Dawson were optimistic about the ACDADS fix, which cheered him up. He turned in a little before midnight.

Then he lay wide awake in the darkened stateroom, brain buzzing like a cycling relay. Through the hiss of the ventilators, he could hear an occasional clank as the boatswains finished rigging something. His eye returned to the green luminescence of his clock. In four hours—no, three and a half now—reveille would go. And it would be time to find out if all their work would succeed . . . or go for nothing.

He forced himself to close his eyes.

HE was jerked awake in the dark by the phone. He heard the cursing from the bunk below as his roommate groped for it, listened, then said, "It's yours." Dan leaned over and the smooth curved plastic found his hand.

"Dan? This is the XO."

"Yes, sir." He blinked sleep scum off his eyeballs, trying to make sense of the clock. "Is it . . . is it reveille yet, sir?"

"No," said Vysotsky. "It's only oh-three hundred. But I need to get you on your feet, give you a quick heads-up to what's going on."

"Okay, sir, what's going on?"

"We're not doing the battle problem today."

"We're not?"

"No," said the heavy grating voice. "We're still getting under way, but not for that. That's all on hold now. There's been . . . a little change of plan."

IV

THE EXODUS

30
At Sea

THE sun came out for an hour around noon, briefly gilding turbulent swells the color of new cane leaves. Then waned again, veiled by high wispy clouds, aligned as if radiating from some far-off point beyond the view of the fifteen people in the two small boats that tossed and rolled in the grip of the sea.

Tomás had put up the mast pole, a piece of pipe stolen from the sugar mill, and set the sail. The wind was strong and steady, and as soon as the crazy quilt of stitched sacking climbed the pole, it bellied out, cracking and slapping. But after half an hour of shouting and adjusting ropes, both craft were scudding along, zigzagging as Augustín fought the tiller.

As they gathered speed, something funny happened. The waves were still huge, but they didn't jerk and slam them about as they had before. Now they lifted the boats gradually, the skiff first, then the bigger boat. Tilted them forward, making them race along for a few yards, and then let them down again, where they swayed, the sail slatting and sagging, till the next wave rose astern.

And gradually, Augustín learned to guess what the sea would do, and their rippling trail unrolled across the murky heaving surface nearly in a straight line—headed west.

The people from Batey Number 3 lay in them, heads nodding with each roll, sprawled out with shirts or arms over their faces, legs propped on thwarts or each other's stomachs. They looked like two boatfuls of dead rocking across the sea.

When Graciela woke, she felt dizzy and a backache pounded at her kidneys. She lay inert, feeling the boat roller-coastering forward under her, listening to the sea bubble past. It wasn't uncomfortable, really, except for her wet clothes and the itching where they chafed. Of course, she hadn't been able to stretch out for two days and nights. So that now lying in an inch of water in the bottom of a pitching boat was actually almost comfortable. The backache, sure, but after three times she knew that this close to the *parto*, she could be in a feather bed and her back would still ache.

Then her mind moved beyond and she remembered the day and the night before. She'd left the graves of her children and husband, and Coralía, too, behind forever. A thin sharp knife turned in her heart, bittersweet, relief and regret and longing all mixed up so that she didn't know what she felt. Then, lagging it by only a moment, came fear. She lifted her head, to see a bare thin back, bony shoulder blades like incipient wings. The boy was sitting in the stern, looking out.

"Miguelito."

His head jerked around. "Tia Graciela. *¿Estás despierta?*"

"Help me up, *chico*. Where is grandmother Aracelia?"

"Up front, with Julio and Gustavo." He got his arm under her and helped her onto the thwart. When she was arranged, she turned her head to the others. They nodded back, eyes red and sleepy. She bent, the boat tipping even under that tiny shift of weight, and glanced down. Clear water rolled back and forth over her bare feet.

"More water's coming in. The boat is leaking."

"I bail it every couple of hours. It's not much. Don't worry, Tia."

"You're a good boy, Miguelito." She blinked and rubbed her eyes, realizing only now how hungry and thirsty she was. The sky seemed very bright. The sun struck through the thin high clouds. She seldom got sunburn in the fields, but already her cheeks stung. Moving awkwardly—big as she was, the least motion was difficult—she dipped a corner of her skirt into the water and patted her face and neck with it. That refreshed her, and straightening her back, she looked around.

The sea was so much bigger than she'd expected. It made her feel small and alone, like standing in a field at night, looking up at the stars. But what was that they were saying about other boats? Clinging to the gunwale, she searched nearsightedly around as they rose to a swell. She didn't see anyone else. Then, surprise, she did, a little boat not all that far away. She lifted a hand tentatively, and to her delight the people in it waved back. They were Cuban all right; no one else could smile as lightheartedly out here. Ahead of the skiff, a dripping rope led to the stern of Tomás's boat, and above it, surprising her before she recognized it, was the sail—her sail, the one she'd stitched together out of the sacks the rice came in. The patchwork expanse bulged as if it had swallowed the wind and the wind was trying to get out. She examined it worriedly, but her doubled seams seemed to be holding. Below it, Xiomara caught her eyes. Graciela smiled back, but just then the skiff fell forward off a wave and she felt water spring into her mouth. If only it would stop, just for a moment, she'd be fine. But it never stopped. . . .

"Tia Graciela, you all right?"

She felt Gustavo's wiry arms around her as she retched. It was terrible, being sick when you were this pregnant. She felt miserable, dirty, sweaty, and turgid. Then she felt something else, and her hand dropped to her stomach. Tight as a drum already, it was growing harder.

She clung to the gunwale, staring into the swirling green. She dreaded what she was about to pass through, but at the same time she wished the baby would hurry and come. No, no, she didn't mean that! She had weeks yet to go. If he was born in Miami, he'd be an *americano*, no?

She clung grimly to the wood, and after a time the giant hand that had been squeezing her slowly opened.

MIGUELITO sat in the bow, looking at his hands. He remembered when they'd been a baby's, small and soft and unable to grab anything but his mother's dress. Now she was dead and he was big, and he could do almost anything he wanted with them. . . . Why, he was a man. And someday, they'd be hard and stiff like old Gustavo's, and in the rainy season he'd complain that they hurt, deep inside.

Or maybe that didn't happen in America. . . .

He wondered what it was going to be like. He'd listened on the radio, tuning in secretly to the Voice of America with the high whistle of the jamming. He heard Cuban voices talk about their crossing and how free and rich and happy they were in the great country to the north. It was like eavesdropping on the saints, hearing the testimony of those who had gone to heaven. He'd even dreamed about it last night. Yes, he'd forgotten when he woke, but now he remembered it again.

He'd been drifting in the water, all alone, at night. But as dawn approached, he'd seen a light and started swimming toward it. As the sun came up, the light faded, but he saw land in the same direction, with white clouds stacked above. He paddled weakly toward it, like a drowning dog. The current swept him along the coast and for a long time he was afraid he wouldn't make it, that he'd be dragged past. Now he could make out bushes or small trees. A point of land reached out for him, but the current moved faster. His arms were so heavy. . . . As he rounded the point, he saw a bay, a lighthouse rising from an eminence. He kept swimming and passed the peninsula a hundred yards from the surf, which he heard clearly.

The current changed then and pushed him in toward a stone jetty. The waves jostled him as he drew slowly nearer. But when he reached it at last, the stones were too huge to climb. Barnacles covered them, razoring his hands like broken black glass. The current carried him, screaming, off the seawall's end, around it, and into a harbor.

In the bay, white boats lay at anchor. Beautiful women lay on the decks, sipping fruit drinks in the sun. They didn't look down. They talked to one another as he swept by, struggling, crying out, drowning.

Then all at once, he realized he didn't have to struggle. He didn't even have to swim. He rose from the sea and began walking toward the shore, toward white and gold buildings towering against the blue sky. He could hear many bands playing all together, like at the Carnaval. As he drew closer to the beach, people gathered to greet him—beautiful blond women in bathing suits, strong men with black hair and white teeth. They carried him gently from the water and up onto the sand, speaking rapidly in a strange, beautiful language that had to be English. The sand was white and, to his surprise, soft. He smiled up at the circle of concerned faces. Someone gave him a Coca-Cola to drink. They were so friendly, the Americans.

Then he saw that they weren't smiling; they were laughing. Only then did he realize that he was lying naked before all of them; the women were laughing and pointing. His clothes were back in Cuba. He had to return, go back to his father's hut. . . .

"*¡Hola!*"

He snapped his head around, to see the other boat not far away at all. It had come up on them gradually. His eyes ran over it curiously. It was almost square. Above it rose a curious double mast and a slanted boom with a brown sail. It was green, the part the people sat in, and looked familiar. He sat astonished for a second, then laughed out loud. It was a truck bed. They were using a truck bed as a boat!

"Hello!" he yelled back.

"Where are you from?"

Tomás's bellow answered before he could. "Alcorcón," he shouted.

"Where?"

"Camagüey. Where are you from?"

"Puerto Vita."

"That is far to the east," Gustavo muttered. "Way down in Oriente."

"It's in Holguín Province now," Miguelito told the old man patronizingly. "There's no more Oriente."

"It's still Oriente, boy, no matter what the Communists call it."

"How long have you been at sea?" Tomás shouted across.

"Two days, *chico.* Hey, how far to Miami?"

"I don't know."

"Any extra food?"

"We have just barely enough. Are you out?"

"No, we've still got some *boniatos.*"

"We don't have much for ourselves."

"I understand, amigo. Shall we stay together?"

"Sure. We'll stay in sight."

"*Vaya con Dios,* okay?"

"*Vaya con Dios.* See you in *los Estados Unidos.*"

They waved, and Miguel gave them a salute as the boxy hull turned away, the slanted bow crushing down the waves.

THAT evening toward sunset, an airplane came over—a big one, with a white belly and a long tail like a dragonfly. They waved, but it didn't turn or indicate in any way that it had seen them. It just flew on steadily, then disappeared to the right of the setting sun.

"It's going back to America," Julio said, and the people in the *chalana* looked after it, each thinking his own thoughts.

They ate plantains, then finished the water in the bottle. They passed it around one last time, her, Miguelito, Gustavo, and finally Julio. The young man made a gesture of renunciation, but Gustavo said, "Drink, *chico,* you must stay strong in case we need you." So he took it and drained the last clear fluid, then held it up.

"Empty," he said. Then he turned, cupping his hands, and yelled across the foaming murky track that separated them from the others, "*Hey!* Tomás! We're out of water!"

Guzman came out of the cockpit, hair snarled. He looked like he'd been asleep. "*¿Qué pasa?*"

"We're out of water."

"What, you guzzled that up already?"

"We haven't 'guzzled' it. It was only one bottle, and that was since yesterday."

Tomás looked worried, or angry, but he nodded. He glanced around, looked up at the sky, and then ducked back into the cabin.

He reappeared with another bottle cradled in his stumped arm and began crawling aft, bracing himself as the sail rattled and boomed and the boat pitched. He got to the stern and looked back at them. "Pull yourself up here. Use the rope."

Julio bent to the line and started shortening the distance, hand over hand. Gustavo coiled the soft worn manila neatly as it came in. But when they were only a few feet away, a wave suddenly lifted their stern. They coasted forward, sliding down its slick slant, and crashed into the back of the bigger boat so violently splinters flew. Julio shot forward, almost jerked out of the skiff. "*¡Mierda!* Be careful, *carajo!*" Tomás yelled.

"The water!" Xiomara screamed, pointing, and they all, in both boats, turned and looked at where the plastic glinted and rolled in their wake. Augustín yanked the tiller over, but Tomás put out his hand, guiding him back on course. "It's gone. Nenita, hand me another," he said quietly.

Colón came out of the cabin. He said, so loudly that Graciela could hear him even over the wind, "They already had their water. They fucked up and lost it. No more for them."

"Hand me another bottle, Temilda," said Tomás.

Colón adjusted his pistol belt. "Did you hear me, Guzman? I said, they had their chance."

Tomás glanced at him but didn't argue, didn't respond at all. He took a piece of wire from his pocket and twisted it around the neck of the new bottle the twins passed up. Colón frowned but didn't say anything else. He just stood watching, hands on his hips, swaying as the boat rolled. Tomás looped the wire over the rope, then pushed it down toward the skiff. It hesitated, disappearing under the sea as the line slacked. Then, dragged by the current of their passage, it slid the last few feet.

Julio held it up, flourishing it like a trophy. Xiomara and Nenita, looking back, smiled. But Graciela saw Colón's scowl as he turned away, bent, crawled back into the darkness of the cabin. Tomás had humiliated him, shown the others he had no *cojones*. For that, she knew, a man must have revenge.

THE sunset that night was the most beautiful she'd ever seen. High thin clouds all aligned like the plowed rows of a field. At first they glowed like hot wires, then gradually cooled through copper to gold before fading away at last into black tiger stripes on a cobalt night. Just before they disappeared, she felt something on her thighs. Turning her back to the men, she gestured Aracelia over. Then she lifted her skirt a few inches, exposing a rash on her calves and painful raw patches where the skin had rubbed off her knees.

"Oh," the old woman whispered. She glanced quickly at the men, who were looking at the sky, and unwound her head cloth. She splashed water quickly on Graciela's belly, wiping off the blood and mucus. Graciela gasped at the salt sting.

"How does it feel?"

"Not pain exactly. Like cramps."

"Contractions?"

"It's too early for that."

Aracelia nodded, wrinkled face serene. "Maybe yes, maybe no. Raise yourself." She slid her hands under the younger woman's buttocks, easing the cloth between her thighs, then bound it tightly.

Just then, a rogue gust came over the sea.

It caught Augustín, on the tiller, by surprise. It snatched the sail from the side and slammed the boom around, and suddenly the whole thing, mast and sail and all the ropes and rigging, collapsed and fell, half into the sea, half onto the people on deck. Cries and shouts came from under it.

But even after knocking down their sail, the gust didn't stop. It kept increasing, making the boat heel over crazily, dragging the mass of wreckage. It started to come broadside to the waves, dragging the skiff around after it. Julio grabbed the paddle, looking quickly aft.

Shouting came from the boat ahead. "Pull it in. Roll it up. Get the end of that rope. Is it broken? Augustín—"

Through the failing light, Graciela caught sight of the men struggling with the flapping cloth. Then heard, all too plainly, a long ripping sound as the boom rolled over the side, followed by intense and impassioned cursing. And all this time, the boats were still slowing, still skating slowly around.

"Tomás!" Julio yelled. But Guzman didn't answer. He was somewhere under the flapping, slamming sail.

Then the wave hit them.

It lifted and heeled them and the boat kept going on over, farther and farther. The twins and the Colón kids started screaming. Graciela, horrified, looked for an endless time at the tin bottom of the big boat.

Then the kids screamed again and the wave passed under it and it came back down, rocking back so heavily it sent the water surging out from underneath it in a great wave. "Get it back around!" Julio was screaming, paddling furiously to keep their own stern backed into the seas. "Augustín! Start the motor!"

Tomás appeared roaring from under the sail, pushing up the mast. His shoulders bulged as a hand and a stump levered the heavy pipe back into the sky. The forward rope came taut but the after one swung frayed, worn through. "Grab it!" he yelled. "Okay, tie it to something, *coño, apirate*!"

"The boom's gone, Tomás, and half the sail."

"That's okay; we can fix that."

When Augustín yelled, "Okay, it's tied," Guzman sagged to his knees on the cabin top, one arm around the mast. When he had his breath back, he motioned weakly to take in the remnants of the sail, which was flapping loose, thundering and roaring ahead of the wildly rolling boat.

* * *

LATER, the five people in the skiff sat in the darkness, watching the vanishing ghostly blur ahead. "That was not good," Gustavo said softly.

"It's getting rougher. The wind keeps getting stronger."

"What if the sail falls down again?"

"Tomás can run the engine," said Miguel.

"There're only a couple liters of gas left," Julio said.

"He should just take it down," said Gustavo. "The current's taking us west. This is a big river out here. I used to fish out here, years ago."

"He can't, Tio. Those waves hit us sideways, we're going to turn over. You saw it; it almost happened."

"This river, it ends up in Miami?" Miguel asked them. "How much farther is it to Florida?"

"I'm not sure. It can't be too much farther; we've been going for a whole day."

"Those people from Holguín have been out for two days now."

"Yeah, but they had farther to go."

The men talked deep into the night. Graciela didn't join their conversation. Neither did old Aracelia. They sat together near the bow, near the little pocket the pointed end of the *chalanita* made. And gradually, the men, too, passed into silence, till all was heaving, whistling dark. She lay down in the floorboards, wrapping her dress tightly around her, and listened to the sea gurgling past her ear.

SHE started awake, the scream tearing her throat apart before she even knew what was wrong.

In the black night, the skiff seemed to spin, sliding sidelong down the roaring black chest of a wave. She screamed again, grabbing at something soft to keep from being thrown out of the boat, and then her throat closed and all she could do was moan. Julio yelled and then everyone was yelling. Then, all at once, they stopped, listening to answering shouts across the water, but faint, so faint.

There was the distant pop of a shot, then nothing, nothing but roaring darkness, with the wind blustering and whining as they rose dizzyingly in the black, then dropped, leaving her stomach floating out somewhere above the waves. She felt strength drain from her fingers even as they gripped wet wood. She stared into black, praying for a glimpse of something, anything—a spark, a face, a star, a light. Nothing came.

Then nausea grabbed her again, and this time acid stripped her throat raw and left her gagging. She hit at the wood, feeling her hands bruise but not caring. Then she felt Miguelito's thin arms. He sounded scared, too. "Tia Graciela . . . Tia Graciela. Sit down! You're going to make us go over!"

"They're gone; they're gone."

Julio's voice, grim as the night: "I've got the end of the rope."

Old Gustavo: "Yeah?"

"It's cut."

"That *hijo de puta*. He cut it, the fat one. The son of a bitch Communist *chivato*, he cut our rope."

"Or his fat wife."

"She's a whore, but she wouldn't do that. It was him, I tell you."

"Tomás will come back for us."

"If he can find us. But in the dark, how?"

"We should have had a light—a candle, anything."

Miguelito said, "Maybe he can't come back. You heard the shot. What if they killed Tomás, Julio?"

Julio didn't answer, and Graciela felt panic close her throat again. Oh God, oh blessed Virgin de la Caridad del Cobre, patron of the sea . . . Squatting on the floorboards, she pressed her fists tightly to her face.

WHEN dawn came they were alone. She looked until her eyes hurt, but there was no sign of the others. There were other boats, but miles away, and she didn't think any of them were Tomás's. They were alone now, five people in a little leaking boat.

Gustavo, Aracelia, and Miguelito lay in the water on the bottom, their mouths gaping in sleep. Only Julio was awake. He was staring out fixedly at an oncoming wave, the paddle poised in his hands like some kind of weapon.

Then he bent, dark skin showing through the ragged T-shirt, and abruptly, furiously dug it into the water. The stern rose and the boat started to roll. But Julio dug harder and the stern swung back just in time to meet the sea. It drove under them, heaving them upward with arrogant power. As they rose, the wind punched at them in heavy cold gusts that ripped spray off the ragged waves and blew it in white trailing lines along the green surface.

Then it was past, and her cousin sagged back. She saw the bloody smears his hands had dyed into the handle of the whittled wood. One by one, the others woke, opened their eyes blankly. She dragged herself up, trying to ease the ache in her back. She wasn't hungry at all anymore . . . but so tired. She blinked burning eyes out at the sea. Something was missing, something that had been there before. Then she knew: the birds. They didn't slant along the waves anymore, cocking an eye their way as they went by. There were no birds at all.

They were alone under a vast sky that was sealed now with a low darkness from which filtered a cold mist. On the far horizon, a black ominous-looking wall of cloud barred off half the world. They looked at it speechlessly, staring for a long time as the boat went up and down, spinning and rolling in the whistling wind.

31
The Windward Passage

THE sea, half an hour before dawn. The uneasy, faintly glowing waves grasp at the bleaching sky but fall back with a slapping noise before they reach it. As they break, the wind spatters spray across their glossy black bellies. They shoulder one another like a big-city crowd. Sometimes they merge into a crest. At other times, their meeting makes only a low place on the sea, a patch of illusory calm. Their surface is slaty, save for an occasional flecking of foam.

The sky reflects the sea, lightless and uneasy. The gray clouds writhe as they ride the high wind.

In these last minutes before dawn, lights rise gradually from the sea: red to port, green to starboard, masthead and range brilliant white. They move steadily closer, striking colored sparks off the tossing crests.

A gray shape forms on a gray horizon. It grows, taking on shape, solidity, reality, detail. A low whine joins the sigh of the wind.

Suddenly it looms over the restless water. Wave after wave, still black in the final minutes of night, is sliced and smashed apart under a blunt blade of gray steel. The waves spit silver fragments that skip away, swerving and dipping along the swell lines: flying fish. The sea parts unwillingly, tearing energy from the moving metal with a dull roar like a collapsing cliff. The high gray sides move past, rolling with the ponderous slow beat of a massive metronome.

But as soon as the squared-off counter moves past, the sea sweeps stubbornly in again. For two minutes, it swirls and leaps, frothing white in the growing metal light. A billion bubbles rise and froth and burst. Gradually, it subsides, healing itself with a smooth, gently heaving skin, a shallow smoothness that seethes beneath with whirlpools.

Then another bladelike bow plows it apart again.

HALF a mile apart, in line ahead at a thousand yards' separation, USS *Barrett* followed USS *Dahlgren* on a northerly course at high speed. Far to port, the low hills of Cuba humped out of the sea like surfacing whales. To the east, just visible, was a bank of cloud that was Haiti. The dominant swell swept in from the northeast, but there was a cross swell, too, making the seas choppy and confused.

Gradually, the sun emerged, visible in the intervals between the speeding clouds. First as a tentative lightening over Hispaniola, a gradual brightening that lighted the world from below. Then suddenly squirting up into sight, a swollen, shimmering ball like a condom filled with blood. Rays of red light shot across the water toward the racing ships, coppering masts and rotating radars, then moving down to paint their decks. Beneath the sodden orb the sea seethed like boiling aluminum, and low altocumulus hurtled overhead as if on motor-driven belts.

On the bridge of the second ship, Dan stood behind Cannon as the navigator set his sextant carefully in its box, wedged it under a shelf, and booted up the computer in the nav shack. The screen flickered, then read:

> GOOD MORNING, DICKHEAD. I'M YOUR FUCKING DATA-EATING SLOPPY-PRINTING PIG. I'M HERE TO FUCK UP YOUR MORNING, PISS IN YOUR WHEATIES, AND MAKE YOU WISH YOU'D NEVER BEEN BORN. ENJOY YOUR STAY.

Cannon hit ENTER and the screen blanked. He began typing in GMT, the DR position, star number, observed altitude.

As Dan turned away, the barometer caught his eye. He tapped it, not because that did anything on a modern instrument but because that was what everyone did. Then he raised his eyes to look the length of the bridge. The morning was colorless through the slanted windows. Cold photons penetrated salt-spattered Plexiglas and glanced off waxed wood, gray paint, polished brass, plastic, aluminum. They showed him tired men with pallid faces.

"What's the trend, Dave?"

"Dropping."

"Fast?"

"Something wicked coming our way."

"What's Fleet Weather calling it?"

"A tropical depression now, and still strengthening." The

navigator pulled down the board and showed him the twenty-four-hour forecast. Dan read it, memorizing figures and locations in case the captain asked, then looked out again to the two points of distant land. The nearer was Cuba, emerging now from the westerly darkness. Successive ranges of hills were cut from steadily lighter shades of reddish gray paper. He looked at *Dahlgren*'s slowly rolling stern half a mile ahead; at the whitish river of churned-up sea that led to *Barrett*'s own bow; at the two long streamers of commingled, nearly invisible smoke that blew from the racing destroyers. The sea heaved between them, but the distance never varied. The water was taking on the faintest hint of blue as the rising sun burrowed its rays under the waves. Patches of foam showed here and there, but no streaks yet. He glanced at the relative wind indicator, bent to the radarscope, checked the surface board one last time.

He said to Van Cleef, "Okay, it's five-thirty. I'll be on the horn for a while. Keep a sharp lookout."

"Aye aye, sir."

He pulled the phone off the bulkhead and buzzed the at-sea cabin. Leighty answered with a grunt. "Good morning, Captain. Mr. Lenson here," Dan said.

"Okay, I'm up. How's it look up there?"

"We're passing Punta Maisi, coming up on the oh-six hundred turn. *Dahlgren*'s holding thirty knots—"

"Thought it was twenty-eight—no, I remember you calling me when they went to thirty."

"Yes, sir. The only contacts are Skunk Charlie—bears zero-eight-six, range eighty-nine hundred, closest point of approach at the turn will be over six thousand yards—and Skunk Bravo, past and opening to the south. The morning is overcast, with true wind fifteen knots from zero-four-eight, gusting to twenty, seas four to five feet. *Dahlgren*'s the guide in line ahead, thousand yards' interval."

"What's Fleet Weather got to say about this low-pressure area?"

"It's a tropical depression now, sir." He repeated back what he'd memorized, finishing, "As of oh-four hundred, the center was moving northwest at about eight knots."

"How are we on PIM?"

PIM was position of intended movement, the moving point where the ship should be according to the movement report they'd filed in the hectic two hours between when he'd been awakened and the time the two destroyers had passed Windward Point. He leaned over the chart, at the extremity of the phone cord. "Sir, we're about two miles ahead right now."

"Nothing from *Dahlgren*?"

"Just the half-hour radio checks."

"Any beefs from the engineers?"

"No, sir."

"And the next turn's at six. Okay, somebody at my door. Must be Pedersen with breakfast. Call me if anything changes."

Dan said he would and hung up. He glanced at Van Cleef; the JOOD had his binoculars up to starboard. Dan followed them, caught for a moment a tiny tossing speck silhouetted by an immense bloody sun. It seemed to expand as it rose, growing more malevolent at each appearance between the bands of cloud.

"Skunk Charlie's a small boat, sir."

"Very well."

The overhead speaker of the radio remote hissed and said suddenly, making Van Cleef jump for the signal pad and codebook, "Juliet Papa, this is Lima Lima. Signal follows. Corpen port three-one-zero. I say again, corpen port three-one-zero. Standby—execute. Over."

"I break that to read, turn port, following in my wake, new course three-one-zero."

"Make it so. Give him a roger and turn in the knuckle," said Dan. Van Cleef bawled over his shoulder, "Left five degrees rudder, steady course three-one-zero. Lima Lima, this is Juliet Papa. Roger, out."

Dan called the captain, told him the new course, then leaned against the plot table, feeling *Barrett* lean, then begin rolling as she picked up the swell. He couldn't decide how he felt. It felt good leaving Gitmo. But there was disappointment, too—like showing up at the dentist's office and finding it closed. They'd all been wound up for the battle problem. But how could you tell how you really felt until you knew where you were going? And they didn't know that, not even a hint.

All he knew was that at 0300, reveille had been passed throughout the ship for an emergency under way and that *Barrett* and *Dahlgren* were now en route to the Grand Bahama Passage. But no one aboard knew why, not even the radiomen, which meant the captain was in the dark, too. The only concrete facts were that they'd done an emergency sortie and were now tearing ass for either north Cuba or South Florida.

Or, to be more exact . . . He examined the chart again. Cannon had plotted their PIM. It curved northwest once they exited the Passage, angling gradually left around the tip of Cuba, where it ended, hanging out there in space. But if they continued on that last course, they'd be steaming parallel to the northern coast. Two hundred and forty miles, just eight hours at this speed, and they'd be entering the twisting bottleneck of the Old Bahama Channel—two to four hundred fathoms under their keel but only ten miles wide at Cay Lobos, and reefs on either side. Past that, the wedge of the Cay Sal Bank split the possibilities into two. They could go westward via the Nicholas Channel toward Havana and the Florida Keys or northward via the Santarén toward the east coast of Florida, Bimini, and Grand Bahama Island.

Okay, short-fuze orders, unexpected changes of plan weren't unknown in the U.S. Navy. The unexpected happened—coups, hostage situations, revolutions, disasters—and ships had to be scrambled. But the funny thing was that once they'd exited Gitmo, their readiness condition had actually dropped. They were back to peacetime steaming now, with five watch sections and no weapons manned.

That meant there couldn't be any sort of military threat.

Finally, he had to admit he was beat. He checked the scope again, ran his binoculars across *Dahlgren*'s stern—a high rooster tail obscured her, then parted, blown downwind—and around the horizon. Nothing but the points of land, the two contacts, both falling astern, and the two destroyers tearing along to the north, alone in the waste of waters. No, he didn't like the looks of that sky.

He stood motionless before the windows, looking out as the last shadows fled. The forecastle brightened to where he could see individual wash-down nozzles, bolt heads in the missile launcher, the faint uneven weld seams in the deck plating. The boatswain, silver pipe dangling around his neck, brought the scope hood out from the charthouse and fitted it over the radar repeater. When he was done, Dan put his face to it.

Still nothing . . . He stretched, then leaned against the plot table again. Getting under way unexpectedly, there'd been no time to plan exercises, drills, the other things the XO and the ops officer generated to occupy the watch standers' free time. So once the confusion and hurry were over, they floated in a void of unscheduled time.

Gradually, other thoughts reemerged from the outer darkness, things he'd shoved out of his mind during Reftra—such as Leighty, such as his own position. He had an uneasy feeling he hadn't heard the last of the Naval Investigative Service.

Barrett didn't pass reveille at sea. The captain felt people could be trusted to get up on their own. So the first word passed was "titivate ship" at 0700. A little later, Cannon came up again, talked to the boatswain and Van Cleef. Then he saluted Dan and said he was ready to relieve.

THE wardroom was packed. Pulling out a chair, Dan said, "Permission to join the mess, XO." Vysotsky nodded without speaking. Dan ordered scrambled eggs and French toast. Lauderdale, Quintanilla, Martin Paul were back in short sleeves. After wearing long sleeves for weeks at Gitmo, their bare upper arms looked strange.

The exec said hoarsely, "Excuse me, gentlemen," got up from an empty plate, and left, carrying his coffee cup like a live grenade. It had a skull and crossbones on it and the letters *XO*.

"So what's the latest?" Dan asked the operations officer. Quintanilla shrugged.

"Nothing official."

"Okay, anything unofficial?"

"I heard something in the spaces about a spill," said Giordano, lifting his cup as Antonio carried the full pot past.

"An oil spill?"

"Tanker hit an oil rig in the Gulf of Mexico. It was on the news on the radio. Maybe we're riding to the rescue."

"You know the first thing you hear's always bullshit."

"That's a Coast Guard mission, not ours."

"You wanted scuttlebutt. Felipe?"

"I'd guess something to do with this maneuvering Castro's doing in the UN. But I don't know how that would relate to us, or having us up north rather than down south."

"We need better rumors than that," said the XO, coming back in. Dan thought Vysotsky looked very tired. "You guys are falling down on the job, all I can say."

"Hey, XO, one question."

"Shoot, Dwight."

"CINCLANTFLT pulls us out of training for some crisis action thing before we do the final battle problem. But then whatever it is, it's over. Do we have to go back to Gitmo? Or do they check us off on the requirement, based on our performance up to when we left?"

"Good question. It'd probably depend on how long we were out and how close going back would crowd us up to the deployment date. Final decision would be up to the training people on Admiral Claibourn's staff. Don't throw anything away, though. We could get a message at noon, turn around and go back, do the battle problem tomorrow."

A knock, and Chief Erb came in with the message board. They fell silent as Vysotsky silently read and initialed it. When the radioman left, he cleared his throat. "Interesting," he murmured.

"For Chrissake, XO—"

"Okay, it says to drop speed to twenty knots to conserve fuel, but we're still headed northwest. They want us and *Dahlgren* to break out our landing-party stores, ready ships' boats, and prepare to embark or refuel helicopters. Norm, Dwight, we need to file a report on status of food, fresh water, JP-four, diesel, gasoline, batteries, habitability items. Dave, we'll need a medical-stores inventory, too. We need to come up on International Marine Distress, one fifty-six point eight megahertz, one fifty-six point three, one fifty-seven point one, one-fifty-six point sixty-five, and the emergency CB channel. There's more." He glanced at his watch. "I'll read it at officers' call. Let's go."

DAN filled two pages in his wheel book with things to do, then started delegating them to his chiefs and officers. Whatever was in the wind, it was going to take a lot of supplies and a lot of radio communications.

When he had everything farmed out and working, he stopped in CIC and stood in front of the combat direction system's screen. The system was up, and he studied the NTDS symbology. Gradually, he noted other units being sortied: a unit from Key West that broke as Patrol Hydrofoil Squadron Two; others were Coast Guard, and there were two NATO friendlies. He started to identify them, then didn't. Time was elastic at sea. How slowly the minutes crept by on watch, and how quickly they sped when too much had to be done.

He headed aft, looking into one compartment after another. In the computer room, Shrobo and Dawson and Hofstra were on the screens again. They glanced his way with their usual glazed gazes as he pulled up a stool.

Suddenly, Dan felt guilty. Shrobo was still aboard. No one had remembered him during the hectic hours before getting under way. He could have been left ashore at Gitmo, either to await their return or be flown home. He couldn't blame anyone else; he should have thought of it.

"What's it look like, Doc?"

The civilian shoved himself back from a keyboard and drew his hands from the top of his skull down to his chin. "Like doing a crossword puzzle backward, in Greek." He leaned back farther, and Dan caught his stool just before it went over. "Thanks.... Like wandering down one of these passageways and opening this door and then that door, and there's a glimpse of something for just a fraction of a second. Then it's gone." He blinked. "Is it light outside?"

"Yeah, it's light." Dan stood up. "Let's go out, get you out of here for a couple of minutes."

When they emerged onto the midships platform, the overcast had clamped down all around the horizon: a darker patch ahead, a slanted haze beneath—a rainsquall. When Dan leaned over the rail, he could see *Dahlgren* rolling heavily ahead, mast tops nodding from side to side. *Barrett* rolled, too, but more slowly, and the sea slipped past, littered with sargasso weed looking like what was left after you ate a bunch of grapes. Dan ran his eyes around the seals on the Harpoon canisters as Shrobo detached his glasses and lifted his naked face. "Smells clean out here," he said. Then, when Dan didn't answer, he added, "I mean, without the poison we're always sucking in with every breath on land. I suppose it's still there, but the dilution factor . . . Do you know anything about the immune system?"

"The what?" For a second, he thought Shrobo was still talking about ACDADS. "Oh. You mean the human immune system?"

"Uh-huh. My wife's allergic to any form of chemical contaminant—like the stuff on mattresses, new carpets, the scents on toilet paper, dyes. . . . There are more people like that than we suspect." He went on about chemical emanations from building materials, pesticides, fertilizers. "She can't even read the newspaper—the ink. There's a place called Portsmouth Island, in North Carolina. It was abandoned years ago; there's never been any spraying or other chemical contamination. I'm thinking of starting a colony there."

Dan said, "Look, Doc, I owe you an apology."

"An apology?" Shrobo opened his eyes.

"This diversion, mission, whatever it is . . . I should have arranged to leave you in Gitmo, arranged for the base people to fly you home. I'm sorry. It slipped my mind."

Shrobo shrugged. "It's a break from being an administrator. But I'd like to call home if I can, let Alma know what's going on."

"I'll set you up with the comm officer. We should be in range of the Key West marine operator pretty soon."

"Thanks." Shrobo blinked in the pale radiance. "You know, you can almost feel it out here, the energy."

"It is pretty bright."

"I meant another kind of energy. Every sphere—like our planet—contains within it two opposed tetrahedrons. Their intersections produce access points, or chakras. One of those dimensional gates is in the middle of what we call the Bermuda Triangle."

Dan looked sideways at him, realizing that the thick glasses, the medical smock, the neurotic preoccupation with his health aside, Shrobo was still one weird bird. You couldn't deny he was brilliant, but after three weeks aboard he still had to have someone take him to the mess hall. And a *Kidd*-class didn't have that complicated a layout.

"So, how's the system fix going? I see we have NTDS back."

Shrobo blinked. "Do they? I've been concentrating on the virus. The interesting thing about it is that it seems to be self-erasing."

"What?"

"Oh, this is a very interesting guy we have here. If you really want to go into it . . ."

"Sure," said Dan. He owed the guy that, to listen.

"The virus operates in the following sequence. One: It establishes itself by writing its basic program—what I call the 'infector'—to memory, with several backups in various portions of the memory. Two: It 'unzips' the actively hostile portion of the program and writes it to additional areas of operating memory. Three: Running in main memory, not continuously, but in short bursts between lines of the executing program, it actively destroys data by deleting portions of existing code. Four: It masks the damage by replacing the erased code with randomly generated garbage, mimicking the format of the original data." Shrobo paused. "Clear so far?"

Dan nodded.

"Okay. Then, and unlike any virus I've ever heard of before, step five: It erases itself."

"You said that before. But I don't understand. Then what's the problem?"

"Because it leaves behind its toxins—the garbage written to the tape. It rezips itself to the spore form and writes the infector to several portions of the tape. Then it erases itself from the operating memory."

"Whew."

"The end result—about a minute after you first boot it—is an infected and degraded tape. The damage accrues so gradually that it may take a while even to notice—especially in the case of the sonar system, which uses deep algorithms to process the signal. That's why you noticed it first in the weapons-control module. You actually get a physical output there, which you can visually observe to be faulty." He fitted his glasses back on again, looked at Lenson. "Any questions?"

"Jesus. Okay, one—this garbage it writes. Can you at least write us something to detect and delete that? Then we could figure where it is by what it leaves behind."

Shrobo smiled mischievously. "A parity check, you mean? I tried. This virus generates the same total of ones and zeroes that are in the original line of code, only they're totally scrambled."

"This is a real bastard."

"It's the most cunningly designed program I've ever seen. It's very difficult to investigate. If the program's running and you attempt to stop it to read its internal code, it erases. So far, all I've managed to do is establish its overall length. Eighty lines. A masterpiece of compression."

"Where would something like this come from?"

"I have no idea. But whoever wrote it was damned good."

Dan stared down into the sea as it all reverberated around in his mind. Finally, he said, "How about this built-in booby trap? Can you write a program that activates that? Make it blow itself up?"

"Good insight. That was one of the first things I tried. The self-destruct feature doesn't work in the spored form. Only when it's unzipped. But Matt and I are still working on it."

"Matt? . . . Oh, Petty Officer Williams."

"That's one sharp kid you've got there. He's been a big help. We'll keep you and the captain advised how it goes."

"Okay. Thanks. Anything else I can do for you?"

"Feel that," said Shrobo.

Dan hesitated, then gripped the proffered bicep. It felt flabby and soft. "Not bad, huh?" the scientist said. "The workout room—weights, stationary bike."

"That's good."

"And I think we're getting close to cracking this thing. It's not St. Paul on the road to Damascus, but I think we're getting close."

"Anything you need, let me know."

"Attention, please," said the 1MC, and they both fell silent, turning to listen.

"This is the captain speaking.

"As you know, we've been under way since early this morning, headed north and then northwest around the tip of Cuba. We have just received a message clarifying where we are going, and why.

"The message directs us to proceed to the north central coast of Cuba, between Cuba and the Florida Keys. Our mission is to be available for on-scene tasking in the vicinity of Boca de Marcos–Anguilla Cay area, in reference to a possible mass boat lift.

"There are no further details on the mission, but there are preparatory taskings that have been passed down via the appropriate department heads. It looks to me like a humanitarian operation. It should not compromise our combat readiness or our ability to return to Guantánamo Bay, which I would anticipate after our activities here are complete.

"I'll keep you informed as more information comes in. Carry on."

DAN made his excuses to Shrobo and left him standing at the rail, blinking up at the sky as if at a huge screen filled with interesting new data. He picked up his morning traffic, the Teletype clatter coming through the little grilled door as the duty radioman slid it open, slid his pile through, clicked it closed. As he leafed rapidly through it, the 1MC's hollow voice echoed around him: "Haul over all hatch hoods and gun covers." They were entering the squall.

He decided to go aft and see how the inventory of helo stores was going. He wondered what exactly they'd have to do in a boat lift. He wondered what they'd find two hundred miles ahead, and which way the storm would decide to go. As he headed down the passageway, absently noting that the red "occupied" light was on again over the door to the crypto vault, he couldn't shake a growing feeling of unease.

ON the far side of that door, a clock hummed to itself in the isolated quiet of a steel-walled cave. A diffuser hummed a steady drone, breathing cold air on the close-cropped head of the man who sat at a bolted-down desk positioned between two large safes.

He sat scratching his bald spot within a windowless steel-sided cubicle surrounded on all sides by the ship. An arm's length away, a heavy system of levers and dogs were locked into welded sockets. The single massively built access was airtight and watertight. Once locked down, it could not be unsealed by anything short of a cutting torch, and even that would take hours to burn through nearly a foot of hardened armor steel. At the upper and lower edges, springed pins were set to trip if it was opened without the proper combination, setting off alarms throughout the ship.

The other three bulkheads were lined with stacked racks of publications, bulletins, films, and data tapes. They stirred uneasily as the ship rolled, restrained by fiddle boards and shock cords. Some were tactical, outlining the way the Navy would maneuver in war or how it would coordinate operations with the other services and allied navies. Others were intelligence, carefully setting forth everything that was known and speculated about possible enemies around the globe. And still others had to do with communications procedures, security, and how to use, maintain, and repair the classified equipment aboard.

The whole room was shadowy. There was a fluorescent light in the overhead, but it was dark. The only light came from the bulb of a single lamp, set low to illuminate the surface of the desk.

Rubbing his head slowly, the officer seated at it was looking at his notebook, doing nothing in particular, just thinking.

Finally, he reared back, stretched, looking around the interior of the compartment. Then he reached out—everything was within reach; he didn't have to get up—and spun a dial.

The safe came open with the muffled clank of heavy pins disengaging.

Inside it were more publications, racks of them. They were technical manuals for the KL-47, the KWR-37, KW-7, KY-36, KW-21 . . . for all the message, voice, and computer encipherment systems

Barrett carried. There were spare cards and parts and the specialized tools required to diagnose malfunctions in complex cryptographic equipment, as well as the bulky red-bound books that contained the daily key lists for each system.

He peered in for a few seconds, running his gaze down the spines. Finally, he took one out. Placing it on the desk, he flipped through the pages till he found the one he wanted. It was a complicated schematic diagram, stamped at the top and bottom with threatening red letters. Then he reached back into the safe, feeling around till his hand closed on a delicate sphere of thin glass.

Taking down a rag from behind a cable, he carefully unscrewed the hot bulb from the lamp, plunging the vault for a moment into darkness impenetrable and complete. No tiniest ray of light leaked in. Not the slightest chink or crack had been tolerated when the vault was built. Then the lamp came back on, three times as bright as before.

Centering the diagram under the 150-watt bulb, he reached back again into the safe for a small camera. He was starting to load it with film when he paused.

He thought, Why am I doing this?

Did he need to do any more of this? Ever again?

He sat unmoving for a few seconds, then decided that he really didn't. Whatever happened, the time for that was past forever now. He closed the camera and put it back into the safe. He slammed the book closed, weighed it in his hand for a second—a lead insert in the spine gave it considerable heft—then slid it back into place.

He slammed the safe shut with a clang, pulled the handle down to lock it, and spun the dial. Last, he carefully took the oversized bulb out of the desk lamp and replaced it with the standard one.

He stood motionless again, holding the still-hot, oversized bulb. Would there be any reason he might need it again? He couldn't think of any. The long masquerade was drawing to a close.

He hooked the trash can out from under the desk with his shoe. A moment later, the imploding bulb burst and rattled against the inside like the explosion of a tiny shell.

32
The Santarén Channel

THE world roared. Gone mad, the wind was no longer wind but an irresistible power so violent that even the gigantic waves it had built cowered before it, cringing as it stripped the white crowns from their heads and flung them across the sea. The flying spray mingled with torrents of rain to make what she breathed, even lying facedown in the bucking, rolling skiff, as much water as air.

The black wall had grown steadily as it approached, and with it the wind, until at midmorning, with the sky lightless as night, the rain started—rain as if an enraged God had abrogated his word to Noah and determined again to drown the race of men. It was so heavy and continuous that she could only breathe by making a mask with cupped hands over her mouth. The rain whipped her back as she lay gasping and choking. The gradually sinking boat reeled and leapt so madly that only wedging their bodies beneath the thwarts kept them from being shaken out.

The wind increased, and increased . . . for hour on hour, till it became one prolonged shriek, till the world, unable to endure, began to break apart. The waves smashed over them, and for long seconds she couldn't breathe at all, just stared at her hands through the green water. The mad shaking and roaring went on and on, till there was nothing else inside her head at all, just the insane wind, the steady crash of the sea.

Then the wind increased.

SOME time later she felt another body pressed close to hers. She opened her eyes in the midst of pandemonium.

The sky was black. She'd never seen night in the day. She could only dimly make out the person whose face was pressed against hers. It was Julio, his eyes streaming water, hair a black pressed-down slickness, mouth an open O. The side of his face streamed blood.

"I can't hear you," she screamed, and couldn't even hear herself.

His head turned away, and she felt something rough brush her hands. She flinched, then realized what it was.

She let him pass the rope under and around her. It dug into her flesh. But now she could relax the terrible tension in her arms. She no longer had to hold on.

With relief came utter weakness, as if her body, no longer needing to resist, had surrendered. A black wall at the edge of her consciousness swept toward her, flickering with lightning. Shaken, battered, she slid downward into lightless caverns bigger than the sea, an abyss that closed around her like welcoming arms.

WHEN she came back to consciousness, the rain had stopped, but the wind had reached a fury that made everything that had come before seem pitiful, slight, and only a prelude to what now seemed the destruction of the world. She raised her head and peeped into it, like a smelter peering into a fiery furnace.

There was no sea, no air, only a frothing airborne foam that boiled in the black light like seething milk. Whenever the flooded boat rose to a crest, the wind clawed at it, trying to careen and tumble it away, smash it apart into boards, bodies, splinters. She was alternately weightless and incredibly heavy, either gasping salty liquid air or crushed breathlessly beneath the solid sea. She gagged and strangled, fighting against the ropes before animal fear subsided and she remembered they were there to hold her aboard the only solidity in this howling waste. Still choking and coughing, she tried to lift her head again—into a terrifying world of gray-black clouds, driven like mad horses by the flickering lash of lightning. The boom and roar of thunder was the only sound the horrific howling of the wind could not blot out. A strange pale penumbra glowed and shimmered around each corner of the boat, and she stared, blinking as cold spray razored her eyes, before she realized it was the wind itself made visible, streaming at unimaginable speed around anything still projecting above the welter of boiling foam.

A black head thrust itself suddenly up from it. Under an incandescent sheet of lightning, she made out Miguelito's blank eyes, his mouth dilated in an expressionless gasp—so bright, she could see the black rot of his teeth and the molded curves of the back of his throat. Another motion and her staring eyes flicked aft. Julio, cheeks drawn back in a rictus of effort, was bending into the paddle as foam covered him like a blanket drawn up to his chest. Every muscle in his thin arms stood out. Behind him, old Gustavo was staring aft at an oncoming wave. Then the glare flickered and ran down into the sea, and they all disappeared, sucked back into nonexistence, and the black came back with a clap like the thunder.

She thought, We're going to die here.

And somehow it didn't seem hostile or threatening. She thought of Death now with yearning, as a black peace where storms could reach no more. It couldn't be so bad, Death. Did not Armando, the dead children, her own mother wait there for her and the child she carried?

At her feet in the dark, the scrabble of nails, the old woman. She was dragging herself up inch by inch, pressing her bony old body close. Graciela could feel her pelvis, her ribs as they dragged across her own. Their faces touched, and the ancient fingers dug into her arms like talons.

Then, to Graciela's slow wonder, she felt the old woman shove herself upright. What was she doing?

Then the lightning came.

The flash showed her old Aracelia kneeling in the madly plunging boat, gaunt body swaying, hair blown straight back by the wind from her transfigured hollow-cheeked face. Her hands were raised in supplication or curse. White-rimmed eyes stared up at the roaring clouds. Her mouth was open, screaming soundlessly in the shrieking fury—no, not screaming, but her lips were moving in prayer or charm, but *speaking to something.* Graciela felt horror move in her soul. She followed the old woman's locked gaze. Black churning clouds, the flickering curving underbelly of the storm like huge crushing rollers in a great mill. But what did the old woman see? What scarred, glaring *orisha,* what enraged ancient god of Africa riding on the lightning flashes, beating the drums of thunder?

The skiff plunged over a crest and dropped as if there were nothing below them for a thousand miles. All at once, the sea seemed to open and then close, sealing its lips over them, swallowing them like a great fish.

Graciela's whole body contracted. Her fingernails ripped into the wooden bottom as it rolled over her, as the whole sea turned itself upside down. Then there was no light at all, only a green flicker from below, above, from all around her, lighting up the screaming yet soundless face of the old woman, eyes staring open, hair streaming, *below her.* . . .

They were upside down, capsized, sinking, and she was tied in. . . .

With a tired, logy toss, the boat surfaced again. The howl of the wind was muffled now, and the spray drummed hollowly on the bottom, above her head. She opened her mouth, hoping for air, but as the foam melted, it seemed to bleed away through the wood, leaving her only water to breathe—salt water, bitter and warm in her mouth. Her chest heaved and her hands scratched and tore, gouging out palmfuls of splinters, her nails snapping without pain as the buried, panicking, dying animal tried to dig its way to the air.

Someone was beside her, kicking and struggling, too, against the sea. But her open eyes caught only dim underwater shapes, outlined and frozen by the ghostly luminescence of lightning. She sagged, exhausted, unable to fight any longer. She opened her mouth to the sea.

The boat came up and the edge of it caught the wind. The terrible shriek reached her only distantly as she sank away. Then the cord at her arms and thighs came taut and she was pulled upward. She fought it, wanting to sink into the peaceful green. Were those faces down there? Yes, there were her father and mother, and old Abuela, Grandmother, reaching out their arms for her in the streaming green-gold light.

Suddenly, one of the cords went slack. Her arm fell free and she beat the water with it weakly. The other cord tugged, and she saw in another flicker-flash two sets of legs kicking madly above her, then felt arms around her, pulling her up.

Then all at once, the remaining cord tore at her again, cutting into her flesh like the edge of a dull machete, and she was ripped bodily from the sea's womb and grave and thrown up and across a hard narrow blade of wood. Back into the roar and howl, but also back into something resembling air. Her throat unlocked and she coughed and gagged as the flooded hulk rocked slowly from side to side.

Just then, the lightning detonated across half the sky, a solid blue arc of vibrating flame that lighted the whole of her heaving, shrieking world. In its hellish light, she saw a thin brown hand reach up through the seethe and welter of sliding sheets of foam. Then, fingers still extended, it slowly slid beneath the surface of the sea.

IT wasn't as if the storm ended after that. It didn't. The waves were as huge as ever, and now, with the boat half-submerged, they passed over as much as under it. The waterlogged *chalanita* rose as each one rolled in, but too slowly, and the sea covered them for long seconds, sealing them like flies in green jelly. But then it passed and the hulk swam slowly upward, and they could gasp and breathe for a little while before the next. Nor did the rain stop. But the hellish wind slacked a little. The racing black clouds still hurtled past above them, but as if to a destination farther on and not to concentrate their fury on this one small spot of ocean. The lightning flickered on, but in the distance now.

They clung to the half-submerged wreck, exhausted, staring at each other or at nothing: Graciela, Miguelito, and old Gustavo, his white hair streaming water. He looked exhausted, a hundred years old.

Julio hadn't come up again.

Graciela realized now what he'd been doing in those last moments under the overturned boat. He was trying to right it. But with her tied in, he couldn't without lifting her deadweight out of the water, too. That was why he'd unlashed her arm, so he could get the gunwale high enough that the wind, catching its edge, would do the rest, finish flipping it upright again. Then somehow he'd managed to thrust her up and out of the water, back into the little pocket of wet wood that was their only protection against the sea.

Only he'd already been tired, fighting all night to keep their stern to the swells. That last effort had exhausted him, and he'd slipped away . . . and Aracelia, too. The old woman was gone without a trace. Graciela remembered her open mouth, fixed horror-stricken eyes, hair streaming out as if still blown by the wind as she fell slowly into the flickering black.

The three who were left clung silently to the wreck, looking out over a barren, chaotic sea.

Sometime later, Miguel crawled and splashed toward her. He put his mouth to her ear. This time, she could just make out the words he shouted at the top of his lungs. She shook her head, close to fainting, then opened her eyes again and thrust her hand inside her dress.

Miracle of miracles, the bottle was still there. She pushed it toward him and he scrambled forward and wedged it in the little overhang at the front. Then he looked back at her.

"Tia? This might give you some shelter."

It was only a tiny niche, but as soon as he said this it seemed infinitely desirable, somewhere she'd be safe and protected. He helped her untangle the line and move up over the thwarts. She fell, hurting her knees, but kept crawling with awkward, fierce determination till she reached it and curled herself in.

Gustavo crawled aft to counterbalance her and the two men huddled in the middle of the boat, carefully, so as not to turn it over. A wave submerged them. The waterlogged hull rolled, started to turn over, then came slowly back as Miguel threw himself across to the other side. The water drained away and the old man yelled, "No paddle. Can't keep her right."

Miguel: "The food's gone, too, and the bailer."

"Julio should have tied all that stuff in."

"He used the line for Tia. And how could he tie the paddle in? He was using it till we went over."

Gustavo rubbed his face. Salt caked his eyebrows. "I think the worst part's passed over. If we can keep afloat one more night, maybe another boat will pick us up."

"I haven't seen anybody since the storm started."

"They're out here; we just can't see them. We can't see a hundred *varas* in this."

Miguel wondered why the old man kept using the old words, the old ways of measuring. Then, suddenly, he understood. That was why he was old: He refused to change. Looking at the old man's reddened eyes, his thin bare shanks, he promised himself to remember this secret. A little later, his head fell forward and he nodded slowly to the pitching, fast asleep.

LATE that day, the wind rose again, though not to the madness of the storm's climax. The rain came back with it, the low gray clouds lashing them with cold silver whips. Spray and rain mingled, as if the sky and the sea were quarreling over who could punish them more. Graciela crouched like a hunted animal into the enclosing wood of the boat's bow. And like an animal, she wished for the concealing dark.

Miguel and Gustavo were bailing, back in the waist. They had no bailer, so they were simply throwing water out with their hands. As they worked, they yelled to each other. She wasn't really listening, but now and then the wind brought her a snatch.

"You think they're out there? Or could they have gone down?"

"I don't know."

"I miss them."

"Me, too, *muchacho*. But maybe we'll see them again in Miami."

"You think so?"

"*Si Dios quiere.*"

"You think we'll make it, Tio Gustavo?"

"If God wills," said the old man again. "Do you think this water's going down at all?"

"I don't think so. Should we keep on bailing?"

"It can do no harm."

"Have you ever been to America?"

"I saw Tampa once—fishing, back before the revolution."

"What did it look like?"

"Like any land. Like Cuba."

"No skyscrapers?"

"I didn't see any," said Gustavo. "Of course, they might have built some since then."

Miguel was silent for a while. Then he said, "Do you think they'll send us back?"

"Send us back?" the old man sounded surprised. "Why? They're friendly people, the Americans. And there are other Cubans there. They'll help us. No, I don't think they'll send us back."

"I won't go back," said Miguel. "Never."

The old man didn't say anything to that. He shielded his eyes, and rain ran off his fingers as he peered into the squall. "I thought I heard something—a motor or engine."

"Another airplane?"

"Maybe not. Over there?"

"I don't see anything," said the boy. He turned slowly, running his eyes along the ragged waves.

"*Coño,* it's getting dark," he said.

And Graciela put out her hand, groping, to seize someone or something. Her mouth came open without her direction and an agonized low moan vibrated in her throat.

It can't be, she thought with that corner of her mind that no matter what she felt, no matter how afraid she was, still looked on with bemused detachment at the strangeness of this life on earth. Not yet. This was too early, weeks too early. She waited through the minutes, praying for the pain not to return.

When it came again, it was like a wave, only not outside, but within her body. It started as a tightening, then grew into a pressure, squeezing, twisting tighter and tighter. She panted for air as it reached its peak. Then the wave passed and the knot loosened slowly and she could breathe again and open her eyes, to see the boy and the old man peering in at her warily.

"Are you all right, Tia?"

She felt her salt-dried lips crack as she smiled at them. They were afraid, even though all they had to do was watch, and maybe help a little. But this was something men never knew. A passage through which they could never step. It was strange, but even here she felt as she had when it first began, the other times—as if the baby brought with it some mysterious glory. Or maybe just that soon it would be over, one way or another. Ahead lay pain and fear and maybe at the end nothing but sorrow if the child didn't live. But that euphoric glow, like a long swallow of *aguardiente,* warmed her icy hands and seeped like slow fire along her legs. If only the old woman were still here to help.

"It's starting," she gasped. "It's coming."

"What is coming, Tia?"

"The baby, Miguelito. The baby."

The wind rose again as a wave drove the lonely boat upward with dizzying speed, lifting them all, boy and old man and woman, once more toward the steadily darkening sky.

33

August 3

THEY caught sight of the first one late in the morning.

Dahlgren and *Barrett* had run northeast for the entire day and night, making this their second day out of Guantánamo. Dan and Leighty and Quintanilla were standing on the wing, holding their hats against the blustering wind, when the lookout leaned over the rail of the flying bridge. "Sir," he said, and all three officers' heads jerked up. "Look out there around zero-three-zero relative. I think you'll see a boat."

Dan lifted his binoculars, and the ring of sight caught it right away: a white triangle amid the heaving gray of a running sea. A sail . . . a wave lifted it and for an instant his eye froze and plucked from motion an elongated shape. Then it disappeared, sinking again.

"Any more of them?" the captain shouted up.

The lookout didn't answer, hunching his shoulders into his binoculars. Then, without a word, he extended his arm and swept it from port to starboard, taking in an immense arc of sea.

Leighty hung his cap on the speaker tube and pulled himself up the ladder. *Barrett* took a roll as he got halfway up, and he crouched and gripped the handrail, then recovered and kept climbing. When he reached the Big Eyes, he uncapped them and swung the huge pedestal-mounted binoculars slowly around the horizon, tracing the same arc drawn by the lookout's arm.

"XO, to the bridge," he shouted down.

"Aye aye, Captain. Boatswain! Call the exec. If he's not in his stateroom or ship's office, pass the word."

Vysotsky pounded up a few minutes later. Dan told him the captain was topside, and he disappeared up the ladder. Simultaneously, the tactical radio remote spoke inside the pilothouse. Dan stayed on the wing in case Leighty gave another order, but he could hear the message coming over. It was from *Dahlgren.* "Speed ten," Van Cleef yelled out.

"Give them a roger and drop to two-thirds."

Another white pyramid broke the gray to port, and Dan swept his glasses around the horizon again. He counted five sails now, lurching and swaying across the leaden sea. He bared his teeth. According to Fleet Weather, over the past twenty-four hours the storm had curved, angling off northward. Good from their point of view, but there were a lot of people sweating it out in South Florida, Dade and Broward. So the center shouldn't pass directly overhead, and they'd be in the navigable semicircle.

Still, it wasn't good weather. They were registering forty knots on the wind indicator, and *Barrett* was rolling heavily as she came beam to the swells. He didn't even want to think what it must be like in a small boat.

"Let's try reporting in," Leighty shouted down. His voice was a thin cry above the keen of the wind.

Dan shouted back, "Aye aye, sir," and went inside. The coordination net was on remote number two, a clear, unscrambled VHF circuit. That would make range essentially line of sight mast to mast, around thirty miles at a guess. He motioned to the boatswain to dog the leeward door. Clearing his throat, he popped the handset and said in a slow, distinct radio voice, "Any station this net, this is USS *Barrett,* DD-nine ninety-eight. Over."

A decisive tenor answered almost before he was done. "USS *Barrett,* this is USCGS *Munro,* WHEC-seven twenty-four. Over."

"Uh, *Munro,* this is *Barrett,* reporting in on this net." He gestured frantically at Chief Morris, who read the ship's current position off the chart as Dan repeated it into the mike. *Munro* came back with her position. Dan told Van Cleef to get that down to CIC, make sure she was properly identified on the surface picture.

Leighty came back in as *Dahlgren* reported in. He reached for the message board as he listened. Dan pulled his own copy of the OTC's message out of his shirt pocket and rescanned it, refreshing his brain.

Since this was a humanitarian operation, the Commander, Seventh Coast Guard District, had designated *Munro's* commanding officer the officer in tactical command of the boat-lift monitor mission. As the other ships reported in, he assigned them to picket positions in a gradually narrowing bottleneck leading from the north coast of Cuba to the Florida Keys. They were to direct and assist the refugees, providing food, water, and navigational advice, and "fulfill a police mission as required." If they judged a craft too badly found to proceed, they were to advise the crew and passengers to turn back to Cuban waters. They were not to take refugees aboard unless foundering was imminent.

Okay, Dan thought, that was pretty straightforward, except maybe for the part about telling them to go back. He refolded the message as Van Cleef said, "Sir, they're getting thicker up ahead."

Dan stepped to the window. His binoculars stopped halfway to his eyes.

He didn't need them now.

As he'd checked their orders, *Barrett* had coasted on, not fast, but now she was surrounded. Ragged sails dotted the heaving sea all around them. He stared out, transfixed and appalled. There had to be a hundred boats in view now, and more poked over the horizon each minute. It looked like a regatta, as if everyone in Cuba had set sail in whatever they could find that would float.

"Slow to five," said Leighty. "Hoist the battle colors. Stand by the motor whaleboat. Away the casualty and assistance team."

Suddenly, the bridge, previously quiet except for the crackle of the speakers, was filled with voices. "Engines ahead one-third. Indicate pitch for five knots."

Ping, ping. "Engine Room answers, ahead one-third."

"Very well."

"Away the motor whaleboat, Section I provide. Away the Cat Team, muster on the flight deck—belay my last, away the Cat Team, muster on the fantail."

"Bridge, Main Control. Request permission to go to split plant ops."

"Permission granted," said Leighty. Van Cleef hit the switch on the 21MC to relay that to the engineers. At that moment, *Munro* came back on the air. Dan whipped out his pencil and got the signal down on the margin of the chart. "This is USS *Barrett.* I read back: Take Station Bravo, conduct channelization operations, and render assistance in accordance with your zero-two-zero-seven-three-zero-zulu. Maintain guard on this net and other nets in accordance with paragraph five. Report hourly at time fifteen. Over."

"This is USCGC *Munro,* roger, out."

Chief Morris read off, "Station Bravo: East corner, twenty-two degrees, fifty-five minutes north, seventy-eight degrees, thirty-five minutes west. Southwest corner, twenty-two degrees, fifty-two north, seventy-eight forty west. Northeast corner, twenty-three twelve north, seventy-eight forty-seven west. Northwest corner, twenty-three zero-nine north, seventy-eight fifty west." He had it already penciled in, but Dan stretched over the chart with dividers, making sure. The area was twenty miles long and five wide, oriented along the east side of where the Old Bahama Channel bent north to become the Santarén. Leighty leaned in over his shoulder. Dan felt him pressing against him as the captain's finger moved along the outboard limit of their patrol area.

"Shit. He's got us thumbtacked right up against the reef."

The captain was right, Dan saw. Along the inner edge of their area, the sea shoaled precipitously from 180 fathoms to 3.5. Along the vast light blue shallow-water sprawl of the Great Bahama Bank, rocks and shoals were marked with tiny crosses: Larks Nest, Copper Rock, Wolf Rocks, Hurricane Flats. Not a nice position, he thought. Reefs and flats to the north, Cuban territorial waters to the south. Obviously thinking along the same lines, Leighty asked Morris, "How far is it to Cuba, Chief?"

"From the southwest corner, twelve miles, sir."

"Shit," Leighty muttered. "And as the storm goes by, the wind'll swing around to put us right on those rocks. . . . Okay, we'll just have to keep a close watch on the fathometer. Ask Mr. Paul to give me a call about the anchor. Give us a course, Chief; let's get headed over there."

They wheeled slowly north and cranked on speed. Leighty limited them to fifteen knots, saying he didn't want to run over anyone—if a boat didn't have a sail up, they might not see them till they came out of the swell line. Dan asked if he should double the lookouts. Leighty said that was a good idea.

The captain started for the ladder, then hesitated, brow furrowed. "I meant to ask them something when they came up on the circuit—the political end."

"How do you mean, sir?"

"I mean, what exactly we intend to do with these people. Do we turn them back? Or are they political refugees?"

"I don't know, sir. Sorry, I didn't think to ask that."

"It'd help to know. I'm going to call them back on a scrambled net, see if the OTC has any dope on that. Be down in Combat."

"Aye aye, sir."

Leighty had the door open when the lookout phone talker said, "Aircraft to port, bearing two-seven-zero, position angle two." Van Cleef went out on the wing and reported back, "Multi-engine. Looks like a P-three."

Dan looked at Leighty, who was still lingering. The captain blinked, apparently thinking. Dan hit the intercom. "Combat, Bridge: We have a P-three in sight up here."

"Bridge, Combat: We're talking to him. He's from VP-ninety-three out of Key West. He's reporting surface contacts to the OTC."

"Roger."

"Captain's off the bridge," the boatswain bellowed. Dan rubbed his face, looking at his watch: still forty-five minutes before his turnover.

"Somebody waving to us, to starboard," the phone talker said.

"What's that?" He turned quickly.

"Wait one . . . Sir, somebody waving at us. Bearing zero-four-zero."

"I've got him," Van Cleef said. Dan lined his glasses on his and saw them, caught for an instant on the crest of a wave.

"Head on over there, sir?"

"Yeah. I'll call the captain." He reached for the intercom.

BARRETT pitched slowly, heavily, as the little boat danced crazily in her lee. Dan, leaning out, signaled to the fantail. A crack, and the orange thread of a shot line bellied in the wind and fell across the boat. When a tow line was across and they were trailing astern, he said, "Pass to the linehandlers: Haul them in and stand off about fifty feet."

"Petty Officer Bacallao, lay to the fantail," said the 1MC.

Dan had taken the conn back from Van Cleef, anticipating tricky maneuvering. With props turning at zero pitch, *Barrett* was essentially a huge sailboat, and she tended to turn downwind, which would be uncomfortable, to say the least, for the refugees. He had to juggle the engines and rudder to keep her bow into the seas, which swept down in impressive-looking ranks from the north. Closer to the reefs, the short fetch should shelter them, but out here they were building to a size that made the little craft astern pitch and heave sickeningly.

"Ready to relieve you, sir."

He returned Cannon's salute but told him to stand by, get the rhythm of the sea before he took over. A few minutes later, Dan handed over the binoculars, calling out to mark the passage of responsibility—hastily, because the helmsman was already wrestling the bow around again. Cannon stepped to the centerline, shouting orders, and Dan backpedaled out of the way.

He jogged aft and emerged on the helo deck. Aft of him, the weather decks stepped downward. He ran across the flight deck, feeling it slant under him so that his progress was an arc, not a straight line, and clattered down two more ladders to join a clotted knot of khaki and denim on the fantail.

A strange-looking craft rode the swells a hundred feet off, undulating as the waves passed under it. Two men were stretched out atop it. "Let me see those," Dan muttered to a chief with binoculars.

With seven magnifications, he could see the stitching in the canvas stretched over what were obviously old inner tubes. Some had gone soft, wobbling at every blow of the sea. The two clung grimly to sewn-on handholds. "Jesus Christ," he heard the chief mutter. There was no engine and only the snapped-off stump of a board that must have been their mast.

He looked around. The captain and the Spanish-speaking petty officer, Signalman Third Bacallao, stood by the rail, looking down. Bacallao held a loud-hailer. Behind them were several boatswain's mates and Ensign Paul.

And behind them was Harper, a short-barreled riot gun at port arms. With him were the rest of his security team, all armed. Catching his look, Harper gave him a wry little smile.

"Ready for anything, right, Chief Warrant?"

"That's my job, sir." Harper nodded toward the sea. "Looks like the fucking America's Cup out here."

"Sure does."

"Yeah, we ought to get some pictures. Then when anybody tells you communism's so great, show them these guys. Imagine wanting to get away from something so bad that you'll go to Miami."

Dan stared down, overcoming his shock at their craft long enough to study its passengers: two emaciated men of indeterminate age. The white-eyed faces that turned upward from time to time could not be read in terms of the emotions he knew. Bacallao turned the bullhorn on and off, making a loud clicking noise, watching the captain.

"But what happens when they get there?"

"Yeah, good point. Too fucking many Cubans in Florida already."

That wasn't what Dan had meant, but Leighty was saying something. When he stopped, making an abrupt gesture toward the men below, Bacallao lifted the loud-hailer and shouted a question. They responded with weak cries. Dan moved up a couple steps to hear the petty officer translate. "They say they have food but no more water. They don't know which way to go. They want to know how far America is."

"Mr. Paul, send them down some water. Chief Warrant Officer Harper—"

"Here, sir."

"Jay, we need to break out some of that landing-party gear. I want compasses, ponchos, groundsheets. Get it all staged up here; there're going to be a lot more boats in this condition."

Harper hesitated. "Sir, I'm on the security team."

"I don't think we need to worry about their taking over the ship, Mr. Harper," said Leighty. His eye caught Dan's and he smiled faintly, then turned back to the rail and the emaciated men on the oversized air mattress. Then he turned back and waved Lenson up.

"Did you ever get through to the OTC?"

"On what, sir?"

"On the political question—whether they'd be repatriated, held, whatever."

"Oh. No, sir, I didn't. I'm sorry, I misunderstood—"

"That's all right; maybe I didn't make myself clear."

The sky broke open in a spatter of rain. Cold, heavy drops clattered down from the whirling gray above to the heaving gray deck. The boatswains had slid down plastic jugs and the Cubans were drinking, holding grimly with one hand while the other held the containers to their lips. Water ran down thin throats.

"Think they'll make it?" Leighty muttered.

Dan looked around at the sea. The shelter of *Barrett*'s towering sides had damped the waves, but the raft was still going up and down so violently, he could barely follow it with his eyes. Outside the lee, the seas were high and cruel. He could only imagine what they looked like to the men below. The Cubans were shouting something now. Their voices arrived all but drowned in the roar of the wind, inhuman, shrill, and distant, like the piping of seabirds.

"They might, sir. The wind's bad, but the Stream's with them. You can go a long way in a small boat. Look at Captain Bligh."

"Bligh was a seaman. And he had a longboat, not something stitched out of canvas and inner tubes." Another man joined them and Leighty said, "George, what odds you give 'em?"

The exec stared down, mouth tightening as he watched the light raft soar skyward. As it reached the crest, Dan leaned forward, fingers going white on *Barrett*'s sturdy lifeline. The wind had caught and lifted the corner. For a moment, it teetered on the brink of capsizing, or maybe just dumping everyone off and soaring away downwind, skipping from crest to crest like a runaway balloon. But one of its occupants rolled over just in time, plunging the errant end so deep green water covered it and him. They clung grimly as the raft rode down the glassy back of the wave.

Vysotsky said hoarsely, "I don't know. Fifty-fifty?"

"That high? That thing's not going to hold air forever." Leighty snapped to the interpreter, "Ask them what they are. Fishermen? Sailors? What?"

Ballacao said, after an exchange that was interrupted when the boat veered dangerously close to the side, "They say they worked in a cigar factory, sir."

Leighty suddenly looked angry. "Okay, that's it. Get them aboard."

Heads snapped around on the fantail. "Sir?" said Dan.

"I said, get them aboard. Jacob's ladder to port. Get moving!" he snapped at the astonished boatswain's mates. "Have heaving lines ready in case one of them slips."

Beckoned aboard, the men hesitated, then unshipped lengths of board and began rowing furiously. The boatswains hauled in on the line. Ensign Paul jumped forward, shouting, but too late. The raft was pulled under the counter, out of sight. For a terrible moment, Dan thought the screw had gotten them. But they must have jumped at the last minute, because they appeared pale and shaken at the top of the ladder. The sailors hauled them aboard, where they stood dripping and shuddering, looking around apprehensively. Up close, they were younger than Dan had thought at first. Their inflamed eyes seemed to pulsate as they looked around. Raw bloody patches showed at ankles and knees, where the canvas had rubbed. "Get the chief master-at-arms," Leighty snapped to Vysotsky. "Get them some clothes. Find a space to bunk them. Have the corpsman look them over before they eat."

One man, cheeks hollowed around a cigarette, started suddenly toward the captain. Leighty shook his head brusquely and started off. "Sink the raft," he called over his shoulder.

"I'll take care of it, sir." Harper unslung the riot gun.

Leighty went forward, apparently back to the bridge. Shortly thereafter, white sea shot from the screws and *Barrett* got under way again, into the teeth of the wind.

Dan stood under the outstretched barrel of the five-inch, wondering if he would have the guts to put to sea in something like that. They could have no idea of what lay before them—except a damn good chance of dying. But still, they'd done it, and made it. Or at least two of them had.

What horror lay behind them, that they'd risk their lives to escape? He'd heard a lot about Cuba, but now, looking at the men's backs as they were led away, covered with olive drab blankets, he realized how little he really knew. You heard about torture and forced labor. But then you read that they'd conquered illiteracy, distributed land, that medical care was free. . . . In the end, you didn't know what to believe, except that a bearded man in fatigues had come out of the mountains and overthrown a dictator, then become one himself; that the CIA had tried to kill him, and failed; that the Russians spent $10 million a day in aid, and that Cuban soldiers were fighting in Angola, Mozambique. . . .

But people kept trying to escape. And wasn't that, finally, the proof of the matter? They hid in the wheel wells of jets, hijacked passenger planes, swam to Guantánamo, crossed barbed wire and minefields and seas. Only God knew how many of them didn't make it.

He stood on the fantail for about an hour. *Barrett* passed boat after boat, all tossing madly, all headed somewhere between northwest and west. Some passengers waved, but in others they saw no motion at all.

The ship picked her way among them, angling from boat to boat in what seemed like random course changes. But after a while, he figured it out. If the boat had a sail and people waved, *Barrett* proceeded past. If they seemed unusually agitated, had no sail, or the lookouts saw no motion, Leighty hove to and checked them out. The captain came back to the fantail each time, personally deciding whether simply to pass down supplies and give them a quick navigation lesson or to take them aboard. Gradually, a crowd of men and a few women gathered inside the hangar, where Oakes had assembled blankets, water, sandwiches, and hot coffee. The corpsman worked at a table, dressing scrapes and cuts. Some of the crew drifted back and sat around the flight deck, attempting to communicate in broken phrases.

When they finally reached Area Bravo, the clouds to the northeast, toward Andros, glowed with the milky reflected light that meant breaking surf. Cannon recommended a two-leg course along the southwest edge, and Leighty agreed. They maintained steerageway at five knots, rolling about fifteen degrees. The captain watched the sea for a time, then lowered the motor whaleboat. It lay to a mile south of them, and when boats sheered toward it, the boat crew intercepted them. They reported back by radio, and Leighty, running things from his seat on the bridge, decided whether to take them aboard or let them go on. As far as Dan could see, he turned no one back to Cuba, despite what the message had directed.

Additional ships kept reporting in: a British destroyer, HMS *Rhyl;* a Dutch frigate, *Van Almonde;* the Venezuelan gunboat with whose crew Dan had gotten drunk, *Federación. Munro* gave them areas stretching up the eastern side of the Santarén Channel. The hydrofoils from Key West reported in and were assigned stations to the west. Aircraft droned over, and once the whaleboat was vectored south to assist a boat that appeared to be on fire. They rescued the crew and brought them back to the growing group in the hangar.

Dan caught a short nap, knowing there might not be much sleep if the weather kept worsening. The center of the storm was due to pass over Nassau early the next morning. Then it was time for watch again. The wind was whistling in the signal halyards and antennas as he climbed back to the bridge. *Barrett* was rolling in earnest now, taking long swoops as the beam seas marched past.

Harper had the deck. "What's going on?" Dan asked him. "Still steaming back and forth?"

"That's right. Basically, we're just here showing them where to go, keeping them off the rocks. The wind's picking up, though. Looks like the bad shit will pass closer than they thought."

"Great." Dan looked out toward where the seas, black and huge, came roaring out of the afternoon mist. He checked the fathometer next, then checked the reading against their satellite navigation position. He felt slightly less comfortable when he recalled that the satnav software was running on the AN/UYK-7s. Fortunately, they had loran here, too. He confirmed that the quartermasters were taking fixes every fifteen minutes.

"Want to stay off those rocks," he told Morris.

"You got it, sir."

"Captain on the bridge, Jay?"

"Yeah, he's over there in the chair. Got his eyes closed."

"What's the whaleboat doing?"

"We recovered it twenty minutes ago. They're refueling it, putting more food and water and gas aboard. Going to swap out crews and put it back in again, keep it out till dark."

Harper sounded on top of things this afternoon. Good, maybe his counseling had taken effect. Then what he'd said about the whaleboat penetrated. "Till dark? In these seas?"

"That's the word."

"What's the gas for?"

"Apparently, a lot of these boats are out of gas because they've been fighting this son-of-a-bitching wind, and they didn't have much to start with because it's rationed."

Quintanilla, behind them: "Dan, how you fixed for sleep?"

"Not great, but I got my head down for an hour. Why?"

"We need an officer on the whaleboat."

"I'm just getting ready to come on watch. Anyway, is this a good idea? It's awful heavy weather out there."

"That's when they need us. Every gallon of gas we can hand out could save a life tonight. That's what the captain says, and I think he's right. I'll take OOD. Can you do it?" Felipe insisted. Dan shrugged, then added, "Okay. Just let me get my boots on, all right?"

HE got his steel-toed boots, foul-weather jacket, ball cap, and flashlight from his stateroom, then reported to the whaleboat just as the rain clamped down again, heavy and drenching.

The crew was climbing in, getting ready to lower. Dan stood close to the bulkhead, checking the crew. BM1 Casworth was the coxswain, with EM2 Reska, two boat hooks, McMannes and Didomenico, and the translator, Bacallao. Casworth told him he'd already done the inventory. They had two radios, two loud hailers, a hand searchlight with signaling capability, two battle lanterns, spare batteries, an M14, a .45, flares, and a kit of tools to fix motors and patch holes. They had food and water, individual kits prepackaged on the mess decks in taped-up trash bags. Each kit also included a photocopied chart of the Straits of Florida, a pack of Kents, and a butane lighter with the USS *Barrett* crest, the last two items outdated ship's store stock Cash had kicked in. Finally, they had a hundred gallons of P-250 stabilized gasoline in ten-gallon jerricans and two lashed-on fifty-five-gallon drums of diesel fuel.

"How do we transfer it?"

"Pumps and hoses, we float the hose downwind lashed to a life jacket."

"They know what to do with it?"

"We done it six times so far, sir. Seems to work."

"Okay, how about the standard equipage—anchor, grapnel, fire extinguisher, line—"

"Yes, sir. I sighted all that."

"Any other problems?"

"The motor cut out a couple of times. It always started again, but Reska just swapped out the filters. He thinks that'll take care of it."

Dan nodded. He couldn't think of anything else they might need. He moved forward into the rain but stopped at the gunwale just before he stepped into the boat, looking into it, the men waiting, the gear and supplies that covered the floorboards.

He hesitated there, struck by a suspicion he'd done this before.

Then he realized he had. Only the chief's name then had been Bloch, and the coxswain's, Popeye Rambaugh. The crew Rocky, Brute Boy, Ali X, Slick Lassard. A black night with the wind coming off the Pole. And beneath the swaying keel of *Reynolds Ryan*'s whaleboat, a sea black as used motor oil, its surface dull and somehow viscid, gruel-like, as if it were kept from solidifying into black ice only by unending motion. And beyond it, a swell and another swell, and after that, utter dark and a thousand miles of dark till the coast of Norway.

Casworth must have thought he was scared, because he muttered, "It's like they say in the Coast Guard, sir. You got to go out. You don't got to come back."

"Yeah, I know," he said. It was true. Looking down at the seas sweeping away from the ship, he really didn't want to go down there. Then he thought of the refugees, without motors, without sails, some without even boards to paddle with. While he had a stout boat with a good diesel, a good crew, and a ship within call if they got in a jam.

He made himself step over the coaming, grab the monkey line, and nod to the boatswain at the lowering gear. "Lower away," he yelled.

34

SWAYING out over the murky, storm-lashed green, the men on deck shouting and tending steadying lines as the whaleboat pendulumed, Dan thought with resigned dread that he'd never seen a boat launched in heavy seas without confusion, screaming, and near disaster. This time was no exception. As soon as they hoisted away, *Barrett* began a series of vicious rolls. The boat swung, slowly at first, but rapidly increasing its arc. The crew flinched and crouched as it came within inches of slamming into the hull.

He clung grimly to the rough knotted line as the winch drums turned, reeling them slowly downward. If anything let go, it would be all that would save him. The sea looked more terrifying the closer they got, foaming and seething. The frightening thing was that they were still in the lee. As the keel took the water, a wave charged in on the bow. It sucked the boat down, then thrust it up again. The heavy releasing hook clacked open suddenly, jerked free of McMannes's hand, and darted aft, straight for Dan's skull. He ducked as the crewman jerked it back by the safety lanyard. Beside them, *Barrett*'s sides heaved and sucked as the ship rolled. He blinked, unwilling to credit that he'd just caught a glimpse of the bilge keel.

"*Cast off*, you stupid asshole!" Casworth screamed, bent to the throttle. The bow hook, face crimped in sudden fear, jerked the sea painter free. The boat plunged and he staggered, almost dived overboard as the line flew upward.

The motor roared, and the boat heaved, yawed, and toppled, brushing paint and fiberglass and a strip of trim off against *Barrett*'s side as the hulls kissed. Then, gradually, it drew away. The coxswain increased the rudder as they turned, glancing back to check the position of the stern. The wind and rain and spray hit them as they emerged from the shelter of the gray steel walls, drawing a translucent curtain over the fading outline of the destroyer as it increased speed again, moving off, leaving them behind.

Crouched to keep his balance in the bucking, reeling boat, Dan aped his way toward the stern. He had to brace himself with both hands to keep from being slammed into the molded-in thwarts and seats. Casworth gripped the big chromed wheel like a wrestler locked with his opponent. He threw a quick glance over his shoulder, gauging a whitecap as it took shape out of the gray. Suddenly he whipped the wheel hard left. The stern dug and the boat spun just in time to catch the sea dead aft. Dan clutched the gunwale as she rushed forward, rising, then swallowed his lunch again as she dropped out from under his feet. Didomenico, McMannes, Bacallao, and Reska huddled on the thwarts, looking like fat, wet ducks in the shiny green hooded ponchos pulled on over their life preservers.

When he looked back again, the ship was just a shadow in the storm. Then she was gone. Christ, he thought angrily. They couldn't even see the ship, let alone another small boat. He tried the radio and got a loud-and-clear. "How are you doing?" Chief Kennedy's voice asked him. "Over."

"It's rough out here. Over."

"If it gets too hairy, sir, let us know and we'll come over and pick you up. That's from Mr. Quintanilla."

"Uh, *Barrett One*. That's good to know, Chief, but I think we can take this as long as it doesn't get any worse. Where you want us? Over."

"Head out around two-two-zero magnetic. We got a couple of pips out there, we think. We don't have a real good radar picture in all this spray and seas, sir. Just try not to run into anybody. Over."

"Roger, *Barrett One*, out. Casworth! Two-two-zero magnetic."

"Two-two-zero, aye."

They made their way through a heaving, roaring dimness like early dusk. A sea came over the gunwale and soaked them all in warm brine, floating the ration packs into a tilted shoal against the port side. The murky water sloshed over the floorboards, then disappeared, sucked down into the bilge pumps as the motor hammered steadily. Dan hunched his shoulders against the rain and spray, wishing he'd put on a poncho before he was soaked through.

THEY ran out along 220 till Kennedy advised them they were a mile or so out from the ship, right about where the captain wanted them.

On the way, he had time to think about what they were supposed to be doing. He'd reported to the whaleboat without really thinking it through. Now he was having doubts. Too late, as usual, he thought. They were running downwind now, the easiest reach. It'd be a lot rougher trying to maintain position. If Casworth screwed up and broached, it would be touch-and-go if the whaleboat would stay upright. The water was warm, but he didn't relish the thought of going into it in these seas with only a kapok life preserver.

In the second place, he wasn't sure they were going to be able to find anybody, much less help them. The whaleboat didn't have radar, and in this rain and spray, they couldn't see more than a hundred yards. A whole flotilla could drift past, and they wouldn't have a clue.

Finally, he told Casworth to start sounding the horn. If anybody was out here, maybe they'd call out, and then they could find them by steering for the sound.

After an hour, though the seas stayed high, the squalls seemed to slack off. Gradually, the mist thinned. He could see the sky again, low, tarnished, swollen-looking clouds that raced by about two hundred yards above the crests, it looked like. Horizontally, he could see maybe half a mile, but the waste of gray-green sea was empty now. He wondered where the regatta had gone.

Around 1500, a craft appeared to the west, rolling hard in the swells. Casworth spotted it first and spun the wheel to make for it. Dan clung to the gunwale, trying to keep from barfing but realizing it was a battle he was going to lose.

It was about forty feet long, an old-fashioned wooden fisherman with a scabby white hull and faded pink upperworks and a jury-rigged mast lashed upright on the foredeck with yellow plastic rope. It bucked wildly as the waves creamed by beneath it. A streamer of cloth fluttered at its head, almost like a burgee, but actually tatters of blown-out sail. As Casworth maneuvered them alongside, five men came out of the cabin, waving and gesturing them in. Dan told Casworth to hold off while Bacallao checked things out with the loud-hailer. After a spirited conversation, he reported that the boat was out of Neuvitas, that they'd been under way for a day and a half, that they knew approximately where they were, had a working compass and a chart, and knew how to dead reckon. They needed food, water, and fuel. "Gasoline or diesel?" Reska said, rubbing his hands.

They said *gasolina*, and got twenty gallons of it in jerricans and five ration-and-water packs. Dan made sure they knew about the reefs to the north and Cuban waters to the south. Finally, he waved and Casworth pulled away. "*Buena suerte,*" Bacallao called. "*Vaya con Dios.*"

"Those guys don't seem to be in such bad shape," McMannes yelled as the old-fashioned vertical stack puffed smoke and the boat turned its head slowly westward. "Yeah," Dan yelled over the steady roar of the wind. "They look like they just might dock in Biscayne Bay."

THE afternoon stretched on. The wind gusted and dropped, gradually hauling around, but the waves kept rolling in. Didomenico lost his balance and fell against the lashed-in drums, gashing his forehead, but insisted that they stay out. Dan gradually went through the seasickness and got his small-boat legs. They encountered and succored two more boats. One had ten refugees aboard, the other fifteen. He judged they could ride out the night, so he let them go on without taking anyone aboard. Watching them draw away, he wondered what had happend to the rafts. The answer that seemed most likely—that they'd broken apart—he didn't like to think about. He concentrated instead on keeping alert. Each time the whaleboat rose in the gradually waning light, his horizon expanded dramatically to a mile-wide circle of wild green sea. He remembered how cramped the straits had seemed from *Barrett*'s chartroom. Now they seemed immense.

"Whatcha think, sir?"

"It shouldn't get any rougher than this, BM One."

"That's about what I think, sir. It's bad in those squalls, though."

"You're doing a good job, Casworth."

Watching the clouds scud overhead, he remembered that when you faced the wind in the northern hemisphere, the center of a rotating disturbance lay behind your right shoulder. He swiveled in the blowing rain and figured that the storm lay to the northeast. A stroke of luck it hadn't come through here. None of these people would be alive now.

"*Barrett One, Barrett*," the walkie-talkie crackled, startling him. Good thing it was waterproof, since it was resting in an inch of water in the bottom of his pocket.

"*Barrett One*, over."

"This is the XO, Dan. Captain wants the whaleboat back aboard. We hold you out at two-three-seven true, eighteen hundred yards. Over."

"Roger, sir, we're heading back. Over."

Vysotsky signed off, and Dan lurched upright, got a hand on Casworth's shoulder. He shouted into his ear, "Just got the word to recall. Make it about zero-five-seven. We'll call them after we figure we've gone a mile if we don't see 'em by then."

As they turned into the seas, the ride got rougher—a lot rougher as their forward speed added to the impact of the wind and sea. The boat hammered its way up each comber like a bulldozer climbing a hill, then toppled over, hitting with a crash that whipped the hull and threw curving sheets of clear water to either side. Dan's crotch chafed with salt water. His head felt light from the continuous motion. Yeah, it was getting dark. This was the right decision, getting them back aboard. As to the refugees . . . it would be a long, rough night.

He was thinking ahead to hot strong coffee, a hot meal, sleep when McMannes yelled, "Something ahead."

He shielded his eyes. The spray lashed them and he gasped, then squinted again where the crewman pointed. A shape loomed mistily from a wave, then sank from sight.

"Head over there, sir?"

"Yeah," he yelled back. "Didn't look very big, though. Might just be wreckage."

Didomenico bent and plugged in the searchlight. McMannes crouched in the bow with the boat hook, grapnel and heaving line ready by his boots. Casworth flicked a switch and the running lights came on, startlingly bright. Dan realized only then how dark it had gotten. The boat climbed a long swell, dropped with a shudder that made the running lights flicker, then started climbing the next one. The stinging rain started again, whipping out of the gray murk like .22 bullets. The shadow didn't show for a while, then it did, closer. Dan saw that it was smaller than the others they'd seen that afternoon, lower, too. In fact, when he glimpsed it again, it looked awash, barely afloat. He was leaning forward to shout this to Casworth when the coxswain leaned on the horn. It droned out over the heaving sea, ludicrously faint in the roar of the wind. Nothing moved.

"Abandoned," McMannes yelled back. Casworth hesitated, then spun the wheel away.

At the same instant, Dan saw what he'd taken for debris along the gunwale stirring. A moment later, a head came up.

"No! There's somebody there." When he looked back, there were two heads, hands waving weakly.

Casworth was spinning the wheel back, bringing the bow around. "I see 'em, sir. Stand by, Manny."

"Bow hook?"

"Better go with the grapnel. Try not to hit any of 'em with it."

The searchlight came on, and the engineman swept it along the boat as they made up on it.

Dan swallowed, staring down as the whaleboat rose dizzily and the other craft sank, as if they were on opposite ends of a seesaw. These people were in trouble. The boat was wallowing, barely a hand's breadth of freeboard amidships. It rolled slowly as the waves lifted it. No mast that he could see. There was no motor, nor even oarlocks. Ragged dark outlines resolved into ravaged faces as the beam found them.

"We'll take these guys aboard," he shouted to Casworth. The coxswain nodded tightly, squinting as he eyed the narrowing barrier of heaving darkening sea.

SHE hadn't heard the drone of the horn, hadn't heard anything, so deeply was she concentrating on the other waves, the ones passing through her body. They gathered somewhere below her chest, then squeezed downward with relentless and incredible force, a giant's fist pounding the floor of her pelvis. They were too powerful to fight. She could only wait, taking gasping breaths, and endure, praying in the intervals.

So when Gustavo shook her and Miguel, she didn't even open her eyes. She was concentrating on the next wave, which was gathering now, throwing its shadow ahead of it.

"A boat," Gustavo said. "You see it, too. Is it coming toward us?"

"Yes. Yes!"

"I can't tell if they see us."

"They see us all right. There, they are turning on a light. Wave at them! *¡Hey! ¡Aqui, aqui!*"

The wave rose higher, sending the shadow of fear racing ahead of it. She panted, snatching breath as she lay in the warm water, as if being born herself. Sometimes she couldn't tell where the water ended and she began. Maybe the sea and her waves were the same and she was giving birth to some sea creature.

Virgencita, quitame este dolor por favor. Mother of God, take this next pain away. I offer it to you.

She bit down on the twisted rag, moaning as the wave broke over her, submerging her deep beneath a red-lighted tide.

DAN stood as the whaleboat towered above the wreck, then dropped below it as the crest passed. This would be tricky. They hadn't had to lay alongside the other boats and he wasn't sure, considering the violence of the sea, that it was smart to try. Spray ripped free in slow motion from a breaking, shattering sea, fluttered out and suddenly slashed his face, cold-warm, salty, stinging. He squeegeed it off his eyes as the other boat rose again, seesawing with a slow, dangerous, logy rhythm. He really didn't see why it was still afloat. The free surface of the water inside destroyed all its stability. It was pocked with roughly patched holes.

On the bow, McMannes got up as Didomenico crouched, holding to his belt under the poncho. They glanced back and Casworth nodded.

McMannes swung the grapnel in a short arc. It bulleted out, plunged downward, and disappeared into the boat. The two men—one old, one young, Dan saw by the light Reska tried to hold steady despite the crazy bucking—grabbed the line and hauled it in, shouting in weak, croaking voices. "What are they saying?" he shouted to Bacallao.

"Can't make it out, sir."

"We're taking them aboard. The way that thing looks, we may stove it in when we come alongside. Tell them to be ready to jump."

The translator yelled it across, but the words met head shaking, violent motions of negation. "What the hell's their problem?" Casworth yelled. "Tell 'em to get the fuck ready to come over here; we ain't going to save their fuckin' boat. It's fixing to sink."

"He says there's someone else—a woman."

"A woman," Dan repeated. "Great. Okay, where is she? You see anybody else, McMannes?"

"Just those two guys, sir."

"Tell them to get over here. Casworth, try to put the bow right down on their stern."

The older man waved, with a toothless grimace. A cheery, grateful motion of a bony long hand. Then he was slipping over the counter, cautiously but swiftly lowering himself into the water. He grabbed the line as it came taut.

Hand over hand, underwater more than above it, he pulled himself through the wind-ruffled sea. The whaleboat surged and plunged, spray broke over them, and a hand appeared suddenly over the gunwale. McMannes and Reska grabbed it and hauled him in. He sprawled on the floorboards, a bony old guy in torn shorts, one sandal hanging off a swollen-looking dark-skinned foot.

"Okay, the other guy," Dan said to Bacallao.

But somebody was shouting. It was the Cuban they'd just rescued. He fought Didomenico's hand off, jerked his way up, and crawled over the thwarts toward Dan, pleading in loud Spanish. "What's he want?" Lenson asked the translator.

"He insists there's a woman aboard, sir."

Dan looked around at the darkness. It wasn't going to be easy, finding the ship in this. He wasn't looking forward to hoisting back aboard, either. He didn't see any woman. Had the old guy gone off his rocker out here in the storm? But if it was true, they couldn't leave her; she might be hurt or too sick to move.

He knew then, accepting it, that he was going to have to check it out.

"Okay, I'm going over there, see what he's trying to tell us," he said. "If there's anybody else, or if it's all in his head. I'll get the kid, too. Take her in close as you can, Casworth."

"Be careful, sir. Take the forty-five."

"I don't need the goddamn forty-five. Just get me as close as you can without smashing in the side. Here's the radio. Take it; I don't want to drop it when I jump."

While they'd been discussing it, the whaleboat had drifted back, away from the wreck. McMannes had let the grapnel line go when he was helping the old guy aboard. Casworth spun the wheel, tucking the radio into his belt, and kicked the throttle lever forward with his knee. The motor hammered and the bow crashed down. A blast of spray like a car wash sanded their faces. Dan kept his down, shielding it with his hands as much as he could.

There, the wreckage again—you couldn't really call it a boat—a mad bouncing shadow in the rain and spray. Reska's light strobed across the kid, all the way aft. In the instantaneous brilliance, Dan could see everything. Hell, he thought, there's nobody else in there. But maybe the kid was too scared to jump. If he had to, he'd just push him overboard; the guys could pick him up from the water. There was no more time to dick around.

He crouched on the gunwale, one hand down like a sprinter bracing for the start. Then, as the half-submerged hulk passed him going upward, he launched himself heavily and gracelessly out and across.

The gunwale hit him in the stomach, so hard that he couldn't breathe for a few seconds, just hung there with his legs dragging in the sea. The kid had hold of his arms, but either he was too weak or Dan was too heavy, in sodden clothes, life preserver and foul-weather gear and boots, to move. Then with an enormous effort, he levered one boot over the gunwale. The other followed, and he rolled over into a shallow pool of warm water.

The beam of Reska's light flashed in his eyes and lighted the interior for a tenth of a second before it leapt away, the boat dropping like a stone.

The woman was curled up in a little cuddy, all the way forward. The wooden overhang sheltered her. She had a narrow catlike face and dark hair stuffed under some sort of cloth. Her eyes were closed and her mouth was set like a jammed square knot. There was something wrong with her, but he couldn't see what.

Then suddenly, he did: the way her taut fingers dug into the edge of the cuddy, the awkward, tumbled sprawl, the upthrust knees folded against the wet bulge of stomach.

The hulk rolled sluggishly as he crawled toward her, sending a wave traveling from thwart to thwart. He shifted to balance it, and the boat lurched the other way. He turned his head and yelled to Casworth with all of his strength, howling madly into the wind.

"It's a woman. She's pregnant."

The coxswain's voice, miles distant: "Can you get her over here?"

He crouched in front of her, studying her face. The darkness gave him nothing. Then a knife edge of Reska's light caught her squeezed eyelids. He felt her hand where it gripped wood like a C-clamp. A plastic bottle was wedged behind her. Her eyes snapped open for a fraction of a second, seeing him, yet somehow not. Then they rolled back and sank closed again.

He said awkwardly, "Excuse me," and put a hand on her belly. Under the wet rough cloth, it was rock-hard.

"Sir?"

He turned and yelled, "She's having it. Jesus, shit, and this thing's sinking. Throw me something to bail with."

He regretted asking as the whaleboat closed in. Casworth was a good coxswain, but no one could predict these seas, this wind. The reinforced bow loomed above him, then crashed down only feet away, sending a torrent of water over the boat. He screamed and waved them away at the same moment that two hard hats came flying in.

A helmetful of sea was heavy. The water didn't pour out when he upended the helmet. It just blew away. The boat rolled again, almost dumping him out. The motion made him sick, it was so close to going over. But he kept bailing, grimly, till his arms were aching.

Another wave came aboard, wiping out all his work in a second.

The woman moaned again. He glanced at her swiftly. Not more than three, four minutes apart. But they had to move her. The waterlogged, weakened shell beneath them could break apart or turn over at any second. He didn't see how they'd come this far in it. Maybe they'd capsized already. There wasn't a thing in it, no oars, no mast—just the boy with the huge eyes, and the woman.

He looked over his shoulder, to see the older Cuban standing in the whaleboat, shouting. Then McMannes was dragging him down. He popped up again and waved. Dan half-rose, then grabbed the thwart as the boat started to go over. Splinters lanced his hand, but he barely felt it. "What?" he screamed.

"Sir, you better get back aboard."

"Shit! Come on over here and get us! Get over here now; pick us up!"

What the hell was his problem? The whaleboat seemed to be farther away. McMannes was still waving, but he was looking behind him now—at Casworth, who was bent over the console.

Then he heard it. The whaleboat's engine was growling, roaring, and then, making his heart stall—nothing. Then he heard the grind of the starter and a renewed burst of sound.

The engine was missing, cutting out. Casworth was gunning the throttle each time he restarted it, trying to keep it running. But as Dan looked across the raging sea, he shook his head helplessly. He let go of the wheel with one hand, made a quick beckoning motion, then grabbed it again as the boat's head fell off, across an oncoming sea.

The engine stalled and died, and a moment later the lights of the boat died, too, dimming and then going out in falling, fading sparks. The roar of the wind filled his ears. Faint shouts came from where the lights had disappeared. He could distinguish Casworth's roar, McMannes's voice. A feeble yellow beam flicked on and wove around: one of the battle lanterns, but in the immense dark that surrounded them, it looked like a dying firefly.

Dan stared. The next minute, he was tearing at his pockets. His desperate fingers found the narrow cylinder of his bridge penlight. He pulled it free and thumbed the button. The next minute, he cursed. The little lifer lights weren't waterproof. He yelled, but his voice was too puny and faint to carry over the bellow of the wind.

The dim searching beam faded slowly, then winked out. A moment later, it bobbed into view again. Each time it reappeared, it was fainter, and farther away.

Then it vanished.

They were alone, he and the boy and the woman—alone under the sealed-down darkness of the racing clouds, in a heaving, water-filled boat. He stared into the dark, unable to move. The sense of abandonment was too great to grasp. Ten minutes before, he'd been looking forward to a meal, dry clothes, his bunk. Now they were as distant as the stars. He was adrift, abandoned, at the mercy of the hungry sea.

A moment later, he was scooping and throwing water as fast as he could make his arms work. If they went over before Casworth got the engine restarted, he had a life vest, but the others didn't. The Cubans didn't have anything—which meant he'd have to try to hold them up. In these seas . . . He bent and felt with his hand across the bottom of the boat, hoping for line or cord, but found nothing. The wood felt spongy and bits came off and stuck under his fingernails. Shit, no wonder it was full of water! The bottom was as rotten as an old stump.

A wave came out of the dark, hit them broadside, like a huge black bull goring its horns beneath them, then tossing them toward the sky. They rushed upward, the motion and the speed sickening and terrifying with nothing visual to match it against. The wind blasted them with spray at the crest.

The grapnel, he thought. That has line on it. He scrambled aft, pushing the boy aside roughly in his haste to get by.

The rough iron claw was jammed into the stern board, points dug deep. He hauled line in rapidly, measuring fathoms with outstretched arms: five, six, seven . . . eight fathoms. He hoped it was enough. He stripped off his life vest, snapped the straps into D-rings, then half-hitched the end of the line fast to the straps.

He had it lifted, ready to throw it overboard, when he saw the wave coming in from astern: a huge one, towering above the rest. Green-glowing, it grew so slowly, it hardly seemed to move.

He threw the bundled vest into the wind as hard as he could, then threw the loose line over after it. The boat hesitated, then started to rise, but too slowly.

The wave bulged up dark on both sides, then broke apart with an avalanche roar over them, hammering him into the bottom like a nail under a sledgehammer. He clutched and scrabbled mindlessly to keep from being sucked out of the boat. He closed his eyes under black water, thinking, This is it; it's going over.

But it didn't.

Slowly, the hulk pushed itself to the surface again. The wind caught it as it rolled his gasping face reluctantly back to the air. He gasped for breath as his heart throbbed in his throat, waiting to see if they were going to live a few more minutes.

Pushed downwind, yet held back by the floating scoop of the life vest, the hulk swung slowly to present its back to the wind. Now when the waves hit, the stern split them like a blunt ax. The water still rolled over them, but at least it didn't feel like it was going to capsize.

Reprieve, he thought. He dragged a sodden arm across his eyes and blinked around, hoping for a glimpse of the whaleboat's lights. But his eyes found no color, no light, only the cold phosphorescent sparkle of the breaking waves. Either the motor was still dead, the whaleboat drifting downwind without power, or else Casworth had lost them in the storm.

A moan from forward jerked his thoughts from his own problems. A long, animal whimpering, building to a scream that made his scalp prickle.

Yeah, he thought when he reached her. Her arms were rigid, and when his hand found hers, the cold fingers clamped on with inhuman strength. Her nails dug into his flesh like the points of a grapnel.

She was due, and it was coming—now. Another glance at the huddled boy told him there'd be no help from that quarter.

Staring into her face in the dark, he muttered, "I'm here. I'm going to help. Don't worry, it'll be all right."

He hoped desperately that he was telling her the truth.

35

AS he stared into her pain-twisted face, he slowly became conscious of a faint light vibrating at the edge of his vision. He couldn't tell if it was coming up out of the sea, or falling from the sky, or generated somehow by the wind, like static electricity. Darkness surrounded them, yet he could make out outlines and shapes. Strangely grainy, as if he was seeing by the individual particles of light itself, it was just enough to make out the huddled body under the cuddy, the crouching boy aft; enough to sense a wave as it bulged above the stern.

Okay, he thought. First inventory what you have, then you'll know what you can do. It wasn't a long list. They had two hard hats, a flashlight that didn't work, and the clothes he, the kid, and the woman were wearing. They had a grapnel, line, and life jacket, now deployed as a sea anchor. And that was all. Oh, and whatever was in the woman's bottle—water, probably.

It didn't sound like much. But the coolness licking his legs told him what he'd better deal with first.

He groped in the bilges, found the second hard hat, and thrust it at the boy. "Bail," he snarled. The kid took it but didn't move. Dan picked up his own again and began scooping and throwing. After a moment, the kid slid down and started bailing, too.

Next: the woman. Thank God this wasn't the first time he'd been around for a birth. He tried to remember the classes he and Susan had gone to before Nan was born. He just hadn't thought about it for so long, years, and when you piled on the Navy schools and all the stuff you had to memorize . . . Don't think about that now. Remember Lamaze classes in the Navy hospital: lying on the prickly thin carpet, adjusting the pillow behind Susan's back; slides of a baby angled in the womb; a room full of panting women, husbands eyeing wristwatches. Crouched in the heaving, pitching boat, he tried to summon the green-tiled room where they'd awaited the obstetrician.

Only here there was no room, no doctor, no pillow, nothing to work with. He crawled forward on his knees to slump next to her.

"Can you hear me?" he said as gently as he could and still be audible over the storm.

The faint gleam of opened eyes . . . He put his hands on her shoulders and his cheek against her face. She was panting, gasping for breath. The muscles of her arms were like cables.

"Do you speak any English?"

"*No. Mi marido . . .*"

"Okay. You understand, okay? We're going to help you out here. I'm just going to get you a little more comfortable. . . ."

He chattered on, not paying much attention to what he said but trying to sound reassuring. He had to get her to relax. Those rigid muscles were burning up energy she'd need later. He started by massaging her shoulders. His hands brushed the bottle and started to shift it. She moaned and pushed his hand away, so he left it.

He massaged down her neck and shoulders to her back, worked on that for a while, then ran his hands gently over her belly. Then he worked her thighs, digging his fingers in, gradually moving down. Susan had said that helped, forcing the tension out. This woman didn't feel like Susan, though. There wasn't much on her *but* skin and muscle. At the same time, his face close to hers, he mimicked deep, slow breaths.

Gradually, it worked. The locked flesh softened under his hands. Her breathing slowed and her eyes sank closed. He glanced back, to see the boy still bailing.

Finally, he ran his fingertips over her face. Then he straightened and pulled his light out again.

Carefully—because if he lost any parts, that was it—he disassembled it. He shook the water off each piece, the batteries, the reflector and bulb combination, the barrel. He held them up to the wind, thinking maybe they'd dry a little, though the spray was still flying. The red filter seemed useless, so he threw it away, then immediately regretted it. He had so little, he shouldn't be throwing *anything* away.

When he put them all back together and thumbed the switch, he was rewarded by an orange spark. He shook it and it brightened a bit.

Muttering, "Excuse me, got to see what's going on here," he seized the sodden hem of her dress and folded it up over her knees, squeezing the sea out of it.

The red-orange waver showed him a patch of hair above a streaky darkness on the thwart. Something about a mucus plug, bloody show . . . Susan had spent seventeen and a half hours in labor. The nurse had told him that was longer than average. But it could be more, if there were complications.

Complications. God. He turned and yelled to the kid, "Hey, you speak any English?"

The boy didn't answer. Dan shone the light at him for a second and saw that he was terrified. Also that he wasn't seventeen, as he'd thought at first. Now he figured twelve or thirteen, with long spindly legs. "Hey," he said again, making his voice kinder, "We're going to be all right here. *¿Comprende? Buenas. Tout sera bien.*" He knew that last was French, but Spanish was a Romance language, too; maybe the meaning would filter through. And the boy might have been responding to that or just to his tone, but he grinned a little.

Dan turned back to the woman. He wished he knew her name. He started to ask, but just then she sucked a sudden breath and stiffened. He held her arms, reminded her to relax, talked her through it. This time, her hand left the gunwale and searched for his, gripped it so hard it hurt.

When the contraction receded, she lay there, panting, her head thrown back. He said, "How many kids you have?"

"*¿Qúe?*"

"How many kids? Children? *¿Niños?*" He pointed at her stomach, held up one finger, two fingers, three fingers.

"*Este es el cuerto hijo.*"

Graciela could only occasionally see the man who talked to her out of the orange light. She didn't understand who he was or where he'd come from. It had crossed her mind that he was an angel, but this seemed unlikely. She certainly wasn't dead; she felt too much pain. Still, he was here, talking with her, and he sounded friendly.

Then she had to stop thinking about it as the wave gathered again, first in the back of her mind, then moving down her body like massive steel rollers. She tightened her grip on his hand. The angel-devil leaned into her face, telling her something in his strange slow language that only now and then she caught a word of. Then he was breathing with her, only more slowly now, and she remembered the chant old Aracelia had taught her last time, how to breathe to the rhythm of the chant. She concentrated on that as the wave crashed over her, until she couldn't breathe anymore at all.

IN the absolute dark of midnight, he could see—not only the luminescent hands of his watch, soldered together and pointed straight up, not just the weird emerald fire of the sea as it broke around them. It was as if his sight had been sharpened. He didn't think he was dreaming, though he was deadly tired. It was as if he had the eyes of a cat, just for one night.

Or maybe somewhere up there, the moon was out, above the riding clouds. . . .

He and the woman were communicating now. They didn't share a language, at least not a spoken one. But the language of hands, of help, they shared that. Isolated from the rest of humanity, separate and alone, they had only each other.

The boy bailed. He'd been bailing so long, he must be exhausted, but he was still dragging the helmet up and dumping it over the side. The water came in as fast as it went out, but at least it wasn't rising. If the seas didn't get any worse, Dan thought they might make it till dawn.

If they were still afloat when light came, they ought to get picked up. He figured Reska had eventually gotten the engine started again on the whaleboat. If not, they had the radio; the ship would have left station to pick them up.

Conclusion: *Barrett* knew he was adrift out here with two Cubans; they'd be searching for him. There were other ships out, too. Sooner or later, they'd run into one. If they could stay afloat . . . He blinked, realizing he was falling asleep, and sat up and looked around. Darkness, that was all, and the flickering light that ran along the tops of the waves. The world had contracted to the limits of the open boat, as if all that mattered was here: himself, the kid, and the woman.

The good news was that she seemed to be doing okay. He even knew her name now. She'd said it several times, guiding his hand to her chest, as if that was where she truly existed. "Graciela," she'd said. "Graciela Gutiérrez."

"Daniel Lenson."

"*¿Cómo es tu nombre?*"

"Daniel. Dan."

"Dan," she'd whispered, eyes sagging closed again.

"Graciela," he murmured now, still holding her hand. She muttered something back. But her voice was higher. He glanced at his watch. Not much interval now.

Suddenly, she gasped and pointed to a leg. He ran his hands down it, dug into the spasmed knot of muscle. Potassium would help. Wasn't there potassium in seawater? He decided giving her seawater was not a good idea. Maybe a drink from her bottle? He pointed to it, but she shook her head fiercely.

When the contraction passed, she moved her legs slowly. She seemed uncomfortable on the wood, and he took off his foul-weather jacket and padded the cuddy with it under her back.

* * *

SHE lay exhausted, feeling the sea beneath her. But this wasn't so bad, she thought dreamily. The sea was warm on her bare legs. Only her lips hurt—cracked, raw, open wounds. She thought of the water again but didn't reach for it. It was not for her.

The contraction came again. It felt as if she was being forced through the huge rollers they used to crush the cane. The smooth green stalks went in, then came out as an emerald paste as the sweet juice drooled down into the tubs. She remembered the sweet smell, like cut grass and molasses.

The contraction eased, but she knew it wouldn't be long before another took its place. Only a little while now until the baby came. She could feel it move and shift, feel her body mold itself around the insistent heaviness being forced through it. It hurt so much sometimes, she couldn't breathe or even think, but it was comforting to know that soon it would be over.

She remembered the first time, with Coralía. How frightened she'd been, and how sick.

Yes, sick, with chills and the vomiting. They hadn't known what was wrong with her for a long time, and the *sanitario* at the farm had not known what to say. Then Armando had taken her to the hospital in Minas. They told him she had to have a certain medicine but that they did not have it. And Armando had looked at them with a hard look and said, "*I* will get it. Give me a prescription so that I may buy it when I find it, and I will get it for her."

And it had taken him two days to go to Camagüey and get the medicine and come back. Part of the way, he rode on a sugar truck, and the rest he had to walk. He'd walked all night to bring her the medicine. Later when she asked where the radio was, she found he'd had to sell it and borrow money, too, for the medicine; it was foreign and very expensive. Then her time had come, and she'd been so frightened, and then she'd had Coralía. But then she had been sick again and for eight days had not known anyone, so they told her.

The second child, Victoria, she'd come very easily. There had been no problem with her; all the old woman had to do was talk to her a while, then later cut the cord. The only thing that made her sad then was that she knew Armando wanted a man-child, to pass on manhood as it had been passed to him by his father. Who could blame him for that? But he had never said anything or slighted the girls in any way. Yes, a good man. She saw his face again, leathery and lined, the metal teeth startling in his face, as if from another life. But the third child, Tasita, had been difficult again. And when she came, she never breathed or moved at all. So much pain, and then the sweet little face with its eyes closed so peacefully ...

Feeling the wave coming again, breathing fast to make up for when she would not be able to breathe at all, she thought suddenly, *I* can die, too. The last time Tasita, and this time me.

Only it didn't feel frightening now. Now, in the darkness, it felt reassuring. She wouldn't hurt any longer if she died. And for another, she believed.

She thought now calmly, waiting for it to reach her, that made all the difference. Who could really be afraid, thinking that if you died, why then you would be with them again? With Victoria and Tasita and Armando, and her mother, Dona Eli, and her father, José. He had not known the revolution; he'd passed away while Castro was in the mountains. And maybe it was better that way; a man with her father's temper would never have been happy after the revolution. Maybe that was why the *revolucionarios* said that you should not believe. Because without that, then you were afraid, and if you were afraid, you would do as you were told.

Then the crest pressed her down again, and she stared into the dark, arched helplessly in the crushing grip of something more ancient and more cruel than anything one understood until they had to give birth or die.

AND the sea heaved endlessly through the dark hours.

Dan sat beside her, staring into nothingness, and thought, There's something wrong.

He couldn't remember how long it was supposed to take. But if the average was twelve, and this was Graciela's fourth, if he understood what she was saying at all, it shouldn't be taking this long. It had been almost twelve hours now and the contractions were still coming, the times between them varying, but never more than three minutes apart. For a long time, she'd borne them with courage and held his hand. Then she'd passed gradually into irritable querulousness. She'd begged him for something for a long time, but he never understood what it was. . . . Now her hand dangled limply in the water, not moving at all.

She was getting weak, dimming, going out, like the batteries of a soaked flashlight.

He had to do something. But what? He thought desperately of a cesarean, but he didn't have a knife. Anyway, that wouldn't save her, only the baby.

Suddenly, she screamed, a terrified burst of animal sound followed by rapid, agonized Spanish.

He took a deep breath, fighting panic. He'd hoped it would be a normal birth, that he could just coach her and catch the baby when it came. But it seemed it wasn't going to work that way.

Okay, boy, he told himself. It's time to see what's wrong.

He turned the flashlight on and thrust it between his teeth. The feeble glow was no brighter than a lighted cigarette. Leaning swiftly so as not to capsize the boat, he washed his fingers in the clean seawater outside. Not touching anything else, he bent close to her opened legs.

Her hot, strained flesh opened easily to his searching fingers. Inward, inward, sweat prickling on his back. Her inner flesh was slippery with blood and fluid. He set his teeth and kept probing in.

Something hard—hard and smooth and slightly gritty. He moved his fingertips along it and felt the curving.

He remembered watching Nan emerge in the bright green-tiled room: the obstetrician's big gloved fingers showing him the crown of the baby's head; Susan's legs shaking, shaking; and Dan swallowing with sudden terror. He could see the top of the baby's skull. But it was too small. Microcephalic! He glanced around at the nurse's face, the doctor's, searching for the horror and shock and pity. But their eyes were unconcerned, routine, and he gulped back his fear and watched as Susan groaned and pushed again and the baby moved forward an inch or two. He saw then that the head wasn't too small after all; it was just pointed, like the end of a football.

This came back to him, and he remembered Dr. Carter's casual deep voice as he "just widened the canal a little, make it a little easier." How Susan had screamed, then cursed him wildly, but Carter hadn't taken offense, just smiled and patted her leg and said she was doing fine.

"*Bueno. Mucho bueno.* You're doing fine," he murmured now, and slipped his fingers around the crown of the baby's skull.

Something tough and only yieldingly elastic was holding it back. He pried it outward, pressing down on the hard yet at the same time yielding bone, till he got his middle finger under the lip. Graciela was rigid, making no sound at all. Maybe she'd passed out. That would be good . . . or maybe it wouldn't, if she went into shock. Sweat broke down his back again as he started working around it, pulling outward at the membranous ring. The baby's head was jammed against it with enormous force. But he pulled steadily, closing his eyes, concentrating all his attention on the tips of his fingers, trying not to tear anything, just gradually working his way all the way around, top to bottom to top again.

Graciela screamed again, suddenly, coming out of whatever syncope or absence she'd been in. Her muscles tightened around his hand. At the same instant the baby slid forward, jamming his finger against the edge of the cervix, or whatever it was. Then the boat bucked upward under his knees and a deluge of warm water smashed down on them. The deck dropped away, and he cursed wildly and jerked his hand out and pushed himself back, scrambling aft.

When he pulled the line in, there was nothing at the end. The life jacket was gone. The nylon strap dangled ragged where the stitching had torn out of the kapok. He held it, mind desolate. He didn't have anything else to put on it. Already the skiff was drifting around, presenting its beam to the sea. When that happened, they'd go over. His foul-weather jacket? No way to make a scoop out of that.

Out of nowhere, he remembered a light-filled afternoon at the Naval Academy: in the natatorium, fifty guys in the pool treading water, the instructor telling them to listen up, the Navy didn't give you a fifty-thousand-dollar education so you could drown and waste it. He was going to show them how to abandon ship safely, how to swim through burning oil, and how to stay afloat.

How whenever you were in a cotton uniform, you had your own life preserver with you.

He pulled his wallet and keys out, stuffed them into his shirt pockets, and buttoned them. Then he stripped his pants off and tied knots in the ends of the legs. He pulled the belt out of its loops and rove the line through them. Then he bent and put it carefully over the side.

He opened the makeshift drogue with a jerk on the line, then paid out as the stern skidded around. Better, but they were still going downwind fast. By now, the wind should have backed to north or even northwest. They were headed south, right back toward Cuba.

Back to Graciela, to find her into another contraction. He waited till she was done, breathing with her, saying whatever came into his mind—that she was doing fine; they'd be picked up soon; the ship would find them at dawn. Then, when it passed and she sagged back, he dilated her a little more. Warm fluid trickled over his fingers.

HE jerked himself awake, feeling instantly confused, then frightened, then guilty—as if he was responsible for this, for everything.

Graciela moaned again, and he sat up and pressed the switch on the flashlight. The filament didn't even redden. He dropped it into the water that sloshed back and forth across her opened bare legs.

Then realized he didn't need it.

The sky was still dark, but here and there were streaks lighter than the rest, faint rays, not yet what you'd call dawn, but like the ribs of a fan unfolding behind the gray clouds. The seas rolled endlessly toward them, black and gray in the distance, then translucently emerald as they towered. They crested but didn't break, passing silently beneath the boat. It took a while before his slowed mind realized the reason.

The wind no longer roared, no longer drove the sea mad with its siren song. Only a steady breeze cooled his face as they rose once again, and he looked across a world of water toward a distant black bank of departing cloud. He lifted his wrist and licked greasy salt film off the face of his watch.

Dawn crept toward them across the sea.

Graciela lay sprawled in her nest under the cuddy. Her hair straggled wet and tangled from beneath the cloth. It covered her face. Her cracked lips were bloody, and blood and shit darkened the water that rolled between her open legs.

The kid was sleeping, too. In the growing light, he looked even younger than Dan had thought last night. Dan looked back at the sky. Was that blue? He stared at it, unable to decide if it was clear sky or just a glimpse of a higher, paler cloud cover. If it was blue . . . He suddenly felt a surge of hope. It was barely possible that they might make it through this. Stay in the Stream; try to attract somebody's attention, either a Coast Guard cutter or even one of the larger refugee boats.

Then he saw the shark.

It must have been circling them for a while, because when he first noticed it, it was quite close. It slid down the side of the skiff, the tip of its fin making a faint rippling noise. He could have reached out and seized it. Instead, he just watched, sitting on the spongy floorboards in the growing light, watching it move past and off until he could no longer see its dark long form beneath the green sea.

Then he noticed something else. Looking down to where his weight rested on the bottom. As the boat surged, filaments of green light opened along the boards. There wasn't anything holding the boards together, and when the frame of the boat worked, they opened up. He put his hand down and felt the cool upwelling current between them.

"*Ayúdame*," Graciela whispered.

He crept forward on his hands and knees, trying to keep his weight on the thwarts, afraid to put his feet on the rotten bottom. The boy slept on. When he took her hands, they were icy.

SHE lay spent, empty, melting into the blackness beneath her.

She knew dimly that she was dying. The child was not going to be born. She'd held back a little strength, husbanding it for what she knew would come: the last, incredible, impossible task of pushing the baby out. But that time had come and gone, and the baby had not. It was locked inside her, and together they would die.

She'd thought that if this happened, she would call on the Virgin, but she knew now that no one could help her. The life was being crushed out of her, like a dog caught beneath the wheels of an oxcart. She'd seen that once at the *cooperativa.* She opened her mouth to scream, but she had no breath left in her. She couldn't see. The red mist blinded her.

Her last conscious thought was of her own mother. So many years before ...

Then there was nothing but the mist—no thought, no body, only something that watched without self, without anything but the watching. As it gazed, the red mist slowly began to whirl. As it gathered speed, a black opening appeared at the end of it. It grew swiftly larger, with nothing beyond but the black. She hurtled toward it with incredible velocity, knowing that this was the final and utter obliteration only in the last instant before it occurred.

WHEN he turned back her clothing again, he could see the baby. The top of its scalp showed wet and glistening, with little dark whorls of plastered-down black hair. But that was all. All these hours and it hadn't emerged. He didn't know how long it could stay like that and still be alive. Maybe it was dead already. Kneeling, he ran his fingers again around the taut barrier of restraining flesh. It locked the child in no matter how hard the uterine muscles shoved. He tried again to pry it apart, but he couldn't even get his fingertip under it now. If that was all that was holding it back . . . Graciela was exhausted, her breathing almost invisible. Blue shadows lay under her jaw. Her wrists looked bruised and bloodless, fragile against the swollen bulk of her body. He could see she was dying. "A knife," he muttered, rubbing one hand uncertainly against his chin-stubble. His dry lips were caked with salt. Christ, he was thirsty.

But he didn't have a knife. He didn't have anything sharp at all. The baby was stuck, and it and she were going to die here, and probably all four of them when the rotten planks split apart. Their fishy friends would see to that. His hand slipped down from his chin—and stopped.

An instant later, he was fumbling with his collar. The little nipples that held his collar insignia popped free and sank, to shine quietly brassy on the dark submerged wood.

Two pointed pins glittered in the glowing light.

He bent one back on the thwart, leaving the other sticking out, and gripped the silver bars firmly between thumb and forefinger. He didn't want to do this. He was no doctor. But she'd been in labor since the night before. She was exhausted. Like what they said about tactics: When it was time, you had to act, whether what you did was right or wrong. Or you'd inevitably lose as your opponent acted and you did not.

Now, at this moment, he knew his opponent was Death himself.

A moment later, blood welled up, dripping into the water and uncoiling like falling silk. It dripped, then trickled, then gushed out.

"Shit," he muttered. He'd cut it and the baby still wasn't moving. Graciela didn't react at all. "God damn you! Don't do this. Help us! For once—"

The baby turned slightly under his clutching fingers.

He panted, set the pin again, and bit his lips as he cut deeper. Then he stopped, horrified as the split suddenly widened of itself. A fresh burst of blood came from the tearing flesh. Jesus, he hadn't meant to do that. . . . But the head moved again. It was turning, as if the baby was trying to burrow its way out. He adjusted her legs, moving them as far apart as they'd go, and lifted her hips.

Suddenly, the baby's entire head slid out amid the blood and mucus. It was blue. Little eyes bulged beneath closed lids. Graciela groaned and threw her head back. Lenson dropped the pin and seized the little shoulders, eased them to the left.

With another gush of fluid and blood, the baby squirted out onto his lap, all at once, in a tumbling rush. It was very small and an astonishing shade of blue-green, with a pointed large head and tiny closed eyelids. It slid off his leg and into the water, slick as a fish. He grabbed desperately and got it, then dropped it again from clumsy numb hands. Finally, he captured the small body across his lap. One tiny froglike leg was tangled in the cord. He unlooped it, then stared down at perfect little fingers, a flat nose, tiny lips. It was a boy. And it didn't move. Shreds of dark tissue and streaks of blood, a bluish discoloration on the neck. He glanced at Graciela, but she looked dead. Blood trickled from between her legs. He stared at the flow, trying to think of some way to stop it. Blood in the water, leaking through the bottom, all those fucking sharks . . . But nothing came to mind.

He opened the baby's lips and cleaned the mouth out gently with his little finger. There was material in the nostrils and he got that out, too. Then he fitted his mouth over its face. The taste of salt and blood. *Blow in.* Just a puff or he'd rupture the tiny lungs. The little chest rose under his hands. *Let go.* The little ribs sank. I waited too long, he thought savagely. If only I'd thought of that, the pin, hours ago.

The little boy shuddered under his lips, struggled to suck in a breath.

A thin catlike meow, a piping, querulous cry pierced the rush of wind.

36

WHEN the sun rose at last, it looked down on a great wrinkled canvas of emerald and turquoise and indigo. The seas drifted across it, and seabirds dipped along their crests. Only the occasional shadow of a high cloud obscured the surface.

Below its searching rays, a half-sunken boat drifted in silence, tossing slowly, like the torn fragments of sargasso weed that marked the wake of the storm. Its occupants didn't move. They lay in motionless bundles as the light grew steadily brighter.

Dan woke to the baby's cry, thin and piercing as a seagull's. For a long time, he just left his eyes where they were when they opened: on the sky. How marvelous it was, clear and so pale it looked as if it had been scrubbed with abrasive cleanser.

Later, he lowered his eyes to the waves. He examined their shape and counted the seconds between the passage of two crests. Down to four feet, he thought. A good long period. And judging by the wind, they'd drop a lot more this morning.

The storm was over.

A pilot flame of hope ignited. He sat up, testing the balance of the half-submerged skiff, then cautiously stood. When he had his balance, he pivoted slowly, searching all around the horizon. The added height of eye gave him a horizon of about three miles, though of course he'd see anything that projected above the surface, such as a ship's upperworks, at a much greater distance. But to his disappointment, his eye snagged on only a single sail far to the west. To the south, clouds, and below them a flat smudge that could only be the Cuban coast.

Sitting down again, he did a little dead reckoning in his head. He came out with a position somewhere in the Nicholas Channel.

He didn't see any sign of *Barrett*, or of the whaleboat, or of anything else that looked like help.

That was the bad news.

The good news lay snuggled in the woman's arms, covered with her drawn-up skirt. The baby's eyes were closed. One tiny hand was curled knuckles and all into its mouth, and its cheeks worked slowly. Beneath it, he noted with pride the slow rise and fall of Graciela's chest.

She opened her eyes as if feeling his. They looked at each other across the length of the boat. Then she smiled faintly and her lids sank slowly closed again.

He must have slipped away again then himself, because the next thing he knew, the boy was shaking him. The sun was in his face and very hot. The baby was crying, and Graciela was rocking and humming to it. He grunted, sat up, and checked the horizon again. Nothing at all this time; the sail had sunk into the west.

"Bail?" The boy made a motion with the hard hat.

"Yeah, go ahead, buddy. Hey, what's your name, anyway?"

When he got across what he meant, the kid said his name was Miguel. Dan told him his. That about exhausted the conversation. He swallowed, realizing again how thirsty he was. He eyed the water that swirled around his feet. Clear as it looked, it was salt.

When he turned back to Graciela, he saw she'd unbuttoned her dress and was nursing. The baby's head was small and still pointed, covered with swirls of dark hair. It reminded him of Nan just after she'd been born. He swallowed again on the sharpness of memory, remembering her learning to crawl . . . to speak . . . the way she hugged him in the morning on the rare days he'd been home. Maybe it would have worked out if he'd just been around more. . . .

He had to put that aside. He'd screwed it up, or maybe Susan had, or maybe it was just accident or fate and no one's fault, but whatever it was, he couldn't alter it now. At least if he didn't make it back, they were taken care of. His serviceman's life insurance was still made out to Susan, and she'd get his pay and allowances. So Nan would be taken care of. That was the important thing.

From aft came the regular splash as the boy bailed. Jesus, it was actually getting calm. The wind just kept dropping. He watched the water roll within the confines of the gunwales. He put a boot cautiously on the floorboards and saw clearly now how the boards separated under the weight. The only thing keeping them afloat was the residual buoyancy of the wood. But wood didn't float forever. It got waterlogged, and by the looks of it, that wasn't far away. He toyed for a while with various schemes for making it watertight again, but he couldn't think of anything that didn't require stuff they didn't have, plastic sheeting, or fiberglass, or canvas.

God, it was quiet. The waves made lapping sounds as they struck the boat. The muffled sucking snorts of the baby made his cracked lips curve. Then he licked them. It had rained last night, but he'd been too busy to think about collecting it.

"How are you doing?" he asked Graciela.

SHE understood what he asked, not the words, but what he meant. So she didn't try to answer in words, just smiled. The child tugged on her breast, and she shifted, making it more comfortable.

She'd been thinking again about Armando. Right after they'd met, she'd been so jealous. He was older and had been married before. That woman was white and attractive, so people said. She'd gone away; no one knew where, just that one day she was gone. Armando might have known why, but he always said he didn't.

They'd met at the dance, and matters had progressed from there. But she'd been jealous, maybe because he'd been married before, or more likely just because she was so much in love, she wasn't thinking right. Yes, you didn't always think straight when you were young. Afterward, you saw that, but by then it was too late to make things right again.

Anyway, she remembered a few months after the ceremony at the *registro civil,* he'd said he would be out till very late, and she'd thought instantly, *El tiene otra mujer.* She knew who, too: the telephone operator, the new girl sent from Havana when the man who ran the phones had left for the north— "*el Norte revuelto y brutal,*" as the propaganda called it. And suddenly, rage had possessed her. She'd gone to his mother's and taken down the machete from the wall, the one his grandfather had used when he fought to free Cuba from the Spanish. It was old but still sharp, and she hid in the reeds along the road Armando would have to take to come home that night. She'd waited, trembling with rage, imagining how he would come walking along with *her* and she'd kill them both, hit them both so hard that blood would flow like a red river.

She'd been so angry that when she saw the shadow moving along the road, even though it was just one person, she'd leapt out and screamed at him. A terrible thing—she did not like to think now what it was she had screamed. Then she'd rushed at him, swinging the machete, trying to kill him. She would have, too, only he took it from her somehow, right out of her hand, and then ran. Yes, he had run from her, silently, without speaking, without explaining, along the dark road, until she became exhausted and had sunk down into the dirt, weeping in frustration and rage.

Only when they'd come for him and taken him away had she understood that what he'd been doing that night and all the other nights had nothing to do with lust and everything to do with love—

for her and for their country. She'd had to live with that, till years later he came back so strange and silent, back covered with scars.

The baby lost the nipple and snuffled and moved his head in little jerks, searching like a blind kitten until she guided him to what he needed. Then she lay back in the sunlight and closed her eyes, feeling its need and glad to give, yet anxious lest she not have enough. She remembered nursing Coralía like this . . . and then, suddenly, the pain of memory: Victoria. Victoria had had understanding from the day she was born. Graciela could speak to her and see in the baby's eyes that she understood. The child spoke perfect Spanish when she was a year old. She could not help feeling that Victoria was watching her now with her blue eyes. Yes, blue eyes for the child. She still couldn't believe she was dead. Because she could talk to her right now, in her heart, and Victoria replied in her perfect Spanish, *Mama, el niño es muy lindo. Tengo un hermano.*

Yes, you have a brother. Your father must be proud. You know he was proud of you, but a man wants a son, just as a mother wants a daughter. It is natural; no one can blame us in this.

She thought, Truly, what does it all mean, Victoria's death, Armando's, this great suffering that has come to our country? We were never rich. We always worked hard. Why had this great trial come to them, that they were imprisoned and starved, driven to trust themselves to the merciless sea? She didn't understand it. And what lay ahead for her and the small greedy one at her breast? Death, or life? More suffering, or perhaps in America a little bit of happiness—for the government in all its might and power simply to *leave them alone. . . .*

She was rocking and humming to the baby when she felt something jolt against the bottom of the boat, directly under her. She looked down but caught only a sliding glimpse of something dark.

GREAT, he thought, staring over the side. Half an inch of rotten wood between us and them. He sat up carefully, so as not to disturb the boat's precarious equilibrium, and searched the horizon again. Flat, blue, empty. Where the fuck was *Barrett*? Or had Leighty given him up? Decided he'd read the wrong diary, and so—no, he couldn't believe that.

The shark came back and bumped them again, harder. He swallowed. Something heavy had lodged in his gullet, like a sodden lump of undercooked pancake.

The boy had stopped bailing. Dan reached over for the hard hat and set to work scooping out the clear water. Shit, it was coming in as fast as he dumped it out.

The worst of it was that he couldn't think of anything else to do. He couldn't stop the leaks, couldn't go anywhere. They had no sail, no motor, not even a scrap of wood to paddle with. He couldn't signal for help; they had no matches and nothing that he could burn if they did, no mirrors, nothing. All he could do was wait and bail. And he really wasn't sure if doing either wasn't just a waste of time.

When he looked back, he was surprised to see she was crying. There was no change in her expression. Not a line of the weathered face had altered. But tears made glistening tracks on her cheeks, slowly drying to white salt. He looked at her in the immense silence, the brightness dazzling off everything, so that his own eyes burned, but he didn't think that was what was making her cry. What could he say? So much separated them. He knew nothing of her life, why she'd left Cuba on this crazy venture, in a rotten, leaking boat.

"It's going to be all right," he said. Her eyes flicked to him, then dropped again.

SHE tried again to recall where this man had come from. In a brown shirt and no trousers. An insignia of some kind on one point of his collar and another on his chest. Gustavo was gone. Julio and Aracelia were gone, too, but she remembered what had happened to them. She remembered the boat turning over, the terrible storm—though already it was fading, as if it had happened years before. She seemed to remember this man helping her, too. Hadn't he helped her in the night?

She thought then, Why wonder? Why not just ask? "Miguel."

"*¿Sí, Tia?*"

"Where is Gustavo?"

"The motorboat took him, Aunt."

"The motorboat . . . yes." She didn't know what boat he meant or what had happened to the old man. The baby sucked harder, and she shifted it to the other breast, hoping it was getting something. "Who's this?" She pointed furtively.

"That's an American sailor."

"But how has he come to be with us?"

"He came from the motorboat, during the night."

She nodded, giving up. She still didn't understand, but it wasn't important. Everything that mattered, she held in her arms. She bent and kissed the close dark wet curls, nuzzling the soft, sweet-smelling head over and over.

* * *

HE started awake again sometime later and realized he was burning. His face and the backs of his hands and most of all the tender flesh of his bare legs itched and flamed. His throat ached with thirst. The sun glared down from directly above, a soundless white flame that covered a quarter of the sky. He had to do something, cover himself at least. He leaned and looked over the side.

When he pulled in on the line, his trousers came sagging wetly out of the water like a long-drowned body. He expected shreds, but they were unharmed except for a broken belt loop. He coiled the line carefully on the floorboards. You could do a lot of things with fifty feet of line. Then he pulled the wet material on over his burned legs. He glanced at the sun again, then immediately away. Its heat was incredible, reflected and focused off the calming sea into their faces. At last, he pulled off his shirt and draped it over his head and arms in a tent effect. That helped, and he sat back, looking again at the others. The boy lay on his stomach, motionless, the bottoms of his bare brown feet toward Dan. Graciela sat propped against the cuddy. She was still nursing, the little dark head nestled against her.

She brought the child away and looked down at it, then kneaded her breast, looking anxious. She glanced at him quickly. Dan stayed motionless, the cloth shading his eyes.

She reached behind her, felt back into the cuddy, then slowly drew out the bottle, glancing at him again as if confirming he was asleep. He swallowed involuntarily as his eyes fastened to the clear liquid sloshing inside the plastic.

Quietly, she unscrewed the cap and lifted it to her lips. And a sudden cynical anger tightened his jaw, followed, a moment later, by a cynical voice in his head asking him what else he expected. She was just like everybody else, thinking of herself first. What was so surprising about that?

But when she lowered the clear plastic, her cheeks were still distended. She glanced at Dan again, then handed the bottle to Miguel, prodding it against the boy's legs till his hand came up. Then, still not swallowing, she turned the edge of her skirt back from the baby's face.

Bending her face down over it, she put her lips to its mouth.

He felt suddenly shamed, disgraced, as if he'd accused her and been proven wrong. He'd thought she was hoarding the water, keeping it for herself. While actually she hadn't taken any. She'd given it all to the baby and the boy. . . .

She lifted her head, looked again at the bottle, now back on the thwart where Miguel had set it. She licked her lips slowly. But when she reached out, it was to place it firmly behind her again.

Then her eyes caught his, saw that he was awake and watching. She brought the bottle back out and held it out to him.

And quite suddenly, staring at what she was offering him, he understood something he hadn't before: what love was, stripped to its barest and most essential elements.

Sitting there motionless, he saw abruptly through a surface that only partially made sense into a depth of meaning that underlay and explained everything. It was like unexpectedly comprehending a language you'd heard spoken around you all your life but had never learned. As he never had. Had never understood, or only glimpsed for a second or two. Only now, in this silent moment, did he finally comprehend how he had denied the best part of himself, the only portion that could regenerate all the rest, to Susan, to Beverly, to his parents, to all those who had loved or tried to love him.

It was as if a light had been turned on back in the dark corners of his soul, and he saw with sudden clarity the dust and rubbish that had accumulated there.

She still held the bottle out to him, and he couldn't stop himself from taking it. He yearned to swallow it all, down to the bottom, and lick the drops out from inside. Instead, he took one mouthful and made himself hand the bottle back.

He took his shirt and dipped it in the water at their feet—the evaporation gave a cooling effect—and draped it carefully over Graciela's and the baby's bare heads.

"*Gracias*," she whispered.

"It's nothing. Thanks for the water."

"*¿Cual es tu nombre?*" she whispered.

He didn't speak Spanish, but he understood that. "Daniel."

"Daniél."

"That's right. Call me Dan."

She smiled faintly and pointed to the baby. "Armando Daniél," she said, and let her eyes drift down, drift closed against the harsh, brilliant sunlight.

He was still looking at her, still dwelling in that timeless place of understanding, when the boat rasped and bumped as something grated again against the frail disintegrating boards.

THE sun dwelt at the height of the heavens, burning down remorselessly, sparkling off the waves. They rocked lazily in the center of a bowl of light. Gradually, the insight, the sense of peace and happiness ebbed as heat and thirst reoccupied his thoughts. Where the hell was *Barrett*? And where were all the other ships and planes that were supposed to be out helping the refugees? Where was the fucking Coast Guard when you needed them?

He was nodding again when suddenly the boy was at his elbow, shaking him, crying, "*¡Ay, mira! ¡Mira!*" He grunted and raised his hand to brush him away, like a fly.

"*Barco,*" the boy said. Then, in English, dredged up from where Dan had no idea: "A ship. A ship!"

He jerked upright and craned around, stared upward at what was closing on them. Gray and huge, it towered up into the pale sky. Brown haze boiled the air above its square stacks.

Behind him, the Cubans talked excitedly, happily. The boy pointed to him, talking rapidly to the woman as he touched Dan's insignia. Dan shook his hand off, still staring upward.

It was a ship all right.

But he didn't stand, as the boy did, and tear off his torn T-shirt. He didn't wave or shout.

He felt suddenly cold as he looked up at the sheer flaring bow, the high pyramidal gray superstructure, each level crowded with fire-control directors and search radars. From forward to aft, his eye moved slowly over antisubmarine missile launchers, rocket launchers, surface-to-air missiles, torpedo tubes, guns.

He knew that silhouette well, had studied it in the recognition manuals. It wasn't *Barrett*, or any other U.S. ship.

It was a Soviet *Krivak*-class destroyer. At first, it had been crossing their horizon and the extension of its course in a straight line would have sent it past a mile away. But someone had noticed Miguelito's excited waving. Pitching deliberately, the long gray hull shortened as it came around, sharp, high bow still throwing up a creamy wave that glowed in the sunlight as it steadied, heading directly for them.

37

EVEN through his shock, he had to admire their shiphandling. The sea crinkled aft along the hull, then a backwash at the stern told him they'd backed engines. The high gray block of the forecastle slid between them and the sun, casting a shadow that sank slanting into the sea. He lifted his eyes unwillingly.

A *Krivak*—a new class, the most advanced destroyer type the Soviets had. He noted the distinctive break halfway up her sheer and the large white Bloc-style hull numbers: 812. *Krivak*s were officially frigates, not destroyers; they were half *Barrett*'s displacement, but as usual with Soviet combatants, they were very heavily armed. He noted through numbness the four-tube surface-to-surface missile launcher flat along the forecastle deck; the two reloadable antiair launchers; two 100-mm guns on a low afterdeck. This smaller ship matched *Barrett* missile for missile, gun for gun. The intel data said they had advanced electronics and sonars, too.

His memory's prattle ceased as the boy grasped his arm again. Dan shook him off, still staring up. The bridge: looking down from it were impassive men in blue. Binoculars glinted. Sailors stared curiously from the rail. A party of men stood around a launcher. Yeah, midmorning, about time for the daily systems tests. . . . Suddenly one of the men on the bridge pointed. The binoculars came up again, and several more officers emerged onto the wing.

A puff of topaz haze emerged from the stacks, hovered for a moment above the upperworks, then blew down. It smelled just like *Barrett*'s turbine exhaust, familiar, yet in these surroundings disorienting and disturbing. Unable to move, he watched the bow nudge closer. Was that the stir of a bow thruster under the surface?

As gray steel eclipsed the sky, he heard shouting, then looked up again to sailors with AK rifles lining the rail. He half-rose, then saw the ladder. A sailor tossed off the last lashing and put his foot to it. It fell, unrolling, splashed into the water a few feet away from the bobbing boat, and swayed, clattering tantalizingly against the hull.

The man on the bridge pointed down, directly at him, then swept his arm up in a broad gesture of invitation—or command.

"Daniél?"

He half-turned, to see Graciela and Miguelito staring at him, puzzled. Obviously, they thought this was his ship. Crap, he couldn't think, couldn't decide what to do. Which was better, to stay out here, possibly to drown, or to be rescued by the Soviets? Two *Krivaks* had been reported with the battle group to the west. This was either one of them or a reinforcement steaming to join. Either way, once on their deck, Graciela, Miguelito, and the baby would be headed for Cuban soil again. He couldn't see them wanting that. Then, too, she was in no shape to climb that ladder. He turned back, spread his arms, and shook his head. He made signs for eating, signs for drinking.

His answer was a threatening shout, followed by a clacking rattle of bolts charging the first round. Then the short barrels came over the lifeline to steady on them, like cold black eyes on steel stalks.

"Wait here," he said to Miguel. "Here. In the boat. *Comprenez?*"

"*Aquí, sí.*"

At least, he thought as he slipped over the side, the shark had glided off as the ship made up on them. It was probably hanging around a few hundred yards off, waiting its turn.

The sea was a warm bath. He crawl-stroked clumsily in his soaked clothes the few yards to the end of the ladder, seized it, and started pulling himself up. He felt either astonishingly heavy or incredibly weak. The ladder swayed under his weight. It didn't really seem as long a climb as it ought to be. In fact, he reached the deck above too soon for his taste. The sailors were falling back in a semicircle, and one was helping him over the lifeline.

He stood dripping on the fantail, looking around. Scared as he was, mouth dry and heart pounding, he reminded himself to observe. No one he knew had actually stood on the deck of a Soviet warship. Anything he could describe—if he ever returned, that is—would be valuable. He stared into the eyes of the sailors. Only one had on the old-style blue jumper. The rest were just wearing flat white hats, rather grimy red-and-white-striped undershirts, leather belts with big tarnished buckles, paint-stained, scuffed boots; obviously they'd been working on deck just before the ship hove to. The Kalashnikovs looked serious, though, short rifles with big curved magazines.

Here came the brass: a paunchy gray-haired man in a white undress shirt and a combination cap, looking angry, and a younger officer trailing behind, blond, mouth anxious. Dan made the older one as either the captain or the exec. He started talking at once, glaring at Dan.

"Good morning," said the younger officer, translating.

Dan cleared his throat to keep his voice from shaking. He felt wet and dirty and slovenly, but he came to attention. Out of nowhere came the thought, I'm glad I got my pants back on before these guys showed up. "Good morning," he said, and saluted the older man, who hesitated, then returned it.

"The commander would like to know, this uniform, you are U.S. Navy?"

"That's right."

"What are you doing in boat with criminals?"

"My ship was rendering assistance to these refugees. We were separated in the storm."

"Your ship, her name?"

He stared at the guy—call him a lieutenant; they were about the same age—then at the "commander." What was the Geneva Convention rule about this? The Code of Conduct? Hell, he thought then, we aren't at war. How could the Russians get them to *Barrett* if he didn't tell them he belonged to her? Finally, he said, "What do you plan to do with us?"

"Your ship, her name."

"USS *Barrett,*" he said. Then, hearing a shout from below, he stepped to the rail and waved down at Miguelito. The kid waved back, looking, Dan thought, scared now, as if he realized something was wrong. He turned back to the Soviets. "See that woman in the boat? She had that baby last night. She can't climb a ladder. You need to lower a boat, put her in it, then hoist her aboard. That's how I'd do it."

As the lieutenant was translating this, a black man in fatigues pushed through the sailors. He had a pistol on his hip and a red star on his fatigue cap. And his Russian had a Hispanic sound. He and the commander had a short, rather angry talk. Fatigues looked over the side, sneered in disbelief at the skiff, then at Dan, who thought, I've got to learn some Russian, I really do.

"Can we get them aboard?" he asked the lieutenant. "They have no water and no food."

When the Cuban heard this, he seemed about to burst. He spat something short and angry at Dan, then stepped to the lifelines. The holster unsnapped and he whipped the pistol out.

He was actually aiming down when Dan lunged. He didn't have anything definite in mind, just to stop him from shooting, but somehow as they were wrestling there at the rail, the Russians so taken aback that for a moment they did not react, the gun squirted free, escaped both their hands, and spun away and down, making a modest-sized splash between the frigate's hull and the skiff. As they watched it vanish, a small dark shape tumbling down into the blue, Dan gulped.

The Cuban swung around and punched him in the stomach, and he bent over, gagging. Then there was a lot of shouting and hands grabbed him. When he got his head up again, the sailors were holding him and the Cuban apart. Shit, he thought, I didn't exactly make a foreign friend with that move. The Cuban looked ready to kill him. Maybe he'd just been bluffing, or showing off. But then, maybe not. Maybe he had orders to shoot deserters, or whatever the regime considered people who tried to escape.

While he was thinking all this, the commander shouted up to the bridge. A hand lifted in reply, and a moment later Dan heard the whine of the turbines spinning up. "No!" he yelled, lunging against the arms. He tried to drag them with him toward the lifeline, not really thinking what he was going to do, maybe jump overboard to Graciela and Miguelito and the baby. But five Russian sailors didn't drag. Still struggling, he saw the sea begin to move past, the skiff drop aft and whirl bobbing in the pale green whirlpools of the wake, saw a thin dark arm lift, fingers splayed out in pleading, or farewell.

NO one hit him again, but they kept their hands on him as they prodded him forward along the starboard side. Still breathless—the Cuban had gotten him right where it paralyzed you, just below the breastbone—he tried to keep observing, as much to counteract panic as anything else. His legs were shaking and he couldn't see too well, yet at the same time he saw and heard everything very clearly indeed. He kept listening for shots but didn't hear any.

He noticed the raised fantail structure first—all the way aft, rather awkwardly situated in the line of fire of the number two gun at depressed elevation. So a small boat would have a good chance of surviving a run in from directly astern. Markings for a helicopter pad on top of the structure, but its purpose was unclear—an enclosed mine-laying rail, possibly. Past the guns, he noted wide decks, nonskid in good condition. Sailors turned from painting to watch him being paraded by. They looked young. There didn't seem to be many senior enlisted around.

Up a deck, his escort releasing his hands so he could climb. Now he got a close look at the SA-N-4 launcher. Soviet antiaircraft missile launchers were usually dropped into a well to protect them from weather and ice. Even the type drawings in *Jane's*, studied during slow hours in CIC, showed them retracted. But this one was being worked on. No cover plates off, just plug-ins, so it wasn't major repair. Probably just what he'd thought at first, an operability test. A mass of equipment midships . . . no, he wasn't going to see that; one of the seamen was undogging a door.

Inside the skin of the ship, the impression changed rather abruptly from modern arsenal to something both oddly cozy and less technologically impressive. The air was warm and laden with the strong smells of Slavic food. The overheads were low and he noted more exposed cabling than U.S. practice tolerated. Partitions were riveted instead of welded. Everything seemed to be steel or wood, even where American designers used aluminum or composite to save weight. The wood surprised him. It wasn't permitted aboard U.S. ships at all. The bulkheads looked like they could use a good scrub-down and fresh paint, but damage-control gear was complete and the hoses new and the fittings glistened with fresh grease. A general announcing system spoke hollowly, and he heard the men with him discussing it. They pointed him at a ladder, clattered after him, and continued down two more decks.

Deep within the ship now, in a narrow white-painted passageway. He caught quick glimpses through successive doors of a machine shop, what looked like a stores office, a fan room. Blue flash curtains stirred as the ship rolled. Then a door was unlocked with a jingle of keys and he was pushed in. When he tried the knob, it was locked.

He looked slowly around at a small windowless compartment that was all too obviously a brig. Most U.S. ships didn't have them anymore. But modern Soviet frigates obviously did. It was as bare as any bread-and-water disciplinarian could wish. A narrow pipe-framed bunk was chained up to a bulkhead, and there was a sink, but no mirror, no can, no towel. A single bulb burned under explosion-proof glass. He unlatched the bunk and let it down and sat on it, feeling suddenly weak and sick.

The door unlocked and he caught a glimpse of an armed sailor outside as a skinny, pimpled Mongolian-looking kid in a stained apron slid a steel tray onto the floor, giving Dan a curious glance as he backed out.

It held black bread, thick and still warm; six slices of salami, the chunks of fat thicker than the chunks of meat; and a heavy mug that when he gulped thirstily from turned out to be not water, as he'd assumed, but straight raw vodka. He coughed it out explosively and peered into the cup. Actually, he wanted it, but maybe he'd better keep his head straight till he found out where things were going. He set it aside and ate the bread and salami dry.

Then he waited.

While he sat on the bunk, a lot of things went through his mind. Would Graciela and Miguel and Armando Daniél make it without him? Unless someone picked them up today, he didn't think so. He wasn't in such a great situation himself. Would the Soviets torture him if they thought he had useful information? Unfortunately, he knew quite a few things that fell into that category—details about Navy sonar processing, the complete weapons load-out of *Kidd*-class destroyers, ranges and characteristics of sensors, the tactics carrier battle groups practiced against multiple Backfire attacks.

Yeah, he knew some things that might interest them. Making it worse was that no one knew the Russians had him. As far as the U.S. Navy was concerned, Daniel V. Lenson was currently missing, presumed lost at sea. The Soviets could keep him, take him back to the USSR. And no one would ever know.

Half an hour later, he heard voices outside. Dan stood up, clenching his fists, expecting the Cuban in fatigues, an angry confrontation. Instead, it was six sailors with cameras. He smiled rather foolishly as they glanced at the light above his head, set their apertures, clicked away. Then the guard started yelling, obviously telling them that was enough, get the hell out now they had their pictures. The door locked again.

When it opened an hour later, the guard was at attention, assault rifle gripped stiffly across his chest. The blond officer, the one who had translated on deck, looked curiously in, then said something to the guard and stepped inside, nodding to Dan. The door stayed open. He felt grateful for that. One thing was quickly becoming evident, that Soviet combatants didn't have very good ventilation.

"I am sorry, the fight. Our Cuban comrade was angry to lose his pistol."

"Uh, I can understand that."

"He will have much papers, much explanation to make on return, why he lost it."

Dan nodded. He felt like saying that if the bastard hadn't threatened women and children, he wouldn't have lost his gun, but that might lead to renewed disputes, and he didn't want those. If at all possible.

"That is why the captain has forbidden him to see you; he is angry. You understand?" He picked up the mug, glanced at Dan. "You don't like vodka?"

"I'd rather have water."

"*Voda. Skaray,*" the lieutenant yelled out to the guard, who looked startled and vanished. To Dan, he said, offering his hand, "I am Captain-Lieutenant Gaponenko. First name, Grigory. Your first name?"

"Daniel."

"Very good, your family name and rank please?"

"Lenson, Daniel Lenson, Lieutenant, U.S. Navy."

"Your serial number and unit, please."

Dan told him and Gaponenko noted it down in a black wheel book, writing out the roman letters rather laboriously. "Now. Again, what you were doing in boat with worms."

"With what?"

"Our Cuban comrade, that is what he calls those who desert their motherland. Why were you in boat with them?"

"I told you. We were rendering assistance in the storm. By accident, I was separated from my ship's whaleboat and left with the boat you saw."

"Your ship does not search for you?"

"I'm sure they are, but you found me first."

"So you are adrift, you say. You have papers proving you are U.S. officer?"

Dan recalled his wallet, still buttoned securely into his shirt pocket. Odd that they hadn't searched him. He took it out and opened it carefully. From a mashed wad of cards and receipts, he extracted his green ID. Laminated, it had held up to the water pretty well. Gaponenko examined it curiously, then turned it over and looked at the back. His lips moved as he read.

"So, what do you plan to do with me?"

"With you?" The Russian shrugged. He held up the card. "I take, make copy. All right?"

Dan had been steeling himself for an interrogation on *Barrett*'s combat systems, speed, and capabilities. He'd already decided that he was going to present himself as the supply officer. After going through the audit, he figured he could fake being Norm Cash. But Gaponenko hadn't asked him what his job was aboard ship or whether *Barrett* carried nuclear weapons. He just wanted to copy his ID card. "I guess that's all right," Dan said cautiously.

"This *Barrett*, she is where?"

"You mean her station?" He reflected on this and again couldn't see any good reason not to answer. "On the north side of the Old Bahama Channel. Due north of Cayo Caiman Grande."

"That is far distance east of here."

"The storm must have taken us west, that and the current."

"How long you adrift?"

"Me? Overnight. Maybe . . . fifteen hours." Jesus, now that he thought back on it, it seemed like a hell of a lot longer. Then, with a stab of anxiety, he remembered *they* were still out there, no food, no water at all now. . . . "The others in the boat, the 'worms' you call them, you didn't help them at all."

Gaponenko scowled at the bunk. "We did not help them, or hurt them."

"But international law requires you to assist people in distress at sea."

"We assisted *you*," Grigory pointed out, slightly nastily, Dan thought. "Although I do not hear you even say thank you. Why should we help those who abandoned their country? Let them do for themselves; that is the way they wanted it." He stood up as the guard reappeared. "Here, this is gasified water."

Dan said, "Thanks. And, uh . . . thanks for picking me up."

"Anything you want else?"

"No, I guess not . . . except, when do the political people arrive?"

"Who?"

"The secret police. The commissar. Isn't there one aboard every ship? Is he going to interrogate me?"

"Oh, commissar. Yes, I am the *politruk*. You want to be getting more interrogation, that is what you say?"

"You?"

"Yes, you want me to interrogate you more so? I can do, you want." Then he saw Gaponenko was joking, and he smiled and shook his head. "All right," the Russian said, beckoning to the guard. "Now, no one is going to harm you, but we don't expect you, you see? The captain has to inquire instructions, you understand? Otherwise, there may be trouble. Cannot let you out. I saw you looking at things. You would allow Soviet officer to look around your ship, the *Barrett*? If I come aboard someday?"

He was starting to understand Russian humor. "No, probably not."

"How is the *Barrett*? She is good ship, happy ship?"

"Oh, relatively," said Dan, thinking, I sure as hell would like to be back aboard her, happy or not.

"We have dinner later. You sleep now."

"Just a minute," Dan said. Gaponenko halted but glanced at his watch. "This ship, it's a *Krivak*, right?"

"That is the NATO designation. Not what we call it, of course."

"Of course. It's very attractive, well maintained. Uh, what is its name? I told you the name of my ship—"

"Oh, that is what you want?" He shrugged. "It is written on the . . . on the . . . it is written on the back part of the ship; it's no secret. This is the *Razytelny* you are aboard. All right? How hot it is here. . . . I leave this door open, but don't go out. Don't talk to the guard. Now, you sleep."

HE slept, eventually, but his dreams were crazy mishmashes of Nan being attacked by tigers, himself defending her with his bare hands. Of being back in the boat—a knocking against the bottom, then the black fin breaking through. . . . He woke in rigid terror, to find the overhead light still burning but turned down from outside to a dull red heat, like a waterlogged flashlight. He stared at it for a long time, sweating, till finally, without foreknowledge or even expectation, he fell again into the black.

"PREHADETYE! Edeetee skaroy!"

Before he was really awake, his reflexes shot him out of the bunk and dropped him to the deck. One of his legs cramped and he almost fell as it buckled under him, but he caught himself on the bunk frame and hobbled out into the passageway as the sailor with the gun gestured angrily. What was going on? Now, the midnight interrogation? Still groggy, he let them half-lead, half-push him down the passageway to the ladder well.

Outside, he blinked and lifted his arm to shield his eyes from the morning. He couldn't believe he'd slept the night through. The flood of brilliance actually hurt them, like tacks pressed into his corneas. The overarching sky was intense blue, and *Razytelny* was cutting through it at a brisk pitching pace, blowers whining and flags snapping in the breeze. Steaming into the wind. Then, as the guard led him aft and down toward the stern, he saw why.

"Z'dayss. Na prava!"

The flutter-clatter of rotors grew louder as the helicopter made another pass only a couple of hundred feet above their heads. A flag broke on the mast, and the aircraft banked sharply left. He shaded his eyes, thinking perhaps it was an SH-2 or a Huey, but then his heart faltered as it came out of the sun and he saw that it wasn't an American helicopter at all. But as it closed, he saw the Dutch roundel, blue and white and red, and his heart started beating again.

Gaponenko was standing by the after mount, hat under his arm, watching the helo steady up. He caught Dan's eye and nodded curtly. He didn't seem nearly as friendly with others watching, Dan noticed.

The copter settled in a clattering roar that backed the watching sailors and officers away. Gaponenko gestured angrily at him, and Dan set his face, too, catching on to his role, and ran, bending into the rotor wash, and hauled himself up into the helicopter. He'd expected fair Dutch faces, but the passenger compartment was solid Cubans. More refugees, he suddenly understood. But his weren't among them. Then the blades sliced the air and the horizon tilted and *Razytelny* and the knot of stolidly watching Russians slowly slid off and away into the rolling, tossing sea.

* * *

"*BARRETT*," he yelled to a crewman, who nodded and spoke into his chin mike. They stayed low, and the seas flashed by. He wedged himself next to a window and looked down, anxiously searching for a half-awash skiff. But nothing showed on the furrowed sea except one lonely inner tube, adrift all by itself. Twenty minutes later, the helo landed on a ship that Dan guessed to be *Van Almonde*, the Dutch frigate. They hot-refueled, with everyone aboard and the engines still turning, took off again, and shortly thereafter the familiar silhouette of USS *Barrett* poked over the curved sea. As she wheeled, growing quickly larger, he saw a crowd of people moving off the helicopter deck, another throng in varicolored clothing covering the stern.

AFTER he'd explained everything to Leighty and Vysotsky in the captain's cabin, he stood momentarily irresolute in the passageway. The air-conditioned, filtered air felt great; the faint smells of paint and ozone smelled like home. Even the slow roll of the deck under his damp boots was familiar and reassuring.

He'd stepped out of the helo, to see the open hangar filled with watching faces. And Vysotsky, there to meet him, had explained. *Barrett* was packed with refugees to the extent that right now they outnumbered the crew. These were the people he'd seen crowding the deck and fantail as the Dutch Lynx came in to land—471 old people, men, women, children, babies, plucked from dozens of foundering craft or the water itself and flown or boated to *Barrett* from the other ships involved in the relief effort.

And more were coming. In his cabin, the captain told him that Commander, Seventh Coast Guard District, had ordered all ships to transfer their rescuees to *Barrett*, except for those needing immediate medical care; the latter would be flown directly to Miami from the small airport at Key West. *Barrett* would detach tomorrow morning and head up the Straits to Miami, where Customs and Immigration was making arrangements to concentrate and process the refugees. Straight shot from Area B to Port of Miami was 190 nautical miles, an awkward distance, so Leighty had decided to proceed relatively slowly, stay out overnight, and go to sea detail around 0700 day after tomorrow. Their orders called for refueling at the terminal and a night of liberty for the crew, then they'd probably come back on-line, since the human flood showed no signs of abating.

The scuttlebutt hummed beside him, the compressor starting up, and he bent to it, sucking icy water till the back of his throat ached so badly he had to stop. He was thinking now of the strained and oddly formal interview that had just concluded. The captain seemed embarrassed as he explained how he'd searched through the night, finally finding and recovering the whaleboat but losing the skiff in the darkness and the storm. Dan said he understood; visibility had been nil. Both officers frowned as he told them about Graciela's delivery and nodded as he'd explained what he'd had to do.

Things chilled, though, when he told them who had picked him up. But after an exchange of glances, Vysotsky had seemed interested in his impressions of the *Krivak*, and Leighty had directed him to draft a message summarizing his evaluation of *Razytelny*'s combat and damage-control readiness, his descriptions of the interior, his sense of the relationship among officers and crew, and the attitude of the Soviets toward an American.

He straightened from the bubbler, conscious now that his thirst was slaked that he was hungry, too. But most of all he wanted a shower, a shave, and dry clothes. What he had on chafed painfully, and the salt crystals didn't make things more comfortable. A water depletion be damned, long, hot freshwater shower, clean khakis . . .

Instead, he went down and aft, through the interior passageway, and came out inside the helo hangar. It was a mob scene. He picked his way through spread-out blankets, crying children, the sad bundles and wet crumbling suitcases that represented everything someone had managed to salvage of a life. A dolorous Latin refrain throbbed on a guitar. Then Dan saw him, sitting alone. He stood in front of him for a moment before the old man looked up.

"Gustavo?"

The old man stared blankly at him before Dan realized he didn't recognize him. He said, "I'm the one who was in the boat with Graciela and Miguelito."

"*¿Qué? ¿Graciela, Miguelito?*"

Okay, he had his attention now, but he didn't speak any Spanish. Dan glanced around, and a young woman got up from her blanket. "You want to speak to him? Tell me what you want to say. But slowly, please."

"Thanks. Please tell him . . . tell him I was left in the boat, after he was picked up."

She translated and the old man immediately stood, pouring out a torrent of questions. "Are they alive? Where are they? Did they come back to the ship with you?"

He explained lamely, conscious of the old eyes gradually turning disappointed, of the others who had gathered to listen. When he got to the part where he'd been forced to leave them, the old man looked at the deck and sighed.

"He thanks you for the news, and for helping with the birth. He knew the baby's father, he says. He will continue to pray for them all. Perhaps God will still bring them safely to land. You will pray with him? he asks."

Dan nodded, bowing his head. And the people around them quieted, too, some crossing themselves as the old man looked up into the dim overhead of the hangar, speaking to his God.

V

CAY SAL

38
Miami, Florida

TWO days later, he leaned over the wing, binoculars dangling from an aching neck, as the linehandlers backpedaled from underneath the crane-suspended brow. A warning tone beeped with monotonous insistence as the gangway seesawed in the breeze. The refugees stood along the deck-edge nets, watching in the glaring sun as one end of the steel ramp anchored itself on *Barrett*'s deck and the other descended slowly, clanging and grating at last on the hot, scarred asphalt of Berth 5, Platform D, Dodge Island, Port of Miami.

A ragged cheer went up, and a smile touched his lips. To him, to the others watching from *Barrett*'s bridge, this was just a cluttered workaday slab of sheet-steel piling and rolled asphalt, transit sheds and rail lines and secure areas with hundreds of containers stacked under the baking sun. To the people embracing and dancing, it was what that first glimpse of the Statue of Liberty must have been to his ancestors. Not that long ago, not long at all in the short history of America . . . and off to the west, windows flaming back the morning sun, stood the skyscrapers, not of Manhattan but of downtown Miami.

The run in had been straightforward. He'd picked up the sea buoys off the beach and run in through Government Cut, then turned left at a gantry crane at the tip of Lummis Island into the South Channel. Following the occasional pointed finger of the pilot, he'd come right to 296, gradually shedding speed till they spotted their berth just past the banana terminal. Even the wind had cooperated, pressing them gently in the last few yards until the lines went straight down to waiting hands on the pier. He looked out through the open windows, relishing a beautiful Florida day.

The trip up had been uneventful, too, except for a fight among the passengers. One man had pulled a machete, and another snatched a fire ax off the bulkhead. The respective families joined in, and Harper had to call away the security team to disarm all concerned. Aside from that, it had been forty-eight hours of hotel services: hot food, blankets, rationed water, medical care, and movies on the flight deck after dark.

And now *Barrett* was moored bow toward the city, stern to Miami Beach, starboard side to. He went out again to check the placement of the spring lines and whether enough slack was left for tide. As usual, the Navy was berthed at the ass end of nowhere. Across the island, he could see the upperworks of a brand-new cruise ship and two huge containerships. The sticks and stack of a break-bulk moved slowly across the roofs of the passenger terminals, headed out to sea.

"Mr. Lenson."

He turned, to see the captain leaning back in his chair. "Yes, sir?"

"Weren't the Immigration people supposed to be here when we pulled in?"

"That was my understanding, sir."

"I don't see anybody. Let's see if port control's heard anything."

"Aye aye, sir." He was picking up the handset when he saw the gate go up and the yellow school buses turn in past a huge transfer shed. "I think they're here, sir."

Leighty picked up the J-phone as Dan thanked the pilot and asked Morris to show him to the quarterdeck. He made sure Casey Kessler was finishing up the checkoff list, then called down to Main Control to secure the engines. By then, the captain was off the phone. Leighty glanced around the flat expanse of Biscayne Bay, dotted with sailboats and motor yachts headed out to sea, and swung down. "Go ahead and secure," he said to Dan, and disappeared.

The 1MC said, "Now secure the special sea and anchor detail. Set the normal in-port watch. On deck, watch section one."

Vysotsky was suddenly beside him. Dan started; he hadn't seen the executive officer arrive. "Where's the captain? Do you see his car yet?"

"He just went below, sir. A car?"

"The port people are supposed to have a sedan here for him and a pickup or a station wagon for a duty vehicle. There should also be some people from Tracor Marine to look at the evaps."

"I'll find out, sir."

"Okay." Vysotsky passed a hand over his cowlick, but it sprang right back up again. "Just so you don't have to ask, we'll pass liberty by divisions to expire on board at zero-six. Make sure everybody gets the word to exercise caution. There's been some racial tension here lately. I'll be in the captain's cabin if you need me."

"Aye aye, sir." He revolved in his mind what had to be done but didn't come up with much. The guys had worked hard for four weeks; they deserved a break. He decided to let them all go, except of course the duty section.

Vysotsky left the bridge. Dan called port services and found the woman responsible for the vehicles. She said they were at the agency; all *Barrett* had to do was send someone over to pick them up. She would call Tracor and find out what the story was on their team. Dan called to Kessler, "Casey, you CDO today?"

"Yeah, why?"

He told him about the cars, then called Vysotsky and told him it was being worked. After which, he went out on the wing, checked the lines and rat guards again, then looked aft.

The first Cubans were filing off, a slow-moving line that inched down the brow. Security types in brown uniforms watched in the heat. Men and women clutched their possessions. Children clung to hands and skirts. Not one looked back at the ship as they climbed slowly up into the buses.

Harper appeared, lean in rumpled khakis, fore-and-aft cap cocked jauntily. "So, what's the plan? We gonna let the guys rampage?"

"Liberty by divisions, Jay. Start at eleven. Warn them to be careful; the exec said something about racial trouble."

"Good enough." The chief warrant started to turn away, then completed his rotation 360 degrees. "Say, some of the guys from the department are going to get dinner, then hit some reggae bars. Want to come? Get off the ship, rub bodies with some significant female companionship?"

"I have a place to go first, but maybe we can link up later. Where's dinner?"

"Place called East Coast Fisheries. Sounds like a canning factory, but it's supposed to be the best restaurant in town. Mitch Miller's gonna rent a car, but I don't think it's more than a mile; you can walk it or take that bike of yours if you don't want to wait for a taxi. After that, we'll head out to Coconut Grove."

"Well, don't wait on me. But I'll try to make it." Dan remembered another loose end. "Hey, how about checking with Dr. Shrobo before you make libs, find out if he wants to go home or what? We may have to make some calls, get him a ride to the airport, whatever. I don't want to overlook him like we did last time."

"Roger, wilco," said Harper.

THAT afternoon, he stopped on Biscayne Boulevard, just outside the gate, feeling conspicuous in his trop whites, and raised a hand for a cab. Taxi after taxi went by; the traffic was heavy, but none stopped. He wondered if it was the uniform. This was another decade, but no one who'd worn a uniform through the seventies would ever feel entirely comfortable in public in one again. But it might give him more clout where he was going. Finally, a Yellow pulled over. The driver looked Hispanic, and when Dan asked him, "Say, you know where they're taking the refugees?" he flicked dark eyes at him in the rearview mirror.

"You mean Freedom City?"

"I don't know. Where they're taking the people who just came in from Cuba."

"That's it, but it's way the hell west of town, Krome Avenue."

"Can I get there on a twenty?"

The cabbie flipped the meter on and pulled out, and Dan settled back, looking out at a changed city.

He remembered the Gold Coast from years before, driving down with Susan during his summer leave: St. Augustine, Disney World, the Space Coast, Palm Beach, the Everglades, Key West. They'd taken A1A most of the way. How bitter recollected happiness became.... He looked out, trying to stop thinking about it. He didn't remember all these new buildings. Miami was booming all right.

"So, what's the Navy think about the trial?"

"I don't know; we just pulled in. What trial?"

"Some nigger on a motorcycle, he resisted arrest, took two cops on a high-speed chase, then ran himself into an abutment. So what's Dade County do? The cops are Cuban, right? So it puts *them* on trial. The verdict's coming out today."

"Is that so?" He stared out, only half-listening as the driver railed on. Looking down from the highway, he saw cafés, bodegas, outdoor markets. One sign read, ENGLISH SPOKEN HERE. Then gradually the city fell away, till they were in open country, scrub forest, fields of what looked like cane.

Then he saw new chain-link fence and buses and trucks idling on raw dirt. "Krome Avenue," said the driver. "Where you want out, at the gate?"

Dan peered out, heart sinking as he saw what he'd feared: hordes of people, guard towers, barbed wire.... "Yeah."

"Want me to wait?"

"No. Thanks." He paid and got out and stood outside the gate, adjusting his ribbons. A convoy was coming in, charter buses flanked by Florida State Police with blue lights flashing. Scrub brush grew in a trash-littered ditch, then there was the fence, so new that straw was still stuck to its concrete footings.

When the convoy was through, he went up to the gate. A guard in a sweat-stained uniform faced him through a metal-bar turnstile he made no move to open. He wore a badge and a revolver. His name tag glittered in the sun. It said STANT. "Help you?" he grunted.

"I'm looking for someone."

"Detainee? Guard?"

"Uh, detainees. They're Cuban. Might have just come in." He cleared his throat at the hostile stare. "I'm on a Navy ship docked over at bayside. We were picking up refugees in the Straits. There were two, three people I wanted to check on, see if they made it."

Already, Stant was shaking his head. "When they get in?"

"I'm not sure. But this is where they all come, right?"

"No. They're routing them to Army camps now—Eglin, Fort Chaffee, Indian Town, all over the country."

"But isn't there a central registry—"

"What? No, no, no. This ain't the *Navy,* Captain. What you're looking for flat don't exist. See those trucks? We're taking in three hundred a day. They've got sixteen thousand in tents in Key West. We are totally overwhelmed."

"How about your roster, then? I can check that and see if she's here."

"There *ain't* no list, I told you. Shit, half these people change their names anyway once they hit the United States."

"You mean you don't know who you have in there?"

"Well, some. But others, hell, we got no idea." Stant seemed to overcome some internal bitterness. He unlocked the turnstile and waved Dan into a guard shack. "Sorry, I been on eighteen hours now. You want to come in, you can look at what we got. But it ain't much. I mean, this caught everybody by surprise. It's like there was a signal on the twenty-sixth of July and all of a sudden everybody hauled ass for the beaches. At first, they were sneaking out. Then they realized nobody was stopping them, so they all started coming, and now two days ago we find out fucking Castro's opened all the jails. We're getting nutcases, murderers, smugglers, homos, psychopaths, you name it."

"What, he's releasing criminals?"

"You don't get news out there on your ship, huh? Pretty clever, he gets rid of his deadwood and sticks it to us at the same time. FBI's got teams flying down. Now they got to decide who's kosher and who they better hold on to. Give us two months and we'll have it sorted out, but right now it's a madhouse. You ask me if Juan McSanchez is here, all I can give you's the old Customs and Immigration salute." He shrugged and pulled a printout from under a counter. "This here's all we got, and I'll tell you now it's a week out of date."

"Well, can I go in and look?"

"No can do, sir. Orders are no visitors, not even family. We can't guarantee safety. We got just enough personnel to man the gate. You got a name, I can put the word out, have them show up here. That might take all day, though."

"But how do they contact their families?"

"Over there." The guard pointed; Dan saw lines at a row of pay phones. "They get two free calls—anywhere in the country. They got relatives or friends, they come down and pick them up. After the paperwork and shots, and after they get their green cards."

"Can I leave a message?"

Stant nodded. "Sure. No guarantee your friends will get it, but we'll put it out down the grapevine, like I said."

He wrote her a short note, telling her who he was, where *Barrett* was, asking her to call. He folded it, wrote "Graciela Gutiérrez" on the flap, and handed it over. After a second, he took out his wallet.

"Forget it; put that back." Stant tucked the slip into his uniform pocket. "I'll get it to her, if she's here."

Stant let him out and went back inside the shack. Dan stood irresolute, still not convinced there was no way to find her.

He drifted along the fence and came to a section that paralleled the road. The grass within was foot-worn to bare dirt, and men stood along it smoking. Most ignored him, but one wiry mustached man perked up and gestured him closer. He jittered from one foot to the other, rubbing his hands against his folded arms as if he was cold, though the heat was penetrating.

"Say friend, got a cigarette to spare?"

"No, sorry. I don't smoke."

"Speak English good, don't I? Used to live in San Antone. You looking for somebody?"

"Yeah."

"Who? Maybe I can help."

"Gutiérrez? Graciela Gutiérrez?"

"Oh sure, I know her. Want me to get her for you?"

Dan stared through the fence into the man's eyes, then looked behind him at dozens, scores, hundreds of men dawdling aimlessly along the fence line, talking or just staring out at passing cars. A tattooed teenager urinated against the trunk of a burnt-looking palm tree.

"You know her?"

"Oh sure." Tobacco-stained fingers probed the mesh. "Pretty girl, I know her, sure. Give me a dollar, I'll get her for you. Or find you another girl—"

"Thanks anyway," said Dan, and paced on, ignoring the shouting, the transition into no-doubt-obscene Spanish. Past the gate area he could look in to where row on row of tents stretched back across the sandy soil. They were going to have a hell of a mosquito problem this close to the Everglades. He saw smoke rising from cook fires, people standing in line holding paper bags, children running, men sitting on overturned cans playing cards. Gradually, he realized the camp was far larger than he'd thought. Only then did he accept, reluctantly, that there was no way to find out if she'd made it or not. It was chaos on the far side of the wire.

They'd fled Cuba looking for freedom. And here they were penned up again.

He only hoped Graciela and Miguelito were among them.

WHEN he got to the restaurant, he found everybody together at a table in the back: Harper and Horseheads; Cephas, the departmental yeoman; Chief Miller, Harper's second in command on the security team. "Had a little errand," he apologized as they moved their chairs to let him in. "Then I had to go back to the ship and change."

"That's okay, sir. Glad you could make it. Casey was gonna be here, too, but he's got duty."

"What's good?"

"Steak, seafood. We already ordered. You'll pay, but it's good."

Dan thought unhappily that after the two taxi rides, he had only four dollars left. Harper looked different, and it wasn't just the thick gold chain around his neck and the shirt unbuttoned to show his chest hair.

"My God. Is that a toupee?"

The chief warrant patted it fondly. "Ain't you ever seen this? My liberty rug. Actual tests prove it doubles my batting average. So, what you ordering?"

"Maybe just a salad."

"Oh, right, you're the guy owes his fillings to the fucking lawyers. Why don't I pick it up this time? Hey! Slick Hips! Martini's your drink, right?"

"Well, okay. Thanks," Dan said. "I'll pay you back next week. Straight up, two olives. And a glass of water on the side."

"Hey, we got mail, didn't we? You hear from your fucking ex, your little girl?"

"No." The question reminded him that he hadn't heard from them since they got under way from Charleston. "I got to find a card, get her a toy or something. Her birthday's next month."

"Buy her something nice, something that'll make her remember her daddy. How old's she again?"

"Five."

"That's a nice age," said Harper. "I remember when my girls was that age. Cute as shit. They'd run through the house after their bath, their little buns naked, laugh and shriek, Bonnie'd chase them.

. . . But shit, I hardly ever saw them, I was out hustling bombs and beans and bullets. I counted it up once when I was in Westpac. Out of a year, I spent seventy-two days at home. The Navy's not the sweet deal they make out in the recruiting posters." Harper paused. "Although there are advantages. Japan, the Philippines."

"I've heard about Olongopo—"

"Shit, not Olongopo. Watching those kids dive off that little bridge into Shit River for pennies. Forget it." Harper shuddered.

"I liked the double-oh-seven," said Cephas. "When I was a seaman deuce, we'd all go see Maria. She'd do that with the pickle—"

"Maria, yeah, she'd pick it up from a beer bottle, then lean over and fire it at the audience. Great show. But I hate Olongopo. Guys selling monkey meat on the street, the little kids saying, 'I love you Joe, no shit. Oh, you cherry boy?' We used to go to Subic City. We had a bowling team. We were always in and out trying to fix the fucking winches. We'd go up there and there was this little two-lane alley and we'd just get fucking plastered on San Miguel and bowl. Sometimes when it rained, the fucking alley would flood, but we didn't care; we'd bowl till the ball wouldn't go through the water." Harper shook his head dreamily, then recalled himself. "But that's long ago and far away. Used to be you could have fun in port. Now it's just grind, grind, grind. You're lucky if you get a night ashore."

"No shit," said Horseheads. "It's like being in prison."

"Only prisoners get color TV and all the sleep they want."

"You got that right, Ed. It's tough on marriages, tough on families. Bonnie's kind of a slob, but you got to hand it to her, she did all right keeping things going when I was away. But now Emily's starting to act up. . . ."

Dan sat half-listening, thinking how his own marriage had self-destructed; about Susan's infidelity first, then remembering what the chaplain had said: that infidelity was a symptom, not a cause, that happy wives and happy husbands didn't need to send signals like that. Could it have worked if he'd been around more, like Harper said? Had Susan been right after all—could they have made it if not for the Navy?

"They ought to pay us more, too," said Cephas.

"Hey! Over here, Sweet Cheeks!" Harper rapped the table for another round. He stared after the waitress. "Shit, I've seen more meat than that on a butcher's apron. Yeah, you can't do it anymore on just your paycheck."

"You've got a nice house," said Dan. "A boat and everything."

"Because I got the bars, a way to make a little extra on the side. Otherwise, I'd be living in some apartment complex, driving a fucking Honda, and Bonnie'd be shopping at K Mart. And I wouldn't have *Blow Job*. Shit, that's what you need," he told Dan. "Remember at the beach, we were talking about how you wanted an apartment? If you had the dough? A place to take a girl? You don't want an apartment. You want a boat. Get them a little drunk, get them seasick, and then take 'em down in that V-berth. . . . All right! Here comes the food."

AFTER dinner, they went out, to find a parking ticket on Miller's rented Dodge. Horseheads crumpled it up and stuffed it in the glove compartment as Harper started the car. "Where to?" said Dan, still not sure he was in the mood. The faces at Krome haunted him.

"Coconut Grove. Skids looked in the paper; there's a hot group at The Yellow Man."

"Skids" must be Cephas, though he'd never heard the yeoman's nickname. "I didn't know you liked Jamaican music, Jay."

"I like anything that attracts young fresh pussy."

"Good point."

The club was at Mayfair-in-the-Grove, a high-rise Spanish-style shopping complex. They took an elevator up from the basement garage. Hammered copper and brass doors opened on tiers of expensive-looking shops. The terraces were paved with brick and cooled by tiled fountains and tropical foliage so lush it looked unreal. Dan glanced around, then up at twinkling lights he only belatedly recognized as stars. The plaza was open to the sky.

The Yellow Man wasn't just packed; the line snaked out the door and past Lord & Taylor. Harper was right; there were scads of women. Some young, some older, though well cared-for, all expensively dressed in silks, leathers, metallic bustiers, velvet jeans. Gold jewelry hung from every possible point of attachment. There was a lot of joking and laughing, a lot of Cuban accents. Dan felt out of place, uncomfortable, but Miller struck up a conversation with a woman behind them. She giggled when he introduced himself, and said, "Do you boys reggae here often?" She told them "Yellow Man" meant mulatto, that the old song "Yellow Bird" was actually about a mulatto woman. Dan wondered if this was so, why there were no blacks in the line, or anywhere here, for that matter. Except for Cephas, of course.

Harper slipped the girl who seated them a bill and they got a table far enough from the band to hear one another, but still close to the action. A harried waitress appeared, and they ordered margaritas and rumrunners and Barbancourt rum with lime and tonic.

Dan sat listening to the music. It was hot, fast, but he couldn't seem to get into it . . . as if he wasn't really here, ashore, in a place designed for people to spend money and have fun. He was someplace else. But it was hard to say where . . . as if he'd been jerked too swiftly through too many different places in the last month. Charleston, Gitmo, the Passage, adrift in a tiny boat; *Razytelny*, *Barrett*, and now Coconut Grove, listening to the Buffalo Soldiers singing an a cappella version of "Ninety-Six Degrees in the Shade," the lead singer in a metallic crocheted hat with dreadlocks down to his waist like Bob Marley. And as each scene flashed by, unanswered questions popped up like "no sale" tabs in an old-fashioned cash register: Strishauser and Billy; Sanderling's death; the captain's truthfulness; whether they'd have to return to refresher training; Graciela's fate . . . none of it settled, as if nothing ever was settled, only left behind. . . . No wonder he was fucking disoriented. . . .

Harper was shouting something and he leaned, cupping his ear. "What?"

"I said, it's bullshit. All this talk about us and the Soviets getting ready to go to war any minute, it's bullshit, that's what it is. You know?"

The chief warrant was back on another of his ultraconservative hobbyhorses, apparently. Dan nodded noncommittally and Harper yelled, "What we'll probably do, next war, it'll probably be both of us against China or something. Want me to prove it?"

"Sure," said Dan, curious as to how he was going to do that.

"I'll tell you. Remember when they captured the *Pueblo*? They got operating cryptographic machines. Okay, you say, so we stop using the KW-seven, right? We go to a new machine? Wrong. We kept right on using it. So, you think anybody really cares?"

"Well, they must," said Dan. "Why else are we out steaming all the time, they're building a six-hundred-ship Navy—"

Horseheads snickered, and Harper said sharply, "Get real, shipmate. Even you ain't *that* innocent. Who makes bucks off that? The goddamned shipbuilders, the politicians, the labor guys. Remember I told you, the only thing the government can do is redistribute money? That's how they scare us, so we let them reach in and pick our fucking pockets: the fucking Russkies are planning to sucker punch us. Well, I flat just don't believe it. They bogeyman us, so we tax the shit out of our people, and we bogeyman them, so their generals can keep churning out tanks and shit. 'Scuse me, but it's all so fucking obvious, it makes me want to laugh."

"Wait a minute," said Dan. "You were telling me—remember when we were out on the rifle range, and you were telling me how feminists are actually Communists, trying to wreck the family and—"

"And that's all absolutely right. But you tell me. You were aboard that Russki tin can, right? Did those guys hate your guts, want to hang you from the yardarm?"

"No."

"What were they like?"

"Just people. People like us, I guess."

"There you go. It's the assholes in charge. They'll use the NAACP and the fucking bra-burners to bore from within. But are they going to screw themselves, start a war, make us nuke 'em? I don't think so." Harper drank moodily. "It's a shell game. Only problem I got with it is Ronnie talks trickle-down, how come none of it trickles down to us?"

"No shit."

"You remember we were talking about that in Gitmo. About the movie, the guys that found the treasure—"

"Yeah, I remember."

"You still think the same? That you'd go for it, you could take home a big piece of loot and nobody'd know? Then you could get that boat, help your brother through school. . . ."

Dan nodded absently, looking across the dance floor. The lanky warrant officer was one of those people you couldn't argue with. It was easier just to nod and move on to something else. But he wished Harper hadn't said that word.

Cephas got up and put some quarters in the Pac-Man. Miller and Harper joined them, and Dan sat with Horseheads, who was tossing back the free popcorn. He stared into his drink, mood darkening by the second.

That word: boat. Shit, shit, *why* had Harper said it? Because when he had, it was not some glossy yacht that flashed in front of Dan's eyes, but splintered, dark-sodden thwarts; the hull boards opening and closing like breathing lips. And looking back at him, Graciela, the baby, the boy. . . . He'd lived, and they . . . He perceived himself suspended above a black pit of despair and guilt. Why had God plucked him from death, fed and rescued him, and let them fall astern, rocking in the wake under the empty sky? How had anything he or they ever done deserved that?

"Jeez, what's the matter, sir?"

"It's nothing, Ed. I was just thinking about those refugees."

"They're okay now."

"I mean the ones that didn't make it . . . or that probably didn't make it. . . . I don't know. Shit, I don't feel so good."

"You better throttle back on those."

"Yeah, maybe you're right." But still he lifted it and drank, the liquor burning its way down his throat. Two or three more and he'd forget.

Cephas and Harper came back with two girls, Jay bragging about his score. "That's not such a challenge, you got a little eye-hand coordination," he told the yeoman. "Angela here, she's got it down. Dan, Mitch, this is Angela, and this is Lori. Where you girls from?"

"Coral Gables."

"Shit, you played it before. You got the technique down."

"Hey, cowboy, I never seen the fucking thing before. You just make the little guys eat each other. What kind of technique can there be?"

"Yeah, you ought to be good at that, boy."

"Boy! Hey, you see any boys around here, just blow 'em up to man-size."

"Sorry, I choke on small bones."

The girls giggled. The blonde, Angela, was about nineteen, with curly damp hair streaming down over her tank top. She looked drunk, and her nipples showed through the damp cotton. Lori was blond, too, but thinner, and her pupils looked frozen, as if she was on something powerful. Already, Harper was cupping her butt casually. "One for you. But you'll pay, you'll pay," he told Cephas. "Hey, Dan, want to play Pac-Man? Angela's ready for some stick action."

"No thanks."

"Dance with Lori; she wants to dance."

He shook his head. Harper said, "Jeez, what's the matter? Let's get this party rolling. Here, babe, take this and go over and get us some more drinks. Get the lieutenant a margarita, what he's drinking ain't working."

Cephas lighted a cigarette and waved the match out, looking around. The beer seemed to be overcoming his reticence, and he started talking. Dan only half-listened at first. He worked every day with the departmental yeoman, but he'd never gotten close to him. Now he was surprised to hear him say, "You know, sir, I know how you feel about your ex. I been divorced two years now and I still hate the bitch."

"Tell him the nut," said Harper. "How you're still making money off her."

"Oh. Oh, yeah. I'm not married anymore. But I'm still drawing BAQ."

BAQ was basic allowance for quarters, the extra pay married servicepeople got. "How you do that?" said Horseheads.

"All you got to do is take the marriage certificate in and show them in the ship's office; it shows up on your next check. I just never told the fucking Navy I got divorced."

Dan tensed. What Cephas was describing was fraud. The girls came back with drinks. Jay shoved one across the table, but he didn't look at it. "You mean you're living aboard ship and still drawing BAQ for living ashore?" he asked the yeoman.

"Cool your jets, loo-tenant," drawled Harper. "Jesus, did you see him tighten up? Look. The poor son of a bitch makes what, four hundred a month? It don't hurt anybody he makes another hundred. Shit, who does it hurt? You could do that yourself if you wanted."

"No, I couldn't. It's against regulations," Dan said. He was angry now, at himself as much as at Cephas. Knowing about something like this and not taking action on it was a violation in itself for someone in the chain of command—as he was. But turning a man in on the basis of a confidence exchanged over drinks . . . that wouldn't play very well, either, in terms of building trust within the department. You stupid asshole, he raged at himself. Didn't you learn anything from that episode with Lassard on *Ryan*?

ACROSS the table, the lean man in the toupee and glasses examined Lenson's flushed, angry face with satisfaction.

Snookered, Jay Harper thought. The self-righteous prick done snookered himself. And not a fucking thing he can do about it. Lori came back with the drinks and he ran his hand up her back as he sipped Jack Daniel's, rolling it past his tongue and sighing. The good stuff. He'd better enjoy it while he could.

Lenson mumbled something about a head call and stood up. Harper waved the glass, smiling after the lieutenant's rigidly retreating back, barely restraining the impulse to give him the finger.

"Is he pissed off?" Cephas said anxiously. "He looked pissed off. Should I of told him that, sir? Is he gonna put me on report?"

"Cool it, shipmate. He can't do nothing to you."

"He can tell the disbursing officer."

"If he does, I'll take care of you. You know that."

"Yeah. Yeah! Thanks." The yeoman gave him a happy, relieved, grateful smile. "I really appreciate it, sir."

"Don't mention it." Harper looked away, running his hand absentmindedly up the inner thigh of the girl who leaned on him. Young pussy, he thought. Wet and tight. Unlike his fucking wife. Forget her, he thought. With a little fucking luck, he'd never see that bitch again.

With a little luck . . .

Miller, back from playing the machines, looked worried. "What's the matter, Chief?" Harper asked him.

"I'm broke dick. Shot my wad."

"How did you do that?"

"It was a bet. On the Pac-Man. A guy said he could—"

"You're kidding. Somebody sharked you at Pac-Man? Where the fuck did that last hundred I loaned you go?"

"Shit, I had to rent the car. I told you that. And you're riding in it, too." Miller pushed his hand out, rubbing his finger and thumb together. "Come on."

Harper grunted. Glancing at the girl, he pulled out his wallet, fanned out a handful of fifty-dollar bills. He snapped off two and handed them to Miller.

"Thanks."

"Goddamn it," he grunted. But the chief was already headed away, back toward the machines.

"He gambles too much," said Cephas, looking to Harper for confirmation. "Doesn't he?"

"Hey, everybody's gotta do something. Him, he can't pass up a fucking bet. Me—it's good looking women." Harper snapped off another crisp note, held it up for a second in front of Lori's blank eyes, and handed it to her. "For getting us the drinks, Sweet Cheeks," he said. She took it without a word, but he felt the gentle pressure of her leg increase.

Cephas was a goddamn lost puppy. His family had screwed him up somehow. Harper'd had to listen to the story, but he didn't have to remember it. The guy was so hungry for affection, he'd do anything he was told. Miller was a pain in the ass in another way. So he was Cephas's sea daddy. And the loans gave him leverage, a handle, on the gunnery chief.

Everybody had a handle, he thought, running his hand up the girl's thigh to the crack of her tight-fitting jeans. All you had to do was find it, find out what they needed, then figure out what they had to give you, or what they had somebody else needed. Anyone who could understand that could make it in business, in the Navy, anywhere. It was so simple. How could you not understand that? How could people be so fucking stupid?

He threw back the last swallow of bourbon, snapped off another bill, and held it up in two fingers. Cephas was watching him in admiration.

"Go get us another round, bitch," he said to the girl, watching her and smiling.

DAN was back at the table, still feeling black, when Miller came back and stood by them, looking back toward the bar. "The fuck's the matter with you?" Harper asked him.

"I was watchin' the TV. There's something going down."

"What?"

"I don't know. First was about some trial, a verdict. Then they said something about Cuba. You think we should better call the ship?"

"Something about Cuba," repeated Harper. "What? It's on the TV, you said?"

Dan got up. He didn't say anything to them, just went to the phone booth by the bathroom and pulled his wheel book out with the quarterdeck number. It was busy, but on the third try he got through. "USS *Barrett,* quarterdeck watch speaking, sir. May I help you."

"Lieutenant Lenson. Heard there was something up."

"Yes sir, we're putting out an emergency recall. Where are you? Get all the guys you can find and get them back to the ship ASAP."

"What is it? Some kind of—"

"I can't say, sir. Just get everybody back you can, pronto."

He hung up and stood in the hallway, listening to the Caribbean rhythms. Then he went back in, to see the others gathered around the television set over the bar.

39

LESS than a mile away, Thomas Leighty stood with his hands in the pockets of his suit slacks on a littered, dimly lighted street, trying to ignore the distant yells of a group of drunks. A pickup truck sheered by and a beer bottle came hurtling out of it. It missed him, but not by much.

Maybe, he thought, I should have taken the official car. But he hadn't felt right about driving it for personal use. Now, looking around at the ominously empty street, he wondered if that had been the right decision.

"Oh, new in town? Sure, a couple places you can go," the waiter had said as he dined alone. They'd made eye contact a couple of times, then got to talking. "What do you want? You don't want one of these back-room suck-off places, like the baths."

"No, no baths."

"Someplace nice. That's what I like, too. What do you want, music? There's Monty Trainer's and 27 Birds—"

"A club. Someplace quiet."

"Where you can be yourself. I know . . . there's Uncle Charlie's, out on U.S. One. But you're not that far from the Double R." He'd smiled slowly. "Then there's my place . . . We could have a drink, listen to some music. I won't be off till one, but I'll give you my number, just in case you're a late-nighter."

Now he stood tensely outside the Double R. The street was quiet after the raucous passage of the truck. The bar was unobtrusive, almost unnoticeable unless you knew or had been directed to it.

When he was at sea, there were long periods of time he didn't think about sex. He might admire another man's body, but distantly, as one admires a piece of sculpture without the desire to possess it. Then they'd put into port, and he would know it would be that night. And he'd dress carefully and stroll out. Where no one knew him, he could show a different aspect of himself. Something he couldn't do in Charleston.

But at the same time, there was the fear. The NIS knew about Sanderling. They suspected him, he knew that, and he found himself examining the shadows behind him. Being seen in a gay bar was "frequenting," "associating with known homosexuals." It could be the last nail in his coffin.

So that left him with the choice, he thought, standing alone on the dark street. He could do the smart thing—turn around and leave. Or he could wait out here and try to make contact as someone came out. He felt exposed here, though. Since overhearing the conversation on the fantail, he had a recurrent nightmare of standing on a corner like this and being recognized by someone from *Barrett.*

The last choice, of course, was just to go in.

Finally, he cursed himself for a coward and a fool and crossed the street and quickly pushed the door open, to find himself confronted by a bulky citizen guarding an inner door. "This is a private club, sir."

"I can't go in?"

He was examined up and down. "Provisional membership's five dollars."

He was sweating, but he kept his back straight as he strolled in. You didn't look directly at anyone, not at first. You weren't here because you wanted someone. You were just here for a quiet drink. Only later would come the subtle checkout, but if they met your eyes, you still turned away. Only to glance back a few moments later. Instead, he examined the decor. The walls were bare wood. The lighting was from wagon-wheel lamps. The bar area was separated from the dance floor by a wooden split-rail fence, like a corral. The sound system was playing Tammy Wynette.

Gradually, he realized that all the men were cowboys—all in western dress, pointed boots of leather or snakeskin or armadillo, heavy silver jewelry, ten-gallon hats, plaid shirts, bandannas. He felt out of place in his suit and tie. He didn't like to feel conspicuous. He almost left, but then seated himself firmly at the old-fashioned bar and ordered a gin and tonic from a bartender in handlebar mustache and sleeve garters.

Eventually, his heart rate slacked off. He tapped a quarter on the bar, musing again over the refugee operation. Apparently, he'd made the right decision, taking people aboard—despite the original orders. Because once the storm hit, that was what everybody had done, British, Dutch, Coast Guard. Navy Regulations, Article 0925, and NWP-9 were explicit about what a commander had to do faced with vessels requiring assistance. Not that there were things he'd do differently if they were ordered back to station. For one thing, he needed a different personnel mix—more Spanish speakers, more medical personnel, including a female corpsman. A dedicated habitability load-out—by the time they docked, *Barrett* was completely out of soap and toilet paper, not to mention sanitary napkins, diapers, and baby supplies, none of them standard stock items aboard U.S. Navy warships. It had all gone into a lessons-learned message he'd shot up to DESRON SIX that morning.

When he looked up again, everybody was streaming out onto the dance floor. An older man stepped up to a microphone and, yes, it was Square Dancing Night at the Double R. That and the fact that no one at all had spoken to or even looked at him made it easy to pay quietly for his half-finished drink and leave as the do-si-dos began to echo off the rafters and the cowboys, grave and reserved and stiff, nodded to one another and began spinning one another about, heavy boots clunking on the scuffed wooden floor.

"YOU know Uncle Charlie's?" he asked the driver of the Yellow. The man, a Cuban, closed his eyes briefly, then opened them. "Byrd Road, U.S. One. A fag joint."

Leighty didn't answer, and after a moment the driver shrugged and pulled out. "So, what you faggots think about the trial?" he said after a mile or so.

"Excuse me?"

"The trial, what you think about the trial?"

"I don't know. What trial?"

The cabbie told him there'd been a police-brutality decision due that day, and they'd just found the cop innocent. "For once, they did justice. But the niggers don't like it."

"We heard there was some . . . racial polarization," Leighty said carefully.

"Call it whatever you want, but I ain't taking no fares to Northwest tonight."

They both fell silent as Leighty looked out. Coconut Grove looked paradoxical, oxymoronic, with expensive, grand houses cheek-to-cheek with falling-down shacks. Uncle Charlie's was across from a Porsche dealership, a peachy brown plain-fronted building, again with no sign at all, no lights out front, no windows, either.

Yes, he thought the moment he entered, this is more like what I'd hoped to find. No leather, no cowboy affectations. Just tables, soft rock, low lighting, and people talking to one another at the little tables. Women and women, men and men, men and women dancing casually. He went through to the bar, ordered another gin and tonic, and sipped it standing up, listening to scraps of conversation, arguments.

"Hey, I think Anita's right. You know? That you can be cured. Only trouble is, I don't want to be."

"Okay, next: Are we going to have the same mimes this year? We have applications from five groups. What kind of feedback did we get about those guys in the green tights?"

"View the planet as a large brain, along with the racial unconscious—"

"No, at Bananas. He was standing there looking out at the bay and I came up and said to him, 'What is that you have on under your slacks—' "

"I bought it at three fifty; now it's at six twenty-five. The point is not to hold out for peak, okay? It's capital gain per quarter you want to use as a measurement."

"I have never used one. Amyl nitrate is not good for the human heart—"

"He said he hated my dog, but he still jumped in to save her when she fell in the pool."

But the glances he got were unfriendly—in fact, rather hostile—and the conversations stopped as he went by and eyes flicked up to him and narrowed. So he didn't try to join any of them, just kept walking, looking for an empty table, but there didn't seem to be any.

"Hi. How are you? My name is Evans."

He turned to a younger man with sandy hair over his ears, direct, slightly sad blue eyes, pouting lips, and teeth that should have been straightened. The Palm Beach look, white shoes, white belt, arms muscular under a tennis sweater with the sleeves pushed up, heavy gold link ID bracelet, gold Rolex.

"Hi. Thomas."

"How are you, Thomas? I haven't seen you here before."

"Haven't been here before. New in town."

"Uh-huh. Are you a cop?"

Leighty smiled. So that was it. "You're direct, aren't you? No, I'm not a cop."

"Something about you, the way you hold yourself. Something . . . authoritative. You're military, aren't you? There are a lot of retired Air Force here, older guys. They came down here during the war and liked it and came back when they retired."

"Why do you need to know anything about me? I just came in for a drink. I'll never be back."

"The ship," said Evans suddenly.

"Excuse me?"

"There's a Navy ship just docked today. You're off it, aren't you? I was in the Army myself. Artillery, in Germany." As he started to respond, Evans held up his hand. "Wait . . . I understand, all right? Say no more. Have your drink. Circulate. Enjoy your night on the town. Have you had dinner yet?"

"Thanks, I'm okay."

Evans patted his back and moved away, nodding to the others, exchanging quick hugs. Leighty stood there feeling threatened, warned, vulnerable. Maybe it would be better to go, after all, if he was that conspicuous that someone could pick him out like that, tell exactly who he was and where he'd come from.

He was strolling toward the door when Evans returned and took him into the back, to a table in the dimness, and introduced him to a couple of people and then left. Jason and Kurt, if he caught their names right. "These are some of the Air Force people I told you about. Tom here is Navy, guys. You can tell each other war stories, okay?" Patting him again, Evans dashed off.

And actually that was what they did, tell war stories, and gradually he relaxed and eventually even had a good time. But he didn't feel anything for them, or meet anyone interesting until he was leaving the club and heard footsteps behind him. He turned, going tense, ready—for what, he didn't know.

He was younger than Leighty, a bit chubby, friendly and anxious. He said his name was Vernon. "I think we're complementary," he said. "I like older men. Not that you're old, but you have a presence, you know? I saw it when you came in. Did you see me? By the door? Then I saw you talking with Evans, but I knew you wouldn't hit it off with him . . . well, I just knew. What do you like to do? I pretty much like to do just about anything. I'm pretty flexible, but I don't like anything rough."

He stood in the dark, listening to the other persuading, hearing the anxious tone in his voice. "Want to go to the Sailing Club? I'm a member; I have a friend who leaves his boat unlocked. Or we could go into the park."

He stared at the pale face hovering in the dark. He both wanted the boy and did not, was both attracted and repelled. Another one-night stand, or not even that, half-hour acquaintance. After which he would feel both complete and incomplete, satiated but guilty. While at home, he had someone who cared, a family. . . . He thought with reflective sadness that he was caught between two eras. Thirty years ago, he could have denied what he was, even to himself. Thirty years from now, he could probably be free. . . . But this was a time of transition, of change, and no matter what he did or how he lived, he would probably always have this feeling of uncertainty and impending retribution. And nothing he did or did not do would ever change that.

The seesaw whine of sirens sounded in the distance, crying over the dark streets. "All right, Vern," he said, touching his wallet and keys lightly through his slacks. "Show me the way to the park."

40

STARING up at the grooved steel, Hank Shrobo wiped his hands on his shorts. Wet hands were dangerous, the guys told him. Could make the bar slip. Interesting how a small amount of moisture increased the coefficient of friction, while more lowered it. Without a word, the man behind him handed him a piece of rosin.

"Okay, how much?" Shrobo asked him.

Iron clanked. "Try her with this. Hundred and fifty pounds."

"Too heavy. I've never done that much before."

"I'll safe for you. You were pumping a hundred and forty yesterday. You been at this a while; you ought to be scaling up. Come on, give it a try. Just remember, don't try this without a spotter, okay? Specially when the ship's rolling."

He stared up at Williams's inverted face, then muttered, "All right." He reached up and got his hands set, then yanked the weight off the stands.

It came down hard, almost crushing his chest before he got his arms set and started pushing back. To his surprise, it went up. Not easily, but it rose as his muscles strained. His elbows locked and he steadied it above his clenched teeth, arms trembling.

"Relax your jaw; that doesn't help you lift. Go on, do a few reps. Till it hurts. You got to tear them muscle fibers; then your body fixes them twice as strong. Go on.... That's good, another.... Okay, I got it." Williams's strong hands closed like leather gloves over his and guided the bar back into place on the rests. "Take a break."

Panting, he sat up, and the exercise room's stark white walls, the well-used Nautilus machine, the racks of weights in welded brackets along the bulkheads, all returned to vertical. Others worked in tense self-absorption on the inclined board and the treadmill, and the punching bag made a steady machinelike rattle. He knew their names now, or at least the nicknames they went by among themselves as they grunted under masses of iron: Hemmie, Lightbulb, Baby J. Williams had introduced him, and although he felt inadequate around them, weak and pale beside their swelling chests and dark massive arms, they seemed to accept him.

"How'd I do?"

"Real good, Doc." Williams squatted in boxing shorts and Nikes and poked him painfully. "You know, you getting some development. Keep this up when you get back shoreside and you'll be more comfortable walking around in that body of yours."

"I never felt uncomfortable."

"I know, I know. Okay, let's grab a shower, see if any of the guys want to hit the beach."

AS he pivoted slowly under the hot water, his mind turned, as it did almost every waking minute and most sleeping minutes, too, to the problem at hand.

Since his last discussion with the captain and the assembled officers, he and Williams and Dawson and the other DSs and ETs had been full-time on the Crud. Or at least they'd started off full-time. But gradually, the others had dropped behind as he entered a shadowy forest of theoretics and speculation. First the chiefs, then the others had made excuses or found something else to do, until finally only Matt Williams was with him.

He was more and more impressed with Williams. The slow-spoken petty officer had no real education beyond the rather sketchy Navy data systems training, but he made up for it with an uncanny insight into programming. He wrote the search routines that Shrobo sketched out directly in assembly language, skipping the CMS-2 compiler. That wasn't so extraordinary. He had several people fluent in ULTRA-32 back at Vartech. But then he'd seen the kid stare, tranced, at the rippling, winking lights on the face of the computer and push the stop button at the exact instant the operating system handed off to the navigational module. He'd realized in that stunned second that he'd seen a human being read machine language in real time. Still, he reassured himself, it was more of a trick, like being able to multiply large sums in your head, than a valid intellectual achievement.

Which was what he'd felt he was on the brink of in the last few days: a breakthrough, something far more radical, more fundamental, and more far-reaching than patching up Elmo to aim the missiles properly again.

Standing motionless under the hot water, he went over it all again in his mind.

A week before—how long ago it seemed—he'd first recognized that the virus operated in a five-step sequence. One: It wrote its basic program, the "infector," to memory. Two: It "unzipped" itself to activate the hostile portion of the program, and wrote it to additional areas of operating memory. Three: Running in bursts of approximately three-hundredths of a second, so rapidly that it wasn't visible to the operator, it destroyed data by deleting portions of the existing code. Four: It replaced the erased code with randomly generated garbage, mimicking the format of the original data.

And step five, unlike any program he'd ever heard of before: It rezipped itself to the spore form and wrote the infector to several other portions of the tape, continuing the insidious process of destruction at the next reboot.

Since then, while the ship's officers had been distracted by this refugee thing—he heard about it, but it wasn't his concern what the ship did or where it went; he had not even breathed open air for days—hour by hour, night after night, he'd hammered at the elusive virus's structure.

But the deeper he went, the more difficult further progress became. For one thing, the UYK-7s were the first militarized thirty-two-bit machines. Unlike most computers, they used a binary logic procedure called the "1's complement." Each bit in the original word was complemented to invert the register contents. One drawback of a 1's-complement machine was that it was possible, under certain conditions, to register a negative zero. This was an illogical thought, and computers finding themselves thinking illogical thoughts created an error condition that was very difficult to debug. The virus took advantage of this to mask itself. Not only that, it seemed to have privileges that pointed to a spawning out of the executive program. It knew the demand entrances; it used cycle stealing to move itself around.

But gradually, as day followed night, he'd crept into the initializing code. This preceded the zipped portion, and though it wasn't easy, it was possible to decipher it gradually, with patience.

And he knew now he had to. He and Williams had gotten some of the modules cleared and running in isolation. But that was only a temporary fix. They couldn't sterilize the programming and expect it to run clean for more than a few hours. They could compare code with listing, cut and patch and paste till their eyes fell out and rolled around on the deck, but as soon as they ran a data tape, the virus would emerge from one of its fiendishly chosen hiding places and reinfect, degrade, destroy.

Isolation was not the final answer.

He had to read the virus, all of it, in order to build a program that would prevent it from ever returning.

This was because his ultimate aim was to create a search string for the Crud.

A "string", in computer jargon, was any given sequence of characters, whether instructions or numerical data. A "search" string was a program that ran through the machine like a rat-catching snake, looking for that particular sequence. If he could break and read the virus's infector, then he could write a search string that would automatically scan the contents of the computer's memory for it—like reading the Bible with a Hi-Liter in hand, marking a given word wherever it appeared. Except that a computer could do it far more rapidly. A relatively simple search routine could rapidly locate a given string wherever it was hidden, even amid hundreds of thousands of lines of code, and insert break points to stop the program there.

And just now it occurred to him that once he had that, it would be relatively simple to add programming to delete and overwrite the virus automatically, then mark the module and line so that the DSs could patch what would now be simply a blank space in the code.

He smiled under the needling water; sometimes ideas came that way, instantaneously, from nowhere. Once you knew everything about the problem and had concentrated on it for days, answers came mysteriously, generated by some deep processing that went on whether you were awake or asleep, only lighting an occasional indicator in the high-level interface that was the conscious mind.

But the next moment, he frowned. He was getting ahead of himself. In order to write a search string, he had to be able to read the virus. And after a certain point, he couldn't. Whenever he tried to unzip it, it erased, vanished utterly as a dream, leaving only meaningless and dysfunctional nonsense where before had stood the stark inhuman beauty of machine language.

Even more unsettling, he still had no idea what the zipped code actually did—except for one thing.

He suspected now that what lay curled at its inmost heart, a black spore in a tightly spun shell of trick and trap and encipherment, was a 1's-complement negative-zero random-number generator, a blasphemous and demonic incantation that was the ultimate negation of all logic, all rationality, all causality, and all order.

No doubt about it, whatever twisted and evil mind had come up with this thing, it was clever.

After days of trying unsuccessfully to slip past the Crud's defenses, he'd gone back to the weight room and started walking on the treadmill. He'd walked for four straight hours. And gradually he had reverse-engineered the virus himself, redesigned it from scratch, as if *he* was the hacker, trying not to defend but to penetrate the AN/UYK-7 and its resident programs.

He decided that he would have built the virus as follows. The first part of the program would be an execute instruction that would trick the host computer into unzipping and running the infector. Second would be the infector proper. And the third part would be the self-eraser, the portion of code which re-spored the infector, scattered it through the host programming, then deleted the original virus. Williams, when he explained this to him, had pointed out that the first section probably also included an instruction that went immediately to the self-erasing feature if the inserting mechanism was interrupted or tampered with. That was what had frustrated their efforts to read it.

So the petty officer had helped, but Shrobo had wished more than once for someone of his own caliber to bounce ideas off of. If they hadn't been at sea, he'd have picked up a phone and called Fred Cohen at USC. But Mainhardt had warned him not to discuss *Barrett*'s decreased combat capability. Anyway, the more deeply he thought his way into the problem, the less he wanted anyone else in on it. It was taking on an epic quality in his mind—a chess match against some anonymous and evil Dr. Fu Manchu, both of them battling on the frontiers of information-processing theory. If he could crack it, defeat the virus, there was a paper in it: a classy, seminal publication that would be referred to again and again for decades to come.

Now, still standing motionless under the shower, he suddenly realized he was thinking like an academic. Of course, he *was* an academic, but he was in business now, too. And there was more than a technical paper at stake.

He leaned against tin, suddenly gripped by a lightninglike premonition of the future. No modern ship or plane could fight without computers. If viruses could infect and disable them, why then scan and detection programs would have to be written, updated, and serviced.

Who better to win the contracts that were sure to be let than his own company, built on a solid theoretical foundation, combined with demonstrated Navy troubleshooting?

And then beyond that golden mountain, taking his breath away, loomed up a whole Himalaya glittering with diamonds. Military computers were a small market. But a program written to search out viruses in an AN/UYK-7 or a USQ-20 could be quickly compiled to sanitize DECs or VACs or IBMs, and there were thousands of business mainframes. If viruses could infect military systems, they could infect business applications, too. Companies could create special strains and release them into their competitor's systems, destroying customer databases and essential information. No one could afford to be without a safeguard.

A face stuck itself through the plastic curtain, and he flinched and covered his privates. That was something he couldn't get used to, the total disregard for privacy aboard ship, men dressing and going about with members and bellies dangling obscenely. He supposed there was a sort of nudist-colony naturalness about it, but . . . "Hey, you about ready? Thought you done gone down the drain. The guys all duded up—"

"Oh, sorry. I was thinking. Guess I'm using too much water, too."

"Don't sweat that; that's Miami water. Have a pool party." Williams disappeared and Shrobo rinsed down and went out into the compartment, holding his towel carefully lest it come undone, into fifty or sixty men dressing and boasting to one another what they were going to do in town. He found his bunk and got his suit on.

"Oh *man.* Whatthefuck you wearin'?" said Hemmie, stopping.

"My gray suit. It's the only—"

"You coming with us to the Zone, you ain't wearing *that.* Come over here to our bay. Lightbulb, he's tall as you. Maybe he got something to fit you there."

THEY didn't get a taxi, as he thought they would, just stood on Biscayne Boulevard, keeping him back out of the light, till a white Impala with two girls in it stopped. It had no rear window, just transparent plastic sheet taped across the empty frame. Hemmie leaned in, talking to them for a long time, then stood up and waved the rest of them into the back. The women did a double take at him. "Who he? Who the skinny white guy?"

"Friend of ours, from the ship. He's cool, baby."

"Sure you wants him out with you? After what they done downtown today?"

"Who done what downtown?"

"Them fucking cops that killed that brother. He run a red light, they pulled him over, then beat him to death with they fucking flashlights. Now the jury just said, let them spic motherfuckers go."

"They treats *us* like dogs. Then some peoples come in from overseas, gets free food, treats *them* just like kings. People is talking crazy, ain't gon' take shit no more."

Shrobo muttered, "Say, where exactly are we going, Matt?"

"Just up to a place Hemmie knows, have a few drinks. Be cool, my man. Ain't gonna be any trouble." And up front, the woman was saying indignantly to Hemmery, "Shit yeah, I know where Liberty City is. I live there."

* * *

HE gazed out, noticing that the streets looked empty; there weren't even many cars out. But pretty soon, he started thinking again about the virus. He was staring blankly out the window when they pulled over. Baby J passed a couple of dollars to the women and the sailors all got out. Lightbulb stuck his head back in, sweet-talking them, but finally let them go, shaking his head. "This it?" he said, looking around.

Hank looked up and down the street, coming part of the way back from his abstraction. Spray-painted graffiti stroked steel-curtained store fronts. The streetlights seemed dim and far away. Several women were parading slowly back and forth under the closest one. A line of men sat on a wall in front of a detached house, looking their way. Hemmie said, "Yeah, this is it. This is a jumping place, man. The Zone. Don't need to look far to find a good time here."

"Uh, is this safe?" Shrobo asked Williams.

"Hemmie say so. He used to live here."

"How long ago?" said Shrobo, but they were walking toward the house, and he either had to follow or stay out in the street alone. As they neared it, Hemmie up front kicking empty cans out of his way, the men got down off the wall. Hemmie called out; they stopped. There was a short conversation. Then he turned and waved them on. "I tol' you, this is cool. It's a guest house, okay? I know the guy they work for."

Inside the "guest house," stuffing leaked from brown sofas. Wires and pipes showed through holes in the walls. It smelled of vomit and something else nasty he couldn't identify. But it felt safer, with iron grilles on the windows and the men sitting beside them looking out. A shotgun leaned in the corner. A black-and-white TV flickered on the floor. They went through a hallway into the back, past a room filled with large, dented blue plastic barrels, then down some steps into a basement.

This felt more welcoming, cozy and dark and thick with the smells of beer and people. An air conditioner hummed cold into the smoky dark. Smoke gave him respiratory problems, but he decided not to object. A bar was the first thing you hit past the stairs, then things opened out. It was bigger than he expected. He got angry looks as they wedged themselves in, but then they'd look at his clothes, see Hemmie and Williams and Lightbulb and Baby J with him, and look away or back at their drinks.

"Table here."

"Doc, what you want?"

"I don't know, maybe an orange juice."

"Johnnie Walker Red," Hemmie said.

"I don't want an alcoholic drink."

" 'I don't want an alcoholic drink.' Well shit, you ain't been asked what you wanted; you is being *bought* a drink."

"All right," he said, unwilling to contradict them. Their voices were louder, more confident here than in the computer room.

"That's the stuff."

"We gonna make a man outta you yet. A sea-man."

"Don't worry," said Williams, catching something in his expression. "These guys is just unwinding. They don't mean nothing."

"Thanks, Matt. I know that."

"You look stronger, though. That training is building you up real good."

When the whiskey came, he sipped it cautiously. "What's the matter?" said Hemmery.

"It's too strong. I'm not drinking it."

"Hell you ain't. I bought it, you gonna drink it."

"Hemmie," said Matt.

"I bought it, he—"

"He *ain't* gonna drink it, nigger, that's all. Why don't you drink it and I'll get him a beer."

"I ain't going to drink after him."

"Then just pour it in your glass. How about a beer, Doc?"

"Do they have any?"

They chuckled at that for some reason. "I imagine they do," said Lightbulb. "I imagine they got any old thing you might care to want. Hey, look, pool table."

Baby J came back with three Colt .45 malt liquors in bottles. Lightbulb examined his. "Ain't never had one of these. Seen they commercials on TV."

"It's just beer. It's all just fucking beer, is all." Williams shoved one toward Hank. "There, drink that an' shut up, okay?"

They sat around talking for a while, the sailors mostly bitching about various personalities aboard the ship and he listening, once in a while nodding. Then he gathered his courage and got up. The bartender looked at him curiously but took his money. Other dark faces turned toward him, then away. He got three Colt .45s and two Johnnie Walker Reds and carried them carefully back to the table. Hemmie and Williams had found cues and were playing pool by the light of Bic lighters. He left their drinks with them and sat companionably with Lightbulb and Baby J, none of them talking, just watching the crowd and every once in a while lifting their arms and taking a drink.

Gradually, he started feeling comfortable. He wondered if Williams was right, what he'd said in the weight room—what was it?—about feeling uncomfortable in his body.

It was true. He'd denied it, but it was true.

He'd always felt weak and too tall and awkward. When he decided he'd never be able to play basketball or even bowl without throwing gutter balls, he'd given up, not even sixteen then, and tried to compensate with his brain.

But maybe it didn't have to be that way. Alma would be surprised when he got back without the belly she'd remarked on sharply more than once. He felt his arm surreptitiously. Definitely harder. Maybe even Gwen would notice.

He thought about that for a while, a pleasant little fantasy about his secretary. But gradually, staring into the shifting smoke, his mind drifted back to its preoccupation. He could dream all he wanted about fame and Navy contracts, but he still had to crack the Crud. And so far, it was smarter than he was.

He finished the beer, but instead of putting the bottle down, he held it up, slowly rotating it as he looked through it toward the single light in the basement, a bulb on a cord above the bar. Then his eye refocused and he made out a series of letters and numbers molded into the bottom. He'd never noticed that bottles had data molded into them. Probably in case something was wrong with that batch of glass. He set it down carefully on the tabletop.

The angled light from the single bulb shone through the glass and through the glass top of the table. Underneath it, on the grimy sealed-in tablecloth, he could make out the faint shadowy image of the letters and numbers, doubled by their passage through the two refracting and reflecting interfaces.

I'm drunk, he thought. Why am I staring at this?

He glanced to the left and saw that Williams had come back and taken Lightbulb's place. Baby J was gone, too; just the two of them at the table now. Williams was looking at the bottle, too. For some reason he didn't understand, Shrobo suddenly felt uneasy.

"What's wrong?"

"Nothing. What are you looking at?"

"The table," Williams said slowly. His eyes didn't move. Unwillingly, Hank looked at it again, seeing only the faint doubled reflection. First, the reflection of the numbers on the glass, under the bottle; then, beneath them and fainter, the shadows of the same numbers, almost but not quite exactly beneath the first iteration. And around them was nothing but the crowded darkness, filled—he couldn't say quite why—with steadily increasing tension.

"That's it," Williams whispered.

A shiver ran up his spine. Why is my mouth suddenly dry? he asked himself. Why is my heart pounding? He coughed nervously, wishing the men at the bar would stop smoking. "That's what?" he said.

"That's how we going to read it," Williams said. He pointed to the bottle.

Shrobo leaned to peer, but there was nothing else there. "Oh," he said. "You don't ever stop, do you?"

"You're the same way."

He said unwillingly, "What have you got? You think of something?"

"Maybe."

"What?"

"See, we can . . . read the initiating sequence. But we can't read the zipped portion because if you try to unzip it, it erases."

Shrobo felt as if it was he being left behind now, stopped at an invisible line he could not cross. It was an unfamiliar feeling and he didn't like it. He said, a little sharply, "Right. So what?"

"So instead of trying to read it, we write to it."

"We write to it?" Shrobo blinked at the tabletop. His throat itched. His eyes burned. But he was still staring at the two lines of letters and numbers . . . of alphanumeric data . . . shining faintly, the letters traced of light superimposed on those traced in shadow. . . .

Then he saw it, too—all at once, stunning in its beauty. He said slowly, "We write over it. We write *the same code* over it."

"That's right."

Williams smiled, eyes still on Shrobo as he went on with growing excitement. "Yeah! If we write over the entire virus perfectly, it won't erase. There's no reason to; it's simply a substitution of a zero for a zero or a one for a one throughout. We're simply writing over it, with the same programming."

Standing above them chalking his cue, Hemmie said, "But ain't that the point? That you don't know the program? So how you gonna write it over itself if you don't know it to start with?"

"What the Doc means, I think," said Williams, "is that we start with the section that we know and . . . iterate random numbers after that. Try a one, then a two, then a three, and so forth. There are only ten choices for the next number. We run through all ten till we find the one that *doesn't* make the virus erase itself. Then we know that's the next sequence. Do that with the next number, and the next, and the next . . . till we get to the end, and that's the virus."

"Exactly," said Shrobo. "It isn't intellectually rigorous or elegant, but it should work, given time."

"A long time. That's a lot of substitutions. And every time, got to set the whole problem up again when it erases."

"Only an average of five times, till we get the next number," said

Shrobo. “An AN/UYK-seven processes—what, ten-to-the-fifth operations a second? Say a complete iteration of the whole substitution/replacement process takes a minute—”

“More than a minute. If a permutation—”

“Don’t look at it as a permutation, Matt. It’s a series. And it’s not that complicated; we’re not inverting any twentieth-order matrices here.”

“No, but figure—you got to print out every bit as you crack it. That will slow you down to the pace of the Teletype.”

“Why? You just save it to a separate register—oh, I see what you mean. Any decode becomes live virus. You’re right, we’ve got to print to hard copy.” He pulled out his calculator and punched it. “Okay, even including all that, I figure we could have it cracked in less than a day, if we ran full-time.”

“Which you can’t, and besides, you got to write the program first.”

“We’ll start as soon as we get back.” He sat back, feeling a queer mix of triumph and resentment. Williams had seen it first. But he’d known his unconscious was trying to tell him something. He’d have had it himself in just a second or two longer.

He was on his fourth beer when a noiseless murmuring wave eddied through the underground room. Heads turned toward the door. He noticed it but didn’t really think about it till Lightbulb said, chalking his cue casually, “Hey, where’s everybody going?”

“I don’t know.” Hemmie got up. “Lemme see.”

When he came back, he was looking around. “We better see if there’s another way out of here.”

“Why? What’s going on?”

“Some trouble out on the street.”

“Kind of trouble?” The others got up and so did Shrobo. “Kind of trouble?” Williams asked again.

“I don’t know, just trouble. Guy at the bar says we better get Doc out of here.”

“This way,” called Hemmie, and they moved after him. They fumbled through a door, an unlighted corridor that smelled of piss and mice, then up a set of steps. The door resisted briefly. Then wood cracked and it flew up and they were out in the warm air in an alley, the sky blocked off to either side except for a narrow ribbon of stars glimmering directly above. They ran, Hank panting along last, just after Lightbulb. Then the street opened out ahead, like a horrible carnival of noise and light and motion.

Glass sparkled over the pavement. There was a choking smell of gasoline and smoke. An eerie flickering lighted the street. Directly in front of them, a car with windows smashed into heaps of jewels was tilted up on its side. Two bodies lay where they’d been dragged out. Around them a crowd yelled and danced, chanting something he couldn't make out. They waved bottles and bricks and pieces of pipe, and now and then one of them would dash in to beat the motionless bodies, then dance back.

As they stared, a white Impala without a back window came down the street. It crept slowly around the turned-over car, nosed the crowd apart, then rolled on, bumping over one of the bodies. It stopped, backed up, drove over it three times. The wheels crushed the head.

"Shit, shit, *shit*, what is going on," muttered Baby J.

"Cover Doc's face, man. Quick. Them is white boys, there on the ground."

Shrobo felt them pushing him down. Then a hand covered his mouth. He choked and coughed, started to wipe it off, then understood what they were doing. He helped rub the ash in over his cheeks, his forehead.

"We got to get out of here."

"Shit, I wish we was in uniform."

"Not me, man. I just wish we didn't have—"

A shot boomed out somewhere, and they realized they'd been hearing them since they came out of the basement. In the distance, but growing louder. "Oh, shit," moaned somebody.

Baby J shoved him and he started to run. They sprinted past the crowd. Then a side street opened up, almost lightless. They panted down it, only to halt at a dead end. The roar and crackle of flames, and an orange glow wavered through the empty windows of an abandoned building.

"Which way to the ship? Shit, we got to get back to the ship," said Lightbulb.

"Hemmie? You got us into this, you motherfucker. How the fuck do we get out of here?"

"Through here," yelled Hemmery, pulling at a sheet of rusted corrugated metal.

They squirmed through onto a littered concrete floor that smelled of shit and smoke, then out another hole onto the street beyond. Here, store fronts had been smashed open. People inside were heaving out boxes. Others were carrying out armloads of coats and dresses. The night glistened in pieces on the asphalt. Broken mannequins, black and white and brown, lay in the gutter.

A patrol car turned the corner. The looters waited till it was almost on them, then scattered. The police emerged warily in riot gear.

Suddenly, a shot cracked directly over the sailors' heads, from a window or a roof, and one of the police spun and collapsed. The others ducked, propping their barrels over the hood and trunk. A ragged volley, flashes, and pellets whacked and whined around them as they ran.

* * *

THEY fled through burning streets and back alleys till they found railroad tracks. They picked their way along the sleepers until the weird yellow glow of the interstate expressway rose ahead of them. When they climbed a chain-link fence out of the switchyard, they found themselves on damp grass while traffic went by overhead. They straggled up the embankment, holding their sides.

Behind them, the crescendo of sirens and the popping of shots was building. Something huge was on fire off to the west, immense clouds of inky smoke flickering from beneath, like a smoldering volcano.

They crested the slope and jumped the guardrail, to find themselves on the I-95/A1A interchange. Williams started trying to wave down cars, but they speeded up instead of slowing. Police cars keened by, headed toward the sound of gunfire. Then a truck veered right at them, and they scrambled over the rail as it roared by, spitting gravel, the driver's fist thrust out the window.

IT took two hours to walk back to Port Boulevard, sticking to cover, running when they had to cross a lighted street. East of Gibson Park, two Hispanic-looking men in a van fired a pistol at them but missed. When they got to the causeway, they found it floodlighted and empty, the gates closed and locked. Port security cars were parked across the road inside. As they trudged up, the guards deployed with drawn revolvers, shouting out at them to leave.

"We're from the Navy ship. Let us in."

"Go to hell. Keep your hands in sight! Get out of here or we'll call the cops."

Shrobo thought Williams sounded tired as he said, "Okay, Hank. Here's my ID. Wipe your face off so that it looks nice and white. Then go up there and tell them to let us in."

41

DAN stood on the wing, clutching at the splinter shield and looking back at a city on fire. A ceiling of smoke masked out the stars, towering above the lights as they slowly dropped astern. Even from out here, he could hear the rattle of gunfire, the seesaw lament of dozens of sirens floating across the smooth reflective water of the last hour before dawn. My God, he thought. What was happening to Miami? To the country?

Then his mind leapt, not to what they were leaving behind but to what lay ahead.

Barrett was on her way to sea again. The orders said "Get under way on receipt of this message," but Leighty had held on until the last possible minute to get as many men as possible back aboard. Even then, Ensign Steel had come running across the hardstand, weaving between the containers, then hesitated, seeing the lines in and the ship already beginning to move ahead, the black water churning between steel sides and steel bulkheading. Then he'd backed off, getting set for a run and leap. But Leighty had leaned out, motioning him angrily to stay put, not to jump. And luckily, he hadn't. He just stood watching, a bereft figure growing gradually smaller and more distant under the salmon pink pierhead lights until they lost sight of him as they rounded Lummis Island and steadied up for Government Cut.

Which they were sliding through now, the Art Deco buildings on South Beach a wall of pastel light drifting noiselessly and smoothly down the port side. Beyond their distinct geometries, the huge hotels of the Strip glittered like a column of great liners. Dan took off his cap and wiped sweat from his forehead. He was glad he wasn't driving. The fresh sea air was clearing his head, but he still felt drunk.

"This is getting to be a habit," Cannon joked when he went back into the pilothouse.

"What is?"

"Getting under way on short notice."

"Oh, yeah. Seems like it." He looked around the darkened, silent bridge, at the shadows of officers and men at their places; the softly glowing indicators at the helm console; the compass card trembling in its alcohol bath, steady, steady, quiet, quiet, as the lights moved past; the captain's motionless silhouette forward of the chart table. Whatever was happening astern, whatever might happen ahead, here at least was an island of order, sanity, dedication. He lowered his voice a little more. "Where we headed, Dave?"

"Back to Gitmo."

"*What?* You're shitting me. They did an emergency recall just so we could—"

"Cool it, cool it. I was joking." The navigator broke off as Morris fed him a round of bearings on Fisher Island, the North Jetty, and the Miami Beach Light. Dan waited as he passed the fix to Kessler. "We're going to Cay Sal," Cannon muttered, pricking off the distance to the next turn.

"I heard something on the news about that. That's down where we just were."

"Right. West of Area B, where we were stationed." Cannon jerked his head aft. "Pub one forty-seven, page nineteen. I just looked it up."

Dan went back into the chart room. He pulled the curtain shut and clicked on the light, waited for the red flicker to steady, then searched the shelves for the Coastal Pilot.

> 2.11 Cay Sal Bank and environs—Cay Sal Bank (23° 50'N., 80° 05'W.) is an isolated and comparatively extensive shoal water area in a somewhat central position with Santaren Channel separating it from Great Bahamas Bank W side, with Nicholas Channel setting it apart from the NE coast of Cuba and with the Straits of Florida dividing it from the U.S. mainland and the Florida Keys. It is roughly in the form of a triangle and has a number of above-water landforms scattered everywhere along its edges save along its S or Nicholas Channel side, where, however, a cursory examination has reported the existence of numerous rocky heads.
>
> . . . Cay Sal (23° 42'N., 80° 25'W.), in the SW part of Cay Sal Bank and the only inhabited landform is about one mile long. It consists of an approximately circular, low-lying islet which, rising to a narrow range of sand hills on its NE side, has in its interior portions a large salt pond commonly replenished by

heavy wind-driven seas that broach the islet along its SW side. It is covered with stunted palm trees and marked by several buildings standing on its W side. Indifferent to poor anchorage is available in 12.8m (7 fm), sand, in a position charted close W of the islet where the play of tidal and ocean currents can be considerable. . . .

Interesting, he thought. But it sounded totally godforsaken—no port facilities, an undependable-sounding anchorage. There wasn't even any mention of fresh water.

When he looked out again, the glow and blaze of Miami Beach was slipping astern and the great dark sea was opening its jaws ahead. He staggered as the deck began to roll, denting his shoulder on the corner of the plot board. It occurred to him that it wasn't doing his professional image any good hanging around breathing margarita fumes, so he felt his way gingerly to the ladder down.

Halfway to his stateroom, he changed his mind.

Somehow he wasn't surprised to find all the lights on in the computer room. He stood among the humming gray slabs of the mainframes, looking at Doc DOS's back as he hunched over the monitor console. The air was icy, electric. For a moment, he thought Shrobo was alone. Then Matt Williams's voice echoed from the equipment room. "Which listing did you say?"

"Module thirty-five."

"Hi," said Dan when Williams came out. "Did the other CE division guys get back in time, do you know?"

"Far's I know, sir," said the petty officer. Dan noticed he was still in civvies. The cuffs of his trousers were ragged and his sneakers were caked with ash and mud.

"We're back at sea. Time to shift back into uniform, Petty Officer Williams."

"Yes, sir," said Williams absently, staring at the screen. Dan didn't insist. If anything big was building, this was where he wanted them, and what they wore was distinctly secondary. "Is the system coming up?" he asked them.

"We're cracking it," said Shrobo. The civilian pushed his stool back from the console, but the legs caught on the rubber matting. Dan caught him before he went over backward. Then he sniffed. "Do I smell alcohol?" he said to Williams.

"We was cleaning the tape heads, sir; that must be what you smell."

"Uh-huh. You said you were cracking it?"

"That's right." Shrobo pointed to the screen. "We finally figured out how. A powerful as hell decryption algorithm."

Dan couldn't see anything but flickering numbers, so fast that they were only a blur. Only once every minute or so did they freeze, suddenly, and the printer in the corner whirred to life and tapped out a single digit.

"How does it work?"

"Well, Lieutenant, let's just say it's an overlap strategy, executed with a random system of replacement. We can't unzip the Crud without destroying it, so we decode it by an empirical, brute-force method." Shrobo examined him through his glasses. "I can go into more detail, if you like."

"No, that's good. Does this mean we'll have Elmo back in operation pretty soon?"

"What?" Shrobo blinked.

"The combat system. Will it—"

"Oh. Yeah. Yes, we should have it all broken in a couple of days. Then we build a search string, a search-and-destroy program. It will automatically delete and overwrite the Crud where it finds it. Q.E.D., your virus is history."

"Good," said Dan, but he didn't make it too enthusiastic. So far, they'd "fixed" the thing three times. No point in celebrating till it actually ran clean for a while. "But for the time being . . . if we're required to go operational, we'll just run with the reduced-capability program. Okay? Till you tell me you actually have Version Three sanitized."

Neither of them answered. The screen froze, the printer whirred up, and one letter tapped out. He went over and looked at the output, but it was in hex—just a string of ones and zeros, in groups of four: 1011 0100 1111 1110. "What is this, again?" he asked them.

"That's the . . . zipped code, sir—the part we couldn't get into before. It'll . . . take a while, but we'll have a printout of the whole thing."

"Okay, great," Dan repeated. He looked up, but they were huddled around the monitor like obstetricians at a difficult birth. He gave up and went below.

"OFFICERS' call."

The 1MC woke him three hours later. He blinked, still lying in his bunk, then jumped out, cursing, and threw his uniform on. As he pounded up the ladder, he thought, I'm getting sick of this. Always late, feeling like shit. He only vaguely remembered the night before, dinner, the reggae bar, drinking, the long conversation with Harper, more drinks. What had they been talking about? He forgot it as he slid into the front rank. Vysotsky gave him a disapproving look. "Mr. Lenson," he noted hoarsely.

"Morning, sir."

The ship plowed through a green and blue morning, pitching to southeastern seas. The wind was warm and brisk. Far to the west, Florida was a green smear. The intakes were whining and Vysotsky had to shout. "Now that everyone's here . . . Listen up, you'll want to put this out to your troops. Why we had to cut short our liberty.

"We are now en route to the Florida Straits area, west of the Cay Sal Bank, in order to join a task force being formed there.

"Background is as follows. Due to the current, many of the refugees leaving the north coast of Cuba were set in large numbers onto the Cay Sal Bank. That's a group of low cays, rocks, and reefs midway between Cuba and Florida. Uninhabited, except for a few fishermen. They're part of the Bahamas, but Cuba has tried to dispute ownership based on historic claims.

"Late yesterday, Cuban forces landed on Cay Sal and Elbow Cay. Havana has announced that they landed to 'restore order.' Elbow Cay is only fifty miles from U.S. territory. It's ideally situated for a number of things, including radar stations and drug running.

"I understand there are diplomatic protests and so forth being made, but that's it in a nutshell.

"The reason for the formation of the task force is that, as you know, the *Kirov* and her associated escorts have been in port in Cienfuegos for the past few weeks. That force has now sortied. It's reported heading west, presumably for the Yucatán Channel. We suspect its ultimate destination is . . . the Cay Sal Bank."

Vysotsky gave it a few seconds, letting it sink in. And the warm wind, the speed of the ship as it crashed southward seemed suddenly ominous.

"There'll be a meeting of all tactical action officers in CIC right after quarters. We'll be going over the operation plan and rules of engagement that came in this morning. As far as the troops go, we need to tell them it's time to put the things they tried to teach us at Gitmo into effect. We'll go to Condition Three around noon and expect to reach the rendezvous point around fifteen hundred. Postpone as much routine work as you can, and make sure we're battle-ready, including prefiring checks.

"Now, I know there'll be loads of questions, but I'd rather have you hold them till the department heads get their brief and get the guys turned to."

DAN shaved quickly, put a fresh shirt on, and took his foul-weather jacket along when he went back up to Combat. When he got there, Cannon and Giordano were already waiting. Herb Lauderdale was going over the radio-remote setup with Chief Kennedy. Quintanilla came out of Sonar carrying a message board. Norm Cash and Burdette Shuffert showed up a few seconds later. CIC had no real briefing area, so they gathered around the darkened glass tabletop of the dead-reckoning console.

"Attention on—"

"Carry on," said Leighty, coming in behind Vysotsky. He was still in trop whites, but they were rumpled. Dan realized he'd been up all night long, presumably studying the execute order and the other messages that had started to follow it. One thing the U.S. Navy did was communicate, he thought. Usually to excess. The sheaf on Quintanilla's clipboard was already an inch thick. The operations officer looked tired, too.

"All right, Mr. Quintanilla, why don't you kick off," Leighty said.

"Yes, sir." Quintanilla put his clipboard carefully on the glass.

"Okay . . . The situation is basically what the exec put out a few minutes ago at officers' call. The *Kirov* battle group has left Cienfuegos, presumably intending to round the western tip of Cuba, then turn north. We're joining an ad hoc task force gearing up to block them if they try to intervene in whatever develops at Cay Sal.

"The, uh, opposing forces are as follows. The *Kirov,* a nuclear-powered battle cruiser; *Tallin,* a guided-missile cruiser; two *Krivak*-class frigates; and accompanying them, one *Boris Chilikin*-class replenishment ship. There may be a *Victor*-class nuclear attack submarine in company. This group's most effective weapons are the SS-N-nineteens on *Kirov.* Range, two hundred and forty nautical miles; guidance, inertial navigation with active radar homing. Closer in, both *Tallin* and the two *Krivaks* carry SS-N-fourteens. We estimate their range at around forty miles, so they're basically the equivalent of our Harpoon. Again, the greatest threat is the SS-N-nineteens. *Kirov* can launch a wave of twenty, programmed to arrive simultaneously from different directions. They come in at Mach one point six and carry a fifteen-hundred-pound high-explosive warhead."

He cleared his throat and flipped to the first tab in the clipboard as Dan thought about what nearly a ton of high explosive would do to a thin-skinned ship like *Barrett.* "This is the execute order from Commander in Chief, Atlantic Fleet to Commander, Carrier Group Two, directing him to activate Task Force One forty-two. Effective at oh-one hundred this morning, we are working for Rear Admiral Keith Larson. His flagship will be USS *Lexington.*"

"Not *Lexington!*"

"The *training* carrier?"

Vysotsky grated, "The ops officer is trying to brief. Do you mind, Mr. Giordano?"

"No, sir. Sorry, sir."

"*Lexington*'s the only carrier available on short notice. The others are all either deployed or in the yards for overhaul. At least she's close, Pensacola. She's embarking aircraft now.

"My impression, sir, is that this is a hastily scraped-up force. So far, it consists of *Lex*, us, and *Dahlgren*, two reserve frigates, *Voge* and *Bronstein*, and a tanker, *Canisteo*. Also one of the action addressees on this message is the *Munro*, although it's not really clear how the Coast Guard's going to fit into the command organization."

They discussed the cutter for a few seconds. Quintanilla pointed out that Coast Guard ships, though they had guns, were limited in communications capacity, could not come up on NTDS, and had no real antiaircraft capability. "She might end up being more a liability than an asset, sir."

"There's our missile sponge," Lauderdale joked.

"We'll see," said Leighty. "Continue with the brief."

"PHMron Two, a squadron of hydrofoil gunboats out of Key West, is also assigned in support."

Dan chewed the inside of his cheek, digesting all this. *Barrett* had just undergone a "chop," a change in operational control. For commissioning, shakedown, and work-up, she had reported to Commodore Niles. But the Navy assigned forces for a specific contingency by task organizations, set up in advance and activated only when needed. Now they were under the operational command of Admiral Larson, embarked on the carrier. Captain Leighty was in charge of task group 142.1, the screening destroyers. Other task groups were the carrier itself, the air group, the oiler, and the PHMs.

That the carrier was *Lexington* was worrisome. *Lex* had a great and long history, but she was no longer a front-line unit. Her home port was Pensacola, where she served as a floating airfield to train naval aviators. She had an old engineering plant known for frequent breakdowns. If it faltered now, Dan thought, not only could she not steam; she might not be able to launch aircraft, either. The catapults were steam-driven.

Now, Quintanilla said, "Apparently, the mission is to deter the Soviets from intervening on the Cuban side while we isolate the forces that are already there . . . and I guess try to persuade them to withdraw peacefully. Intel estimates there aren't more than a couple hundred on the cays. Castro's probably waiting for our reaction. If we do nothing, he'll reinforce, raise the Cuban flag—you can see where that's going.

"From the other traffic, the Joint Chiefs are bringing up readiness as rapidly as they can in the CENTCOM/Caribbean area. But the fleet is spread thin, with two extra carriers deployed to cover Iran. Our group will buy time while *Kitty Hawk* is pulled from stand-down and associated cruisers and destroyers are assembled from Charleston and Norfolk."

Giordano said, "Felipe, any sense of what's driving this? What the Cubans hope to get out of it?"

"I'd be speculating. Politically, it doesn't make a lot of sense. Since the missile crisis, they've tended to avoid direct confrontation. The Cay Sal islands are Bahamian, not ours, but they must know we'd react violently to an occupation so near our coasts. It's not much to risk a major showdown over. There's really nothing there but a few rocks."

"So why are they pulling our chain?"

Quintanilla said carefully, "Maybe Castro's trying to embarrass the President. He hates us, and this is just his way of telling him, Welcome to the big leagues. Whatever, if the *Kirov* group can join up, it'll be that much more difficult to kick them off the islands. We're supposed to keep that from happening, I guess."

"Okay, that's the mission and the forces," said Leighty. He stood there a moment more, leaning against a fire-control console. Posing again, Dan thought sarcastically. "How about the rules of engagement?"

"Sir, I've made copies." He passed them out and went over them line by line. Then glanced at the captain. "That's all I have, sir."

Leighty put both hands on the glass and looked down into it. Then he spoke, seemingly to the gears and machinery dimly visible through the transparent surface.

"So that's the situation. We're headed south now and will join up with Lady *Lex* sometime this afternoon.

"I don't need to remind you that we're not all that used to operating in formation—especially at night. Either Commander Vysotsky or myself will be on the bridge at all times when we're in company. That doesn't mean the officer of the deck is relieved of responsibility. We won't be doing your job. But we'll be available on a second's notice. Inform us instantly if you're in doubt, and we'll drop what we're doing and help out.

"For the TAOs." His eyes picked out Dan, Quintanilla, Lauderdale. "Every other confrontation we've had with the Cubans, they've backed down. But our job is to prepare for the worst, so let's do that. Felipe went over the rules of engagement. I want you to memorize them. There's not going to be time to look things up to see whether or not we fire. There's no doctrine that says we have to wait for them to shoot first if it looks like we're going to be attacked. This could be a first-salvo situation. The side that gets a solution and fires first is going to clobber the other guy.

"Dwight, we've got to be ready to fight fires and flooding. Your new damage control officer, Lohmeyer, he up to speed yet? He drew some flak at Gitmo."

"He's learning, sir. I got the chief backstopping him. We'll be ready."

Leighty spoke to the glass again. "*Barrett* will be the most capable ship in this task group. I anticipate carrying most of the radio nets. Mr. Lauderdale, review identification procedures with all your console operators. Make sure we have electronic threat profiles for the *Kirov, Tallin,* and the escorts. They can also target by video downlink from maritime reconnaissance, so we need to stay alert for overflights.

"Dan, we're going to need all weapons systems at Condition Three, ready for a heavy missile engagement. I want VT/IR ammo to the transfer trays in the five-inch, Phalanx loaded, AAW war shots in the loader drums. Have Mr. Horseheads test the chaff launchers and report to me. I want to see Mr. Kessler about our sonar. As soon as we break from here, get me an up-to-date status on ACDADS, what modes we can operate in, how many targets we can handle—"

"I can brief you on that now, sir." He was glad he'd stopped in the computer room. Glad, too, that the news seemed to be good.

"All right, stay afterward and bring me up to speed. Anything else, gentlemen?" He waited for a moment, eyes still searching through the glass. "Thank you. Now let's get ready for this operation."

42

24° 25' N, 85° 01' W: The Eastern Gulf of Mexico

HE sat tensely in Combat, monitoring the progress of the tracking drill. Watching the bent backs of the weapons coordinators, engagement controllers, petty officers manning the radars and weapons and tracking consoles. They muttered rapidly into handsets or mikes, chanting an accompaniment to the green flicker of the consoles. Cold air roared from the diffusers. His ears skipped from one conversation to the next. *Voge*'s helicopter was making low runs from various quadrants, acting as a radar target for the antiaircraft-capable ships. At the same time, the combat air controllers were shaking down their tracking and handoff procedures. He followed the polyphonal murmur with only one mental ear. Tonight something underlay it that had been missing at Gitmo. Now each man knew he was preparing for battle.

The formation had gradually taken shape over the past day and evening. During the transit south, then west around the tip of Florida, *Barrett* had fallen in with *Dahlgren*. As they made westing the rendezvous point moved, too, jumping northwest. South of the Tortugas they'd linked up with *Bronstein*, then finally reached the new rendezvous, Point PAPA, 143 nautical miles due north of Cabo San Antonio and 110 miles due west of Garden Key. *Voge*, the other frigate, had come over the horizon an hour later, and following her, at last, *Lexington*. *Munro* was not in sight, but a message came in shortly thereafter reporting her position off Key Largo. Dan wondered whether he should call the staff watch officer on the carrier and ask if they could expect her to join and, if so, when.

A figure moved through the gloom, lifted a hand in greeting. Burdette Shuffert picked up the battle group commander's standing orders and slid into a vacant seat to read himself in. The tactical action officers were in three sections, Quintanilla, Dan, and Shuffert. They relieved each other an hour before the bridge stations turned over. The Soviets knew U.S. watch procedures. Overlapping minimized the likelihood of being taken by surprise.

Dan slid down and went into Sonar, into a cramped blue-lighted shrine with the acolytes fixed in adoration on the sonar stacks as above their heads Barbie twirled, ignored. Fowler glanced up from the passive-tracking console. "Mr. Lenson, howzit going?"

"Okay, Chief. Everything working?"

"Looks like it at this end."

"My guys have got sonar processing up and running on a separate computer. Dedicated to you."

"That's good, sir, we might could need it with a Victor out there. Remember that contact we had west of Haiti? That could have been the boat that's supposed to be with this Soviet battle group."

"I was thinking the same thing, Chief." Dan watched the pen etch slowly along. "What's predicted range?"

"Uh, not too good. It's shallow here. Lots of biologicals. We're probably not going to get a good bottom bounce, either. Here's the prediction sheet, you want to look it over."

"Uh-huh." He ran his eyes down it. "How's the situation between you and Mr. Harper?"

Fowler molded an invisible soap bubble. "He seems to be acting more reasonable now, sir. Since you straightened him out on whose equipment this was."

"Good. Well, stay alert, but pace yourself. We could be out here for a while." Dan looked around again, then drifted back into CIC. He checked the electronic-warfare console over Hiltz's shoulder, then got himself a fresh coffee and stirred in lumpy yellow powdered creamer. He looked at the TAO chair but sat at a momentarily untended console instead.

He tapped keys and got the long-range plot, a picture of the formation and its surroundings out to two hundred nautical miles. Around the central cluster of the formation was open water, the Gulf of Mexico. If they had to fight, at least they had sea room. A few surface contacts flickered north of them. As he spun the track ball, hooked each one, and pressed the readout button, the system identified them and gave courses and speeds. Tankers, apparently, en route to the offshore oilfields of Louisiana. Far to the southeast, some surface and air activity near the Cuban coast. He picked up the interphone and asked Hiltz what he had in that direction.

When he felt satisfied, he tapped keys for the short-range plot. Now the carrier symbol occupied the center of the screen, a silently pulsing amber circle. *LEX*, said the readout. 220 013.5, course and speed.

Dan stared at it, his mind suddenly vacant. The glowing wheel seemed to spin as the data refreshed second by second. The howl of the wind grew in his skull. His hand crept up without thought or knowledge to knead the old burn tissue that fissured his shoulder.

How the freezing men had screamed, floating in the dark. Then *Kennedy*'s deck-edge lights had brightened, coming around. They'd thought, to rescue them. But then they'd steadied up, the massive towering bow filling the night, looming above the drifting, burning *Ryan*. . . . He sucked breath and jerked his eyes off the screen, rubbed them violently until green coruscating patterns blotted out the afterimages. The carrier wasn't the only thing he had to worry about now. Fifteen hundred pounds of high explosive arriving at one and a half times the speed of sound would tear *Barrett* apart just as thoroughly, leaving them dead in the water, sinking, on fire—

Shuffert, at his elbow: "Ready to relieve, sir."

He took a deep breath, grateful for the interruption, and masked his apprehension with a gulp of coffee. Had to control his fucking imagination. Nothing was going to happen. They and the Soviets would hang around out here for a few days and make threatening gestures at each other till the diplomats came to some face-saving compromise. "Hi, Shoe. Sit down. Let's look at the formation first."

He briefed the AAW officer carefully and thoroughly. Forgetting to tell his relief something could cost lives. He began with the formation, the screen stations, the capabilities of each unit and any equipment problems or limitations, the status of the weapons systems and sensors.

"What about helos?"

"We don't have enough to keep one overhead continuously. As FASWC, the captain has directed two four-hour searches. The rest of the time, a fifteen-minute standby on deck."

"They flying armed?"

"Two Mark forty-sixes."

Shuffert nodded and Dan went on. "The carrier's guide, offset from the center of the formation. *Canisteo* here." He swept his hand across a great semicircle, subdivided electronically into glowing segments of arc. "Screen stations: *Voge* as a backstop; *Dahlgren, Bronstein, Barrett* out front. Notice *Bronstein*'s set farther out along the threat axis. She's got a towed array sonar streamed and is also going to act as a radar picket."

"She's not NTDS-equipped."

"No. Link Fourteen." This was a Teletype readout plotted by hand. It meant that the older frigate would react more slowly than the rest of the force and that reports from her would come in more slowly, too.

"I don't think that's very good tactically, is it?"

Dan shrugged. "It's a trade-off. The captain decided to put her out there to take advantage of her sonar."

"Okay. What have we got on the away team?"

"Last report has *Kirov* at twenty-one degrees north, eighty-five degrees thirty minutes west, steaming slowly for the Yucatán Channel. They're not being reported on NTDS yet."

They covered the rest of the intel data and predicted sonar ranges and modes. Dan reviewed the comm plan, engineering status, and the rules of engagement. Shuffert said quietly, "Do we have release authority?"

"Yes. The captain wants us to contact him or the XO if at all possible. But if we've got missiles incoming, we have authority to fire in self-defense."

"How's NTDS holding up?"

"We've got solid Link Eleven with the carrier, *Dahlgren*, and *Voge*. Like I said, *Bronstein* has only the Teletype. She's reported some glitches, but they're copying data."

"Okay, I relieve you." Dan nodded and started to hit the 21MC to tell the captain he'd relieved, then didn't. "I'll go up. Something I want to ask him."

"Okay." Shuffert was already hunched forward, head turned a bit, listening, Dan knew, to the muffled murmur that came from all around him.

HE stopped for a quick whiz in the little urinal near CIC, then ran up the ladder, making his heart pump and thud after four hours of sitting.

The bridge was completely dark. Even the indicator lights had been masked with tape, until only the dark-adapted eye could detect them. His weren't; the green brilliance of the iconoscopes burned away night vision. He brushed past someone standing near the door, felt his way past the helm to the chart table, and from there groped forward to the smooth leather back of the CO's chair. His outstretched fingers pressed something soft before he jerked them away from the captain's leg.

"Who's that?"

"Sorry, sir. Mr. Lenson, properly relieved as TAO by Lieutenant (jg) Shuffert."

"Very well. You'd better lay below, grab some sleep."

"Captain, I wanted to ask about *Munro.* We still don't know if she's going to be in the screen. I can call the staff watch officer—"

"No!" The captain's tone softened. "Sorry. I mean, I'm glad you're on things like that, but don't bother. She's not part of One forty-two point one in the comm annex to the op order. I think we can conclude Admiral Larson's got some other plan for her."

"Uh, all right, sir."

Harper's voice from the dark: "All engines ahead standard, indicate pitch and rpm for fifteen knots."

"Sir, did Mr. Horseheads report to you on your chaff question?"

"Yes. Thank you."

Another shadow. When it spoke, Dan recognized Norm Cash. The supply officer said, "Captain? We've got a major problem, sir."

"What's that, Norm?"

"We're out of cartridges for the copier. Ordered some in Miami, but when the guys open the box, it's for Xeroxes, not Savins."

Dan felt his way to the starboard side and looked out the slanted square window. His vision was returning. He cupped his hand against the Plexiglas, then stepped around and through the open doorway, out under the stars.

They sparkled across the sky like sequins tacked across black velvet by a master dressmaker. The warm night breeze breathed in his ears. From below came the steady roar of steel plowing water. He leaned back, to see the lookout outlined against the Milky Way. For once, he wasn't dicking off, but searching the horizon. Somebody must have told him the first hint they might have of an incoming SS-N-19 "Shipwreck" missile would be the reddish flare of its exhaust, like a hovering, slowly brightening comet.

The night-orders message had them steaming in the area of Point PAPA, on a course angled across the wind, so the carrier could turn and launch aircraft within minutes of an alert. Their current course was 210. That would put her off their starboard quarter, nearly astern. He craned over the splinter shield and saw it—not only the dimmed running and deck-edge lights but the sudden yellow blowtorch flare of a jet being catapulted off, afterburners lighted. He could imagine what kind of confusion reigned over there, operating aircraft from a ship that hadn't done it in years. But she was getting the planes off. In Combat, Dan had watched them orbiting a hundred miles out, two F-4 Phantoms under *Barrett*'s control.

Sweeping his eyes across 180 degrees of darkness, he picked out four more sets of lights—running dimmed but not totally blacked out yet. On his left hand, so distant that only her white masthead light was visible: *Bronstein*, the older frigate, built in the early sixties and light on defensive armament. She had a good antisubmarine suite, though, and could most likely deal with a Victor; Leighty was probably right to put her out there as an ASW barrier, though it was cold-blooded. In an air attack, she'd have to depend on *Dahlgren*'s and *Barrett*'s missiles for cover.

On the far side of the formation, red sidelight burning below masthead and range: *Dahlgren*. She and *Barrett* were spaced symmetrically on either side of the missile-threat axis to cover the other ships, and especially the carrier, with their long-range weapons.

The next lights, seemingly twinned, although they were separated by some distance, were the carrier and the oiler. Roughly centered in the protective ring of the screen, neither carried defensive weapons worth mentioning, though, paradoxically, *Lexington* bore the most powerful striking arm of the force, her aircraft; and without the fuel, parts, ammunition, and stores *Canisteo* carried, the other ships would have short legs indeed.

Last, a faraway twinkle like a low star: *Voge*, a more modern frigate, armed with Sea Sparrow missiles, five-inch gun, and a good antisubmarine suite. Leighty had placed her to the northeast, behind the carrier and the oiler, to guard against end runs.

Standing there, looking at the force spread around him, he could see in advance exactly how it all would go. Or at least how it was supposed to go, according to the best estimates the U.S. Navy had been able to muster over the past forty years.

For hastily assembled though it was, Task Force 142 was a textbook example of the Navy's fighting doctrine as it had remained with startlingly little change since the end of World War II.

In the "air age," the Navy's leaders had concluded that power resided not in a single massive vessel, nor in a phalanx of identical units, but in a mix of specialized ships deployed in a mutually supporting formation. Destroyers, cruisers, and frigates were its shield. Its sword was the aircraft on the flattops' decks. The old capital weapon, the battleship gun, had limited range and tactical flexibility. But attack aircraft could strike hundreds of nautical miles and target not only enemy ships but land-based installations, airfields, communications.

Ever since, moving endlessly across the face of the waters, these powerful yet mobile concentrations of self-contained force had gradually made obsolete the old necessities for bases and garrisons. Where U.S. interests were threatened, there the carriers could go, and the far-flung twinkling of lights he contemplated now was a microcosm of the great battle groups deployed now across the globe. That had kept, in large measure, what modicum of peace the world had enjoyed since 1945.

It still seemed a reasonable disposition for offensive operations. He had every confidence in the aviators. He'd seen them train; he knew their courage and skill would put ordnance on target. But given TF 142's limited defensive assets, he didn't feel terribly confident facing a brand-new nuclear battle cruiser and her escorts. For if the U.S. Navy had a standard formation, they were the ships designed to defeat it—*Kirov* and her associated screen units, now only a few steaming hours distant.

What if it really came to fighting? Harper scoffed, but did that mean it couldn't happen? Men at Pearl Harbor and Jutland and

Trafalgar, too, had probably laughed at the thought there could be battle, that they could be dead and their ships wrecked.

For just a moment, looking out, he had a moment of self-doubt sharp as terror. If it came to war, how would he react? But then, the next moment, he shook his head slowly. He already knew the answer. It had scarred his body, tried his soul. But that much, the doomed *Ryan* had given him. He might—he *would*—be afraid. But he knew he'd stand his ground. He'd do his duty, even in the face of death.

He thought with a sort of suspicious wonder, Could that be how life worked? That whenever it took something, it gave you back—

"Mr. Lenson, you out here? Captain asked if you were still on the bridge."

"Yes, sir," he said, back inside. He could make out Leighty now, a small silhouette against the window.

"Dan, how's our NTDS, sick or well?"

"We seem to be well; we've never had any problem with the Link Eleven module."

"And the Link Fourteen?"

"*Bronstein* reports glitches, dropped data. I recommended they tune their equipment, maybe try the secondary frequency."

"I want you to keep close tabs on your systems. Inform me immediately if there's any degradation, or any significant improvement."

"Aye aye, sir. Um . . . what do you think's going to happen? Are they going to try to come through us?"

"Don't know. If they do, I'm not sure we can stop them. It's as if they waited till all our first-line carriers were deployed, so we'd have nothing left to fill a hole down here." Leighty didn't speak for a few minutes. Then he said, as if musing to himself, "It's not good to be weak."

Dan couldn't think of anything to say to that. He was turning away when the captain added, "Could you get me some coffee, please?"

"Yes, sir."

When he came back with it, Leighty said, "Thanks. So you think we're about as set as we can be."

"I'd say so, sir."

"I meant that, about getting some sleep. I was talking to some Royal Navy officers once. They told me, if they ever had to fight us, they'd hang back for a week before they attacked. We'd be so spun up by that time, we'd be asleep on the consoles."

"Probably true, sir. That's how we operate all right."

"Not aboard *Barrett*. Anyway . . . what are your plans after this tour, Dan?"

"Plans, sir?" He blinked dully at the figure above him.

"You have plans, don't you? I thought you were Academy-issue, career track."

"I guess so, sir."

"You don't sound very positive."

"Well, I haven't been thinking about it lately, sir. Been kind of down in the weeds with the combat system, and . . . and personal stuff, too."

A speaker over their head crackled, "All units Alfa X-ray, this is Whiskey Foxtrot. Radio check. Over."

"Do you have that, Jay?"

"Yes, sir, I got it. This is Delta Tango, roger, out."

"You mean your divorce?"

"I wasn't thinking of that, but that, too, yes, sir."

"Well, you need to start thinking about your career. Combat systems on a *Kidd*-class . . . that's good to have in your jacket. Leave here as a senior lieutenant, do a shore tour, staff duty somewhere, postgraduate work, you'll be right in line for XO."

"Maybe, sir. If I get picked up for lieutenant commander." He had a momentary impulse to lay it on the line, tell the man above him he doubted he'd stay in that much longer. Then his lips closed again in the humming dark. He didn't like this man; he didn't trust him. He no longer wished even to talk with him.

"If you want to discuss it sometime, let me know. Maybe I can help."

"Aye aye, sir," Dan said, thinking, And what price would I have to pay?

"Get that sleep now."

"Aye aye, sir."

TWO decks below, the Teletype tapped out a single zero and fell silent. The figures on the screen froze, then disappeared.

Hank Shrobo looked up slowly from the empty screen. He blinked, detaching his glasses from one ear, then the other. He carefully rubbed what felt like grit out of his eyes. He sighed, shoved the stool back, and felt for his shoes with his toes. He picked up his mug and was startled to find it half full of icy black liquid. Sharp cracks came from his spine as he straightened.

"Matt," he croaked. "Matt?" There was no answer, and after a moment, he looked around.

Chief Dawson was standing in front of the mainframes, arms folded, watching the play of lights as the programming ran. "Hi, Doc. Coming up for air?"

"Finished, that's what. Where's Matt?"

"Think he just went to the—no, here he is." The compartment door thumped open, then the dogs grated as it closed again.

Williams came into the light. He was in uniform now, but his face was ruined, slack and sleepless. His gaze met Shrobo's, then moved to the screen and then the printer. His head snapped up. Without a word, he jumped to it, tore off the two-foot length of paper, and smoothed it out on the test bench. Together they stared down as if at the Dead Sea Scrolls.

"There it is."

"Just like we figured—eighty lines."

They gazed at the rows and columns of ones and zeros for a few seconds. Then Williams cocked his black ballpoint. He etched slashes between the four-digit groups of the first line. Then, gnawing his lip, he began writing the hex equivalent below each group. Shrobo went back to the monitor for the plastic-laminated "Repertoire of Instructions" card.

"Got it? Okay, first group." Williams read it off.

"That's 'initiate input/output chain from one forty.' "

"Okay. Next instruction . . ."

" 'Decrement BCW for XJ instruction.' Are you writing this down, or am I?"

The door thumped open again, but they didn't look up.

DAN could tell just by looking at them that something had happened. He hoped it was good. "What's going on?" he asked. "Sorry. Didn't mean to startle you."

"This is it. Here it is!" The black petty officer flourished two pages of green-and-white fanfold. "We're starting to decompose it to CMS-2."

"Great," he said, but when he looked around the space, he saw only two computers running and three dark, shut down. "What do you have on number one?" he asked the chief.

"That's sonar processing, sir. The isolated NTDS and Link Eleven modules are running on three."

"What about the op program? The weapons module?"

"Still down, sir."

Dan was suddenly so angry, he could not speak for a moment. Finally, he managed, "Who ordered the weapons-control module taken down?"

"Dr. DOS thinks it's not a good idea to run it now."

"Is that right. How long has it been off?"

"Two, three hours, sir."

Dan wanted to lash out, but he controlled himself. Missed communications somewhere, that was all. He cleared his throat, took a deep breath. "Great, you've cracked it. So all you have to do now—correct me if I'm wrong—is to write a program that goes: 'Look for this first string here'—B-four-F-E, that it?—then, 'Look for this last string' and, 'Delete all between them.' That'll search out and delete everywhere the virus is hidden. Bingo, you patch any missing lines and it's good to go. Then you scrub down the drum memories, the data tapes, everything runs smoothly, and we're back to C-One readiness. That right?" He fixed his gaze on Shrobo. This time, he was going to get an answer.

"It's not exactly that simple—"

"But you can write a string search, right? Isn't that what you were going to do? We need it, Doc. Yesterday."

Shrobo blinked. Lenson was disturbed, he could see that. But he was getting annoyed, too. How did anything ever get done aboard this ship? Everything was hurried, superficial, cosmetic, with no regard for underlying principles. He said rather coldly, "I don't think you understand what Mr. Williams and I have just accomplished here, Lieutenant."

"I understand you've decoded the virus. But it's still in there, right?" He pointed to the gray cabinets. "If it reactivates, our weapons systems are useless, right?"

"I believe it's more important to understand exactly how it does what it does—whatever that is."

Dan felt his temper slipping. "Okay, I'm sure you're right theoretically. But do *you* understand where we are and what we're doing out here?" Or had Shrobo been down here so long that he was really clueless as to what was going on topside, at Cay Sal, and a few hundred miles to the south? Shit, maybe he didn't know.

"Look. Maybe nobody's explained this to you. We're off the Cuban coast, looking down the throats of a Soviet battle group. They've got missiles with double our range and three times the warhead weight. We need the operating system, the whole system, operating at peak performance." He swung from the civilian's rather hostile gaze to the DS2's. "Petty Officer Williams, do you understand that?"

"Yes, sir, I grok that. But what Doc here is saying—"

"I *hear* what he's saying. I'm not deaf! I'm thrilled you got it solved, okay? But we don't have the time right now for theoretical investigation. *Write the fucking routine!* Get Elmo running in mode three. Then you can take all the time you want to figure out the fine details."

"Sir, I think Hank—Dr. Shrobo is right. What he's saying, we don't know yet what the thing is actually doing in there."

Dan lost it then. "That's enough! I want a search routine and I want it now. Chief, explain it to them. The Soviets are three hundred miles south of us. They're trying to decide whether to come through our line or not. We're the only ship here with a credible missile-guard capability. We've got to have it running before the showdown or the *Kirov* is going to mow us down. And we'll be on the bottom, along with these computers and your theories, too."

There, Dawson got it at least. The chief straightened. "Will do, sir. I'll get everyone down here, get them on it."

"Keep me informed. I'll either be in CIC or in my stateroom."

"Gotcha, sir."

"And get that goddamned weapons-control module loaded. Right now."

"Aye aye, sir."

He turned from their hostile eyes, satisfied now they'd obey. It shouldn't take that long to write the routine. With ACDADS running, they could face a wave of missiles with some hope of surviving, protecting the carrier, then striking back.

Then the 1MC speaker on the bulkhead hissed and popped, snapping their heads around. Only emergency word was passed after taps, and it was almost midnight. For a second, they heard nothing but frenzied cries. Then the clang of the alarm, followed by BM1 Casworth's voice, strangely high-pitched, as Dan had never heard it before.

"Now general quarters, general quarters. All hands, man your battle stations. This is *not* a drill."

43

AS he reached Combat, he expected the sound level to be high. And true, every radio circuit was crackling, every Teletype clattering. But it wasn't noise. Data was coming in, being processed, going out. There was a continual rapid murmur from the console operators, the tapping of keys, but no shouting, no running, no confusion. Thanks, Gitmo, Dan thought. Whatever was happening, they were ready.

He reached Shuffert at the same moment Vysotsky did. "What's happening?" the XO snapped.

"Trying to find out, sir, but I think *Dahlgren*'s been hit."

"Hit!" Dan instinctively marked the time: 2343.

"That's a guess, sir. I'm trying to confirm." Shuffert reached for the 21MC. "Bridge, Combat: Anything from *Dahlgren* yet?"

"No answer on the tactical net. Ditto fleet common."

"Have the signal bridge try them flashing light."

"We're supposed to be running dimmed, Shoe."

"Use the infrared filter. And keep the lookouts alert; we could be next duck up at the shooting range."

"Bridge aye." The intercom clicked off.

"Who sounded GQ? Why?" Vysotsky demanded.

Shuffert blinked rapidly. "I did, sir. We were night steaming, everything same as when you were here, Dan. Then suddenly we got a voice report. *Canisteo* saw a streak of fire go past them. Off to the north at first, then it moved south, across the formation, they said. Then our lookout reported a flash from the direction of *Dahlgren*."

"Combat, Bridge: No answer from *Dahlgren* to flashing-light query. Also, we can't pick up running lights on them anymore."

Dan hit the key twice, acknowledging, as the tactical circuit speaker said in a deliberate bass, "Foxtrot Uniform, this is Whiskey Foxtrot. Over."

Clicking his eyes to the call-sign board, Dan confirmed that "Whiskey Foxtrot" was CTF 142, the task force commander, and that he was calling *Dahlgren.* Could even be Admiral Larson on the circuit. But whoever it was, the other destroyer didn't answer.

"NTDS?" Vysotsky grated.

"Sir, *Dahlgren*'s dropped out. She's not responding to the network query."

"Do we still have radar video?"

"Yes, sir, she's still there, but she's not transmitting."

Dan swung on Hiltz. "EW, what you got?"

"No threat signatures, no seekers, sir. I've been going up and down the spectrum."

Leighty came in as the 21MC said, "Combat, Bridge: All stations report manned and ready." He snapped, "Hiltz! Any rackets?"

"None, sir. Mr. Lenson just asked me that."

"Anything on the long-range plot?"

"Air plot, negative contacts, sir."

"And no one's reported any submarine contacts."

"No, sir," said Dan. Just then, the tactical circuit intoned, "All stations Alfa X-ray, this is Whiskey Foxtrot. Message follows; execute to follow."

"Copy it; copy it," Leighty said.

"Echo November One tack two. Foxtrot corpen nuco juliet alfa, juliet sierra, bravo victor. Tack. Zulu X-ray two tack three. Over."

Lauderdale, from the darkness: "Captain, I break that: Prepare for enemy attack. Coming to flight course one-three-zero. Formation course one-three-zero, speed twenty-seven. Preparing to launch aircraft."

"She's getting her strike off."

"Roger it, somebody."

Dan grabbed the handset, but just then Van Cleef's voice said from the bridge, "This is Delta Tango; roger, out."

The deliberate voice came over the air again, repeated the message, then said, "Standby, execute."

Dan touched Shuffert's arm. "Okay, I've got it. Go take the AAWC." The black officer nodded, tapped Chief Alaska's back, slid into his seat in front of the antiair-weapons-coordinator console. Dan swung himself into the TAO chair as Leighty hit the 21MC. "Bridge, this is the captain. Get moving; get around to the new course. Keep a sharp eye on the carrier. Use left rudder to come around—that is, *left* rudder."

"Bridge aye, sir. Left rudder, coming to one-three-zero."

Leighty, standing in the middle of the compartment, was speaking rapidly in a low voice, almost as if to himself. "All right. First things first. Dan, get on the HF command net—"

The HICOM was a high-frequency channel that went direct to the fleet commander. But even as Leighty spoke, it crackled into life. "Flash, flash, flash," said the same deliberate voice that had just put out the message on the tactical circuit. "All stations this net, this is Alfa X-ray, Station Papa in the Gulf of Mexico. Radiant. I say again, Radiant; time twenty-three fifty-one Romeo." It repeated the message and authenticated it. Two stations confirmed receipt, the single-sideband transmissions making them sound as if they were talking through a flute.

"Dan, are our Phalanxes in automatic? All weapons stations manned? As soon as we have a clue where that missile came from, I want a Harpoon out there."

"Aye, aye, sir. CIWS is in automatic mode. Sir, based on the fact that we have no air or surface contacts in range, I call that as a submarine-launched missile. Victors aren't supposed to have them, but our intel could be wrong. I recommend all screen units go to active search."

"Okay, do it."

He put the word out through Kessler, at the ASW console. A moment later, the outgoing sonar pulse sang through the now-vibrating fabric of the leaning ship. He glanced at the rudder-angle indicator above his head, to find it at left full.

"Combat, Bridge: *Lexington* is launching aircraft."

It's started, he thought. There was no time to think it, but the knowledge filtered between the race of precautions, reactions, orders he had to give. A knowledge that obliterated everything else, that condensed a numb dread into his bones. *Radiant* was the proword for "I am under surprise attack." The equivalent of "Air raid, Pearl Harbor." Now the bombers and escort fighters were catapulting off *Lexington*'s decks toward the Soviet battle group.

They were at war.

Yet something was missing. The screens were blank, where there should, by all rights, be a coordinated wave of missiles overwhelming and obliterating their defenses. All the tactical references and briefings, the discussions and drills agreed. The Soviets didn't have the command and control to feint and maneuver. They'd open battle with a single crushing mass assault. The first blow had descended; surprise had been complete—but where were the other missiles? He stared at the plot, thoughts skittering across its surface as across ice, seeking a purchase but finding none. A one-shot attack made no tactical sense.

"Sir," said Mallon from the big SSWC scope. "*Dahlgren*'s turning."

"Say what?"

The petty officer put his finger on the pip. "Coming around to the new course. Lagging behind, but they're not dead in the water."

"They've still got power, steering control, then."

"But something hit them. That flash. Then they dropped all their comms."

The beep and squeal of the scrambled circuit caught his ear. He reached up to adjust the volume as a breathless voice said, "CTF One forty-two, this is *Voge*, over."

"CTF, over, make your transmission short."

"This is *Voge*, reporting accidental launch. Over."

"CTF One forty-two, say again, over."

"This is *Voge*, reporting accidental launch of one of our Sparrow missiles. It is . . . possible that the missile impacted USS *Dahlgren.*"

"Oh Christ," Dan heard somebody whisper. He couldn't see who. "Christ," the voice said louder. It was Vysotsky.

"This is CTF One forty-two." A pause, then the same voice again, but gone hard: "Investigate and report back as soon as possible. Out."

Several minutes later, just past midnight, *Voge* came back up. She confirmed that one of her RIM-7E Sea Sparrow missiles had been fired accidentally on an approximate bearing of 215. They were investigating to determine the cause. Glancing at the maneuvering-board sketch of the formation taped by the TAO's chair, Dan said, "That could put it on *Dahlgren* all right."

"Oh my God."

They stood and sat frozen in place around the slanting, vibrating space. Dan knew they could still be under attack, the word from *Voge* could be wrong. But presently, Larson—it had to be him—came back on the HICOM and canceled his Radiant message. He added a code group that Dan didn't recognize but that must mean "equipment failure, accidental firing." Dan didn't envy whoever had to account for this.

Canisteo reported flames off her starboard quarter.

Not long after, Larson ordered *Barrett* alongside *Dahlgren* to investigate and report, rendering assistance as necessary.

HE was on the bridge when *Barrett* drew alongside, the helmsman warned to be ready to sheer away instantly if the other ship started to come around. *Dahlgren* had way on, but she was only making about ten knots. Calling in speed adjustments, micrometering the rudder a degree or two right or left, Leighty conned slowly up on her until the two ships rolled along together, side by side, less than a hundred yards apart.

The other destroyer was a long black mass lighted only by flame and the firefly searching of battle lanterns. The fire was centered in the high, slightly out-thrust bridge area. Then the wind blew the flames back, and he saw the sickening writhe of buckled plates, the gape of holes punched through the thin superstructure plating. There didn't seem to be any forward director.

"Flashing light from aft."

He shifted his attention back along the dark length of the ship, to see a lamp blinking from abaft the after stack. He caught the last few letters: *A-T-I-O-N*.

The signalman shouted down, "Signal from *Dahlgren*. 'I am still on station.' "

"That's after conn."

"Their radios must be out."

Dan had an idea. He went back inside and found the bridge-to-bridge walkie-talkie in the chart room. Sure enough, someone was calling them on Channel 13. "This is *Barrett*," he said, turning the volume up so the others could hear, too.

"Ah, this is Lieutenant Abbott." Dan remembered a huge soft hand gripping his, an indignant voice: "I resent comparin' me to some faggot. It's natural bein' black." "I have control from emergency conn. I don't get any response from the bridge."

"What happened, Lieutenant?"

"Ah, I don't know. I was down in Combat, getting ready to take over the watch. All at once, there's a hell of a blast. Guys go down, fragments come through the overhead. Power, lights, everything dies. I don't think there's anybody left on the bridge. They're fighting the fire up there now. I came back here to try to keep us in formation, fight the ship. We don't have any radars up, but if you can pass us oral designations, we can fire in local control."

Dan thought about how to tell him, but to his relief Leighty took the radio out of his hands. "Lieutenant, formation course is now one-two-zero true. I believe that will be about one-two-four by your magnetic compass. Speed is twenty-seven, but I don't think we'll be at that much longer. You can secure your men from battle stations and turn everyone to, to fight the fire. We are not being attacked. You were struck by a missile from *Voge*. An accidental launch."

"A what? Accidental—"

"*Voge*'s missing one of her Sparrows. *Canisteo* saw it crossing the formation in your direction. The guidance must have enabled and it guided into you."

"Oh Christ." The transmission clicked off and on. "All those guys blown away up there. You saying it was a screwup? Jake and Larry and Ming—all the guys, the lookouts—"

"Take it easy; we'll stay with you. If you need help, we'll put people aboard. We will close in and get water on the fire from here. Go ahead and check, then call us back. *Barrett* out."

A deep howl, a thundering rumble, and they looked up, to see five double cones of flame pass slowly between them and the stars. Then, spaced seconds apart, three more groups. The strike was orbiting while Larson decided whether to call it back aboard. Dan felt both sick and grateful. At least planes were recallable. If it had been missile-to-missile, their own salvo might already be on its way now, beyond recall. And the result . . . war by accident, wanted and intended by neither side.

HE went back down to CIC, following what was going on alongside through an occasional eavesdrop on the damage-control circuits. *Barrett* stayed with the stricken ship, gradually edging in while her damage controlmen got hoses rigged to the 03 level, midships. From there, when they were close enough, they could pour foam across and down into the cratered inferno that was *Dahlgren*'s bridge area.

At 0032, the carrier began taking the air strike back aboard. Now the atmosphere turned edgy again. The missile burst over *Dahlgren* had cut the formation's long-range antiaircraft defenses in half. And until the attack aircraft were refueled, *Lex* couldn't launch another strike. If the Soviets wanted to clobber them, this was their chance. Dan hovered behind the petty officers on the scopes, scrutinizing the blank airspace to the southwest. He wondered what Gaponenko was doing, the other officers and men on the *Razytelny*. Were they hovering over their consoles, too? Anxiously inspecting each sparkle on their screens for the first sign of an incoming bomber? Or were they even now listening to the shriek and thunder of their own missiles going out?

"Man, this sucks," muttered Lauderdale.

Dan said, "We ought to have some other way to hit them . . . besides aircraft."

"We've got Harpoon. And the Standard, in antisurface mode."

"Harpoon's okay, but sixty miles isn't that far. And you've got to have a helo up to provide targeting. Standard's an antiair weapon; the warhead's all wrong. I mean something big and long-range," Dan said. "Then if anything happened to the carrier, we could still carry out some kind of attack."

"Where would you put it? How would you target it? And where would you get the money?"

Three good questions. Finally, he said, "We keep throwing money at the carriers; maybe we should use some of that for a backup. I don't know where you'd put it, though, or how you'd get targeting data." He stood thinking about it after Lauderdale went back to his console. It kept his mind from other things, such as wondering whether the SS-N-19s were on their way.

BUT nothing showed; the scopes and plots stayed empty.

At 0112, *Dahlgren* came up on the VHF again. She wanted to make a damage report, but the walkie-talkie was too short-range to reach *Lexington.* Dan arranged for Lauderdale to copy the reports and relay them to the task group commander on the scrambled net. Abbott reported that the fire was out. Four men were dead, seven wounded. They also had five people down with smoke inhalation and burns.

"Is your commanding officer there?"

"He's in sick bay. One of the smoke casualties. I think he'll be all right, but right now he's out of commission."

"How's your damage look?"

"I just got back from forward. The bridge is wrecked. It looks like the warhead went off just above it. The forward director's knocked out. The ASROC launcher suffered fragment and water damage. We may be able to reactivate CIC, at least partial capability."

"Radars?"

"Have to get back to you on that."

"Can you take a helicopter aft?"

"Yes, sir, believe so. We have power and lighting restored aft."

"Good. Get your wounded ready for evacuation. What else do you need?"

"Yes, sir, I'll start them moving back to the fantail. I think we can cope battle-damage–wise. We could use more canisters for the OBAs, though."

"Stand by to receive aircraft. We will disembark your wounded. Out."

Lauderdale passed that on the VHF. As soon as he signed off the secure net, *Voge* came up again. "*Voge* actual," her commanding officer. Dan listened with fascinated horror as he tried to explain to Admiral Larson how the accidental firing had occurred. The ship had been at Condition III, with weapons-control stations manned. An internal drill had been under way, one that included simulated launching of the point defense missiles, but safety interlocks had been in place in the weapons-control program. The missile should not have fired.

"Then why *did* it fire, Captain?"

"We're working on getting you a solid answer on that, Admiral. Right now, I don't have one. Over."

"Very well. I'm launching a helo shortly to evacuate *Dahlgren*'s wounded. After they're aboard, I'm sending it out to you with a staff officer, to assist with the investigation. This is CTF One forty-two actual, out."

Dan stood motionless. Around him, the circuits and the men were quieting again. *Barrett* had secured from general quarters. He really ought to turn in. But he knew he wouldn't sleep. He couldn't stop thinking about Prince's last riposte on the old destroyer's quarterdeck. The golden boy, deputy brigade commander. His friend.

Graciela, Miguelito, the baby, Sanderling . . .

How close death was out here! It flowed around them like the dark and bitter sea itself, patiently awaiting the smallest breach—a failure of man or machine, a storm, a broken cable—to stream through, wiping out all plans, all dreams. But wasn't life itself like that, its end only the hesitation of a heart away, a missed step, the turn of a steering wheel; only that separating you and all you held dear second to second from obliteration, separating love from never-ending loss? And knowing that, how mad war seemed. How insane to plan anything but fiercely clinging to those you loved before the inevitable annihilation. There was so much he didn't understand. But this, he told himself as he leaned tiredly against a console, yes, this he believed he was starting to understand at last.

44

THE rest of the night passed without further alarms. *Barrett* stayed in company with the stricken destroyer till just before dawn, when they separated again. Sunrise found them miles apart, back in their assigned stations; found the task force steaming unhurriedly across a rolling, empty blue Gulf. Still waiting.

Dan went up to the bridge a little after the sun popped up. He'd traded breakfast for another half hour in the rack, but a doughnut wrapped in a napkin was jammed under his hat. He stopped at the top of the ladder and looked searchingly around at the sea, the sky, the formation. *Lexington* was port side to them, about eight miles away. Another sunny, cloudless day roofed the Gulf of Mexico. A light easterly wind harried up three-foot seas blue as the indigoed cloth they sold in bolts at the Old Slave Market.

Downtown Charleston, Beverly, Sibylla, his motorcycle . . . it all seemed like something he'd read about in a book a long time ago. Hell, he thought suddenly, guiltily, I never did write back to Billy.

Jay Harper was leaning against the radar repeater, pursuing his own contemplation of the empty sea as it slipped past. At Dan's "Good morning, Chief Warrant," he started, then returned a curt nod.

"Anything hot?"

The rangy warrant shifted his belt higher on his hips. "No, everything cool, very cool. Steaming as before. Barometer steady. Been a quiet watch."

"How's *Dahlgren* doing?"

"Can't see any damage from here. Course, you're looking at her stern." Harper took off his cap and rubbed his bald spot as Dan lifted the proffered binoculars. The gray dot off their bow jumped closer, details almost painfully distinct: whip antennas erect at her stern; after launcher vertical in the air-ready position; a light haze boiling the clear air above her stacks.

"She's keeping up."

"Well, she's still there." Harper looked vaguely around the bridge. "Shit, I need to get my head down. . . . I don't know why they don't just detach 'em and send 'em home. She ain't gonna do us any good out here now."

"Captain up?"

"He was in his chair till oh-three hundred. I gave him a buzz a little while ago, but he hasn't come up yet." The chief warrant polished his glasses with a bit of lens paper. "How you feeling, shipmate? Got over them margaritas yet?"

"Yeah. No more of those suckers for me."

"You know, we hadn't of got called back, we'd've ended up down and dirty with those girls. That Lori was a piece of action. We were out on the dance floor; she was squirming around like a worm on a hot shovel. And that other bitch, I could see you getting ready to come in your pants just staring at those tuning knobs of hers."

"Maybe." Sober, it didn't seem as exciting, but he had to admit, Angela had been hard to look away from. Harper was probably right: They'd have ended up in bed. But then what? Just chalk up another score, the way the chief warrant did?

"Hey, reminds me, I ever tell you why the Polack divorced his wife an' married the shithouse? He said the hole was smaller and the smell was better."

Dan grunted and steered the conversation back to the weather forecast. Finally, he disengaged himself and went down to Combat. Dark and still, a good sign. The tactical circuits were silent except for a distant hissing like an ice storm. Dan walked around, turning them up, then down again to make sure they were on. "Okay, what you got?" he asked Quintanilla.

"A new player and new op plan. Came over the wire two hours ago."

"A new player? Somebody to replace *Dahlgren,* you mean?"

"No. Would you believe, they're back up on the link, got their air search back up, too? Just got off the horn with them. They're still conning from aft, but CIC's manned up again and weapons-wise they're just about back at C-One, except for the missing director."

"Nice work," said Dan. "Who's the new player, then?"

"Nukie boat. *Scamp,* SSN-five eighty-eight. A significant force addition."

"Yeah, that'll help. When did she slide in?"

They discussed the employment of the submarine for a while. Subs didn't operate in an integrated tactical structure. They fought independently, their movements and attacks only loosely coordinated with surface and air forces. Dan hoped their orders included a brief surface-and-radiate, or some other more or less overt reconnoiter of the *Kirov* group. Just the knowledge a U.S. nuclear attack boat was in the area would have a chilling effect on the Soviets' movements.

"More news. Lot of stuff happening. *Inchon, Spruance,* and *Valdez* were headed for Brazil. They're turned around, ETA in the Caribbean day after tomorrow. CINCLANTFLT's delaying *Eisenhower*'s and *Virginia's* overhaul, and the Air Force is moving tactical wings down to Florida. Okay, let's talk about hydrofoils."

"Wait a minute. What about the bad guys? Any sign of them reinforcing?"

"Nothing in the traffic. It'd take them a long time to get here if they did. This is our backyard, but to them it's halfway around the world."

"What are they doing?"

"The One forty-two oh-seven hundred sitsum shows them still steaming in the same area. *Lexington* has an E-two up; we've got long-range surveillance now. That'll help our early warning time."

"Yeah, good."

"Overall, it looks to me like they missed the boat. They should have come up and kicked our ass when they had the chance. Oh, the op order." Quintanilla rapped the red-and-white-striped Masonite cover of the Secret board. "Forwarded to us for info only. This isn't a USN ball game. Probably a good idea in terms of avoiding escalation. They call it 'Operation Tempest.' Royal Bahamian Defence Forces, backed by British and Canadian destroyers and—get this—*Munro,* are going to cover a landing in the northern part of the Cay Sal group. That leaves the back door open for the Cubans to make a graceful exit to the south. Next step, they'll send a Bahamian police detachment into Elbow Cay, covered by one of the destroyers. They will politely tell the Cubans, 'Thank you for maintaining order. We'll take care of the refugees. You may now get the fuck out of our territory.' "

"If they don't?"

"Then things get serious, I guess. But by then, we'll have the beef on scene to make things turn out the way we want. At least locally."

"It still doesn't make sense, Felipe. What do they get out of it? Other than proving they can jerk us around?"

"I don't know. Who knows why that asshole does anything?"

"Which asshole?"

"I don't know which asshole." Quintanilla sounded as if he was getting tired, too. "Let's talk about hydrofoils. I want to get relieved sometime this week, okay? Admiral Larson has them stationed here, east of us. That way, they can move west to our support if *Kirov* shows any signs of moving north, or else head east to cut the Cubans off from reinforcement and resupply if the landing turns ugly. . . ."

When Quintanilla was gone, Dan sat in the big leather chair, trying to stay awake long enough to finish his doughnut. Having a submarine on their side made him feel more confident. The news about other ships on the way was good, too. Hell, he thought, we get Ike and *Virginia* here and we'll be able to take on two *Kirovs*. The Russians weren't crazy. They stepped back when they were outnumbered. This whole thing might just end up without the two sides blowing each other out of the water.

AS he rose from the console, Hank Shrobo's head felt like a helium-filled balloon slowly rising toward the ceiling. His legs felt shaky, foreign, as if they'd just been grafted on.

"That it?" Dawson asked, still regarding the screen.

"You saw it. A complete run-through, no hang-ups."

"Congratulations," Matt Williams said, clapping him on the back. Then he staggered around and finally sat down on the deck. "Jeez, I don't feel so good all of a sudden."

"It's ROE syndrome," said Hank. "Return to Earth. Common among programmers. Okay, Chief, you understand the trouble-shooting procedure now? I might ask you and Matt to write it up, something brief we can put out interim, till we get a new section for the manual."

"I think so."

"I'll go over it once more. The antiviral program's loaded on computer number three. You bring up the module you want to scrub on computer two, then put it in maintenance mode from the MCC. Three will then take control of number two and start scrubbing whatever's in it line by line. Each time it hits a piece of virus or a flawed sector, it'll delete it and break to the screen. You poke in the marked lines from the listing, then hit 'run' again. Got that? We scrubbed the op program first, then sonar. You can do the others. Except the Link Eleven module, it's always come up clean."

"Got it. But what if it comes back?"

"That's the other program. I call it Antibody. Later, we'll integrate it into the exec, but for right now just load it before the op program goes in. Matt wrote it in Ultra-32, it doesn't take much memory. Load the O.P. right on top of it. It doesn't do anything unless it sniffs virus. Then it runs a search-and-delete, marks the line number, and logs out an error condition. Eventually, as you run all the data tapes and subprograms, it'll filter all the Crud out and you'll have a virgin system again." He stretched again, his mind moving on, now that the job was complete, the problem solved, to what was waiting for him back at Vartech. "Any more questions? Okay, I'm going to go find Lenson, tell him we've got it licked."

HE found the lieutenant in the dark room they called Combat, looking bored. Shrobo stood beside him for a while, watching the displays. Finally, he said, "Lieutenant."

"Oh." Dan turned his head slowly. Powdered sugar sparkled on the front of his uniform, even his hair. "Hi, Doc, what you doing up here?"

"Came to report. Finished the scan program. It runs. Your ACDADS is now fully operational."

"It works? Confirmed? Because I've heard this before—"

"This time it's a guarantee."

"Wait a minute," Dan said. "The CO's going to be happy to hear this." He picked up the J-phone, but a strange voice answered from the captain's cabin. "Who's this?" he asked.

"Seaman Pedersen, sir. In here makin' the bunk up."

"Oh. Skipper there?"

"Hold on."

"Captain, what is it?"

"Sir, Mr. Lenson. Dr. Shrobo's just reported that he's finished the scan program. He says our problems with ACDADS are over. Did you want to have him—"

"Yes, bring him in. No, wait. You're in Combat? I'll be in in a minute."

Five minutes later, Leighty appeared in the doorway. He looked fresh and dapper, hair combed back wet, clean khakis, gleaming shoes. He nodded to Shrobo and said in a friendly tone, "Dan tells me you've got everything running again."

"Just about, Captain."

"Call me Tom, all right? Hank?"

Shrobo cleared his throat, impatient, now that it was all solved, to get through the official congratulations and get to work on his paper, get a skeleton draft down while everything was still fresh in his head. And then go home. "Sure. Tom. We finished the antiviral program early this morning. The op program is sanitized. So is the sonar module. The procedure's simple enough that your men can run it on their own now to filter the others."

"So the whole ACDADS is operational again?"

"The exec program is. The others will come on-line one by one through the day. There's also another, smaller program that will operate continuously to keep the Crud from recurring."

"This sounds like a permanent fix."

"On this virus, at any rate. Other viruses, we'll have to go through the same procedure of breaking it first, then writing a search program. Eventually, though, I may be able to write one that detects any foreign replicating programs and penetrates, decodes, and deletes them automatically." He reflected. "There might not be memory space in the current generation of computers. But there will be soon, with the AN/UYK-forty-three series."

"That's great news. Thanks for all your help. Uh, I'll be writing a message saying how much we appreciate all the time you've put in cracking this thing. If there's anything else I can do—"

"Can I get a ride back to Virginia Beach?" Shrobo asked him.

"There may be a COD flight, a carrier onboard delivery plane, between *Lex* and Pensacola. We'd have to get you shuttled over there."

"I'll check it out, sir, see if we can set it up," said Dan. He asked Shrobo, "You want to go right away?"

"As soon as I can, yes. I've been away too long as it is. Also, I want very much to put some of my systems analysts on this bug. I want to try to figure out where it came from."

"What's your guess? Some kind of amateur hacker?"

"That's what I thought at first. But now I'm not so sure. It has to be somebody who knows UYK-sevens. Somebody who knows Navy computer systems. Somebody who knows a hell of a lot and is very smart indeed."

"Whom could that be?" Leighty asked him.

"When we figure it out, you'll be the first to know," Hank told him. "Now, if you'll excuse me, I'm going to get some sleep."

SHUFFERT came up to relieve him at eleven. Dan wolfed lunch, then checked his spaces. Everything seemed normal, so he went down to the office and cleared up his in box. He bagged his laundry, then went down to the barber shop for a trim. On the way back, he passed the ship's store. It was open, so he went in and bought a new lifer light and batteries. Then he remembered Billy and bought a USS *Barrett* T-shirt, size small, a USS *Barrett* belt buckle, and a Camillus stainless-steel Navy pocketknife and put them in the mail to him. No telling when it would go out, but when it did, they'd be in it. At 1530, he pulled on his shorts and running shoes, went up to the hangar, and did some stretching exercises. He jogged around the flight deck for half an hour, the rough black nonskid canting slowly under his feet, the horizon rolling up slowly, then down again beyond the deck-edge nets. He did some push-ups and leg lifts, then walked for a while, cooling down and letting the sun bake his bare chest, bare shoulders. The only mar on his peace was when he looked at the waves and reflected that he still didn't know what had happened to Graciela and the baby.

When he went back to relieve Quintanilla, the ops officer was reading a message. One of the radiomen stood beside him, waiting to take it back. "So, what's the news?" Dan asked him.

Quintanilla handed him the board. "Press your eyeballs to this," he said. Dan scanned down an update on Operation Tempest. The Bahamian Defence Forces, three boats and fifty men, backed by *Rhyl*, the British destroyer previously assigned to the refugee assistance operation, and *Gatineau*, a Canadian destroyer, were landing on Anguila, the next island up the chain from the Cay Sal group. Dan initialed it, muttered, "Good luck, guys," and handed it back to the radioman.

All through his watch, update messages came in every hour. The combined Caribbean Commonwealth forces, as they were now being called in the messages, completed the landing, picked up ten refugees, then reembarked for their next stop, Elbow Cay. So far, there was no sign from the Cubans either of preparations for resistance or preparations to depart. It looked to him, from reading the messages and measuring distances, that the showdown would take place at dawn.

THAT night, he came suddenly awake out of a sound sleep. He didn't know why, but he knew something had changed. He fumbled in the dark for the phone, dropped it clattering down the bulkhead. His roommate grunted. "Sorry," he muttered, dialing CIC by feel.

Lauderdale answered. He said that yeah, formation course had changed; they were headed east now.

"Any change in the situation?"

"Yeah, that's why we turned. The Cubans are pulling out."

"Is that right?"

"That's what the last report from the Commonwealth force says. They're postponing the morning landing on Elbow Cay to let them evacuate. They'll leave Cay Sal itself as soon as the Bahamians have a police presence there."

"How about the Russians?"

"The *Kirov* battle group has turned south. Southeast, actually. Anyway, away from us."

"Jesus. At the same time?"

"Yeah. Obviously coordinated."

"Huh. So that's it?"

"I guess."

He hung up and lay there, staring into the dark. Was this really how the whole crisis, the whole face-off was going to end? Just sort of evaporate, fizzle out? Everybody turn around, go home, live happily ever after? He couldn't quite believe it.

45

TWO days later, Dan pulled his chair out from the wardroom table as Antonio flicked a breakfast chit in front of him. He yawned as he picked up the stub of pencil and stroked off pancakes, egg, sunny-side up. Someday he'd get a full night's sleep again—maybe when they got back to Charleston. Check in at the Q, not leave a forwarding phone, then just turn the air conditioning up and the lights off. . . .

TF 142 had left Point PAPA on a course of 105, opening the range between the two forces to the east as the *Kirov* group opened it to the south—both sides gradually retiring but keeping a close eye on each other. *Lexington* kept her reconnaissance and CAP aircraft in the air. *Barrett* stayed at Condition III with weapons systems in standby. But the atmosphere in CIC was noticeably less tense. The radarmen were already discussing the chances of pulling liberty in Key West.

For the last forty-eight hours, *Lexington* and her escorts had remained in the Straits of Florida, monitoring the situation and sending out an occasional fighter sweep to demonstrate presence. But the Cubans left Elbow Cay peacefully. The Bahamian police landed on Cay Sal itself the next day, and the invaders left there, too. Dan had watched their patrol boats creep across the screen, headed south, back toward the Cuban navy base at Mariel.

That had been yesterday. Today, the task force, its mission fulfilled, was breaking up. *Dahlgren* had detached first, headed for a long stay in the yards. *Canisteo* had departed after a last alongside refueling of *Voge*, *Bronstein*, and *Barrett*. This morning, the remaining ships were simply waiting for the signal to disband and their orders as to where to proceed from there.

"See the news, Mr. Lenson?"

"The what?"

"The bird farm puts out a paper every day for their crew. Mr. Van Cleef figured how to get it sent over to us by radio. Ain't electronics wonderful?"

It was three stapled pages, a summary of stateside and international news, sports scores, the Dow Jones. Dan got coffee and read through it. The papers were applauding the successful resolution of the Cay Sal crisis. The *Los Angeles Times* called it a "showdown." They said, "The US Navy and the Soviets went eyeball-to-eyeball a second time, and once again, the USSR blinked." The *Chicago Tribune* said, "A scratch force of Navy, Air Force, and Coast Guard, hastily assembled from training duties and reserve bases while front-line units were deployed to face Iran, held the line until Castro understood he could not expect acquiescence in this latest adventure." He smiled wryly, reading the excerpts. They were heroes this week; next week they'd be villains, fools, and wastrels again.... A volcano had exploded in Washington state, killing an eighty-three-year-old man who refused to evacuate.... The rioting and looting in Miami was still going on. Whole blocks of the city were burning. The mayor had called in the National Guard and they were searching for weapons at roadblocks, but Liberty City was a free-fire zone. Snipers were shooting at anyone who moved, black or white. Chief Dawson had told him about Williams's and Shrobo's narrow escape the night the rioting began. Dan wondered whether they'd actually been safer out here at sea, facing the Russians, than if they'd stayed in Miami or North Charleston. He remembered warning his men to buddy up going ashore in a foreign port. Now stateside was the most dangerous liberty of all. He noticed there was nothing at all about the Cuban refugees. They were last week's news. Just as Task Force 142's vigil, the insanity of courting war over a couple of specks of useless sand, Larry Prince's meaningless death—all would be forgotten in a week or two. Erased, as the wave marks on the sand were obliterated by the next tide.

So what was the lesson? he asked his coffee. The yellow specks of creamer floated up, swirled in tiny whirlpools, dissolved. Perhaps it was an answer, but he couldn't decode it. What was he supposed to conclude from all this? Should he see his dad when they got back? Forgive the bastard before he died? Get serious about Beverly Strishauser? Leave the Navy and go back to school, get a degree in something useful, like civil engineering?

"Pancakes, sir."

"Thanks." He set his quandaries aside and dug in, tuning into the conversation around him, the officers enjoying a second cup of coffee and a few minutes of bullshit before quarters.

"No way," said Dwight Giordano. The engineer looked, Dan thought, the least worn of them all; he'd stood normal watches through the entire crisis. So that now his habitual harried look seemed relaxed next to those who had stood endless bridge and CIC watches. "They'll never send us back. Are you nuts? There're other ships scheduled now. Five bucks says they bless us and say, 'Go and train no more.' "

"I'm not taking any bets, but we've got to go back. You can't graduate without passing the battle problem," Quintanilla insisted.

"Why not?"

"That's what they said from the start. It puts everything together, shows whether you can make the band play in tune."

"They can't figure? Look at *Dahlgren*, those guys fucking saved their fucking ship."

"They already passed. We haven't. If we'd gotten hit and put out a fire, stopped flooding, treated casualties, maybe then we could ask for some kind of waiver."

Obviously, they were talking about Gitmo—whether, now that the boat lift and the Cay Sal crisis were over, *Barrett* would be required to finish refresher training. "What I heard," he said, just to bait them, "is because our training was interrupted, we'll have to do it all over again from the beginning."

"Get out of here."

"That's just crazy enough to be right."

Kessler said, "This was more real than Gitmo. This was real-world operations. I say they'll waive it."

"You just want to get home, Casey. That ain't your brain talking; it's fifty million backlogged sperms."

"Shit yeah, I'm ready to go home. We've jumped through our grommets enough on this fucking cruise."

Vysotsky cleared his throat from the door. They glanced at him, then went on to other topics, such as how the syrup was holding out.

"NOW quarters, quarters for morning muster and inspection. Officers' call."

The exec's grating voice rose above the murmur. "Okay, listen up. We have the word on where we're going."

"Shut up, goddamn it," somebody muttered in the back. The mass of khaki shuffled, quieted.

"Okay, listen up. We will out-chop from Task Force One forty-two on signal this morning. At that time, we will set course once more for Guantánamo Bay."

The mutter rose again to something near anger. Vysotsky's shout cut through it like a load of gravel being dumped. "That's *enough*! Pipe down! We will not be at Gitmo long if everyone turns to and remembers what they learned a week ago. We'll do one day's refresher work-up, then do the battle problem the next day. If we pass, we'll be headed back to Charleston by Friday."

A voice from the rear. "What about Guadeloupe?"

"We no longer have time to make liberty in Guadeloupe. We have predeployment inspections, maintenance assistance, and a multiship battle group work-up scheduled. Then we'll be deploying." He waited. "Any other questions? The senior watch officer will be posting a five-section watch bill this morning. We'll transit the Windward Passage tonight and get into Gitmo tomorrow morning. All right. Today . . . I know everyone's tired, but we've got to get the ship cleaned up. We've let things go for the past few days and we need to do basic titivation. Also, restore the ship to readiness for the battle problem. Check your fire-fighting gear for proper stowage. Planning board for training will meet at fourteen hundred. . . ."

After the XO broke them, Dan walked a few paces away, into the shadow of the helo hangar. Not yet 0800 and already the sun was intense, glaring off the water at a low angle till it brought tears to his eyes. He waited as his division officers and chiefs gathered—Harper and Dawson and Mainhardt; Kessler; Chief Fowler, nervously patting emptiness; Ed Horseheads, grinning at nothing; Chief Glasser; and Burdette Shuffert and his two chiefs, Alaska and Boyer.

"Okay, you heard it," he said to them all. "We need to put it out to the troops, make sure they understand what's going on and why."

"They aren't gonna like it."

"Yeah, that's gonna take morale to about minus twenty."

"Tell them we're almost home. Two days in Gitmo, then we'll be headed back."

"Dan?"

"Yessir." He turned; it was Vysotsky. "Sorry, I forgot to mention about Dr. Shrobo. Tell him we've got his transportation set up out of Gitmo. He's to have all his gear together, ready to hop off and ride over to Leeward Point as soon as we touch the pier in the morning."

"Aye aye, sir. Okay, let's turn to."

He went along with Horseheads to see how the enlisted took it. There was considerable griping, but that was acceptable. It had bothered him once, as an ensign. But now he knew bitching and moaning was more or less the normal situation. It was only when you got dead silence that you were in trouble with American enlisted men. That meant they no longer trusted you. Satisfied, he went down to the department office, greeted Cephas, and set to work on the ever-growing pile of administration and reports.

* * *

ALONE in his cabin that afternoon, Thomas Leighty stripped plastic off a fresh khaki shirt. Hands moving with the deftness of long practice, he pinned silver oak leaves to the collar, an inch and a half in and centered on a line bisecting the angle of the points. Then, above the left pocket, the five rows of uniform ribbons, combat ribbons, unit commendations, achievement medals; and, in careful priority, the gaudy scarlet and yellow and gold decorations from a government that no longer existed. Above that, one-quarter inch spacing and centered, he attached the crossed swords of the surface warfare insignia. And above that, pinned centrally and another quarter-inch up, the small-boat command device that every time he pinned it on made him remember the growl of engines, the distant popping of AK-47s, and the omnipresent smells of delta and river.

Slowly buttoning it, he looked at himself soberly in the mirror.

Regarding him was a face he had always thought of as expressive, handsome, almost aristocratic. The touch of gray at the temples only added to it now. And the pull-ups and exercise kept his body slim, well-muscled, honed beneath the uniform. He carried himself well, and just that conveyed an impression of self-confidence. What had the young man in Coconut Grove called it—Vernon, that was his name—something about him looking authoritative? He didn't recall now exactly what the word was he had used. But he understood. He understood how that could appeal to a younger person.

His eye moved to the clock. Four more minutes.

He extended his hand, noticing a faint tremor. Yes, he was excited. He was afraid, too.

He'd only slowly become aware of the glances that the young steward had been giving him. Only over weeks had he noticed him lingering after his work was done. Pedersen was only twenty, not long out of boot camp, and he had a refreshing shyness about him. Tall and lithe, dungarees tight where they should be tight and flaring above polished shoes—that was what he'd noted first, just that he looked shipshape and seamanlike. But gradually, Leighty had noticed other things about him: something graceful about the way he moved; a little extra inclination in the head when he spoke to him; a glance that lingered the fraction of a second too long. Could he be mistaken? He didn't think so. It happened, but not often.

It was the same way it had started with the young technician—Sanderling. That, too, had started with small things, eye contact, a smile, the sense that he was being examined as he bent over a message board. Then it had moved on to a first-name basis, at least Leighty used the younger man's first name, and then to something that he really should not have permitted. He knew that, but he couldn't say even now he was sorry. Only that he hadn't gotten close enough to the boy to understand how close he was to self-destruction.

Now he stood waiting for the call.

It had happened casually. Not at his instigation. Last night, just as dusk was falling. He'd been in his chair on the bridge. They were alongside refueling, and he couldn't go below for dinner. Pedersen had brought him up a covered plate and stood beside him as he ate, Leighty glancing out occasionally to check on Lenson's conning as they approached the oiler, matched courses and speeds, and sent the first line arching over. And Pedersen had asked him casually what he'd done in Miami. He hadn't told him. But the memory of the park had risen up in his memory. And the boy, Pedersen, had said, "I had a good time, Captain. I met some other fellows. We had a good time," looking at him as he said it.

"Would you like to see some pictures," Pedersen had asked then.

And Leighty had responded, before he could think about it or stop himself, "Sure. Bring them up sometime."

"Is there any time we could look at them and not be disturbed?"

And he'd said, "Yes, early in the afternoon," thinking they'd be independent steaming by then. He could make sure they weren't disturbed. And he'd looked after Pedersen as he'd moved gracefully off the bridge, carrying the covered tray, Leighty feeling the excitement beginning in his body.

Yes, it had been the same with Sanderling—the dawning awareness, the tentative gestures of friendship, and then the electric suddenness of mutual recognition. But then when the boy had died, he'd looked down at the pale white patch sinking away beneath the water and found himself feeling nothing, absolutely nothing. . . .

Now he looked at himself in the mirror and felt his heart pounding. He looked rapidly away, evading his own eyes, around the room, as if searching for an answer in the commonplace things he saw every day: the rudder-angle indicator, the brass lamp, the desk, the portrait of his wife and child. . . . He'd never been passionately attracted, but he loved her. But when you wore the mask so long, learned that role so perfectly, it was not easy sometimes to tell which was you and what was that alter ego you pretended to be. His boy? Yes, he loved Dougie. He loved his daughter, too. There was no question there. But even from that, he could not draw strength now.

He could not pray to be changed. He wouldn't change. He wasn't even sure now that he wanted to. But there was one thing he could do, one thing he could say, that might make a difference.

The trouble was that he knew he wasn't going to say it.

The phone buzzed discreetly. Mouth dry, he picked it up quickly.

It was him, the man he'd dreamed of for days. "Yes?" he said. Then he caught sight of himself in the mirror. He cleared his throat, and said more loudly, "Captain."

"Captain? Is that you?"

"Yes. It's me."

"This is Joe. Seaman Pedersen. Chief just let me off duty. You want to look at those pictures now?"

Leighty closed his eyes. He reached deep inside himself but found no strength there. He opened his eyes again and caught the remote gyro indicator on the bulkhead. And despite his inner turmoil, a part of his mind compared the course it showed to the one the navigator had briefed him on; found that it matched; and only then released him to himself and sat back, satisfied.

But it had told him who he was, who he really was, in this uniform, this cabin, aboard this ship.

He wasn't gay. He wasn't straight. He wasn't even Tom Leighty.

He was the commanding officer of USS *Barrett.*

"I decided against it," he muttered.

"You what?"

"I changed my mind, Joseph. I've got too much on my desk. I'm busy, don't have the time, understand?"

"Oh. All right, sir." The voice was disappointed but relieved, too, he could tell. Maybe even as relieved as he felt. His legs trembled. A click.

He looked at the number card beside the phone and dialed quickly, waited, spoke again, his voice stronger now, surer.

"Dave? Captain here. Look, I want you to replace Seaman Pedersen as my steward. I don't care who; he's been up here too long. No, no, he's been doing a good job. I just think they ought to be rotated occasionally."

He hung up again and looked at himself. From the mirror, his other self peered back.

Slowly, sadly, it smiled at him.

LATE that night, the bent, gawky green-suited figure sat alone in the silence of the wardroom, staring down at a printout.

The unzipped code from within the virus. Line after line of binary, and under it, handwritten in red, was its translation into the AN/UYK-7 machine language. Here and there, arrows called out connections to op programs and other modules. But then came a section that had no call-outs, no connections.

He sat alone, head propped on his arms, staring down at it.

This is strange, Hank Shrobo said to himself.

He'd expected, once he broke it, to be able to read it all. And most of it, true, he could. At the center and heart of the infector, just as he'd intuited, nestled a random-number generator. Other elegantly concise sections activated cycle stealing, privileged memory access, and negative-zero error conditions. But still one section remained that he couldn't penetrate. It just didn't make sense. It wasn't even machine language. It was just gibberish.

But why, when the rest of the virus was so short, so efficient, designed with the beautiful, elegant deadliness of a shark? Was it a message of some sort? Something that once had made sense but had changed in the thousands of replications the program had gone through since? Mutated? Evolved?

A thrill of something like fear ran up his back.

"Doc. Understand you've got it all fixed."

One of the officers was pulling out a chair opposite. Shrobo only glanced at the young face, neither Lenson, nor Harper, nor one of the senior officers. He didn't recall the man's name. He nodded, wishing the fellow would go away and let him ponder.

"What's that?"

Hank shifted irritably in the chair. "It's a printout of the virus we just broke."

"Is that right?"

"But I don't understand it—not this section of it here." He put his finger on it, glanced at it, looked up at the overhead, then frowned down again suddenly.

He moved his fingers slightly, so that only a portion of the code showed between them.

Then, forgetting the man across from him, he fumbled for his pencil.

Let's see, he thought, keeping his excitement under control until he could test the hypothesis that had just assembled itself. He and Williams had read the long string of ones and zeros by dividing them with slashes every thirty-two bits. Those were the byte divisions for the AN/UYK-7 computer. Then they'd broken those down further into four-bit nybbles, the basic digits of a hexadecimal counting system. With four bits per digit, thirty-two bits per byte, that gave eight digits per byte. This was a word of Ultra, which could be read and understood by human and machine alike.

Now he proceeded differently. Beginning where the gibberish started, he divided the ones and zeros into sections not of thirty-two, but of thirty. Then he subdivided these into nybbles.

He stared at it.

He was looking at machine language, but not for the UYK-7. For a second, his mind was blank. Then he recalled from some dim recess that . . . hadn't the granddaddy Navy mainframe, the CP-642, been a UNIVAC? A real kluge, a dinosaur, tubes, the works. Sixteen bits. Then had come the AN/USQ-20. That, too, had been a UNIVAC.

Not only that. It had been, he suddenly remembered, a thirty-bit-word system.

"What is it?" said the man across from him. Shrobo started, then said, annoyed, "Nothing. Just had an idea. It must be for the older machine."

"What?"

"This section of code here, it must be for the old USQ-twenty. I don't know the instruction set; I can't tell what it does . . . but what is it doing here?" He was talking to himself and now, forgetting the man he left sitting at the table, he got up and started pacing around the wardroom. It was like deciphering a page of modern German and finding one paragraph in Sanskrit. Unless . . . was it possible that the virus was older than he thought? The USQ-20 was a 1960s-era machine. Could it have evolved . . . shit, there was that word again. He didn't like to think about virtual viruses that *evolved.*

But like it or not, he forced himself to consider it now. Had he found the remnants of an older, more primitive form? Like mitochondria within human cells, remnants of ancient bacteria, now part of the machinery of the host? Was it possible that the virus had been around since the 1960s and only recently become virulent? Retaining at its heart the original bit of code, like the original DNA that each life-form on earth carried deep within its cells, tracing back its origin to the Adam cell, the common ancestor?

And did that mean that it was no longer a bug, a glitch, an annoyance? . . . Did it mean that he was faced now with a new form of life?

Not really knowing what he was doing, he went slowly out into the darkened, red-lighted passageway. The listing fluttered from his numb fingers. He turned back, picked it up off the deck, thrust it into the pocket of his scrub greens.

Eyes distant, he drifted aft and down through the ship. Seamen slid around him as he passed through their compartments, grinned at one another. "Doctor DOS." "He's floating, man." "He's somewhere else."

Finally, he blinked, staring at a familiar door—the weight room. He smiled to himself. Why not? Maybe it would clear his mind.

He flicked the lights on in the emptiness. The swollen scuffed leather of the punching bag pendulumed slowly as the ship side-stepped around it. The endless belt of the treadmill lay motionless, dusty footprints marking its worn surface. The familiar stark walls, the gray all-weather carpeting tilted slowly around him as he took off his shirt, selected a bar, and began racking the clanking iron disks onto it. When he had 180 pounds, he twisted the keeper nut tight, set the bar on the steel guides with a grunt, and pegged the reclining board to the proper height. He wondered for a moment if he should wait for a spotter, then decided he didn't need to; the rolls weren't that bad.

He rosined his hands slowly, staring at himself in the mirror. Hemmery and Lightbulb were right: He was gaining definition. Suddenly, he thought, I'll miss those guys. They weren't his intellectual equals. But they'd been . . . friends. They'd accepted him, taken him along on liberty. Hell, they'd saved his life.

He slid under the bar, took a breath, and began.

He did a set, putting everything aside to concentrate on powering the mass of metal up and down smoothly, then guided the heavy bar carefully back onto its guides and shook his arms out. A hundred and eighty pounds, yet he felt strength still in his biceps, his shoulders, his chest.

The 1MC out in the passageway hissed.

"Good evening. This is the captain speaking. I wanted to say a few words before taps about our operations over the past week, and a few words about tomorrow.

"Today, we completed our operations with Task Force One forty-two. And we did so with distinction. There was real danger, and I'm proud of the way every man faced it. I think we all discovered something new about ourselves. *Barrett* was fully prepared to fight, and I'm convinced we would have won.

"Tonight, I would like everyone to get as much rest as possible. We have only one challenge remaining on this cruise, and that is the battle problem. After all our training, I don't anticipate it will be that difficult for us to get a top grade. I know we'll look as good on the grading sheets as we've proven ourselves at sea.

"Thank you, and good night."

As the silence returned, Hank looked up at the tiny grooves, the handholds on the steel rod of the bar. Tiny particles of chalk and rosin clung to it, directly above his eyes.

The captain's remarks made him think back over the last few days. It *had* been dangerous. Obviously, because people had died on the other ship. But how could that have happened? There were safety interlocks in the software to preclude accidental firing.

Then he remembered what Lenson had told him had happened aboard *Barrett*. The first indication of any problem—the first sign of the virus, though of course they hadn't known that—had been a malfunction in the weapons systems. The missiles had failed to respond to midcourse correction guidance. The gun mounts had slewed out without direction.

Hadn't the same thing happened to *Voge*—an unexplained weapons-system failure? Only this time, it had launched a missile. The Sparrow, shorter-ranged than the *Barrett*'s Standards, carried its own radar guidance. Once activated, it would search for, acquire, and home on any radar return within its seeker head acquisition arc.

And *Voge* was an older ship, as was *Lexington.*

Shrobo wondered now if they were old enough that . . . He frowned. Could they be old enough that they would still be equipped with the USQ-20? The older computer was slow. It didn't have the memory of the UYK-7. But it still ran the basic software satisfactorily—the same software that *Barrett*'s computers were running. A different operating system, different machine language, but built on top of that was the same syntax of CMS-2, responding to queries from the net control station on the carrier, then transmitting its computerized tracking data to the other ships in company. . . .

Transmitting its data . . .

He got up vaguely and hunted around and found two more ten-pound weights. He slid them on either side of the bar, relocked the keeper nuts, and fit his long body back onto the bench. It would impress the guys if he could tell them he'd pressed two hundred before he left tomorrow. As he got his hands set, he heard the door open and close, then a rattle as someone began to set up the Nautilus. He didn't look to see who it was. His mind was somewhere else, and his body, preoccupied with the weights, yet another place. He sucked a breath, as the lifters had taught him. Then he gripped the bar again and started powering it upward, the energy growl starting deep in his chest.

Transmitting . . . the net control station polled each participating ship in turn. In response, their computers sent track data, range and bearing on their contacts, back to the central computer, which then retransmitted it to the other units.

The bar slowed halfway up.

Suddenly, staring upward blankly, he saw it: what the mysterious section of code did.

That last section of the infector wasn't garble at all; it was a machine-language program written for older, thirty-bit machines. Why was thirty-bit code in *Barrett*'s computer, a thirty-two-bit machine? Not because the virus had originated in thirty-bit machines. Because it had been written to operate in either of the two computers in the fleet.

How would it get from one to the other? Not by tape, because the tapes were different; the programs were different. You couldn't run a thirty-two-bit tape on a thirty-bit machine.

There was only one answer: It was being passed *by radio* from one NTDS unit to another. That was the explanation of the "accidental" firing. The Crud had infected *Voge*'s computers, and presumably also those of all the other ships in the task force via radio—via the Link 11.

Suddenly, he realized he'd done it. He was pressing two hundred pounds. His arms shook as they suspended the bar, the massive iron weights above him at arm's length. The slow roll of the ship made them sway gently from side to side. He fought to control them, sweat bursting out suddenly on his face and under his arms. The shaking grew, took his shoulders and chest. Gradually, gradually, he let it sink. Slowly, fighting for control, he lowered it millimeter by millimeter, till at last it engaged back into the rests with a double click of steel against steel. He dropped his grip, blew out, and relaxed, letting his hands fall to the carpet, shaking the fatigue out onto the floor.

It was incredibly devious . . . subtle . . . but it would work. Oh, yes, it would work. He should call it not the Crud, but the Plague. And now that he knew, all sorts of other unexplained phenomena suddenly made sense, such as that it had never showed up in the Link 11 module. It had been there, but dormant, undetectable, as it propagated itself over the radio net. Every time an infected ship transmitted, the virus traveled silently along with the good data. Leaping from one ship to another across miles of sea, burrowing into the memories, the tapes, gradually corrupting, degenerating, destroying every piece of programming it touched. Till billions of dollars in weapons and sensors, and the work and devotion of thousands of men, were useless, impotent either in defense or attack.

This was no random bug. Nor was it some hacker's amateur hatchling.

It was a weapon.

He had to tell someone. They had to warn the other ships who'd been in the task group—shut them down now, stop broadcasting, before the pestilence spread.

He heard a sound behind him, a clank as iron was set down on the machine. Then two hands appeared directly above his eyes. He stared up, oblivious to everything as his mind whirred on, spinning out insight, dropping level by level into deeper and deeper knowledge.

To the realization that if *Barrett* was transmitting such a signal, someone had had to introduce the virus in the first place. Someone who had access to her computers. In all probability, someone who'd been aboard when the Crud began.

He caught his breath, suddenly seeing that they might still *be* aboard, watching him try to break the code. He had to tell Lenson that, had to tell the captain. Who could it have been? There weren't many people with the combination of knowledge and access. In fact, he could think of only a few. No—actually, he could only think of *one*.

He didn't realize until it was too late that someone standing directly behind him had taken hold of the two hundred pounds of iron, lifted it off the rests, and was holding it directly over his outstretched throat.

VI

THE PASSAGE

46
The Windward Passage

A frantic peeping, as if a cricket was being crushed, pulled him from confused and frightening dreams through a fuzzy black tunnel into his bunk. Dan groped for the clock and got it shut off. For a few seconds, his heart still hammered, till he remembered that the crisis was over, the face-off past, that there had been no war and no battle after all. Lying back, he yielded to the temptation to stay cocooned under the sheets, the warm blanket.

Then he remembered: He had the watch. He groped for the handhold and swung his legs out, dipping bare soles inch by inch into the darkness till they rested on the cool tile floor. Red light bled faintly around the joiner door. He flicked his desk light on, pulled khakis from a hanger, ran a hand over his chin. Then noticed the clock again. He'd have to shave later. He found his cap, stuck his flash in his back pocket, and shut the door quietly behind him.

The ship slept around him as he threaded the passageways, swimming through corridors of dim red light like a diver picking his way through a flooded wreck. Surrounded by the familiar hum of machinery, the uneasy creak and slam of a ship in a seaway.

The bridge was pitch-dark, as usual. The big square windows shone faintly, framing tilting blocks of stars. The helm console hummed and ticked to itself. The fathometer flickered. Tiny jeweled orbs shone from the corners like the eyes of watching creatures. He felt his way across it, noting the course as he passed the helm gyro: 250. The surface tote board showed only one contact, past and opening. He closed one eye and bent to the surface scope. It was set to close range. The mountains and bays of Punta Maisi sparkled like kryptonite foil along the edge of the picture. They were rounding the island, transiting the Windward Passage, the channel between the easternmost point of Cuba and Haiti.

A yawn grew in his throat. He was rubbing his mouth with the back of his hand when he became conscious of a shadow in front of him. He didn't know how long it had been there. "Who's that?" it said.

"Lieutenant Lenson," he snapped, sliding past it to the chart table. He felt for the light and clicked it on.

The shielded scarlet glow pulled from nothingness the outlines of the Oriente coast, a bow of shoal stretching out from the headland of Punta Maisi, the tiny triangles of loran fixes. Thirteen miles off the coast was the faint pencil line of *Barrett*'s intended course, laid off by Dave Cannon. It paralleled the north coast at 120, then turned south to round the point with two course changes. Dan bent forward, blinking to clear his gaze as he studied it. The next course change would be at 0500. His fingers walked off the distance to the Guantánamo Bay entrance. He judged they could make it on time.

He studied it for a moment more, still rubbing his eyes, then clicked the light off. He started to swing away, then frowned.

He turned back, clicked the light on again, and studied the pencil trace again.

According to the chart, they should be headed due south now, course 180. They weren't scheduled to come west to 250 until 0500.

But the course he'd noted sliding past the helm, that hadn't been 180. Had it? He thought it had been 250. A faint unease made him clear his throat, check the chart yet a third time. Everything was probably fine; he was just groggy. But he'd better—

"Dan."

Harper's voice, from across the chart table. Dan blinked. He hadn't realized he was there. "Evening, Jay. Calm tonight."

"Yeah, pretty calm."

"This Punta Maisi light, it in sight? You getting bearings on it?"

"Oh, yeah, we picked that up about an hour ago."

"I'm just about ready to relieve. One question." He put his finger on the penciled course. "This turn west to two-five-zero. That's not supposed to go till oh-five hundred, right?"

"Right."

"What course are we on now?"

"Two-five-zero."

"We're on it now?"

"That's right," said the shadow. It came a little more into the backwash of light. Funny, though, he still couldn't make out Harper's face.

"Uh-huh," Dan said. "When did we come to it?"

"At oh-three-thirty."

"Making better speed than we thought, huh? You got a fix and had to correct?"

"No."

Dan sucked a tooth, the sense that all was not well growing. "Did my watch stop, then? I've only got oh-three-fifty."

"That's right," said Harper. "Oh-three-fifty. That's what I've got, too."

Dan found himself getting annoyed. Harper had better not be dicking off again. With a shoal to the west, they could get into trouble fast. He turned his head. "Quartermaster of the watch," he said sharply.

No one answered, but he felt someone behind him, the faint radiated warmth of another person's body. Then something hard rammed into his spine.

Across the chart table, Harper said, "You win the prize, shipmate. It's oh-three-fifty, and we're on two-five-zero early. That thing sticking in your ribs, that's a forty-five. Just like this one here in my hand."

He stared, unable to react or even think as the service automatic emerged into the red light. The hole in the end of the barrel looked big enough to put his thumb into. "Put your hands up," the chief warrant said. "And don't get any smart-ass ideas; we already had to kill one guy tonight."

His first thought was that it had to be a joke. Harper loved to play jokes. But holding a gun on someone was off the scale, even for the King Snake. And now, as the chief warrant moved forward, Dan saw why he hadn't been able to make out his features. He was wearing a balaclava, from the foul-weather-gear locker. The olive drab wool covered his face, his whole head, everything but his eyes.

"What exactly are you doing, Jay?" he said through a suddenly dry mouth.

"Simple, shipmate. We're taking charge of this shrimp boat."

"Uh-huh, right."

"Hard to believe? Look over there." Dan didn't move for a moment, and whoever was behind him pushed him so hard, he almost fell. "Open the chart room door," Harper said to no one Lenson could see.

The curtain slid back, and he saw where the rest of his watch section had gone. The lookouts and helmsmen were crammed together, looking out into what to them must be the darkness. They looked frightened, and he saw why. Just as the curtain rattled closed again, he caught the outline of a shotgun.

He was moving toward them when Harper's hand shot out to stop him. He halted instantly. "Uh, don't you want me in there? With them?"

"No," said Harper. A snap sounded. Dan recognized it as a safety going back on. The chief warrant moved away, into the darkness. He said over his shoulder, "Come on out on the wing, Hoss. We got a couple things to discuss."

* * *

THE stars were a brilliant scattering of diamond dust, the Milky Way a silver band like an immense ring. Far off to starboard, a powerful beam glowed into life, wheeled through the black, then faded slowly away. Punta Maisi light, marking the headland of Cuba, Dan thought. It ought to be on their quarter, falling astern. Instead, it was abeam. They were headed under the point, into the vicinity of the Bahia de Ovando. The bow wave made a crashing noise below them. Everything was so normal, so routine, that part of his mind tried again to convince him this wasn't happening. While another, very frightened part insisted that it was.

Harper's voice again, clearer now, and as the beam swept past again, Dan saw that the warrant officer had taken off his mask. His bald spot glowed like a monk's tonsure. He rubbed his face, but the other hand, the one with the gun, held steady on Dan. "So, you probably wonder just what the fuck is going on."

"That's kind of an understatement."

"It's technically known as a mutiny. I looked it up. First one in the U.S. Navy since 1842."

"A historic occasion," Dan said. "Look, I haven't done a fix, but we're headed in toward a shoal area—"

"Don't worry about that. We ain't gonna hit any shoals. History? We'll probably make some headlines, yeah." Harper sounded as if the prospect pleased him.

If this was a joke, he was fished all right. Dan found his legs trembling so badly, he had to grip the splinter shield. "Great, but . . . What's the point, Jay? You can't go pirating around the sea lanes. The Navy will be out here on your ass tomorrow."

"That kind of depends on where I'm taking her, doesn't it?"

He thought about that. And gradually, he began to understand.

"Let's see, where could we go?" Harper mused. "Someplace the Navy couldn't follow us—where, if they tried, they'd find themselves in a shitload of trouble." He thrust an object at him, and Dan flinched back before he realized they were the binoculars. "Oh, yeah, I *know* where they are this time. Look out there. Tell me what you see."

He adjusted the glasses by feel and laid them where he figured the horizon ought to be. He stared at the distant dancing glints for a long time, till he was sure.

"Well?"

"Two surface contacts, bow-on, coming this way."

"Gunboats. They'll escort us in."

Dan tried to steady his voice. "This has all been figured out, then."

"Yeah, all figured out," said Harper. He sounded cheerful about it, upbeat. "We've pretty much got it all down cold, even drilled it a couple of times. Okay now, we don't have a heck of a lot of time before they get here. You want to hear what I've got to say? Because I need something."

"Why ask me for it? Whatever it is?"

"Because I think you'll be interested. Okay? Want to hear it or not?"

Dan hesitated. "Go ahead," he muttered.

"First some background. Right now, we're two miles inside Cuban territorial waters, and going farther in every minute. That's a violation of international law. The U.S. is major, major in the wrong, okay?"

"But you steered us in. You turned early. Where's the captain? Did you tell him you turned?"

"Cool your jets, Hoss. Forget about him; we're taking care of him. Look, it don't matter how, being here's a no-no, okay? Now, these guys, these coastal PTs, they're coming out to see what the hell we're doing. Then they're gonna escort us to Santiago. That's the closest big port." Harper moved a little closer. "That's where you come in. Thing is, I'm gonna need help. I've got mucho shit to keep tabs on. I need somebody to handle things up here. They won't know the ship, how to run these variable-pitch props. I need somebody to conn us in, get us alongside the pier without bashing into things, scratching up this nice new paint job."

Through the numbness, horror was creeping now. It wasn't enough that Harper was taking over the ship; he was counting on him to help. He started to refuse indignantly, then stopped. "So you're thinking I'll do that? Conn us in?"

"That's the idea, yeah."

"So, what's in it for me?"

"Now you're talking!" Harper slapped his shoulder. "Okay, remember the one big score you wanted? One big batch of money, without having to worry about taxes? Even if it was illegal. Remember?"

The conversation at the beach at Windward Point came back to him then. Had he really said that? He supposed he had . . . but not meaning what Harper assumed he did. Harper thought he could be bought, that he'd help take over the ship. Only the pointed gun kept him from bulling into the lanky shadow, smashing him to the deck with his fists.

Then, suddenly, the fire curtain came down, isolating his brain from his feelings, leaving him still trembling, but coid now, ice-cold.

"You've got other people helping you. How many? Or is it just the guy on the helm?"

Harper chuckled. "Oh, we got lots of guys. Thirty total, set up in teams—the bridge team, engine room, and the security teams are going through the berthing compartments." He glanced at his watch. "We started forty minutes ago. Most of the crew's locked down already."

"Where? We don't have a brig."

"Told you, I thought this through. We don't got a brig, but we got magazines, no? You lock people in there, they're not going anywhere. And if they make too much noise, we pull the flood valve and drown their asses." Harper looked out to where the beam lashed out, flicked overhead, dimmed away—noticeably brighter now, and higher. Dan felt the imminence of land like an encumbering shadow.

"For Christ's sake, slow down. The shoal reaches way out from that point."

"Drop to one-third," Harper yelled into the pilothouse, and Dan heard the ping of the engine-order telegraph. The running lights were closer now, but for some reason they seemed dimmer. Then he realized why. The sky was growing pale. Dawn was on its way.

Harper swung back, tone crisp. "Anyway, we've got the ship now. We have all the small arms. We got the bridge and Main Control. Just a couple loose ends and we'll be ready for an orderly turnover."

A shadow. "Call for you," it said in a muffled growl. Part of the disguise, Dan guessed.

Harper took the proffered phone. "Yeah. Here. What? He's not in his stateroom? Well, track him down. We don't want him roaming around. . . . Yeah, sure, if he resists . . . okay." He hung up.

"Who was it?"

"Vysotsky. We'll get him, though." Harper was silent a moment, then cleared his throat. "Well, what do you say? Gonna help us out?"

Dan had been thinking furiously during the interruption, putting things together. It enraged him that Harper thought he'd betray his country. But he didn't want to get locked below. It wasn't an attractive prospect, being battened down in a magazine while a scratch-manned ship felt her way into an unfamiliar port.

And he was beginning to realize something else: That he—and maybe now the executive officer—might be the only men uncommitted to Harper's plot still at large.

The more he knew, the better chance he'd have of limiting the damage. So he didn't answer directly. Instead he said, "I still don't quite get it. You're planning to turn the ship over to the Cubans?"

"Isn't that what I said?"

"But what do you get for it? And what do they want it for? Oh—wait a minute. The ACDADS."

"ACDADS?" Harper sounded amused. "Shit, no. The other side

got a complete set of program tapes the first time I saw them, way back in precommissioning. How else you think they could have built the Crud?"

Dan stared at him openmouthed.

"Never mind. You don't need to know why they want it, okay? All you need to know is what I want you to do, and what you get out of it."

"Yeah, that was my second question. Shit, mutiny's still a capital offense."

"All taken care of." The beam flickered around again, and yes, Harper was smiling. "Like I told you, all in the plan. Here's the scenario. The Cubans take the ship into custody. They take the crew off. But not everybody goes quietly. Some guys make trouble. And they're gonna get knocked around.

"Those will be *my* guys. Throw in with us, they'll beat you up enough to make it look like you were forced to conn the ship in. It'll hurt, but no permanent damage. What do you end up with? Later on—after everybody's repatriated—each of my guys gets mailed fifty thousand dollars in an unsigned money order. Every year after that, you get another installment. Tax-free. Nobody ever knows."

"That's for what? For turning the ship over?"

"That's right."

"How about you? How much do you make?"

"Not a thing."

"Come off it."

"I'm serious. See, I won't be coming back," said Harper. "Look, I can read the handwriting. I don't want to get left out in the cold. I'll be 'killed resisting boarding.' The body will be lost at sea. You get what that means."

Dan said slowly, "You're a hero."

"Bingo, you got it! Shit, they might even name a ship after me. Bonnie gets my pay, insurance, and allowances. Me, I go on to a privileged life with a changed name as an intelligence adviser, plus two million bucks in back pay they been holding for me."

"What about your bars?"

"My what?" Harper stared, then burst out laughing. "My *bars*! You still don't get it, do you? I been working for the Reds for twenty years now, shipmate! There aren't any *bars*!"

Dan said slowly, "You're a spy."

"Now you're hittin' on eight cylinders."

"And you've been at this for a long time. Feeding them"—he remembered Byrne's suspicions then, the hints and forebodings—"feeding them—what? Tapes for our fire-control systems. And what else?"

"Whatever I could get my hands on. A lot of stuff, when you're classified materials custodian." Harper shrugged. "If you're gonna be a spy, shit, might as well be a good one."

"How'd you get into this, Jay?"

"Back in Vietnam. When I was on the *Milwaukee*. One time in the radio shack, the guys were talking about what the stuff we had was worth. 'The Reds'd pay a bundle for this one'—that kind of stuff. And it occurred to me that maybe they would. Only thing was, I didn't just daydream about it. And you know what? They did."

Dan still felt appalled. But now he'd had time to think, he realized there was only one thing for him to do. He had to try to take the ship back. He didn't know how. But he seemed to be the only one in a position to do anything. His mind kept coming back to that. The loyal men, if what Harper was saying was true, were all locked below. Anyone else abovedecks was one of his evil dwarfs. Could he figure a way to wreck Harper's plan? He'd have to pretend to cooperate, keep his eyes open, and hope an opportunity presented itself soon. The lights had separated, one drawing forward of the beam, the other aft. Soon they'd be under close escort.

It would be a dangerous game against armed men.

"Okay, enough questions," Harper told him. "I can't wait any longer. You in or out?"

"You say we'll be paid?"

"Cash. No tracks."

"And they'll never know I helped."

"Right. All you got to do is play along, let them punch you around a little. Might even get a medal out of it. Help your career, you know? It hasn't been looking so good up to now, I hear."

Dan kept his voice flat, trying to keep hatred and near nausea from showing in it. Minute by minute, he understood more and more. And saw ever more clearly how imperative it was that he stop the traitor and spy.

He said in an even tone, "Okay, sounds good. Count me in."

A flash from the thinning darkness, and Dan jerked his eyes up, startled, to see a plume of white water collapse back into the darkling sea ahead. "Shit!"

"Take it easy! All in the plan. They'll fall in on the quarters at two hundred yards. Steady as you go. I'm glad you're with us. . . . This is Mr. Harper. Mr. Lenson has the deck," he shouted in. The helmsman nodded silently. Then, to Dan, he said, "Okay, shipmate. Set us a course for Santiago."

* * *

HE stood by the chart table, sweat trickling down his back. Harper and the other man had left the bridge, herding the captives from the chart room below. Leaving him alone on the bridge with the mutineer with the riot gun. Harper hadn't offered Dan a weapon. Obviously, he didn't trust him that far. The growing light showed him the masked face behind the helm console. Dan had no idea who it was. A big guy, well built. Enlisted, apparently, but he'd taken off the dungaree shirt. All he wore was his white undershirt, tails out, and dungaree trou—that and the mask.

"What's the course?"

"Uh, come left to two-three-zero." He looked back at the chart, aligned the parallel rulers, and applied himself to navigation for a while.

Harper had told him to stay inside the twelve-mile limit. He struck off a track that would get them safely past Punta Negra. Then they could come right off Punta Caleta to shape a course for Santiago, the next Communist-controlled harbor past Guantánamo Bay. He walked out the distance with his dividers, realizing it wouldn't take long to get there. He hoped the Navy got their shit together, sortied whoever was pierside at Gitmo, came out to get them.

The only problem was, he didn't think they knew a mutiny and capture was in progress. He glanced around the bridge in the growing light, inspecting the radio remotes from the edge of his sight. Raw copper gleamed at each one. The cables had been snipped through. He didn't see any of the walkie-talkies; Harper had probably heaved them over the side.

Then he remembered with a truly doomed feeling that even if he could notify someone, there weren't any warships in Gitmo. They'd been suckered north, off Cay Sal. The big shell game, he understood it now; remembered an afternoon in the sun, too much beer, plastic cups on the cockpit seat. "Classic misdirection. Make 'em think they've won. Then, when they lift the last cup—nada. They're dicked."

Harper had been telling him all along what was going to happen. He just hadn't understood the code.

Barrett was naked before her enemies.

He looked out to starboard, to see the little gunboat tucked in close, two hundred yards, like a guard escorting a prisoner. Another to port. Little guys, maybe *Zhuks* or P-4s. He wasn't as familiar with small craft as he was with larger combatants. But they had mean-looking automatic guns. This close, they could sweep *Barrett*'s topsides with a withering storm of fire.

As he calculated the time to the next turn, he thought swiftly over what Harper had told him. How much of it should he believe?

Because some of it just didn't compute, once you thought about it. Such as, why would the other side need *Barrett* at all? If what he was saying was true, he'd already given the Reds everything they needed: design details, tapes, even—he tensed as another piece snap-fit into place—yeah, even MAM cards, the actual tuning circuitry on their fire-control radar. He'd wondered who else could find something like that useful. How about . . . somebody designing a way to jam it?

Marion Sipple's death made sense now. The former department head had probably caught on somehow, stumbled over Harper or one of his associates in some situation beyond plausible denial—and been killed, slugged and dumped off the brow in dry dock. The thefts had been cover, a smoke screen Harper had deployed to shift any suspicion to the dead man himself.

Just as, he realized with a chill, it was perfectly possible for Harper to use him to put *Barrett* alongside the pier in Santiago, then kill him. And orchestrate his men to shift all the blame to Dan Lenson, already suspected by NIS, already known as a disgruntled and insubordinate junior officer.

He jerked his mind back from his personal problem to the bigger one at hand. There had to be some reason they wanted the ship itself—something Harper could not photocopy or photograph or walk off the brow with. But what? Not nuclear weapons; *Barrett* didn't carry any. But why else would you actually want to capture a Navy ship? The last time that had happened, it was the *Pueblo*—

Dan gripped the edge of the chart table, suddenly dizzy. Yes, the *Pueblo.*

Just as Jack Byrne had said that day at the squadron headquarters, sitting in his office after they had met Commodore Niles. You needed two things to read encrypted message traffic: the key list *and the encrypting equipment.*

In 1968, the North Koreans had captured USS *Pueblo,* claiming she'd violated their territorial sea. He'd only been a midshipman then, but he remembered. There'd been a KW-7 aboard her. Her crew had been repatriated, eventually, but *Pueblo* had never been returned to the United States.

And Harper had had access to KW-7 key lists.

Conclusion: The Soviets had been reading U.S. message traffic—for years. No wonder their AGIs always turned up for fleet exercises!

But now the KW-7 was obsolete. The Navy was phasing in new systems. If the Soviets got them, they could keep right on reading Navy comms into the next century.

If there was a war, they'd win it.

But those weren't Soviet ships out on their quarters; they were Cuban. He could see the flag now as the sun rose. Cuba was a satellite, but they weren't puppets. Seizing a U.S. warship was a major risk. What did they get out of it? He didn't have an answer to that, or even a suspicion.

His thoughts, running like a rogue torpedo, circled back again now to the *Pueblo*'s capture. He remembered how contemptuously Navy people had talked about it. Why hadn't her skipper fought back? they'd asked one another. Or scuttled his ship? Where were his guts, his brains, his balls? Well, now he was in the same situation, and so far he wasn't doing any better. Technically, he had the conn, but any order he gave to increase speed or attempt to break away would be futile—unless he could overcome Riot Gun somehow. And as for scuttling . . . *Barrett* had destruct charges. But with the crew locked below . . .

"Steady on two-three-zero," the man behind the helm told him. "Are you navigating?"

Dan cleared his throat. "Yeah," he said. He bent to the pelorus and sighted along it at the left cut of the headland, swiveled to take a bearing on the light. It was fading as day grew but still visible. Holding both bearings in his mind, he went to the chart table. The fix showed them due east of Punta Negra. Two-three-zero looked good for at least the next twenty minutes.

He didn't know how it all hung together. But he had to admire how beautifully Harper had positioned himself. Only the CMS custodian had ready access to codes. No one but a combat systems department member could have stolen MAMs kits and sabotaged program tapes. And Harper had volunteered to lead the ship's security team, giving himself access to small arms, ammunition, equipment, keys—everything he needed to take over a ship. Dan understood all the security drills now, too late. Harper had been rehearsing, using the excuse of honing their readiness for Gitmo, but really planning how to take *Barrett* over quickly and efficiently.

A distant howl. His breathing stopped as he listened, not daring to hope. Then he dropped the dividers and leaned forward, staring around the sky.

Two black specks swept toward them. Jets, but the flat nose intake, the stubby backswept wings told him they weren't American. The MIGs came on low to the water and swept over their mast tops, rattling the glass in the windows with a low pass. Yeah, he thought bitterly, everything was in the plan, even the air show.

He'd known Jay Harper was smart, but he'd wondered sometimes how motivated he was. Now he understood. He'd been motivated all right, but not by what Dan had thought.

Because judging by the standards of traitors, spies, and murderers, he rated a 4.0 right down the line. Dan sucked air through his teeth, then forced himself to plot another fix, knowing that every minute that went by made it less likely they would escape.

HE held the new course for half an hour. The bridge felt lonely, solitary, with only one other man where usually there were six or eight. No one was working on the forecastle. No sounds came from the signal bridge, no rattle of shutters or shouted commands. It felt spooky. Harper called twice to check on them, insisting on speaking both to him and the helmsman each time. He didn't say where he was calling from. The headland slowly slipped past, tan hills and, rising behind them, green mountains, the Sierra Maestra. The MIGs circled overhead, and to either side the gunboats rolled in the golden sparkle of *Barrett*'s wake, dogging her steps like border collies herding a sheep.

As dawn flooded the world with heat and light, he made out something on the horizon ahead. Gradually, it drew closer, taking on a shape he recognized with dread and apprehension: the long, straked hull, low and gray, and reflected beneath it, in the eerily calm, slightly undulating mirror, the pyramidal superstructure, bristling with guns and missile launchers. . . . As the two ships closed on converging courses, he lifted his binoculars to confirm the hull number.

Yes, he thought then, though he'd known it the moment he saw her upperworks over the curve of the sea.

Gut heavy with foreboding, he looked across the water at the *Razytelny*.

The 21MC clicked on. "Bridge? Harper here. You make out a Russki destroyer ahead, shipmate?"

Dan leaned forward and pressed the key. Through numb lips he said, "Yes."

"Okay, great. Stop engines and heave to."

"All stop," he told the man behind the helm. He heard the double ping as the engine room answered.

Barrett coasted ahead, gradually slowing. The helmsman let go of the wheel and stepped back, but Dan told him to stay where he was and keep her head steady as she lost way. He went out on the port wing, into an already hot, calm, airless day, looking down on a smooth oily-looking sea. Cuba was a jagged darkness to starboard, more distant now as they left the point behind. High clouds hovered behind the mountains like tethered blimps. He propped his elbows on the splinter shield. Holding the binoculars with the tips of his fingers, he centered them on *Razytelny*.

A crinkling of the sea at her bow told him she was making five or six knots, steaming nearly parallel to *Barrett* on a gradually converging course. Sailors moved purposefully about her decks. Forming up? Yes, falling into ranks. A bustle of activity on the boat deck.

A chill ran up between his shoulder blades as he realized that the Soviets were mustering a boarding party, getting ready to take possession. Yet it was not so much frightening as uncanny. A sense of déjà vu, as if this all had happened before, only strangely reversed. . . .

Then he remembered: It had—on an Arctic night, the sea black and rough and freckled with ice, and he and the Kinnicks getting ready to lower *Reynolds Ryan*'s motor whaleboat. It had been raining then, an icy, freezing diagonal mix of rain and sleet that pelted down out of invisible clouds, soaking their foul-weather gear in seconds. The seamen had crushed and shoved past him into the boat, settling on thwarts sweet-smelling with glycol antifreeze. Loose ice had slid around the floorboards. And across the water, that time, the madly rolling hull of a surfaced submarine.

Today, everything was so strangely mirror-imaged, he wondered if a mysterious nemesis had arranged it as revenge. The sea was hot and bright and calm. And this time, the Russians were coming to him.

Suddenly, he realized the last seconds were ticking away. The Soviets were taking their time, but once forty or fifty armed sailors had boarded, taking *Barrett* back would be impossible.

He felt something very like panic, and at the same time, a fatal resolve. Even if Harper didn't kill him, once they got to Cuba, they could expect the standard treatment for those who fell into Communist hands: prison, starvation, humiliation, beatings, interrogations, pressure for confessions, endless propaganda, mock trials. It might be months before they were released or exchanged. It might be years.

He'd thought about it, and he just flat wasn't going to go along with it. He just wasn't going to let them take his ship without a shot fired in her defense.

He turned his head slowly, checking the helmsman with his peripheral vision as he bent to examine the radarscope. His only chance was to charge this masked son of a bitch. If he had to die, he'd die trying to kill him. And that was most likely exactly what would happen. He didn't have good odds, alone against an alert, armed man.

But it was all he could think of to do.

He leaned back slowly, looked casually into the chart house, then strolled in. The helmsman's eyes followed his every step. He came out again, crossed to the starboard wing, noting exactly where the man stood, where he'd propped the shotgun against the console. If only he could make him step away from the wheel. The door to the starboard wing grew slowly ahead of him like a bright portal to another life. Through its shining oval, he saw the sparkling sea, the distant violet and green of a forbidden land. What a calm, beautiful day. Legs, hands tingling numb. So scared. He hoped Nan had a good life. He hoped she remembered her daddy.

"Where you think you're going?"

He took a deep breath. One more look at the sea, then he'd come back in and do it. "Gonna take a bearing; I can't see my marks from inside anymore," he called back.

The guy nodded. Dan stepped over the knee-knocker into the sunlight. How warm it was on his hands, his lifted face. He smelled flowers, grass, the land. How beautiful the world was. His lungs pumped, getting ready. His heart accelerated, preparing to fight and die. When he went back in, he'd take three steps, pivot as he passed the chart table, and charge. He knotted the leather strap of the heavy binoculars surreptitiously into his fist. If he could slug this asshole with them before he got to the gun, he might live through the next sixty seconds. He glanced out and aft, back toward where the gunboat rolled uneasily, keeping pace—and into George Vysotsky's intent blue eyes.

For a long moment, he couldn't speak, just stared. The XO was crouching below the level of the window, a few feet aft of him. His blond hair stuck up in a ragged cowlick. His bare feet, pale toes splayed, were dug into the wooden gratings of the deck.

In his right hand, extended toward Dan, was a long gleam that he recognized after a puzzled instant as a saber.

"XO," his lips shaped, but his voice died in his throat. He remembered the helmsman, just inside. He glanced back. The masked head was bent, concentrating on maintaining course as the slowly dropping speed reduced the effect of the rudders. The shotgun lay propped against the console.

Obviously, he hadn't noticed the executive officer yet. But it was a nasty dilemma. If Dan spoke, the helmsman would hear it and look up. But if he didn't say something right now, it looked like the XO was going to run him through. He was already moving forward, point extended. "You bastard," he hissed. "You one of them? *Are you*?" The point glittered, rising toward his throat. Dan couldn't breathe. He couldn't take his eyes from it.

"No," he whispered. He motioned frantically. "No. Keep it *down*, XO!"

"What are you doing up here, then?"

"Shut *up*!" But he could see his voiceless whisper, his desperate and furtive gesticulations weren't getting across. Vysotsky wasn't listening.

He had to speak or the exec would kill him. But he couldn't speak, because then Vysotsky would die.

In that interminable frozen instant, while his brain fought with itself, the point pricked into his throat. Dan closed his eyes. He stood motionless, waiting for the lunge.

Then, when it didn't happen, he opened them, to see Vysotsky rise slightly from his crouch, peep quickly through the bottom of the window into the pilothouse, then drop again.

Dan turned his back on both of them, set up the bearing ring, and bent to sight through it. His hands were trembling so badly it took several tries to get a cut on Punta Caleta. He had a crazy desire to jump over the side. But there was nowhere to swim to, and jumping wouldn't help recover the ship. Just then, one of the MIGs circled back, not as low as the first pass, but the thunder gave the exec auditory cover to mutter, "I couldn't sleep. Felt uneasy. Then I heard people moving around outside my cabin. I hid just before they came through my door."

Dan murmured through motionless lips, "They were waiting for me up here, when I came on watch."

"The guy at the helm, he one of them?"

"Yeah. He's got one of the riot guns."

"Is it loaded?"

"I think so."

"He's forcing you to conn?"

"Yeah. What you want to do, sir?"

Vysotsky murmured hoarsely, "We've got to take the bridge back, then turn her head to seaward and get the hell out of here. They can sink us if they want, after that. At least she'll go down in deep water."

"Look, if we work together, we can maybe take this guy. I'll distract him. Then you come in from the wing."

"Can I trust you?"

"You can trust me, sir." The MIG dwindled toward the hills, and he lowered his voice. He bent as if to take another sight, knowing he couldn't linger out here much longer.

"There's another guy loose," Vysotsky's hoarse whisper floated up. "I caught a glimpse of him down near the boat deck. Had his back to me. I didn't see his face."

"One of them?"

"I don't think so. He was in coveralls, but he wasn't wearing the hood."

"Lost steerageway," the helmsman shouted from inside. Dan turned and saw to his horror that he'd moved away from the wheel. It turned lazily this way and that.

Without another look at Vysotsky, who was crouched with the

blade gripped in both hands, Dan stepped back inside. He said, "Try to keep her head southeast as long as you can."

"I did. Told you, we lost steerageway."

Dan got to the far side of the console. He lifted his hand to his cap, took it off, the motion drawing the man's eyes. He said loudly, angrily, "Oh yeah? Mark your head."

The tone worked. The eyes in the drab wool mask dropped, seeking the compass. *Now, XO,* Dan thought, wanting to look toward the door but knowing he couldn't. Do it *now.*

From outside came the clack of a wooden grate being stepped on.

The helmsman's eyes flicked up instantly from the gyro and widened as Vysotsky bulled through the doorway. A second later, the short ugly barrel of the twelve-gauge came up as Vysotsky charged, screaming, his blade whipping down in a shining arc of steel.

The blast blew the exec off his feet, shattering the window behind him white around the pellet holes. Blood splattered like rain against the captain's chair, the radar repeater, the double-ought buckshot gouging the housing to bright aluminum. Vysotsky hung on the gyrocompass stand, staring not at the man who'd shot him but at Dan. "You bastard," the gravelly, hoarse voice said. "You goddamned traitor. May God strike you dead."

Lenson stared at him, frozen, as Vysotsky's eyes went dull and the sword clattered to the deck. Faintly, Dan heard someone yelling from the deck below, from the open ladder well.

He cursed himself, understanding too late that he should have charged at the same instant Vysotsky had; one of them would have made it. He started to step forward, but from behind the console came the clang of the empty shell being ejected. "Leave him alone," the masked figure shouted. "Don't touch him. Get back."

Dan lost it then.

Lost it and charged, right into the gun. The masked eyes widened. The muzzle came down from where it had been pointed at the overhead as the second shell was jacked into the breech, came down, but not quite fast enough to be aimed at him when it went off, right past his ear.

He slammed into man and gun with a full body block, elbow in his throat, and the impact and the recoil of the shotgun carried them locked together back into the bulkhead, into the coffee mess. Stainless pots and mugs clanged and spun to the deck. Dan got in a punch, hammering the other's head back into a corner of the 1MC panel.

The other man wedged a knee between them, got an arm across Dan's face, and started forcing him back. The shotgun clattered to the deck at the same time he chopped Dan across the bridge of the nose, a short blow that didn't hurt as much as it would have if he'd had more room to swing, but it still made him gasp. As he staggered back, Dan grabbed at the other's head, an instinctive clawing to keep them locked together. If the other broke free, he could get the gun. He had to stay on him until one of them went down for good. But instead of flesh, his taloned fingers snagged wool, and the balaclava came off in his hand.

He stared into Casey Kessler's eyes, astonished—till the ASW officer levered him off suddenly, and he reeled, staggering backward.

The steel edge of the helm console caught him right in the kidneys. He screamed at the sudden obliterating pain. Kessler swayed in front of the door leading aft, dragging an arm across his face, bleeding from a saber cut across the scalp. Then, as he started toward Dan again, his boot struck the stock of the shotgun. He stared down, blinking through the blood, then stooped.

Bent double with the pain in his back, Dan shoved off the console into a low, crabbed tackle, hitting Kessler as his extended fingers brushed the gun. He crashed backward, but his head snapped forward as it hit the jamb of the open door with a crack. The lieutenant turned away and ran, staggering a few steps down the short passageway behind the bridge, then suddenly faced Dan again, punching him painfully in the cheek. Dan, still unable to straighten, hit him as hard as he could in the belly, driving him back another step down the passageway. Then he bulled forward and butted him in the chest.

Kessler screamed, arms windmilling, and toppled backward into the ladder well leading down to the next deck. Aluminum crashes and heavy thumps and thuds came back up. But Dan wasn't listening. He was crimped over, fists to his knees, panting hard and staring at a nothingness flecked with pinpoints of light. His ear was still ringing from the blast. He felt like he was going to pass out. Then he heard someone yelling below him. "Hey. Hey!"

"Yeah?" He lurched forward, grabbed the rail at the top of the ladder, looking down.

Kessler lay facedown on the polished green tile outside the captain's in-port cabin. Standing over him was another man without a face—just an olive drab head, with eyes that now looked up at Dan through the peep sight of an M14 pointed at his chest.

47

AT the bottom of the ladder, Kessler moaned and stirred. Lenson stared with terrible fascination at the rifle. Why didn't the man fire? He'd seen him knock Kessler down the ladder. Why didn't he shoot?

Then, to Dan's astonishment, he let the barrel drop. "What happened?" he yelled up. "I heard shooting. Would've come up, but I'm supposed to stay here."

He looked down at himself, bleeding and disheveled, and suddenly understood. In his hand—still clutched where he'd yanked it off Kessler's head—dangled the olive drab hood.

Harper had compartmentalized his teams, so that not even they knew one another. Clever, clever, Dan thought. But maybe also a weak point.

Kessler grunted and tried to hoist himself up. "Stop him," Dan yelled. The rifleman jumped back, then brought down the rifle butt savagely.

Dan swallowed with a dry throat. With a last glance around the bridge—at Vysotsky's body, his blood painting the deck like spilled primer; at the vacant helm droning to itself—he pulled the balaclava over his face, then went forward to pick up the shotgun. Remembering *Razytelny,* he checked her through the shattered Plexiglas. She was hove-to now, a half mile away. A boat lay alongside; the boarding party was climbing down into it. He returned to the ladder, cursing as pain kicked his kidneys, and started crabbing his way down.

"Sons of bitches tried to knock me down, take my gun," he growled. "Almost made it."

"I heard two shots."

"I got one of them—the XO. Where's Harper?"

"I thought he was up there with you."

"No." Dan got to the bottom and shifted his grip to the barrel of the shotgun. "What, he's got you guarding the captain?"

"Yeah. I was in there with him, then I heard the shots."

"He in there now?"

"Yeah."

"Shit! Look out!"

The other whipped around, and as soon as his back was to him, Dan swung. The stock cracked, but the guy went down.

Dan stepped over him and tried the door—unlocked. He slid in, closing it behind him. He felt incredibly alert now. Colors seemed brighter. Sounds seemed louder. He wanted to think, wanted to try to get his mind around some things, such as Casey Kessler being one of *them.* But there wasn't time to think. His only advantage was that no one knew he was free yet. But what should he do? Maybe Leighty would know. "Captain," he whispered. "Captain!"

Puzzled, he looked around at an empty cabin. His eyes snagged on the porthole, swinging slowly, undogged. Beyond it, sky. Not much of an opening, but Leighty wasn't a big man. Could he have escaped through it? Was he the one Vysotsky had seen on the boat deck? He moved toward it, letting the shotgun droop.

Then he stopped, going rigid as an edge dug into his throat. "Don't move," Leighty whispered into his ear, pressing it deeper. Dan couldn't tell what it was, but it felt slicing-sharp. "Drop the gun or I'll cut your head off."

"Sir, it's Lenson. I'm on your side."

"Drop the fucking gun."

Dan threw it onto the sofa. Eyes still on the porthole, he muttered again, "Sir, I'm on your side. If you'll open your door . . . I just took out your guard. Just got free myself a minute or two ago. That was the shooting you heard."

Leighty didn't answer, but the door opened, then closed. Then footsteps came back, quick and light. Dan felt the shotgun placed back in his hand.

When he turned, the captain was checking the M14. A letter opener was tucked into the belt of his whites. Trop whites, white shoes, ribbons, the uniform he wore every time they went into or out of port. He looked small and fine and freshly shaven and the weapon seemed too large for him, like a boy with his father's gun.

"First thing, we have to get to the 1MC," Leighty said. He released the operating handle and the breech slammed closed. "Who's on the bridge?"

"What for, sir?"

"To announce what's going on—that this isn't a security drill, that someone's actually trying to take over the ship."

"Sir, it's past trying. They've got it." He explained as quickly as he could about Harper, his spying, passing key lists and classified equipment, how Dan suspected him of killing Sipple to cover his tracks. The captain's face stilled as he listened. "He's got thirty people with him. They drilled this in advance. Everybody else is locked below. More bad news—we're being escorted by gunboats and MIGs to Santiago. And there's a Soviet destroyer off the bow, getting a boarding party ready."

Leighty touched his teeth with his knuckles. "And you think we're the only ones free? How about George? Felipe?"

"Sir, the only other loyal man I've seen was Commander Vysotsky. And he's dead; he died on the bridge, fighting. I wouldn't be here without him."

"I've been doing some thinking while they had me locked in here. I've also been doing some listening."

"Listening, sir?"

Leighty nodded into his bedroom, and Dan saw the phones on the bulkhead. "On the internal circuits. There's not much going on. In fact, there's no chatter at all. From that, I deduce he doesn't have thirty men. If he did, he could set a normal under-way watch. And I can't believe he'd find that many disloyal men aboard, whatever he offered. Where'd that figure come from?"

"From Harper."

"It's smoke, bluff. You've seen—what, three, four?"

Dan thought. "Maybe four. It's hard to say who you've seen twice. The ski masks."

"That's a smart tactic. But I don't buy thirty. I don't think he's got more than six or seven. And maybe less."

"You might be right, sir." He'd been banging his brains against that, too, wondering who Harper could have turned. And he'd come up with a few names. But Leighty was right: Thirty sounded way too high.

"We've got to stop him, take the ship back, and beat off the Russians and Cubans."

Dan said, "Sir, I was thinking, too, when they had me up there conning at gunpoint. If we could get the conn and weapons systems back, we could try to fight our way out. But I don't think we can hold the bridge. Even if there aren't thirty, there are more than there are of us. I think we should try to disable her, buy time. Eventually, somebody's going to notice we've missed our ETA, start looking for us."

"Does anyone know we've got a problem? Did we get any comms off?"

"No, sir, I don't think so, but we were supposed to pick up the pilot off Leeward Point at dawn. They've got to wonder where we are. If we could get to the engine room, disable the engines—"

The captain said slowly, "The reduction gears are the most vulnerable point. Get the covers open, dump in some tools—then when they turn over, they chew themselves apart. We wreck those, she's not going anywhere." Leighty eyed him. "If we get separated, or one of us doesn't make it, the other keeps going. Agreed?"

"Yes, sir." He felt relieved to have an order to follow, to be back under command. He crossed to the door, cracked it, and peered out. Then he checked his twelve-gauge. The butt was cracked, but it should still fire. His mouth was raspy-dry, but he seemed to be getting used to the idea he could die any minute. If Jay Harper was around the next corner, great, let it be.

"All right, let's go," said Leighty, slipping past him.

DAN bent to check the guards as they stepped over them. They'd be out for a while yet. He pulled the balaclava off the one he'd slugged and held it out. The face under it he only distantly recognized; it wasn't one of his men. Leighty hesitated, looking at it. "Your shirt, too, sir," Dan prompted. Finally the captain stripped it off and threw it back into his cabin. He pulled on the olive drab wool.

"Let's go," Leighty said again. But instead of heading aft, toward the engineering spaces, he ran forward.

"Shit," Dan whispered, but he followed.

He expected Harper and his entire crew. But the pilothouse was still empty, the helm still humming untended, throttle at stop, 55 rpm, zero pitch. To port, one of the gunboats lay to, rolling, although the sea looked calm, the Cuban ensign hanging limp and then stretching out and then returning to curl around its staff. Then he saw the first boat of armed sailors headed toward them from *Razytelny*, drawing a widening V over the mirror-skinned sea.

Leighty straightened from Vysotsky's body and saw them, too. "Ahead full," he yelled, sprinting out onto the wing. Dan grabbed the handles and rang up "ahead full." The bell pinged as Main Control answered.

A shot whiplashed, making him jump. He saw Leighty aiming again, the rifle propped on the splinter shield.

He couldn't tell if it was the captain's intent or if his sights were still set point-blank, but both bullets fell short, raising brief spurts of foam between *Barrett* and the oncoming boat. Whichever it was, it wavered, then came right, rocking, as it sheered off.

Suddenly foam shot out from beneath the gunboat's stern, and it leapt ahead.

Leighty spun and ran back inside. "That should slow down the boarding process," he shouted as he went by. Dan followed, almost falling as he tried to change direction on the slick tile.

Downward and aft now, ladder after ladder. Dan wondered how

far they'd get. The reduction gears were all the way aft and five decks down. Harper had said he had a team in Main Control. He and Leighty would have to deal with them somehow to destroy the gears.

They clattered through the 01 level, ran aft, and rounded another ladder. Aft again now past the locked doors of the ship's offices, the dark display windows of the ship's store, the mess deck, tables and serving lines echoing empty. It was day topside, but the interior was still at "darken ship," and the dim red night bulbs cast long shadows. Ideal cover for an ambush. He'd never expected, ever, to have to fight *within* his own ship. Leighty was ahead now, pounding into the dimness. Dan wished the captain would take it slower and make less noise. Fingers slippery on the shotgun, kidneys jabbing him at each step, he trotted after him. Leighty seemed to be banking on speed, hardly glancing down side passageways as they ran. Granted, they had to reach the engine room before the Russians recovered and boarded. But he'd have felt better if they'd advanced leapfrog-fashion, covering each other.

Two detonations shook the deck, muffled, but not gunshots. He didn't know what they were.

Three men burst around the corner of the barber shop. Masks covered their faces. Seeing Lenson and the captain, they slowed but didn't shoot. Dan grinned tightly under the hot wool. They still didn't know they were being challenged, that there were loyal men still free aboard USS *Barrett.*

Leighty fired from where he stood, right in the middle of the passageway. Navy M14s weren't set to full automatic, but he fired so fast, it sounded like a burst. The men scattered instantly, rolling to cover behind bulkheads and doors. One ended up behind a scuttlebutt, inadequate cover. Dan dropped to one knee and fired, and he abandoned the watercooler, scrambling backward.

Muzzle flashes lighted the passageway as they returned fire. Dan rolled to the side and came up against a gear locker. As he wrestled the heavy watertight door open, a bullet clanged into it, right opposite his head. And suddenly, he couldn't see. He was down, clawing at his eyes.

Leighty was still standing out there, trading shots with men behind cover. "Shit," Dan muttered, blinking the passageway partially back into focus through tears and maybe blood. What was he trying to do? He thrust the muzzle around the door and pumped three loads of buckshot down the passageway, flinching each time it jolted his shoulder before it clicked. Oh no, he thought. "Captain! Get back here!"

"It's Leighty," someone shouted. "And another guy. Just two of 'em, I think."

He heard a reply but couldn't make it out. He stuck his head out again. "Captain!" Another bullet hit a bulkhead fire station, raising a smoky cloud as it punched through a hose. He smelled burning rubber and gunpowder. "Get back here! I can't cover you!"

All at once, the firing stopped. Leighty stood alone in the center of the passageway. Smoke drifted toward the overhead, ghostly in the red light. Dan's ears were ringing and his eyes were running fluid. But he was alive. So far.

Leighty came walking back. Dan couldn't believe he hadn't been hit. The captain looked behind the door. "You okay?"

"Paint chips in my eye. But I'm out of ammunition."

"Me, too." Leighty glanced back down the passageway, and, peering out, Dan saw that it was empty. "I don't think we'll get to the engine spaces. They pulled back in that direction. I think it was Harper giving the orders. They're probably going to—"

A tremendous explosion sent them diving to the deck. It was followed by a rattling sound. The scream of a small-caliber shell accompanied another terrific bang and clatter. Dan realized the rattle was fragments going through joiner work and light bulkheads.

"They're shooting at us."

"Hitting, too," said Leighty, but he didn't sound unhappy. Dan understood perfectly. As long as they were firing, the boarding party would have to stand off. And the more damage they did, the less use *Barrett* would be when they got it into port. "I wish we could make them torpedo us," Leighty added. "That'd be perfect. No, shit, I forgot, they've got guys locked below."

A change in the vibration, a lean of the ship made them both glance up.

"They're heaving to again," Dan said. The engines could be controlled either from the bridge or the CCS, in the engine room. He took slow, deep breaths. His gut didn't like it down here in the shadows. It couldn't believe there wasn't someone behind him, and he had to keep checking to reassure it. "How about the magazines? See if we can take out the guards, let some of our people out? They could fight the boarding party with axes, hoses—"

"Maybe," said Leighty slowly. "Or maybe they'd just get gunned down for no good reason. I'm wondering if maybe we'd just better get the word out we need help. You said the remotes were cut on the bridge. Did you try CIC or Radio Central?"

"No, sir."

"I know, I should have thought of it when we were up there. But maybe we ought to go back, try to get a Pinnacle out somehow."

Dan didn't answer. He was struggling with a question of his own. Leighty had stood in the middle of the passageway with three men firing at him. Yet he'd emerged without a scratch. And that made another doubt recur. When he'd stepped into his cabin, Leighty had presumably been under guard. But if he was really being guarded, why hadn't the mutineers tied him up?

Was this some sort of charade? But he only said, "Whatever you think, sir. You lead, I'll follow."

"Radio, then," Leighty said. Still carrying the empty rifle, he started jogging back up the passageway. Dan looked at his own weapon, almost threw it away, then decided to keep it. Even empty, it might buy him a couple of seconds if they met more of Harper's Judases.

Leighty was almost out of sight. The captain still didn't seem to worry about noise. Or was it because he knew they weren't going to shoot him?

Sweating again, he forced his tiring body back into a run.

THE door to Radio stood open. Always locked, window barred with steel, now it hung on one hinge, bent and mutilated as if hacked open with a pickax. As he stepped through, Dan saw why. A shell had come through the side and exploded inside one of the receiver cabinets. Broken circuit cards and shattered parts littered the rubber deck and were embedded in the overhead. The compartment stank of explosive and burnt plastic. He found a relatively undamaged-looking transmitter and tried to power it up, but without success. He kicked a rack of power supplies in helpless anger.

He turned, to find Leighty watching him. "I don't think we're going to be getting any messages out, sir."

"The bridge, then."

"They'll be there by now, sir."

Leighty said, tone strangely gentle, "You don't have to come, Dan. In fact, maybe it's best you don't."

"What's that mean, sir?"

"I'm going to take this ship back. Or else."

"Don't worry, sir. I'll be right behind you." As much, he added to himself, to make sure of Leighty as anything else.

But as they stepped out of Radio, they heard shouting from the next deck down. The captain hesitated, then, motioning him to follow, broke into a run. Dan jogged after him, trying desperately not to make any noise.

Then he tripped, and the shotgun clattered away. And someone shouted, "They're up ahead. Spread out. Safeties off."

Leighty jerked a door open, held it, waving him on violently. Dan scrambled up, expecting a bullet in the back at every step. But finally he reached the captain and ducked through. Leighty eased the door shut, then quickly dogged it from inside. Steel, Dan thought, touching it; that might hold them for a little while. And he turned, to find himself back in CIC.

HE stood there listening to boots hammering past in the passageway, watching the captain lash the dogging lever down with phone cord. The shouts swelled in volume, then faded. But it wouldn't take long to discover they weren't on the bridge. Then Harper's men would backtrack, checking each space.

Combat was cold, deserted. The plot boards cast a soft yellow glow. Green radiance shone from the screens. Back by the TAO chair, a red light blinked on, just for a moment, then blinked off. The radio remotes glowed like little colored flames. For a moment Dan hoped—until he picked up a handset and pressed the "transmit" button. He got nothing, no receiver hiss, no *pop* of outgoing carrier wave. Of course not; the transmitters were wrecked. The Cubans had put three or four shells into the vicinity of the radio room, then stopped firing.

"They're dead," he told the captain. Leighty, still facing the door, had set aside his rifle. His hands dangled empty. Dan looked around again, this time for a place to hide. The storage lockers, for life jackets and gas masks. They could hide there. But only until *Barrett* docked. They'd have to come out sooner or later.... into imprisonment.

The red light flashed again. Dan frowned, then moved cautiously toward it. But when he reached the spot where it had gleamed, between the TAO chair and the weapons-control station, he didn't see it anymore. Then it winked on again, accompanied by a nearly imperceptible hiss.

It was the call light on the 21MC. Somebody was calling on the intercom but not speaking. He pressed the key. "Combat," he muttered.

"Who's that?"

"CIC. Who's calling?"

"Mr. Lenson! This here is Petty Officer Williams."

Dan felt a sudden light-headedness. He sat down at the console. He glanced back to check that Leighty was still guarding the door, then muttered, "Where are you, Williams?"

"Here in the computer room, been here the whole time. Locked the door when I heard shooting. You know Doc DOS is dead? I kept hitting the button for Combat. Been waiting for somebody to show up there. Who there besides you?"

"Me and the captain. That's all. What did you say about Dr. Shrobo?"

"He's dead. Me and Lightbulb found him in the weight room. It looked like the weights fell on him. But then all this started, so I don't think it was no accident. Some son of a bitch killed him. What's going on, sir?"

"It's a mutiny, Willie. Apparently Mr. Harper's been working for the other side . . . for a long time. They've taken over the ship. Who else is with you?"

"Just me, sir. Just me . . . an' Elmo."

Dan stared at the speaker as his mind raced. Finally, he called in a low voice, "Captain?"

He explained quickly. Leighty looked puzzled at first, then determined. He reached past him to the intercom. "Petty Officer Williams, recognize my voice?"

"Yessir, Captain."

"We'll try it. We'll handle things from here. Let's hope they're just a little bit slow on the uptake."

"Okay, sir, I'll start the load."

Suddenly, a thunderous pounding came from the door. Dan swallowed. Harper's turncoat security force had figured out where they were. Okay, the start-up procedure . . . His thoughts were interrupted by Leighty's hand on his shoulder, by the captain motioning him out of his seat. "I'll take the console, Lieutenant. You get the systems panel up."

Dan ran three steps to the systems-monitoring panel that connected the weapons-control consoles in Combat with the computers in the DP center. As it came up, the "on-line" lights told him the panel was controlling number three AN/UYK-7. The "bootstrap start" light told him Williams was loading the ops program. He set the switches on the control/indicator panel to "master clear" and "high speed," then set up mainframe number two as default computer.

"Captain?"

"I'm up on the WDS. I'm a little rusty. Tell me—"

"Display control panel, on your upper right, switches are at the top. CRT, center; IFF on; challenge on. Radar Select, leave it wherever it is."

"Check."

The hammering grew louder and Dan saw Leighty turn his head. He spoke louder and the captain looked back to the console. "Next: upper left, the category select panel. Put all the switches that have an *S* position to *S*. Everything else, turn them from off to on."

As Leighty complied, Dan ran his eyes over his own panel again. Now the "start" light went out, telling him the op program was loaded, and the "start" button began to wink. He depressed it and it changed to a steady glow. Simultaneously, the fault-and-alarm display began pulsing, one second on, one second off. ACDADS was running.

"Check," said Leighty. "Now the action entry—"

"Your lower left. Set the mode switch to 'weapons direction, master.' To the right of that's another three-position switch—"

Then two things happened at once. The first was a loud thud from outside, then another shot, this time followed by a clang as the jacketed bullet penetrated the steel door and ricocheted into a console. Great, Dan thought. Sooner or later, they'd hit the dogging mechanism, or cut the wire lashing that held it closed.

The second was that one of the status lights, up to now cycling steadily one second on, one second off, began flashing rapidly. He jerked his eyes to it. Not a malfunction yet, but an abnormal condition. Sweat itched down his back. If this didn't work, and work perfectly, they were all going to die—he, Leighty, Williams, and all the men locked helplessly below.

Leighty got up. He said quietly, "I'll take the door. If they come in, they might not shoot at me. They didn't before."

"Yes, sir," Dan said. He wanted to ask him just why he thought they wouldn't shoot, but there wasn't time. Instead, he hit the intercom. "Williams!"

"Here."

"Abnormal condition light on computer three. Should I switch to backup?"

"No. Hit your fault jump."

He studied the panel frantically, then stabbed the button. "There, it's on."

"Now go to your mode select, on the console—"

Another shot from the door was followed by light and the screech of yielding metal. Men burst in at the far end of the compartment, men in olive drab hoods, weapons in their hands. Leighty stepped out in front of them, hands raised and empty. "Wait," Dan heard him say. "Wait. It's me, the Captain. I want to—"

A burst of fire, and he staggered back, arms flung out. Dan stared, then remembered what he had to do. He leaned across to the console Leighty had just left. His groping fingers found the three-position mode switch, clicked it over.

"Set to mode three, full automatic," he muttered. Then he stood, turning, to face the guns.

WITHIN the computer's humming circuitry, no thought took place. Only calculations. It was only a machine. It could not think, or feel anger, or desire revenge. It could only receive input, process data, issue orders.

But properly programmed, it could act as if it felt all these things.

The first to notice anything was the pilot of one of the MIGs. He saw a light flash on on his warning panel, heard a high-pitched whine in his earphones, overriding the transmission he was making just then to the Cuban air force base at Siboney.

Suddenly the ship below him seemed to come alive. White water churned suddenly, shooting out from the screws as her propellers went from idle, zero pitch, to 100 percent ahead. A shimmering haze blasted from the stack as the turbines jumped to full power.

On the bridge, a hooded man staggered back as the ship leapt suddenly ahead. Recovering, he jumped to the helm console, pulling back the throttle, cursing as *Barrett* surged past a boatload of startled faces below. The first men of the boarding party were already climbing Jacob's ladders toward the forecastle, assault rifles slung over their backs. Now as the destroyer gathered speed, they dropped off into the sea, one by one, shaken off, dragged off by the water, or simply letting go in surprise and consternation.

The man stared disbelievingly at the throttle, then racked it ahead and back again. The ship continued to accelerate. The rudder-angle indicator swung over to hard left, though the wheel itself did not move. He pressed buttons on the console, then kicked it. The ship ignored him. The deck slanted under him, the rumbling vibration increased, and he heard a *whine-and-stop, whine-and-stop* through the overhead directly above.

Bells began shrilling all over the ship. From above, forward, and aft, they blended in a high, wavering chorus, like cicadas swarming.

On the forecastle, the twin arms of the Mark 26 launcher suddenly pivoted to point straight up. Two heavily-armored blast doors flicked open as lightly as camera shutters. Two shark-finned shapes appeared as if created instantaneously from nothing, thrust up from below faster than the eye could follow.

The launcher swung down and whipped around with startling quickness, aiming the coned noses of the missiles off to starboard. At the same moment, the long, tapered barrel of the five-inch gun trembled tentatively, quivering as if, Pinocchio-like, it had been touched magically with life. It rose, hesitated, then swiftly rotated, its muzzle dropping to track along the horizon as *Barrett* continued her hard-left turn.

The Cuban gunboat came into view.

Suddenly, a deafening bellow shook everything on the forecastle, vibrating the glass in the windows, accompanied by a dazzling white-hot torch flame that an instant later flung itself into the sky, blotting out all sight in an impenetrable cloud of acrid yellow-white smoke. Still accelerating, the destroyer drove forward through the haze while the bells continued their discordant scream. With another ship-shaking roar, a second shaft of fire climbed rapidly to port. Once in clear blue, it built a long pillar of opaque smoke, tipped at its end with a white arrow that slowly turned, glittering as its fins flexed.

Ahead of it, a silver dot twisted frantically, the sun flashing off aluminum wings. The white shape shrank as it closed in. Then both vanished, replaced by a sudden irregular cloud of fire and black smoke. Fragments of glittering metal rained down from it, tumbling lazily toward the shimmering sea.

The men on the gunboat stood frozen at their weapons. They were ready to fire, but they had no target. A wall of white smoke lay across the sea, opaque, sharp-smelling, choking. Their sights searched back and forth across it, uncertain, blinded.

Then a towering blade of bow crashed out of it, tossing back huge curtains of spray to either side. As two more missiles shot up into the light, a huge ball of orange flame crashed from the muzzle of the five-inch. At the same instant, both Phalanxes, already aimed by radar, motor-driven barrels spinning themselves into a tubular blur, began firing so rapidly, the ear made out not individual shots but a continuous deafening drone.

And from aft, still all at the same moment, came four unevenly spaced howls, one, two, pause, one, two, as four Harpoons exploded from their canted launch tubes. Each rose a few hundred yards into the air, nosed over, then steered into a curve that ended locked on its target: either the Soviet destroyer or one of the Cuban gunboats.

Thirty seconds later, the battle, if it had ever really been a battle at all, was over.

DAN clung to the console, facing the masked men. For a long moment, no one spoke, listening instead to the hellish din of departing ordnance. Then he pointed at the console video. One after the other, the symbology for hostile aircraft and hostile surface ships flickered and changed, from "target," to "engaged," to "destroyed."

"You just lost," he said quietly. "Put down your guns. It's over."

"We're not surrendering to you," one of them snapped, but his tone was uncertain.

"You don't have a choice. We're on our way out of here. Jay?" He waited, but no one answered. "Where's Harper?"

A sullen voice said, "Don't know."

"I know he's the ringleader. If you surrender now, I'll go to bat for you, say you didn't understand how far he meant to go and that you . . . cooperated when I explained the situation. Otherwise, you're going to a court-martial for mutiny and murder, with nobody behind you." He gave them a second to think about it, then barked, "Now, put them down!"

One by one, they bent and laid their arms beside the unmoving body of Thomas Leighty.

THE captain was breathing, but with difficulty—hit in the lung, the classic sucking chest wound. Coldly angry, Dan ordered Chief Miller to give him first aid. As the hoods came off, other faces were revealed. Some looked ashamed, some defiant, others almost blank. Men he knew: Cephas, Horseheads, Antonio. Officers, chiefs, enlisted. Men Harper had somehow suborned, blackmailed, tempted . . . "If the captain dies," Dan muttered, letting each finish the sentence in his own mind. He gathered up the weapons and carried them up to the bridge. Keeping one of the shotguns, he dumped the rest over the side. Then he raised his head, blinking into a hot, raw wind.

Barrett was tearing through the water at flank speed. Behind her lay Cuba. Behind her, too, smoky columns towered up into the crystal blue. Looking back, Dan could see both gunboats listing and burning. A patch of brownish smoke drifted several thousand feet up, slowly dissipating. No other sign of aircraft. *Razytelny* lay still hove-to, a haze rising from her superstructure. At first it looked like stack gas. Then he saw the twisted wreckage the Harpoons, set to detonate high for a mission kill, had made of her radars and antennas. He remembered standing on her decks, surveying the curious faces of her crew. A seaworthy ship, manned by competent men—but just a little too slow on the draw. The green hills were already dropping below the horizon as *Barrett* ran south at almost forty miles an hour. She wasn't undamaged. Holes smoldered in her stacks and hangar, and smashed mast members hung down. But she was going like hell. Looking aft, he saw that the after five-inch was still tracking the Soviet frigate.

He went inside, looked at the helm console, then checked the radar, wondering if he could trust the ship to take care of herself for a little while longer. She had open water in front of her, at least a hundred miles till they'd have to start thinking about avoiding Jamaica. Finally, he called the computer room. Williams answered, "Here, sir. How did it go? I didn't . . . hear anything hit us."

"I think we're out of the box, Willie. We laid down a hell of a lot of ordnance, most of which seems to have hit, and are now hauling ass out of Dodge. Give Elmo a pat on the back for me. How's he holding up?"

"Running solid, sir."

"Great. Now, look at your watch. If you don't hear from me in ten minutes, leave ACDADS running and get down to the magazines. Let everybody out. Tell them what happened and get them to general-quarters stations as soon as possible. Oh, and better load the sonar module, too. I don't know where the Victor is, but I'd rather not be surprised."

"Where are you going?"

"Somebody's got to find Harper. He can still fuck us up if somebody doesn't defang him."

"Use some help?"

"Thanks, but I need you to keep things running. Call you back in ten minutes. If I don't call, you have your orders."

"Aye aye, sir," Williams said. Dan clicked twice, signing off, and checked the shotgun. The .45 was easier to handle in tight quarters; the M14 had more power, but in a gunfight between him and the chief warrant, his two-second analysis edged him to trade accuracy for coverage. Four rounds in the tube, one in the chamber, safety off. He was turning for the ladder when his eye caught the 1MC. He hesitated, then ran his finger down the switches and unhooked the mike. A moment later, his voice rang out over all topside and interior speakers.

"This is Lieutenant Lenson. To all hands: The mutiny has failed. As the senior surviving officer on deck, I am now taking command of USS *Barrett*. We are commencing a sweep of the ship. Anyone throwing his weapon and his hood over the side now and reporting immediately to his general-quarters station, might just not get picked out of the lineup when we go to trial. You decide. The only one we want is Chief Warrant Officer Harper. Anyone still bearing arms after this announcement will be shot on sight."

As soon as he hung the mike up, the intercom clicked on. "Dan? You up there? The King Snake here."

He lunged across the pilothouse. "Where are you, you son of a bitch? I hope they still hang people for this. The exec's dead; the captain's shot—"

"Nobody would have gotten hurt if you'd gone with the program, shipmate."

"I'm coming after you. Where are you, you asshole?"

"Just head aft." The intercom grille chuckled. "I'll head forward. Catch you somewhere in the middle, okay?" A double click, and the transmit light went off.

The quickest way aft was topside. Dan ran through the deckhouse passageway and out into the open area between the stacks. He dodged across, eyes searching the spider-work steel above him, using the empty Harpoon tubes for cover when he could. He hesitated at the after deckhouse, then decided to go for height and see if he could spot Harper before the chief warrant spotted him.

His boots hammered aluminum treads till he reached the top of the hangar—in the open again, the intakes roaring like a huge fan, exhaust blasting out of the stacks. From up here he could feel the ship roll as the rudder cycled, see the snake wake ACDADS was steering to confuse any fire-control solution. A white storm tumbled and leapt behind her as she cut through the blue Caribbean at maximum power. He sucked air for a second, then ran on, stopping this time just outside the safety arc of the Phalanx. The automatic 20-mm was on, live, radar and motors cycling. The intricately looped belt of brass cartridges gleamed in the tropical sun. From time to time, it jerked slightly right or left. He hoped it didn't start firing while he was standing below it. Leaning over the rail, shading his eyes, he searched the fantail, the flight deck.

A bullet sledgehammered the rail by his hand. He flinched back, and another sabered the air where he'd stood. He caught only the instantaneous glimpse of a figure below him, standing in the center of the flight deck where the white lines crossed. He dropped to all fours and wormed backward, grimacing as he saw blood welling from his hand. Once out of Harper's sight, he got up and ran back to the ladder. The flap of sliced skin peeled back as he slid down the handrail, but it didn't hurt yet.

Two choices from here: port or starboard. Instead of taking either, he jerked open the door into the upper level of the hangar.

Inside was a short passageway lined with storage racks, then a ladder down to the interior. He checked that the hangar door was closed, bobbing his head out and then back quickly; it was. Slinging the riot gun, he handed himself quickly down the vertical ladder, stamping it with bloody handprints, and sprinted across the cavernous empty space till he could peer out a slotlike observation window at the flight deck.

It was empty, and he swore softly. He'd hoped for a shot at Harper while he was in the open. He pulled the door open and leaned out, scanning the deck swiftly, only exposing himself for a moment.

The heavy 230-grain .45 slug crashed into the window, showering him with glass. He ducked, shielding his face with his arms. Maybe I should have kept the balaclava, he thought. No, what I really need is a bulletproof vest.

Harper was not only a far better shot than he was; the match-grade Colt automatic was a more accurate weapon. Maybe he'd screwed up by taking the shotgun. He needed to get closer, a lot closer.

He hit the door running, crouched, and caught the tall figure at the far corner of the helo pad. He was bending, getting ready to climb or drop down to the next deck. Dan braked, leveling the shotgun, but before he got a bead Harper saw him, ducked, and dropped suddenly below the edge of the flight deck.

At least he was moving him aft. Harper couldn't allow him a shot at close range, and he couldn't break back around Dan without giving him one. The other man was now on the 01 level, the fifty-foot-long step down between the flight deck and the fantail, which held the aft launcher. Its arms towered up, holding two live Standards like a javelin thrower ready to cast. The warning bell was still screaming. Dan hoped the ship didn't decide to fire. The booster exhausts were pointed right at him.

He dragged sweat from his forehead, trying to think. Harper, masked by the deck edge, could move forward around the port or starboard sides, or continue aft. Dan decided to go up the middle. He ran to the edge, leaned over, gun shouldered, and caught Harper's back past the launcher pedestal, disappearing down the ladder to the fantail. He swung, jerking the trigger as the bead crossed his back. The gun jolted and through the blast he saw pellets smoke paint all around Harper. He couldn't tell if any hit, though.

Now his hand hurt like hell, and the stock was slippery with blood. He could feel it on his face, too, sticky where he'd tried to scoop sweat from his eyes. They itched as if there was still grit in them. The sun was incredibly bright, burning directly off the calm, flat silver that surrounded the fleeing ship—like a flashlight a child persists in pointing into your eyes. Nan had done that once, giggling as he told her to knock it off, that it wasn't funny, as he balanced on a ladder trying to fix the burned-out light in the kitchen—

This wasn't the time to reminisce about his daughter. He ejected the smoking empty hull, jacked another shell in, and ran for where Harper had vanished.

From the top of the ladder he looked down on the entire fantail, the whole of *Barrett*'s wide, square stern as it canted shuddering into a zig, making empty powder canisters roll across the dark gray nonskid till they wedged against scuttles or lifelines; the lines laid out for mooring; the white-painted markings of the aft helo pad; the lowered spears of whip antennas; the after five-inch, unmanned, like all *Barrett*'s guns and launchers, but quickened now with that uncanny servomechanical mimicry of life, barrel gradually elevating as it maintained its vigilance against the receding enemy.

It seemed vast and eerily empty as he edged down the ladder, twitching the muzzle from side to side. His injured hand burned on the trigger. Where was Harper? The only cover back here was the smooth gray fiberglass bulge of the gun shield. He suddenly dropped his eyes, looking straight down through the ladder steps, but he wasn't there, either. The only place left was the far side of the gun mount.

He forced unwilling legs into motion again, clattered down the last few steps, and launched himself toward the mount. No cover out here at all, nothing but wind and sun and space. He ran, sucking for breath, dragging leaden legs behind him, expecting the hammer blow of a slug every second. But he got there safely and kept going, circling the gray curved shell, eyes fixed ahead. At some point, he was going to encounter Harper—either the other's back, in which case he lived, or his face, in which case he probably wouldn't. Every step seemed to take minutes. His eyes burned; his hand burned. The shotgun swung awkwardly and far too slowly.

On and on, his boots thudding into the deck, hot air sawing in and out of a parched throat. Through the mount's shadow, and the sun blazed directly into his eyes. Ahead, too, lay the vanishing horizon, toward which the long barrel still rose. Beside him the gun twitched and moved, correcting its aim with a hydraulic whine.

He slowed, realizing he'd circled the mount and found nothing. Then halted, panting, staring around. His back crawled, but when he glanced back, the deck behind was empty, too. He had no idea where Harper had gone. Forward again? Had he slipped past him, gone up the port side—

"Dan."

He jerked his head around, to see Harper aiming directly at him, eye steady over the extended pistol. The warrant was standing back by the safety lines, at the very stern. So still that his burning, blinking eyes, searching desperately for motion, must have slid right past him. It was too late to react, too late to do anything. He watched Harper's trigger finger whiten.

"Hold it," someone shouted.

When he looked toward the ladder, Dan saw with a numb lack of astonishment that it was Gary Lohmeyer. The ensign was still in his Engineering Department coveralls, but now he had a badge pinned to them. He looked older without his round glasses, and the callow, confused look was gone, too. Now he looked very competent indeed. As did the snub-nosed revolver braced on the rail. He shouted, "Naval Intelligence. Drop it, Harper!"

When Harper glanced away, Dan got the shotgun on him. The muzzle jumped with his panting and heartbeat, but he kept it as steady as he could.

Harper was still holding the .45 in front of him, but at waist level now, midway between the two men confronting him. Beyond, on the far horizon, the plumes of smoke were thinning. Either the gunboats had finally gone down or they'd put out their fires. Dan couldn't see *Razytelny* anymore, and only the very tops of the far blue hills. To Lohmeyer, he yelled, "Intel, huh? You showed up awful goddamned late."

"Hell, Lieutenant, I couldn't tell who the bad guys were till just now."

"I suppose you think you got me cornered," Harper said, obviously speaking to one or both of them but looking down over the safety line into the wake. "Well, guess what? I'm not surrendering.

How long you gonna stand around scratching your balls? Let's get it over with."

"I'm not going to shoot you down, if that's what you mean," Lohmeyer called. "This is an arrest. Throw the gun down."

"Fuck you, keyhole peeper."

"Let me talk to him," Dan yelled. The train warning bell was still ringing shrilly, making it hard to communicate or even think. And below that was the thunder of the wake, the rumble of the madly spinning screws just beneath them.

Lohmeyer shook his head, holding his aim. "You want to try? Have at it. But if he doesn't put the gun down in thirty seconds—"

Dan yelled, "Give up, Jay. You lost. You can't shoot us both. And I don't think you want to."

"Lose? I didn't *lose.* I won; I won big. I just stayed in the fucking game too long, that's all."

"Sounds like losing to me."

"Have it your way, Lieutenant. Just remember, you're looking at the greatest spy America's ever known. Maybe the greatest in history. If there'd a been a war, the Russkies would have won it. All because of me."

"What are you talking about? You gave them a lot. But not that much."

"You don't know the half of it," shouted Harper, still looking over the lifeline. The wake seemed to fascinate him, and Dan had to admit, it was frightening this close. Hard to ignore, like Niagara roaring past just below the guardrail. Eighty thousand shaft horsepower at 100 percent pitch kicked up a rooster tail fifteen feet high, churned the sea white for a hundred yards back, left spinning green whirlpools rocking crazily far behind. "They were reading everything, Hoss. Not just the KW-eight. *Everything*—secure voice, fleet broadcast, even satellite comms. They always knew exactly where the carriers were. They wouldn't have needed reconnaissance. They were targeting right from our messages."

Dan didn't say anything. It was probably true. God knew, they'd have to change everything after this, all the codes, everything. Harper had damaged the Navy beyond anything he could have imagined. But maybe he hadn't damaged it beyond repair.

With his free hand—the one that wasn't holding the .45—Harper was working at the fastener that held the safety line in place.

Lohmeyer cut in. "Harper. Harper! Listen! It's not hopeless. The Navy'll probably cut you a deal."

"A deal? Why?"

"We don't know what you turned over. We don't know what's compromised and what's still safe. No promises, I don't have the authority to make them. But you cooperate, they'll probably cut you some slack."

The stern rumbled and shuddered and canted as the ship threw her rudder to the other side. Harper staggered but kept the .45 up. He could still shoot either of them, Dan thought. The shotgun was getting incredibly heavy, but he had to keep it steady, had to keep it pointed at the arrogant, complacent face.

Harper yelled, "What, give me eighty years instead of life? No thanks. I'll make it simple for you, okay? Everything I ever saw that was worthwhile, I turned over. I decided when I started, if I was going to be a fucking spy, I was going to be the best and the biggest. And I was. The fucking best there was."

He was still working at the lifeline with his free hand. Dan watched, feeling sweat and blood dripping off his own fingers. The shotgun was dragging downward despite everything he could do. And Lohmeyer couldn't keep him covered forever, either. This couldn't last much longer. He couldn't tell if the agent was serious about making a deal or just trying to talk Harper into surrendering. After what he'd seen, knowing about the men Harper had killed, he didn't have a problem with shooting him. But he'd probably get shot in return. He was closer than Lohmeyer; Harper would aim for him. He hoped the intelligence agent had been trained for situations like this. He shouted, "Jay, listen. You bastard! Go for his deal. At least you'd be alive."

"That ain't being alive. Let me tell you something."

Harper turned his face to the sky, turned it as if to follow the arch of the heavens. Behind him, smoke billowed up as if from burning Sodom. Then his far-off gaze steadied. Following it, Dan saw the stars and stripes at the mast top, rippling and snapping in the hot breeze *Barrett* made for herself.

Looking up at it, Harper slowly raised his free hand in a salute.

"You know, I love this fucking country. You think that's funny? It's true. Everything I ever got, it gave me. And I appreciate that. I really do. Nothing I ever did hurt this country, no matter what they'll try to say. I didn't want to hurt Marion, or Sandy, or the Doc. Remember that, Dan. Tell them that when they come looking to write books about me."

Dan stared at him openmouthed, then felt his face tighten with rage. "That's horseshit, Jay. You killed people. Probably more than we'll ever know about. Everything you've ever said to me is fucking horseshit!"

"You got a point there, Hoss. But you bought the pile, didn't you?"

"Why did you do it? Why?"

"'Cause they paid me, that's why."

"Was that really it, Jay? Was that really all?" The riot gun was shaking now as his tired muscles shuddered. And as what Harper was saying hit him, deep in his stomach, making him want to kill him, then vomit.

Harper didn't answer for a few seconds, staring down into the racing sea. Finally, he said, sounding tired, "It was . . . at first. Then it got to be something else.

"It made me somebody, Lieutenant. Everybody thought I was just another hard-ass warrant counting the years till he retired. I'd train these kids, fresh out of the Academy and OCS. They don't know shit, but they put on lieutenant, lieutenant commander; they go on up. And I stay down in the division, pushing buttons, pushing paper. . . . But really I was on the inside. I used to say to myself, If *they* only knew that everything they're doing, everything they're planning, the other side's reading it the next day. *Because of me.* I was more powerful than the admirals. More powerful than the President. He didn't know what I knew. He couldn't do what I could do. That more like what you wanted to hear?"

Shouts drifted back to them on the wind. Glancing up, Dan saw crewmen looking down from the flight deck. Williams had followed his orders. . . . "Okay, that's it," called Lohmeyer. "Put up or shut up, asshole. Get rid of the gun. Get your hands up."

The chief warrant didn't move. He was looking down again. Dan was close to crying, although he didn't know why. He wanted to see Harper die, but still, they'd been shipmates, and part of him still didn't understand. He said, "Don't do it, Jay."

He didn't quite see how, but the toggle came out at last and the lifeline sagged to the deck. Leaving a space of slanting blue horizon, and nothing between the thin, balding officer and a twenty-foot fall into the foaming wake.

"Later, shipmate," he said, and swung himself out by one hand. Then he leapt outward and fell into the maelstrom. Dan ran forward, stopping only when his boots hit the deck-edge coaming, staring down into the shaking white roar where the sea sucked endlessly downward, foaming and whirling, never relinquishing anything it received.

VII

THE AFTERIMAGE

Epilogue
Guantánamo Bay Naval Base

STANDING on the bridge wing with Van Cleef and Quintanilla, Dan watched the pier gradually slow, then stop, as if the solid crust and core of the planet had backed engines instead of *Barrett*. The hills and administrative buildings, shops and fuel bunkers overlooking Corinaso Cove looked familiar in the brilliant sunlight. Familiar but also strange. He only slowly realized they were deserted. The only activity visible was a small group waiting on the pier, a few official vehicles parked at its foot.

"You're going to have to give her a touch more. The breeze is setting you off."

"Ahead one-third; indicate pitch for three knots," Van Cleef called into the pilothouse.

Dan swept his good eye—the other was bandaged; the cornea had been scratched—along the ship. Maybe they weren't exactly coming in with all flags flying, but they were still under command, and still a fighting ship. Radio was a shambles, but the radiomen and electricians had gotten the satellite transceiver up, getting off reports to Commander in Chief Atlantic Fleet, Commander, Naval Forces Caribbean, and Commander, Guantánamo Bay Naval Base. Inside the pilothouse, Dwight Giordano sat in the captain's chair, boot tossing nervously. The engineering officer had taken over as acting CO, and Felipe Quintanilla as acting exec.

"All engines stop. Left full rudder. All back one-third . . . all stop." As *Barrett* eased to a halt a few yards off the battered timber and concrete, Dan leaned out again. A moment later, heaving lines arched toward the waiting linehandlers. A whistle blasted. "Moored. Shift colors." On the forecastle, the starred patch of blue cloth climbed the jackstaff, touched the apex, then slowly descended to half-mast.

"We've got visitors. I'll be on the quarterdeck, Dan."

"Yes, sir," he said, saluting Giordano with a bandaged hand. He saluted back, looking awkward, and left the bridge.

Dan scanned the faces below. One of the waiting vehicles was an ambulance. When the brow settled into place, the first across were the wounded—Leighty, Kessler, and the engineer Dan had slugged—and then the dead—Vysotsky, a gray-blanketed shape on the Stokes litter, and Hank Shrobo. Dan leaned back, shading his eyes. The leading signalman took his glance upward for an order, and the third substitute broke atop the signal hoist.

Yes, the captain was ashore, and Dan had no idea if he'd be back. He didn't feel good about those litters sliding into the ambulance. But it could have been worse. They still had the ship. And there might have been more casualties, a lot more.

Several sets of whites separated themselves from the waiting party and headed for the brow. Dan raised the binoculars. "Boatswain. Boatswain! Rear Admiral, United States Navy . . . Commander, Naval Base, Guantánamo . . . Commander, Destroyer Squadron Six, arriving."

HE stood outside the wardroom, fiddling with his hat, feeling suddenly bone-tired, exhausted. He looked again at the slip of paper Jack Byrne had handed him.

> This intelligence debriefing is a non-formal fact-finding panel. You are hereby assured that all information obtained from you during the debriefing will be carefully safeguarded and held exclusively as privileged information. It will not be used in any way, directly or indirectly, in any judicial, nonjudicial, administrative, or other disciplinary proceeding to be convened subsequently to this board. However, neither is it an offer of clemency or protection from or during such proceedings, if convened.

It was signed by Rear Admiral G. H. Mason, CINCLANTFLT Inspector General.

The door opened and Quintanilla came out. Dan gave him a questioning glance, but Felipe didn't meet his eyes, just held the door. He went in, came to attention, uncovered.

"Sit down, Lieutenant," grunted a deep voice, a voice he knew. He took one of the chairs, looking in turn at an unfamiliar admiral, two middle-aged men in civilian suits, a captain who must be the base commanding officer, and at Commodore Barry Niles, USN, Commander, Destroyer Squadron Six. The little eyes perused him, sleepy and bellicose, mustache downturned over grim lips. No

Atomic Fireballs were in sight this afternoon. The red light of a cassette recorder was another eye examining them all. Dan expected some reference to their previous meeting, but Niles only rumbled, "You understand the purpose of this debriefing?"

"Yes, sir."

"This is not in any sense a court of inquiry, or a court-martial. It's a fact-finding body." He went on to explain what the piece of paper had already said. Dan didn't interrupt, just waited. And when he was done, he said, "I understand, sir."

Niles conducted the interview; only from time to time did one of the others pose a question or encourage Dan to elaborate on something he'd said. But the commodore was thorough. He went through the background, then the events of the previous day. Dan had to explain everything he'd done, and why. The men who listened did not respond, either sympathetically or otherwise. They just listened intently as he described his forced conning of the ship; how Vysotsky had died and he'd overcome Kessler and then Leighty's guard; how he and the captain had tried to disable the engines and failed, tried to get a message off and failed, and finally turned the fight over to the ship. He gave Dr. Shrobo credit for getting ACDADS back on-line in time to frustrate the attempted capture, and Matt Williams for getting the program running. They seemed especially interested when he described *Barrett*'s performance in mode three against the Soviets and Cubans. One of the civilians passed a note to the chief of staff, who read it, nodded, and folded it into his pocket.

"And you're satisfied Harper was the ringleader," Niles rumbled.

"Yes, sir."

"How many other men were involved?"

"I believe no more than six, sir. Three enlisted, one chief, two officers. I never saw more than that."

"You'll be called on to identify them."

"Yes, sir, I will do that with pleasure." He intended to keep his promise—to request that their surrender be taken into consideration when sentence was passed—but as far as he was concerned, Harper's confederates were still mutineers and still accessories to murder.

"Any other questions, gentlemen? . . . I believe that is about all we have for you at present, Lieutenant," said Niles. Dan started to get up, but the commodore was still speaking, heavily, deliberately, in his slow, precise diction.

"Let me advise you of our intentions. We are not going to advertise Harper's success as a spy. To do so would only play into the Soviets' hands. Nor do I think it will serve any purpose to publicize the fact that there was an armed confrontation. The Soviets and Cubans know what they tried to do. The message is going to come through loud and clear to them that their side was left dead in the water. We feel that the wisest course now is to deescalate. Fortunately, this all took place in an essentially closed arena. We can seal the lid on it pretty effectively, I believe. At least till enough time has passed that it will be of less than immediate concern. That is why we cleared the waterfront before your arrival. We will be asking the officers and crew of *Barrett* to assist us in downplaying the incident."

Dan thought it over. Niles hadn't asked for his opinion or whether he thought this was a good idea. It sounded more like an order. So all he said was, "Aye aye, sir." And that seemed to be what was expected, because the commodore put his big freckled hands on the table like a sea lion getting ready to climb out onto the ice, reared back, and said, "One last question. Commander Leighty . . . wounded but expected to recover. What, to the best of your knowledge, was his involvement?"

"I don't believe he was involved, sir. Other than in trying to take his ship back once he realized what was happening."

"He was in no way associated with the plot, the attempted mutiny, Harper's espionage?"

"No, sir. I once suspected . . . I suspected him, but I believe now that I was mistaken."

Niles's little eyes glowed like dark stars. He rumbled, "Concerning this suspicion, was or is there anything about Captain Leighty that this board should know? Anything contrary to the ideals of naval service, or the behavior expected of a naval officer?"

Dan sat without speaking while thoughts struggled in his mind. Less thoughts than opinions he'd believed without examination, assumptions he'd assimilated over years in an organization that valued conformity and conservatism as core values. And set against them was the reality of a man standing up for his ship when all he could expect was death. Putting his life on the line without hesitation or doubt, because it was his duty.

"No, sir," he said, holding the commodore's eyes. "The skipper's one of the finest officers I've ever known. I would be proud to serve with him again."

OVER the bare, foot-worn ground, the woman carried the baby wrapped in a clean undershirt, cradling its head against her breast. The blankets the soldiers had given them were warm, but too rough for a newborn's skin. Its eyes were squinted closed against the glare, its thumb jammed firmly into its mouth. Around them the camp clamored with shouting, music, the kettledrum clamor of garbage cans being rolled across gravel. Lines were everywhere: for the showers, for the washing machines in the big tent, for the strange little plastic outhouses where for just a few seconds you could be alone before someone banged impatiently on the door. And there were lines to speak on the telephones to relatives and puzzled strangers, after struggling to deal with operators and snappish government clerks who spoke no Spanish. Graciela stepped over power cables snaking through the dust, wandering across the open square, going nowhere in particular, holding the child tightly.

She did not remember much after the gray ship had left them behind, taking the American away. She must have become delirious after that, for she truly didn't remember the white boat with the red stripe that Miguelito had said finally plucked them from the waterlogged skiff. She had not been well then, no. Half-crazy from lack of water, loss of blood—she didn't even remember who had sewed her up, or when, on the boat or in the first camp. The stitches were still bleeding, but she was healing. And thank the Virgin, she still had her milk.

She'd been at this camp for a month now, long enough to see many people come and many leave. She never ceased searching the faces of the new arrivals, never ceased asking each party for any news of a boat from Camagüey, from Alcorcón. But to no avail. She did not want to believe it, that they could be gone—young Julio and old Aracelia; strong Tomás and beautiful Xiomara; resourceful Augustín. Could the sea really have taken them; could it be true that she would never see any of them again? And Colón and Nenita—well, she could not pretend regret if he was dead, but she had not disliked Nenita; they could have been friends. Nor had she ever heard anything of old Gustavo again. It was said that there were many camps. So there was still hope. But it was queer to reflect that of all those who had sat on the hillside that night, only she and Miguelito might remain.

And sometimes at night, the sea still roared in her ears. She dreamed she was back in the *chalanita*, helpless in the storm. She wondered if having known *la mar* in its rage, it had become in some mysterious way part of her, the way she would always carry Armando in her heart, and Victoria, and Coralía, and now Armando Daniél; or if it was more like the mystery of possession, as if the sea, called by blood sacrifice like a god, mounted and lent its aspect from then on to those it had spared. Thinking of the sea in this way, she could envision, grasp, almost accept that those she loved had gone to it; for the sea was at various times like all of them—strong, beautiful, resourceful, and treacherous and evil; sometimes a friend, then suddenly an enemy. Being all these things already, how natural that it could contain them all. For whatever we are, she thought, so, too, is Death. And that, perhaps, is why Death needs us all.

And now she was in *los Estados Unidos*. And really it was strange and at the same time not so strange. On the way to the camp, she had marveled at the huge buildings, the colors, the clever signs, the beautiful cars and huge trucks and wide roads. The people looked pale but healthy, and clearly they were all rich. But here she was still surrounded by Cuban voices, Cuban faces, Cuban music, the smells from the cook tent of cumin and bijol and black beans simmering in the big stainless pots. But here no one called another *compañero,* unless, of course, one forgot, then laughed, embarrassed, making it a joke. Most foreign of all was that there was no fear. At first, it was exhilarating. Then gradually, one noticed the gates, the barbed wire. So that although you did not have to go to propaganda lectures, or sign petitions, or join any organizations, this was not exactly *la tierra de libertad.* The soldiers would not even let her help cook. So all she did was eat in the big tent and care for Armando Daniél and take her walks around the camp, watch the colored television where everyone was wealthy, even the black people, and once a day go to where a woman gave them lessons in how to speak American. "Good morning," she said to the baby. It opened its eyes and peeped up at her, then closed them again. "Good mor-ning," she murmured to herself, looking toward the gate.

"There you are," called a man, and she recognized Orlándo, the one who worked with the soldiers, or for them—it wasn't clear, but he was a man of authority. He was educated and spoke to her condescendingly. But now he was motioning to her to come to the gate. Another man was waiting there. Three small children stood beside him, but no woman. Graciela looked critically at the children. The teeth of the oldest were rotten, brown. That was from the sweet condensed milk the peasants gave their children; you set the can on a burner till it turned to caramel, then the child ate it all day, a treat. She had never let her girls do that. Orlándo asked her loudly, "Señora, have you received your documents yet?"

"*Sí,* yes. I have the green document."

"Are you ready to leave?"

"What? To leave?"

"You said you didn't know anyone in the North, no relatives to come for you. Fine, my job is to find you a home anyway, you see? One cannot stay here forever. There is a woman here from a place called Tallahassee. It is in Florida, not near here, but up in the north. It is still warm, though; it doesn't snow. A small city. They have a Cuban social club. The club will place you with a family and help you find a job. She can take two more people. Do you want to go and live in Tallahassee?"

"Why not?" she said. "Wait a minute, I will find Miguelito and get my things. Just wait, *por favor.* Do not let her go; I will be right back."

The woman was Cubana all right. Plump, no longer young; as she smiled her face creased into wrinkles like an old piece of leather. Her name was Maruja. The name of the man with the children was Alejo. He helped Graciela and Miguelito put their clothes in the trunk of the car. It was a huge car, not new, but the engine sounded loud, very strong. The woman was talking a mile a minute about how much Graciela and Alejo and the children would like Tallahassee. She seemed to assume they were husband and wife, that Miguelito was their oldest. Afraid that contradicting her might cause them to be placed back in the camp, Graciela smiled and nodded and said nothing. The little girls looked up at her. They were cute, despite their terrible teeth. Graciela patted the rusty fender. She said hesitantly to Maruja, "Is this your car? Do you own this beautiful car?"

"This is my car, yes."

"They gave it to you? The government?"

"The government!" Maruja guffawed. "You will learn, they do not give you cars here. This is not communism. Here, you want, you have to earn. Me and my sister, we own a little grocery on Railroad Street. That's where you'll live, over the store, if you want. You can help us in the mornings, until you learn some English. There is also a nursery; a plant nursery; they always need workers. Or you can be a maid. It is not the easy life, here."

"I can work," said Graciela. Alejo nodded, too, eyes darting around the interior as he slid into the backseat with her, and Miguelito got into the front, observing carefully as Maruja inserted the key and started the engine.

Hugging the baby, Graciela snuggled into the plastic cushions. How comfortable it was, how soft. Then her eyes widened. Wonder, cold air inside the car! An open bag of potato chips lay on the floor. A rosary swayed from the mirror. The little girl beside her sat motionless, brown eyes wide. And like the child, Graciela, too, stared with her mouth open as they bumped forward and the gates swung open, and leaning back into the torn upholstery, she sped forward into the cruel, generous, licentious, gaudy, and tumultuous country that was to become her own.

DAN sat in the cramped booth, in the telephone building up the hill from the pier area, searching his pockets for coins. He arranged them on the shelf as at the far end of the line the phone began to ring. He tapped a quarter nervously, reading the ballpointed graffiti: I WANT TO BLOW LARGE BLACK DICKS and USS MONONGAHELA, CAN DO. How far should he commit himself? He realized now that he'd never given her a chance. He'd decided before they first went to bed that it wasn't going to last. Now, though, he'd come to understand love took more than that. To receive, you had first to give.

To be loved, you had to be willing to love. He owed her an apology, to begin with; then, when he got back, honesty. No more lying, no more cheating. Maybe then what he hoped for could start to grow.

"Hello?"

"Hi. Bev? It's Dan."

A pause, then: "Dan. Where are you?"

"Guantánamo. Cuba. Calling from the phone exchange here. I, uh, sent Billy some things. A T-shirt, belt buckle . . ."

"Oh yes, he got those. He enjoyed them."

"How are you? I'm sorry I didn't return your calls before we left. A lot was going on. And I was confused."

"I sensed that."

He took a deep breath. "Anyway, I'm sorry. I think I've got things more together now. I realized I missed you." *I, I, I,* he thought; *ask about her, you dolt.* "So I thought I'd call, see how you were doing."

He listened to the static of the long connection to the mainland, the faint voices of other people talking. He could even make out the words: "No, I didn't get that. When did you send it?" But he didn't hear anything from Strishauser. He said, "Are you still there?"

"Yes, I'm still here. Dan—I had an abortion."

"What?"

"While you were gone. It was your child. I tried to let you know. But I realized I couldn't count on you. Maybe it was unfair to think I could. So when you didn't call me back or write, I went to the clinic."

"Beverly," he said. He couldn't think of anything to add, and the lines hissed again. The closed booth seemed to be swaying through space. It didn't even sound like her voice as he remembered it. It was calm, reasonable, final.

"You don't need to say anything. It was my decision and it's over. Sibylla went with me. She came in and held my hand. But I don't think we should see each other again."

"I'm . . . sorry. I'll be back in Charleston soon, before we deploy—"

"I don't think it would be a good idea. Please don't call me again, Dan. Or Billy. I think I knew you wouldn't want to make it permanent. You might have done it for the baby, but sooner or later you'd have felt trapped; it wouldn't have worked out. Maybe it's no one's fault. I hope you learn to love again. Get over Susan, and find somebody who's right for you. And that you have a good life. But I don't want to see you again. So . . . good-bye."

He sat there shaken, gripping the receiver, listening to the seashell hiss, the sound of the empty sea, and of his own blood singing in his ears.

And in himself, he sensed the darkness lurking, and living, burrowing and burgeoning, even as he sat immobile in shock and horror. And knew finally and irrevocably that that shadow presence would always be part of himself.

For all men wore masks, and most tragically and terribly of all, even to themselves; and of all masquerades, the bitterest and most destructive was that of one's own virtue. So you could not distinguish the just from the unjust by the uniforms they wore, or the words they spoke, or by what they were called. They could be judged only one by one, by what they did. Evil lived in each man and woman, and above and before all, he knew now, in his own heart. Like a virus, that corrupted and spread until a program was written to filter it out. That was the only battle worth fighting. A war no one could deter, or avoid, or win . . . only refuse to surrender. The war that would never end, that would continue till the final passage into darkness, and perhaps also, just perhaps, into the light.

THE starving, ragged men on the timber raft had seen no one else for days. For a time after they set out, there had been other craft around them, scores, hundreds of them; but gradually all had drawn ahead of the clumsy raft, dropping one by one below the curving sea. Then the storm had come, blowing them far to the south and west.

When the sky had cleared again, the wide sea was empty. They'd lost their plastic tarpaulin sail, had no oars, no engine, no compass. For days now they'd seen no other boat, no hint of land.

Now they were too weak to paddle, even if they had known where their goal lay. They'd brought water but no food. They'd tried to catch fish and birds, but without success. Now they were starving. The raft rocked gently on the quiet sea, like a cradle, like a coffin.

Suddenly, one man stirred. Then he spoke. And the others woke, sat up painfully, shading their eyes, looking where he pointed.

Far off, birds wheeled and darted above something floating on the shimmering surface.

Paddling with their arms and a piece of driftwood, they slowly made up on it.

It was a body. Eyes pecked to jellies, so swollen only a few rags of khaki clung to it. They pulled it close to the boat and stared silently. Then came discussion, low, painful murmuring through cracked, bleeding lips. For a long time, they argued under the broiling sun. Finally, silence fell again. Then a shared murmur arose, each, in his own way, asking forgiveness, and giving thanks.

With a faint rasping noise, one of them began whetting a knife.

THE SECRETARY OF THE NAVY
TAKES PLEASURE IN PRESENTING THE
SILVER STAR
TO LIEUTENANT DANIEL V. LENSON
UNITED STATES NAVY

FOR SERVICE AS SET FORTH IN THE FOLLOWING CITATION:

FOR CONSPICUOUS INTREPIDITY AND GALLANTRY IN ACTION DURING OPERATIONS IN THE WINDWARD PASSAGE AND CARIBBEAN OPERATING AREAS WHILE SERVING AS COMBAT SYSTEMS OFFICER, TACTICAL ACTION OFFICER, AND OFFICER OF THE DECK ABOARD USS *BARRETT* (DDG-998). LIEUTENANT LENSON PERFORMED HIS DUTIES AS COMBAT SYSTEMS OFFICER AND OFFICER OF THE DECK IN AN EXEMPLARY AND HIGHLY PROFESSIONAL MANNER DURING HUMANITARIAN ASSISTANCE OPERATIONS IN THE FLORIDA STRAITS AREA, FLEET OPERATIONS IN SUPPORT OF OPERATION TEMPEST, AND IN RESPONDING TO SERIOUS CHALLENGES TO THE RIGHT OF FREE TRANSIT OFF THE PEOPLE'S REPUBLIC OF CUBA. AS TACTICAL ACTION OFFICER DURING TRANSIT OF THE WINDWARD PASSAGE, LIEUTENANT LENSON WAS INSTRUMENTAL IN EXTRACTING HIS SHIP FROM A THREATENING SITUATION OF ACTIVE HARASSMENT DURING WHICH HIS COMMANDING OFFICER AND SEVERAL OTHER CREW MEMBERS WERE SERIOUSLY WOUNDED AND TWO MEN WERE KILLED. SUBSEQUENT TO THIS CONFRONTATION, THOUGH PARTIALLY BLINDED BY SMALL-ARMS FIRE, HE PERSONALLY TOOK THE LEAD IN PURSUING AND SUBDUING AN ARMED AND DANGEROUS CREW MEMBER. BY HIS INITIATIVE, COURAGEOUS ACTIONS, AND COMPLETE DEDICATION TO DUTY, LIEUTENANT LENSON REFLECTED GREAT CREDIT ON HIMSELF AND UPHELD THE HIGHEST TRADITIONS OF THE UNITED STATES NAVAL SERVICE.

FOR THE PRESIDENT,
SECRETARY OF THE NAVY